D0562661

Praise for Shannon McKenna

"Sensual, hard-hitting love scenes, and underlying themes of hope, faithfulness and survival."
—*Romantic Times* on *Extreme Danger* (4 starred review)

"A passionate, intense story about two people rekindling lost love in the middle of a dangerous, heart-pounding situation. Intricate story-lines give the book depth and power, tying in the edge-of-your-seat ending with flawless ease."
—*Romantic Times* on *Edge of Midnight* (4½ starred review)

"Wild boy Sean McCloud takes center stage in McKenna's romantic suspense series. Full of turbocharged sex scenes, this action-packed novel is sure to be a crowd pleaser."
—*Publishers Weekly* on *Edge of Midnight*

"Highly creative, erotic sex and constant danger."
—*Romantic Times* on *Hot Night* (4½ starred review and a Top Pick!)

"Super-sexy suspense! Shannon McKenna does it again."
—Cherry Adair on *Hot Night*

"A scorcher. Romantic suspense at its best!"
—*Romantic Times* on *Out of Control* (4½ starred review)

"Well-crafted romantic suspense. McKenna builds sexual chemistry and tension between her characters to a level of intensity that ex-plodes into sexually explicit love scenes."
—*Romantic Times* on *Return to Me* (4½ starred review)

Shannon McKenna

Tasting Fear

BRAVA

KENSINGTON PUBLISHING CORP.

www.kensingtonbooks.com

BRAVA BOOKS are published by

Kensington Publishing Corp.
119 West 40th Street
New York, NY 10018

All Kensington titles, imprints and distributed lines are available at special quantity discounts for bulk purchases for sales promotion, premiums, fund-raising, educational or institutional use.

Special book excerpts or customized printings can also be created to fit specific needs. For details, write or phone the office of the Kensington Special Sales Manager: Attn.: Special Sales Department. Kensington Publishing Corp., 119 West 40th Street, New York, NY 10018. Phone: 1-800-221-2647.

Brava and the B logo are Reg. U.S. Pat. & TM Off.

ISBN-13: 978-0-7582-2863-5
ISBN-10: 0-7582-2863-5

First Kensington Trade Paperback Printing: August 2009

10 9 8 7 6 5 4 3 2

Printed in the United States of America

Prologue

John was stoked. This job was going to be easy money.

He parked in the shadow of a tree—not that his quarry could see him parked around the corner. The stupid old fuck was probably congratulating himself for being so crafty. Marco Barbieri's plane from Italy had landed five hours ago, and the old man had been riding taxis in big, useless circles around the boroughs of New York City ever since. He'd changed cabs five times, but he always took the traitorous RF blip with him, the one planted deep in the trolley of his carry-on suitcase.

And it had led John right to the small upstate town of Hempton.

Served the old fart right for trusting his domestic staff back at his crumbling palazzo in Castiglione Santangelo. All it took was money to get the device planted in Barbieri's suitcase. Not even that much money.

John slunk along the spiked wrought-iron fence that lined the street, staying in the shadows of overhanging shrubs. The taxi was pulling away, turning the corner. Barbieri climbed the steps slowly.

Triumph pumped through John. He'd found the elusive, long-lost Contessa. Marco Barbieri's runaway bride. She'd be a shriveled hag now. Too damn bad, but she was still the key to the treasure chest. Marco Barbieri himself knew jack-shit. He was played out, ripe for the coroner's slab, but the Contessa was another story. She would know what his boss needed to know. Why the fuck else would she have run?

John's hands twitched with eagerness.

The door opened. A square of light, a tall, thin silhouette of a woman. The two figures stared at each other, motionless. John squinted in the dark. Too far to be sure, but saliva still pumped into his mouth.

They were speaking. John wished he'd been able to plant a listening device. Fuck it, he'd just get the woman to repeat their conversation, word for word. A few minutes with John's talents, and the old bitch would walk on her hands and bark like a dog if he told her to.

He enjoyed that part of his work a bit more than he should, but whatever. No one ever knew how much he enjoyed himself on the job except for his victims. And they certainly weren't telling.

He pondered ways and means as he composed himself to wait. Killing Barbieri in front of the Contessa would put her in the right mind-set for his interrogation, but it might also make a mess. John could wait when the situation warranted it, but his employer had been waiting for decades already. Nothing could be served by more waiting.

He drifted like a big dark ghost up the stairs, pulling on the mask. Unnecessary, since the Contessa would not live out the night, but John had found that wearing the mask unleashed him in some obscure way. He became superhuman. The essence of Death. Just putting it on made his body buzz with unholy anticipation.

He heard voices behind the door, the click of locks being disengaged. John slunk to put his back to the wall, reining in the hungry blood-drinking beast inside him. No knives, no guns. Barbieri's blood spilled here would narrow John's options afterward.

The instant the old man stepped out the door, John was in motion; grab, wrench, a strangled grunt, a wet crunch of a spine snapping, like a chicken with its neck wrung for the pot.

"Marco!" The old woman sprang out the door at him. "*Stronzo!*" she shrieked. "*Assassino! Aiuto!* Help!" She clawed at his face.

He lunged back, startled, dropping Barbieri's limp body to the floor. Her shrill cries choked off as he knocked her into her house, onto the floor. She scrambled back, crablike, and squeaked as he landed on top of her, knocking all the air out of her. He clapped his hand over her trembling mouth. Feeling her fragile rib cage hitch and jerk, seeking air. The fine, soft wrinkled skin beneath his palm. He pinned her flailing hands in the vise of his thighs. Her long white hair had come loose. Her shirt was torn. Her thin, frail body vibrated with stark terror.

He drank it in, grinning. Guzzling it. Terror. A heady liquor.

"Not as fresh as I like," he remarked, lightly. "You must've been good-looking a century ago. But I'm a professional. I'll manage." He yanked out the first implement that came to his hand, a hooked blade, and waved it in front of her eyes. "So, Contessa. Let's talk about the sketches. Where are they?"

Her eyes froze wide. "D-d-don't know wh-where."

He narrowed his eyes at her. "Oh, yes, you do," he said through clenched teeth. "And you'll tell, Contessa. Believe me. You'll tell."

Something like amusement flashed in her eyes, in spite of her fear. Something cynical, ironic. She gave him a little head shake. *No.*

As if she were laughing at him. The uppity dago bitch actually dared to laugh at him. Like she thought she was smarter. Better.

Killing rage flooded him like rocket fuel. He was going to know everything in her head. He would carve it out of the snotty old whore, chunk by chunk. He reared up, twirling the blade in his fingers—

And realized she was no longer looking at him at all. She looked at the ceiling, gasping. Her face was white, her lips purple. He rolled off her, dismayed. Sure enough. Her freed hand went to her chest. Clutching. Oh, Christ, no. A fucking heart attack. He leaned over and stared into her face. "You stupid, troublesome bitch," he said loudly.

She focused on him, and his heightened predator senses felt her, slipping away to where he couldn't follow. He saw a fleeting hint of triumph in her eyes before they rolled, went blank. Unconscious. He wanted to howl. Dying, to spite him. And now old Barbieri was dead, too. The boss was not going to be happy.

Searching Barbieri's suitcase and briefcase yielded no insights. They'd fucked him but good. He touched the Contessa's throat. Dead as a doornail. He suppressed the urge to mutilate their corpses.

The austere room was empty but for a writing table and some carefully lit art pieces. Three envelopes lay on the table.

He snatched one up. Stamped, but not yet sent. The one he held was addressed to a Nancy D'Onofrio. He ripped it open and squinted at the fine, delicate antique cursive script.

My dearest Nancy,
*   What I have to tell you will come as a shock, and I'm sorry to tell you in a letter. I wanted to tell you all in person, but after my cardiologist appointment last week, I see now that I do not dare to wait until I can get all three of my girls together in one room . . .*

Girls? John's head lifted like an animal scenting new prey. His eyes lit on a shelf crowded with photographs.

He strode over. Sure enough. Three young women smiled out of the picture frames. Pretty girls. Each hot, in her own dick-prickling way. Too young to be the bitch's daughters. Granddaughters, more like.

Fresh meat. And their addresses, written right there. Handy.

He stared at the images, breathing hard. One buxom, curvy girl with curly dark hair was curled up in a window seat, reading. Another mahogany-haired sylph was holding up a calico cat beneath her chin, smiling. A slender redheaded waif sported a slinky evening gown, gesturing toward a huge abstract sculpture behind her. All had sparkling eyes, rosy lips, expanses of smooth, unmarked skin like untrodden snow. Hot blood, blushing beneath. Curves and hollows, for him to pinch and squeeze and bite. Those girls would walk on their hands and bark like dogs for him, too. He would find those sketches, make his pile of money, and have a fine, juicy old time doing it.

So much saliva exploded into his mouth he began to dribble. He licked his lips, wiped his chin absently. Wouldn't do to make it easy for the forensics techs, leaving a puddle of genetic material for them to test.

Finally, this job was starting to get interesting.

Outside the Limit

Chapter
1

"Are you girls going to be all right?" Elsie's white brows knitted anxiously above her faded blue eyes. "I can stay, you know."

Nancy plastered what she hoped was a calm, reassuring look on her face as she gently nudged the old lady out the door. She gave Elsie's wrinkled cheek a kiss. "We'll be fine. We just need some downtime."

"But . . . but I'm sure Lucia wouldn't have wanted you girls to be all alone, at such a terrible time," Elsie fussed.

"We have each other, Auntie Elsie." Nancy's sister Nell grabbed the elderly neighbor's hand. "Thanks for the casserole. You've been wonderful. Lucia was lucky to have you for a neighbor. We all are."

When Elsie was finally nudged and flattered out the door, Nancy collapsed against it, sliding until her butt hit the floor. "God. It took forever to get rid of them all. Lucia must have known everyone in town."

Nell sank down to join her. Vivi flopped onto her back onto the scratched floorboards. She clapped a hand over her eyes to block the late afternoon sun. They were all in black, for the graveside service, and Vivi's fiery locks seemed the only color in a room leached of color.

Nancy stared at her sisters, feeling empty. She always felt as if Lucia's house was a benevolent entity, enveloping and protecting its people. Now, it just felt tired and old. As if the life had been sucked out of it.

Well, it had. The warmth, the benevolence, the life that had been Lucia. The house was just a house, faded and creaking with age.

Nothing like a funeral to pop the bubbles of one's imaginative fancies. She was desperately glad Vivi and Nell were there with her.

Nell blew out a sharp breath. "I can't believe it," she said. "I hadn't been up here to see her for over a month. I thought, we'll be celebrating her birthday soon enough, so I just took on extra shifts and put it off."

"Me, too," Nancy said wearily. "I've been swamped. Two albums to cut. Mandrake going on tour. Blah blah blah. Who gives a shit, right?"

"Lucia's birthday was today," Vivi said. "We should have been drinking port wine, eating one of those grape focaccias she made. Funny. I hated that thing, but I'd give anything to be crunching grape seeds in my teeth, telling her to get with the new millennium and make fudge brownies. Getting the lecture about the importance of tradition."

"God, Vivi, please, no," Nancy pleaded. "Don't get us going."

The warning came too late. Vivi's face convulsed. The grape focacia set the three of them off. For the umpteenth time.

They carefully avoided each other's eyes when the sobbing eased down. Nell's fingers found Nancy's. "I'm so sorry you had to find her alone," Nell said. "I don't know what I would've done if it had been me."

"Same thing I did," Nancy said wearily. "Called nine one one. Fallen to pieces. I was already nervous. I'd called her two evenings in a row. She didn't pick up. Not like her. So I guess I was braced for it."

"The asshole might have called an ambulance when he saw she was having a heart attack," Vivi said. "The bastard murdered her, even if the coroner did decide not to call it that. Natural causes, my ass. Since when is being scared to death a natural cause?"

"Ironic, isn't it?" Nell mused. "The thief takes the jewelry, the stereo, and the TV, and leaves the Fabergé picture frame and the Cellini bronze. Ignorant dickhead."

"Speaking of which. We can't leave Lucia's fine art here," Nancy said. "You're the sculptor, Vivi. Why don't you take the bronze?"

"Yeah, a priceless Cellini satyr would look great on the dashboard of my van. Right next to the air freshener and the plastic Madonna."

"I thought you were through with the crafts fair circuit," Nancy said. "Didn't you say you wanted to stay in one place these days?"

Vivi shrugged. "Theoretically. Maybe someday. I guess two studio apartments in Manhattan the size of gnats' asses aren't much better than a Volkswagen van for museum-quality art exposition, huh?"

"No way," Nell said. "All I've got are books. Volumes of epic poetry don't have much direct trade value for crystal meth or heroin. How about you, Nance? Isn't your block protected by the Hells Angels?"

Nancy shrugged. "Yeah, but even so. The crack houses the next block over do not inspire confidence. So, what? A safety-deposit box?"

"We can't put Lucia's precious *intaglio* writing table in a safety-deposit box," Vivi said. "Damn."

The three of them dubiously regarded the table in question.

"Should we get an alarm?" Nell suggested, her voice full of doubt.

Vivi harrumphed. "Seems silly, since the house is empty."

"I'll go out tomorrow and buy a plastic tablecloth," Nancy said. "Something hideous, for camouflage. I'll take the bronze, and you take the picture frame, Nell, until we come up with a better plan."

This attempt at brisk practicality petered out into sad silence. Vivi rolled onto her side. Nancy slid her hand into her sister's long, silky mane.

"It feels so strange," Vivi said quietly. "She was our foundation, wasn't she? Now she's gone, the world's lost all its structure."

Nancy tugged Nell into the embrace. "We'll make a new structure. We've got each other, right? That's what Lucia would have said."

The group hug was a sure detonator for another sob explosion. The doorbell jangled in the middle of their sobfest, making them jump.

"I can't handle another condolence call," Nell whispered, mopping her face. "Check the peephole. Don't make any sound."

Nancy peeked out. A bored-looking young man stood there, holding a box. "Looks like a delivery guy," she told her sisters.

"More flowers?" Vivi asked.

"No, it's a smallish white box." Nancy pulled the door open. "Yes?"

"Special hand delivery from Baruchin's Fine Jewelers," the guy said. "For Lucia D'Onofrio."

"She died a week ago," Nancy said. "Today was the funeral."

The guy blinked rapidly, mouth open. This scenario was not covered by the very simple flowchart in his head. He looked helpless.

Nancy took pity on him. "I'm her daughter. I'll sign for it."

"Ah . . . ah . . . lemme call my boss." He called, muttered for a moment into his cell, passed the clipboard, waited as she scrawled her name. "Uh, sorry for your loss," he mumbled, abashed.

Nancy took the box into the house. "Baruchin's Fine Jewelers since nineteen thirty-eight," she read. "Anybody else want to do the honors?"

Vivi and Nell exchanged nervous glances. "Go for it," Nell said.

Nancy pried open the seals. Inside were three small identical leather boxes. Nell flipped open each box. They leaned over. Gasped.

A rectangular gold pendant was inside each box. Each was adorned with a delicate cursive letter, each done with a different color of gemstone. The *N* for Nancy was done in tiny sapphires, the *A* for Antonella in rubies, and the *V* for Vivien in emeralds. Diamond brilliants clustered around the letters for contrast. Each pendant had a halo of white, lacy white gold openwork swirling above the top of the rectangle. They were exquisite. It was cruel. The three of them turned away from the table and totally lost it. For at least ten minutes.

Finally, Vivi dragged a shredded Kleenex out and blew her nose. "She was going to give them to us on her birthday," she said.

Nancy nodded, loosening the *V* from its velvet nest. She reached around Vivi's neck, fastening the clasp. She did the same for Nell, and then her own. "We'll wear them always," she said. "In her honor."

Vivi fled to the kitchen, clutching her pendant in her hand.

Nell clutched hers, her wet eyes faraway. "She saved us, you know," she said. "At least me and Vivi. Maybe not you, Nance. You were born grown up. You could have saved yourself from the cradle. "

"Ouch," Nancy said sourly.

"It's a compliment," Nell said. "I respect and admire you for it."

"Right. Stolid old Nancy," she muttered. "Hit me over the head with a brick. I barely even blink."

"Wrong," Nell snapped. "Solid. Solid is different from stolid. You're tough. Not flaky. Tough is sexy. There's nothing sexy about flaky."

Nancy grunted. "Yeah? Ask any of my ex-fiancés."

"Hell, no." Nell made an exaggerated pantomime of spitting on the ground. "Not unless you want me to slug them out for you."

Vivi burst out of the kitchen, eyes alight. "I found it!" She waved a yellowed scrap of paper in one hand and a wine bottle in the other.

"Found what?" Nancy asked.

"The recipe! For that horrendous grape thing! *Schiacciata all'uva!* We even have some grapes, with seeds! Elsie left some with the casserole. The recipe's in Italian, but you read Italian, right, Nell?"

Nell adjusted her glasses, took the paper out of Vivi's hand, and peered at it. "The measurements are metric, but we can find a conversion table online with Nancy's BlackBerry," she said.

Nancy was bemused. "I thought you hated the grape thing!"

"Oh, I do," Vivi assured her. "But that doesn't matter. It's the perfect thing for Lucia's wake. Just us three all sniveling together, a couple of bottles of port, and the gross grape focaccia."

Nancy grabbed her and hugged her hard. "Okay," she whispered.

None of them were good at pastry, but they put their hearts into it for Lucia's sake. Their ragged version of *sciacchiata all'uva* was a far cry from Lucia's elegant traditional Tuscan dish, but whatever. The oven timer did not go off. The smoke detector did. But the quantity of port they had drunk made them indiscriminating enough to actually eat some of it. It was as wonderfully awful as ever, especially burned.

They toasted Lucia until dawn, alternately laughing and crying at the impenetrable mysteries of life and death. The cruelty and the beauty of it. *Il dolce e l'amaro*, as Lucia would've said. The bitter and the sweet.

Nell leaned out of the passenger-side window of Vivi's gaudily painted Volkswagen van the next morning. "Take-out dinner, eight o'clock, my place," she reiterated forcefully. "Be there."

"If I can," Nancy hedged. "I've got a million things to take—"

"To take care of, yes. You always do, but you still have to eat," Vivi scolded, leaning over Nell's lap from the driver's side.

"If you're not there, we'll think you don't care," Nell warned.

Vivi's taillights glowed in the morning mist until they turned at the corner and were gone. The sky was heavy with bruised-looking clouds. Nancy's head felt bruised, too. No surprise, considering the port they'd sucked down in their drunken revels. Cathartic, yeah, but this morning she felt like something scraped off the bottom of a shoe.

Too bad. Time to get busy and do all the normal things in her crazy schedule, plus everything that had been put off last week because of Lucia's death and funeral. Fortunately for her, frantic activity was her favorite coping mechanism, considering her career choice—an agent manager for singer-songwriters and folk bands. Back in college, she'd wanted to be a musician herself. She'd learned, to her cost, that she didn't have the chops for it, and decided to make the best of it, and help the musicians who did. And *that* she *was* good at. Damn good. She had just the detail-minded, dogged determination for it.

She had nudged her handpicked group of folk artists and ensembles out of the pub and coffeehouse concert series circuits and into theaters and more prestigious folk festivals. They were getting better record deals, more airtime on radio stations. Some were poised to break into the big time. If that happened, her hard work would start to pay off. This was the last push toward that glorious day when she could hire a staff, instead of being a one-woman agency. She'd been working sixteen-hour days, sometimes working nights as well, for years.

But that was fine with her. A woman zipping around at three hundred miles an hour, six hands waving like a dancing Shiva, a cell phone in every one of them, did not have time to feel this sour, sucking hole of grief inside her. Or at least, if she did feel it, it would be on the periphery of her consciousness, not smack-dab in the center.

Even so. She pressed her hand against the ache in her middle. It was going to take some crazy scrambling to distract herself from this.

First, something hideous to cover the writing table. She got into her car, zipped down to the dollar store, and stood in the aisle for several minutes pondering the merits of hideous florals or plastic plaid in dull hues of beige and taupe. She concluded that in the understated simplicity of Lucia's front room, the quietly ugly beige and taupe mumbled "Don't notice me," whereas the checks and hideous floral squawked "What's wrong with this picture?" Or perhaps she was giving the burglars too much credit. As if those drugged-up bottom-feeders were going to be listening to what plastic tablecloths whispered to them.

It was raining when she got back. She held the package that held the tablecloth over her head as she darted up the steps.

"Excuse me, miss?"

The deep voice jolted her, and she let the package drop. It slid down the stoop, landing at the feet of a man who stood there. He stooped to pick it up. Rain sparkled on the spiky tips of his short brown hair. He stood, looked up, and her breathing stopped. Everything stopped. Time stopped. Or seemed to.

"Sorry to startle you." His words started the clock again.

That's okay, her lips tried to say, but her lungs were still immobile.

She gave him a jerky nod. Her glasses were spotted with rain. She dried them on her sweater. Even out of focus, he was amazingly good-looking. No, good-looking was too pallid a term. Cut it down to just "amazing."

She couldn't focus in on any particular detail. His broad, strong-boned face was wet with rain, but it was his eyes that did it to her. Beard stubble accented all his chiseled planes and angles of his jaw. His eyes were silvery green, the color so bright it seemed to catch the light and reflect it back. Huge shoulders. Fabulous thighs, nicely shown off by faded jeans, although she'd bet money he wasn't conscious of it. She'd also bet money that he had an ass to match.

He looked solid. Strong. Balanced. Like a rock, an oak, the earth.

He observed her for a timeless moment as the rain pattered down, and she had the sensation that everything important about her was written in a language that he could read in a glance.

She put her glasses back on. In that moment of grace before they spotted up again, she flash memorized every detail. The sweep of the dark hairs of his brows, the grooves that bracketed his mouth.

He wiped rain off his forehead with the sleeve of his wool shirt.
"Are you Nancy D'Onofrio?" he asked.

This epitome of manhood knew her name? She nodded, wishing she hadn't opted not to wash her hair. She'd slicked it into a tight bun. The peeled-onion look. She was still in yesterday's funeral black, and her breath must reek of liquor, considering how hungover she felt.

This guy, by contrast, looked clear eyed, clean living. He'd probably gotten to bed at ten and was up at five to meditate, or do yoga or some such. He probably drank something austere, like green tea. Not the sugared-up, high-test espresso she guzzled to get revved for her crazy days. She saw him in her mind's eye. Shirtless, in a yoga pose.

And, God, what was she even doing having thoughts like this, at a time like this? How freaking shallow was she, anyway?

Distraction, came the answer from a calmer place deep inside. He was eye candy. Fantasy material. Better even than frantic work as a way to not think about the ragged hole in her life. Her eyes were fogging up, and the guy's mouth was moving, and had been for some seconds already. And she'd just been staring at him.

Mouth open, no doubt.

". . . Mrs. D'Onofrio here?"

Ah, God. Not again. Irrational anger flared inside her. Why was it always her goddamn duty to announce it to the world? She'd been the one to find Lucia's body. She'd called the cops. She'd called her sisters. She'd told the neighbors. She'd told the delivery people. She'd written the obit. Could somebody else please take a fucking turn?

Not his fault, she reminded herself. She shook her head.

"Lucia's dead," she croaked.

The man's face went blank. "Oh, my God," he said. "When?"

She swallowed hard, rubbed her eyes under her glasses, and tried again. "Last week," she said thickly. "The funeral was yesterday."

He was silent for a long moment. "I am so sorry," he said finally.

There was no good response to that. She'd learned that this week. Painfully. Nancy sniffed and said, "Me, too. Who are you?"

"I'm Liam Knightly," he said. "I'm the carpenter. I'm here to start the work on the house."

"Work? On the house? What work?"

"She didn't tell you about the renovation she was planning?"

"I hadn't spoken to her for a couple of weeks before she died."

"Me, neither," he said. "We set this date weeks ago."

Nancy shook her head, bemused, and stared at his big truck.

"Not a word?" Knightly wiped rain off his face. "Would it make you nervous if I stood under the awning with you? I'm getting drenched."

"That's fine," she said distractedly. "That is, do you want to come in? For a cup of coffee, or tea? If Lucia has tea. Or had, I guess I should say." Babbling, again. She hated that. So damn stupid.

His eyes gleamed with a smile he was too polite to allow to emerge. "Thank you," he said. "One moment. I'll go tell Eoin to wait."

"He can come in, too," she called. Hmm. His ass was as fine as his quadriceps had suggested that it would be. More so, even.

"No, he's shy. He'll be fine in the truck." Knightly jerked open the driver's-side door and exchanged a few words with whoever sat on the passenger side. A few graceful strides brought him back up the stairs. It took forever to get the locks open. Her hands felt clumsy and thick.

The funeral smell of lilies and other florist shop herbiage was intensely strong in the front room. Knightly followed Nancy through the house. She snapped on the light and had a bad moment when she remembered that they had trashed the kitchen last night. Every surface was covered with spilled flour, shreds of dough. Grapes were squished on the floor. The scorched remains of the *schiacciata* looked sad and unkempt on the serving plate. Lucia's fine-cut crystal liquor glasses were sticky with port. The bottles lay empty and forlorn under the kitchen table. He must think her a total lush. And a slob, too.

"We had a wake for her, last night," she felt compelled to explain. "Me and my sisters. Up all night, with port wine and Tuscan pastry."

He nodded. "A good thing to do."

Nancy touched her aching head with her fingertips. "Felt that way at the time. So what was I . . . oh, yes. Coffee. Or tea." She started rummaging in drawers. "Which do you prefer?"

"Tea, please. If Lucia has it. Or had it, I should say."

She whipped her head around, suspicious. Was he teasing her?

The smile in his eyes disarmed her. She was almost betrayed into smiling back, but a vague sense of inappropriateness stopped her. "I thought you'd pick tea," she murmured. "What kind? Green? Herbal?"

"Black tea," he said. "With sugar and milk, if you have it. I'm Irish. I get the tea thing from my folks."

"I'm Irish, too," she confessed, for some odd reason. Like he cared.

He looked perplexed. "With a name like D'Onofrio? And Lucia . . ."

"Was Italian, yeah. Right down to her toenails." Nancy yanked a green canister of Irish Breakfast tea out of the drawer. "Will this do?"

"That'll be fine," he assured her.

"She adopted us," Nancy continued, rummaging for a teakettle. "She took us in as foster kids. I was thirteen. Nell and Vivi came later. My name was O'Sullivan, then." The pans rattled as she shoved them around. "O'Sullivan was my mother's name. I don't know about my father. He could have been Italian, or anything else, for all I know. The way things went, I was lucky to have a surname at all."

"Hey," he said. "You don't have to tell me all this, if you don't—"

"I was so glad to be adopted by Lucia." She kept talking, a tight, vibrating quaver in her voice. "So proud that she wanted me. I've been a D'Onofrio for more than half my life. So I guess I'm Italian now, too." She yanked out a saucepan that was nested in the other pans and ended up pulling the whole cluster out of the shelf. They hit the floor, clanging, rolling. Nancy stared down, saucepan dangling from her hand, and felt his hands at her elbows. He gently steered her until she was in front of a chair, then pulled her back until she was forced to sit.

"I'll take care of this." He pried the saucepan out of her fingers.

He ran water into it, set it on the stove, and lit the gas. Then he gathered up the pans and slid them back into the cupboard. Without seeming to search, he assembled sugar, mugs, spoons, milk. He pushed the mess aside on the table, draped a tea bag in each cup.

Nancy pressed her hand over her mouth and let him do it.

Knightly poured the hot water, then sat down. After a few minutes, when she made no move to drink, he stirred some sugar and milk into the cups and nudged hers toward her. "Go on," he urged. "Tea helps."

She tried to smile, and took a cautious sip. Tears kept slipping down, one after another. Tickling. Dangling from her chin.

"She was a wonderful lady," Knightly said gently. "Pure quality."

Nancy wished she'd left her hair down, but it was slicked back, every wisp, and her wet face was naked, shrinking in the cold, gray light.

"Yes," she whispered. "She really was."

The sounds of the morning shifted into the foreground. Cars going by, rain sluicing down against the window glass. Steam rose, curling from the two cups. Liam Knightly reached out and took her hand.

Her first instinct was to yank it back, but she didn't want to be rude, and he'd been so nice about the tears, and the tea. And besides. He had a nice hand. Big, warm, graceful. His grip made her hand tingle.

"I lost my mother, six years ago," he offered.

"Oh. So, um. You know," she said. "How it is."

"I know how it is," he echoed.

Tears blinded her again for a while. He sat with her, sipping tea. Holding her hand. Usually silence felt like emptiness that needed to be filled. Knightly's silence made space for her to breathe. Space for tears, for her silly meltdown. He wasn't put off. He was in no hurry.

It was strange, but she didn't want it to end.

It occurred to her that this was the most intimacy she'd had, besides hugs from her sisters, since her last fiancé's defection. Ah, hell, maybe before. The chaste way that Liam Knightly was holding her hand was more subtly erotic than anything she'd ever shared with Freedy.

That passing thought made her blush. She mopped her eyes and felt a square of cloth being tucked into her hand. She glanced at it, bemused. "I didn't know people still used these."

"I'm old-fashioned," he said. "My father liked them."

She dabbed her eyes with the crisply ironed cotton, wishing she looked prettier for him. Feeling stupid for wishing it.

"What happened to Lucia?" he asked.

The question jolted her out of her self-absorption, and thank God for it. "A thief broke into the house. She was here, alone. The shock and fear must have provoked a heart attack."

His mouth tightened. "That's terrible."

"I was the one to find her," she told him. "Two days later. I'd been calling. She hadn't been answering. So I came to check."

"Ah, Christ. That must have been terrible." His hand tightened. "Did he . . ." He hesitated, clearly afraid to ask. "Had he hurt her?"

She gulped her tea and shook her head. "Not as far as they could tell. The chain on the door was broken. The TV, DVDs, and stereo were gone, and the computer. And Lucia's jewelry." She forced herself to sit up and pulled her hand away. "Let's get back to practical matters."

His subtle smile flickered. "If you like. There's no rush."

"I imagine you're losing money right and left as the clock ticks."

"I'm self-employed," he replied. "I choose not to see my time that way. There's time for tea and condolences for a lost friend."

"Ah." Well, hmmph. Just call her just brittle and shallow and tense, why didn't he. "Um, thanks. Anyhow, I have no idea what kind of arrangement you made with Lucia, but—"

"How about if I just tell you?" he suggested mildly.

She retreated behind her tea mug. "Ah, okay," she murmured.

He pulled a square of folded paper out of his pocket. It proved to be a floor plan of Lucia's ground floor. Several notes and edits had been made, in Lucia's distinctive, elegant script. It hurt to look at it.

"We chose this date to start the work a month ago," he said. "She was going to make the changes to the ground floor that you see on that plan, build a new deck, put in new teak flooring, do over both the bathrooms and the kitchen, redo the stairs, enlarge the upstairs closets, finish the attic, and put in some skylights."

"Ah . . . wow," Nancy said. "I am so sorry that it, ah, went up in smoke. I imagine that makes problems for your work schedule."

He shook his head. "I'll be all right. I have plenty of work, and for this job, I'd hired only one assistant. But I have a truck full of building materials parked outside, and another full load in my barn back home. Bought and paid for. And that stuff's not smoke."

She was startled. "Bought already? Lucia bought it?"

"Yes. Twenty-two thousand dollars and change," he said.

Nancy's jaw dropped. "Twenty-two . . . my God! Is it refundable?"

Knightly gazed into his cup. "No," he said, reluctantly. "I knew a guy who was going out of business and liquidating his stock. I took Lucia there a few weeks ago, and we picked out supplies at a quarter or a third of the list price. No refunds. The lumber's all cut."

Nancy rubbed her forehead. "Oh, lovely. This is all I need right now," she muttered. "Twenty-two thousand bucks' worth of lumber, flooring, tile, and bathroom and kitchen fixtures dumped on my head."

"I'm sorry," he said. "I liked her. I was trying to save her money."

"Well, thanks for that," she muttered, with bad grace.

He drummed his fingers against the table. "You've got a couple choices," he said. "You can try to sell the stuff on eBay, or craigslist. Or you can go ahead with the renovation. It'll boost your property value. Though I have no idea who owns the house." He paused, delicately.

"My sisters and I," Nancy supplied.

"Then all you have pay now is labor and a few odds and ends. You'd recover that and more in increased property value," he said. "That way the investment won't be wasted. If you intend to sell the house."

Nancy chewed her lip. "We don't 'intend' anything," she said. "The funeral was yesterday. We have no plan. We have no clue. None."

He lifted his hands up. "I'm sorry. I didn't mean to pressure you."

His quiet tone shamed her. This was not his fault. It was hard to think clearly. She kept losing the thread, getting muddled and lost. "My sisters should know this. Would you excuse me while I call them?"

He set down his cup and rose to his feet. "Certainly. Would you like me to leave while you make the call?"

"No, no. It's fine. Sit down." She waved him back down and dialed Vivi's number. Nell, the impractical scholar and bookworm, had no cell phone. She considered cell phones evil, annoying, and probably carcinogenic, and refused to accept one even as a gift, which drove her sisters nuts. This, of course, amused Nell to no end. Naughty Nell.

"Yeah?" Vivi picked up, her voice sharp with alarm. "You okay?"

"I'm fine. It's just that I've discovered a new wrinkle." Nancy outlined the situation and waited while Vivi relayed it to Nell.

Her younger sisters conferred. Vivi came promptly back with the verdict. "Our combined opinion is that if Lucia wanted it done and went to the trouble of buying all the supplies, we should respect her wishes. But I don't have any cash on hand to help pay the crew." Nell said something emphatic in the background. "Neither does Nell," Vivi added.

"Okay. I'll look into some loans, then. Later, babes."

"Eight o'clock tonight," Vivi reminded her, in a steely tone.

"Right." Nancy snapped her cell closed. "So," she said. "My sisters and I are disposed to proceed, but we're broke. Lucia had some money, I assume, but we don't know how much, or when we'll be able to access it. I can look into taking out a personal loan, but in the meantime . . ."

"I'll just get started," he said. "Pay me later, when you sort it out."

She was startled. "Uh, are you sure that's wise? I don't even know when I can get the cash. I wouldn't want to get you in a bind."

His shrug was nonchalant. "I can cover the costs for a couple of weeks. It's just me and Eoin to pay, for now. Then we'll see how it goes."

"On . . . on just my word?"

His eyes gleamed over his cup. "Your word's good."

"You just met me fifteen minutes ago," she pointed out.

Knightly glanced at his watch. "Eighteen minutes," he said. "Eighteen minutes are enough. For you, anyway."

His eyes had a magnetic pull that wiped her mind clear of coherent thought. All thoughts but one.

Oh, Lord. She had no business getting all trembly thighed. She was grieving, wobbly, her judgment shot to hell. Probably imagining all these vibes flying right and left. Or maybe not, and that was worse. He was way too big, for one thing. Too much of him. She avoided men who sent out alpha-dog signals. Like the plague. And perfect though Knightly's manners might be, mellow as he might act, there was no mistaking one of those men. She could spot one disguised in any costume: a suit, a military uniform, jeans and a work shirt. The force field of his machismo hummed against her skin, all the more dangerous for how subtle it was. Not that it was a bad thing. It was just the way he was, like having brown hair, or a nice ass. But even so. She had to run the show when it came to relationships, romance, sex. That detail was nonnegotiable. And a guy like him would definitely want to be on top.

Um. Figuratively speaking, of course.

Her eyes skittered around, fell on the plastic tablecloth. Something to do. She grabbed the package, ripped open the cover, and headed for the living room.

Knightly followed her, sipping from his mug in that leisurely way of his. Nursing the damn thing. She had long since nervously gulped her own tea down. He watched her unfold the tablecloth and shake it out. The sharp stink of new plastic overwhelmed even the scent of funeral flowers. She started to position it carefully over Lucia's *intaglio* writing table.

"I know it's none of my business," Knightly said. "But why are you covering that table with that god-awful thing?"

Nancy paused and pulled the plastic away. "My sister and I are taking the smaller art pieces home, but none of us has a place for the table," she told him. "I figured the tablecloth was camouflage, if burglars should come again. Worth a try, anyhow. Did Lucia tell you its history?"

"She told me the SS officers used it during the Nazi occupation," he replied, "that they used her father's palace for their headquarters."

Nancy was startled. Lucia had not usually been so forthcoming about her family history. "The Nazi officers were the ones who made these graffiti," she said, tracing some of the brutal scratches carved into the delicately carved tangle of flowers.

"Incredible," he commented. "A piece of living history."

"Lucia's father was actually a count, you know?" she told him. "The Conte de Luca. Which means Lucia was technically a countess, even though she lived almost all of her life here, in New York."

She was babbling, but it felt good to talk about Lucia. Like a pressure valve opening, letting off a tiny bit of steam.

"I'm not surprised she was a countess," Knightly said. "She looked the part. That lady was a class act."

Nancy blinked back another rush of tears and shook the tablecloth into place with an angry little jerk. "Yes, she was." She positioned the jade plant carefully in the center. "There. Who would guess?"

"It looks butt ugly," he said judiciously.

"Thank you," Nancy murmured.

Knightly laid his hand on the table, as gently as if it were a living thing. "I'd love to study it someday. Figure out how the guy did it."

"Did what?"

"Made something that's still intact and still so beautiful after four hundred years. That's talent." He turned, and took his cup back into the kitchen.

Nancy's eyes fell upon Lucia's shelf of photos as she gazed after him. She waited until he appeared again in the doorway. "How did you know who I was?" she demanded.

His subtle smile lit his eyes. "Lucia showed me pictures of you," he said. "She told me all about you. Bragged you up."

A dark suspicion dawned in her mind. "Bragged me up?" she repeated slowly. "What do you mean? What did she tell you?"

"That you work too hard, and let everyone take advantage of you. That you live in an apartment surrounded by Hells Angels, crackheads, and the criminally insane. That you come across as bossy and managing, but you'd give the shirt off your back to a stranger in need—"

Nancy winced. "Oh, no. I see where this is going."

"And that you're definitely not married," he concluded. "She also told me you'd be here for her birthday. She wanted to introduce us."

"Oh, God." Nancy turned pink. That manipulative schemer.

Lucia would never have done this to her if this guy was taken. A swift glance at Knightly's left hand confirmed that he wore no ring.

A glance that he intercepted. His subtle eye smile deepened. Her mortification deepened, too. "I'm, ah, sorry about that. You being put on the spot, I mean. Lucia couldn't stand it that I'm single."

"Yeah, that was my impression. It is really strange, though."

She covered her hot cheeks with her hands. "What's strange?"

"Strange that you're single. You're not what I expected."

Don't ask it. Don't ask it. Don't. "Ah . . . what did you expect?"

"Well, she told me you were beautiful. I could see that from the pictures. But she didn't tell me how beautiful. Photos can't show that."

Beautiful? Oh, God. Strange, wild energy crackled through her nerves, as if he had touched her.

Out of nowhere, she started to imagine how it would feel if he did.

She started to vibrate. Strange that she was single? Whoo-hah. Little did he know. She forced her voice not to shake. "Don't flatter me."

"Who's flattering?"

She looked away, flustered. She had no idea what to say to him.

"I'm sorry," he said quietly after a long moment. "I can't believe I just said that to you, right now. It's a bad time. Please forget I said it."

"Um, it's okay," she murmured. Right. Like she could.

The easy, unexpected intimacy she had felt with him before was gone. Knightly's face was cool and distant as they exchanged numbers. He and his assistant, Eoin, would unload supplies that day and start the kitchen tomorrow, though she had to clean stuff out of it first. They set a time to meet for the following morning, and that was that.

It gave Nancy a pang to hand over Lucia's house keys to a man she'd only just met, but the thought of having someone in the place was obscurely comforting. She hated the thought of the house lying empty and bereft.

After that exchange, there was no good reason to hang around. She put the carefully wrapped bronze sculpture into the car and took off. She felt uncomfortably guilty for being irritated with Lucia for setting her up. At the same time, she was missing her desperately. She felt so raw, so shaky. Desperate to glom on to something else to think about. And God knows, she'd been twitchy about the whole issue of dating and romance even before Lucia's death. It occurred to her that Lucia had probably filled Knightly in on her daughter's string of romantic disasters. The thought made her cringe.

The first time her fiancé had dumped her had been bad. The second time, worse. The third time, she'd gotten philosophical about it.

Maybe she would have to resign herself to never having children. Content herself with a series of cats. Or do what Lucia had done. Adopt some half-grown kids who needed a home. There was more than one way to have a family. The center of a woman's life did not have to be a man. And men didn't seem to enjoy being in the center of her life. By all accounts, it was a prickly, uncomfortable place to be.

Nancy's sisters and Lucia had despised Freedy, Ron, and Peter. But was it their fault they'd fallen out of love? You loved someone or you didn't. She didn't want to be married to a man who didn't.

She wiped her eyes on her sleeve. She must lack some innate womanly skill. She should have practiced gazing up through fluttering eyelashes, hanging on their every word. Puffing up their egos.

But she'd always been too busy managing their careers, making them take their vitamins, making sure their socks matched.

Freedy had said that she was too controlling. Ron had told her that she was too driven. Peter had told her that she was too prosaic, that she just couldn't join him in that place full of dreams where he needed to live in order to make the magic happen. She lived in another world, he had explained.

Huh. He sure hadn't minded her finding lucrative gigs for him from that other world. Too bad watching her scurry around to do the scut work for his career had been such a turnoff. Prosaic Nancy, the detail freak. And that damn cell phone of hers, ringing all the time, shattering his precious creative trance. Oops. So sorry.

Not that she was bitter or anything.

The strange, raw mood fostered brutal honesty. She stared, hot-eyed, out the windshield. The problem with her fiancés had been sex. Sex had always been problematic for her. She did not like feeling vulnerable, squished, or squeezed. Being overwhelmed in any way, physical or emotional, made her run away in her head. She became unreachable and detached. Instant Popsicle.

Her lovers, not surprisingly, had gotten impatient with this.

The thought of having one of those tense conversations about intimacy issues with Liam Knightly made her cringe.

After Freedy's defection, she'd sworn off romance. Celibacy was less painful. No bikini waxing, scratchy lingerie, or contraception.

But the intensity of Knightly's gaze made her feel as if he'd seen something in her she'd never imagined she could be. She wanted to see him again, to see if it was a fluke. A trick of the light. A passing spasm.

An experiment doomed to failure, of course. The guy was way too big. And he exuded an aura of controlled power that made her feel vulnerable even when she was fully clothed and an entire room away. She could only imagine how that vibe would feel if they were naked. Skin to skin. And oh, *shit*—

She screeched to a stop at the red light.

She, Nancy D'Onofrio, the born multitasker, couldn't even think about the man while driving.

Chapter 2

Liam followed Nancy's car with his eyes. Her taillights were a thread of connection until the car turned. He wanted to sprint to the end of the block, catch another glimpse. He didn't. He had that much self-control.

Though that was about as much as could be said for it.

He let his breath out. Jesus, Mary, and Joseph, he hadn't seen that one coming. He ran down the steps, and got into the truck. Eoin, the Irish kid fresh from County Wicklow who worked for him, gave him a questioning glance. "So? What are we doing?" he asked.

He shrugged. "We're getting on with it."

Eoin's blue eyes widened. "The daughter wants to go ahead?"

He nodded, squeezing his hand around the sense memory of Nancy D'Onofrio's cool, slender fingers. Eoin caught the vibe, the sensitive, curious little bastard, and shot him a sidelong glance.

"Daughter's a looker, eh?" he commented.

"She just put her mother in the ground yesterday," Liam snarled.

Eoin mumbled something apologetic that made Liam feel like hypocritical shit. Like he had a right to scold, after what he'd said. What the fuck was he thinking, coming on to a woman who'd just buried her mother? Still wearing her funeral dress? Red-eyed from crying? She probably took him for one of those slimy opportunists who preyed on grieving women. Idiot words, popping out of his mouth like they were spring-loaded. Telling her how beautiful she was. Christ, his tongue had probably dangled out of his head like a slavering hound while he said it.

Lucia D'Onofrio had been a classy old lady. Funny, smart, with a sharp, cutting sense of humor. She'd reminded him of Mom. He'd known Lucia for only a few weeks, but even so, her death made him feel as if something had been taken from him. A fucking burglar? What a stupid, offensive shame. It made him restless and furious.

"Ah . . . what are we doing?" Eoin asked cautiously.

"Waiting for the goddamn rain to ease off," Liam retorted.

Eoin flinched and averted his face.

Liam cursed, softly. "Sorry," he said. "I'm just . . . it pisses me off. About Mrs. D'Onofrio. It's not your fault."

"It's okay." Eoin's voice was long-suffering. "Don't worry about it."

Liam felt Nancy D'Onofrio's business card in his pocket and pulled it out. Her name was printed in bold, curvy letters that stood out sharply from the creamy paper. Just like the woman. Bold. Curvy.

He stuck the card in his pocket before Eoin could catch him fondling it. Usually he didn't care for women who dressed in black. He found it affected. Nancy didn't look affected. Her tight tailored black dress made her skin look pearly pale and her red-brown hair redder. That tight bun showed off every finely molded detail of her face. Only a woman with amazing bone structure could get away with a look that severe. The secretly sensual governess look. And he wanted to play her horny, unscrupulous lord of the manor. Sign him up for that.

He could have looked at her face for hours, always finding something new to admire. And her cheek looked so fine, so soft.

Not affected. Sharp, elegant, to be reckoned with. A female ninja assassin. The perfectly formed girl who undulated in the opening credits of a Bond movie. A fantasy woman.

Yeah, and paying the crew out of his own pocket for an undetermined interval, that was a fucking fantasy, too.

But he couldn't let a chance to see her again slip away. She was so elusive. So wounded and wary. Going after her would be like catching fish with his hands. Christ, what an idiot he was. He scared himself.

He flung the car door open. "Let's get started," he growled.

Eoin peered up at the rain running down the windshield, started to say something, thought better of it. He sighed and followed him out.

Liam gave himself the grim mental lecture while they unloaded. Pursuing a woman like Nancy D'Onofrio would be a waste of time. He didn't want a citified, high-strung workaholic for a lover. He'd thought long and hard about what he needed in a woman. No, a *wife*. Enough dicking around. He wanted someone in line with his life-style. He didn't need to look further than his own parents to see what happened when you messed with that rule.

His mother's cherished dream had been for a big, noisy family, but his father had been driven by ambition. He'd had no time to spend with Liam, was never there for meals, was always gone for holidays.

Liam's mother had begged, schemed, and nagged for years until she realized that he would never change. She'd made him leave at last, keeping Liam with her. He hadn't seen his father since that day. Not that he'd seen that much of him before. He'd been eleven years old.

His mother eventually did find the kind of man she wanted, but Liam never forgot her disappointment. He'd taken the lesson to heart. When it came time, he knew what to look for. He was a set-tled person. Ambitious, in his own small way, but he liked living in the country, running his business, keeping his own hours. He liked playing seisìun in Irish pubs with his fiddle and flutes, downing a few pints with his friends now and then. Growing his garden, tend-ing his orchard of walnuts and apples. Someday he'd like to buy a couple of horses, when he could afford a bigger piece of land and had kids to ride them. He'd like to build his own house on that land. A big, comfortable, rambling place. Full of kids, noise, color. Life.

He'd thought a lot about the woman who would fit into his per-fect life. She didn't have to be a raving beauty. He wasn't hung up on that. It was more important that she be kind and good-natured. Maternal and craftsy. That she like cooking, canning. Baking her own bread.

But his balls didn't give a damn about his long-term contentment. They wanted what they wanted, and they wanted that slim, spicy ninja girl with those big, mysterious eyes behind her trendy glasses and the ridiculous high-heeled, pointy-toed boots on her tiny feet.

No way did Nancy D'Onofrio know how to make bread. He'd be surprised if she could boil an egg. Her type lived on carrot sticks and sushi. The result was nice, though. He liked how her back was so straight, head high, chin up. He liked the jut of her shoulder blades, the smart way her short jacket fit. The delicate shape of her upper lip, the lush swell of the lower. He wanted to smooth away the anxious crease between her brows. Those shadowy hazel eyes were full of sadness. Secrets.

Problems. Sadness, shadows, secrets, those equal problems. The voice of reason shouted at him from a distance, but he was too lost in his fantasy to listen. She could use more flesh on her bones. He would love to see ten more pounds on her.

Crash. Thud. He'd knocked over flower arrangements with his boot. Bruised white lilies scattered across the floorboards. He laid his boxes on the pile that was forming in the middle of the floor, gathered the flower heads up, and threw them away. The sweet, heavy smell of lilies reminded him of Mom's funeral.

It didn't matter how alluring Nancy D'Onofrio was. By her own mother's admission, she was a compulsive workaholic. Genetically engineered to make him angry and miserable. But his gonads weren't thinking about the lecture. They were too busy thinking about her ass in that tight skirt. The tits were nice, too. Small, but with a personality all their own. Nipples that poked audaciously through the fabric of her dress. No bra. Wow.

Aw, Christ, enough. He was thirty-seven years old, and he still hadn't found his mellow earth mother. He was looking around, in a relaxed sort of way, hoping destiny would kick in. He didn't want to force it, but time was wasting, if he wanted a big family. And he did not have the energy for a casual affair. He hated the flat, dull feeling when one of those scratch-the-itch flings had to end. Too fucking depressing.

The morning passed, in grim, sweaty, wordless silence. Two trips, back and forth to Latham, loading and unloading. It was late after-noon by the time they were through, and when they got back to his place, they were exhausted and ravenous, having skipped lunch.

He put on a kettle to make a pot of tea for himself and Eoin, who boarded in his basement. Eoin got busy cooking some hamburgers, or so it seemed. Charred as they were, it was hard to tell, but the sliced tomatoes, ketchup, cheese, and bread on the table were all clues. Liam lunged for the gas and turned it off. "Making lunch?"

"I made one for you, too, if you fancy it," Eoin said timidly.

"Keep the flame a bit lower," Liam advised.

Eoin's freckled face flushed. "Sorry."

"Speaking of stoves, I found you a secondhand electric range. After we eat, maybe you can help me haul it down into the base-ment."

"Great," Eoin said. "Now I can make myself a cup of tea without bothering you."

Liam grunted. "It was never any bother."

"Thanks anyway," Eoin said earnestly. "For the place, the work, the stove." He laid the shriveled burgers on the table. "Are you going to the seisìun at Malloy's on Saturday night?"

"I might. You keen to go?"

"God, yes," Eoin said. "I've been working on that new tune of yours all week. I want to try it out with the lads."

"Fine, then. Malloy's on Saturday," Liam promised.

Malloy's was a good seisìun, from ten until two Saturday night in an Irish pub in Queens. A motley but talented group of regulars got together every week to mainline Irish tunes. Liam almost always went with his fiddle and flutes, unless he was too worn out from work, but young Eoin was religious in his zeal. And he was damn good on his Uilleann pipes. Liam had never heard anyone better. The kid should go pro.

But people had to work, so the tunes and the Guinness had to wait. Which reminded him that Saturday followed Friday, the day he was starting work on the D'Onofrio house. He would see her to-morrow.

Maybe he would go early and help her. He could lift boxes for her. Wrap dishes in newspapers. Eoin could come later. Excitement swelled at the idea of being alone with her.

"Are you okay? You look a bit off," Eoin said.

Liam swallowed with difficulty. "Nah, just remembering something that I have to do. Ready to haul that stove down?"

"Sure thing," Eoin agreed.

Liam kept himself busy, hooking up the stove in Eoin's lair, washing up the kitchen, sweeping debris out of the bed of the truck. Cleaning rain gutters. Soaping the squeaky bottoms of his underwear drawer.

That was what clued him into the stark truth. He sat there on his bed, the drawer on his lap, his underwear scattered around himself, and contemplated it.

He was so fucked.

Beep. Beep. Beep. John Esposito rolled over on the couch and punched the button to silence the alarm. Yes, fuck you very much, it was five to midnight, and the big guy was about to check in. He'd set the alarm to be sure he was alert. He had to be razor sharp to deal with Haupt.

Truth was, he almost never slept when he was on the job. He didn't miss it, either. Stalkings, interrogations, punishments, executions, they stoked him like petroleum fuel. He loved his work. When the gig was over and the fee was safely tucked into his offshore account, he slept two weeks straight.

He peered out the window, across the street. A glance at the monitors of the vidcams he'd installed the other day while the Countess was gasping her last on her living room floor confirmed that nothing was happening in the empty house. Eight vidcams. Living room, kitchen, bathrooms, basement, and three upstairs bedrooms.

He stood up, stretched out his shoulders. Any second, Haupt would call. John knew very little about the man. Only that he paid well, and that job failure would be very dangerous for John's health. John could live with that. He held himself to high professional standards. That was why he charged the big bucks.

The terms of this job were complicated. Not a cut-and-dried hit.

John preferred to have half up front, but Haupt had only given him a third, plus expenses. The rest of his fee was contingent upon a successful outcome, but the promised sum was so large, he'd decided it was worth it. He hadn't factored in what a pain in the ass Haupt was going to be. It was worse than dealing with his own mother.

His employer had been unimpressed with John for letting the Countess slip away, but was it his fault the old bitch croaked on him before he questioned her? Was that a reflection on his professionalism? In his line of work, he'd never bothered to learn CPR. Wily old hag. He wanted to punish her. Women did not thwart him, ever.

His only consolations were the Countess's three extremely fuckable daughters. He couldn't decide which one he liked the best. They might try to thwart him, too, in the course of this job, if he was lucky.

And if they did, oh, man. He was so very ready for them.

He'd video-streamed a segment of last night's drunken henfest in the kitchen to Haupt, but the humorless had prick been unamused. All that had interested the boss last night had been the jeweled pendants.

The three identical letters that John had taken from the Contessa's house made cryptic references to some necklaces, but had offered no clear explanation. John had studied every piece of jewelry he had taken from Lucia D'Onofrio's bureau, to no avail. None of it relevant to the fucking letter. He'd had the stuff delivered by courier to Haupt, but the old bastard hadn't made any more sense of the jewelry than he had.

It seemed logical that this new delivery of pendants was significant. Goddamn letter, full of cryptic clues designed to annoy the shit out of a straightforward professional. *"Music will open the door."* What the fuck did that mean? *"It's up to you three to decipher the key together,"* the stupid hag had written. *"Consider beauty, faith, and knowledge, and above all, love—the key to all secrets worth knowing."*

Fucking drivel. Beauty, faith, knowledge, and love? Not his field of expertise. He'd faxed the thing to his employer, who had been unable to make anything of it, either. But John hadn't exhausted all possibilities yet. Given incentive, the daughters could probably figure out their batty old mother's letter. And he had all the incentive necessary in the black plastic box under the bed.

Crafty bitch. Fucking with him from the grave. He flexed his knuckles. He wanted to wrap them around her stringy old neck and squeeze. But her daughters' necks were velvety soft, he reminded himself. He could punish Lucia through them and have a juicy old time doing it. He took the cell in hand. His internal stopwatch had warned him that the time had come. Five till midnight—four . . . three . . . two . . . one . . . *Beeep*. Right on cue. John punched "talk." "Yes?"

"What do you have to report?" came the soft, accented voice. "Something more interesting than weeping, bingeing females, I trust?"

John meditated for half a second upon the number of zeros that would be printed on his final bank draft. "Only that there's a carpenter crew coming tomorrow morning to start renovating the place."

"Renovating? Now?" The usually soft, dead-calm voice on the other end of the line rose in pitch to a gratifying squeak. "Did you search again?"

"As requested. I went through the place after the carpenters—"

"What? Carpenters? You mean they have already begun?"

"They unloaded their supplies," John said. "Tomorrow they start."

"Did you get the paperwork on the pendants, at least?"

At least? What was this "at least" shit? As if he'd failed? Asshole.

"Of course," John said, his voice flat. "I found the delivery slip with the jeweler's store address. I also found his home address."

"And?" The German waited.

"Ah . . . and what? It was past business hours, and the guy was probably eating dinner, or fucking his mistress, so I figured I'd wait—"

"Wait? For what? For the carpenter's crew to rip the house apart and find what you are unable to find? What then, John? What then?"

John's mouth worked. The asshole went on before he could reply.

"Assume that the pendants are part of the Contessa's puzzle. The daughters know nothing. The Contessa is dead, thanks to you—"

"I did not kill her!" John protested. "I just started to—"

"The only person who could conceivably know more is the jeweler," the German said. And? So?

John blew a breath out flared nostrils. "All right. Tomorrow I'll—"

"Never put off until tomorrow what you can do today."

"You mean . . . now? But it's past midnight, and I—"

"I know exactly what time it is. Past midnight is an ideal time for an interrogation. It's an ideal time for many things. As you know, John."

John reordered his mind around this new imperative. "You are implying an, ah . . . ultimate solution?"

The man sighed, as if John was being tiresome. "When you were recommended, I was told that I would not have to micromanage."

John ground his teeth. "I will take care of it."

"I do not want that crew in that house until we know more."

A muscle twitched in John's cheek. "I can't stop it without making a mess," he said. "I could arrange an accident for the carpenter . . . ?"

"No. No more bodies unless it is necessary. A break-in, some vandalism. Delay the work. Search again, not that I hold up much hope after your failure so far."

"Yes," John said tightly after a pause.

"Very well, then. Until tomorrow."

The connection broke. John laid the phone down. Back to work.

He dragged his black plastic box out from under the bed. It was full of curiosities that he'd acquired over the years, devices he'd made and adapted himself, even some original antiques. He selected some tried-and-true favorites and loaded his kit bag. The thought of the job ahead, his knives and picks, the jeweler screaming, begging . . . ah. He needed something to kick him up. But first, the bitch Contessa's house.

He selected the lock drill. Even if the contents of the house were inanimate, smashing them would feel good.

It was a precursor of warmer, softer, juicier things to come.

Chapter
3

Nancy took a bracing gulp of her coffee, finished typing the latest edits into Peter's CD liner notes in her laptop, and closed the program. She was already late. Moxie flung herself at Nancy's feet and writhed. She picked the cat up and buried her face in the animal's fur. Her kitty had been feeling neglected, and now Moxie had to spend yet another day alone while Nancy cleaned the stuff out of Lucia's kitchen.

She had not asked her sisters to come help. Not that they could have, today. Nell was working, as always, teaching classes all morning and waitressing all afternoon, and Vivi was working a crafts show upstate. Of course, Nancy herself had a triple workday that she was canceling out to do all this. But the truth was, she preferred to see Liam Knightly alone. Nothing got past Vivi's and Nell's sharp eyes. Nancy didn't want her sisters intercepting any smoldering glances, catching any stray waves of throbbing sexual heat. They would draw their shrewd conclusions, and, God forbid, tease her. Or worse, worry about her.

First order of business, to dress. The jeans and T-shirt she'd thrown on after her shower were perfect for cleaning and packing kitchenware, but they were utterly inadequate for facing Liam Knightly.

Moxie sprawled, purring, on a growing heap of rejects on the futon couch as Nancy yanked item after item out of her closet.

She finally settled on snug black pants and a white cotton blouse, nipped in at the waist, primly buttoned up. Just the last button left open, so that the beautiful sapphire N at her throat showed, a tiny glint of color. Crisp, no-nonsense, yet subtly feminine. She fixed her hair twelve different ways. In a paroxysm of disgust, she fell back on her old standby: slicked back with styling gel into a gleaming braid. She spritzed on hairspray to underscore the no-nonsense message of the tough hair. Some cover-up under her eyes, brown mascara, a dab of sandalwood oil to infuse the look with an air of sensual mystery.

She stared into the mirror wishing she could make the anxious crinkle between her brows disappear. What was she trying to accomplish, anyway? A come-on, or a back-off?

Hell with it. It was 8:20 already, and she was wasting the guy's time with her stupid, crushed-out primping. She perched her glasses on her nose and gave herself a hard smile. Ta-da.

She picked up Moxie and buried her nose in the cat's soft fur again. "Time for me to scram," she whispered. "Sorry. I'll make it up to you."

Her cell phone buzzed. She almost ignored it, late as she was, but ingrained professionalism prevailed. Or maybe obsessive paranoia. It depended on one's point of view. She hit "talk." "Hello?"

"Nancy? This is Liam Knightly."

Moxie fell to the ground with a squawk as Nancy's arm went boneless. "Ah. Um, hi," she stammered. "Are you already at the house?"

"Yes, and I—"

"Oh, God. We must have crossed wires about the meeting time. I'm so sorry. I'm running a little late, because of some—"

"Nancy." He cut her off, his voice grim. "There's a problem."

"A problem?" A weird, creeping, cold began to spread its tendrils out to her belly and her limbs. "What do you mean, a problem?"

"There's been another break-in."

Another break-in? "That's not possible," she whispered.

"I was driving by on my way to breakfast, to see if your car was there," he said. "I wanted to pass a broom through the place before you saw it, since Eoin and I tracked in mud yesterday. I saw the door was open, so I thought maybe you drove a different car up. Then I looked inside."

His eloquent pause chilled her blood. She was starting to shake. "And?"

"It's bad," he said shortly.

She was crumpling. On her knees, her hands holding the floor away from herself like it was trying to rise up and hit her in the face. Her cell lay next to Moxie's bowl of kitty crunchies. Fish-shaped pellets were scattered on the black-and-white tiles. The floor was cold against her hands. Liam Knightly's urgent, tinny voice came through the phone, from where it lay on the floor. She let her hip drop to the floor so that she could support herself on one hand, and picked up the phone.

"Here I am," she gasped out. "Sorry. Dropped the phone."

"Jesus! You scared me! Are you okay?"

"I'm good," she croaked. "Did you, um, call the—"

"The cops? Yeah. They're on their way. You were my second call."

Unreasonable panic seized her, ballooning inside her into something monstrous. She saw Lucia's body lying on the ground, her wide-open eyes, her livid face. "Don't go in! Get away from there," she told him wildly. "Right now! What if whoever did it is still inside?"

"I'll be okay," he soothed. "I won't go in. I'll leave that for the cops."

"It's just a goddamn house." The words made no sense, she realized, as they flew out of her mouth, and oh shit, her face had dissolved again. "It's just a goddamn house. That's all. That's all!"

"Yes. That's true," he said. "Hey, Nancy? Answer me!"

She tried, but her throat was vibrating too much. She made a wordless sound, just so he would know she was still conscious.

"Nancy, give me one of your sisters' phone numbers, okay? You shouldn't be alone. I'll call one of them for you. Give me the number."

He thought she was going batshit on him. Embarrassment stiffened her spine. "No. They're busy. I'll be out there as soon as I can."

"No!" He sounded appalled. "You're upset! You should not drive!"

"I will be *fine*. I'll see you in an hour and ten, barring traffic."

"Hey! Wait! Nancy—"

She hung up on him and lurched over to the kitchen counter. The little espresso pot had a mouthful of powerful coffee in the bottom. She poured it into a cup, cold though it was, and dosed it with sugar.

Her cell began to tinkle. She checked. It was him. No freaking way was she answering now. Ten rings. A pause. Ten more. Take that, buddy. Then, the chime of a text message. She opened it. It said,

At least take a goddamn taxi pls

She snorted. Like she had a hundred and twenty bucks to burn. She tossed on her jacket, legs wobbling. This news had taken all the starch out of her, but it gave her a feeling of unfurling warmth in her chest that he worried about her. She cherished the feeling.

Silly though it was. Bossy though he'd been. Sweet of him.

She spent the drive up to Hempton trying to figure out why she'd flipped out like that. It was just a deserted house. A break-in was upsetting, expensive, a rotten inconvenience—and that was it.

Lucia was no longer in that house. The very worst that could possibly happen had already happened.

So why did she still feel so scared?

Liam lurked in his truck and watched cops and forensics techs trooping in and out of the D'Onofrio house. Finding the house trashed had been a shock. Weird, for lightning to strike the same place twice, just a week after Lucia's death. He felt strange, queasy, like he was missing something important. Something that kept flitting out of sight before he could focus on it.

Maybe that was a result of not having slept. Around two-thirty a.m. he'd given up and headed to his furniture workshop. The detailed work of joining without glue or nails was one of his favorite activities. It put him in a mellow, focused place that he liked. The next best thing to sleep. Currently, he was working on a dining room table big enough to feed a dynasty. Sometimes he fantasized, in a vague, hopeful way, about his future wife while he worked on it, imagined how it would feel to see his wife and children gathered around it.

The fantasy usually gave him a connected feeling. Hope for the future. He'd figured that working on that table would be just the thing to chill him out. Hook him back into reality. His real, bedrock values.

He'd bombed out, big-time. He hadn't been able to picture his future wife. She was a fog of bland possibilities, whereas Nancy D'Onofrio stood out, brilliantly sharp and clear. Every vivid detail of her, burned onto his retina. Those soft, cool fingers. At a certain point, his unruly mind had gone wild with erotic fantasies involving Nancy and the dining room table. Her, perched on the edge, graceful legs spread wide. Him, on his knees, with his face in her muff and his tongue as deep inside her as it would reach, licking up her lube. Her hands wound into his hair. Writhing and whimpering.

He was still twitching from the aftereffects. Whew. Working on that dining room table was never going to be the same again.

He'd gotten out of the house before Eoin was up. The first thing he'd done was to drive by the D'Onofrio house. And the bitch of it was, she wasn't even in the damn house. Oh, no, it was enough for him that she'd been in it the day before. That she'd be in it again today.

Jesus. How sick was that. How stupid.

Well, he'd paid for his sophomoric bullshit. He got to be the dumb-ass who bore the bad tidings. That was what happened when a guy started nosing around in a woman's messy, complicated life.

Even so, he was quietly glad it had fallen out this way. Better him than her. If she'd been that upset to hear about it on the phone, it would have scared her out of her wits to see the condition of that house in person and alone, with no warning. And no wonder, for the love of God. After finding her mother there dead, just a week before.

Nancy's small, battered black Volkswagen Jetta pulled in behind his truck. His heart rate kicked way up. She'd driven. Stubborn female.

She didn't spare him so much as a glance when she got out. The wind fluttered her white blouse, but did not budge a wisp of her smooth hair. Her body was so graceful. Her profile stark and pure as she stared at the house. Her face was terribly pale. She looked like she might faint.

He got out of his truck and folded his arms over the heavy thud in his rib cage, as if she might hear it. As if the woman didn't have more serious things to worry about than his horn-dog crush. She turned at the sound of the car door. Her chin went right up.

He went for it. "So you drove."

"Of course," was her cool retort. "I can't afford a cab."

He let his silence criticize that decision, and a flush of anger bloomed on her cheeks. "Did you call your sisters?" he demanded.

"Not that it's any of your business, but no. Not yet. Nell's teaching and doesn't have a cell anyway, and Vivi's upstate doing a crafts fair. I'll tell them about it later, when I know exactly what happened."

He grunted. "Hmph. Just wondering why it always seems to be you who has to take care of the messy details."

"It's not their fault!" she snapped. "They're perfectly willing to help! They're just busy! And you had my number, not theirs."

Her head was high, her eyes snapping. Excellent. She looked much better. Nothing like putting a man in his place to perk a woman up.

"Uh, yeah. Of course," he murmured, suitably subdued.

She trotted up the stairs with a spring in her step that she hadn't had before. He caught up with her, looked at the marks under her eyes that the makeup did not hide. He wanted to take her hand, offer her his arm. But her hands were clenched, knuckles white. Bracing herself.

He followed her in. She looked around. The place had been brutally trashed. Every piece of furniture had been upended, every sofa cushion and pillow slashed, every breakable thing crushed. The tiles he and Eoin had hauled in were everywhere. Lengths of lumber were scattered around like huge matchsticks. There were jagged holes in the walls. Every picture had been flung down and lay shattered on the floor. A photograph of Lucia and her three daughters smiled up from the floor, covered with shards of glass.

Nancy bent down and reached for the pieces. Her hand shook.

"Please don't touch anything yet, ma'am," said the evidence tech working the scene, a middle-aged woman. "It might be better if you waited outside. Until we've finished."

"Oh. Um, let me just take a look," Nancy said. "I'll be quick." She took a step farther into the room and let out a low cry of distress when she saw what lay at her feet. It was impossible to identify, a formless tangle of wire and chunks of broken glass and stone.

"Oh, no," Nancy whispered. Her voice shook. "This is . . . this is a sculpture that Vivi did for Lucia, years ago. 'The Three Sisters,' she called it. It was one of Lucia's prize possessions." Then she turned and saw the *intaglio* writing table. Her hand flew up over her mouth. "Oh, my God."

The plastic cover she'd bought had been tossed aside, and the plane of the table itself smashed in. The two pieces lay collapsed in upon themselves, splintered edges ragged. The four-by-four that had been used to break it lay in the midst of the broken pieces. The jade plant was in pieces on the floor, dirt and leaves scattered everywhere.

Better judgment, common sense clamored at him, but he ignored them. He reached out and took her hand.

Nancy's fingers curled gratefully around his. A rush of sustaining energy flooded into her body through his hand. He was so solid. An oak that would never bend or break. The romantic metaphor almost made her smile. It was lifted right out of the haunting ballad that Enid had just cut for the album, a song Nancy had finished helping mix in the studio only a few days ago. Of course, the oak in that particular folk song did break. The girl was left barefoot in the snow with an illegitimate baby in her arms. Just a little something to think about.

She stared down at the ruined table, thinking about the vast sweep of history that it had seen. Lucia's family line and this historic table had both come to an abrupt, violent end, here in this room, within a week of each other.

As if the table could not exist without Lucia.

One thought kept coming back, circling around and around in her mind. She opened her mouth, and voiced it. "He wasn't satisfied the first time. He's still angry."

Liam slanted her a cautious glance. "You think it's the same person? From what the cop said, it's a very different kind of crime."

She shook her head. Anything she said was going to sound like grief-stricken rambling. She pressed her hand hard against her mouth as she stared at the ruined table, painstakingly crafted by some nameless artisan hundreds of years ago—smashed by a brain-dead hoodlum.

It felt as if someone had defaced Lucia's grave. Ugly and vicious and very personal. She shuddered.

Liam's hand tightened. "Want to go outside? Get some air?"

She snapped herself to attention. Shook her head.

"I am so sorry," he said. "It really was a beautiful thing."

She nodded, swallowing hard. "Yes, exactly. A thing. On the one hand, it's a precious heirloom. On the other, it's just a thing. Made out of old, carved oak wood. That's all. I don't know how to feel about it."

"You don't have to choose. Both things can be true at once."

She was startled and moved by the comprehension in his eyes. She looked away quickly, but discovered that there was noplace to rest her eyes in that room that did not hurt to look upon.

"I, uh . . ." He stopped himself, looking doubtful.

"What?" she demanded.

"I could try to repair it," he said slowly. "I've done a lot of furniture restoration. My mother was into antiques. I wouldn't expect payment for the labor. I'd consider it a privilege to work on that thing. But even so, you might be better off contacting a specialist."

She stared at him for a moment. "I accept," she said.

"Not so fast," he warned. "I couldn't make guarantees. It'll never be the same as before. There's a lot of damage, and it would take a while. With something like this, I'd go one splinter at a time. You'd better talk it over with your sisters and see if you—"

"Yes," she said, with flat finality. "I want you to do it."

He studied her face. "Well, whatever, then. I won't hold you to it, though. Not until you talk to your sisters."

"I'll hold *you* to it." She glared, daring him to rescind his offer.

"Uh, okay," he murmured. "Whatever."

She was clutching his fingers with all her strength. Heat flooded into her face. She whipped her hand away. "Sorry." She headed toward the kitchen. His light footfalls came after, crunching broken glass.

The kitchen was just as bad. Cupboard doors had been torn off their hinges, the cupboards' contents hurled to the floor with a violence that had shattered the floor tiles. The table was upended, the chairs were tossed, every dish was smashed. The garbage they'd forgotten had been dragged out from under the sink, the plastic bag slashed open, its contents spread wide.

"Well. Guess I won't have to go looking for any packing boxes," Nancy said, her voice thin. It was such a silly thing to say. She clapped her hand over her mouth, stared down at the floor.

That was when she saw it. A crumpled piece of white bond paper, and something written on it, in Lucia's elegant, slanted antique handwriting. She snatched it up, heart thudding. Some helpful soul had swept up the garbage for her, and thrown away this as well.

"Nancy, hey. You're not supposed to—"

"Yes, I know." She shook coffee grounds off the paper. The page was covered with scribbled handwriting, marked up with small edits, some words crossed out, others scribbled in:

will come as a shock to you girls, and no doubt you think me Machiavellian and foolish for creating this elaborate system of checks and balances, but after what happened to my father, after what this thing did to my marriage, I feel I cannot be too careful. Just please know this: I made these arrangements not because I do not trust you, but because I love you, and because you love each other. Love, like any precious thing, should be protected by every means possible. The older I get, the more I understand that it is the only thing worth protecting.

Then a couple of lines, both of which had been savagely crossed out, as if Lucia had been frustrated, searching for the right words:

The necklaces are the key to

You must use the necklaces together to discover the secret of

The writing continued with a new paragraph:

You are each in your own unique way great lovers of beauty—music, literature, and the visual arts, and so I devised the

And the page ended. She could hear Lucia's soft, accented voice echoing in her head.

"What is that?" Liam picked his way across the rubble.

"It's a letter." Her voice cracked, broke. "To us. From Lucia."

She held it up for him. He scanned it rapidly and met her gaze, his mouth grim. "Wow," he said. "That's very weird."

"A draft," she whispered. "It's a first draft of a letter to us."

"Right." He paused, thoughtfully. "But if this is the draft . . ."

"Then where the hell is the finished version?" she finished.

They stared at each other. She wanted to grab his arm, for balance. The ground beneath her was just a thin crust of apparent normality, and beneath it, an abyss of dark, shifting possibilities.

"Why didn't we find the finished letter?" she demanded. "Why?"

He pondered it. "Could she have mailed it to you?"

"Eight days have gone by. It takes two, four at most, for a letter to get to the city. It was an important letter. She was putting a lot of thought into it. This did not get forgotten, or lost in the mail. No way."

He finished the thought. "You think it got lost in some more sinister way."

"'After what this thing did to my marriage'?" she quoted softly. "What thing? What the hell is this thing that she's talking about?"

"Maybe it's what she installed the safe for," he suggested.

She glanced up at him, startled. "Safe?"

His eyes widened. "She didn't tell you?" Nancy's blank face answered his question. He whistled silently. "A few weeks ago, she hired me to install a hidden safe. In her closet upstairs. That's how we met. Sorry I didn't say something before. I assumed you knew."

The woman from the forensics team came into the kitchen and frowned at her. "Miss, I asked you please not to touch anything."

"I found something." Nancy held out the letter. "The investigating officer needs to see it. Please, be on the lookout for more pages."

The lady twitched the sheet of paper out of Nancy's fingers with her own gloved ones. "I'll bring it to her attention. Since you can't keep your hands to yourself, could you wait outside until we're finished?"

The lady sternly escorted the two of them out onto the stoop, and they looked at each other, feeling abashed as naughty children.

"I want to look at that safe," Nancy said fretfully. "Not that I could open it. I don't have the combination. I don't imagine you . . . ?"

He shook his head. "Lucia had to choose the combination herself."

Nancy chewed her lip. "I wish I had a copy of that letter. God knows when they'll let me see it. I wanted to show it to Nell and Vivi."

"One second." Liam went to his truck and pulled a paper from his dashboard. He plucked a pencil from his shirt and scribbled against the hood of his truck. He handed it to her. It was the text of Lucia's letter, written out in a bold, angular cursive script.

"It's maybe not word for word, but that's the gist of it," he said.

"That's incredible! Do you have a photographic memory?"

"Not really. In an hour, I wouldn't be able to write more than a rough paraphrase. And it has to really interest me. Otherwise I don't retain a damn thing."

Nancy broke eye contact and busied herself folding the paper into a pocket-sized square. "Well, thanks for being so interested, I guess."

"Anything to do with Lucia and you interests me. Don't thank me for something involuntary."

"Involuntary?" She let out a self-conscious snort. "Like sneezing?"

"More like breathing."

His low, quiet response abruptly halted that very bodily function to which he was referring. She shoved the square into her pocket.

"Um, great. Thanks. Since they're not going to let me in, I might as well—"

"The investigating officer's going to want to talk with you," Liam said. "I told her you were on your way. She should be back soon. You haven't had breakfast, have you?"

She floundered, thrown off course. "I . . . um . . . huh?"

"Breakfast?" His subtle smile gleamed. "First meal of the day? Familiar with it?"

"Ah, I've . . . I've had coffee," she offered.

"You've got me beat, then," he said. "There's a diner up there on the main strip. We could get some food before you talk to the cop."

She started groping for excuses. *Calm down, birdbrain. At mealtimes, normal people get food without reading any big, hidden meanings into it. Lighten up.* Her stomach wasn't in line with the lecture, though.

"Lunch would be great," she said faintly.

Chapter
4

Nancy regretted her decision when she was seated across from Liam in the pink, madly mirrored interior of Luigi's Diner. She wished she'd left her hair loose, worn contacts instead of glasses. Something low cut. Not that she had any cleavage to speak of.

He just waited, sipping his tea, and after a couple of minutes of that, her control snapped. "What is it?" she demanded. "What the hell are you waiting for? What are you looking at?"

He discreetly looked away. "I was looking at you. You look . . ."

"What?" she snapped. "Unapproachable? Unfeminine?"

His mouth twitched. "No, not at all."

"What, then?" she almost shouted.

"You look good, Nancy." His voice was velvety, soothing.

Nancy wrapped her arms across her chest. "Sorry. Those long, significant silences of yours are making me twitchy. I appreciate you being nice, but tell me the truth. I look like hell, don't I?"

His eyes narrowed. "You look stressed and scared. But that doesn't keep you from looking good. I'm sorry about the long, significant silences. They're hardwired into me. I'm not much of a chatterbox."

"That's okay." She stared down into her coffee and fished Liam's copy of Lucia's letter out of her pocket. "I am scared. I'm scared that things didn't happen the way the cops said they did. She wrote this letter, but we didn't find it. And your classic butthead burglar looking to trade a TV or a diamond for a hit of crack or meth—that guy is not going to take this letter. That guy does not give a shit about this letter."

Liam nodded. "No. You're right. He doesn't."

His quiet agreement rattled her even more. She realized she'd been hoping that he would talk her down from this terrifying line of reasoning. "So who did take it? And what the hell is this 'thing' she's referring to, and what's the deal with these pendants? And if she had this great big hairy family secret, why did she not tell us before?"

Liam cleared his throat. "Maybe she was—"

"And what did it do to her father? And who the hell knew she was ever married? I mean, married? What kind of mom just sort of forgets to mention that little detail to her daughters, even if they are adopted?"

Liam waited patiently. People were starting to peek. She was making a scene. She hunched down over her coffee cup. "I'm sorry," she said. "Flipping out on you in public. The breakfast date from hell."

"You're a great breakfast date," Liam said. "We're talking constant entertainment. I'm in no danger of boredom when I hang out with you. It's just one humdinger after another. I can't wait for the car chase."

She exploded in shaky, snorting giggles that splattered coffee over the table, and to her horror, over her blouse as well. But when she peeked up from sponging her collar, he looked pleased with himself.

"You know what freaks me out the most?" She tried to keep her voice down. "It's the responsibility. I have nothing to help the cops. Just hints about a secret, and some mysterious, sinister 'thing' that I've never heard of. I don't know what or where it is, just that somebody appears to want it. And that somebody might have . . . might have killed my mother."

There it was. She let out a long, shaky breath. She'd said the unsayable, and Liam just accepted her words calmly, without reacting to them or negating them. She hid her face with hands that shook. "If somebody hurt Lucia, I have to do something about it. I can't just lie down, let it go. But what? And to whom?"

He was quiet for a long time before he spoke again. "What's with the necklaces?" he asked. "Do you know what she's referring to?"

Nancy held up the pendant that glittered at her throat. "I assume she's referring to these. They came the day before yesterday. Special hand delivery from the jeweler's shop. Evidently she'd commissioned them for us before she . . . before it happened. Mine's an *N*, for Nancy. Nell has an *A*, for Antonella, and Vivi has a *V*, of course."

He leaned forward, peering at the pendant, and she unclasped it and handed it to him. He examined it from every angle and passed it back to her. "Very pretty," he commented.

"Thank you," she said, reclasping it. "That's what I thought. It's just pretty. No mysterious keys that I can see. And it was probably expensive, but not outrageously so. Several hundred dollars, maybe."

He drummed his fingers thoughtfully on the table. "It might be worth a try to talk to the jeweler," he said.

She nodded. "Yes. I most certainly will. Today."

"I'll take you," he said.

"Oh, no, don't worry about it," she said quickly. "I have my car, and you must have all kinds of things to do, so—"

"Nope. Nothing. I was going to work on Lucia's house today. I can't, so I'm just kicking my heels. And I wouldn't miss it. So really. Don't fight me on this. Trust me. You'll lose."

Whew. There it was, a naked challenge. Right out there in the open. She blinked as she looked at his set jaw, his narrowed eyes. Ahem. There he was, Mr. Alpha Dog. Woof. This was the part in the script where she crisply gave him to understand that he was not the boss here, and that he was not dealing with a fluttery pushover, and that her decisions were entirely her own, thank you very much. Buh-bye.

The words just didn't come out. A strangled silence took their place. Having company today would be so very nice. Having big, tough, hard-muscled, keen-eyed protective company would be even better.

So. Maybe . . . just maybe she would let him have this one. A chunk of meat for a hungry wolf. Just this once, mind. Never again.

"Um. Let's . . . let's talk about something else," she said.

He lifted his teacup, eyes smiling at her over the rim. Pleased with himself. "Whatever you like," he said magnanimously. "Be my guest."

His expression made her squirm on the plastic cushion.

"So what do we talk about, then?" she demanded.

His lips twitched. "Anything you like. You were the one who wanted to change the subject. I was fine with the subject."

"Don't start with me," she warned.

"I'm not," he said. "Try to relax." He reached out, pausing as she flinched, and touched her forehead with the tip of his finger, massaging the anxious crease between her brows as if trying to erase it.

"Oh, that. That's always there. That's just part of my face," she said with a shaky laugh. His boldness made her feel . . . naked.

Weird. She hadn't known there was a good side to that feeling.

"So, Liam," she said briskly. "Tell me about yourself. Lucia told you all about me, and that puts me at a disadvantage."

His smile vanished. She felt a flash of regret for killing the moment. She hardened herself. She had to be tough, and careful.

"What do you want to know?" he asked.

"Whatever is relevant. You're not married, engaged, or seriously involved. Lucia wouldn't have thrown me at your head if you were."

"True enough," he agreed.

"So what's wrong with you?" she demanded.

"What do you mean?" He looked mildly curious, not annoyed.

Nancy shrugged. "You'd think a guy like you would've been taken by now. You must be, what, thirty-seven? Thirty-eight?"

"Thirty-seven," he said.

"Thirty-seven," she repeated, in a wondering tone. "How have you escaped the noose for so long?"

"I don't see it as a noose. But I haven't met the ideal woman yet."

Her cell phone rang as the waitress arrived with their food. The manager of the venue in Indianapolis where Peter was performing in three weeks, calling to postpone the date. Nancy made a note and promised to get back to him as soon as she had checked the artist's availability. She hung up and gave Liam a thin smile. "So, back to this ideal woman of yours. What's she like?"

"You really want to know?"

"Hell, yes," she assured him. "I'm fascinated. I'm all agog."

Liam swallowed a mouthful of omelet and washed it down with tea. "Okay," he said. "My ideal woman is a great cook. She likes to bake bread. She wants lots of children. Would consider being a stay-at-home mom. She's relaxed. Likes flowers. Loves to hike and garden."

Nancy's heart sank. *Cut it out, loser.* She had no designs on the guy, so why should it matter if she was the opposite of his ideal woman? She couldn't tell a pumpkin from a hollyhock. Lots of children? What a concept. Although she hadn't completely given up hopes of maybe at least one, someday. And cooking? Bread? Hah.

Liam went relentlessly on. "She puts home and family first. She's content with simplicity. She's sincere, and genuine."

Nancy tried for a breezy tone. "I get her vibe. Earth mother. Dips her own candles. Makes her own soap. Carves her own toothpicks."

His lips twitched. "Uh, that's the general idea, I guess."

She forced out a brittle laugh. "Well, good luck. I didn't know they were even still making that brand of female. I bet you'd have more luck shopping for used and vintage models." Her cell rang again. A presenter of a concert series in Portland, Oregon, wanted Mandrake's promo packet. She took down his data in her organizer.

"You know, that thing has an off button," Liam informed her.

Nancy gazed at him blankly. "What's your point?"

He sighed. "Never mind. You haven't touched your sandwich."

Nancy looked down at her turkey club. "I'm not really hungry."

Liam examined her face with a frown. "Try to calm down a little," he said. "See if you can get down at least half of your sandwich."

"I don't want to argue about my sandwich. I want to know more about this ideal—"

"You're not going to find out a damn thing worth knowing if you come at me with that attitude."

She set down her coffee, taken aback. "I didn't mean to offend you."

"I'm not offended. I'm pissed off. There's a difference."

She stared down into the puddle of coffee while Liam finished his omelet with undiminished appetite. Finally, she looked up. "I'm not sure what just happened," she said. "But I have a feeling it was my fault."

"All I know is, one minute I was talking to you, the next minute I had an uptight, bitchy stranger in my face, wearing a Nancy mask."

"Sorry." She blinked back a startling rush of tears.

"Don't be," he said. "Come on, Nancy. Indulge me. Eat some of your sandwich. Please."

Oh, for God's sake. What did she have to lose by obliging him, anyhow? She picked it up and took a bite. His dimples flashed.

They talked, carefully and politely, about neutral subjects. She managed to eat almost three quarters of her sandwich, which made him happy. When the bill came, he snatched it from her hand and looked personally offended when she tried to pay. Wow. She'd never met one of those guys before, although she'd heard that they existed in the wild.

After they left the diner, Liam opened the truck door for her, climbed in, and started the engine. "So where's the jeweler?"

The paperwork was buried in the rubble at Lucia's house, but the name, Baruchin's Fine Jewelers, was burned into her mind. A consult to her BlackBerry located it as a couple of towns away. The time it took to drive there was spent in conversation that was calculated to keep her calm. It wasn't working. She got more distracted as they drew nearer.

They pulled up in front of the storefront. The metal sliding doors were down. Closed, on Saturday at noon. Prime shopping hours. Everything around was open and bustling. Odd.

Nancy's neck prickled unpleasantly as she got out of the truck. There was a small restaurant, Tony's Diner, next door. Nancy headed in and slid onto a stool at the counter. Liam joined her.

A middle-aged lady sporting a high red bouffant came over with a coffeepot. Nancy smiled and held out her cup. "Yes, please. I have a question. I need to speak to the jeweler next door about a delivery. I was wondering how long they've been closed. Is he on vacation?"

A splash of hot coffee slopped out of the pot and onto Nancy's thumb. She jerked back with a gasp. The bouffant lady's face crumpled. She set her coffee down, covered her face, and fled into the kitchen.

Nancy glanced at Liam. He was frowning. She sucked on her scalded thumb. "That's not a good sign," she said.

"Sure isn't," he agreed.

After a minute, a bent, scowling elderly man with bushy white eyebrows, wearing a paper cook's cap, came out of the kitchen, wiping his hands on his apron. He scanned the counter and headed straight for them. "You folks was askin' Donna about Sol Baruchin?"

Nancy nodded. "I don't actually know Mr. Baruchin personally," she said, a little nervously. "I needed to ask a professional question—"

"Old Sol's dead," the old man said heavily. "He got murdered."

The cold, weighty silence seemed to grip the whole room. Everyone was frozen, listening. Not a spoon clinked.

"M-m-murdered?" Nancy echoed, in a tiny, shaking whisper.

"When?" Liam asked.

"Last night, sometime. Him and his wife and his mother-in-law, all three. Christ, the mother-in-law was bedridden. Musta been ninety, ninety-five years old. Goddamn animals. I got this cop buddy, comes here for breakfast. He tipped me off about it. Frickin' horrible mess."

Nancy covered her mouth with her hands and tried to process this information. It wouldn't seem to go in. Everything was blocked.

"Sol's been having breakfast and lunch in this joint every day for the last thirty-five years," the old man said dully. "Donna's all broke up. Christ, it's hard enough at my age, with friends dropping like flies from heart attacks and strokes, without some sick bastard murdering 'em. So, anyhows." He shook his head, his wrinkled mouth compressed into a grim, bluish line. "Sol's shop ain't gonna be open anytime soon, miss."

She tried to answer him politely. Nothing came out.

Liam smoothly filled the gap for her. "Thanks for the information," he said. "I'm sorry for the loss of your friend."

"Yeah. Yeah, thanks." The old man turned and shuffled back toward the kitchen, his shoulders bowed.

Nancy lurched out into the street, desperate for a gulp of air, but it was even worse out there, with the murdered Baruchin's shuttered shop staring at her morosely from behind heavy, gray, metallic eyelids. The effect was chilling. "Let's get away from here," she gasped.

"Where to?" Liam unlocked her door, hoisted her in.

"Anywhere," she said.

Liam took her at her word. He was rattled himself by old Tony's bombshell, and as soon as he pulled out onto the street, he was on autopilot, his mind racing. He was actually surprised when he found himself pulling up under the big maple that shaded his own driveway. Whoa. This was going to be tricky, in her present mood.

Nancy looked around herself, as if waking up from an unpleasant dream. "Where are we?"

"My house," he said.

Her gaze cut nervously away from his. "Oh. I didn't even see where we were going." She twisted her hands and stared at the water that trickled down the windshield. "That poor guy," she whispered. "And his wife, and her mother, too. God. How awful." She looked back at him, her eyes haunted. "It's not a coincidence."

He hesitated for a long moment, unwilling to freak her out further, but honesty prevailed. "No. What happened to Lucia was bad enough. And after the break-in, the necklaces, the letter, and now the jeweler killed, I don't know. I'm no expert. But it doesn't smell good."

They sat there in the rainy gloom, watching the drops of water coursing down the windshield, the waving green foliage surrounding them. He reached out for her hand. It was as cold as ice. He chafed it.

"Come in," he urged her. "Let me make you a cup of tea."

She stared down at her hand, clasped in his, but did not pull it away. "I'm the opposite of your ideal woman," she blurted.

His jaw clenched. "I know," he said.

"So, um, where does that leave us?" she asked quietly.

He looked up at the dripping trees, the heavy clouds. "At the moment, it leaves us parked outside, in a truck, in the rain."

Her face turned deep, warm pink. "You want me to come in?"

"Only if you want to," he said. Hah. He lied. He wanted her to come in more than he wanted his next lungful of oxygen.

"I hardly know you," she whispered.

"We can fix that," he suggested. "Come in for a cup of tea. Tell me about yourself."

"That's very nice of you. But it's not a good idea to have a first date in one's own private space," she said primly.

He started to grin. "Is that what it would be? A first date? Doesn't breakfast count?"

She looked flustered. "I don't know. Second date, then. What would you call it?"

He drummed his fingers on the wheel. "I'd call it a cup of tea."

Nancy wrapped her arms around herself. "I don't think breakfast counts. It wasn't premeditated. And a first date—that is, um, any first encounter—should take place on a mutually agreed-upon neutral ground," she told him. "A public place, like a bar, or a restaurant. And just a drink, not dinner. Just to see how it goes."

"Oh. Is that how it's done?" He pressed a kiss against her fingers. "Tea's a drink, right? And I really think breakfast counts as a date."

"No," she said, sounding slightly breathless. "No way. We're nowhere yet. Breakfast doesn't count. Intention is everything."

"Now that is the God's own truth." He reached out and stroked her cheek. It was as soft as he had imagined.

She made a low, inarticulate sound. He was dazed by the warmth of her, the downy softness. The delicate details.

He leaned forward, in tiny increments, until their faces nearly touched, and commenced a slow, careful dance of advance, retreat. Feeling her breath against his cheek, stroking her jaw. Tracing that elegant jut of delicately sculpted cheekbone beneath her smooth skin.

He waited, sensing her caution and her longing. Waiting patiently until the two found their perfect balancing point, and . . . ah.

Her eyes shut as he tasted her lips. So lightly. So carefully.

He gasped at the contact. Oh, Jesus, she tasted like light. Incredible, electrifying. Her lips, so soft and shy beneath his.

He explored her face with his fingertips, stroking her jaw, her pale throat. She dragged in a sharp breath as he slid his hand down her back, settling on the curve of her hip. Her nipples poked against her blouse. His fingers ached to caress them. He touched the first button, tugged it. It came loose, revealing the hollow of her throat, a warm cloud of some exotic, woodsy scent. He wanted to gulp it in. Lick it up.

He pulled her closer, kissed her jaw, then her throat. His lips brushed the warm gold of the little pendant Lucia had given her. His hand brushed down over her breast, just close enough that the nipple barely brushed his palm. The little nub was hard, tight.

His arm tightened. He felt it, the second that it happened. A door, slamming down between them in her mind. One moment she was melting in his arms, fingernails digging into his shirt. Out of nowhere, tension gripped her, and she arched away, stiff and brittle as a stick of balsa wood. He was so in tune with her, he actually felt alarm jangling through her, like warning bells clanging. As if the fear were his own.

He forced himself to let go. It was as hard as bending metal.

He eased back, hands clenched. Giving her the space she needed. He was doing it again. Pushing her. It was a piss-poor time for this. She was a complicated woman, grief stricken, stressed out, and he was a jerk-off for forcing the issue. Out of his fucking head. He struggled not to pant. Fists clenched. Slow breathing. *Don't even look at her. Don't.*

He looked away. Minutes ticked by, measured by drops of water making their meandering way down the window of the truck, by ragged, labored breaths that he struggled to keep silent.

At length, he heard her rustling, the soft sounds of fabric shushing together. Buttoning her blouse, getting herself in order. A cough. Clearing her throat. "Ah . . . um, Liam? That was, ah—"

"Amazing." He stared fixedly at the lean-to, the pattern of the carefully stacked wood for his fireplace. "But you choked."

She looked at her lap. "I'm sorry. I didn't mean to lead you on. Look, I need to get back. I need to talk to the cops about that letter, and the jeweler, and clue my sisters in, and you've been really great, and I appreciate the company, but I . . . but I'm, ah—"

"Scared," he said.

She sighed. "Not of you." Her voice was muted. "You're a really good guy. I know that. It's just . . . well, everything."

"Yeah?" Anger twisted in him, hard to wrestle down. "Everything's not here in the cab of this truck, Nancy. It's just me in here with you."

She looked at him with big, beseeching eyes. He stared back, unrelenting. "It's just a cup of tea. It's not the end of the world."

She made a sniffing sound. "Right. You know exactly what would happen if I went into your house, Liam."

"Do I? Yes, actually," he said reflectively. "I can see it. I'd pull up a chair for you. Put the kettle on the stove. Rummage around in the pantry for that tin of ginger butter crisps. Ask if you take milk or lemon. Ask leading questions about your childhood. Say nice things about your eyes, your hair, your earrings. Try my best to be witty and charming."

"Really?" A smile flickered on her face. "Is that what you'd do?"

He nodded, willing it to be true.

"It sounds nice," she said demurely. "But I . . . oh, never mind."

Yeah, she didn't have to say it. He saw that alternative scenario, too. The one where he ripped the clothes off that slim, lusciously curved body, pinned her up against the wall and nailed her, deep and hard, until they both exploded. His heart thudded. His ears roared.

Cool it, bonehead. The moment was so fragile, so uncertain. She was intensely sensitive to his every word, his every goddamn thought.

He caught her eye flicking to his lap and darting nervously away. Yeah, the boner of the century, trying to rip the seams of his jeans loose. Aching with each heavy thud of his heart for the soft touch of that cool hand. Heat burned into his cheekbones. He gave her a shrug that said, *yeah, and so?* He couldn't control his physiological responses, but he could, by God, control his behavior. He wanted her to know that, but there was no good way to say it. Better to keep his mouth shut.

"I just need for things to be . . . under control," she whispered. "I have enough to be scared of right now, without piling it on, you know?"

He rubbed his hand against his face, feeling around instinctively with his senses for a way through this labyrinth. He did not want to turn around and go back. No. He could not. That wasn't even an option.

He flung the door of the truck open. The rain on the earth had released a deep, sweet, spicy perfume, and drops pattered heavily down onto him. He circled the truck, and stood outside the passenger-side door, staring at Nancy's huge eyes through the rain-spotted glass. He mimed rolling down the window. She did so, frowning in perplexity.

"What the hell are you doing out there in the rain?"

"Continuing our conversation. You need control. Control it, then. The car door's the limit. I won't violate it. I swear upon my sacred honor that I will not touch any part of you that's inside that door."

She looked away, embarrassed. "Oh, God, Liam. You don't have to play elaborate games like that with me. You're getting soaked."

Like he gave a shit. "That's my problem, not yours," he said.

"But it makes me feel guilty!" she protested.

Ah. Yes. This was progress. "The guilt is your problem," he informed her. "I can't help you with that. Sorry."

She laughed at him. Something primitive inside him capered with glee. *Yes.* It was working. She was lightening up. Praise God.

"So?" Her eyes sparkled. "You're just going to stand out there and get drenched, then? That's silly."

"It's a crafty attempt to disarm you with my gallantry," he told her. "Is it working? Are you charmed?"

She wrinkled her nose at him, leaned out the window a little. "I think you're out of your mind."

His grin stretched all the way around his head. "You're charmed," he said. "And you're outside the limit. Any part of you outside the plane of the window is fair game, remember? The tip of your nose and your forehead are at serious risk. This is by way of a courtesy warning."

"Very gentlemanly of you," she said demurely.

"I'm trying like hell," he said, with stark sincerity.

And she didn't pull back. In fact, she leaned a tiny bit farther out. And her fingers were curled over the side of the door.

He jerked his chin toward her hands. "Outside the limit."

Her lips formed words that didn't quite make it out of her mouth, so she swallowed, and tried again. "I . . . I know."

His heart started to thud again. The rain was increasing, its soft, patter beading his face, and hers, as well.

Over the limit. Fair game. She'd been warned. She knew.

He reached out, as slowly as if she were a bird that would take flight at any sudden movement, and touched the backs of her cool, slender fingers. So pale. Wet with rain. Unexpectedly, her hands turned beneath his. Excitement jolted through his chest. Palm up, like flowers, blooming beneath his hands. Opening, offering. Yes.

He leaned closer. The rain whispered, murmuring, pattering tenderly against every new leaf. She glowed like a South Sea pearl, that faint blush of pink, barely a hint of color in her pale cheeks. Her huge eyes were wide open and luminous. Greenish brown. Leaves in the water. Dilated pupils, deep and endless. A sprinkle of ruddy freckles on her nose, now that he was close enough to see. A frivolous detail that made her beauty more believable, more approachable. More kissable.

He studied every drop of water beading her forehead. Followed the grain of her eyebrows, the jut of her cheekbone. Perfect. Radiant. He was dazzled. Lost. His wits gone. Like they'd never been.

She extricated her hand, and touched his face from cheekbone to jaw. The trail of her finger was a path of light, moonlight on water, a beckoning shimmer. Rain dripped into his collar, soaking his shoulders. Rain defined the dimensions of this sensual liquid otherworld. Pearly gray, green, silvery, glittering cool. And beneath it, secret hidden heat. The blush in her cheeks, the warmth of her lips. Wet with rain, sweet with rain. Her scent, escaping him every time he tried to inhale it. Elusive, alluring. Driving him mad. He swayed. Their lips touched.

The kiss pierced through him, broke something open. He started to shake and clutched the edge of the door to steady himself. Moved, by a shy, cautious, trembling kiss. Tears started into his eyes. Luckily, his face was already wet. He closed his eyes, tasted her, felt her. The delicate texture of the inside skin of her lips, the flick of her shy tongue. He drank it up. Like fine liquor. So sweet, for being given, and not taken.

The cell phone could have been ringing for hours by the time he registered it. He never wanted to come back, but the sound was a grappling hook that dragged her away from him. He begged her, in his mind, to turn the goddamn thing off. Stay with him. Let this magic go on.

She pulled away, groped for her purse. Avoiding his gaze. "Hello?"

She listened to a loud burst of talking on the other side, and her eyes flicked up to him. "Just a sec, Eugene. Um, Liam? This is going to take a few minutes. You might as well get back into the truck."

Yes, it was definitely over. *Fuck.* He stood there, fists clenched. She was paying no attention. She was all business now.

He got into the truck, feeling stupid and dismissed. Chump asshole. Winding himself up into thinking he was on the verge of something important.

But not more important than a fucking phone call.

"Thank God you picked up. We've got a disaster on our hands!"

Eugene was the fiddler from Mandrake, her Afro-Celt fusion band. She avoided looking at Liam as he got back into the truck. "What's the matter?"

"It's Dennis! He's deserting! The stinking rat bastard!"

"Calm down, and let's take this step by step."

"He just got a gig with a touring show of Riverdance! He's blowing us off, a week before the tour! The gigs in Boston and Albany and Atlanta all specified Uilleann pipes in the contract! We can't show up without a piper!" Eugene's voice cracked.

"Calm down," she said again. "This is bad, but we'll fix it."

"How, Nance? Every piper we know is booked solid those weeks! I've already made seven phone calls! We're completely screwed!"

"We'll fix it!" she insisted. "I'll be back tonight. When I get home, I'll call you and we'll work something out. Don't panic."

She listened with half an ear to Eugene's carrying-on, her body still quivering. After all her resolutions to be tough. Making out madly with a stranger in his truck. Getting swept away, too, toward God alone knew what. His house, his couch, his rug, his bed. She hadn't been swept away since . . . well, never. Swept away was not in her repertoire.

She'd never known anyone that good. She'd never known that good existed. She was squirming, hot. Practically desperate for it, and after some gallant moves, a light kiss, one single collar button undone.

He'd barely touched her. How had he done that?

She jerked her attention back to Eugene before she lost the thread. "All this work for nothing," he moaned. "I can't take it. I'm going back to school. I'm going to be an accountant, like Mom wanted."

"You're not going to be an accountant," Nancy soothed with practiced ease. "It's too late for that. You're not fit for any work but being a fiddler now, so get yourself a cup of tea, and calm down."

"Where the hell are you, anyway?" Eugene demanded.

Nancy's eyes flicked up to Liam's impassive face. "Later," she said, clicking "stop." She dropped the phone back into her purse.

The rain was slanting in her open window. She rolled it up.

"I'll take you back to your car," he said. The warmth was gone from his voice. She missed it.

They were silent for the twenty minutes it took to get back to Lucia's house, and every minute that passed, she felt like she shrank further into herself against his quiet reproach.

When they arrived, he parked behind her car. So much had happened since she'd been there last, though it had been less than two hours. The whole gamut of human emotions blazing through her. She was wrung out, hollowed. Practically transparent.

She stared up at the shabby old house, bright yellow crime scene tape festooned across the door, and started rummaging for her car keys.

"Thanks for the ride," she said. "And for keeping me company when we went to Baruchin's." *And for the most mind-blowing sexual arousal I ever felt.* She wanted to say something else, after having been so altered by that amazing intimacy, but his face looked closed, and the words stopped in her throat before she figured out what they were.

She flung the door open and slid out of the truck. Her legs almost buckled. She steadied herself on the door and hurried over to her own car. She tried to unlock it, but the key fell from her stiff, cold fingers, splashing into a small clear puddle in the cracked old sidewalk.

Suddenly, he was beside her, fishing the keys out of the water, wiping them on his jeans. He opened the door and helped her inside. She sat down heavily in the driver's seat, glad to be off her feet.

"You need protection," he said. "Twenty-four seven."

She made a derisive sound to mask her nervousness. "Isn't that a shame. In a perfect world, I might agree. But I live alone, and I work."

"You could stay with me," he said.

She gaped at him, speechless. "I . . . what?"

He shrugged, looking vaguely abashed. "It's a solution."

"But I . . . but what about your own work?" she demanded.

"I cleared my schedule for three weeks for Lucia's house," he said. "I'm overdue a vacation. I'd take some time for this. Just say the word."

"But your assistant—"

"I can find Eoin work on someone else's crew in five minutes," he said brusquely. "Don't worry about Eoin. He's covered."

That finished all the obvious objections to the outrageous proposal. Now, she had to get down to the truth. "Liam. We don't have the kind of relationship where I could move in with you. Not even close."

"You need protection," he repeated. "Something bad's happening."

She shivered. "Well, maybe so, but that's not the point. I just met you yesterday. All we have is . . . well, I don't even know what we have."

"We had breakfast," he offered.

"Do not make fun of me," she flared. "This is not a joke." She groped for something else to say, but she was lost. The silence was fraught with exquisite tension.

"It wouldn't be much of a leap," he said.

"What leap? What are you talking about?" she asked crabbily.

"From where we are to the kind of relationship where I could offer for you to stay with me. There's a gap of"—he held up his thumb and forefinger with barely any space between them—"about that much."

Oh. Whoa. Shivery tingles chased themselves across the entire surface of her body. "I've known you for one day."

"Time is an illusion," he said.

"Don't give me that lofty metaphysical crap. It just pisses me off."

"Okay. Just the facts, ma'am."

She grunted, unwilling to be cajoled. "So is this an exchange of goods and services? I shack up with you, in return for what?"

"No! Do I strike you as such an opportunistic pig, then?"

"Whoa!" His anger gave her something to push against. "Excuse me! Maybe it's just me, but I couldn't help noticing a certain wave of hurricane-force sexual energy coming off you, Liam!"

He wiped rain off his face, frowning. "Sorry. It's been a strange day."

"Tell me about it," she agreed fervently.

He crossed his arms over his chest. Big arms. A lot of chest.

She hadn't touched his body yet. And he was being so careful with her. Like she was made of glass. Which was exactly how she felt. Fragile, brittle. On the edge of disaster, poised to fall. No need to go take a running leap for it. "Things are strange right now, and it's a bad—"

"Strange times call for bold gestures. Brave risks."

She snorted. "I'm actually not that brave."

"Bullshit. You have stainless steel for a spine. Like your mother."

The mention of Lucia made her grope for her box of tissues.

He waited for a moment. "I'm not a cop or an investigator, Nancy. I'm just a carpenter. I can't promise to help you solve this. But I can make damn sure that nobody messes with you. That, I can commit to."

Her eyes dropped, heat infusing her face.

"Let me help," he urged. "At least think about it."

Oh, yeah. Think about it she would. Every waking second. "Thanks," she murmured. "I'll bear that in mind."

He crouched until his face was level with hers. "And stay with your sisters. Do not stay in your apartment alone."

"Liam, you cannot imagine how tiny our living spaces are—"

"Please, Nancy. Please. For me."

The low intensity of his voice moved her. He really cared. He wasn't just throwing his weight around. "Okay," she heard herself say.

"Swear it," he said. "On your mother's grave."

She flinched. "Oh, for God's sake—"

"For Lucia's sake. She would want you to be safe."

She sighed. "I swear, on my mother's grave, that I will stay with my sisters tonight," she said, through gritted teeth.

"Indefinitely. Until we know exactly what the fuck is going on."

"You aren't shy about bringing out the big guns, are you?'

"Not in the least," he said flatly. "Not when it's this important."

"Fine," she snapped. She shut the car door. Manipulator.

He knocked on her window. She rolled it down. "Now what?"

"Is an Irish pub in Queens neutral ground?" he asked.

Nancy blinked. "Huh?"

"You said a date had to be on neutral ground," he said. "I'll be at Malloy's, on Queen's Boulevard, tomorrow night. Ever been to a seisiun?" He waited for her nod, and went on. "Malloy's is a good one. The Guinness is good, the players are good, the food's good. Irish stew, burgers. The seisiun's from ten until two. I'd like to see you there."

"Huh. This is backward," she told him. "First you invite me to live with you. Then you ask me out."

He shrugged. "I try to be original." He sank down onto one knee, his face level with hers at the open window. "You're over the limit."

She gave him a jerky nod. A grin flashed over his face, and he leaned forward and touched his lips to hers. The burst of delight made her body clench and thrum.

"I've never felt anything like that," she whispered.

"Me neither." He stroked her cheek with his thumb. "You're cold. Turn the car on, and get the heat going," he said. "You're going to wait for the investigating officer?"

"Yeah, might as well," she said. "Since the evidence techs don't want me in the house till they're done."

"Okay. Tomorrow night, then." He smiled at her as he backed slowly away. Then he climbed into his truck and drove away.

She touched the tip of her tongue to her lips, still tasting him.

Chapter
5

"Once more, from the top." Vivi stretched out on Nell's battered sofa, propping up her slender legs. Her gilded toenails gleamed in the flickering candlelight. She peered at her photocopy of Liam's transcription of Lucia's letter with a frown of intense concentration. "So something bad happened to her marriage, and to her father. But what? When did she come to America, anyway?"

Nancy pondered that as she petted the wildly purring cat curled in her lap. "Nineteen sixty-five or before, I think. She taught art history at Beardsley for thirty-five years before she retired. And that was over eight years ago."

"What was the name of the town she came from?" Vivi asked.

"Castiglione Sant'Angelo," Nell replied. "In Tuscany." She turned the Fabergé picture frame that held the old photograph of Lucia's father. "Maybe that's why she changed her name, from de Luca to D'Onofrio. Because of what happened to her father," she mused. "I asked her once why she changed it, but she didn't want to talk about it. You know, I asked her to go to Italy with me once, to do an art and architecture tour, back when I was an undergrad. And she snapped my head off. I was so taken aback, I never mentioned it again. To anyone."

"Huh. So let's run it down again," Vivi said. "The things we did not know about and still don't." She totted them off on her fingers.

"Her father. Her marriage. The mysterious object. The system of checks and balances designed to protect our sisterly love. Whatever the necklaces are the key to. Then, to make things even more interesting, we have the mysteries of the purloined letter, the murdered jeweller, and the pissed-off burglar. That's a lot of mysteries. Makes a girl hungry." She rolled up onto her side and reached for a slice of the pizza on the coffee table.

"I wish we had access to Lucia's papers," Nell fretted. "I'd like to go through her old letters and photographs."

"The meathead trashed Lucia's office files," Vivi reminded her.

"He might have missed something," Nell said stubbornly.

Nancy held out her hand. "Can I see that photo for a second?"

Nell handed it to her promptly. "Sure."

Nancy studied the somber, hawklike face of the late Conte de Luca. His intense, deep-set eyes were so much like Lucia's, they made her chest ache. "I wonder when he died," she murmured. "He looks like he was in his fifties. Maybe there's a date on the back." She fumbled with the back of the delicate silver and gilt frame until she loosened the little hook that held it closed and pried the back of the frame loose, shaking the contents into her hand.

She sucked in a startled breath. They all stared, frozen, at what lay in her hand. Not one photograph, but two. And something else, besides. A small, carefully folded square of yellowed paper.

Nancy gently pushed Moxie out of her lap and scooted over toward the lamp. Nell and Vivi scrambled to look over her shoulder. Moxie stalked away, tail high, deeply offended.

"Oh, wow," Vivi breathed softly, as they stared down at the picture. "That's Lucia. Just look at her. What a bombshell."

The young, beautiful Lucia had dark curls clustered over her shoulders and wore a smart little hat. Her lips were painted into a bold fifties Cupid's bow. She gazed up into the face of a tall, handsome young man, who clasped her waist and gazed down as if he were hungry to kiss her. Nancy turned it over. On the back, in faded, brownish ink, was written, *Venezia, Carnevale, 1957.*

"Who is this guy?" Nell murmured. "Maybe he's the missing husband. What's on the paper?"

Nancy unfolded the delicate, yellowing paper. It was lightweight airmail paper, covered with fine, faded script. She held it to the light. "It's in Italian," she said, passing it to Nell.

Nell fumbled for her glasses and pushed them up her nose. "It's dated April of 1964," she said, and began to translate.

Beloved Lucia,

I do not know why I continue to write while you continue to be silent, but I cannot seem to stop myself, undignified though I must seem, begging on my knees for your return to our life together.

I understand how shocked and horrified by what happened to your Babbo, but you must believe me, it was like a knife to my own heart as well. If I could change the terrible events of the past for you, I would, at any cost. But I cannot.

But this is not a reason to abandon your home, your family, your nation. You will never heal in a foreign land. You cannot run from this pain, my love. It will follow you wherever you go. Of this, I am sure.

You have always been obstinate. It is a part of your strength, which I love and admire. But true strength must be tempered by softness. Compromise.

But why do I waste my ink? You are resolved to be cruel and immovable. I try to accept this, but still, I cannot swallow it. I enclose this photograph, in hopes that it will remind you of happier times.

I continue to try deciphering your father's map. I have once again completely excavated the palace gardens, this time draining the lake, in my search which you hold to be both stupid and pointless. My efforts were entirely in vain, as I am sure you will be gratified to know.

Ah, God. Forgive my acid tone. I miss you desperately. For the sake of the children we might still have together, please, Lucia, come back to me. Come home.

> *In faith,*
> *Marco*

The sisters stared at each other after Nell stopped reading, eyes wide with shock.

"Wow," Vivi whispered. "That guy knew how to lay a guilt trip."

"I bet that's why she never married," Nell said. "She had men chasing her, up into her seventies, but she blew them all off. She must have still been in love with this Marco. How romantic."

"And how awful that they spent their entire lives apart." Nancy stared at the photo. The innocent happiness radiating out of the young couple made her stomach hurt. "And all because of some horrible thing that happened to the Conte. Between the years of 1957 and 1964."

"And do you think . . . that this horrible thing could possibly be connected to the horrible things happening now?" Vivi's voice was timid.

Nancy folded the letter delicately back into its original creases. "Well, this Marco had a map," she said slowly. "And he was looking hard for some hidden object. In Lucia's letter, she refers to "this thing," plus what happened to her father and what it did to her marriage. So, yeah. I can't imagine how, but yeah. Somehow, they're connected."

"And this is not good news," Nell said. "Since we're clueless."

"At least the letter I found in the garbage makes it clear that the 'thing' she's referring to isn't the trio of necklaces that she gave us," Nancy said. "The necklaces are the key. So maybe this secret thing is in that safe that the carpenter installed."

"Yeah, the one we have no combination for." Nell held up her pendant. It spun, tiny rubies and diamond chips winking in the light of the candles she'd set around her studio apartment in SoHo. "I guess we could count the stones, try the different sequences we come up with as possible combinations to the safe," she said thoughtfully. "But that doesn't use our love of music, literature, or the visual arts. It seems blah and obvious. Lucia had a much more devious personality than that."

Nancy tucked the photograph and the letter carefully back into the picture frame. "She was gearing up to tell us more when she was killed."

"Killed?" Vivi put down her slice of pizza, and swallowed the mouthful she had with a pained gulp. "God, Nance. You really think . . . ?"

"The jeweler and his family get whacked the night that the house is trashed, before I can talk to him about the necklaces? Hell yes."

Nell reclasped her pendant around her neck, her dark eyes worried. "I've never seen you this way, Nance. You'd say you were fine even if you were bleeding to death. I about dropped my teeth when you asked to come over here tonight. Not that you aren't more than welcome. I'm scared, too, and damn glad to have you."

Nancy fidgeted. "Oh, that's just because I swore a vow," she blurted. "I would've been perfectly fine at home."

"Vow?" Vivi straightened up, her eyes wide. "What vow? To whom?"

"To Liam." Nancy picked at the fabric of her jeans, regretting her incautious words. "The carpenter who was going to do the remodel."

Nell and Vivi exchanged significant looks. "He made you swear not to stay alone?" Nell asked. "This is the carpenter who flash memorized Lucia's letter? My. He certainly is taking a personal interest, isn't he?"

If they only knew. "I guess you could say that," Nancy said.

"Tell us about this carpenter," Nell prompted. "I'm picturing a potbellied guy with a bushy beard and a red nose and twinkling eyes. Like a young Santa. Jeans slipping down over a big, hairy ass. Am I close?"

"Um, no," Nancy admitted, with a snort. "Light-years."

Her sisters exchanged knowing smirks this time. "So?" Vivi asked. "No potbelly, then? No big, hairy ass?"

"No," Nancy hedged. "Lean belly. I can't speak for the hairiness of his ass, but shapewise, it was, well, proportional, let's just say."

"Proportional, hmm?" Vivi purred. "Height?"

"Maybe six two," Nancy admitted.

"Six two," Nell said dreamily. "Eye color? Blue, right?"

"Wrong. Very pale green. Like a dollar bill."

Nell and Vivi grinned and gave each other a high five. "She remembers his eye color!" Vivi crowed. "It's serious!"

"Oh, shut up," Nancy muttered.

"Let's celebrate." Nell popped open another beer. "At least the guy isn't a musician. That's a step up, at least."

"Actually, he invited me to a seisiun in Queens tomorrow night, so he's some sort of musician. Although I have no clue at what level, or even what instrument."

"Invited you? To a seisiun?" Nell's voice rose to a squeak.

Nancy squirmed. "Not a date. It's just a seisiun. We're talking a couple of pints in a grotty Irish bar, and Irish tunes until our eyes cross. A date is a bigger deal. Dinner, drinks, dancing, a show."

"Yeah, like you're such an expert," Vivi said. "What bar?"

Nancy stared from one to the other. "Oh, no. Don't you dare."

"What bar?" both sisters demanded in unison.

"I'm not telling. Forget it."

"Fine," Vivi said. "We'll go through other channels. I'll call . . . Let's see . . . Eugene. We'll tell him you have a hot date in Queens tomorrow night, and ask him for a list of the seisiuns tomorrow in Queens, and Nell and I will take my van and make the rounds until we get lucky."

"Oh, God, Vivi," Nancy started to protest. "Don't."

"And then we will roast you, babe. We will have no mercy. None."

Nancy closed her eyes, her face hot. "Don't tell Eugene," she begged. "He's a terrible gossip. I'll never hear the end of it."

"So give it up," Vivi said, merciless.

Nancy gritted her teeth. "It's at Malloy's," she admitted. "Ten to two. I haven't decided yet whether or not I'm going."

"Oh?" Vivi's eyes were innocently wide. "Six two, green eyes, perfectly proportional ass? You are *so* going to that seisiun."

"Whether or not, it's my business," Nancy bitched. "We'll see how you like it when I hunt you down on a date to embarrass you!"

Nell looked pained. "Like it's going to happen in this century."

Something in Nell's voice made Vivi and Nancy give their sister a careful second look. Vivi hoisted herself up onto her elbow. "Why shouldn't it?" she asked. "You're gorgeous, smart, sweet. A prize. What's not to date?"

Nell shrugged, her gaze sliding away. "I don't know. I'm one of those girls who only gets crushes on unattainable men. Protecting myself by making sure I never have to deal with a real relationship, blah, blah."

"Who?" Nancy demanded, her voice hard. "Unattainable how?"

"It doesn't matter. You don't know him."

"Is he married?" Vivi demanded.

"No!" Nell snapped. "I mean, that is to say, I have no idea. He doesn't talk to me. But he doesn't wear a ring, so I guess probably he . . . oh, hell. Never mind. It couldn't be more irrelevant."

But the damage was done. Nancy dug in her teeth. "Who is he?"

Nell threw up her hands. "No one! Just a random guy who comes into the Sunset Grill for lunch every day. I have a monster crush on a guy I serve lunch to. Believe me, it's as stupid and pathetic as that."

"Did you write your number on the check?" Vivi asked archly.

Nell rolled her eyes. "If I'd ever established eye contact with him, that would make sense. But he's never even looked at me. And I mean that literally. He just looks into his laptop. It looks like code."

Vivi flopped back and put a pillow over her face. "Oh, God. A techno-geek. You poor, poor thing."

"Well, how about you, Viv?" Nancy demanded. "Romantic prospects? Any news? 'Fess up."

Vivi looked pained. "Hell, no. I'm making celibacy into a high art. After what happened with Brian, I still don't have the nerve to."

"That was six years ago!" Nancy snapped. "Get over it already!"

Vivi's soft mouth tightened at her sister's sharp tone. "Believe me," she said flatly, "I have tried."

Something in her Vivi's voice made Nancy back off. She studied her sister's tight, averted face, suddenly.

But Vivi just waved her hand, brushing the subject away. "Forget Brian," she said briskly. "He's a putz. Nancy's carpenter with the proportional ass is way more interesting. I can hardly wait to check him out."

"Me, neither," Nell said, with relish.

Moxie rose to her feet and started kneading Nancy's thigh. Nancy popped the top off another beer. "God help me now," she muttered.

Nell nudged her sister's arm. "We don't mean to torture you," she said gently. "Well, actually we do, but it's so nice to have something frivolous to smile about, you know? Bear with us. We've been so sad and confused lately. Your proportional-assed carpenter is hard to resist."

Nancy squeezed Nell's hand. It was true. It was nice to hear her sisters laugh. To chatter and bicker about men, dating, stupid crushes, nice asses. Silly, nonessential things. Nothing earthshaking.

Although the earth had definitely shaken during that kiss in the rain. Nor would she characterize that kiss as frivolous, or lighthearted. Oh, no. Calling that earthshaking was putting it mildly.

She wouldn't show. He was sure of it, but like an idiot, he kept checking his watch every half minute or so since he'd walked into Malloy's and took his fiddle, flutes, and whistles out of their various bags and cases. He took a swallow of Guinness and wondered why he tortured himself. After all, the woman's cell phone alone would drive him insane.

He could hardly believe his idiocy. Offering himself as an unpaid bodyguard? Getting all up on his high horse when she called him on his bullshit. Oh, sure, he'd keep her safe. Nobody would mess with her while she was snug and warm in his bed, pinned to the mattress beneath his heaving body. No problem. He'd keep her plenty safe.

But his eyes kept drifting to the entry door. He wanted to see her again. Hear her voice. He liked the way her mind worked, the way her brow furrowed when she was thinking. Those big leaves-under-the-water eyes. The way she wrinkled her nose when she was disgusted, which appeared to be fairly often. And when he kissed her, God. The rain that fell on him yesterday should have evaporated into pure steam.

"Yo! Earth to Liam! Come in, Liam!" Mickey the guitar player brayed into his ear. "Do that set of reels you did last week that ends with 'The Tinker's Bride,' okay? I want to try out a new accompaniment."

"Sure." He took another swig of his pint. His watch said 11:07. He had to just get the hell over it and concentrate on the music. He tuned up his fiddle.

They'd just launched into "The Tinker's Bride" when she walked in. He felt her even before she pushed through the crowd. A smile spread across his face. By the time she made it back to the table, it had become a grin. He started speeding up. The other musicians gave him panicked looks, dropping out one by one until only Eoin played with him. They finished with a flourish, to appreciative hoots and hollers.

She looked soft tonight. Amazingly, her hair was shiny and loose, surprisingly wavy, hanging long down her back. She was wearing jeans and a snug, low-cut red T-shirt that made her skin look pearly and glowing and showed off the perfect shape of those pert, suckable tits.

Her eyes were cautious behind her glasses. Liam put down his fiddle and made his way over to her as the group tore into "The Redhaired Boy." Her eyes widened as he leaned over and kissed her. As if he had the right. She smelled incredible. Her lips were so soft.

She swayed back. "Whoa," she said with a nervous laugh. "You don't waste any time, do you?"

"Fuck no." He slid his arms around her, kissing her again.

It started happening again, like yesterday. The world fell away, narrowing down to just Nancy and his own pounding heartbeat. He could barely hear the music. He forced himself to pull away, glanced over his shoulder, to a circle of grins, smirks, and nudges. Eoin lifted his pint, his face discreetly curious.

Nancy's face was pink. "Did I mess up?" he asked her.

"I'm not used to a guys just grabbing me," she said.

"Oh. Uh, sorry." He ached to grab her again. "Did your other boyfriends ask nicely before they kissed you?"

"I don't think so," she said doubtfully. "I don't remember. To be truthful, I don't think it was ever much of an issue."

He looked baffled. "Dickless wimps. What was their problem?"

He was rewarded by an startled crack of laughter from her, and he grinned, delighted with himself. "Can I get you a drink?"

"You said the Guinness was good?"

"Best this side of the Atlantic." He elbowed his way to the bar and got her a pint. She sipped, and sighed with an expert's appreciation.

"I thought you wouldn't show," he admitted.

She licked foam off her lip. "I don't know if it's a good idea."

"Me neither, but I don't care," he said recklessly. He dragged another chair to the musicians' table and sat her down next to him, taking her hand. He wound his fingers through hers to warm them. In the confusion that followed the end of the set, she leaned over to him. "I want to hear you play!" she shouted.

Her breath against his neck made his head swim. He picked up his fiddle, Mickey called another set, and they were off. It was a good group. Guitar, fiddles, bodhran, accordion, and Eoin, locked in a trance of perfect happiness, his fingers flashing as he played his Uilleann pipes.

Nancy clapped vigorously as they finished the set, and leaned over. "You guys are great!" she said, her eyes alight with pleasure. "You kick ass with that fiddle, Liam! Where did you learn to play?"

"My stepdad played the fiddle," he replied. "He got me into it when I was a kid. And I picked up the flutes and whistles a few years back, just for fun. I'd rather mess around with them than watch TV."

"You're hot," she said. "Did you ever consider going pro?"

He used the excuse of having to talk over the noise into her ear to kiss the soft skin behind it, and smell the scent of her shampoo. "For about ten minutes," he admitted. "Figured that would take all the fun out of it."

"Hmm. I guess that's one way of looking at it. Who's the piper?"

"Oh, Eoin? He's my cousin. Second cousin, actually. Fresh from County Wicklow. He works for me. Lives in my basement. Good kid."

"He's fabulous," she said.

"Yeah, isn't he just?"

That was all there was time to say before they plunged into another set of the reels. After the set she leaned over to him. "Would he be interested in touring with a hot band that gigs a lot?"

He blinked. "Who, Eoin?"

"I don't want to put you in a bind. But he rocks." Her eyes glowed.

The world was warm and generous tonight, and so was he. "Ask him. I'm sure he'll be thrilled. He lives to play those pipes."

They played a set of slip jigs as she talked into her phone, a big happy smile on her face, like a kid with a new toy. She sat down, looking satisfied. "This is the answer to my prayers. Matt and Eugene are on their way over, but I'm sure it's a done deal, if he's interested."

"You work fast," Liam said wryly.

She looked troubled. "You sure you don't mind me stealing him?"

He shrugged. "I've just found him a fill-in job. Nothing big."

Her face relaxed. "I love it when things work out perfectly."

"Me, too," he agreed, leaning over to breathe in her subtle fragrance, let her glossy, perfumed hair brush against his face.

A stocky redheaded guy with a guitar and a skinny guy carrying a fiddle pushed their way through the crowd about a half hour later. Their eyes fastened on Eoin, lost in the rapture of a set of fast jigs, his eyes closed, bellows pumping. They nodded to Nancy. The redheaded guy's eyes lingered curiously on Liam, who was still smelling her hair.

"That's Matt with the guitar, and Eugene with the fiddle," she said in his ear. "I'll introduce you after the set."

Matt and Eugene pulled out their instruments and dove into the seisìun. Nancy patted Liam's hand and extracted her own. "I have to go talk to Eoin," she said, with a smile. "Be right back."

He watched, fascinated, as she made her way through the crowd. She waited until the end of the set, tapped Eoin on the shoulder, and started talking in his ear. Eoin shot him a bewildered look. Liam gave him a thumbs-up. Nancy spoke again, and Eoin's freckles disappeared in a deep blush. She made her way back to Liam and sat down.

"I'll let the boys take it from here! He's shy! Needs some convincing!" she yelled, as the players tore lustily into "The Abbey Reel."

Some time later, Liam noticed a man across the bar lifting a pint in salute. It was Charlie Witt, a cop from Latham who'd been partnered with Eddie, Liam's stepdad, back when Eddie had been on the force. Charlie was a good guy. Past retirement age, but he kept on working.

An impulse struck Liam, and he leaned over to Nancy's ear, nuzzling his nose into her soft hair, sucking in a greedy chestful of that sweet warm scent that made him want to lick her all over. "There's a guy I want to talk to over there," he said. "Will you come with me?"

Nancy gave him a puzzled nod. They slid out of their chairs, and he clasped her hand and led her through the crowd just as the lads all followed Eoin's lead and struck into a raucous reel.

Nancy's fingers curled around his. Her hand was so small. He wanted to kiss it. Drag her out of there. Find someplace private.

He shook Charlie's hand, introduced Nancy, and got a congratulatory thump on the shoulder from the old man as Charlie looked her over. "You got yourself a dish," the older guy said. "Treat her good, huh? Or else I'll steal her for myself."

The next reel had a couple of bodhrans thundering along, so Liam had to speak right into Charlie's ear. "I need some advice."

"Anything for Eddie's kid," Charlie shot back.

"Remember that elderly Italian American lady in Hempton who died in a burglary attempt about ten days ago? D'Onofrio?"

Charlie's smile faded. "Yeah, heard about that. Fuckin' shame. They say the house got tossed again, even worse this time."

"I was the one who reported it yesterday," Liam told him. "And Nancy is Mrs. D'Onofrio's daughter."

Charlie looked at Nancy again, his round face grave. He jerked his chin toward the back of the bar. "Let's go where there's less noise."

They followed Charlie into a quieter room, with a pool table and a pay phone. Charlie slid into a booth and took a swig of the pint that he'd brought with him. "I don't know a lot about that case," he warned them. "It ain't my case, or even my town. I just heard about it because my partner, Henry, is hangin' out with one of the evidence techs."

"I just wanted your take on it," Liam said.

He outlined the facts for Charlie, with a few interjections from Nancy, clarifying and explaining. Charlie read Lucia's letter, peering through his bifocals for several minutes, and scowled, chewing his lip.

He looked at Nancy. "Your investigating officer knows about this letter, miss? You told him about the connection with the Baruchins?"

"It's a her, Detective Lanaghan, and I told her about both things yesterday," Nancy said. "And the letter was bagged by the forensics team. They might have even found more of it by now. God, I hope so. It's our only hope of knowing more."

Charlie shook his head. "Bad couple of weeks for senior citizens around here. The D'Onofrio lady, the clotheshorse. Now the Baruchins."

"The clotheshorse? Who's he?" Liam asked.

Charlie scowled. "Nobody knows. Strangest shit I ever heard. Kid finds a body in a vacant lot in Jamaica 'bout a week ago. Some guy in his eighties, neck snapped. No ID, but the guy was dressed head to toe in Italian designer clothes. Like, ten thousand bucks on the guy's back. Steffi got on the Internet, did some pricing. His shoes alone would have cost two thousand bucks. But if he's a rich bigwig, why doesn't somebody report him missing? And if he's a crook, his prints or DNA would turn up some priors, right?" He shrugged. "Nothing. It's like the guy never existed. But somebody popped him, and now somebody pops Baruchin and his wife and mother-in-law, the same night that somebody comes back to the D'Onofrio house and searches it again? It stinks." He gazed at Nancy. "You're absolutely sure you don't know what these clowns are looking for, right, miss?"

Nancy's lips tightened. "Absolutely not. Unless it's these necklaces, and Lucia's letter indicates that it is not. The necklaces are the only connection to the Baruchins. Believe me, if I knew more, the first thing I would do would be tell the investigating officer."

"You and your sisters should stop wearin' those necklaces, if somebody might be willing to kill for 'em," Charlie said bluntly.

Nancy's hand shot up and clutched the thing, as if someone were trying to tear it away. "It . . . they were Lucia's last gifts to us," she said.

"Yeah. Could be the last gifts you ever get." All the breezy good cheer was gone from Charlie Witt's ruddy face. He was dead serious.

Nancy stared back, polite but defiant. "Lieutenant Witt—"

"Call me Charlie, honey."

Nancy gave him an incandescent smile. "Charlie. In the first break-in, the forensics team found a set of fingerprints on my mother's writing table that did not belong to her or the three of us. Do you suppose they might try comparing them with Baruchin's prints? Or this mystery man? To see if they were ever in my mother's house?"

Charlie looked doubtful. "I don't see why it would have occurred to anyone, but why not? I'll call Detective Lanaghan tomorrow, talk to her. Just remember—don't expect any quick or easy answers."

"Of course not," Nancy murmured.

Charlie turned to Liam with a thoughtful frown. "I wouldn't let her out of my sight, if I was you, kid. Not for a second."

Liam nodded. It was a relief to have his own instincts verified. He hoped Nancy was paying attention. "That's what I figured," he said. "I'm still working on selling that proposal. She's not convinced."

"Work harder," Charlie advised, his voice hard. He looked over at Nancy, his eyes lingering on her décolletage. "Not that it would be such a chore to keep your eyes on that, now, mind you."

"That it wouldn't be," Liam heard himself agree, though the look on Nancy's face indicated that he was going to pay for it.

"Kinda hard to take your eyes off her as it is," Charlie commented.

"Could you two gentlemen please stop talking about me as if I weren't here?" Nancy asked, her voice very crisp.

Charlie blinked. "Honey, was I objectifyin' you?"

Nancy snorted. Charlie took it as encouragement. "Had this girl-friend once. Always said I was objectifyin' her when I pissed her off."

"Charlie," Liam broke in, "put the brakes on."

"Never did figure out what the hell she was talkin' about, but boy oh boy did she ever have a nice pair of round, jigglin'—"

"Charlie!" Liam snapped his fingers in front of Charlie's face.

Charlie subsided. "Sorry. Uh, well. Anyhow. Guess I better be heading on home to the wife." His eyes rested on Nancy as he took his final swallow of beer, and then his eyes cut to Liam's half-empty pint of Guinness. "I'd switch to coffee, if I was you, kid," he said quietly.

They went back to the music table after Charlie left. Liam took Charlie's advice and switched to coffee. Even so the night quickly took on a dreamlike quality. He was drunk on a different intoxicant, one far more potent than beer. The music thundered, and Nancy's slender hand, now relaxed and warm, was clasped in his, fingers entwined. They didn't talk much, with all the noise, but it didn't matter.

At a certain point in the evening, he noticed a disturbance in the energy of the group. The driving tempo of the music never faltered, but all of the male members of the group around the table except for

Eoin were rubbernecking at something behind him. He took a look, and the mystery soon resolved itself. Two strikingly pretty women stood there: a slender waiflike girl with big gray eyes and a mop of long, fire-red hair, and a brunette with flashing dark eyes, lush curves, and full lips. Both of them were standing right by the musicians' table, smiling. At him.

He glanced down at Nancy, perplexed. She was rolling her eyes. She gestured for him to lean down toward her mouth. "My sisters," she called into his ear. "They wanted to check you out. And to roast me."

Her sisters. Well, hot damn. That gave him a warm feeling, and a rush of energy that kicked up the already brisk tempo of "The Three Wishes" to a dangerous driving pace. He looked up at the sisters and gave them a big "here I am, so check me out" grin. They gave each other wide-eyed looks and giggled. They took turns whispering into Nancy's ear and giggled some more. Nancy turned brick red. He loved it.

He was sorry when they left not long after, before he had a chance to chat, but he hoped there would be another chance soon to charm them and get them on his side. In a less noisy environment, maybe. Dinner, maybe, at his place. When Nancy was there with him. Soon.

Liam looked at his watch when the musicians started packing up, astonished to find that it was well past two in the morning. Eoin was already wangling a ride to his next seisiun, hopeless tunehead that he was.

"I should be getting home," Nancy said.

"I'll walk you to your car," he offered.

"Oh, no. I found such a good parking spot for it yesterday that I couldn't bear to move it. So I took the subway."

He stared at her for a horrified moment. "You're joking, right?"

She looked uncomfortable. "Uh, no," she said. "Believe me, it was perfectly safe. The trains were crowded when I came out, and it's not like I can get into any trouble on a crowded Uptown Six. Then the Seven train got me within two blocks of here, and it was pretty full, too. I take the subway whenever I can. It's so much more efficient, and I—"

"You're not taking it tonight," he said grimly. "I'm driving you home."

"Oh, no. Don't worry about it. If it makes you feel any better, I had every intention of cabbing it back, given the weird—"

"Have you not been listening at all? Did you hear Charlie? I know you're not stupid, so are you nuts? Do you have a death wish?"

She looked abashed. "No, not at all. I just try to get through my days as best I can," she said tightly. "What about Eoin? Didn't he come with you?"

"Eoin's fine. Your friends are taking him to a late-night seisiun in Brooklyn. He'll play tunes all night and wake up God knows where."

She bit her lip. "It's out of your way. Really, a cab would be fine."

The woman had no grip on reality. She wasn't used to a guy giving a damn whether she got home safely any more than she was used to being kissed.

Tough shit. She was just going to have to get used to it.

Nancy clasped her hands nervously in Liam's truck. Alone with him in the dark, her doubts came rushing back, mixed with a dose of simmering lust. Funny. She had thought herself in love with Freedy, Ron, and Peter, but she'd never felt like this with them.

Like a live wire with the plastic casing peeled off.

She searched for something neutral to talk about. "I can't believe what a stroke of luck it was to find Eoin. How old is he, anyway?"

"Twenty-one, if I remember correctly."

"Just a baby. Looks like he hit it off with Matt and Eugene, too. And he's available for the tour, thank God. Does he have a green card?"

Liam hesitated. "We're working on it," he said guardedly.

"We can help," she assured him. "Uilleann pipers are rare. It's a specialized skill. We'll write letters to the INS about how desperately they need him for this gig or that. It may take a while—" She shot him a glance. "Why are you smirking? Do I amuse you?"

He pulled up at the Midtown tunnel toll booth, batted away her handful of dollars, and paid the toll himself. "You're a sweet girl, Nancy."

Nancy's cheeks grew warm. "I'm not doing anything altruistic. Drafting Eoin into Mandrake is business. He's saving my ass."

"And the green card?"

"That's in my best interests, too," she retorted.

"Why does it embarrass you when I tell you that you're sweet?"

She thought about it for a minute. "It makes me feel like you're condescending to me," she finally said.

"It makes you feel vulnerable, you mean."

"Don't tell me how I feel, please. And don't psychoanalyze me," she snapped. "I'm not in the mood."

"She's back," he said. "The tough broad with the attitude. But you don't fool me. You're tough, yes. But sweet as honey. And I'm not condescending. Not at all. I salute you for it."

She was speechless. The naked, exposed feeling was unbearable. The tunnel spat them up into Midtown, and she was intensely grateful for the necessity of giving directions.

"Take the FDR Drive south, to my place." She held up her hand at his expression. "I swear, I kept my promise. I'm camped out at Nell's, but I had to take my cat, and I didn't have enough arms to carry all her stuff yesterday. I need food, I need toys, I need kitty litter. I'm sorry to inconvenience you, but—"

"It's no goddamn inconvenience."

That response squelched further attempts at conversation. She just muttered "right" and "left" at the appropriate times until she indicated her own door in Alphabet City. He drove on past without stopping, and found a parking space three blocks down.

Nancy was disconcerted. She hadn't expected him to find parking. God knows, she never did. She'd expected that he'd drop her off at the stoop and wait as she hustled upstairs. But here he was, parked.

Liam Knightly, at her apartment, at three in the morning. It flung open doors in her mind that she just wasn't ready to look through.

She lost patience with herself. For God's sake, the man had just driven forty minutes out of his way to take her home in the middle of the night. The least she could do was to offer him coffee for the drive.

"Do you, uh, want to come up for coffee?" she asked.

"Yes," he said.

The word reverberated, invested with infinite shades of meaning. Her knees went rubbery. "My apartment isn't neutral ground."

His eyes gleamed. "I'll be good."

Hah. Loaded words, if there ever were ones.

Liam slung his fiddle and flute and whistle bag cases over his shoulder and took her arm. He looked around at the block of cramped turn-of-the-century brick town houses as if he expected the garbage cans to animate and attack them. She hauled out her house keys. The bulb that lit the stairs was dim, flickering. The place looked so shabby at three A.M. She actually wanted to apologize for her apartment building. Make nervous excuses about real estate prices in Manhattan. She stopped herself. As if. Their footsteps echoed on the stairway. She groped for something to say to break the tension, but her brain had ceased nonessential functioning.

So when the black-clad guys hurtled around the corner of the landing above, she just stared, mouth wide.

Too startled to scream.

Chapter
6

"Aw, *fuck*," Liam hissed. He flung her behind himself. She hit the wall with a grunt. Big. Dark clothes, stocking masks. Meant business.

He was in the air and spinning before his conscious brain kicked in. His heel connected to the chin of the closest guy, who reeled back, right into his companion. It gave Liam a second to regroup—and register the knife that appeared in the first guy's hand. He danced back, keeping his eyes on the blade, evading his opponent's lunges, but the landing was small. He had to keep that blade away from Nancy.

His opponent lunged again, jabbing high. Liam parried with his forearm, glad he wore the leather, and rammed the guy's arm against the wall. The knife clattered to the tiles. He spun to jab a knee into the gut of the guy bolting toward Nancy, but the first attacker did a foot sweep, scooping Liam's legs from under him. He stumbled against the wall, took an elbow slam to the ribs. In his peripheral vision, he saw the fiddle case slashing through the air. *Crack*. A masculine grunt of pain, limbs flailing, thuds. The second guy was falling down the stairs. Good.

But the first guy was diving for Nancy. She didn't have time to load another swing with the fiddle case. The asshole barreled into her, knocking her against the wall of the staircase. Her legs gave, she slipped, and they toppled in agonizing slow motion, careening downward, out of Liam's line of vision.

He hurled himself down the stairs, so fast his feet may not have even touched them. She dangled under the bastard's meaty arm, her body slack. Stunned. Liam plowed into him with a shout and looped both arms around the guy's neck. The other attacker was nowhere to be seen.

Nancy's weight thudded to the floor. The door yawned open, and shadows spun as the guy took a flying somersaulting leap into the dark off the stoop and took Liam spinning with him, over his head.

The world twirled and spun. A battering rain of blows: head, shoulders, back. Pain followed pain in such quick succession, Liam barely had the time to perceive them. Then, a half second sprawled together on the sidewalk, trembling and panting. Christ, the guy's breath was foul.

Then, the masked thing twisted against him like some huge, muscular serpent and slammed an elbow into Liam's ear. The fight exploded into movement again. They grappled, grunted, heaved. Liam slammed a hand up under his attacker's chin, knocking his teeth together. The guy was huge, but Liam whipped the man's knife hand back with the strength of desperation, ramming it into the rails of the wrought-iron fence beside them that separated the garbage cans from the sidewalk. And again.

The knife fell. Liam jerked part of his weight out from under the guy so that their bodies were crossed. The other man attempted to use his thick legs for traction, spreading them wide. Liam's hand flashed down, grabbed the guy's balls. Squeezed, with all his strength.

The guy screamed. Liam lunged for the knife on the sidewalk, scooping it up, and rolled up to his feet in a wary crouch, brandishing the blade. The other guy leaped up, too, still wheezing in pain. *Yeah. Come at me now, pig fucker.*

Would be a fine joke on him if the guy pulled a gun.

The man hesitated and backed away. He turned and began to sprint, booted feet pounding the pavement. Liam started after him, but was brought up short, as if there were a rope around his neck. Every hunting instinct screamed to run down his prey.

Nancy. She had not stirred from where the guy had let her drop in the entryway, and the door was flung wide open to the night, and it was three in the morning, off Avenue B, and he had no fucking clue where that first guy had gone.

The guy darted around the corner. It was quiet and still.

Both men, gone. Liam's jaw ached with frustration as he leaped up the steps of the stoop and sank down next to her, heart pounding.

He brushed the thick, glossy hair off her face. "Nancy? Are you okay?" His voice was breathless, quavering. "Talk to me, Nancy."

"I'm okay." Her eyes fluttered open, and she dragged herself up onto her hands and knees. "I think. Are they gone?"

"Yes." He helped her up, scanning for injuries. She looked dazed, disoriented, and as pale as a ghost, but there were no obvious marks on her. She let him pull her to her feet, and they held each other for a long moment, swaying and correcting, clinging to each other for balance.

"Wow," she whispered. "That was . . . wow."

"Like I said," he said into her ear. "One humdinger after another."

Her laughter had a choppy, hysterical feel. He held her closer, stroking her shaking back. The first time they'd ever embraced, he realized. Strange, that they'd waited so long. Two days, he remembered. They'd known each other for two fucking days. God. It felt like forever.

"We should call the cops," he said.

Her face contracted. "Oh, God."

"I know," he said. "But it's not like we have a better plan."

"Let's get up to my apartment," she said, sounding exhausted. "I need to sit down. And my purse and cell are somewhere on the steps."

They gathered up her stuff and his instruments as they climbed the stairs. A peek inside the fiddle case showed that the tough fiberglass had done its work well, cracking heads on the outside, protecting the instrument on the inside.

The door didn't look forced, but he took the key from Nancy's stiff, trembling fingers and opened the door himself, hesitating.

"Light's over the stove," Nancy forced out, through chattering teeth. "Yank the string."

Shock, he thought. She was acting shocky, and she, by God, had the right to. He peered inside suspiciously.

There wasn't much to the place. He could take it in in a single glance. A long narrow room with a barred, grilled window at both ends, a tiny water closet in the back behind the tiny kitchen. No place for an attacker to hide. He pulled her inside, grabbed an afghan off the couch, and wrapped it around her. She landed with a *whump*, on the couch, legs giving out. He turned on the light that dangled over the kitchen corner.

"You swing a mean violin," he said.

He got a wavering smile and a peek through those long, dark, curling lashes. "I did what I could," she said. "But you . . . My God, Liam, where did you learn to fight like that?"

"My stepdad was a cop and a Vietnam vet," he said. "A Marine. He taught me the basics. I did some training on my own, too, later."

"You were amazing," she said.

"I let him get away," he said sourly. "Amazing would have been knocking the dickhead out and tying him up, so we could give him to the police. After we pounded some answers out of him."

"So you think this is connected to . . ." Her voice trailed off as the expression on his face answered her. She shrank into the couch. "Oh, God. My sisters. I have to warn them. Where is my phone?"

He helped her find it, and handed it to her. "Here. Breathe deep," he advised. "Calm down."

Liam put on a saucepan of water and rummaged for tea bags while she talked to her sisters. Some excavating had uncovered a cheap brand of stale tea, but he was more concerned with getting sugar and caffeine into her than in the subtleties of flavor. When she hung up, he held out a sweet, milky cup to her and took the phone. "Let's trade."

She sipped it slowly while he called 911. His whole body ached and hurt, but he had no one but himself to blame. This was what happened when a guy poked his nose into a woman's big, hairy problems. He'd done it voluntarily. In fact, he'd insisted.

When she'd drunk her tea, he took the cup away and sank down in front of her. Her hands were cold, in spite of having clutched the hot cup. So smooth and slender. He rubbed them and contemplated a uniquely scary thought. This woman's life was a fucked-up, deadly mess.

And there was no place on earth that he would rather be than right in the middle of it.

Liam kept Nancy's teacup loaded with sugary tea during the whole police routine. He did most of the talking, for which she was grateful.

And that was the least of what she had to be grateful for. If not for him, she would be dead. Or something else that was very bad. Something she didn't even want to contemplate. It kept backhanding her afresh when she tried to think about something else, or better yet, not to think of anything. Those guys had not been trying to rob or kill her.

Those guys had been trying to abduct her.

Shudders of retroactive horror kept rippling through her, at how close she'd come to an unspeakable fate. But why her, for God's sake? Why on earth? She had two hundred and seventy eight bucks in her checking account, after paying her rent.

After a while, she drifted loose. She was floating in a faraway bubble, and the two policemen talking to Liam in her apartment were in another one. Their voices were tinny, a radio chattering in another room.

Only Liam held the cord. He could reel her back in to himself if he wanted to. Otherwise, she'd stay in her bubble, thanks very much.

The police finally left. She and Liam had declined to go in for medical observation, in the face of strong disapproval from the female officer, but enough was enough. She wanted peace and quiet.

Liam sat down next to her, touched her cheek.

"Nancy," he said.

That "don't freak out on me" tone made her brace herself. "Yes?"

"Those guys who attacked us. They were trying to—"

"Kidnap me, yes. I figured out that fun factoid all on my own."

"No need to snap," he replied. "Just factor that fun factoid into your future plans."

"Plans?" Her voice rose to a squeak. "What plans? You think I'm capable of planning? Someone killed my mother and tried to abduct me. And murder you while they were at it. I noticed that, too."

"Calm down," he soothed.

She hissed out a long sigh. "I'm sorry. I'm scolding you, and you don't deserve it. You saved my ass tonight. Don't think I've forgotten it."

"Anytime." He fished a cat toy out from under his leg, a jointed wooden snake. "How can you keep a cat in a place this cramped?"

The disapproval in his voice stung. "It's better than the life she had on the street! She was half dead when I found her, and I spent fifteen hundred dollars getting her sewed back together, plus getting her spayed, and shots. And I spend a fortune in kitty litter and niblets."

The silence that followed stretched out too long to bear. When she looked up, Liam had a gleam in his eye. He was trying not to smile.

"What?" she asked crossly. "You're giving me that look again."

"Bet getting the cat fixed up was a hard-assed, self-interested business decision, right?"

Nancy gave him a cool stare. "You're bugging me, Liam."

He gazed back, unrepentant. "Get used to it."

He picked up Lucia's bronze Cellini satyr, turning it carefully in his hands. "You think this thing is safe here?"

She bristled. "Probably not, considering what just happened, but is anything safe anywhere?"

"A good point." He set the thing carefully down. "Probably not."

"I guess I should put it in a safe-deposit box," she said. "It got all the way through the Nazi occupation without getting appropriated. The Conte wrapped it in burlap and buried it in the kitchen fireplace ashes. It would be ironic if it got stolen now and traded for crack."

"The Conte?" Liam's sharp gaze bored suddenly into her eyes. "Lucia's father hid art from the Nazis?"

"Everything he could. I think they got most of it, but— Oh, hey! You don't know about the letter, do you?"

He frowned. "What letter?"

"We found an old letter last night, and a photo, in the Fabergé picture frame at Nell's apartment." Nancy quickly outlined the contents of the letter to him.

Liam listened, his face impassive. When she finished, he turned again to stare at the Cellini bronze. "Maybe there's something else that was hidden from the Nazis, like the satyr," he said. "Except that it's still hidden. And the old count died before he told anyone where it is."

Nancy chewed her lip. "But then why are they attacking me?" Her voice quivered again. "I don't know anything."

"They don't know that."

Dark spots started swimming before her eyes. "Oh, God. That would suck. The worst of all possible worlds. If it's true, they'll never stop. And I'll never, ever be able to give them what they want."

"Put your head down." Liam pushed her head between her knees.

Nancy did so and concentrated on breathing. When she dared to sit up again, he had a small, thoughtful frown in his eyes. "Don't think about it anymore," he said gently. "Please. Don't faint on me."

So give me something else to think about, you doofus, she wanted to yell. She contented herself with a slightly hysterical crack of laughter.

He looked around her apartment. The cramped room was crammed with floor-to-ceiling shelves, cassettes, CD racks. A desk dominated the room, with a computer, a fax, a scanner. A file cabinet, copy machine, and water cooler were crowded around it. Liam patted the back of the couch where they sat. "Does this thing open up into a bed?"

Her hackles were on the rise, as she sensed a criticism in formation. "Yes, it does," she said. "Anything else? More pronouncements about my apartment, my life, my choices? By all means, Liam. Express yourself."

"So this place is an office. With a couch for those occasional moments when you want to assume a horizontal position," he said.

Yeah. Like, right now. With you. She groped for a smart-ass retort, but an unexpected insight took form in her mind as she looked into his eyes.

"You're pissing me off on purpose," she said slowly.

His face was impassive. "A couple of zingers to get you going. It kicks up your blood pressure. I like to see some color in your face."

She covered her face with her hands. "I must look like death warmed over. Or not even. Death served right out of the fridge."

"No." He reached out, pulled her hands gently off her face. "You're beautiful, Nancy. You shine. Like a jewel."

She was moved, embarrassed, mortified. Charmed beyond belief.

"It's sweet of you to say so," she managed.

"Sweet has nothing to do with it."

She giggled. "Now who's defensive when I call him sweet?"

"You don't believe me." His voice was incredulous.

A hot blush stained her face. "I, uh, appreciate the compliment. Really, I do. But it's not a matter of believing or not believing. It's just that beauty is such a subjective thing. So it doesn't mean anything."

He looked baffled. "Subjective, my ass. What's not to understand? Beautiful is beautiful."

She rushed on. "What does it mean, to tell someone she's beautiful? Men have told me that I was beautiful before. They changed their minds when they met someone they thought was more beautiful. By comparison, I suddenly became less beautiful. That sucks, by the way, when you look into your boyfriend's face and realize that your stock just went down the toilet."

"Nancy," he said gently.

"Who knows what a person sees when he looks at another person? It changes with his mood, the weather, what he ate that day! How beautiful would I look to you after I'd annoyed you for a while by popping my knuckles, or slurping my soda, or whatever grates on you? Telling me I'm beautiful is meaningless. So don't do it. You'd have more luck coaxing me into bed if you stayed away from the whole subject."

"You think that's what this is about? Just getting you into bed?"

She swallowed over a lump in her throat. Doing it again, with him. Babbling nonsense, like an idiot.

"Be quiet for a second." His voice was as soft as drifting smoke. He reached out and plucked a spray of miniature orchids out of a vase on the end table by the couch. She'd bought them the week before, in honor of Lucia, who had always loved them. Deep pink, spotted with purple, luminous and mysterious. "Are these beautiful?"

"Yes," she said without hesitation.

"How do you know they are?"

She chewed her lip, sensing a trap. "I don't know. I couldn't say. I'm not the poetic type. They just are."

He tucked the sprig back into the vase and stroked a petal with his fingertip. "That's my point. You don't have to be poetic. Just look at them. Shut up, and really look at them. And you know. You feel it. Right here." He put his hand on his chest. "They just are."

She gazed at him, hypnotized as his finger stroked the lambent curve of the blossom.

She tried it. Exactly what he suggested. She shut up, the talk, the worries, the fear, the clamorous noise in her head. She just looked at him as he touched that flower. He gazed back at her, those clear, light eyes endlessly patient, and gentle. Waiting for her to get it. He reached out, touched her cheek, as softly as he'd touched the flower.

And suddenly . . . *ah*. She got it. She knew. Right in her chest, just like he said. Oh, yes. He was beautiful. He shone. Like a jewel.

The realization pierced, burned, like a knife in her chest, turning.

This was against all her rules, all her better judgment. The power dynamic was whacked, wrong. He was the one who had saved her. He was the one offering protection and comfort. She was the one who was desperately in need of it. He had everything, she had nothing. She couldn't even guarantee him a good time in bed to compensate him for his trouble, with all her sexual hang-ups. A crass assessment of the situation, but there it was. She called it how she saw it.

She preferred to have something concrete to offer a man that would keep him connected with her after the initial flash of desire flickered and went out, as it inevitably did. Not that the trick had ever worked that well before, considering her romantic track record.

Liam didn't need her. She had nothing to offer him but herself, and when he lost interest in that, she would be toast.

Liam sensed the direction her mind was running. She could tell by his thoughtful frown. "What's wrong now, Nancy?"

He sounded exhausted. Fed up. She didn't blame him a bit. She was a piece of work. Nothing but problems. Her mind raced to come up with a plausible lie. Letting him see how small she felt would just embarrass them both.

She shook her head. "Nothing," she whispered.

He let out a sigh, and leaned back, laying his head against the back of the couch. Covering his eyes with his hands.

That was when she noticed the condition of his hand. His knuckles were torn and raw, encrusted with blood. God, she hadn't even given a thought to his injuries, his trauma, his shock. She'd just zoned out, floated in her bubble, leaned on him. As if he were an oak.

But he wasn't an oak. He was a man. He'd fought like a demon for her, and risked his life, and gotten hurt, and she was so freaked out and self-absorbed, she hadn't even noticed. She was mortified.

"Liam. Your hand," she fussed, getting up. "Let me get some disinfectant, and some—"

"It's okay," he muttered. "Forget about it."

"Like hell! You're bleeding!" She bustled around, muttering and scolding to hide her own discomfiture, gathering gauze and cotton balls and antibiotic ointment. He let her fuss, a martyred look on his face. After she finished taping his hand, she looked at his battered face and grabbed a handful of his polo. "What about the rest of you?"

"Just some bruises," he hedged.

"Where?" she persisted, tugging at his shirt. "Show me."

He wrenched the fabric out of her hand. "If I take off my clothes now, it's not going to be to show you my bruises," he said.

She blinked, swallowed, tried to breathe. Reorganized her mind. There it was. Finally verbalized. No more glossing over it, running away.

"After all this?" Her voice was timid. "You still want to . . . now?"

"Fuck yes." His tone was savage. "I've wanted it since I laid eyes on you. It's gotten worse ever since. And combat adrenaline gives a guy a hard-on like a railroad spike, even if there weren't a beautiful woman in my face, driving me fucking nuts. Which puts me in a bad place, Nancy. I know the timing sucks for you. The timing's been piss-poor since we met, but it never gets any better. It just keeps getting worse."

"Hey. It's okay." She patted his back with a shy, nervous hand. He was usually so calm, so controlled. It unnerved her to see him agitated.

He didn't seem to hear her. "And the worse it gets, the worse I want it," he went on, his voice harsh. "Which makes me feel like a jerk, and a user, and an asshole. Promising to protect you—"

"You did protect me," she reminded him.

"Yeah, and I told you it wasn't an exchange. You don't owe me sex. You don't owe me anything. And that really fucks me up. Because I can't even remove myself from the situation. I'm scared to death to leave you alone. And that puts me between a rock and a hard place."

She put her finger over his mouth. "Wow," she murmured. "I had no idea you could get worked into such a state, Mr. Supermellow Liam Let's-Contemplate-the-Beauty-of-the-Flower Knightly."

His explosive snort of derision cut her off. She shushed him again, enjoying the feel of his lips beneath her finger. "You're not a jerk or a user," she said gently. "You were magnificent. Thank you. Again."

He looked away. There was a brief, embarrassed pause. "That's very generous of you," he said, trying to flex the wounded hand. "But I'm not fishing for compliments."

"I never thought you were."

She placed her own hand below his and rested them both gently on his thigh. Her fingers dug into the thick muscle of his quadriceps, through the dirty, bloodstained denim of his jeans. Beneath the fabric, he was so hot. So strong and solid.

She moved her hand up, slowly but surely, stroking higher toward his groin. His breath caught, and then stopped entirely as her fingers brushed the turgid bulge of his penis beneath the fabric.

Here went nothing. "I think I know what you mean, about the hard place," she whispered, swirling her fingertips over it. Wow. A lot of him. That thick, broad, hard stalk just went on and on. "Or was this what you meant when you were referring to the rock?"

His face was a mask of tension, neck muscles clenched, tendons standing out. "You don't have to do this," he said, his voice strangled.

Aw. So sweet. Her fingers closed around him, squeezing. He groaned, and a shudder jarred his body. "I can't seem to stop," she said.

"Watch out, Nancy," he said hoarsely. "If you start something now, there's no stopping it."

She stroked him again, deeper, tighter, a slow caress that wrung a keening gasp from his throat. "I know," she said. "I know."

He reached out, a little awkwardly and clasped his arms around her shoulders. He stared into her eyes as if expecting her to bolt.

He pulled her close, enfolding her in his warmth, his power.

Suddenly, they were kissing. She had no idea who had kissed whom. The kiss was desperate, achingly sweet. Not a power struggle, not a matter of talent or skill, just a hunger to get as close as two humans could be. He held her like he was afraid she'd be torn away from her.

She tugged his shirt up, and he wrenched it off. She almost purred when she saw him half naked. His skin was pale, and his lean, sinewy muscles were sharply defined in the dim light that dangled over the kitchen stove. So hot. He smelled like soap, sweat. Then he pulled her tight T off, and she was just as exposed as he was, blinking through her mane of tangled hair. She was goose-pimpled by the chill that hit her skin, scorched by his eyes, his roving hands. Her nipples tingled where they touched his chest.

Shyness gripped her, but it was nothing like her usual cold feeling when the iron-plated doors slammed shut in the distance, shutting her lover out and her own small, numb self deep in. No, this was altogether different. She wasn't numb. She was shaking apart. About to fly into a million pieces. It was marvelous and unbearable. She crossed her arms over her chest, eyes squeezed shut. "Can we turn off the light?"

He froze for a few seconds. "Don't hide from me," he said.

"Oh, I won't, I'm not," she assured him, through trembling lips. "It's just that I'm . . . it would be easier for me."

He started to speak, and she cut him off before he could ruin it. "I don't want to stop, I swear," she said forcefully. "Just the light."

He hesitated, as if trying to read some secret language in her face.

"It's because I really care about this," she blurted. "I'm trying to . . . I'll use every trick I can think of not to shut down with you."

Ooh. Smooth move, Nance. Big turnoff, laying out her sexual problems to a prospective lover before she even made him come.

But Liam didn't look put off. "All right," he said. "First, let's put down the bed, though. I don't want to do that in the dark."

Oh. She'd forgotten that detail. A few deft tugs and wrenches with Liam's big muscles, and her rickety old futon bed was flat and ready for business. The mattress was already dressed with a sheet beneath the couch cover, which he tossed away. Then he went to the stove and yanked the string. The room was plunged into a million shades of gray.

The darkness hid nothing. The grays took on subtle meanings, shaded nuances, and he was a fulcrum of deeper gray in the midst of them, an enormous, brooding presence. Every hair prickled on her body at his proximity, every sense was attenuated to its limit: eyes straining in the dark, lungs pulling in deep breaths for his scent, ears attentive to the pad of his bare feet. Hungry to touch his skin, to taste his salt.

He unbuckled his belt, kicked off his shoes, shucked pants and briefs and socks with quick businesslike movements that the darkness loaded with pure eroticism.

She stared at his body, the curves and angles and contours in the shadows, the jut of his big penis. She shoved down her own jeans, peeled them off her ankles, and waited for him, her legs shaking.

She sensed him moving closer, but it was still a shock when his arms circled her. She convulsed with delicious shivers. His chest pressed to her breasts, the stroke of his hand trailed down the curve of her back, the swell of her hip, fitting her against him.

His cock prodded her leg. She could hardly breathe.

He bent his head, kissing where her neck met her shoulder. "You're not going to shut down," he said, part command, part triumph.

"No," she replied, astonished to realize that it was true. She wasn't. In spite of the terror they'd just been through and her tedious list of hang-ups. Usually, the harder a lover pounded at her stone walls demanding to be let in, the thicker her walls became. With Liam, there was no wall. Or there might be, but it didn't matter, because he was miles inside, and driving her ever deeper into her own self, deeper than she'd ever been. Every sensation, every emotion was a revelation. The thrill of leaping into a star-studded nowhere and the pleasure of coming back to a home she'd never known she had, all at once.

He pulled her down onto the bed and arranged her so she was wrapped around him, perched on his thighs, arms looped around his shoulders. Her nose buried in his sweat-stiffened thick, spiky hair. His cock pressed against her belly, his arms were tense and shaking.

Tenderness for him melted her inside, a hot shimmer around her heart that just got brighter and hotter. She slid her hand down between them and curled her fingers around his cock. She stroked, greedily exploring, teasing, milking him.

"Slow down," he whispered. "I don't want to come yet."

She let up her grip, just slightly. "When, then?"

"You first." He slid his hand down, tracing the divide of her bottom and stroking the wet, exquisitely sensitive places with an unerring fingertip while he situated her just . . . so . . . so that his penis was rubbing against her clit, while his fingers delved tenderly inside, and that slow, throbbing pressure, that slick, swirling caress turned her inside out, making her shudder with rapture. She almost fainted.

Liam hung on to her, lungs hitching. Trying not to let his fingers dig in too hard, leaving marks on her perfect skin. So soft. A marvel of nature, every detail graceful and perfect. Naked in his arms.

She was the most perfect creature he'd ever seen. That climax, a small supernova, right in his arms. He wanted to kneel at her feet, suck her toes, lick her arches, kiss her ankles. Thank her for existing. Make the whole world bow low whenever she walked by.

He rolled her slowly down onto her back, his finger still deep inside her clinging pussy. He folded her legs wide. She gazed up at him, with those huge, fathomless eyes, her hair a swirling mass against the sheet. So responsive, gasping and sighing at every caress. His finger was in ecstasy in the hot, clinging vortex. She was lifting herself, shoving against his delving hand, silently begging for more, deeper, harder.

His cock ached. She did a swirl twist of her fingers around him, and pulled. *Ah.* "I won't be able to wait if you do that again," he warned.

Her lips curved in a smile so lovely, it made his heart hurt. "Who asked you to wait?" she said.

He panted, his existence measured by heartbeats throbbing in his cock. "I wanted to make you come about ten times first," he told her.

She shook with breathless giggles. "That sounds like fun, but I'm too wound up for anything lazy and drawn out. I just want you."

Praise God, they were on the same page. He took her at her word and groped on the corner of the bed, where he'd laid a condom. He ripped it open, rolled the thing on, and leaned over her, balancing on one hand while he carefully nudged his cock into her slick opening.

What followed were the most excruciatingly wonderful moments of his life. He was big, she was tight and small. Her pussy hugged him. She arched, offered herself, wiggling to accommodate him. Damn. He should have insisted, gone for the ten orgasms. Gone down on her for an hour or so.

But with each shove, he slid deeper, felt her relax around him, her nails digging into his shoulders. He was dazzled at her alabaster pale body, so fragrant and smooth. Her arms, clutching him. Those perfect breasts, with the puckered dark nipples that he hadn't even had a chance to properly feast on. No time. So much to do with her.

A man would need a lifetime for it all.

"Are you okay?" he asked her.

She had to try about three times before she could get words out of her throat. "I . . . I think I'm going to fall apart."

He tried to warm her with his body without crushing her. "Is that a good thing or a bad thing?"

"I don't know," she said, through chattering teeth. "It's an unprecedented thing."

"Ah. Well. I guess . . . that's good," he offered. "I hope."

"You're huge, by the way," she said.

"I'm sorry," he said helplessly.

"Don't apologize." She slid her hands down his back, dug her fingernails into his ass, pulled him deeper. He couldn't talk. He was too busy trying not to come as they rocked, looking for their rhythm.

They found it, and were off. Much harder and faster than he'd meant to go, but he felt possessed. She twined around him, hanging on, jarred by every thrust. Wild horses were thundering through his body, but she was with him, holding on. Riding the crest. Not trampled by it.

The orgasm jolted through him, each jolt blasting him deeper, wider, wide open to the stars, the wind. Naked and exposed.

When it subsided, he was the one who felt trampled. Humbled and destroyed. So shy, he didn't dare look into her face.

The sky had brightened while they'd been busy, and he made out leaves rustling and moving in the pearly blue light outside the window.

Nancy cupped his face with her hand, pulling it around.

He rolled onto his side to face her, and they clasped hands, bodies still joined and slick with sweat and lube. Speechless. Eyes locked.

This time he was the one who couldn't handle the long, significant silence. He was afraid he'd hurt her, scared her. He got up, got himself a drink of water, gulped it thirstily. He hesitated a moment, and got one for her, too. When he brought it back to the bed, she was sitting up, her slender body curled in a graceful pose like a mermaid on a rock, legs tucked to the side. He handed her the glass, and she held it up to her cheek for a moment. He steeled himself, and asked it. "Are you okay?"

She nodded. A soft smile curved her lips. She didn't speak. It was driving him crazy. "What?" he demanded. "What the hell is it?"

She laughed, softly. "That's funny, from you," she said. "I'm just using your trick." She saw the bewilderment in his eyes, and explained. "You know. Shutting up, and just looking at you. Feeling it, here." She put her hand on her heart. "I like the way it feels."

He squirmed, inwardly. "Oh. That's not a trick. It's just the truth."

She nodded gravely and drank the water, looking over him with a frank approval that brought a blush to his face. His dick responded, too, standing up proudly. Not yet. Ten more orgasms. And they'd see how things went. He took the glass of water, placed it on the lamp table next to the bed, and then grabbed her and tugged her to the edge of the couch. She sensed his intention and grabbed his hair. "Liam—"

"Shhh." He shoved her thighs wide. Her cunt was beautiful, juicy and plump and soft, adorned with a soft fuzz of ringlets wet with lube. He kissed his way up to the good stuff, and moaned with pleasure when he tasted her juice. Sweet and hot, slick and earthy. Fucking delicious.

Her phone rang. They froze. "Do you usually get calls at this hour?" Liam demanded.

"Unfortunately, yes," she murmured.

Her machine clicked and whirred. A man's voice came on the line. "Nance? Pick up, if you're there. You have to come to the studio and listen to this great new order I came up with for the CD."

Nancy reached for the phone that still lay by the couch. Liam leaned back. The guy's voice went on ". . . try your cell phone next—"

She picked up. "I'm here, Peter."

"What took you so long to get to the phone?" Peter demanded.

"It's five in the morning, or haven't you noticed?" She perched on the edge of the couch. "What do you mean, change the order?"

"I thought of a great new—"

"You've done this to me three times! If we don't get those liner notes to Shepard by nine-thirty, the CD won't be in the catalog at all!"

"But it makes more sense if I put 'The Road to You' at the end!"

"Tell me about it when I get there." She hung up and looked around as if waking from a dream. "I forgot the liner notes. My mind was wiped." She shot Liam a guilty look. "I'm sorry, but I've got to get moving. I've got a million things to—"

"No," he said.

She froze, eyes tightening. "Excuse me?"

Rage was bubbling hot inside him. "What would it take to convince you that you can't go bouncing around, la-di-da, and do your fucking errands like nothing even happened?"

"They are not 'fucking errands'! This is how I support myself!"

"You can't support yourself if you're dead." The words were a blow, as he'd meant them to be. "You're coming up to Latham with me."

She let out an incredulous laugh. "Am I? Thanks so much for discussing this decision with me."

"You don't have any grip on reality," he told her.

"It's you who needs to get a grip." Her voice shook. "Don't think that I don't appreciate what you did last night. But don't think that it's all up to you, now, either, understand? I have a life, and I have to—"

"That's what I'm trying to help you protect," he said. "Not your work, Nancy. Not your career. Your *life*. Do you know the difference?"

"This city is swarming with millions of people—"

"Two of whom came at us with a knife last night."

"Do not be sarcastic. I'll be with people the entire day, and I'll take cabs. I have to be in midtown by nine-thirty sharp, and I—"

"I'll go with you," he announced, his voice grim.

She struggled to marshal her arguments. "Liam, I'll be racing from pillar to post, and I can't concentrate if you're watching my every—"

"Deal with it. Or come back with me to Latham." He could tell already from the look on her face that he'd played his cards all wrong.

"Yes, and do what while my livelihood goes straight to hell?" she demanded. "Spend my days lolling in your bed, with my legs in the air? I'm sure it would be fun, Liam, but it's not a long-term solution."

"I never said it was," he said, but that was the wrong thing to say. Her soft, pink mouth went all pinched and tight.

"I see. Of course. Just a temporary thing," she said. "Sexual entertainment while you amuse yourself with your bodyguard hobby."

Shit. "Nancy, that's not what I meant. I'm just saying you can't—"

"It's not up to you." She stood there, auburn hair tousled out to here, eyes blazing, so beautiful it hurt his eyes. He grabbed his clothes.

"This is the biggest production company I've ever done business with. If I flake out on them, they'll never take me seriously again."

He finished tying his shoes. "Don't try to justify yourself to me," he said, his voice clipped. "Because you can't." He shrugged into his jacket. "Get dressed," he said. "I'll take you to your recording studio."

Her chin went up. "I can get a cab."

Two strides put him right in her face, one hand tilting her head back, the other digging into the soft, smooth swell of her ass cheek.

"Don't push me any further," he warned. "Give me this one. You owe me a hell of a lot more. But you will—give—me—this."

Or else. Her throat bobbed. They both heard the sexual menace in his tone. He had never used his size and strength to intimidate a woman. Never dreamed that he was capable of it. But look at him, actually wondering what he would do if she kept defying him.

His rock-hard, throbbing dick had some very good ideas.

She wrenched her chin away. Started getting ready. He was so relieved, he almost sagged to the ground. He'd bluffed her.

But the predatory beast inside him was as disappointed as hell.

Chapter
7

"**I** don't see what the point was of you schlepping down here if you're not even going to listen," Peter said crabbily.

Nancy rubbed her eyes. Peter's handsome face swam into focus. "Peter, please," she said wearily. "I haven't slept, and I risked death and abduction last night. Spare me the attitude."

"I very much doubt that anyone was trying to abduct you," Peter said with a sniff. "I mean, why would they? You're having delusions of grandeur. Do I need to brew some coffee, or can you stay conscious long enough for me to run this new song order by you?"

"Hit me with it," she said, dragging herself to her feet. "I'll stand. Easier to stay awake."

"Good idea," Peter said. "My thought was to put 'Glory Road' at the top. Hit 'em with everything we've got, bada-bam-bada-boom. Once we've got their attention, 'The Slippery Slope.' Then Enid's a cappella intro to 'The Far Shore.' And then, we'll put . . ."

Despite her best efforts, Peter's voice faded into background noise. Nancy shifted her weight from one foot to the other, thinking of Liam's eyes when he left her. It made her want to bawl. But she couldn't throw her whole life into the air and leap into his pocket. She couldn't.

She shook the memory away, keeping her eyes fixed on Peter's refined, ethereal good looks that had so attracted her back in college. They had met freshman year and formed a band: Peter on lead vocals and guitar, herself on acoustic bass, Henry on drums, Chad on keyboards. She'd worked herself to the bone finding gigs, planning spring-break tours. She'd fancied herself in love with Peter, and he loved her, too. At least, he'd assured her that he did, even on the day that he and Henry and Chad had sat her down and told her they were looking for a new bass player. Someone with more natural rhythm.

"We need somebody with a jazz background. Someone who can lay down a really killer bass line," Peter explained earnestly.

"Oh," Nancy squeaked, trying not to cry.

"It's not that we don't love you, Nance. What we're trying to say is, everybody should do what they're best at," Henry coaxed.

"Yeah, and what you're best at is finding gigs, Nance!" Peter encouraged. "You should be the band's business manager!"

"Yeah?" Nancy sniffed.

"Yeah! We can't do without you!" Henry said eagerly. "It's like, you take care of us, you know? Like how you always make sure that Chad's shirt doesn't clash with his pants before he goes on stage. Like the way you find gigs. That's what we need! Bassists are a dime a dozen. We can find a bassist anywhere!"

Peter patted her shoulder. "Come on, Nance, be a sport."

"I'm trying, I'm trying," she said dully.

Yes, she'd tried to be a sport. She'd tried again, years later, when Peter fell in love with Enid. He'd used almost the same words as when he'd dumped her as a bassist. "It's not that I don't love you," he'd said, patting her shoulder. "It's just a different kind of love. The love I feel for Enid is, like, she sets a match to my heart, and poof! I go up in flames. A match to my heart. Cool image." He began to hum, and stopped when Nancy burst into tears. "Oh, God. Don't do this to me," he begged. "It's not like we had this grand passion, you know? Come on! Be a sport."

She had choked back her tears, and been a sport for Peter and Enid. She'd been a sport again, when Ron dumped her for Liz. And damned if she hadn't been a sport yet again, for Freedy, when he jilted her for Andrea. She was a professional sport. A real trouper.

How crushing the loss had felt then. How far away, how insignificant it felt now. After losing Lucia. After facing death in a nylon mask and a switchblade. After making love to Liam.

Ron, Freedy, Peter. They were like dimly remembered games of hopscotch and tag from kindergarten. She blinked. Peter was yelling her name. "Nance! For God's sake! Are you having an epileptic seizure?"

"I'm fine," she said faintly.

Peter's frown became a pout. "I need your feedback, and I don't feel like you're there for me! Listen while I play the new order for you."

Nancy braced herself for the raucous burst of percussion that opened "Glory Road." Halfway through "Devil's Bargain" she zoned out again, staring at Peter's ethereal beauty. It struck her as effeminate and insubstantial. Liam's stern masculine beauty was imbued with strength, whereas Peter's had an air of fragility. In fact, her instinct had always been to protect Peter from harsh reality, to buoy his confidence. To manage his career so he could make a living doing what he loved.

There was nothing fragile about Liam. She would never have to make sure his socks matched. She would never need to find work for him. Strange. All these years, she'd been so busy frantically trying to earn what love and attention came her way. It had never even occurred to her how immensely sexy self-sufficiency was in a man.

Her revelation brought her no pleasure, however. If anything, it made her more miserable. He was so angry and hurt by the fight they'd had. He probably never wanted to see her again.

The final strains of "The Road to You" were dying away. Peter was staring at her expectantly. "So?" he prompted. "What do you think?"

Exhaustion rolled heavily over her. "It's fine, Peter."

His face fell. "Just fine? That's all you can say?"

"I need a nap," she said. She flung herself onto the couch, and slid instantly into sleep. Peter's scolding babble faded to black.

At some point during her nap, a vivid dream came to her. Liam was sitting on a chair, lit by a beam of sunlight, playing a haunting melody on his fiddle. In the unaccountable way of dreams, she knew the lovely tune was for her. She woke up smiling, into Enid's face. Enid knelt by the couch, waving a cup of coffee under Nancy's nose. Nancy's smile faded, and she struggled into a sitting position and grabbed the coffee. "Thanks, Enid."

Peter walked briskly into the room. "Sorry to drag you back to the real world," he said. "But it's eight-ten, and you're going to have to move your butt to get those liner notes redone in time before we head up to meet with Shepard."

The familiar pressure settled on Nancy's chest—and suddenly, she thought about the dream. Something clicked in her mind.

The painful pressure lightened, like magic. This was not life or death. The liner notes, the meeting—they were insignificant, in the grand scheme of things. Close encounters with sex and death did wonders to reorder a girl's priorities. "Not," she said, sipping her coffee.

Peter and Enid glanced at each other. "What do you mean, 'not'?" Peter asked, his voice cautious.

" 'Not' meaning that you and Enid have to move your butts, not me. As of this moment, the liner notes are no longer my problem."

Peter's face was blank. "What are you talking about? We have to deliver the layout to Shepard this morning, and if we don't—"

"You, Peter. Not we. I've revised those notes three times. The disk is in my purse." She dug it out and handed it to him. "Change it on your computer. Deliver it to Shepard yourself. I can't go today."

"Can't go? Are you nuts?" Peter looked horrified. "Nance, I don't do desktop publishing! I'm an artist, not a secretary!"

"You could always leave the album order like it was, if you get desperate," she suggested. "It was fine before."

"You're not coming?" Enid's limpid blue eyes widened with outrage, to the point of bulging, Nancy noticed with detached interest. "What's gotten into you? What are we supposed to say to Shepard?"

"Call and reschedule, if you don't want to go alone." Nancy suggested. "Or tell him that I'm having some personal problems."

"What personal problems could be more important than—"

"Being attacked by masked kidnappers. Being threatened with death and dismemberment," Nancy said. "Just for starters."

"Oh, please, Nance. You don't even care if the album gets into the catalog or not?" Enid sounded wounded.

"Of course I care. But you guys have to do your part. I'm done pulling rabbits out of hats. I have to go. Peter, get your shoes on. You have to come back with me to my apartment."

"Today? Why?" He sounded outraged. "Nancy, don't be ridic—"

"You owe me," Nancy said, her voice steely. "I work my ass off for you. I almost got killed last night, and I promised a friend I'd get company everywhere I go. And that means you're up to bat. Lucky you."

Peter rolled his eyes. "Your timing is—"

"Plus, I need help packing my computer and scanner and printer into the car. I'm going up to Latham for a while."

Enid and Peter exchanged shocked glances. "Latham?" Peter repeated. "Now is not the time for country air! Tonight's the gig at the Bottom Line with Brigid McKeon! The liner notes are due, we're going on tour in two weeks, the FolkWorld Conference is coming up—"

"It's really not that far," she assured him, patting his shoulder. "And I'll be in touch. By e-mail and cell. It's really no big deal."

Peter accompanied her with bad grace, but she ignored his sulking. Outside, it was a beautiful morning. A brisk wind made the bits of garbage dance and swirl cheerfully over sidewalk grates.

She snagged them a cab back to Avenue B on the first wave.

Peter stared stonily out the window, leaving her free to be self-absorbed. Peter usually required a lot of attention, but she wouldn't be capable of giving it to him today if she wanted to. And she couldn't be bothered. She felt strange, manic. Something had happened to her last night. She had changed. She wasn't sure exactly what the change was, but she liked it. She was going to pack up every piece of her life that was portable, collect her cat, drive up to Latham, and throw herself on Liam's mercy. And a couple of other choice body parts.

Doubt clutched at her. No way could it work. A guy like him, with his mellow country lifestyle, his earth mother ideal. A busy, citified madwoman like herself. Besides, he was so angry at her. And there were the armed abductors and angry burglars. Add a murdered jeweler to the mix, a mysterious letter, a deadly hidden object, and yikes. Having Nancy D'Onofrio for a girlfriend was quite a proposition.

Problematic didn't even begin to describe it.

But at least she no longer felt like she would disappoint him in bed. Oh, no, she knew just exactly what she wanted to do to that big, strong body. She thought about the look in his eyes when he told her how to look at the flower. The feeling that pierced her. The sweetness. It made her heart catch, and her lungs squeeze, painfully.

She was going to Latham. And if she got her heart crushed to a fine powder, well, whatever. It wouldn't be the first time.

But it would definitely be the worst.

Eoin shuffled up the driveway to Liam's house at 2:00, red eyed and shamefaced, like any guy would who had been guzzling Guinness all night and had faced the new day without sleep or a shower.

Liam looked up from the chopping block. He'd been trying to unload excess adrenaline and misery by chopping wood. So far with limited success. "Look who the cat dragged in," he commented sourly.

Eoin flushed. "I was playing tunes with the lads at this pub in Sheepshead Bay, and I lost track of the time. I had to hitchhike back."

Liam grunted. "Hear you've got a new job."

"Uh, yes. I'm going on tour with this band, Mandrake. Next week."

"Congratulations," he said.

"Don't think I don't appreciate—after all you've done for me—"

Liam held up his hand, and Eoin choked off whatever he was about to say. "It's okay, Eoin," he said wearily. "You should be making music. You're doing the right thing."

Hope dawned on Eoin's pallid face. "You're not mad?"

"Do you want to work for Matigan until you leave, or don't you?" Liam demanded. "If you're too busy, I need to let him know right now."

Eoin straightened his thin shoulders. "I'd be glad to work," he said with dignity. "I start rehearsing Sunday. I can work until then."

"Go get some rest," Liam said. "You look like hammered shit."

Eoin hesitated. "So. Ah. Liam. Is, ah, something happening? With you and Mrs. D'Onofrio's daughter, I mean?"

Liam shot him a look that made Eoin spin on his heels and bolt.

Inviting her to the seisiun had been his first mistake. Taking her home was the second, though he'd paid for that by getting pounded by masked assholes. But the crowning stupidity had been fucking her. Now he knew what it felt like. And he could think of nothing else.

He was begging for the trouble he'd spent the first eleven years of his life watching. Bitterness that ate away love until it was gone. Was he programmed to repeat this bullshit? Was he fucking doomed?

Memories rolled into his mind, sickening and vivid. The vacation to Niagara Falls his mother had planned, a last-ditch effort to unite them as a family. The bags were packed, train tickets in his mother's clutch purse. She'd been waiting, dressed in her eggshell blue pantsuit. But when his father walked in the door, Liam took one look and knew that it wasn't going to happen. Dad had done it again. You could count on him to let you down the way you could count on the sun to rise.

"It's about time you got here," his mother said, reaching for her coat. "We'll have to hurry to catch the train."

"Something's come up, Fiona," his father said flatly.

His mother laid her coat down, her face carefully expressionless. "What do you mean, something's come up?"

"There's a problem with a shipment, and I have to go look into it."

"Why can't you send Martin, or Brady?"

"You want something done right, you got to do it yourself."

"That doesn't apply to your family, however," she said frigidly.

His father's mouth became a hard line. "I make sacrifices to keep you in style, Fiona, and all I ever get from you is whining and nagging."

"Did I ever ask you to make these sacrifices? No, Frank. All I want is to see you more than once a month." His mother's voice shook. "All I'm asking is that you keep your word and go with us to Niagara."

His father's fists clenched. "God, Fiona, why can't I make you understand? It's my responsibility—"

"Go, then. Just go. Your bag is right by the door." She walked stiffly out of the room. Her back was very straight, but her face was crumpled.

His father looked at Liam, immobile on the couch. "Sorry, son. When you've got a family of your own to support, you'll understand."

"Go to hell," Liam said.

Frank Knightly's face darkened. "Don't speak to me that way. I'm your father. Show me some respect."

"You're not my father anymore," Liam said in a cold, very clear voice. "You're a terrible father. You're fired."

His father stared at him, grabbed the suitcase, and walked out. That was the last Liam had seen of him. Twenty-six years. A lifetime.

Liam shook himself back to the present, and savagely attacked the kindling pile again. Fuck this. Fuck it all. No way. Not him.

He looked around some time later at the sound of a car. Nancy's Volkswagen Jetta came buzzing down the driveway. He clutched the ax handle as she got out of the car. Wishing he'd bathed.

She was elegant in faded low-slung jeans that clung enticingly to her hips and a charcoal high-necked ribbed sweater that showed off a discreet strip of flat belly. Her hair was wound into a loose braid, backlit by the sun like a halo of fire. She looked gorgeous. And nervous.

"Hello." She gave him a tentative smile.

Liam crossed his arms over his chest. Her smile faltered.

She opened the back door of her car and pulled out a cat carrier. A plaintive meow issued from the white plastic box. Her cat? He peered into her car windows. The backseat was piled high with stuff.

Suitcases. Computer equipment. What the fuck? Was she actually planning to . . . Oh, sweet Jesus. She was. His heart started to gallop.

"What are you doing here?" he demanded.

She'd known this was going to be hard. Nancy stuck out her chin. "I was under the impression that you'd invited me."

"Yes, and you blew me off."

His icy tone chilled her. "I did some thinking this morning," she said. "I realized when I got to the studio that I'd made a mistake."

"What changed your mind? Another ambush?"

Nancy threw up her hands. "For God's sake, I'm sorry! I made a mistake! Can't a person be allowed to make a mistake sometimes?"

He shrugged. "People make them whether they're allowed to or not."

"Cut out the snide remarks, Liam. I'm trying to be serious."

He was grimly silent. "Yeah. That's what I'm afraid of, Nancy," he said finally. "I think that for us, getting serious would be a bad idea."

Nancy fought for control of her face. Be a big girl. Be a sport. God knew, she had the practice. She knew the next part of the script by heart. *Okay, forget it, then. Forget I ever said anything. Have a nice life.*

The words wouldn't come out. She was going to get a freaking backbone, and try a little bit harder, damn it. She cleared her throat.

"So, Liam. Are you done punishing me yet? Because this part is really boring and irritating, and I'd like to move on to the good stuff."

The darkness in his eyes changed, like clouds shifting in a turbulent sky. "I'm not punishing you," he said. "Just being clear." He waited a moment, trying hard not to say it, but in the end, he couldn't help himself. "And what exactly do you mean by the good stuff?"

She looked over his big, gorgeous body, the opened shirt sweat stained, showing his ripped, cut pecs. "If you have to ask . . ."

Liam started to speak, bit back the words, and closed his eyes. "I'm not a person who takes this kind of thing lightly."

"I know," she whispered. "I'm not, either."

Liam's hands clenched. "We're going to hit a wall, you know."

She ached to touch his face. "You're so sure?"

"I feel strongly for you," he said. "But I see that wall in the distance, just waiting for us."

Nancy swiped tears from her face with the back of her hands. "Maybe you're right," she said. "But you know what? I don't care."

A ghost of a smile touched his lips. "No?"

"No. Let's just go for it. Full speed. We'll hit that wall together."

"If this is because of those guys who attacked you—"

"I'm glad you mentioned that," she broke in. "This was a point that I wanted to make. I appreciate your offer to protect me, but that has nothing to do with the fact that I think you're really special, and I want to spend some time with you." There it was, bald as an egg.

She waited for the verdict.

And waited, and waited. It was agonizing, to go this far out on the limb, and just stay there, fighting for balance. One last, desperate sally before retreating in despair. She sucked in a deep breath.

"And there is, ah, one more little thing," she said.

He looked like he was bracing himself. "Yes?"

She cleared her throat again. "I'd, ah, like to give you a blow job."

His face went blank. Probably wondering if he'd heard correctly.

"I hope you're not too shocked," she added. "But the last two days have sort of burned away all my maidenly shyness. I can't promise any world-class fellatio technique, but I still think that performing oral sex upon you right now would be the absolute highlight of my day."

Liam blinked, coughed. "Ah . . ." He turned, and swung his ax in a big arc. It landed in the block with a sharp *thunk* that made her jump. He grabbed her cat carrier and headed toward the house.

"Follow me," he said.

Chapter
8

Nancy trailed after Liam, up the steps of the wide wraparound porch. She was so dizzy with the success of her last-ditch ploy, she barely even registered the details of his home. Just an impression of airy rooms, big windows, sparse and graceful furnishings. He knelt down and flipped the lever that opened Moxie's carrier. The cat stalked out, sniffed his hand, and padded away to investigate, tail high.

Nancy wanted to break the tension, but the purposeful way that Liam strode through the dining room with his back to her discouraged speech. She scurried after his long strides. He'd started up the stairs without turning to see if she was being pulled along in his wake.

It looked like she would be making good on her rash offer. Her toes were curled with lust at the thought, but she hadn't pictured going down on him when the weather conditions were this, well . . . stormy.

He stopped outside a door. "I'm sweaty. I need to take a shower."

"No," she said. "You don't."

He gave her a doubtful look. She waved him in the door. God forbid she lose her nerve, or lose her moment, or miss her window of opportunity. Besides. He looked great, just like that. Gleaming with sweat, hair damp and spiky. Salty and virile and vigorous.

He opened the door and beckoned her in.

The room was stark in its simplicity. An antique brass bed sported a beautiful green Irish Chain quilt. An earth-toned Navaho rug lay on the gleaming wooden floor. Musical instruments from around the world decorated the white walls. There was a straight-backed chair, a narrow, upright antique chest of drawers. A turn-of-the-century steamer trunk. Old-fashioned, sparse, simple and neat.

Sunshine blazed through the open window, lighting up a bright rectangle on the rug. Liam slowly, deliberately went and stood in the middle of that patch of sunlight. An aggressive, wide-legged stance.

So, then. No banter, no chitchat, no lead-in. He was still pissed, but he wanted his blow job anyway. Well, fine. That felt weird, but she was getting comfortable with weirdness in these strange days.

Now all she had to do was act like a femme fatale. It couldn't be that hard. She'd seen it done in films. But her breath was coming fast, her palms were damp, her knees were jittery. Her thighs kept squeezing around a melting pulse of aching heat at the idea of taking him into her mouth.

A slow, deliberate striptease would be the thing, but she was dressed wrong. She needed more pieces, more complicated lingerie, snaps and straps and ribbons and laces. As it was, she could only let her purse drop to the floor and peel off her sweater with slow, sexy deliberation. She walked toward him until the patch of sunlight illuminated her body below the neck. The chilly breeze from outside tightened her nipples to puckered little brown nubs.

She twitched her braid over her shoulder, pulled out the elastic, and unraveled the braid. Her hair stuck to her damp hands and flew up all around her face, electric and wild, floating around her like Medusa's locks.

The jeans came next, the appallingly plain white cotton panties, and there she was. Stark naked but for her dangling garnet earrings and Lucia's sapphire pendant. He stared, eyes burning. Not a word.

"Do you, ah, want to sit down?" she asked, timidly.

He shook his head.

Nancy drew in a deep breath and reached for his belt. It took forever to get the thing undone, but he did not help. His hands were clenched into big fists held rigidly at his sides. The emotion in his face vibrated around him. She felt its pressure against her skin.

She went on to his jeans, shoved them down with his briefs just far enough to free his cock. It sprang up into her hands, hot and huge and hard, the thick knob at the end dripping with pre-come. So. No lack of enthusiasm on his part. One less thing to worry about.

She moistened her hands by swirling them around the slick fluid that gleamed on his big cockhead and gripped him, moving up in a long, tight slide. He arched, jerked. His short, shocked groan sounded as if it had been captured in his throat and wrestled into submission.

She sank down to her knees on the rug without even thinking about it. Partly it was her rubbery legs giving way, partly it was raw hunger to taste him, to make him shudder and gasp.

His cock bobbed in her face. She was kneeling right in that patch of brilliant morning sunshine, and its brightness blinded her. The sun was hot, but cool air moved from the open window. The combination was a subtle caress, a million little thrills, like fluttering strokes with feathers or silk. She stroked, gripped him. Lashed him with voluptuous strokes of her tongue. His hands slid into her hair, gripping it hard. His body shook, rigid. She was so excited, she felt faint.

She went at him with everything she had; licking and lapping, stroking and swirling with her hands. Flicking at the sensitive slit at the end of his glans and savoring the slick, salty fluid that dripped from it.

Then she pulled him into her mouth.

It took a little while to get comfortable with his size, but she was extremely motivated, her entire body buzzing. Somehow she figured out how to relax, take him deeper. The sensual choreography all came together in her mind, and it was like something she'd always known. Always loved. She sucked him deep, pulling on every outstroke, torturing him with a swirling twist of her tongue.

His hands tightened their grip in her hair, and he pushed her face away from him. She wiped her mouth, and looked up into the stark, tense mask of his face. "What?" she asked.

"I need to fuck you," he said.

She blinked. More welcome words were never spoken. She felt lit up like a Christmas tree, about to spit sparks, catch fire. She stroked his balls with her fingertips, just to enjoy the abrupt shiver of pleasure that racked his big body. "Do you have a condom?" she asked.

"Bedside table drawer, by the wall," he said.

He made no move to get one, just hoisted her to her feet. And waited. She tried not to stumble. She should be doing a hip-swaying sashay, but it was all she could do to stay on her feet. She started to circle the bed, but stopped short, gazing at that expanse of quilt. A real femme fatale would not waste an obvious chance to strike a hot pose.

Her stomach quivered, but she clambered up onto the bed on her hands and knees and crawled across. Arching her back. Going for sexy, sinuous. She fumbled in the bedside table drawer for the condoms.

The effect on him was instantaneous. The bed squeaked and sagged, and there he was, arched over her, his hot body covering her back, his cock swinging and bobbing against her inner thigh. She almost lost her balance. He reached out over her shoulder, snagged the long string of silver foil packets out of the drawer.

She tried to wiggle, shift, turn herself, but he held her in place while he ripped a packet open and applied the condom. Her breath came fast and nervous through her open mouth. Uh-oh. She'd miscalculated.

Oh, please. She'd presented her backside to him. The guy could hardly be blamed for taking her up on the invitation. But this sexual position made her feel particularly vulnerable and small. Plus, it hurt. Deep inside. Just another of the long list of things that shut her down.

No. She was not going to spoil this. Not for him, and not for her. She was not chickening out. She wanted him more than she'd ever wanted anything. And she would . . . get . . . through . . . it.

She braced herself for it, but there was no painful, invasive shove. Just his enormous warmth poised, motionless over her, warming her, waiting. His hot, soft lips endlessly caressed her nape, her spine. He slid his hands between her legs, circling her clit with clever fingers, with slow, lazy strokes. Petting until she squirmed against his hand, breathless and desperate.

When he finally nudged inside, she lunged back to take in more. He gripped her hips with a low, admonishing murmur, kissed her shoulder blades, licked her spine. Her inner flesh clenched around his thick shaft. He shoved deeper. She'd never felt so full. Every part of her that he touched responded, glowing. She squeezed harder, squirming, clawing her way closer. . . . He shoved as deep as he could go. . . .

And she disintegrated into countless blissful, shimmering motes of light, with hot, bright jolts of pleasure pulsing through them, on and on.

His breath panted, hot and rhythmic against her back. He set his teeth against her shoulder, licked her sweat. "Ah, God. That felt so good," he muttered hoarsely. "Do that again. Please. Do it forever."

"Anytime you like," she told him, with a shaky laugh. "I can't seem to stop. Not when you touch me. It's crazy."

He made a strangled sound deep in his throat, gripped her hips, and began to move. It took on a wild, frenetic momentum. She clutched the bars of the brass bed to brace herself, her face shoved in the pillow to stifle the cries that jerked out at each slick, driving stroke and swivel of his thick shaft. He felt wonderful, stirring her into a creamy froth. And it didn't hurt. Her body had resculpted itself to cherish every thick, throbbing inch of him, and melt with delight while doing it.

She came, again and again, until she was wilted, boneless into the bed, flat on her face, panting. Too spent even to beg for mercy.

He let go and let his own climax wrench through him.

They lay together for a few minutes, floating in a timeless dream measured only by a burst of birdsong and the flickering shadows of clouds passing over the sun. He was squishing her, but the pressure felt good. So what if her lungs could only expand to 10 percent of their capacity? Who needed air, after sex like that?

But after a moment, he stirred and rolled onto his side, still keeping her clamped against him. His penis still inside her.

Her cell phone rang. His body went tense. Nancy leaned down, fished the cell out of her purse, and checked the display. Peter. Hah. As if. She dropped it back into her purse, letting it ring on unanswered.

She turned her head, enjoyed his startled expression.

Liam smiled, a slow, wondering smile. "That must've cost you."

"I would turn the thing off completely if it weren't for my sisters," she said. "I don't want to be out of touch with them."

"You can give them my landline number," he suggested.

"Thanks," she said demurely. "That's very generous of you, Liam."

He snorted at her sarcasm and nuzzled his nose into the nape of her neck. "God, you smell good," he said. "Like something good to eat."

"Vanilla sandalwood essential oil mix," she explained.

"It drives me crazy," he said.

She arched herself like a cat, glorying in his response to her. "So, Liam. Are you done being mad at me?"

She peeked back over her shoulder after a long silence. He looked thoughtful. "I don't know yet," he said. "I was pretty upset. I think we're going to have to have a whole lot more sex before I work it all out."

"Okay," she said cheerfully.

His chest jerked with laughter, and he extricated himself, pulling off the condom and heading toward the door. "Have to get rid of this."

She feasted her eyes on his gorgeous naked body when he came back into the room. The pattern of dark chest hair arrowing down to his groin, the powerful muscles of his legs and thighs, his heavy arousal, rising proudly out of a thatch of thick black hair. Mmm. Already. Wow.

"Are you hungry?" he asked. "I could fix you something to eat."

"I'm not hungry," she said. "Not for food, anyway."

He came closer until he was standing right by the bed, his cock rigid and high. He lifted the quilt, tossed it away, and stared down at her naked body. "Ah, God," he said softly.

She caressed his cock, the pulsing, swollen red heat of it. He grasped her hand, bent to kiss her knuckles, then turned it over to kiss her wrist, her palm, each finger. He pressed the back of her hand against his cheek with reverent tenderness.

She reached out for him, drawing him down. He plucked another condom from the string, readied himself in a few deft moves, and mounted her, thrusting inside in a seamless slide that made tears start in her eyes. His arms circled her, and they clung, rocking for what could have been hours. She lost all sense of time. The sunlit room was a magical space, dust motes doing a lazy dance of joy above them. The breeze rustled the trees, making wind chimes tinkle and clank. His face filled her whole world. His weight, deliciously sensual between her legs, pressing her down into the bed, in a slow, maddening, pumping pulse and swirl. She could look into his astonishing eyes forever.

They moved together faster, kissing with an ardent hunger that made her heart swell. Every place his body touched her was like a kiss, specific, hot, deliberate, and she lifted herself against him, reaching for perfection. Without warning, it burst upon her. He cried out at the same moment, and they were flung together into that long fall, fused.

They came back to reality slowly. He untangled himself, stroking her back. "Was, uh, everything all right?" he asked hesitantly.

She laughed. "It was great, and you know it."

He rolled onto his back with an ironic grunt. "I have my moments of doubt," he said. "I was just afraid maybe we're overdoing it."

"You don't say." She laid her head on his solid chest, practically purring as his arms closed possessively around her. "You're amazing," she said lazily. "I've never been able to . . . well, you're amazing."

He lifted his head, eyes curious. "Never been able to what?"

She tried to gloss over her thoughtless gaffe with a laugh. "I just don't usually have this wonderful a time in bed, that's all. I tend to shut down if things get too intense. But with you, it doesn't happen."

He ran his fingers through her hair. "Why does it happen?"

"Who cares, since it doesn't happen with you?" she said brightly. "I'd much rather not dwell on my stupid, tedious—"

"Why does that happen to you, Nancy?" he demanded, relentless.

She sighed. It would seem that Liam would not be guided around this particular crack in the pavement. "Well, I've got a theory."

"Let's hear it."

She gathered her composure, hoping without much hope that

talking about her hang-ups would not invoke them back into being. "I told you about being in foster care, remember? It was the last home I was in before Lucia. I was thirteen. A nice family in Larchmont. I felt lucky. It was better than a lot of places I'd been. Until their son came back from his freshman year at college. Big guy. Body odor problem."

Liam's face contracted. "Oh, Christ."

"Oh, don't get scared. It's not that bad," she assured him. "He never actually . . . well, luckily, there were almost always lots of people around, and I shared a room with other girls. But he would take every chance he got to pin me against walls and in dark corners and rub his erection against me. That was usually all he had time for. Thank God."

Liam's hands were clenched. "What a piece of shit."

"He was working up to it, though," she went on. "It was only a matter of time. And he was his mother's firstborn darling. She was never going to believe me over him. Which was sad. I really liked her."

She stared up at the ceiling, twiddling with a piece of the quilt, lost in unpleasant memories. Liam nuzzled her with his lips. "And? So?"

"I told my social worker," she concluded, with a sigh. "She confronted the mother. The mother took his part. Called me a nasty lying slut. I got a new placement. With Lucia." She rubbed his hair, comfortingly. "So you see? My luck turned. But I carry some of that old stuff around with me, I guess. I never go for guys who are significantly bigger than me, for instance. I hate being pushed around, or squished. Makes me freeze right up." She hoisted herself up onto her elbow to stare down at his muscular body, and petted his massive chest. "You're a big exception," she added, in a wondering voice. "Very big."

His penis was long and hard and red, standing up against his belly. He shot her an uncomfortable look. "Sorry. I know it's inappropriate, after what you just told me. Being close to you just does it to me. I can't help it. Or hide it, either. Since I'm bare naked."

"It's okay," she murmured. "I know you're one of the good guys."

He gathered her into his arms. She melted into the hug. Her arms trembled with the strain of holding him so tightly, but she wanted it to last forever. When they finally relaxed, he brushed the hair off her face and cupped her cheek. "I want to find that guy and kill him," he said.

She was taken aback. "Ah, I don't recommend that, Liam," she said, a little nervously. "I have enough problems as it is."

He traced her eyebrow with his finger. "It feels strange to say it," he said. "I am not a violent person. I've never gone looking for a fight in my life. But I will kill anyone who touches you."

Nancy opened and closed her mouth a few times. "Um . . . I'm not quite sure what to do with that."

His shoulder jerked in a careless shrug. "You don't have to do anything with it," he said. "It just is."

He pulled away and got up, groping for his jeans. Their idyll was over. He was serious again, all business. She admired his ass as he pulled up his jeans. Then he opened his closet, rummaged up high under a pile of thick wool blankets, and pulled down a heavy-looking black fiberglass case. He brought it over and laid it down on the bed.

"What's that?" she asked.

He unsnapped the case. "My stepfather's old service revolver."

She flinched. "What are you going to do with that thing?"

He lifted a sardonic eyebrow. "Keep it close."

"You really think that's necessary? Do you know how to use it?"

He pulled out a box of bullets, flipped open the cylinder, and loaded the gun. "Yes, and yes. I could have used this in your stairwell last night. And of course I know how to use it. Jesus, what a question." He tucked it into the back of his jeans and shrugged on his shirt.

She shivered at the thought of the deadly thing, cold against the warm skin of his back. "Do you have a license to carry concealed?"

He looked directly into her eyes. "I'll arrange to get one. I've never needed one before, so I never bothered."

"But until you get one, maybe you'd just better—"

"Think it through, Nancy," he said. "If the cops catch me carrying concealed, they'll give me a hard time. If the bad guys catch me without it, they'll kill me, and take you. What scenario scares you more?"

Her stomach cramped, into a cold, hard knot, and she doubled up tight around it, hugging her knees to her chest and hiding her face.

After a moment, Liam sat down on the bed beside her and put his arm around her shoulders. "It's just a precaution," he said gently. "I'm sorry it upsets you. But I'll feel better if I'm packing."

She leaned into the hug. She could never get enough of them. She'd been starving for this embrace all her life and never even knew it.

And he seemed just as ravenous. They clung, nuzzling. Offering comfort with their bodies, their warmth, the strength of their limbs entwined. The patch of sun on the floor had moved across the room to the wall by the time he lifted his head and smiled at her.

"You hungry?" he asked.

"That's the second time you've asked me that," she observed. "I'm beginning to think it's a loaded question. Are you?"

"Starving. I haven't eaten since before the seisìun last night."

She hadn't eaten since the morning before that, but she thought it impolitic to say so. "You poor thing. Why didn't you say something?"

He shrugged. "It didn't seem important. Until now, that is."

"Well, let's go feed you, then! Have you got food?"

"I fixed the neighbor lady's porch steps a month ago, and she gave me a lifetime supply of frozen pot roast stew. Get dressed."

"Aw. Why? It feels good to be naked. Are you expecting company?"

"Eoin's around here somewhere. I'm sure he has the good sense to keep his distance, but there are no curtains on the kitchen window."

Liam finally compromised and enveloped her in his big green terry cloth bathrobe. They went down to feast in Liam's big kitchen on rich, savory stew, raisin toast, crisp apples, and wedges of white cheddar. Nancy ate with uncharacteristic appetite. Having a man stare at her like that made her giddy. She practiced her femme fatale act, licking fruit juice off her fingers, and was immensely gratified when he dragged her back up to the bedroom. They came together roughly, a wild collision.

The day went by, a blur of caresses, embraces. The revolver sat on the bedside table. A small, ugly sentinel, grimly reminding her of the fear and sorrow lurking outside this little magic circle.

The sun was low and the light a deep, rosy gold when she opened her eyes and found him twirling a lock of her hair and staring into her face with something like awe. "I feel honored," he said softly.

She gazed at him, muddled and disoriented. "You do? By what?"

"That Lucia thought I was good enough for you."

Nancy's eyes widened. "Oh, please," she snapped, and then suffered a rush of guilt. "Never mind," she muttered. "I loved her tremendously, but I'm furious with her for setting me up like that."

He propped his head up on one hand. "Why? What's so mortifying about her trying to fix you up? She wanted you to be happy."

She shifted uncomfortably. "I know, but Lucia didn't understand one of the basic laws of the animal kingdom. Men only want what they can't have. They chase things that run. So babbling on about my availability is the kiss of death."

Liam gently turned her face to meet his eyes. "I'm not an animal."

"I never said you were, Liam! You're taking this too personally!"

He shrugged. "Don't know any other way to take things."

She rolled back onto her side with a sigh. "I bet you wondered why a reasonably attractive woman would be so desperate that her mother has to find her a date."

He smiled at her and smoothed a lock of hair out of her eyes. "Strike out reasonably attractive and put in drop-dead gorgeous."

She blew a lock of hair out of her mouth, and tried to concentrate. "So, um, anyway," she stammered. "To get back to what I was saying—"

"Incredibly gorgeous," he reiterated.

"Yeah, we've been through the beauty-of-the-flower lecture. I got it, okay? Do you want to hear the rest of this or not?" she demanded crossly.

He crossed his arms behind his head. "Hell yeah. Go for it."

"Lucia wanted save me from myself. She hated all my fiancés."

That got his attention. He jerked up onto his elbow. "All your fiancés? What do you mean, 'all your fiancés'?"

She huddled deeper into her quilt. "She didn't tell you about my train wrecks o' love?" He shook his head, and she rolled her eyes. "I was engaged three times. All three of them dumped me. Not exactly at the altar, but close. Two of them also happened to be my clients."

He looked incredulous. "Jesus. Why? What happened?"

She plucked the quilt, feeling stupid. "They fell in love with someone else at the last minute."

He winced. "Oh, Christ. Ouch."

"Yeah, it sucked. At least by the time Freedy dumped me, I knew better than to get the wedding dress made in advance. I've only got two wedding gowns in storage, not three. One takes comfort in little things." She stared down, afraid to see pity in his face.

"They did you a favor," he said. "And me, too."

"You?" She looked up at that. "How do you figure?"

He gave her a grin. "If you were married to one of them, you wouldn't be here with me right now, and wouldn't that be a shame?"

A little fit of giggles shook her. "You're right. It's just as well. Lucia nagged and nagged about how they take advantage of me."

He shot up. "Present tense? You're still in contact with them?"

"Of course. I told you. Two of them are my clients. Or three, I suppose I should say, counting Enid. I manage her, too."

His jaw dropped. "These dickheads dump you for other women, and you still work sixteen hours a day managing their careers?"

"Don't start," she said huffily. "I have enough to bear from my sisters. We've put it all behind us."

"That guy who called at five a.m., was he one of your exes?"

She hesitated. "Uh, well, yes, as a matter of fact. That was Peter, my first fiancé. He's married to Enid, another singer whom I manage. I introduced them, ironically enough. He's an incredibly talented—"

"Manipulator," he supplied. "Dishonorable, self-indulgent user."

Nancy's chin went up. "You don't know him."

"I don't want to," Liam said promptly. "I know enough."

She frowned. "That's very critical, Liam. You don't hear me making judgments, announcing that you've lived your life all wrong."

"I didn't mean to sound critical."

She snorted. "Sure you didn't. And I don't mean 'Liam, you arrogant, know-it-all bastard' in a rude way."

He reached, grasping her upper arms, and dragged her down on top of him. "I'm saying the wrong things, so let's not talk," he said.

Her face was inches from his silvery green eyes. She was embarrassed to feel her anger fizzling away under the blunt force of his masculine allure. "You can't win an argument by seducing me."

He rolled on a condom she had not noticed him unwrap. "Were we arguing?" he asked innocently, pushing her legs wide. She dragged in a gasp as he thrust inside, caressing her with his hot, thick length.

"Smart-ass," was all she could say before the power possessed them, and all they could do was cling to one another and ride it out.

The haunting sound of the Uilleann pipes woke Liam. Nancy's light weight on his shoulder sent a rush of surprised joy through him.

He turned his head carefully and looked at the clock. 2:17 A.M.

Eoin. That sneaky, sentimental little bastard. Nancy murmured softly and raised her head. Moonlight flooded through the window, illuminating her shadowy eyes. She brushed her hair out of her face.

"How gorgeous. 'The Soldier's Vow.' That's one of my favorites."

"Yeah, Eoin goes for the real heartbreakers," he muttered.

She cuddled up next to him again. "It's romantic."

"It's two in the morning," he growled.

She punched him in the shoulder. "Oh, give in, Liam! There's moonlight, there's music, it's romantic. Surrender, already!"

He silenced her with a kiss. "I already have." He pulled her hand down and showed her the effect she had on his body.

She laughed. "Don't you ever get tired?"

"Not yet. What about you? Are you sore?"

"I'm fine," she said bashfully. "But I'd rather just talk for a while."

"Okay," he said, rolling onto his side. "What about?"

"Let's take it one minute at a time," she suggested gently. They stared at each other in the moonlight as he ran his fingers through her hair. Eoin ended "The Soldier's Vow" and began "The Women of Ireland."

"God, that kid is good," she said. "So he rents your basement?"

"Not exactly. He just bunks there. It's a space to crash."

"You give him a job and a place to stay? That's nice of you."

"Not really. People helped me when I was a kid. This is the best way to pay them back. Besides, he's family. My mom's cousin's boy."

"People helped you how?" Her slender hand trailed over his shoulders, exploring his muscles. It was turning him on like crazy.

He wrangled his attention back to her question by brute force of will. "When I was Eoin's age, I traveled the world. I worked my way across America on cattle ranches. Crewed on a yacht on the Pacific. Worked on sheep stations in Australia. I met lots of people who gave me a meal, or a job, or a place to sleep. It was a good education."

"How did your parents take it?" she asked, fascinated.

He shrugged. "They worried. My stepfather wanted me to be a cop, like him. He was a good man. He taught me music. Carpentry, too. It was what he did for fun." He studied the curve of her cheekbone as Eoin's pipes began to sob out yet another haunting tune.

"Did you ever think of going to college?" she asked.

"Seemed like a waste of money," he said. "Anything you want to learn, you can just go to the library and study up on it for free."

She slid her slender arm around his waist. "I never thought of it that way, but I guess you're right. What's the story on your real dad?"

His body stiffened. "I haven't seen him in twenty-six years."

Her eyes were full of interest. "You don't know where he is?"

"Maybe there was an address with the flowers he sent to Mom's funeral," he said curtly. "I didn't bother to look."

Nancy sat up slowly. "I'm sorry. I guess I hit a nerve."

"It's okay," he said tightly.

She caressed his shoulder. "Do you want to talk about it?"

"I've put it behind me," he snarled, and then felt like shit for using that tone with her, but his gut was clenched. Every word she said pulled them closer to that wall. They needed an emergency detour. He grabbed her arm, yanking her down. She cried out, and he froze abruptly. "Did I hurt you?" he asked.

"No, but—"

He muffled the rest of her words with a kiss, using all his skill and instinct to drag her back into the burning present moment. No future, no past. Just the melody that throbbed outside the window, the moonlight, and Nancy's slender body moving beneath his. So generous, and soft, and strong.

He didn't want to think about the wall they would hit. The look on his father's face as he walked away forever. Lucia's freshly dug grave. Masked attackers in the stairwell, the violence that lurked around every blind corner, the gun on the bedside table. The uncertainty, the danger. And this delicate thing they had. So precious, so fragile. Beset on every side.

She gripped him, crying out as her first climax jolted through her.

Yes. His. The satisfaction that burned in him felt almost like anger. He buried his face against her hair and hung on as his own dark explosion blasted him, mind and body, into blessed oblivion.

He would cheat fate for as long as he could. Fuck them all.

Chapter
9

The sky was pink outside Liam's window when Nancy woke up. The bed beside her was empty, and a shower was running behind the door. She flopped back onto the pillow and studied the room. A photo of a younger Liam sat under the lamp. He had longer hair and a big carefree grin, his arm around the shoulder of a handsome older woman with the same eyes and smile.

She found the bathroom. Took a shower. Muscles she didn't know she had were pleasurably sore. When she came downstairs, bacon sizzled on a skillet, a teakettle was whistling, and Liam was spooning pancake batter onto a griddle. It smelled incredibly delicious.

He looked over his shoulder and smiled. "What kind of tea would you like?" he asked. "I've got Darjeeling and this great Nepali stuff."

"No coffee?" She stared at him in dismay.

"Not in this house."

She plugged her cell phone into a countertop outlet to recharge. "There's got to be an espresso bar somewhere in Latham."

"I wouldn't know," he said, unsympathetically. "Do you like your bacon crisp or chewy?"

"Chewy, please. Could I use your telephone? I want to give my sisters your home number."

"Be my guest," he said.

Nancy forked some wet food into a bowl for Moxie as Vivi's cell rang and rang. She picked up, though her voice was sleepy. "Yeah?"

"Get a pen, Viv. I have to give you a telephone number."

"Omigod. Omigod. Is it the telephone number of that big, tall green-eyed drink of water? Hey, Nell! Wake up! Nancy got laid!"

"Get the pen, Viv," Nancy repeated, with gritted-jaw fortitude.

Vivi hummed ebulliently as she copied down the number that Nancy dictated. "Okay, it's on the fridge. So? Details, honey, details! Is he, well, as vigorous as he looks when you two, well, you know?"

"I absolutely will not discuss that," Nancy said primly.

"I should think not, since he must be right there in the room with you, am I right?"

"Bingo," she whispered.

"So go upstairs, or outside, or whatever, and I'll call your cell," her sister ordered. "You've just got to tell me everything!"

"I don't have my cell on," she admitted. "The battery's dead."

There was a dramatic silence from the other end of the line. "The battery is dead? You forgot to recharge your cell phone? Wait. Who is this, and what have you done with my sister?"

"Oh, stop it," Nancy snapped.

"Well, tell us all about it when you get back," Vivi burbled. "And I mean all. When are you getting back, by the way? Let's do dinner."

Nancy hemmed and hawed for a moment. "Um, well . . . I don't exactly know when I'll be coming back. You see, he's asked me to—"

"Omigod! Nell!" Vivi bawled out. "Get this! Nancy's shacked up!"

"Stop it, Vivi," Nancy begged. "Please. Don't jinx it for me."

"Okay, you big scaredy-cat. Call me when you get the chance, between the bouts of hot bed-play. And say hello from the two of us!"

Vivi hung up, and Nancy clutched the receiver with a hand that shook. A high-frequency buzz, as if every cell in her body was electrified.

Liam's hand touched her shoulder. He took the phone, hung up.

"My sisters say hello," she offered.

"Great. Why do you look so worried about it?"

"Because now they're having this big, happy freak-out about me being up here with you, and it's making me nervous," she snapped.

Liam's mouth hardened. "Nervous? You mean you think they'll be crushed to find out that it's no big deal, then? Just a casual fling?"

Nancy's throat started to burn. She winked back tears. "You're the one who said we were going to hit the wall," she said.

"So I did," he said heavily.

She laid her hand upon his chest, feeling the steady throb of his heart. "It isn't casual. It's a very big deal."

He covered her hand with his own. "How big?"

"Huge," she admitted, surprising herself with her own honesty.

They came together into a tight hug. She buried her face in his chest. They clung to each other, silently agreeing to let the dangerous moment pass. An ominous scent some time later made them look up.

"Oh, God. The pancakes," Liam said, lunging for the griddle.

They feasted on pancakes and bacon. Nancy ate twice as much as usual. They washed up and looked at each other, embarrassed.

"So, ah, what now?" she asked.

His lips twitched. "You tell me, Nancy."

The gleam in his eye was hard to resist, but reality beckoned sternly. "I really need to get some work done," she said.

He looked resigned. "I'll set up an office for you," he said. "I'd give you the spare room, but if you want a phone line, it'll have to be in the living room. I'll go get the stuff from your car."

When he'd hauled in and set up all of her office equipment at the desk, he kissed her. "I'll try to stay out of your way," he said. "If I can."

She tried not to smile. "Don't freak if I turn my cell on, okay? I need to charge it up and check my messages."

"Be my guest," he said magnanimously. "I'll be in my workshop."

Her voice mail was loaded with petulant messages from Peter and Enid, so Peter was her first call.

"It's about damn time!" Peter scolded, the second he picked up. "I've been trying to get in touch with you for twelve hours!"

"Horrors," Nancy said mildly. "What's up?"

"There's no reason to be snotty." Peter sounded hurt. "Enid and

I did the opening act at the Bottom Line last night for Brigid McKeon and the Beltane Beldames, remember?"

"Of course. I sweated for months to get you that gig."

"I figured you'd forgotten, since you didn't bother to come. Well, get this. Brigid liked Enid's voice so much, she wants her to go on tour with the Beldames!"

"Wow," Nancy said. "That's great. Did you tell her to call me?"

"Of course, but you've been unreachable, so I expect you've missed her call. So, what now? It's not like Enid can say no at this point in her career to Brigid McKeon!"

"True. She shouldn't," Nancy said.

"But she can't throw away her solo career to be a Beldame, either! Enid belongs in front of the band, not singing backup!"

She lost the thread when she glimpsed Liam in the doorway, listening. He moved around behind her, out of her field of vision.

"Relax, Peter," she soothed. "I'll talk to Brigid's manager and get the dates, and see if I can switch Enid's concert schedule, or maybe agree to just one tour, and use it as a selling point for her own tour."

She squeaked, startled, as Liam's arms slid around her, cupping her breasts. He started to kiss her neck, and she batted his head away.

"You're up there with some guy, aren't you?" Peter said suddenly. "The graphics are overdue for my album, it's a week until FolkWorld Conference, it's a critical moment in my and Enid's careers, and all you can think of is your hormones? We're talking serious money, here!"

"Speaking of money, remember when I advanced you the registration fees for the FolkWorld Conference?"

"But we still haven't gotten paid for those five gigs upstate!"

She wiggled madly as his hand slid down her belly and into the waistband of her jeans. "Meanwhile, my credit cards are maxed, and you haven't reimbursed me for the last two mailings."

"I can't believe you're bugging me when we've got this huge decision to make. I don't want to talk to you again until you're ready to act professional," he snapped, and hung up on her.

Nancy let the phone drop. "Damn. Now he's furious."

"Good." Liam's hand delved deeper. "Heard the name Peter," he murmured. "Couldn't help myself. Let him stew in his own juices."

"Easy for you to say!" she snapped.

"What have you got to lose?" he demanded. "The cheap bastard doesn't even pay you what he owes you, right?"

"Butt out of things that don't concern you, Liam," she said tartly. "I appreciate all your help, but please do not interrupt any more of my business calls with inappropriate sexual advances."

"Inappropriate?" He grinned. "I'll show you inappropriate."

"Not today, you won't." She stuck out her chin.

"Later, then," he said.

Nancy swallowed, riveted by the hot promise in his eyes. "Later."

The day raced by. She spent most of it on the phone rearranging concert dates and dealing with Brigid McKeon's agency. Liam was unobtrusive, but she was intensely aware of his presence, sneaking hungry glances at the unconscious grace and power of his every movement. More than once he caught her peeking, and his grin made her heart twist joyfully.

Daylight faded. She printed up labels for the next mailing of the new Mandrake promo brochure, exited out of her database, and closed the computer. She hesitated for a moment and turned off her cell. It was the professional kiss of death, but right now, she could give a flying flip. She went to the door that led to his workshop, which was dominated by a large and beautiful dining room table. He'd left the door open.

He was bending over a workbench, sanding some piece too small for her to identify. He looked up, though she was barefoot and had tried to make no sound, and put the piece down.

"You done for the night?" he asked.

She nodded. "Just shut down the computer."

He held out his arms. "So you're all mine?"

She wrapped her arms around him and breathed deeply of the fresh smell of wind and rain and fresh-cut wood that clung to him. "All yours," she promised rashly. "I even turned off the phone."

Silent laughter vibrated his big frame. "Wow. That's huge, Nancy."

"It is, it really is," she agreed. "Shall we think about dinner?"

"In a bit," he said. "First, there's something that I want to try out with you. I've been thinking about it all day. And before, too."

She kissed the triangle of skin at the V of his shirt. "What's that?"

Without warning, her jeans slipped down around her hips and around her knees. He'd sneakily unbuttoned them. Her panties soon followed, and she stepped out of them, giggling. "Liam—"

"Let me just put you right . . . here," he said, hoisting her naked bottom up onto the edge of the table he was making. The varnished surface was cool and smooth against her naked buttocks.

She smothered more giggles, gasping as he pushed her thighs apart. "Um, what exactly do you have in mind?" she asked, breathless.

He sank down onto his knees. "Let me show you."

The week that followed was strange and wonderful, a seesaw of emotional extremes. Her days were spent in the makeshift office in Liam's living room, working, or trying to. She vacillated from wiggling her toes with manic joy and laughing out loud for no reason to worrying obsessively about her sisters, or stressing about the stairwell thugs. And missing Lucia, so sharply she could taste it. Grief left a hard lump in her throat that only Liam's embrace could ease.

It comforted her, somehow, that Lucia had handpicked him for her. Like a benediction from beyond. Her sisters approved of him, too. One night, Vivi and Nell had driven up in Vivi's van from the city to have dinner. Liam had impressed the hell out of them with leg of lamb, new potatoes with herbs, and a good red wine. Gooey chocolate profiterole had clinched the deal. They were blatantly rooting for him. Which was great, but it ratcheted the pressure up even higher.

Nancy and Liam ate all their meals together, and feasting on Liam's abundant home-cooked food was having its inevitable effect. After only a few days, her jeans were noticeably tighter, to her chagrin and Liam's unqualified approval. She'd brought an espresso pot, a bean grinder, and a sizable stash of coffee beans to his house, and with that small but crucial detail taken care of, she was in hog heaven.

On evenings when it didn't rain, they wrapped themselves in a fluffy afghan and sat together on the porch swing, listening to birds, crickets, frogs, wind chimes. Talking about anything and everything, or sitting in a companionable silence. A fearful little voice whispered cynically to enjoy it while it lasted. And goddammit, she would.

Liam was still carrying the gun around, but after over a week had passed with no attacks upon her person, the immediacy of the threat had eased. Nancy was almost ready to broach the subject they were so carefully avoiding. Which was, what came next.

She couldn't stay up here cloistered in his bed forever. And in any case, the time he'd taken off to work on Lucia's house was coming to an end. He had other jobs scheduled after it. The real world beckoned.

Her fantasy was to integrate the two realities, make him a real part of her life. Part of her was cynically sure that it was too much to hope. But oh, she liked the person who she was with him.

She would make adjustments. Be flexible. He was so worth it.

He was showing her how to make soda bread in his kitchen one evening, a pot of fragrant stew bubbling on the stove, when she broke the ice and told him she needed to drive back down to New York.

A chill settled over his face, though his expression did not change.

"What for?" His voice had a strangely distant tone.

"I have to leave Moxie with Freedy's wife, Andrea, when I go to the FolkWorld Conference next week," she explained.

He scowled, suspiciously. "A conference?"

"It's important," she said. "For me and for all my artists. Freedy and Peter and Enid and Mandrake are all performing. Eoin, too. I won't be alone for a second. I'll be surrounded by everyone I know, in fact."

He let out a skeptical grunt. "Is Freedy another one of your exes?"

"Yes, but it's amicable," she assured him. "Freedy has a showcase Friday night at FolkWorld, but Andrea has to work, so she's staying in the city. She promised to look after Moxie for me."

"Why not just leave her here with me?"

She gazed at his unreadable profile and gathered her nerve.

"Thank you. But that, uh, brings me to something I wanted to ask."

"Ask away." He did something efficient looking with milk, mixing the batter with a few competent swipes of a wooden spoon.

She took a deep breath and blurted it out. "Want to come?"

He froze, his hands buried in dough. "To the conference?"

She hastened on. "It's in Boston, at the Amory Lodge. I'll get you a listener's pass. You'd stay in my room, of course. Seeing as how it's a weekend, and you have a job scheduled for next week, I figured, maybe you could drive up Saturday."

"Hmph." He looked unconvinced.

"This is the thing," she went on. "I've been experiencing your life since I've been here, staying in your house, eating your food—"

"Sleeping in my bed."

"Yes, sleeping in your bed, and it's wonderful. But I have my own life. I want you to get to know it the way I've gotten to know yours. The conference will be crazy, and I'll be networking with agents and presenters, and probably we won't sleep. But you'll hear great music and meet great people. And Eoin would be ecstatic. Mandrake's showcase will be his first performance. It kicks off their spring tour."

He gathered the dough into a loose ball, his face thoughtful. "What night is Eoin's thing?"

"Saturday night. At eleven-thirty, if you can believe it."

He laid the dough on the floury countertop, still not meeting her eyes. "I was thinking of taking a few more days off," he admitted.

"You were?" she said hopefully.

"But I was thinking along the lines of running away with you. Someplace where I won't have to share you with hundreds of people. I know a guy on the coast who charters a sailboat. I thought, four or five days, no worries, no looking over our shoulders. No cell coverage."

She snorted. "You do like to push your luck, don't you?"

"To the hilt," he said, eyes gleaming.

Nancy watched his floury fingers patting dough onto the counter. "It sounds wonderful," she said. "But I was hoping—" She bit her lip.

"What were you hoping?" He laid the lump of dough onto a floured baking sheet. He flicked his eyes up, frowning when she didn't answer.

"I want this thing to be real, Liam," she said. "Right now it's a fairy tale, totally removed from my real life. I want to pinch myself to make sure you really exist."

He slipped his arms around her waist, careful not to touch her with his floury hands. "Let me prove to you that I exist, sweetheart."

She swatted him. "Stop trying to distract me. I want my friends to meet you. I want you to hear my artists. I . . . I want this to be real."

"How long is this conference?" he asked cautiously.

"Four days. Thursday through Sunday."

He tapped his fingers on the counter. "How about I come Saturday night, see Eoin's showcase, and experience your life Sunday. Then Monday morning we take off and go sailing for a few days. Deal?"

Her heart soared. "Deal."

"Great. I'll call the guy, make the reservation. And now, let me put this in the oven and wash my hands, so I can grab you properly." He scrubbed and rinsed his hands and pulled her into his arms.

"I'm so glad we're doing this," she said softly. "It makes me feel as if there's hope for us. For the future, I mean."

He stood so still, and so silently, a chill of apprehension gripped her. "Sorry," she said, through gritted teeth. "Forget I said that."

"It's all right," he said in a guarded voice. "I hope it, too."

But he wasn't hoping too hard, from the sound of it. She buried her face against his sweater and hung on with all her strength. As if strength had anything to do with hanging on to a man. She never had gotten the knack, what with her talent for saying the wrong thing at the wrong time. Like the fairy tale about the girl who dropped toads from her mouth. But she would hang on to the bitter end, toads or no toads.

They would have to pry her away from this guy with a crowbar.

John adjusted the angle of the flexible head of the video camera he was threading between the slats of the heating vent, checking the monitor to be sure it would cover the whole miserable little apartment.

He was in a foul humor, and had been for days. Ever since that bruising encounter with that pain-in-the-ass carpenter who had taken it upon himself to be Nancy D'Onofrio's champion. Knightly had been an unpleasant surprise. He'd caused John to lose still more face with his employer, which he could ill afford to do. And for that, Knightly would die. First he had to get this shitbag job behind him. But most definitely later. John planned to make the carpenter his own special little personal project.

He'd already dispatched the worthless turd he'd hired for local backup, but that did nothing to satisfy the bloodlust. That came squarely under the category of taking out the garbage before it began to stink. That was pure practicality. No element of pleasure or recreation.

Back to the task. He looked around Nancy D'Onofrio's wretched apartment. It was clear that she had not located the sketches. But she would be highly motivated to do so. He would be, if he lived like this.

He'd searched her sister Antonella's apartment in SoHo the day before. It was lined with books rather than CDs, but had more or less the same pathetic square footage. He'd searched every nook and cranny. Studied every piece of correspondence. Rigged up watching and listening devices. State-of-the-art stuff. It was nice to have a large operating budget.

The carpenter's house was the obvious next step, but John was waiting for the perfect opportunity. Patience was key to not getting caught or killed. Hard though that was to justify to a demanding boss.

The carpenter never left her alone. No doubt fucking her for most of the day. John didn't blame the guy. He was looking forward to taking his turn. He thought about that a lot as he sat in the woods, staring through binoculars at the carpenter's house, massaging his crotch.

His exhaustive, systematic search of the D'Onofrio daughters' living spaces had turned up exactly nothing so far, which meant that the time had come to start in upon the luscious physical persons of the D'Onofrio daughters themselves. A task he would relish.

He'd given a great deal of thought to where to begin. At first, he'd leaned toward the younger ones, who seemed more careless and distracted. Antonella and Vivien had not yet internalized the threat.

But his instincts prodded him in the direction of the oldest daughter. If one of them knew something, chances are she would know the most. Besides, he was salivating to interrogate her. Having her snatched from his jaws had sharpened his appetite for her to a knife's edge. He lay in bed, sleepless, imagining it. Her, beneath him, begging and struggling. Knightly couldn't afford to hover over her forever.

Eventually, he would falter. And John would be ready.

The phone rang, and he whipped around, irritated to have his happy reverie interrupted. The answering machine clicked on.

"Hey, Nancy?" a woman said. "This is Andrea. I've been calling your cell, but it's not on, so I hope you're checking messages. I'm just calling to tell you that I'm sorry, but you're going to have to find some other solution for Moxie. I decided to take a personal-leave day and drive up to Boston Thursday night so I can see Freedy's showcase. I know I promised kitty coverage, but Freedy and I get so little time together as it is, you know? Anyhow, see you at the conference. Bye!"

Boston? Conference? John went back to Nancy's cluttered desk, and shuffled with his plastic-gloved hands in the paperwork, looking for something that had flickered at the edge of his attention. Ah, yes. There.

A conference program. The FolkWorld Conference. Thursday through Sunday, at the Amory Lodge Hotel. It would be crowded, but she would be distracted. Open to meeting new people, schmoozing.

He tucked the program into his bag. Nancy D'Onofrio was about to have the networking experience of a lifetime.

Chapter
10

Nancy leaned over the counter in the Amory Lodge lobby. "Are there any messages for me?" she asked.

The desk clerk looked put upon. "Not in the past fifteen minutes."

Liam had told her he would arrive around eight. It was a quarter to nine. Peter and Enid's showcase was scheduled for nine-thirty.

She looked up to find Enid bearing down on her in performance regalia: a velvet miniskirt, cleavage bulging out of her black leather vest, her hair a mass of luxurious blow-dried curls. "Peter forgot to pack my new mike!" she wailed. "I just spent a thousand bucks on that thing!"

"You bought a thousand-dollar mike before paying me back for the registration fees?" Nancy asked wryly.

Enid threw up her hands. "I couldn't sing 'The Far Shore' with that piece of crap! It sounds like I'm singing in a public bathroom!"

Nancy sighed. "This hotel is crawling with musicians who have good mikes. Think of someone who owes you a favor." Her eyes flicked to Enid's cleavage. "Shouldn't be that hard," she muttered.

"Hey," came Liam's deep voice from behind her.

Nancy whirled around. There he was, large as life, in a crisp white shirt, jeans, and a long, elegant black coat. Incredibly handsome.

Enid simpered. "Aren't you going to introduce me, Nance?"

Nancy bit down on an impulse to smack her. "Enid, this is Liam Knightly, a friend of mine. Liam, this is Enid Morrow, one of my clients."

"Delighted," Enid cooed, holding out her hand.

He shook it politely. "You must be Peter's wife."

Enid smiled brilliantly. "Nancy must have told you all about us!"

"Of course." He turned back to Nancy. "Sorry I'm late. I hit traffic." He gave her a hard, possessive kiss, right in Enid's face.

An uncontrollable grin spread over Nancy's face. "It's okay. I'm just glad you're here." Her whole body was smiling. Every cell, every atom, every photon of her was happy to see him. He was the handsomest man in the room, probably in the entire hotel. By a factor of ten.

"You're just in time to hear our showcase," Enid announced.

"Wouldn't miss it," he said, with a courteous nod.

"Find Eugene and ask if you can use a Mandrake mike," Nancy suggested. "I think I saw him in the restaurant about ten minutes ago."

A pout marred Enid's heart-shaped face. "Can you take care of it? I have to touch up my makeup and make sure Peter's dressed properly."

"Okay, I'll do it."

Enid scampered toward the elevators, casting a dimpled smile back at Liam. Nancy grabbed his hand and towed him toward the restaurant. "Sorry to rush you, but I've got to catch Eugene," she said.

Liam's fingers curled possessively around hers. "He left you for her?" he asked, in a low, wondering tone.

She tried to wipe the silly, satisfied look off her face. So Enid's sex-kitten appeal didn't affect him. Her mood soared. "Pick up the pace," she urged. "I've only got ten minutes to save the world."

He swung her around a corner into an alcove full of vending machines. "If you've got ten, you can spare one of them to kiss me. That leaves nine to save the world. That's a generous margin."

He kissed her very thoroughly, until she was soft, hazy, and glowing. "What was I supposed to be doing?" she asked, dazed.

He leaned his forehead against hers and kissed the tip of her nose. "The mike. From Eugene. For Enid," he said dutifully.

"Oh, God."

He tagged after her companionably as she ran her errands, and finally they were seated in the back of the hall, her hand tucked securely in Liam's. Peter and Enid were great, and the band that backed them played with energy and precision. When the plaintive strains of "The Road to You" died away, the applause was long and loud. Nancy nudged Liam as she clapped. "What do you think?"

His face was noncommittal. "Better than I expected."

Nancy tugged on his hand. "Let's congratulate them. Come on."

Enid spotted Liam's tall form first, and she bounced toward them, beaming, her eyes expectantly on Liam.

"I enjoyed it very much," he said politely.

Enid took him by the arm, pulling him toward where Peter was still seated, fingering his guitar. Nancy trailed uncomfortably behind. The situation was out of her control, and it made her nervous.

"Hey, Petey! Meet Liam, Nancy's new *friend*," Enid said.

Peter's head whipped around. His eyes narrowed. "Ah, so you're the guy who spirited away our manager the most important week of the year."

Liam gently extricated his arm from Enid's grip. "And you're the guy who left her at the altar and mooches money off her."

Peter's mouth dropped open. He glanced at Nancy, his face both thunderous and betrayed. "Who does this asshole think he is?" he hissed.

Nancy pushed closer, horrified. "Peter, I'm sorry. He—"

"Don't tell me. I don't want to know." He grabbed Enid's arm. "Come on, baby. Let's network." Enid shot a bewildered glance over her shoulder as he dragged her away.

Nancy was aghast."Oh, no, Liam. Look what you've done."

The expression in Liam's eyes was absolutely unapologetic.

She turned her back on him and left, but Liam kept pace beside her. No matter how fast she went, his stride lengthened to match it.

She pretended not to know him in the elevator. She'd known he was opinionated, but this was scary. This was destructive. Once out of the elevator, he stalked beside her with catlike grace to her room door, waiting as she fumbled for the key. She unlocked it and stumbled inside. The door *ka-thunked* shut behind them.

Liam flipped on the light by the door. "Okay," he said in a grim, tight voice. "Go ahead. Let me have it."

"I cannot believe you!" she exploded. "I had no idea when I invited you here that you would do your best to sabotage my professional life!"

He frowned. "I just told it like it was. And about time, too."

"About time for what? To ruin my career?"

He snorted. "No, for a reality check. Peter and Enid are vampires. They suck you dry. And you don't react. You don't draw the line."

"Timing is everything! Right after an important gig, surrounded by concert-series presenters, is not the best—"

"There's never a good time, Nancy."

She plowed on. "Grace. Delicacy. Minding your own goddamn business. These are the earmarks of maturity."

"Fine. So I'm immature." The label clearly did not bother him.

"Liam, if I didn't know better, I'd think you were jealous."

"I'll tell you who's jealous," he said bluntly. "Peter. He's jealous of me, and afraid of losing you. Or at least of losing control of you."

Nancy gaped. "But Peter's got Enid, and besides—"

"I got that jerk's number the minute I laid eyes on him. 'You're the guy who spirited away our manager,' " he mimicked in a whiny voice so much like Peter's, Nancy almost betrayed herself by smiling.

She caught herself just in time. "Peter and I have been friends for years. It's normal that there's some ambivalence—"

"Ambivalence?" His voice was heavy with sarcasm. "He's pissed because for the first time, he doesn't get to have his cake and eat it, too. He took advantage of you the whole time you were together. Then he met Enid, and he wanted her, too, so he figured out a way to keep you both. The perfect setup. You to get the gigs, and Enid to suck his dick and fluff his ego. Nobody's going to give you the respect you deserve for free, Nancy. You've got to demand it. You've got to put your foot down."

Nancy opened her mouth in automatic denial, then closed it.

A dull pain in her belly told her that he was speaking the truth. An ugly, dangerous, ill-timed, inconvenient truth. But she couldn't deny it.

"Maybe you're right," she said slowly. "But that doesn't change the fact that it was wrong of you to say what you said out there."

Liam shrugged. Right or wrong. He did not care.

An aching silence spread out between them. Nancy wanted to howl in frustration. "What the hell do you expect me to do about it?"

"Get rid of them," he suggested matter-of-factly. "Fire them."

She gave a short laugh. "It's not that simple. They're my clients, Liam, not my employees. And besides, they're also my—"

"Friends, right." His voice was heavily laced with irony.

"Yes. Friendship is complicated. You work things out. Over time."

"They suck you dry, and don't even thank you, let alone reimburse you. They're spoiled children. Get rid of them."

Nancy threw up her hands. "Liam, you can't just fire your friends. You have to find solutions, compromises."

"Nope. News flash, Nancy. You don't."

"You're not very good at compromise, are you?" she asked slowly.

He stared back. His silence answered for him.

Nancy clenched her hands. "I can't deal with this conversation right now," she said. "I've got enough to worry about. So please. Either keep your mouth shut around my colleagues, or leave now. Agreed?"

Liam started to speak, stopped himself. He nodded.

She braced herself. "Does that mean you're staying?"

He nodded. She let out her breath in a long sigh of relief. It wasn't the wall. A reprieve. Maybe. She pulled her key card out of her pocket and handed it to him. "Here. You take this, and I'll get another one made at the front desk. Get yourself settled in. Mandrake plays in"—she glanced at her watch—"an hour. Same room as Peter and Enid's showcase. See you there." She opened the door, turned. "Liam?"

"Yes?" His voice was wary.

She searched for words to express the yearning in her chest. She was glad to see him, missed him, wanted him. Maybe even loved him.

"Nothing," she whispered as she slipped through the door.

* * *

Liam strode down the corridor, self-disgust sour in his mouth. Being rude to her ex had been bad enough, but spouting off preachy crap to Nancy was worse. Telling her how to conduct her business. Like he had the right. *Damn.* He mouthed the word as he stabbed the elevator button. A blue-haired old lady gave him a nervous look and a wide berth. Good instincts. He was an animal tonight. Lacking in social skills. What were the earmarks of maturity? Grace, delicacy, minding your own goddamn business? He came up blank in every category.

No more scenes. If he could get through the conference without any fuckups or fistfights, he would be rewarded by four days of solitude with Nancy. The elevator pinged. It was almost time for the Mandrake showcase, so he headed toward the hall.

"Hey, Liam!"

Liam turned to find Eoin leaning against the wall, freckles standing out in sharp relief in his pale face. Liam clasped his hand, which was ice cold. "Nancy told me you would be playing. I've been looking forward to it. How's it going?" he asked.

Eoin shrugged. "I don't know. We've only rehearsed three times."

Liam slapped him on the back. "You'll be great. Don't worry."

Eugene and a tall, skinny black guy came charging down the hall, looking excited and self-important. "Come on, man, let's do it!" Eugene said to Eoin, as they surrounded him and bore him away.

"Break a leg!" Liam called. Eoin shot a final desperate glance over his shoulder. Liam gave the kid a thumbs-up.

He went into the crowded hall. No chairs left. Nancy was on the other side of the room, talking to Matt, the big redhead he had met at the seisìun at Malloy's. She turned, gave him a tentative smile.

He smiled back. Her smile widened, became brilliant. God, she was pretty, dressed up in one of her ninja outfits, hair pulled into a braided bun, earrings dangling down to her jaw. Exotic, elegant. He leaned against the wall and stared. She made every other woman in the room look commonplace. That airhead Enid was insipid in comparison.

The lights dimmed, and Mandrake came onstage to tremendous applause. The lanky black guy laid down a complicated primal-sounding rhythm, and Eoin promptly launched into a fiery Irish reel, followed by Matt and Eugene on the guitar and fiddle, and finally a scrawny blond girl who played what looked like an endless variety of wind instruments.

They were excellent, and Liam applauded after each piece till his hands tingled. The pulsing energy of the music soothed something raw and savage inside him. He was fiercely glad that Eoin had fallen in with this group. They would keep him happy and busy until he found his feet. After they finished, he pushed his way through the crush and gave Eoin a quick, hard embrace. "Great job," he said. "You kicked ass."

Eoin grinned. "Thanks," was all he had time to say before he was surrounded by chattering, congratulating people.

Something poked Liam in the back, and he looked around to find Nancy smiling at him. "Weren't they fine?"

"Excellent." He swept her into his arms. "Sorry," he whispered.

He offered up a silent prayer of gratitude as her body softened, went pliant in his arms. He'd gotten through the crisis. This wasn't the wall. There was still time, still grace. His arms tightened hungrily around her. "Do you have more to do tonight?"

She looked through her eyelashes. "Theoretically, I could network for hours. But I don't have any appointments until tomorrow."

He saw Peter, who was scowling at him from across the room. Liam grinned, baring all his teeth, and nipped Nancy's ear possessively.

"How long has it been since you've eaten?" he asked.

She looked guilty. "Um . . ."

He rolled his eyes. "Nancy, for God's sake—"

"Okay, okay, don't scold. I forgot. So sue me. Let's go get something. Want to ask Eoin and the others if they—"

"No. I want to be alone with you. I missed you." He leaned over, sucked in a whiff of her perfume. "You smell good."

She stood up on tiptoes and kissed his lips. "I missed you, too."

Dinner options were scarce at that hour, but they found an all-night pizza place that delivered. It arrived in their room shortly after, and Liam watched with approval as Nancy enthusiastically devoured pizza.

"Wow," she murmured, licking her fingers. "Guess I didn't know how hungry I was."

"No wonder people take advantage of you. You never eat. It takes energy to put your foot down."

She snorted and grabbed another piece. He made another cautious attempt at conversation. "So the conference is going well?"

"Excellently," she said, fishing for a napkin. "I've given out scads of promo packets. We'll get lots of bookings. And the showcases all went wonderfully."

"I'm glad," he said.

She took a sip of her soda. "I've been thinking about our conversation. In some ways, I think you're right. But in others—"

"Let it go," he offered. "I was way out of line."

She studied him with her wide, brilliant, leaf-colored eyes. "Only somewhat out of line," she conceded gently. She took her cell out of her purse, made a big show of turning it off, and got to her feet. "Have to wash off pizza grease," she murmured, disappearing into the bathroom.

He pinched out the jack of the room phone. This was a delicate moment. He didn't want anyone to interrupt it and fuck it up. He peeled off his shirt, in the interests of saving time, and followed her into the bathroom. She washed her hands and face, patted herself dry. Her eyes locked with his in the mirror. Full of longing.

He longed for it, too. He reached around, trapping her against his body. He plucked off her glasses, pulled her hairpins out, unraveled the coiled braided hair, and smoothed the crimped waves over her shoulders.

He wrenched his belt loose, got rid of the rest of his clothes. Nancy gave him that secret little sorceress smile that drove him wild and glanced down at his stiff, rampant erection. She petted it.

"Ever ready," she murmured. "At attention."

"Fuck yes," he said. "For you. Always."

He tugged the snug black sweater out of her jeans and peeled it off over her head. Her bra was silvery green, a sheer, lacy thing.

"Wow," he said, admiring it. "Look at that. Fancy underwear."

"I thought I might get lucky," she whispered.

He unhooked the bra and tossed it away, ran his hands over her velvety softness, felt the muscles that moved sinuously beneath it. Marveling at the translucent perfection of her small, high breasts.

"I'm the lucky one," he said. "God, look at you. So beautiful."

She just smiled, but her eyes caught his in the mirror, and they both laughed. "See? I'm making progress, aren't I?" she teased him. "I no longer flip out and get all uptight and scared when you say that."

"That's good," he said. "But I want you to know it in your bones."

Her gaze slid away, and she blushed. She didn't know it, though. She liked to hear it, but she didn't buy it. He could see it in her eyes, and it made his chest ache. That he could not get past that invisible barrier inside her. Her caution. So deep, it was beyond his reach.

He could only wait. He slid his hand down over her belly to the downy tuft of hair at her muff, and insinuated his finger against that tender, tight furled slit. Just resting it there. "I wish you could see what I see when I look at you," he said. "It drives me nuts."

Nancy twisted in his arms and looked into his eyes. Her gaze had suddenly become very focused. "Then we'll just keep at it, then. Things take time. Right?"

They stared, gripped by tension. "Right," he said hoarsely.

He turned her, sank down to his knees, and buried his face against the hot, fuzzy ringlets crowning her pussy. He pried her legs a little wider, just wide enough to slide his tongue inside, teasing and fluttering her clit, thrusting deeper to taste her hot, rich flavor.

Hunger swamped his mind, but he kept at it until she shivered and arched and cried out, her body jolting in his grip.

He picked her up, carried her into the other room. He flung her onto the bed. Touching her, kissing her, spreading her out wide and loving her again with his lips and his tongue, again, again. Making her sigh and sob and clutch him, begging.

When he finally fumbled the latex on and positioned himself, she took him in so completely, it felt like flames of pure pleasure were licking him, each stroke an agony of delight more perfect than the last. He clutched her, heartbeat clamoring in his ears.

Things took time. Hell yes, they did. All the time she liked. The more time the better. A lifetime would be fine with him.

That amazing idea lifted him up and blasted him into inner space.

Someone was pounding on her door, and probably had been for some time. Nancy struggled out of a dream that had a great deal of gratuitous pounding in it. Liam stirred as she slid out of bed. She found her nightshirt, and slipped it on as she went for the door.

The pounding had redoubled. She pulled the door open and focused on Peter and Enid, who looked electrified.

"Good God, Nancy, you're not even dressed!" Enid said, dismayed. She peeked into the room, eyes widening when they landed on Liam sitting on the bed dressed only in his jeans. "Remember yesterday at the Exhibition Hall when you were talking to the promoter for the Jericho Arts Center in D.C.? Where Bonnie Blair is opening next week?"

"Uh, yes, of course. I gave him a promo packet. He seemed interested in an opening act sometime," Nancy said, rubbing her eyes.

"Yeah! That's just it! Sammy Phillips with the Phelps Bay Blues Band was opening for Bonnie, but he wrecked his car yesterday, and—"

"Oh, no!" Dismay shocked her to full consciousness.

"Don't worry, Sammy'll be fine," Peter said impatiently. "But he broke his collarbone. Enid and I were having coffee, and the promoter came up and asked if we're free Wednesday! I told him are we ever!"

Nancy was wide awake. "Opening for Bonnie Blair? At the Jericho? You mean *this* Wednesday?"

Enid and Peter nodded violently, identical wide grins splitting their faces. "Is that megaspectacular, or what?" Peter crowed.

"That's incredible," Nancy breathed. "I've got to get on the phone right away to the presenter. To all the venues in D.C., Maryland, and Virginia. I've got to get pictures to the press, I've got to—"

"But that's not all," Enid said. "There's more! Get this, Nance!"

There just happened to be this exec from MGM Studios in Holly-wood staying at the hotel, and he heard our showcase! He loved it!"

"Hollywood?" Nancy rubbed her eyes again. "Excuse me?"

"His name is Maitland Sills, and he's going to put his production department in touch with us! He says 'The Far Shore' is perfect for the closing credits of a big-budget feature film they're doing, star-ring Brad Pitt! And you have to talk to him pronto, Nance, because he's leaving for Logan Airport in an hour. He's got a meeting this afternoon in L.A."

"Holy crap," she said slowly. "Why didn't you call me?"

Enid and Peter exchanged long-suffering glances. "Your cell was off," they said in unison.

"I was going to introduce you to Sills last night after the show-case, but you disappeared," Peter scolded.

"So why not call the room?" she snapped. "You knew my num-ber!"

"Disconnected," Enid said triumphantly.

Nancy's head whipped around to check. Sure enough. No jack in the phone. Liam met her eyes and lifted his big, muscular shoulders in an unapologetic shrug. She felt the tension begin to gather in her neck.

"Time to focus, Nance. No more distractions," Peter said, staring at Liam. "You'll come to the Jericho gig, right?"

"I definitely should," she said.

"It's happening, Nance!" Enid burbled. "We're going to hit big!"

Liam moved around in the room behind her. Nancy suddenly re-membered their sailboat plans. Her stomach took a nosedive. "Oh. I, um, did have plans for the next few days," she said hesitantly. Liam's naked, muscular back was to her. He rifled through his overnight bag.

"Postpone 'em," Peter said carelessly. "This is the chance of a lifetime. We've gotta jump on it with both feet."

"Uh . . . yeah," she said, glancing anxiously behind herself.

Peter followed her gaze, and his face hardened. "He's not coming with us, though," he said. "So don't even think about it."

"Don't worry," Liam said remotely. "Wouldn't dream of it."

Peter made an impatient sound. "Well? Enid will stall Maitland Sills while you get yourself together. Hurry! See you in a few."

Nancy shut the door and turned to face Liam.

His face looked hard. "So we can forget our plans?"

She pressed her fist against her mouth. Shit, shit, *shit.* "I'm so sorry, Liam, but everything has to stop for this gig," she said apologetically. "I'll be on the phone nonstop for days to publicize—"

"I understand perfectly," he said.

Hope stirred briefly. "You do?"

"Of course. I shouldn't have put down a deposit. It was stupid. There's always going to be something more important for you. Always."

Hope shriveled and died. She stared at his averted face as he fished under the bed for his shoes. "Liam, I would love to go on this boat trip with you! We can go when I get back!"

"Something else will come up. And something else after that. I know that tune by heart."

She shook her head helplessly. "We're not listening to the same tune, Liam," she said miserably. "And we couldn't keep up this eternal vigilance routine much longer anyhow. I understand the impulse, and I honor it, but we both have to make money, and this is the biggest—"

He held up his hand. "Stop. You're just making it worse."

Her knees went weak with dread. "We've hit that wall, haven't we?"

Liam dragged a shirt over his head and tucked it into his jeans with swift, economical motions. "We are roadkill," he said.

She lurched forward and laid her hand on his chest. "Liam, it can't be over just because of this. This is stupid. It's just bad timing."

He stepped back. Her hand dropped, with nothing to hold on to.

Her jaw trembled. "I was starting to think we had a chance."

"So come with me," he challenged her. "You can't, can you? Of course not. You've made your choice.

No big deal. Don't sweat it."

"Liam, I've been working for this moment for my whole adult life!"

"Good luck, then." He took the revolver from the back of his jeans, opened the cylinder and shook the bullets out into his hand. He tossed the empty gun into his bag. "You'd better start making those phone calls."

"Wow," she said. "You are the most rigid, uncompromising person I have ever known."

"Remember what I said last night about putting my foot down? That's what it all boils down to."

"And you don't care what gets crushed under your boot?"

He shrugged on his coat. "This conversation is over."

Nancy grabbed his arm. "You can't just cut me off like that!"

He wrenched away. "Watch me." The door thudded shut.

Nancy sank down onto the bed. The silence was deafening.

Chapter

11

John scanned the shifting crowds. His face itched from the fake goatee, and he sweated heavily in the overheated hall as he listened with half an ear to the self-serving prattle of the blond slut singer.

He'd begun to fantasize about shutting her up. Definitively. After she'd delivered the services she was blatantly advertising with the rolling eyes and the heaving tits. At least she wouldn't be chattering for that. He'd keep that shiny pink mouth way too busy to talk.

Where the fuck was Nancy, anyway? He did not want to converse with these idiot musicians any longer than was necessary. He was good at improvising a rap, but his ruse as a Hollywood movie producer was a thin one. Anyone asking the right questions would cop to it in no time.

Fortunately, Enid Morrow was too self-absorbed to ask the right questions. And Nancy herself would never get a chance to ask them. He fingered the tiny little transparent gel capsule in his pocket. A designer drug, exactly calibrated for her size and weight.

But where the fuck was she?

He was anxious to get on with it. Instinct was pricking and prodding, saying *now, now, now*. Even with people around, if he started the job at the right moment and pushed on through, hard and swift and decisive, they would probably be too absorbed in their own shit to figure out what was happening. All they'd notice would be a confusing kerfuffle of motion, a brief swell in the noise level, and *voilà*. Back to normal.

". . . sorry that she's so late this morning. It's totally unlike her," the slut singer burbled.

He smiled and stared at her tits. She obligingly arched her lumbar spine to facilitate his view. "I just hope I have a chance to discuss it with her before I go," he said. "I wanted to present this idea to the meeting with my team in L.A. this afternoon. Get the ball rolling."

"Of course," Enid cooed. "It's like fate! That you happened to be at the hotel by pure chance, and heard us play!"

"Yes, it is." He scanned the room with his peripheral vision beyond the halo of blond ringlets in the foreground.

There! Looking pale and tousled and waiflike, her hair streaming loose. Last night's makeup smudged around her huge eyes. She must not have even taken a shower. Probably had Knightly's nasty spunk still inside her body. That dirty little bitch.

His heart rate quickened, his mouth watered, his dick stiffened. His instincts, his senses sharpening. Ah. He loved this part. She was his succulent little rabbit. He was the hawk, poised to dive and rend.

Enid craned her neck. The effort popped her bosom further out. "There she is! I'll introduce you, Maitland—can I call you Maitland?"

"Of course," he said. She hooked her arm around his elbow and towed him through the room. Aw. How sweet. His new little best friend.

"Hey! Nancy! This is Maitland! He's the producer I was telling you about from MGM Studios!" Enid sang out.

Nancy looked over at her, her face oddly stiff and blank. "Huh? Oh. Enid, hi. Hey, have you seen Liam?"

Enid's jaw dropped for a second. "Um, not lately, Nancy," she said, in a warning tone. "Focus, please. Did you hear me? Maitland Sills? The guy from MGM Studios? Hollywood? Hello? Earth to Nancy?"

But Nancy kept rising onto her tiptoes, her gaze sweeping the room. "Hollywood? That's nice. Could you folks excuse me for a sec?"

"Nancy!" Enid hissed. "Don't be an idiot!"

"I'll just be a moment. I need to check something in the hall." She slipped like an eel through the crowd, and disappeared.

The predator inside him howled and gnashed its teeth.

Enid caught the vibe, and shot him a nervous look. "Um, ah, alrighty, then. I'm sure she'll be right back. Say, how about if you just meet with me and Peter? We can speak for ourselves when it comes to big career decisions. Just come with me." She began to tug on his arm.

Nancy had disappeared. The moment might be lost. The slut singer pulled again, babbling with a smile he wanted to knock right off her doll-like face. She tugged harder. His patience came to an abrupt end. He yanked his arm away, so roughly she teetered, stumbling on her tottering spike heels. "What is wrong with you?" she squawked.

He stared into her eyes. "Get out of my way." He put a vicious punch of venom behind each softly uttered word.

Enid shrank away, stammering.

He forgot her utterly the second he turned his back on her and hurried after his prey, blood pumping fast and hot and hungry.

As Liam strode through the lobby, he avoided the hostile gaze of that butthead Peter Morrow as he strode through the lobby. He felt like he was caught in the guts of some pitiless machine, and it would churn on whether he was smashed to a pulp in its grinding gearwork or not.

He didn't want to leave her alone, with the stairwell assholes gunning for her. He didn't want to leave her at all. But that was not his problem. She'd made that clear. It never had been. She wasn't his wife, his fiancée, even his girlfriend, and she wasn't going to be. Because relationships weren't based on fleeting perfect moments. They were based on solid, firm things. Respect. Compatibility. Shared interests.

Strange, how tired and pat that thought felt. Like he'd thought it a thousand times before, and worn off the nap.

"Liam!" Eoin bounded across the room toward him like a jack-rabbit on crack, his eyes alight like flashlights in his skinny face. He had partied all night long, but he was still revved. "Hey, what's up?" He looked at Liam's bag. "I thought you were staying till tomorrow!"

"Can't," he said, though his mouth felt dusty and dry. "Gotta go."

"I'm glad I saw you, then. A favor before you go, eh? I've been telling Eugene about that set of reels you wrote. I remember 'The Dusty Shoon,' and 'Traveler's Joy,' but not the B and C parts of 'The Old Man's Beard.'"

His stomach curdled in dismay. "I have to go. Another time."

"Oh, man, please?" Eoin entreated. "It'll only take five minutes. Eugene has his DAT to record it. I had this great arrangement worked out, and the lads love it!"

Liam's jaw ached from clenching so hard. "I don't have my fiddle."

"Eugene will lend you his!" Eoin's eyes pleaded. "Five minutes?"

Christ on a crutch. Five minutes of stomach-churning agony. But he didn't want to burden Eoin by telling him that the world had just ended. He let himself be towed into the small conference room and tucked Eugene's fiddle under his chin. Tried to compose himself.

The kid was having such a great time. Let him fly, as far as the air currents would take him. A guy crashed to earth soon enough.

Liam wasn't in the lobby. Nor in the parking lot. Nor in the showcase halls, or the alcoves, or the vending machine corners, or the lounge, or the gift shop, or the restaurant. No. He was gone. It was over.

Sadness settled down, like a smothering blanket. She'd come to depend upon him for feeling good. The world looked wretched and empty, dirt poor without him. And she was so angry. She wanted to break windows, smash furniture.

She couldn't have caved to his demand. It took two to make a compromise. If she blew off an opportunity like this out of fear, she'd never respect herself again. And he wouldn't respect her, either.

"Ms. D'Onofrio? Are you all right?"

Nancy dashed away tears, and looked over her shoulder. "What?"

"Can I get you something?" It was Enid's Hollywood studio exec. Big, beefy guy. Muscle going to fat. He had a sleek black goatee on his broad face, gleaming black hair. His eyes were full of concern.

She tried to orient herself, vaguely remembering that this guy was significant for some reason. She was supposed to be kissing his ass.

"No," she whispered. "Thanks. I'm fine." She dug around in her pocket for a tissue. It was coming back to her now, in little fragmented pieces. The studio exec. The time crunch. The plane leaving for L.A. "I'm sorry," she said. "We were supposed to have a meeting, right?"

"Yes, but it's all right. I can see you're not well," the guy said.

Her spine stiffened with embarrassment. "No, actually, I'm fine. You've got a plane to catch, so let's go to the bar and have some coffee."

But Sills led her right past the bar and into the restaurant. He walked briskly past the few free booths, and sat down in the oddest spot. A table, not a booth, and way in the back. Out of sight of all but a few of the booths, but annoyingly close to the kitchen door, which continually swung open as tray-laden waitresses bumped and bashed their way through with hips and elbows to carry out orders.

The waitress brought them a carafe of coffee. Maitland Sills poured and pushed the cup across the table. "You look tired," he said.

Did he but know. She gave him a wan smile, and took a deep, grateful gulp of coffee.

She knew within three seconds that something was wrong. A numb, crawling feeling spread from the tips of her toes and fingers, creeping inward toward her core. Her heartbeat, louder and faster in her ears. She couldn't move. She was frozen, fighting to keep breathing as the darkness rose. What the hell? Was this a panic attack?

She looked into the eyes of the MGM studio exec. Her insides flash froze. Those dark eyes, fixed and cold. Reptilian. His mouth, so wet. Her eyes fluttered, and in those brief eyelid flickers, she saw like tiny nano-sized film clips the monstrous thing he was beneath his human mask. Something fanged, tusked. Ravenous and foul.

His breath was fetid. It smelled like death.

He leaned forward and pitched his voice low, like a snake's hiss. "Do you wonder what your mother's last words were when she was gasping on the floor, Nancy?" he crooned. "Do you want me to tell you?"

She tried to open her mouth, scream for help. Nothing worked.

A waitress burst through the kitchen door and bustled past them without looking at them. The open door let a wave of clattering sound swell in volume, then diminish again as it swung shut.

He reached across the table, seized the pendant Lucia had given her, and began to twist. The burn of the gold chain tightening around her throat kept her conscious. *Snap.* The chain broke. He pocketed it.

He got up, came around the table, and reached for her.

"Let us by!" John bawled. "Move over! She's going to be sick!"

He shoved his way through the snarl of employees in the restaurant kitchen. Nancy stumbled alongside him, nearly unconscious. He'd plastered her own hand over her mouth to muffle any sounds she might make, clamping his own hand on top of it. Her hair dangled down to hide her face. He dragged her past a waitress carrying a loaded tray, jostling her hard enough to make her stumble.

Plates of eggs Benedict flew, splattered. Shouts of protest. He hustled on, bellowing, "She's going to be sick!" whenever anyone tried to interact with him, and burst out the kitchen entrance. He loped past the Dumpsters, toward the corner and the hotel parking lot.

He dragged her into the shrubbery, still doubled over, and let her drop, right next to a big fiberglass instrument case that he'd planted there four o'clock the previous morning. It was for an upright string bass, and big enough to carry a slender, curled-up, drugged woman.

He made barfing, choking noises, for the benefit of any employees who might have poked their heads out of the kitchen, but it was probably overkill, after the mess he'd made in there. They'd be too busy scrambling to clean up and replace orders to pay attention to him.

He snapped open the case in feverish haste and followed his carefully planned choreography. Rip off goatee and wig. Shove them into the case. Shake out his own shaggy dark hair. Strip off jacket. Replace with a fringed yellow leather jacket. Mirrored aviator sunglasses.

He scooped up the D'Onofrio woman, dumped her slight, limp weight into the wide part of the case, folded and tucked her limbs until she fit. Curled up like a chick in an egg. Soft and helpless. Prey.

He did up the fastenings, peeked out of the bushes, and yanked the rolling case onto the asphalt. Walking, oh so nonchalantly, toward his car. He glanced at his watch. From restaurant table to parking lot, barely over three minutes. Good show. He forced himself to stop grinning. Wouldn't do to get sloppy, or too self-satisfied, or overexcited.

Time enough for excitement later. When it was time to indulge.

A big-name showcase was about to begin. Liam had gotten stuck in the crowd. He shoved his way through the crush, having finally extricated himself from Mandrake's clutches. Something inside him was pulled so tight, it hurt like a bastard. When that part snapped, he did not know what would happen. He just knew he didn't want it to happen in public.

A high-pitched commotion was taking place. He tried to wiggle around it, but the press of bodies filing into the hall was too thick. It was the blonde, the singer who was married to the butthead. She was having a snit fit. He didn't particularly want to know the details, but someone was wheeling a fucking piano into the hall. It blocked his way.

". . . can't believe that guy! That asshole! Can you believe what he said to me?" She caught his eye and promptly directed her outrage toward him before he could turn and shrink away unnoticed. "He shoved me!" she shrieked. "How dare he?"

"Calm down, baby. Don't freak. There are concert presenters all over the place," the butthead pretty boy was muttering desperately.

"Calm down? Screw you, Petey! I was, like, attacked in public, and all you can say is just calm down?" She turned her bug-eyed blue gaze to Liam. "He shoved me!" she repeated. "I almost fell!"

"Who shoved you?" Liam asked.

"The producer asshole, but you know what? I bet he wasn't a producer at all. I mean, he didn't look like one. He didn't have that Hollywood gloss. And he was big and fat, and he had bad breath. Like, nobody's fat with bad breath in Hollywood! And why would he want to talk to Nancy, and not me? I mean, I'm the talent! She's just—" Enid struggled for a word sufficiently dismissive—"administrative help!"

First the hairs on his back prickled, and then icy cold talons sank into his gut. Big fat guy. Bad breath. Wanted Nancy. *Shit.*

He grabbed Enid's shoulders so hard, she squeaked. "Did he go with her? Where did he go?"

She goggled at him. He gave her an impatient little shake.

"Do you mind?" she sniffed, wrenching away. "He went after her, toward the restaurant. She's welcome to him. Rude son of a bitch."

"What does he look like?" Liam demanded.

"Hey!" the butthead Peter blustered. "Don't touch my wife!"

"Fuck off," Liam said, not bothering to look at him. "What does he look like? Hair color, eyes? Talk to me, goddammit!"

Enid was starting to look scared. "Um, black hair?" Her voice had gotten small and uncertain. "A goatee, and, um, a black leather jacket."

He lost the rest, already forging through the crowd amidst shouts and grunts of protest. Fear propelled him toward the restaurant.

He'd lose too much time if he stopped to get the gun and load it. He jogged through the restaurant, checking all the tables. No Nancy.

Think, meathead. *Think.* The door to the kitchen burst open. A harried-looking waitress came bursting out. Behind her, there was some sort of commotion in the kitchen. People were yelling. Good enough for him. He pushed his way through the swinging door. A woman caught sight of him and ran forward, holding up her hands to bar his way.

"Hey! No customers in here!" she yelled. "Get back!"

"What happened in here?" he demanded.

"It was gross," a round-faced girl standing near the entrance con-fided. "This lady was sick to her stomach, and the guy gets the bright idea to drag her through the kitchen? That's so unhygienic! The Board of Health could shut us down for—hey! Where are you going?"

Liam barreled through the people. He slipped, arms flailing, in a long, harrowing slide down the straight-a-way between two rows of range tops, in a slippery skid of yellowish sauce, barely keeping his feet.

He pitched out the door, reeling. Loading bay, garbage. No movement. He took off, heart thudding, for the parking lot.

A harried mother pushing a stroller. A young couple. A retirement age man and his blue-haired wife getting out of a sedan, arguing. Their voices floated over. A big guy in a yellow fringed coat rolling a string bass behind him. No black-haired guy, no black jacket. No Nancy.

He looked again. Nothing else moved. The man and his wife passed. Their babble did not penetrate his mind. He stared at the parking lot, feeling with all his senses. Doubts niggled. Maybe Nancy was in the hall, safe and sound, conducting her business. And he was out here chasing phantoms created by his own overheated brain.

And maybe not. *Big fat guy. Bad breath.*

He gave the yellow-coated man a second look. The guy slowed to a stop and looked around. Sun glinted off his mirrored sunglasses. He looked at Liam for a second, and turned away, but when he started to move again, he was moving slightly faster. Dragging his big instrument case. It rattled and bumped behind him.

The case. The fucking *case.* Oh, sweet suffering Christ.

He took off running. The guy was opening the hatchback of an SUV. He heaved the instrument up and into the back of it, slammed it shut. Glanced at Liam racing toward him. Dove for the driver's seat.

The motor roared. Brake lights came on. Liam was shouting, screaming. The SUV started to pull out. It had to stop and correct. Liam flung himself at the back of the vehicle, yanked at the latch of the hatchback.

It opened. The guy had been in too big of a hurry to lock it. Liam flung himself inside, next to the case. It lay there like a deformed coffin in a hearse. The guy screamed back over his shoulder.

Liam scrabbled for something to grab on to as the guy backed up again, with a violent burst of speed, and then braked abruptly.

Liam slid out the back, dragging the case with him. It toppled, rolled, rocked on the asphalt. *Bam*, the asshole took a shot at him. Liam flung himself to the side. *Zing*, another bullet ricocheted off the asphalt.

A car window exploded. Glass rattled, tinkled. The case was still lying right behind the vehicle's tires. The SUV had stopped moving.

Liam guessed the filthy fuck's intentions and leaped to heave the case out of harm's way right before the SUV roared into reverse and ran it down. They landed between parked cars in the opposite row. He flung himself onto the case, landing with a bone-wrenching thud, in case the bastard stopped to shoot again. Shouts, screams. People had heard the gun.

The SUV peeled away, tires squealing. It tore out of the parking lot, ran a light at the corner, and was gone.

Liam slid off the case onto his ass, shaking. His face was wet. His nose streamed with blood. He turned the case gently right side up and unlatched it with trembling hands, his heart in his throat.

Nancy was curled inside the padded interior, hair over her face. He felt her throat, rejoicing at the pulse. Scooped her out into his arms and cradled her. He brushed the hair off her forehead, murmuring her name over and over. Alive. Not shot. Not broken. Not taken. Oh, God.

He was crying. He couldn't stop. He just sat on the ground, while the commotion buzzed. Rocking her. Holding her.

Until they pried her out of his arms and took her away from him.

Chapter 12

Nancy stared out the window of her apartment from her seat on the couch. It was full dark, but she couldn't be bothered to turn on the light. And she was too tired to wrestle the couch down into a bed.

She should be at the cathedral uptown, where Novum Canticum, her Gregorian chant choir, was having their big New York debut concert. It was an important gig for them, their first well-established classical concert series, and she should be there to support them.

But she couldn't get off the couch. Her ass was weighted down.

They would understand, of course. Everybody was extremely understanding these days. They were treating her like blown glass.

She'd tried to stay too busy to be miserable. How could a woman wallow in self-pity when her cell phone never stopped ringing, and her e-mail in-box never had anything less than twenty new messages? She was surrounded by people who needed her. The hub of frantic activity.

The Jericho gig had been a smash. Peter and Enid were besieged with offers. Record companies that had previously disdained them were making unctuous overtures. Nancy boosted concert fees by a judicious 50 percent and passed out promo packets right and left, wondering why she wasn't happier. It was finally coming together, and that was something, wasn't it? All that heroic effort had paid off. Hadn't it?

No. It hadn't. The horrible events in Boston had laid her pathetic emotional stratagems bare. She'd been scrambling for love all these years. And she only knew that because she'd finally gotten some of it. Just enough to know what it felt like, anyway. And now it was gone.

She'd been better off before. Not knowing.

No, she hadn't earned any love from all her heroic efforts. Love couldn't be earned, or God knew she would have more of it. She finally understood Lucia's impulse to matchmake. Her mother had wanted so badly to find Nancy someone solid. A man she could lean on. The joke was on them, though. Liam was so solid, he was like an outcropping of volcanic rock. Immovable. A cosmic joke, but she wasn't laughing.

She flopped down onto her side, curling around the empty space inside her. Liam had saved her from the guy with the reptile eyes. He'd come to her rescue as heroically as ever, but after snatching her from the jaws of death, he'd decided that his duty as a righteous dude was fulfilled. He'd shaken the dust off his boots and walked into the sunset.

Not a word from the man. Not a call. Not a peep.

She was having nightmares, crying fits every night. She'd stayed with her sisters for the most part, but she'd slipped away from everyone tonight. She needed to be alone. Scary though that was.

The doctors said that it would take a while for the anxiety to ease. The pills they'd prescribed rattled in her purse. She hadn't taken them. All she had were her feelings. She didn't want to cut herself loose from those, too. And she wanted to be sharp, if Reptile Eyes came calling.

She thought constantly about calling Liam, but something always held her back. She'd told him that she loved him, so technically, the ball was in his court. But this was no game. She was too raw, too sad for games. She just wanted to go to him, hold out her heart and say, "Take this. It's yours anyway, you great big idiot. So take it already."

The intercom buzzed. She leaped up, her heart in her throat.

Her sisters both had keys. And Reptile Eyes would not buzz. He would transform into fetid slime, ooze under the crack in the door, and reconstitute himself on the other side like the über-evil Terminator III.

She didn't want to talk to anyone. Just as well she'd left the light off. She curled into a tight ball, and gave the intercom the finger.

Buzzzzzz, it rang, loud and long and demanding. Persistent bastard. She waited. Two minutes. Three. *Buzzzzzz*, again. Curiosity laced with fear dragged her to the window. She leaned out to peek.

Liam stood on the top of her stoop. Her heart leaped, thudded heavily against her ribs. Her legs started to wobble. *Buzzzzz*, he hit the intercom again. He looked up into her eyes, and held out his hands, palm up, in silent entreaty. She shuffled to the intercom like a zombie and buzzed him in.

She unlocked all the locks, of which there were many. She'd added three more to her collection since the Reptile Eyes episode.

She opened the door. He was thinner. Pale, drawn, and deadly serious. In the flickering light from the stairwell, she saw the fading bruises beneath both eyes. A broken nose, Eoin had said, and cracked ribs. Hanging out with her was hard on a guy's health.

She suppressed the concern, the guilt. The desire to fuss.

Her heart was careening at such a fast clip, she felt woozy and faint. She couldn't speak, so she just stepped back and gestured him in.

He shoved the door shut after him, blocking out the light, and she was grateful she'd left it off—until she started remembering the last time they'd been alone, in this room, in the dark. Making love.

He cleared his throat, awkwardly. "Are you all right?" he asked.

She blocked all the automatic babble-mode replies at their source. The "Oh, I'm fine and how are you" bullshit. She had nothing to lose, no reason to lie. "No," she said flatly. "I feel like shit."

He took a step closer. "I'm sorry," he said.

She choked on her laughter. "Oh, are you? I can't sleep. I can't eat. I can't concentrate. I'm scared of my own shadow. I am wrecked, Liam. I am roadkill. So don't ask stupid questions. And don't tell me that you're sorry. Because I don't want to hear it."

"You're going to have to hear it. Because I'm not done saying it."

"Oh, yeah?" She backed up, and her thighs bumped against the couch. She was so wobbly, she sat down with an undignified thump. "Don't tell me what I have to do, because I am so very done with all your arrogant pronouncements and your bullshit ultimatums!"

"I love you," he said.

That cut her tirade off and left her gasping for air. She just hung there, head dangling, hands clamped over her mouth.

Liam sank down onto his knees. He pried one of her hands off her mouth, pulled it to himself, and kissed it, with reverent slowness, like a sacred ceremony. "I'm sorry," he said again.

She didn't know where to start. This thing between them was a maze, a confusion of entrances and exits, full of dead ends, land mines. Her heart shook at the idea that there might be a way through it.

If she could find that narrow, winding way. If they could find it, together.

"Why didn't you call?" she blurted. The question she'd sworn she would not ask had popped up and asked itself, without her permission.

He hesitated, his face turned away. "I couldn't. First, I was numb. Then, I was scared. Then, I was embarrassed. I was just . . . stuck. In a big machine. I had to shake loose of it. It took some time. But I'll regret how long it took for the rest of my life."

That startled a watery smile out of her. "Don't get melodramatic. The rest of your life is a long time." She paused. "I hope."

"Do you?" He slid his arms around her hips and laid his head in her lap. "No matter how long it is, it'll be too long without you."

Whoa. Following up his advantage, the crafty, presumptuous bastard. He'd caught her in a weak moment, and now he was just waiting for her to cave. And oh, how she wanted to cave. So badly.

Nancy put her hands on his shoulders, with a vague notion of pushing him away, but as soon as they made contact, her fingers dug in. His muscles seemed leaner, harder than before. He trembled.

She couldn't push him away. She had no strength for it. She found herself bowing down like a wilting flower. Draped over him, her hands splayed over his ribs, feeling the rise and fall of his breath.

"How's your nose?" she asked.

"Healing," he replied. "No big deal."

"It was for me," she said. "It was huge, for me. You saved my life. Again. Thanks, by the way."

He lifted his head, and frowned. "Speaking of which. You should not be alone here. It's not safe."

She sighed. "Don't start. If it comforts you, my sisters have been babysitting me. I just needed to be alone."

He looked dubious, but let it go. After a moment, he cautiously tried again. "So. Ah, how did it all go?"

"How did what go?"

"The gig. Peter and Enid. Are they megasuperstars now?"

"Not one bit of sarcasm out of you, or it's out the door, Knightly."

He lifted his hands in quick surrender. "Sorry."

She harrumphed, unmollified. "It went well," she said coolly. "It was a big boost for both their careers. And mine, too, incidentally."

"Ah. Well, good. I'm happy for them. And you."

She was appalled to realize that she was trying not to smile at his supercareful, kid-gloves tone. "That's very big of you, Liam."

"I hope they appreciate you now." The edge was back in his voice.

"I think they do. They even paid back the money they owed me."

"No shit?" He looked impressed. "How'd you swing that?"

"I put my foot down. I admit, that approach does have its uses."

He looked away. She couldn't see his mouth, but she could feel that he was trying not to smile. "Funny how you should say that," he said. "Myself, I've been working on the concept of compromise."

"Oh, really?" Her heart thudded crazily. "And how do you feel about it these days?"

He shrugged. "It's not as bad as I thought."

They gazed at each other. She laid her fingertips against the bruises under his eyes, petting them. He seized her hand, kissed it.

"I called my father," he offered.

She blinked, taken aback. "Wow. And? So? How did it go?"

"It was weird," he admitted. "Awkward. But we got through it."

"So? What did you say to him? What did he say? Tell me!"

He kissed her hand again, and again, making her wait. "I, uh, asked him if I should send him an invitation to my wedding."

Her jaw dropped. Too much, all at once. Her throat shook.

"Ah, shit," Liam muttered. "I'm sorry. That came out all wrong. I know I have to propose, and beg and grovel first. And I didn't mean to sound like it's a done deal. It was a . . . a hypothetical question."

"Hy-hypothetical," she whispered.

"Yeah. You know. In case I get lucky."

She hid her face. He waited patiently for several minutes.

"So?" he coaxed. "You are my queen. Everything that's beautiful and fine. I'll spend my life trying to be worthy. Trying not to fuck this up. Please. Say yes. Be my wife."

"I . . . I love you, too," she burst out.

His grin began to spread. "That's a yes? That means I got lucky?"

"That means I love you," she said. "I already have two wedding dresses in storage. I don't know if I could handle being engaged again."

"Okay," he said promptly. "Let's skip the engaged part, and go straight to the married part. I got on the Internet before I came here. There's a red-eye flight for Vegas. Tonight."

She started to laugh, helplessly, tears in her eyes. "Oh, God."

"We can get married by an Elvis impersonator. Spend three days on a vibrating bed. Rent a convertible, drive through the desert."

It sounded surreal. Wonderful. "What about the invitation? For your dad?"

He shrugged. "Oh, that. We can do another wedding when we're back. For your sisters, and your friends. This one will be just for us."

He waited for a moment, and went on, his voice more hesitant. "Your schedule permitting, of course. I didn't buy the tickets yet. Didn't want to seem cocky. It can wait. If you've got work commitments."

"Wow, Liam," she said demurely. "That speech sounds rehearsed."

"It's so obvious?" he asked, rueful. "Give me credit for trying."

Nancy slid her hands around his waist. "Have you been eating?"

"Hey! You stole my line."

"I have to fatten you up," she said. "There's this great little Vietnamese place down the block that has killer noodles."

"Don't you have any noodles here? Spaghetti, linguini?"

"Are you kidding?" she scoffed. "With a name like D'Onofrio?"

"If we make our noodles here, we have the advantage of being able to get naked and sweaty while the water boils," he pointed out.

She laughed at him, tears slipping down her face. "Um, all right."

"That's awesome. But you haven't answered my proposal."

She bit her lip. "Liam. I love you. You love me. Isn't that miracle enough for now? Can't we just be grateful? Let's not push our luck."

He looked mutinous. "I want it all. Every night. In my bed."

"Hmm," she murmured. "I thought you were working on the concept of compromise."

"Yeah, but let's not overdo it." He touched her face, as carefully as if she were one of Lucia's orchids. "I almost lost you forever," he said. "It would have ripped my heart out. I love you, Nancy. I'll never stop loving you. Push your luck with me all you want, and keep on pushing. There's no limit to it. It's bigger than any limits. It's deeper than the ocean."

Something moved inside her chest, swelling until her heart was about to burst. Until there was no more room for fear.

"Yes," she said, and reached for him.

Ask
for More

Chapter
1

It was him again. Right on time.

Nell ducked behind the dessert display case, eying him hungrily over the pecan fudge brownies, tingling from that guilty rush she got whenever she saw him. The only thing effervescent enough to ease the chronic, heavy ache in her middle that she was carrying around these days. She craved the feeling.

He checked to see if his usual table by the window was free. It was. The lunch rush was nearly over by the time he arrived; three-fifteen, regular as clockwork.

He took off his jacket, tossed it on the chair, and seated himself. He pulled out a laptop, opened it, and set to work, face grimly intent. As he had every day Nell had worked the lunch shift at the Sunset Grill.

For weeks he'd been coming every day, and she'd found herself starting to take all the lunch shifts she could, even though she earned way more tips with dinner. Broke as she was, that fleeting, ephemeral rush was worth more to her than the cash. She had it bad.

Considering that the guy remained utterly oblivious to her existence.

She polished her glasses, perched them back on her nose, and fished the order she had just taken out of her short-term memory. She dished up ratatouille for the table of women underneath the aquarium, sneaking peeks as she drizzled vinaigrette and tossed grated beets and sunflower seeds on their salads. She loaded the tray and chose a path through the restaurant that brought her by his table. Close enough to smell the detergent his crisp white shirt was washed in. The next sneaky sweep past him garnered her a hungry whiff of his aftershave. Mmm. Nice. Those shoulders, wow. Flaring out, so broad and thick. Solid-looking. He wasn't movie-star handsome at all, not with that narrow, angular face. She'd studied his features minutely, reviewing them in her dreams and daydreams, but every time she saw the real flesh-and-blood thing, it was a fresh thrill. She loved the severity of his features. That bladelike nose with a crooked bump on it, the black, slashing eyebrows set at a sharp upward angle. His cheeks were lean, with grooves flanking his mouth, and he had crinkled lines around his eyes, as if he'd squinted into desert sun. His mouth was grim, his black hair short, sticking up wildly. She doubted it was due to styling gel. He was not the type to affect messy hair on purpose. This guy could not possibly be bothered.

She peeked at his computer screen from behind his broad, muscular back. It was full of incomprehensible code. She forced herself to march away without looking back. She was going to be realistic and mature and ignore him today. After one more tiny, hungry peek.

Behind the counter, her boss, Norma, looked over from the mushrooms she was grilling. "Here again, eh, Nelly? Can't get enough of that strip steak sandwich, I see. Before I lose you in a romantic haze, hon, I need to ask a favor."

Gack. Who knew her silly crush had been so obvious? Nell grabbed the bread knife and began slicing. "Ask away."

"Easy does it, hon. That knife is sharp. Can't help but notice that you never take your eyes off the fellow. Can't blame you. If I were twenty-five years younger . . . hell, maybe even just fifteen years younger . . ." Her voice trailed off, eyes twinkling, waiting for Nell to soften, but Nell just pressed her lips together and cut more bread. "Looks like a workaholic, though," Norma mused. "Always typing, never a glance at the cute waitress serving him. Take it from an expert. Leave that guy alone."

"Thanks for the advice, but it's not relevant," Nell snapped, tossing bread into baskets. "I'm not getting anywhere near him."

"Whatever you say. Are you free to work an evening shift? Kendra just called in sick. The girl's driving me crazy. Always at death's door."

"Sorry, Norma, but I'm teaching a discussion section tonight for the summer school American poetry lecture course."

"I was afraid of that. Oh well. We'll be shorthanded, but we'll survive. Get some coffee for that hardworking fellow before he starts feeling neglected. Do you absolutely have to wear those glasses, hon?"

Nell snatched her glasses off and polished them defensively.

"Unless you want me to bump into tables! What's wrong with them?"

"They just make you look so, I don't know. Intellectual, I guess."

"Norma, I've got news for you. I *am* intellectual!"

"Don't get your knickers in a twist, hon. Your eyes are so pretty, I just want the world to see them." Norma tucked a hank of curly brunette hair behind Nell's ear, chucked her on the chin, and tugged down the front of Nell's apron so it showed more bosom. "For God's sake, Nelly. Use those assets of yours. Work it. Go on, scram! Get the man's order!"

Nell poured a cup of coffee and scurried out with her order pad, self-consciously tugging her orange apron bib back up over her cleavage. She felt nervous and fluttery every time she took his order. God knows why. He'd never glanced up from his screen. She could take his order stark staring naked, and he would never notice.

She placed the coffee on the table. Without moving his eyes from the screen, he reached for it and took a swallow. "Thanks," he said, in that resonant, distant voice that made her shivery. "The usual, please."

"Okay," she replied. "We have three soups today: minestrone, French onion, and three bean. Which would you prefer?"

A small frown furrowed his forehead, but he didn't look up. "I don't care. Whichever is fine."

"One bowl of whichever, coming right up," Nell murmured, staring at the cowlick in his hair. There was raffish stubble on his tense-looking jaw. His cuffs were turned up, revealing tough, ropy muscles and black hair that lay flat and silky against the golden skin of his forearms.

"Is there a problem?" he asked, fingers tapping.

"Um, no, of course not." Nell fled, flustered, and ran herself promptly into a table edge. She bit back a yelp. She would have a bruise tomorrow. A stern reminder of what happened when one gave in to adolescent urges. The fact that Norma had noticed was proof that she'd let her crush get out of hand. She put the order in and began assembling his lunch. Norma glanced over with professional interest. "The usual, I assume?"

Nell nodded, popping a roll into the toaster grill. She scooped an enormous serving of Knorma's Knockout Coleslaw onto a small plate.

"You're ruining me with those portions, hon. He's not worth it."

"Cut it out, Norma," Nell snapped, preparing the garnish. Thick slices of tomato, radish rosebuds, and carrot curlicues. She tossed on a handful of alfalfa sprouts, hesitated for a moment, and then cut a substantial slice of sweet onion and added it with a flourish, since his breath was neither her responsibility nor her problem. The toaster pinged. She pulled out the roll, avoiding Norma's gaze.

"What soup did he want?" Norma inquired.

"He doesn't care. I'm going to give him the three bean."

"Really? I don't know, hon. Minestrone might be safer."

Nell ladled a bowl full of soup. "He'll learn to express a preference if he doesn't like it," she said in a clipped voice. When she hefted the tray, the soup slopped dangerously near the edges of the bowl.

"Easy does it, Nelly," Norma teased. "He's not going anywhere without his lunch."

Nell gave her a withering look and carried out the guy's soup, head high.

When she served the rest of his lunch, the only place to put the plate was the extreme edge of the table. It looked so precarious. He hadn't touched the soup yet. His long, graceful hands tapped ceaselessly on the keyboard.

"That'll be all," he muttered, staring fixedly at the screen.

Nell headed back to the kitchen, mentally ticking off issues to cover in her discussion section on Emily Dickinson's poetry tonight. The sad plight of women in nineteenth-century America. Poverty. Powerlessness. Arid celibacy. Secret love. Constraint. Corsets. The life of the imagination. Ooh, ouch. It was the story of her life. Except for the corsets.

"Everything go smoothly?" Norma asked in a sly voice.

"No problems." Nell loaded ice water on a tray, marched past Norma with her chin up, and proceeded to trip on the plastic mat.

Crash. Glass broke, heads turned, water pooled, ice cubes rolled. Nell got the dustpan and started picking up shards, mouth tight.

"You're too tense, Nelly." Norma put her hands on her substantial hips and scowled in concern. "You need to get out more."

"Norma, get real! My life is nuts right now!" she flared. "My sister was stalked and attacked by a slobbering maniac, I'm short my rent because of all that lost work after the Fiend jumped Nancy, my thesis adviser is on my case night and day, I can't seem to sleep anymore, and Lucia . . . oh, God. Never mind. Please, just leave me alone, okay?"

Her voice choked off. Tears slipped down her face. She was mortified, but Norma just tugged her up to her feet and enveloped her in a big hug. "Oh, honey, I'm so sorry about Lucia. I didn't mean to stress you. I know you're grieving, and what happened to Nancy is terrifying, but things have worked out, right? Things are calming down, and Lucia would have wanted you to get out, have fun! You know that."

Nell polished her tear-splattered glasses. "I appreciate that you worry about me, but I am not in the mood for fun, and I can't take this lecture right now," she quavered. "I need to get dessert for table six, table eight needs their check, and Monica is taking a cigarette break—"

"Forget I said anything. I must say, though, I'm glad to see you taking a healthy interest in a good-looking guy. It's a good sign."

Nell stomped out to dump broken glass into the trash. Her eyes were red and puffy, but who cared? The black-haired man would never notice. When she refilled his coffee, she asked, "Care for dessert?"

"The usual," he said coolly.

Nell hesitated for a moment, then took her courage in both hands.

"Sure you don't want to try something new? We have strawberry shortcake today, and the pecan fudge brownies are wonderful."

His hands froze over the keyboard as he processed this. "I'm sure they're all good." His voice had a dismissive edge. "Give me the usual."

Nell sighed and went to get a slice of apple crumb pie with vanilla ice cream. As always, when he finished, he closed his laptop, dropped a bill on the table that covered the check as well as a moderate-to-generous tip, and left. The guy had the imagination of a large rock. And the manners of a hibernating snake. To hell with him, anyway.

The rest of the shift was a tired blur. She helped Norma prep for dinner and went to the bathroom to freshen up before her discussion section. She took off her glasses, leaned close to the mirror, and peered.

Norma was right. The round glasses were nerdish. And the long, unstyled mop of dark curly hair was juvenile and nondescript.

She twisted her hair into a knot, letting curly wisps fall down around her ears and jaw. Marginally better. Her eyes were her best feature. Dark, with long lashes and eyebrows that she had to pluck or else they did a coup d'etat and took over her face. A nice mouth, she conceded, if a little large for her jaw. Maybe she should try contacts.

But why was she stressing over her looks, anyway? Who was noticing them? She had bigger things to worry about. She splashed water on her face, hefted her bag onto her shoulder, and sprinted for the bus.

Her discussion group went as expected. A healthy two-thirds of the group actually attended, and out of that number, only three appeared to be sleeping, which wasn't bad, statistically speaking. They had quite a spirited discussion about Emily Dickinson's love poetry. One serious young man with stringy hair said earnestly, "Like, how do you know Emily Dickinson never had, you know, sex? Maybe she, like, had secret lovers! Some of those poems are totally scorching! I can't believe that she could feel like that if she never, you know, got any!"

"Believe it," Nell said without thinking. Fifteen faces gave her speculative looks. She noticed that the young blond man and she had the same type of glasses, and felt a sudden, desperate urge to change her style. "Let's wrap it up for tonight," she said. "I expect a five-to-ten page paper from everyone by Wednesday."

"But I have a physics midterm to study for!" one student whined.

"And I have to write a philosophy paper by Monday!" another lamented. "Can't we have till Friday?"

"Wednesday," she said firmly to a chorus of groans.

Nell trudged through the bustling, congested city campus to the English department offices. The office door opened as she approached, and Maria, a fellow grad student, came out holding a fax. "Hey, Nell. Take a look. I was about to post it. It might be just up your alley."

Nell looked it over.

WANTED

Writer-Editor-Proofreader
for interactive fantasy game project

EXPERT IN <u>POETRY</u>

Good Pay   Flexible Hours
Call 555-439-8218   Ask for Duncan

"Weird, huh?" Maria commented.

Nell looked up at her. "Interesting."

"Thought you might think so. Good night, Nell."

Nell said good night absently. What on earth would a software outfit want with poetry? She scribbled the number, wondering exactly what "good pay" meant to this Duncan. She often picked up temp legal secretary jobs at night, when she was broke. They paid well but exhausted her. She was always alert for a job that would pay enough so she could quit working at the Sunset and live a life that resembled normal, if such a thing existed. Though she'd begun to doubt it, with the bizarre things that had been happening since Lucia's death.

And she wasn't going to think about Lucia, or she'd cry again. She fingered the pendant Lucia had given her. The golden rectangle with its halo of swirling, white gold lacework was warm from her body's heat. A talisman of love, but a shadow of fear clung to it. Her fingers tightened around the thing in a possessive spasm. The Fiend had taken Nancy's pendant. It was stupid for Nell to wear hers around. A blatant provocation, even. But she felt naked and defenseless without it.

She'd compromised by lengthening the chain and tucking the pendant inside her dress, where it usually got wedged between her boobs. She had pepper spray in her bag. And she was going to sign up for self-defense. Maybe she'd even learn to use a gun.

She shivered. Then again, maybe not. Just knowing how to use a gun meant nothing. She had to be willing to point it at someone and pull the trigger. And that tasty, cheerful reflection propelled her straight to her broom closet–sized office, to call Vivi's cell phone. For comfort.

Since Nancy's adventures, she'd secretly begun to consider getting a cell phone, but she was still hesitating, after having made such a big fat deal of how much she hated them to her sisters all these years. After all her pompous tirades on the risk of brain tumors, how sinister it was that a person couldn't have privacy, how aggravating it was that one was constantly on call, etc., etc. She'd feel like a fool with her tail between her legs if she caved now.

But pride and privacy had so lost their charm lately. When evil stalkers with unknown agendas lurked in the shadows, looking foolish didn't seem so bad. It was comforting, when things got weird, to be an electromagnetic frequency away from the people you cared about.

Vivi picked up promptly. "Hey, baby. All's well?"

"Nobody's abducted me lately," Nell said. "How about yourself?"

"Still working. Busy day. I'll wrap it up in about an hour. Then my breakdown, and I take off tonight straight for Wilmington after I grab a bite. I feel weird staying in one place for too long. I want to be a moving target. Sound stupid?"

"Hell no. Drive carefully. Did you talk to Nancy?"

"Yeah, she's with Liam. Still in Denver, with his dad. They're coming back tomorrow, I think. Thank God we don't have to worry about her, at least. That guy of hers is like a Doberman lunging at the chain. Got a customer, darling. Gotta go."

"Okay, later." Nell hung up, stared at the flyer again, and dialed.

"Burke Solutions, Inc., can I help you?"

"Yes. May I speak to, um"—she consulted the tag—"Duncan?"

"May I ask what it's regarding?"

"It's regarding the writing job."

"Oh. Just a sec. Hold on."

Nell drummed her fingers and fretted until a deep, resonant, oddly familiar voice came on the line. "This is Duncan."

"Hello. My name is Nell D'Onofrio, and I'm a grad student at NYU. I'm interested in the writing job."

"Do you have writing and editing experience? Do you know anything about poetry?"

She was taken aback by his brusque tone. "Of course. I'm writing my thesis on nineteenth-century women poets. I lead a discussion section for a summer poetry lecture course, and my graduate seminar focused on Christina Rossetti."

"Ah." There was a thoughtful pause. "I'm supervising the creation of a computer game," he went on. "A mystery quest, with clues encoded in maps, books, poems, etc. I need a writer for the texts."

"Sounds good," Nell said. "The flyer says flexible hours. How flexible?"

"I don't know yet." He sounded irritated. "I've never done this before. It's actually my brother's project. I have meetings all afternoon, so come to the office tomorrow at six, and I'll interview you."

His master-and-commander tone pissed her off. "I'm free at seven-thirty," she said crisply, although she could have probably done six, with a little switching and trading of shift hours. But phooey on him.

"That'll work. Tomorrow, then. My receptionist will give you directions."

Nell wrote down the directions. Strange, but interesting, even if Duncan seemed bossy and arrogant. And tomorrow was Friday. She had nothing better to do after her shift than to go home and jump at the shadows. She shoved a pile of midterm essays into her bag. That'd keep her too busy to work herself into a paranoid frenzy over every sound. Or climb the walls with futile lust, which was almost as bad. No, worse.

* * *

Nell armed the infrared alarm as soon as she went into her apartment. Any breach of the door or window would be instantly reported to the police. It made her feel safer as she heated and ate a dinner of leftovers. She cooked when Vivi was there, but didn't bother when she was alone.

She was nibbling a stale Oreo that she'd found in the cookie stash when the ringing phone made her practically bounce off the ceiling. She had to concentrate hard to slow her breathing and control the shake in her voice as she picked it up. "Hello?"

"It's just me," said her sister Nancy.

Nell sank onto the futon couch, knees trembling. "Oh. Great. How are things? Viv told me you guys were still in Denver."

"We are, with Liam's dad, and his dad's lady friend. I have news. Remember when Liam's friend Charlie Witt told me about that eighty-year-old guy with the designer clothes? The one they found in Jamaica, with his throat snapped?"

"The one they called the clotheshorse? That was just after Lucia died, right?"

"Right. The time of death they determined was roughly the same time that Lucia died."

Nell doubled over, pressing her hand against the nervous twisting in her stomach. "So? What about him?"

"Well, after what happened to me in Boston, Detective Lanaghan decided to take this a little more seriously." Nancy's voice had an edge. "She had his prints compared to the ones found on the coffee cup in Lucia's apartment. As I suggested they do weeks ago."

"And they match?" Nell asked.

"They match," Nancy echoed quietly. "She just called me."

The sisters were silent. Nell forced out a shaky sigh. "It's Marco," she said, with absolute conviction. "Lucia's long-lost husband."

"Yeah," Nancy said. "It must be. He came to find her and got murdered that same night. By the same person who killed Lucia."

Nell squeezed her eyes shut, and pressed her hand against her forehead. It felt clammy. "That poor old guy. How awful."

"At least they're together now," Nancy pointed out, her voice soft. "I think, probably . . . that she loved him. To the very end."

"You could look at it that way," Nell agreed. "If you believed in love and eternity and all that good stuff that's dusted with sparkly haze."

"And you don't?"

"Not right now," she admitted, her voice cracking. "You're madly in love, Nance. You've got sparkly haze happening by the bucketful. But in the real world, it's actually a pretty rare commodity."

Nancy paused for a long, painful moment. "I'm sorry," she whispered. "I was just trying to cheer you up."

Nell felt guilty. Scrooging on her poor sister, whose only crime was in getting lucky in love. "Don't be," she said. "I'm glad for you. Really. So did you tell Detective Lanaghan about the letter in the picture frame?"

"Yes, and she said it's a great lead, but since all we have is the guy's first name and the name of his town, it's going to take a while. She has to contact the local police in Italy, find an interpreter, et cetera. So I started to think, in the meantime . . . since you speak Italian . . ."

"You want me to call the cops there?"

"Would you?" Nancy asked eagerly. "Just to facilitate things?"

Nancy looked up at the clock, calculating time zones. "I can do it tomorrow morning, before I leave for work," she said.

The sisters went through their now obsessive routine of admonishing each other to be careful. When they finally hung up, Nell stared at the wall for a long time, her hand pressed against her mouth.

She was grateful for a job to do. Something that might help, a move that might actually yield some answers. But whatever answers she might find were not going to be comforting. This thing kept getting scarier and scarier. But dwelling on that fact would not help matters.

Nothing to do now but get her ass busy.

A thick sheaf of essays later, she rubbed her eyes, stretched, and flopped onto her bed with a groan. The surface of her bed was covered with books. There was just a narrow strip the size of her body to sleep in. It made her smile, grimly. What a perfect metaphor for her life. She could never take a lover. Where would she put him? Between her complete *Riverside Shakespeare* and her twenty-pound annotated Dante's *Divine Comedy*?

The black-haired man popped into her mind, predictably enough. He was her default mode, whenever she wanted to avoid an uncomfortable thought. She pondered him, wondering why she was so pathetically obsessed with the man. It was weird. She wasn't the type.

Probably because he was so clueless. Emotionally inaccessible to the point of being practically autistic. What could be safer for a coward like herself? She knew nothing about the guy, except that he had a stunning capacity for concentration, and he really, really liked strip steak. And thinking about him was more fun than thinking about that poor old guy, still lying in the morgue in Jamaica. Nameless, unclaimed, unmourned. The cold, stark loneliness of it made her roll over onto her belly and shove her hot face against the pillow.

Maybe tomorrow, she could put a name to the old man who may or may not have been Lucia's husband. Recognition, the dignity of a name. The best she could hope for.

Her eyes started to close, and sometime later, she woke from a dream of the black-haired man. In her dream, weirdly enough, he was smiling at her. A really beautiful smile. His face practically shone.

She'd never seen the guy smile in real life. As she drifted to sleep again, she wondered if he even knew how.

"What is she doing now?"

The sharp tone, loaded with tension and implied criticism, made John Esposito flex his fingers until his knuckles popped. Bloody, murderous fantasies flashed through his mind, red tinged and wet.

He carefully did not turn his head from the monitor, and kept his voice very flat. "She appears to be reading papers," he said.

"Reading? Reading what papers?" Ulf Haupt came hobbling over, his cane tap-tap-tapping against the floor. He leaned down to peer over John's shoulder. John had a fantasy of jabbing an elbow into the decrepit asshole's gut. Hard enough to cause internal hemorrhaging.

"Students' essays," he said, with grim patience. "She's a teacher."

"Essays?" Haupt leaned lower, his head bobbing far too close to John's face, and he leaned away to keep his space.

"Keep watching," Haupt snapped. "She might get another phone call. You must let nothing slip through the cracks. Nothing. Tomorrow, she will make that call to Italy, and identify Barbieri's corpse. This is already a disaster, John. A disgrace."

The old man's shrill, accusing tone put John's teeth violently on edge. "Why?" he demanded. "It'll tell them nothing. I need to take a piss. The stupid bitch hasn't moved in four hours. Watching her is about as relevant as watching water evaporate."

"I'm not paying you to be entertained," Haupt shot back. "Keep your eyes on this one. Since you lost the other two."

"I did not 'lose' the others!" John said, stung. "I know exactly where they are at all times. The youngest one is in Pennsylvania, working at a crafts fair, and the older one is with her fiancé in Denver. If you want me to take the young one, I could drive down to—"

"No. Stay here, where I can direct you, blow by blow. I do not like the results when you are left to your own devices, John."

John bit back what he wanted to say. He loathed having someone look over his shoulder. By the end of this gig, he might just cut the whiny old bastard's throat and punish the D'Onofrio sisters for no recompense at all. Just for having been such pains in the ass.

He stared at Antonella as she tossed the essay in a pile and grabbed another. He was staring almost at the top of her head, the camera being hidden in her smoke detector. A great angle for cleavage, of which she had a goodly amount. She was chubbier than her sisters, with tits and ass to match. He liked that. Something to grab and shake.

The pendant he was supposed to take from her sparkled from that beautiful plump cleft of pale flesh that bulged from the neckline of her gray tank. She had peeled down to loungewear. Gray cotton stretch shorts over her hips. Taut, pinchable nipples poking through her tank.

He thought of her older sister, the one who had eluded him twice. Rage grabbed him deep, and twisted. He glared up into Haupt's eyes. "I'll go get the dumb bitch right now, if you like," he offered. "She's alone in her apartment. I have the code to disarm her alarm. And then she won't make that call to Italy." Anything to get this goatfuck moving.

"No," Haupt said coldly. "You will wait. They will identify Barbieri anyway, now. It's only a matter of time. Discipline, John. She's finally getting back to her normal schedule and back in her own apartment again. And once you take her, you will have to move fast for the other sister."

"I have backup for that. And for following Antonella tomorrow."

"I hope they will prove more competent than that idiot you hired before. I want this done without mistakes that end up on the evening news," the old man lectured. "We lost weeks waiting for the noise to die down. Keep watching." He hobbled out of the room.

John looked back at the screen. Antonella was stretching, tossing her head back. That strong, curvy, flexible body, mmm. He could feel it in his grasp, writhing desperately. He licked his lips. She massaged her temples, a tiny frown between her brows. A headache. Aw. Poor baby. Working so hard. She needed Big John to give her a neck rub.

After which, he would rip those cock-teasing panties off her, stuff them into her mouth, and make her forget all about her poor head.

It was the least he deserved, after all this fucking aggravation.

Chapter
2

"**G**razie for the telephone call, Signorina D'Onofrio," said the inspettore, Osvaldo Tucci, the person at the comissariato who had finally fielded her call. "I do not believe that we have any pending missing-persons reports from Castiglione Sant'Angelo, and to be sincere, without a surname for reference, it will take a long time to—"

"But that's just my point," Nell argued stubbornly. "If he got on a plane for New York weeks ago, why would it have ever occurred to anyone to declare him missing? Perhaps you can cross-reference. I know he was a resident of the Palazzo de Luca. And I know that he was married to Lucia de Luca, sometime between 1957 and 1964, I think. Doesn't that help?"

"I am not familiar with all the palazzi of the noble families in Castiglione Sant'Angelo," Inspettore Tucci said, his voice heavy with professional patience. "There are many of them, and I did not grow up here myself. I was transferred here from Calabria. But I assure you, we will look into this, and get in touch with the Detective Lanaghan as soon as possible."

They closed the call with a polite round of pleasantries, and Nell hung up, frustrated and unsatisfied. Not that she'd expected anything to be easy, or obvious. But it would have been nice.

Lunch prep at the Sunset was as busy as ever, and she was glad. It kept her too frazzled to dwell on poor old Marco's sad fate. Or wonder, uneasily, if Lucia had been forced to witness her husband's murder.

The thought chilled her to the bone.

At three-fifteen, Nell felt a familiar tingle in the nape of her neck. She looked up from the banana kiwi smoothie she was blending. It was him.

Thank God. She welcomed the little thrill gratefully. Her drug of choice. A scary analogy, but damn it, she didn't have much to thrill about these days. She'd take what she could get.

He was frowning at his favorite table, which was occupied. He chose another, pulling out his laptop. Monica jerked her chin in the direction of his table, even though the man had seated himself in her section, not Nell's. Oh, God. Even Monica knew.

Norma tapped her shoulder. "Get that strip steak ready pronto, Nelly. That guy looks hungry."

"I don't want to give him the strip steak," Nell said rebelliously. "Always the same damn thing, every day. It can't be good for him. To say nothing of the nutritional implications and saturated fats, a person needs stimulation, variety, change! Or else they're as good as dead!"

"You're a fine one to talk, sweet cheeks. I have a suggestion for you. Go tap him on the shoulder and tell him he needs a change. Like the tofu cashew stir-fry. Or the curried chickpeas. Or dinner with you."

"You're crazy," Nell said, aghast. "He doesn't know I exist!"

"Whose fault is that? You'd be take-your-breath-away gorgeous if you played yourself up a little bit! Go get the man some coffee!"

Nell stomped out onto the restaurant floor, tired of being lectured, hounded. She set the coffee on the table beside the black-haired man with more force than necessary, slapped a menu down, and whipped out her order pad.

"What would you like? The usual?" she demanded. Monica passed with a tray of sundaes and made audible smooching sounds. Nell glared at her.

The black-haired man frowned into his screen. "Why do you even ask? You know exactly what I want." He sounded irritated.

Nell braced herself. "Good question. One to which I have perhaps given more thought than it deserves. I'm prepared to answer, however."

His fingers slowed their tapping on the keyboard, and then stopped. He reached slowly for his coffee. "Go on."

Nell's heart thumped. "Although I know you want the strip steak, the one day I don't ask will be the day that, out of sheer perversity, you decide you want the bulgur pilaf." She tried to sound breezy.

"Not likely." He looked up. For the first time, she had his full attention. It was dizzying. He looked into her face, eyes narrowed. They were dark, penetrating. Gorgeous. He had unbelievably long lashes.

"Therefore," she continued, "by saying, 'the usual,' I'm killing two birds with one stone. I'm acknowledging that you have a relationship with us, and that we will gladly cater to your preferences. But the fact that I ask at all pays homage to the fact that life is full of surprises—and people do change." She poised her pen over the pad. "Your order?"

He stared at her for a long moment. Blinked. She waited, belly fluttering. "The usual," he said.

Nell scribbled and fled.

Back behind the counter, Norma gave her cheek an approving pinch. "Good start! Not what I told you to say, but he sure took notice! No, don't look now. He's still looking. Practically staring! For goodness' sake, look nonchalant. Look busy!"

"Yeah. Like, play it cool," Monica advised.

"Leave me alone. You're embarrassing me to death. Monica, would you take over his table? I can't face him again," Nell begged.

"Not in a million years," Monica said, heartless. "All yours, babe."

"I'll dip up his coleslaw," Norma said in a businesslike tone. "Put the roll in the grill, and tuck that hair behind your ears. Monica, get a bowl of soup, and pass me those veggies!"

Norma and Monica smartly assembled his lunch and passed the tray into Nell's nerveless hands. The black-haired man pushed his computer to one side of the table and watched as she laid the dishes down. His gaze on her face made her skin tingle and burn.

Nell straightened her spine and forced herself to look into his eyes. "Will that be all?" Her voice was embarrassingly tremulous.

His eyes traveled down her body. Slow, cool, assessing.

She wished desperately that she hadn't called his attention to herself. If he kept looking at her like that, she was going to melt, burn, fly into a million pieces.

"For now," he said simply.

She fled again, and behind the counter, Norma and Monica hooted and cheered in whispers. "He's eating you with his eyes, honey! Don't look! Get the coffeepot and do a round of refills," Norma directed.

"Yeah, chica, you did good. Tomorrow wear something sexier. Say, like, a tight ribbed turtleneck. Sleeveless, 'cause you got good arms. If you don't have one I'll lend you one of mine," Monica offered.

"Ladies, do you mind?" Nell hissed, grabbing the coffeepot. She did as Norma suggested, refilling coffee cups to steady her nerves.

She didn't really have much experience with men. She'd dabbled in college, but this guy was in another league from the unthreatening, callow literary types she'd discussed poetry and philosophy with.

It was embarrassing. Such a brief, inconsequential encounter, but look at her. She'd almost had a seizure.

The moment he had finally taken notice of her, a primitive emotion stabbed through her, part excitement, part naked fear. She couldn't tell if the feeling was pleasurable or not. She had never felt so vulnerable, or so female. And all he'd done was ogle her.

Oh, no, no, no. She would be hopelessly out of her depth with this man. She was backpedaling. Like the dithering scaredycat coward that she was.

She went back to the counter to refill the coffeepot and assayed a sidelong peek. Yup. Still looking at her. Fixedly. Hungrily. Scorching dark eyes. Her stomach jumped up and crowded her lungs. Oh dear.

Norma presented her with a plate of apple crumb pie with vanilla ice cream. "You've got to see it through," she said sternly.

"Norma, I can't. I just can't."

"You must, or I'll fire you," Norma threatened.

"Go ahead. Do your worst," Nell said, putting the coffeepot on the warmer and putting her hands over her very pink cheeks. "I don't care."

"Chica, if you don't do it, I'll start talking real loud about how you have this huge crush on the guy by the window. I swear. I'm not kidding," Monica said, her voice rising perceptibly in volume.

Nell shot her a furious look and took the plate. She approached his table and laid it carefully beside his computer.

"You didn't ask if I wanted the usual dessert," he said. His resonant voice sent a shudder of excitement down her spine.

"I've taken enough risks today," she said, gathering up dishes. "I haven't given up hope of persuading you to try the pecan fudge brownies, though." She scurried, feeling his hot gaze against her back.

He got up, dropped a banknote on the table, and walked out. When the door closed behind him she exhaled and sank down onto a chair.

Monica punched her shoulder. "Good job, chica. That's some flirting to be proud of."

"I wasn't flirting!" Nell dropped her face into her hands. "I tried to persuade him to order something new and failed."

"Right. If it was no big deal, how come you're hyperventilating?" Monica asked.

"Because I'm stupid, okay?" Nell yelled back. "Is everybody on board with that assessment? Anybody need more clarification?"

"Calm down, Nelly." Norma bustled over and patted Nell's cheek. "Monica's right. I couldn't have done a better job myself. He is obviously intrigued. Come in early tomorrow and let me fix your hair."

"Norma, please!"

"Oh, honey, indulge a fond old lady, do!"

"I'm gonna bring that shirt tomorrow. And I'm gonna put some makeup on you, too," Monica said, looking her over with a critical eye. "You need a new look. What's your shoe size? Got any spike heels?"

"For waitressing?" Nell asked, aghast. "You're insane!"

"One must suffer in order to be beautiful," Monica intoned.

Nell jumped to her feet. "I'm going out for a cigarette break."

Monica looked perplexed. "Uh, you don't smoke."

"If I did, I would take a cigarette break now." Nell marched out the back door without taking off her apron and walked down the street through the blaring traffic, her face feverishly hot.

How could she be so susceptible, so flustered? She was almost thirty. All she'd done was serve him lunch. Imagine if she and he actually ever . . . no. Better not to imagine it. She felt faint already.

It had been years since she'd had a relationship. The more time that passed, the harder it got to contemplate. Her sister Nancy at least got out there and tried. She'd been burned miserably three times before she finally landed a winner in Liam. Grit and persistence had paid off.

But Nell hadn't had the stomach to run that kind of risk. She wasn't willing to face the chill, the sad ugliness she knew was waiting if she made a wrong move. Getting used. Getting hurt. Ugh. Brr.

Elena, Nell's birth mother, never had any fear of men. Elena Pisani had been a beautiful woman. She'd used her beauty as currency, being a practitioner of the world's oldest profession. She'd always looked perfect, no matter what the circumstances. Sexy clothing, makeup, and hair, those were the tools and weapons of her trade. Probably that was why Nell had always avoided makeup and wore baggy dresses and nerdish glasses, she reflected. Dressing down blurred her startling resemblance to her mother.

Nell herself had been an unpleasant surprise to Elena, a pregnancy that her mother had unaccountably decided to bring to term. For the first ten years of Nell's life, she'd watched her mother being kept by a series of rich men in various lavish apartments around the country. When it was convenient, Elena brought her daughter along. When it was not, she stayed in a series of boarding schools.

Nell had just been old enough to start to understand the nature of her mother's arrangements with this long string of "uncles" when Elena died suddenly, of an undiagnosed brain tumor. It had taken ten days, from the onset of the crushing headaches to her death under the surgeon's knife. There were no relatives. No life insurance. Her mother had not had any friends to speak of. Her lover had swiftly disappeared from the picture.

Nell had entered the foster system. She'd been ten years old.

Three very dark years followed, years that she tried hard to forget, before Lucia found her. Those years, and having watched her mother ply her trade—they were reasons enough to be reticent about romance.

Not that she was fishing for an excuse. She flinched away from self-analysis. She vastly preferred to study books rather than herself, books being so much more interesting. One thing was for sure, though. Her childhood trauma had forged her into a hopeless romantic. Book junkie. Poetry addict. Her choice had been simple: romantic escapism or brutal cynicism. Romance was better. It was comforting to wallow in the highest, purest sentiments of which human hearts were capable. So what if it was all blather and bullshit. It was beautiful blather and bullshit, and she would dedicate her life to reading it, studying it, and teaching it. To hell with them all.

There was only one problem with that scenario. A real, live guy with all the warts would never fit in with her ivory-tower ideals. Particularly not a guy with no manners, no imagination, and dark eyes that burned with lust.

She didn't want it to be about just lust. Call her stupid, but she'd seen what sex just for sex's sake looked like. It had chilled her blood.

Although, oddly, the dark-haired man's scorching gaze had not.

She couldn't handle this kind of emotional voltage. She had a career to forge, rent to pay, the Fiend to stay alert for. Look at her, wandering the streets without even paying attention to her surroundings. She had to sharpen up, or she'd find herself stuffed in the trunk of a car.

After her shift, Nell changed into her suit and dabbed on lipstick, staring doubtfully in the mirror. She twisted her hair into the tightest knot she could, with all that curly volume. It was the best she could do.

The receptionist's directions to her interview were easy. It was a twenty-minute walk through Midtown. She entered the lobby of a large office building, took the elevator to the sixteenth floor, and found a door marked "Burke Solutions, Inc."

It was a big, well appointed office. The receptionist was a young man with bulging eyes and a bow tie. He smiled as she approached.

"Can I help you?" he asked, hanging up the phone.

"I'm here for an interview with Duncan Burke," she said.

"Another poet?" He regarded her as if she were a rare bug.

"Uh, yes," Nell said. "Why do you ask?"

"You wouldn't believe some of the weirdos who have been coming in. You look relatively normal, but you never can tell. I'll tell Duncan you're here." He pushed a button. "Duncan, I've got another poet for you." He listened, hung up. "I'll take you to his office. Follow me."

Nell followed, waited as he knocked. "Come in," a deep voice said.

The receptionist gestured for her to walk in first. The smile on her face froze as she saw the man who stood up to greet her.

It was the black-haired man.

Chapter 3

Nell's mouth went dry. He stared at her, eyes narrowed. She lowered her outstretched hand. Her stomach was cartwheeling. She pressed her hand against it, and forced herself to drop the hand. It twitched.

"I know you," he said slowly.

Nell whipped up some instant bravado.

"Strip steak sandwich, soup of the day, apple crumb pie with vanilla ice cream, and lots of coffee," she responded.

"You're the waitress." His tone was accusing. He seemed so much taller. Of course. In the restaurant he'd always been sitting down. "You look different."

"I'm not wearing an apron." She resisted the urge to button up her jacket. No need to advertise her self-consciousness. And she'd buttoned her blouse to the top. Hadn't she? *Do not check. Don't.*

"You guys know each other?" the receptionist said, eyes goggling.

"Derek, that'll be all," the guy said.

Derek blinked innocently. "Can I make you guys some coffee?"

"Out, Derek." Derek sidled out the door. Nell and the black-haired man looked at each other for a long, nervous moment.

"You told me you were an expert in poetry and a doctoral candidate at NYU," he said.

"And so I am," Nell replied.

"Excuse me for being personal, but you look far too young."

She had to change her look. "I'll be thirty in October," she said. "Would you like to see my driver's license?"

"Look, Ms. . . . uh . . ."

"D'Onofrio," she supplied.

"Ms. D'Onofrio, I sympathize if you want to break out of waitressing, but I don't hire young women just for scenery. If you're not qualified, don't waste my time. It would be unpleasant for us both."

Nell was speechless. The nerve. And he'd just implied that she was, well . . . pretty enough to be scenery. A compliment hidden inside an insult, or maybe an insult hidden inside a compliment—she wasn't quite sure which. "I gave you my credentials," she reminded him. "And I didn't misrepresent myself in the least. If you'd like to verify my references, feel free. I am more than qualified for the work you've described. I'm interested in the flexible hours. It's difficult to find jobs that fit into a graduate seminar and teaching schedule."

"If you're a teacher, why are you waiting tables?" he demanded.

"Because it's impossible to pay rent on a grad student's stipend," she retorted. "I'm a busy person, but I'm the best you'll find for this project. If you want to interview me, let's proceed. If you intend to keep insulting me, I'll go." She looked him in the eye.

He examined her for another long, harrowing moment, and tapped his pen against his keyboard. "Okay," he said. "Let's proceed."

Nell rummaged in her bag and handed him a résumé. He stared down at it and nodded. "Fine. Pull up a chair."

Nell looked around. The chairs were piled chest high with computer printouts. The black-haired man got up. His sleeves were rolled up, and the muscles in his forearms bulged appealingly as he grabbed armfuls of paper and dumped them on the floor. "Derek was supposed to recycle this stuff last week," he growled. "Sit down."

Nell seated herself gingerly on the edge of the chair.

"We're creating a cutting-edge computer game. More puzzle solving, less blood and guts. At various points in the game, to move to the next level, the player must decipher a map, break a spell, or defeat some magical creature. Instructions for the tasks will be encoded in texts that are stylistically in keeping with the game. I also hope to use stuff that has actual artistic merit. Good stuff. Do I make myself clear?"

"Quite," Nell said.

"We've been interviewing for weeks, but I've been unsatisfied with the pool of applicants. It was my idea to fax colleges and universities. I figured, if I want fancy writing, I should go to the source."

"Sensible," Nell commented. "You said last night that you'd never done anything like this before."

"Right. I'm not a game designer. I design programs with practical applications. The game is my brother Bruce's baby. My mission is to make sure he doesn't do anything stupid. I've invested a fortune in graphic designers and programmers. I can't afford for this thing to fail."

"I see," she murmured.

"Let's get back to what I want from you," he said.

"Of course." The intensity of his gaze made his choice of words seductive. Nell clasped her hands and forced herself to concentrate.

"For example, to move to the second level, the player finds a manuscript that gives him these clues: a silver vial, a scrying pool, and a jeweled dagger. You pour the contents of the vial into the pool to understand where to find the dagger, which leads you to the next level. The labyrinth. Got it?"

"Uh, yes," Nell said.

"So write something that gives clues, but leaves the player to figure out the details. While alluding to the overall quest of the game."

"Which is?" Nell inquired.

He shifted restlessly. "To rescue the enchanted princess." Nell raised an eyebrow. "I know, it's been done," he muttered, uncomfortable. "Maybe we'll come up with something more original later."

"Stick with the princess," Nell said. "That's always a winner. So. A computer game for hopeless romantics. Lovely. Just my cup of tea."

Duncan tapped his pen impatiently. "There's nothing romantic about it. It's for magic and fantasy freaks."

"You don't think rescuing a princess is romantic?"

"That isn't the point," he snapped. "What can you do with the clues?" He leaned back in his chair and steepled his hands, waiting.

She blinked. "You want me to write something on the spot?"

He nodded. Nell pulled off her glasses and polished them. It was easier to look him in the face when he was blurry. "What type of poetry?" she asked, in her most professorial tone. "Early, mid, or late medieval? Renaissance? Classical antiquity? Homer, or Catullus? Chaucer? Spenser? Sidney? Heroic couplets, like Pope? Or something more, say, Miltonian?" She put her glasses back on, blinking as his fierce, hawklike face came back into focus. Whew. Potent.

He scowled. "How the hell would I know? I don't know anything about poetry. That's why you're here."

"You don't have to know anything," Nell said. "The more clues you give me, the quicker I can structure the piece. I'll just choose a style arbitrarily for now. A Shakespearean sonnet, for instance."

He nodded. "Fine. Whatever. Go for it."

He passed her a notebook and a pen. Nell scribbled down the list of elements: vial, scrying pool, dagger, labyrinth, enchanted princess.

She swiveled her chair so he was out of her line of vision, and let the magic happen. The world and Duncan Burke disappeared as she submerged herself into a state of inward concentration.

Twenty minutes later she turned back. "Take a look."

He reached for the notebook. "Finished already? Just like that?"

"It's a familiar exercise. I make my students do it all the time. The best way to study a poet's style is from the inside out."

He read the page she'd passed him, looked at her for a long moment, read it again, pen tapping ceaselessly against the keyboard.

"You want the job?" he asked.

The seductively pretty waitress had the wiles of an Arab street merchant when it came to bargaining. Duncan escorted her grimly to the door after finally agreeing to pay far more than he'd anticipated. She had a high opinion of how much her time and skill were worth. He admired that in a person, if it was backed up by content. Which it was, in her case. She was good. High-quality production, under pressure, while he watched. That was the kind of focused, high-octane energy he liked to infuse into his projects. It was expensive, but it was worth it.

Except for one little thing. Since lunch, he'd been considering asking the cute Sunset Grill waitress out, and this heated fantasy had made his afternoon brighter than it had been for a long time. Now his succulent waitress had morphed into a key employee.

That scenario was no longer feasible. And that sucked.

Derek had the poor judgment to approach him at that moment, his eyes goggling wildly. "So, Duncan, did you hire her, or what?"

"Derek," Duncan said with deceptive calm, "remember when I told you to put the printouts in my office into the recycling bin?"

"Uh," Derek mumbled uncomfortably.

"Put the phones on voice mail, Derek, and do it. *Now.*"

Derek scurried away. Duncan scowled out the window. What the hell was his sloe-eyed waitress doing being a poetry professor, anyhow? How fucking improbable was that? She'd ignored him while she was writing her piece, giving him the perfect opportunity to study the sensual shape of her full lips. He'd wanted to tug on one of those fuzzy dark ringlets, watch it spring back up into shape. Her pinup-girl curviness made his hands clench with the urge to handle her.

It had been a very long time. He'd gotten good at sublimating the need for sex. Dealing with women was so exhausting. The constant shrill demands, the fuckups he didn't comprehend or even remember having committed. The constant demands for him to reveal feelings he didn't feel. Talk of love that always gave him acid stomach. Their endless, perennial need to know "where this relationship is going."

Which was usually straight to hell.

He didn't have the stomach to lie to them. He just couldn't pretend. He got the urge for sex as often as the next guy, but he'd learned to shove it under the rug. Exercise, hard work, cold showers, and as a last resort, his own right hand. But every now and then, it reared up, tossed the rug aside, and bit him in the ass. Hard.

That was his problem, he thought. Today in the restaurant, when she provoked him, the urge had surged. A wild beast, rattling the bars of his cage. His dick had been hard on and off all afternoon.

He grabbed his jacket. He needed air. He had more business to attend to, but the business never ended. He could keep himself busy until midnight or beyond, and usually did. But not tonight.

Maybe he'd go knock around a punching bag in the gym. He'd already spent two hours there that morning, from five to seven, but he needed to unload some excess energy before he did something extremely stupid.

He ground his teeth going down in the elevator. He had a personal code. *Don't fuck the employees* was high on the list of key rules. He might as well just shoot himself in the head right off the bat rather than pull a stunt like that. He'd save himself a lot of time and trouble.

He'd been working out the perfect scenario in his head before she walked in with her goddamn four-page résumé. A secret affair with a woman too young to be seriously husband hunting. A nubile girl who would be content with nights of pounding sex, not a whole lot of conversation, some costly gifts from time to time. Someone who had no connection with his family, professional or social life. No one would meet her, or know about her. She would meet no one. She'd be all his.

A few nights a week, a car service would bring her to his condo, where he would rip her clothes off and make her come screaming until she'd forgotten her own name. Then, coffee and a croissant, and the car service would take her away again. He could shower and get back to work. Refreshed and restored.

He loved sex, under carefully controlled conditions, with no repercussions, no regrets. Hard conditions to create.

So much for his scenario. This poetry professor was not that girl. Twenty-nine was plenty old enough to be husband hungry, and it was clear that she was complicated, demanding, too smart for her own good.

This one would not be content to be a fuck buddy. She'd want to converse. She would insist on connecting with him, on levels that he didn't even know existed. The idea made his head ache. He preferred to know in advance what he would eat for lunch. Much less did he want uncertainty when it came to sex.

The evening air was cool; the street was wet with rain. Traffic blared from the downtown avenues. He picked a direction at random as his internal monologue droned on. It wouldn't be much of an issue, he lectured himself. She'd be working much more closely with his younger brother than with him. Bruce. The charming, flirtatious womanizer. They'd scheduled a meeting with Bruce the following evening to discuss the project. Bruce was going to lick his chops when he saw her.

That thought, unaccountably, irritated the living shit out of him.

He rounded the corner onto Eighth Avenue, stopped, and retreated into the shadow of a restaurant awning. Nell stood at the curb just a few yards away, arm lifted high as she tried to flag down a cab. It swept on by. The river of yellow cabs were all taken. She kept trying. After each attempt, she looked around at all the people who passed her.

He was good at reading body language in a glance. He'd served for years as an NSA field agent abroad, gathering intelligence. He recognized all the tiny indicators of stress that her body betrayed.

She was afraid of something.

Curiosity burned inside him. What could a girl like her possibly have to be afraid of? An asshole ex? That was a classic.

He could rip the fucker's throat out for her, if she wanted him to.

The thought took him by surprise. It had sneaked up on him while he stared at the way that button strained ever so slightly over the swell of her tits. How sooty and long her lashes were. The fey upward tilt to her eyes, her brows. Hers was not a glossy magazine sort of pretty, and that was fine. He'd never gone for the hollow-cheeked, toothpick-legs look. He liked a nice round ass, that deep inward curve at her waist that cried out for the grip of his hands. That Mediterranean milkmaid look: creamy skin, rosy cheeks, bouncing tits. Dimpled knees.

He checked out her knees, but her dowdy skirt was just a shade too long to ascertain the dimple situation.

She finally noticed him lurking and shrank in on herself, clutching her blazer closed. So. She felt the animal rattling its cage, after he had tried so hard to play it cool. "Looking for a cab?" he asked.

"Not having much luck," she murmured. Her gaze skittered around shyly. "It's hard when it's raining."

He gazed at her, unable to stop himself. Fuck all, he'd been through this. He'd drawn his conclusions. *Don't think with your prick.*

But she was afraid, it was late, it was raining, and he really needed to know what the hell she was so afraid of.

And also, incidentally, if her knees were dimpled.

"I'll drive you home," he said.

"Oh, no. Thanks, but I couldn't. It's okay, really," Nell babbled. She leaped, waving her arms at the next cab that went by, even though its meter light was off. "I'll just, ah, walk. Until I find one."

Or the Fiend finds you. She and her sisters had promised each other to take cabs. Not that it had helped Nancy, who'd been nabbed right out of a crowded hotel restaurant. Surrounded by people she knew.

"No," Burke said. "You're not walking. It's late. And it's raining."

She opened her mouth to slap him down politely. Who did he think he was, anyway, announcing what she would do or not do?

Then she looked into his eyes, and the commentary in her mind just . . . stopped. It was dark. No cabs were stopping. Her neck was prickling in the worst way. The business crowd had gone home, and this part of Midtown was dismal and deserted at night.

The man was scary in his own right, but he was not the Fiend. She was not a brainless bimbo, whatever he might think, with that provocative, hiring-young-women-just-for-scenery comment. She could handle him.

She licked her dry lips without thinking and regretted it when his gaze flicked right to them—and stuck there. "Um, thank you." Her voice felt dry, was scratchy.

These were the last words she managed to speak. They walked together in silence. She was strangled by shyness. For God's sake, she'd just accepted a job from this man. They had plenty of things to talk about, but still, her voice was huddled up into a tight, scared ball in her throat. He led her down into the underground parking garage near his office building. She stumbled on the steep concrete slope, clutching the folder that held the game outline she was supposed to study tonight. He caught her elbow and held on to it, all the way to the sleek silver Mercedes that answered his remote beep with a pert flash of its lights.

He helped her into the car and closed the door for her. Her voiceless condition did not improve, even after the necessary interchange about the best route to take to her SoHo address.

After a few minutes of driving, he spoke up. "What are you afraid of?"

There were so many answers to that question, it scrambled her circuits, left her floundering. "What on earth are you talking about?"

"You looked scared when you were waiting for the cab."

His perception made her feel naked. "Ah, wow," she said. "I didn't . . . that is to say, I'm surprised you noticed that."

He slanted her a quick glance. "Why is that?"

Yikes. Now he'd think she was judging or criticizing, and only thirty minutes after hiring her. "It's just odd," she said, evasively. "It's intuitive of you. I wouldn't have thought you were the type."

He frowned into the windshield. "Why not?"

"I don't know," she said, helplessly. "You never noticed anything in your field of vision at the restaurant. You never made eye contact with anyone. You always order the same thing. You have an extremely narrow range of focus. Intuition requires . . . well, openness."

"Openness?" He laughed. "You think I'm closed, then. You and my family. That's Duncan for you. Thick as a brick wall."

"I don't think anything of the kind," she retorted primly.

"I do have a narrow range of focus," he said. "But there's a flip side. Whatever gets into that narrow range, I see. Every last detail."

She flushed. "Well, thank you. I appreciate your interest, but—"

"But you haven't answered my question. What are you afraid of?"

Her chest bumped with nervous laughter. "Good God. You're like a dog with a bone."

"Pit bull, my family calls me," he agreed easily.

She shot him a quick, nervous glance. "Family? So you're—"

"Married? No. I'm talking my mother, brother, and sister. So?"

Nell blushed, both for her loaded question and his matter-of-fact answer. There was no reason not to tell him. There was nothing to be ashamed of. But still, it was scary and flesh creeping, and this guy had just become her new employer. And it was none of his damn business.

He waited. She could feel his insistence in the profound silence between them. He just sat there, motor idling, waiting.

"It's a long, complicated story," she said warily.

"We're stuck in traffic," he said. "Entertain me."

True enough. They were motionless in a gridlocked snarl.

"It started a few weeks ago," she began. "When my mother died."

He shot her a startled glance. "I'm sorry to hear that."

She acknowledged his words with a nod, and went on, simply and sequentially, with the whole crazy tale. The burglar, the necklaces, the mysterious letters. The clotheshorse, the murdered jeweller and his family, the attack in the stairwell, Nancy's attempted abduction in Boston. The crazy, winding story got them all the way down to her apartment.

He double-parked, listening with no visible reaction. The longer she talked, the more self-conscious she felt. He probably thought she was a paranoid nutcase. Or worse, an attention-mongering nutcase.

"So, anyway. That's why I'm scared," she finally concluded. "All of us. Nervous, and scared, and confused. Do you want to fire me now?"

He frowned. "Why the hell would I do that?"

She shrugged, feeling silly, but before she was required to come up with a coherent reply, a guy opened the SUV in front of them, got in, and pulled away—leaving a perfect parking spot. Unheard of.

Burke pulled into it. "I'd better walk you up to your door."

Oh boy. How very gallant of him. If only her heart would stop acting like it was trying to pound its way out of her chest. "Don't worry about it," she told him, with a breathless laugh. "It's a fourth-floor walk-up."

"It's okay," he said. "I work out."

She glanced at his body, strangled another crack of laughter into a dry cough. She led him into her building.

Up, up, up. The stairs never stopped. She stopped in front of her door, glad for an excuse to be that breathless and red. "I appreciate the ride and the company," she said. He nodded, and kept standing there. Like a mountain, a monolith. "I'm not going to invite you in," she blurted out. "Not for coffee, or for drinks, or . . . ah, anything."

"Of course," he said. "You hardly know me." But he did not leave.

"So?" she prompted. "Why are you standing there? What do you want from me?"

"Something I can't have, I guess." His voice was low. He reached out and touched the end of a dangling fuzzy ringlet that had escaped the bun. "I got the strangest sensation today. In the restaurant."

"Yes?" Her lips trembled. She pressed them together hard.

"I got the feeling that you were trying to get my attention."

Duh, Einstein. "Well, I suppose I kind of was," she fluttered.

He tugged the curl, watched it rebound. "You've got my attention."

"Um"—she laughed, nervously—"now that I have it, I'm not sure what to do with it."

"There's a lot you can do with it," he said. "It's multipurpose."

"Ah," she whispered. "Um, really."

"Yeah, really. You'd be amazed." He wound the curl around his finger. "Once you've got my attention, it's hard to shake."

"I noticed that. The way you stared at that computer, a herd of elephants could have trooped by. But I'm not doing anything with your attention tonight. Thanks again, for the ride." She hesitated. "Good night."

"Is your sister here?"

She considered saying yes, just to defuse the tension, but she could not lie to those penetrating eyes. "She's driving to Delaware," she said. "She designs jewelry. She works the crafts fair circuit."

"You and your sisters have a lot of nerve, wandering around all alone when a stalker's out there gunning for you."

She bristled. "We have no choice! We have to make a living!"

"You have an alarm, at least?"

"Yep. Top of the line," she said promptly.

He leaned against the wall. "A dog might be a good investment."

His position crowded her into the tiled corner. "Oh, please," she said. "Not a chance. You have no idea how small my apartment is."

"No, I don't," he said. "And I guess I'm not going to."

"No," she whispered, licking dry lips. "Not tonight."

The words slipped out, their obvious corollary being that he might well get lucky some other night. He smiled. The look in his eyes set off fireworks, in her mind, chest, thighs. Her face felt like it was on fire.

He pulled his cell out. "Let's exchange mobile numbers," he said. "If you have a problem, call. Whenever. Any time of day or night."

"Thank you. That's very kind," she whispered. She groped in her bag for a pen and her little notebook.

He frowned. "Just program it in," he suggested. "You're not going to want to dig in your handbag for a number in an emergency."

"I don't have a mobile phone," she admitted.

He stared at her, as blank as if she'd announced that she was a space alien. "You what? You're insane!"

Nell's chin went up. "Thank you for sharing your opinion."

"Here!" He held out the phone he'd pulled from his pocket. "Take mine, for Christ's sake! I have four more!"

"No, thank you," she said, in her snippiest tone.

He slid the phone into his pocket and studied her face with hypnotizing intensity. "There's just one thing I need to know before I go," he said. "Or I won't sleep tonight."

She tilted up her chin, trying to breathe. "Know what?"

He sank down onto one knee. "Don't panic," he soothed, as shocking erotic possibilities flashed through her mind. She shrank back, shocked, as he grasped her skirt—and lifted. Just a couple of inches. She quivered, trapped. She couldn't retreat, with her back flat to the wall. "What are you doing?" she squeaked. "Let go of my skirt!"

He looked up with a triumphant grin. "Dimples."

She wanted to sink into the ground. Oh, for willowy slender legs, like Nancy and Vivi. Having her chubby knees remarked upon by this guy, of all guys, was just too much to bear. "Oh, God. Get out of here."

"No, no! They're great. Really. I was hoping they'd have dimples."

She shook her head. "I can't handle this. Good night. Get lost." She put all the commanding punch she could behind the word.

He rose slowly to his feet. Up, up, and still up. God, the guy was tall. And broad. And he smelled so seductively good, it was filling her senses. Scrambling her brain.

"You're, ah—not moving," she pointed out to him.

"No," he agreed.

She tried to look stern. A tall order with that tremor in her mouth. "Why not?" she demanded.

He shrugged. "Because you don't really want me to."

The guy's nerve was staggering. "Oh?" she snapped. "You read minds, do you?"

He shook his head, impassive. "No. I read faces, and bodies."

She struggled for a moment with that. She was blushing hotly, which did not help her dignity one bit. "That's very impressive," she said primly. "But my face and body do not make the executive decisions around here."

He leaned closer. "Of course they don't." His voice was a velvety, rumbling caress. "They have better things to do."

She was still groping for a comeback when his lips touched hers.

She gasped at the sparkling rush of energy. The startled heat, unfurling through her body. Spreading out, like a rippling current of water. Too delicious to resist.

She rose up on tiptoe, and it all spun out of control. Before she knew it, she was pinned to the wall, kissing him madly. Forgetting everything except for how sweet, how good it felt. How much more she wanted, how bad she wanted it. He hooked her knee with his hand and pulled it up to clasp his muscular thighs, leaning against her so that the hot bulge at his groin pressed against her tender intimate places, in a slow, deliberate pulse that made her ache and squirm and moan.

His tongue slid inside her mouth, commanding and directing the kiss with implacable skill. His hand cupped her bottom, stroking.

She started to shake, terrified and disoriented. Something was spinning out of control. The heat, the light, the ache began to coalesce, sharpening, swelling into something huge and wild—

It burst, and her startled shriek was smothered against his hungry mouth. He held her tightly in his arms, while shudders of unbelievable, shocking pleasure wrenched through her entire body.

Her eyes fluttered open. His gaze burned her face. Her eyes were wet, her mouth couldn't stop shaking. She couldn't believe herself. A stranger? In her own *stairwell?* Her eyes shut against the pressure. So. That was what a screaming orgasm felt like. She'd always wondered.

He stroked her cheek gently, waiting. "Any new executive decisions coming down the pipeline?" he prompted softly.

All she wanted was to yank him inside. If this is what he could do to her fully clothed, in the stairwell—ah, God. It was too much.

Way, way too much. She shook her head. *No.* She mouthed the word. Had no breath to actually say it.

He stepped back, let go. "Sorry if I went too far," he said. He turned, and headed slowly down the stairs. "Good night."

She stayed there, immobile, until she heard the front door click far below. Then she fumbled with the keys, her hands trembling so hard she could barely hold them.

Once inside her apartment and the alarm armed, she sank down onto the ground as though her legs had no bones, and rocked, hands over her mouth. The keening sounds coming out of her made her throat ache and burn, as if a tuning peg were turning, ratcheting up the tension relentlessly, tighter, higher.

Furious with herself for being such a goddamn coward.

Duncan stared at the screen of the online version of *The Golden Thread Poetry Journal* and sent the pages to print. He reread the series of short lyric poems by Antonella D'Onofrio on the screen while the pages churned out of the machine. It was the tenth time he had read them.

He was baffled by them. Or rather, he was baffled by his reaction to them. It was complete gibberish, of course. He couldn't figure out what the fuck she was getting at, for the life of him. But he liked the way the sequence of words made him feel. He kept rereading them, over and over. Grasping for that elusive feeling. Weird.

And the way it made his dick feel was a damn inconvenience. He stared down at his stubborn boner. He'd already tried to deal with the problem in the shower. Wild, hot water fantasies. Nell, naked and soaked and soapy, pinned to the shower wall, her legs draped over his arms. Whimpering with each deep, slick thrust. He'd come so hard, he practically knocked himself out, so why he should still have a tent pole in his sweats was beyond him. Had to be the poetry, he guessed.

He'd been at the computer since he'd gotten home. He was too wound up and turned on to sleep, so he'd used the time to research everything he could glean about the D'Onofrio saga that could be found on the Internet. He was champing at the bit to call his NYPD source and get some inside details on the case, but it was too early.

So he'd ranged further to pass the time. Reading articles she'd published in various literary journals, about Sara Teasdale, Emily Dickinson, Edna St. Vincent Millay, Sappho. A paper for her graduate seminar. Then there was poetry she'd written and published herself. Guest blog entries on websites that catered to poets, scholars. Online poetry workshops that she critiqued. Outlandish stuff. And they said computer nerds were arcane and weird? Computer nerds had nothing on poets and scholars. This crap was from fucking outer space.

He glanced at his watch. Almost five a.m. Good enough. His friend and ex–comrade in arms was now a detective in the NYPD. Gant owed Duncan his life, from a number of bloody adventures they'd had back in Afghanistan. If he wasn't awake by now, it meant he was getting soft.

He dialed the number. It rang twelve times before the guy picked up. "Who the fuck is this?" said Gant sleepily.

"I need some info," he said.

"Oh, Christ. You. Couldn't it wait till daylight?"

"It's dawn," Duncan said, staring out his picture window at the spectacular New York City skyline, silhouetted against the faint glow of breaking day. "I need the details of an ongoing police investigation, in Hempton. It involves an elderly woman named Lucia D'Onofrio. She died during a burglary in her house, of a heart attack. A few weeks ago."

"Yeah? Why do you want to know?"

He leaned his hot forehead against the cool window glass, and hesitated. "Because I'm interested," he hedged.

"Interested? You wake me up at this un-fucking-godly hour just because you're *interested*?" Gant paused for a moment. "This is about a woman, right?"

"None of your goddamn business," Duncan muttered.

"I knew this would happen," Gant bitched. "You freak. Acting like a fucking monk, for years at a time. It was just a matter of time till you snapped. So it's happened, huh? You're obsessed? You're awake at this hour because you spent the night Googling her life? Poor girl. She has no idea what she's in for. So what does this chick have to do with the old broad who had the heart attack?"

"She's the old broad's daughter. Stop busting my balls and just get me the info," Duncan growled.

"You'll have to wait. I won't call those guys until it's a decent hour. That's called common courtesy. Ever heard of it? Go to bed, Dunc. Or better yet, go jack off, and then go to bed. Later."

His friend hung up, and Duncan let the phone drop and spun the chair back around to read those poems again.

He was unaccountably fascinated. As if some window were opening in his mind, with a view he'd never seen before. He couldn't understand what the fuck she was talking about, but so what? Who cared? He liked the way the words resonated inside him, like a big, deep bell. He'd never felt like that before. Everything buzzing, humming.

It felt strangely, dangerously good.

Chapter
4

"Stop here," Nell directed the driver of the car.

The guy screeched to a halt and took the money with a deadpan face. She was spending a fortune on car services, but there was no help for it. At least there were enough people on the streets that she felt safe walking the rest of the way to the Sunset Grill.

She stared at the hair salon as the car accelerated away. She'd been circling this issue all morning, since she'd wound her hair into the usual thick, fuzzy braid and twisted it into a heavy knot. She caught a glimpse of her reflection in the window, slid her glasses up onto the bridge of her nose, and took another good, long look.

She was hiding behind the glasses, the baggy dresses, the dowdy, frizzy hair. She'd hidden behind the cowardly assertion that looking good was all vanity and nonsense. That she was a lofty scholar who was too intellectual and above it all to care.

What total bullshit. After less than ten lust-charged minutes with Duncan Burke in the stairwell, she cared passionately. She needed every weapon at her disposal to deal with him.

The stray thought made her wince. There it was, beauty as a weapon. The association was programmed into her. She'd chosen plainness because she'd wanted to stay off the battlefield.

But the battle had come to her. There was nothing to do but fight.

She marched into the salon, sniffing nervously at shampoo, perfume, and chemicals. A slight, bald Hispanic man with a pearl-drop earring gave her a toothy smile. "What can I do for you?" he inquired.

Nell stared helplessly. "Do you take walk-ins?"

"When I feel like it. What do you have in mind?"

"I, um, don't know yet," Nell confessed.

The man rubbed his hands together. "Hmm. You're in luck. I just had a cancellation. I'm Riccardo, by the way. Let's take a look."

Nell soon found herself in a chair, her body swathed in a plastic cape. Riccardo's expert fingers pulled the pins from her hair, unraveling it and fluffing it up. He made cooing noises of approval. "May I?" he asked, removing Nell's glasses. The salon became a glittery blur. "Good material here. You really ought to try contacts," he counseled.

Nell harrumphed. "Can you do something that's easy to style?"

"Oh, yes. I'm just going to shape this a bit, and thin out all this weight, and layer this . . . and lighten it, make it more fluffy. See?"

Of course, Nell didn't, without her glasses, but this was the beauty salon of destiny, so she nodded and consigned herself to Fate.

Some time later, she retrieved her glasses and gasped at the result. Riccardo had layered and shaped her formless, kinky waist-length mop into a shiny halo of black curls that framed and flattered her face and still hung halfway down her back. Nell kept putting an unbelieving hand up, feeling the soft, springy texture of her ringlets, the way it fluffed up on top, perfumed with various salves and waxes and goops massaged into it. The price was staggering, but she passed over her credit card without protest. The only problem was the glasses. With her new do, they looked even more ridiculous than before.

One step at a time, she told herself.

Her hair caused a sensation when she walked into the restaurant. Monica wolf whistled. Norma spun Nell around, looking at her from every angle. "Oh, honey! You look as gorgeous as I knew you would!" she exclaimed. "I just wish your mama could see how pretty you look!"

Nell's eyes dampened, and she hugged the other woman tightly.

"Enough of the sentimental stuff," Monica said briskly. "C'mere, Nell. I wanna put some makeup on you."

"Aren't we supposed to be prepping for lunch?" Nell asked plaintively, as Monica dragged her to a chair.

"That's all right, hon. We can open five minutes late," Norma said indulgently. "How did that job interview go?"

"Oh. The job interview," Nell hedged, as Monica tilted her face up and outlined her eyes with black pencil. "It was extremely interesting."

"Oh? How so?" Norma asked, picking the chairs off the tables.

"You will never, in ten million years, guess who it was who interviewed me," Nell said.

Norma froze. Monica's eye pencil stopped moving.

"No way, chica," breathed Monica.

"You don't mean to say . . . You're putting me on, Nelly. I simply don't believe it," Norma said.

"Believe it," Nell said.

There was an incredulous silence. Nell turned around. Norma and Monica were grinning at each other like fools.

"Did he ask you out?" Monica tilted Nell's head back and brandished her mascara wand. "Did he come on to you? Did you kiss?"

The whole heated sequence in the stairwell played through her mind in a timeless instant, and her face went beet red. "As if," she lied. "I've barely met the man."

"Well?" Norma said bracingly. "Take the bull by the horns, honey!"

"It's not that simple," she hedged. "He's my boss now, and I'm meeting with him after my shift here to discuss the—"

"My goodness, you mean he hired you? Mercy! Things move so quickly in this world for an old lady. And just this morning Kendra told me that she has Epstein-Barr syndrome. But all's fair in love and war."

"Norma, you don't understand." Nell wiggled as Monica brushed powder on her face. "Monica, that tickles!"

"Hold still, chica. You're making me smear. Lemme put lipstick on you, and you can look at yourself."

Nell headed to the bathroom afterward. Her reflection made her gasp. Her eyes looked big, luminous. The lipstick was a deep, sexy red. With her hair fluffed into that luxurious mane of black ringlets, she looked . . .

Just like her mother. She stared at herself. Swallowed.

"What do you say, chica? Are you stunning, or are you stunning?"

Nell forced herself to smile at her coworker. "Yes. You're an artist, Monica. Thank you." She pulled her glasses out of her apron.

"Do you have to?" Monica complained. "It ruins the effect!"

"I'm blind as a bat without them," Nell said regretfully.

"Oh well. You look better anyway. Strip Steak's going to have a stroke when he gets a look at you."

"His name is Duncan Burke, and it's not going to happen," Nell said resolutely. "He's my boss. I wouldn't compromise a paying job."

"Oh, excellent! Taboo!" Norma stuck her head in the bathroom door. "The lure of the forbidden! Look at you, good enough to eat. Strip Steak's jaw will hit the floor. Have you thought about contacts, Nelly?"

Nell swept past them, chin high. They giggled like ninnies.

Three-fifteen came and went, with no Duncan Burke, and the afternoon fell flat. Hanging in her garment bag was the oatmeal-cream sweater dress she'd bought for Nancy's engagement party, the prettiest thing she had in her closet. She pictured herself walking into his office in that subtly clinging dress, and shivered.

Yikes. Problematic, for sure. He was her boss, after all. And he was rude, arrogant, and presumptuous. And he suffered from a profound lack of imagination, judging from his lunch habits. Plus, he had a weird, fetishistic thing for her chubby knees. So nothing doing.

Uh-huh. So why had she spent all that money she could ill afford on her hair? Why was her face painted? Why had she brought that clinging dress? She'd tarted herself up for exactly what? Get real.

She tried to drug herself into enforced calmness by mentally reciting the first sixteen lines of the prologue to Chaucer's *Canterbury Tales*, over and over as she worked. The afternoon passed slowly.

At the end of her shift, she sneaked into the back to change. She needn't have bothered sneaking, as both Monica and Norma were waiting outside the door when she came out. Monica grabbed Nell's chin and freshened her lipstick by brute force. "Good luck, chica."

"Be careful, honey," Norma said, her eyes misty.

"And don't forget these." Monica held up a three-pack of condoms, and stuffed them into Nell's purse. "Got 'em for you on my cigarette break. Be safe, always, you hear me?"

She was mortified. "You guys! It's a business meeting!"

She grabbed a cab, despite the warm evening, in deference to the promise to her sisters, and took the elevator to the sixteenth floor. She stood in front of his office, gathering nerve, and reached for the door.

It flew open. She looked up, straight into Duncan's eyes. Her throat clenched.

His eyes flashed down over her body. "It's you."

"You were expecting me, weren't you?" she asked.

"Of course," he said. "Come on in."

She regretted the dress. It didn't cling provocatively, but the way he looked at her made her feel as if she were reclining naked, draped in silk, like Bathsheba in an old painting. *Come and get me. At your peril.* Or hers, rather.

"You changed your hair." His tone was disapproving.

"Why, yes," she said, confused.

He studied her hair, eyes narrowed, and was about to speak again when a handsome young man strode out into the room. He flashed her a dazzling smile and shook her hand, continuing to hold on to it. "Wow. Duncan told me you were an excellent writer, but he didn't say you were so pretty," he said. "Can I call you Nell?"

"No, you can't," Duncan cut in. "Let go of her hand. Ms. D'Onofrio, this is my younger brother, Bruce. Please excuse his unprofessional behavior." He turned and marched past the goggling Derek into the conference room. "Let's get started."

They sat in the conference room. Bruce began. "Ms. D'Onofrio—"

"Nell is really okay," she broke in.

"I prefer that he use 'Ms. D'Onofrio,' " Duncan said.

There was an uncomfortable pause. "Ah," Bruce murmured. "As I was saying, Ms. D'Onofrio, Duncan showed me your writing sample. I was impressed. I take it you've looked over our outline?"

"Of course," she said. She'd been too rattled to think about it last night, after that charged stairwell incident, but she'd glanced over it while drinking her morning coffee, and had been pleasantly impressed.

"So?" Duncan prompted impatiently. "What do you think?"

Nell leafed through the folder. "It's great. The story is involving, and the graphics are beautiful. It's just that I think the choices the player needs to make seem too, uh . . ." She hesitated, reluctant to criticize.

"Too what?" Duncan snapped.

"Too logical," she gasped nervously.

The two men looked at her blankly.

"If you want to appeal to language-oriented, literary types, I think you should play up the romantic, magical elements," she went on.

Duncan grunted. His chair creaked in protest as he pushed himself away from the table. Nell pressed on. "It would be interesting to develop some plot twists based on leaps of faith, to deepen the feeling of mystery, create a sense of wonder. The game's title, for instance. 'The Dagger and the Thorn' sounds so, um . . ."

"Pointy?" Bruce grinned. "Phallic?"

"Um, warlike," Nell temporized demurely. "Masculine. I would recommend something more evocative, more magical. When I read about the sixth-level forest sequence with the lake and the magical swans, I thought of 'The Golden Egg.' "

" 'The Golden Egg,' " Bruce mused. "That has possibilities."

"I like it," Duncan announced.

Bruce whipped his head around, incredulous. "You do? You've never liked anything imaginative or evocative in your whole life!"

"No, not that," he said impatiently. "I mean her hair."

A shocked silence followed his announcement.

Duncan frowned. "So? What are you gaping about? I didn't like it at first, but I've decided that I like it. Is that so hard to understand?"

Bruce spoke up gallantly, after another half minute of shocked silence. "Ah, Ms. D'Onofrio, I didn't have the pleasure of seeing how you wore your hair before, so I can't offer any comparisons, but I can certainly say that it looks lovely now."

"Uh, thank you," Nell said. Her face was on fire.

"And if you've gotten the approval of anybody as resistant to change as my brother, believe me, it's a compliment," he added.

"Shut up, Bruce," Duncan snapped.

"You're acting unprofessional, Dunc," Bruce murmured.

Nell knotted her hands together. "I'm glad you like my hair, Mr. Burke, but I'd rather talk about what you think of my ideas."

"I don't like them," Duncan said abruptly.

Nell swallowed. "Ah," she murmured. "I, uh, see."

"I don't want an interactive fairy tale. I want a fantasy quest. What you're proposing would be impossible to reason your way through," Duncan explained.

"But that's just it! Reason isn't the only tool people use when they're problem solving," Nell argued. "There's an enchanted princess to be won! It should be romantic, surprising."

"He hates surprises," Bruce muttered.

"Shut up, Bruce," Duncan snarled.

"Sheathe your claws, Dunc, you're scaring her," Bruce warned.

"Not at all," Nell lied. "I don't scare easily."

Duncan got up with an abruptness that shot his chair against the wall with a bang. He stalked out of the room.

Nell watched the door fall shut behind him, alarmed. "Did I say something wrong?"

"Oh, not at all," Bruce assured her. "He's just that way. Don't worry. He likes you. Your ideas are fascinating. It's all good."

"Uh, thank you," she said, confused.

"Don't mind him. Duncan's just twitchy because there's been so much change in his company since we started working on my game. Everything's all shaken up. He'll calm down."

"But if he hates my—"

"Nah, he doesn't hate anything. He's just being a dickhead for the pure fun of it. Pay him no attention at all. He can't help himself. He's just programmed that way. He used to be a spy, you know that?"

Nell was startled. "Um, no. I didn't know that."

"Yeah. Intelligence and analysis, for the NSA. Spent a lot of time in Afghanistan, and other nasty hot spots. I'd like to say being a spy was what made him such a tight-assed bastard, but the truth is, he's been like that since we were kids. So don't expect it to change."

"I wouldn't expect anything of the kind," she murmured.

"He's a genius when it comes to algorithms for intelligent database design," Bruce went on. "His biggest client is the U.S. government. Everything's always so damn serious. National security. Terrorist threats. Blood and guts. Something as frivolous as a computer game drives the poor guy nuts." Bruce rolled his eyes. "But he'll feel better about it when the money starts pouring in. He likes money just fine. You just keep coming up with ideas, and you'll be golden."

"Okay," she said. "And you really can call me Nell."

Bruce grinned. "You'll do." He got up, came around the table, and sat down next to her. "So, here's where I think we should start."

A half hour of intense concentration ensued, in which the two of them worked out a prioritized schedule of the texts she needed to churn out first. It looked like fun. She was actually getting excited about it, even if she was probably going to have to skip pesky little details like, say, sleep, in order to keep up with Bruce's schedule. He needed twelve hours' worth of work done by tomorrow evening, with a long waitressing shift cutting right into the middle of it. But hey. What else was new.

Just one thing still perplexed her. "But what about your brother?" she asked, hesitantly. "If he hates my ideas—"

"Ignore him," Bruce advised. "Really. Suit yourself. But work fast, whatever you do, because I've got programmers and graphic artists working on the sixth level, and we need to catch up with the texts." He looked over his shoulder with exaggerated caution, and dropped a gallant kiss on her hand. "Our unprofessional secret," he whispered.

Nell was laughing at him when the door opened.

Duncan stood there, scowling. "What the hell is going on?"

Bruce looked guilty. "Uh, nothing." He glanced from Nell to Duncan and back again. His face took on a thoughtful, calculating look. "Maybe you have the wrong idea," he said. "I'm not . . . say, Duncan, did I tell you about the new girl I'm seeing?"

"No," Duncan said icily. "Nor is it in any way relevant."

"Her name's Melissa," Bruce went on, undaunted. "She's a knockout. I'm totally in love. I've got to introduce you. She's a poetry fan. The ultraromantic type. Speaking of which, I need some personal poetry advice." Bruce slanted a sly smile toward his brother and winked at Nell.

Nell was bewildered. "You need what?"

"Melissa loves poetry, and I want to impress her. What would be a good poem for me to memorize? To, ah, you know, melt her?"

"That depends on her tastes. Before I recommend anything, though, there's one thing I want to know. What's your purpose?"

"Isn't it obvious?" Bruce said, with a roguish wink.

Nell frowned. "Not necessarily. If you mean to genuinely court this woman, then I caution you against presenting yourself as other than who you really are. She'll just be disappointed when she realizes the truth. Which she will. Don't fool yourself."

"I'm not a total Neanderthal," Bruce said indignantly.

"But if, on the other hand, you're not serious, and mean to simply use this woman to, uh . . ."

"Slake his lust?" Duncan offered helpfully.

"To slake your lust, leaving her crushed and embittered, then you're a dirty dog, and don't deserve my help. Either way, I don't want to participate. So forget it. Go read some poetry for real. Expand your horizons. Take a night class. Go to the public library. Good luck."

She crossed her legs and looked at him sternly over the lenses of her glasses. Bruce stared down at her for a moment, bemused, and started to laugh. "You'll do," he said. "You're perfect."

"Thank you for sharing your opinion, Bruce," Duncan said. "That'll be all."

Duncan's voice cut through the laughter.

Bruce choked off his chuckling and nodded hastily. "Uh, yeah. I'm gone. I'll let you guys, uh, work your stuff out, then. Bye."

He left the room, still snorting with muffled laughter. The door clicked shut. The room was profoundly silent. Nell stared out at the cityscape without seeing it, tongue-tied and intensely nervous. Bruce was pleasant, and his enthusiasm heartening, but Duncan was a problem. She didn't have the kind of brazen self-confidence necessary to simply ignore his disapproval. That took brash nerve, and she was coming up short on that commodity, with the Fiend at large. She needed all her brash nerve just to walk out her apartment door every morning. She didn't have any left to spare for wrangling sexy, difficult men. For God's sake. She didn't even have the courage to talk to the guy.

Well, whatever. She sighed. If it didn't work out, she would be no worse off than before. Time to go home, eat a TV dinner, and get to work writing epic poetry about goblins and demons and holy quests. God knows there were worse night jobs. At least it wasn't telemarketing.

She got up, cleared her throat. "Well, I'll just, um, be on my—"

"No. Don't go yet. We need to talk."

Nell's heart thumped. "Okay," she managed. "We do?"

"Yeah. I'm sorry I was rude. My brother was bugging me."

"I could see that," she offered tentatively.

"I shouldn't have taken it out on you," he added.

"No, that's true. You shouldn't have," Nell agreed.

A smile came and went on his face, so quickly, she wondered if she'd imagined it.

He smiled, briefly. "The situation makes me crazy."

Nell cleared her throat delicately. "What situation?"

He shrugged. "This project. I design specialized data sorting and analysis programs. I'm good at that. I understand what they're good for, whom to market them to, what they're willing to pay. Then Bruce waltzes along, with his game idea. I couldn't talk him out of it, and God knows where he would have gone for the money if I'd refused, so now—"

He stopped suddenly, and turned, looking out the window.

She gazed at the sharp line of his silhouette. The shadows in the dim room accentuated the harsh planes of his face.

"And now?" Nell prompted gently.

"I don't know about games. Anything about them. I don't like it."
His voice was clipped. "I like to have all my facts in a row. No surprises."

"Like the strip steak," Nell said daringly.

He considered that, turned and looked at her. "Yeah, I guess."

Nell perched on the table, clasping her hands. "Well, the soup
changes every day, and you've bravely tried a new one every time."

"They're all pretty good." He took a step closer. "I didn't come
to the Sunset Grill for lunch today."

"We missed you," Nell said. Her voice felt breathless, wispy.
"There was a very nice lentil stew you could've tried."

One step closer hid his face in shadow, silhouetting him against
the illuminated buildings outside.

"I don't hate your ideas," he said. "I just automatically contradict
everything my brother says. It's a reflex."

"He shouldn't tease you," Nell said. "Any man who runs his own
business knows about taking risks. What's Bruce risking? He's launching his project using your business as a springboard. What has he got
to lose? You're financing it. You're the one who's put everything on
the line!" She was startled at her own vehemence.

She couldn't see his face, but she got the feeling he was smiling.
"Thank you for saying that," he said. "I appreciate your understanding."

The hairs rose on her arms as he took another step closer. She
could smell the fresh, crisp scent of his shirt. "You're welcome," she
whispered, gazing at his inscrutable silhouette.

"I spoke to Detective Lanaghan today," he said abruptly.

Denise Lanaghan was the investigating officer for Lucia's case.
Hearing her name spoken here, in this context, was disorienting.
"You did what? Why on earth?"

"I wanted to see what progress they were making on the case."

Shock was quickly replaced by anger. "Oh. I understand. You
wanted to see if my story was just so much paranoid bullshit, right?"

He hesitated. "Ah, no, actually. Not at all. A few minutes with a
good search engine was enough to establish that."

She was further outraged. "Oh! So it's true, then? You checked up
on me? You cyber-spied on me?"

"I would hardly call it spying," he said. "I didn't hack into anything private. I just looked at what was lying around in plain sight."

"But why?" she demanded. "Why nose into my life?"

He shrugged, unrepentant. "I was interested."

"Well, this level of interest is making me nervous! And I do not need anything else to make me nervous! Understand?"

He nodded, but did not apologize.

"It's all or nothing with you," she said tartly. "Either you ignore my very existence, or you pin me under a microscope. So, whatever. What did Lanaghan say?"

"Pretty much what you told me last night," he said. "They haven't made much progress."

"No," she said. "The guy's good. He left no trace. No prints, no DNA, nothing. Even the SUV in Boston turned out to be stolen, hours before." The thought chilled her. She shied away from it, groping for something else to think about. "So what else did you find on me out there in cyberspace?" she prodded him. "I suppose you read last term's graduate seminar paper on Christina Rossetti? Or did you dig into the archived transcripts from the message boards at the online poetry forum?"

"Yeah, both," he said. "But my favorites were those five short poems you published in *The Golden Thread Poetry Journal* last January."

That floored her. Her mouth opened and closed. "Ah . . . actually, I was, um, just kidding. About you reading . . . any of that stuff."

"I wasn't," he replied.

The silence stretched out, heavy between them, and he made a sharp gesture with his hand. "Don't get me wrong," he said. "It's not like I can discuss them intelligently. I can't. To be honest, I don't have a flipping clue what you were talking about. In any of those poems."

She was puzzled. "So how did you know you liked them?"

She sensed his discomfort as he fidgeted and looked out the window. "I don't know. I just did. I liked the way they made me feel."

She was startled and moved by the awkward confession. "That's one of the nicest things anyone's ever said about my work. Thank you."

He drifted like a shadow until he stood right in front of her. So close, his aura was interfering with her brain waves.

"You're welcome," he said, his voice low and velvety. "This is the first time in my life I ever got something like that right. And damn if it wasn't by accident. Pure, dumb-ass luck."

"Don't put it in those terms," she scolded, breathlessly. "It's not something you get wrong or right. It's just a matter of paying attention and telling the truth."

He touched one of her ringlets, pulling it out long, letting it spring back, bouncing. "I've got no problems with attention. Or truth," he said.

"Um, n-no, you sure don't," she stammered.

He curled another lock of hair around his finger, stroking the texture. "So, what's my prize for getting this right, Nell?" The deep vibration of his voice made her skin tingle. His breath was so warm. It smelled of coffee, of mint. "Did I earn some points?"

"There you go again," she protested, in a whisper. "It's not about points. Or prizes."

His lips grazed her temple. "It's not?" Then her cheekbone. His voice was a delicate brush of darkest sable over her nerves. "Then what is it about, Nell? Teach me. Enlighten me. I await your wisdom."

Her head dropped back. His hand was ready to support it, warm and strong. Cradling her. "Do not make fun of me," she whispered.

"Oh, God, no," he muttered, and kissed her.

It was like light flashing through her, delicious heat flushing every corner of her body. Like some sinuous, muscular animal thing inside her woke up, a thing that was not afraid of him at all, oh no, not one little bit. That sleek animal part knew exactly what she wanted from him. Knew that he had it to give. Lots of it. Loads of it.

She wound her arms around his neck and demanded it. He made a surprised, satisfied sound deep in his throat and positioned himself between her legs where she perched on the table. Cupping her head with one hand and her bottom with the other.

She'd kissed men before, and been kissed, and had sex, too. Some, not a lot. She'd even enjoyed it, sort of. But never like this. Always before, part of her had stood apart, critiquing, judging. She'd tried to let herself go, experience the magic, the ecstatic passion that poets wrote about, but she'd always stayed so flat, so cool.

With Duncan, there was no problem with letting herself go. Oh, no. The problem was in holding herself back. She wanted to eat him up, strip him bare, ride him hard. He tasted so good. He coaxed her mouth open, and she wound her fingers into his thick, straight hair and moved against him, helpless to stop. He bent her back on the table until she let go of his arms to prop herself up on her elbows. He grabbed her ankles, folded her legs up high, until her skirt rode up and her gartered stockings showed. The ones she'd put on this morning, back when she was still trying to fool herself into thinking she wasn't going to wrestle this guy to the ground and have her wild and wanton way with him. Like, please. Who had she been trying to kid? He was gorgeous. A smorgasbord of sexual delights. So big, so hot. She gasped and pressed back at each grinding shove of his erection against her. He circled against that crazy, hot, delicious, writhing sweet spot, and oh . . . *God.*

Bursts of pleasure rocked her, jolting her mind out of whack.

When she opened her eyes, she found his hand clamped over her mouth. He was grinning. Delighted with himself.

"Wow," he whispered, slowly lifting his hand.

"Oh, God," she croaked, mortified. "Did I . . . make a noise?"

"Oh, yeah. Big-time. Hold on a sec." He pulled away, wrenched the door open. Nell's legs snapped together as a blade of cold light sliced into the room and assaulted her eyes. Duncan poked his head out the door, peered around, and closed it, plunging them into darkness again. "They're gone," he said, and she heard the click of the door lock engaging. "Not a sound. But just in case. Since you're a screamer."

A thread of cold unfurled in her belly. She slid off the table. tugged her skirt over her legs, and found him in front of her. "Oh, no. Don't panic on me now." There was an edge of pleading in his voice.

"I just . . . the locked door, it, ah . . ."

"I'll unlock it, if you want. I just don't want surprise visitors." His hands slid under her skirt and gripped the tops of her thighs, slid slowly up to her groin. "Making you come is not a spectator sport."

"Uh, no, of course not. But I—"

"Shhh," he shushed her, and he seized her again, and they were off, kissing wildly. She gripped his arms and drank him in. Their mouths melded with the sensual sureness of well-matched dancing partners. It was as if they'd known how to kiss each other senseless since time began, with all the excitement of novelty, all the grace and ease of familiarity. She wanted to claw his shirt off, to discover every detail of that big, solid torso, to smell his sweat, to feel the texture of his chest hair, the shape of his nipples, the contours of his muscles.

And his cock. She wanted to grip it, test it, pet it. She reached down, pressed her hand against his flat belly and slid it down over his belt. His hand covered hers and pressed it against the bulge in his crotch. He stroked the gusset of her panties. A murmur of satisfaction rumbled against her shoulder as he found her wet. Very wet.

He kissed her again, his tongue venturing into her mouth to twine lazily around hers, and both of them moaned as he explored her tender folds with a gentle finger, circling and pressing, sliding into her slick opening. She clenched around him, gasping in shocked delight.

"Oh, God," he muttered. "I think my hand is going to come."

"You think you've got problems," she said jerkily.

Then, no more talking. Just deep, ravenous kissing while his finger delved and her hand stroked that massive, hot bulge. Her legs twined around his thighs for balance, and they shuddered and gasped together, tongues twining, wrapped in a tight, trembling knot of desire. Tension rose, until the sweet, keening ache of anticipation shattered.

Pulses of hot delight jolted through her body.

She sagged against him, shimmering and soft. Made of liquid, glimmering with moonlight. He'd undone the fastenings of her garters at some point and was tugging her panties off her legs. She was too limp to react. She hung on to handfuls of his shirtfront and tried to form words with her mouth. "What . . . ah, what are you going to . . . ?"

"I don't have latex," he said. "So I'll do this."

He dropped to his knees and put his mouth to her.

She almost screamed, the sensation was so intense. He felt the flinch and murmured soothing, incomprehensible things against her groin as he rubbed his cheek against her thigh, petting her. His breath felt so soft, like a brush of fine silk, and his fingers were so skillful, parting her, and then his tongue, warm and soft, swirling and fluttering, and the pleasure grew too intense to differentiate sensations.

She collapsed back onto the table, and a tiny part of her brain stood apart for a moment, astonished at how her life had upended itself. Last night, celibate, and crushed out on an unattainable man. Today, spread-eagled and pantiless in his conference room, getting marvellously tongue-lashed by that same unattainable guy.

Yeah, and if she didn't attain him all the way, she was going to collapse into a screaming, writhing human black hole, the hunger bit so deep and hard. She pushed his face away. He looked up in silent question, wiping his mouth. She saw his grin flash in the dimness.

"Mmm," he murmured. "Good. More?"

"What about you?"

His soft laughter tickled her pubis. "I'll live." He paused for a moment, and added, "Somehow." He pressed his lips to her, fluttering his tongue around her clit in a way that sent her spinning into a dizzying vortex. The man was amazing. And her body was a fire gone wild in a fireworks factory. She pushed his face away, struggled up onto her elbows. "Please," she whispered. "Make love to me."

He stared at her, and she wished she hadn't used a silly romantic euphemism. It made her vulnerabilities so obvious. She should have just said, "Fuck me." It would have been clearer, more honest. They'd both know where they stood. Or sprawled, as the case may be.

But she couldn't. Such a blunt, crude phrase would not come out of her mouth. Romantic, old-fashioned idiot that she was.

He gripped her hips, fingers digging in. "No latex," he repeated.

She gulped in air and exposed herself still further. "I have some."

He froze. "No fucking way."

"Um, actually, yes. In my purse. My co-worker bought them for me today, as a joke. She was roasting me. I never thought I'd—"

"Where's your purse?"

"On the chair, I think, on the other side of the—"

He'd already yanked it open and flung its contents onto the table. He found the box, and seconds later he was back, opening his belt and opening the shrink-wrap in a show of manual dexterity that would be dazzling if she'd been in any condition to appreciate it. She caught a glimpse of his big, thick phallus as he sheathed it, and then he pushed her back down onto the table and folded her legs up high.

The bulb at the end of his cock seemed impossibly big, pressing against her. He slid it tenderly up and down the length of her labia, caressing her with it until he was wet, and she was squirming against him, in silent pleading. And he drove slowly inside.

Duncan counted back from ten, holding his breath. Please, God, not yet. He breathed the climax carefully down, but the second he opened his eyes and looked at her again, spread out beneath him, he was in trouble again.

So beautiful. Fuck. His body shook with excitement. The jealous, eager grip of her pussy was an agonizing torment. Each stroke was another torturous lick of the lash.

He was glad he'd gotten her good and wet, or he'd never have gotten inside. As it was, each stroke was slow, pushing against the hot, plushy resistance of her body that enveloped him, throbbing with the heavy beat of her heart.

Again . . . and again, and finally the tight, careful strokes relaxed and they found their rhythm of deep, swirling, rocking thrusts, punctuated by wet slaps of contact, his labored breathing, her breathless gasps. She was working up to another climax. And now his own orgasm was crashing down on him like a falling meteor, the sky was in flames, but God knew how, he held it off . . . until she took flight.

They soared together, through that inner nowhere. Fused.

He collapsed over her, panting. His mind wiped clean. He'd never imagined feeling so close. Feeling the essence of her, in the heart of that burning, twisting glow. So beautiful.

His eyes fluttered open. He was pinning her soft body onto the hard table with all the weight of his torso. He lifted himself hastily up.

Her face was turned away. He felt shy, humbled. He didn't know if she'd felt what he'd felt. The postcoital crash chilled him with doubts. He pulled out of the excellent, tight clutch of her body.

The condom was a problem. No way in hell was he leaving it in the trash can in the conference room. He rummaged on the table for the drugstore bag the box had been in. Peeled the condom off, sealed it up. Tongue-tied as a thirteen-year-old boy who'd just had his first lay. He hastened to shove his still-turgid dick back into his pants, and fasten them, with some discomfort, over the bulge, before he even dared to look at her.

She'd straightened her clothing in the meantime, too. She'd pulled her panties back on. Her stockings were up, skirt tugged down. She was fastening her garters. Waiting for him to speak first.

Damn. Women were always the talkative ones. This was the first time in his life he'd ever longed for one of them to break the silence.

"Are you, uh, okay?" he ventured. She nodded. He kicked himself for his lack of inspiration. So much for that stellar, brilliant attempt.

"That was incredible," he offered.

"Yes," she agreed.

He was heartened. "I didn't mean for things to happen so fast between us," he said.

She stifled a soft, whispery giggle. "Me neither," she murmured.

It looked like she wasn't getting all emotional on him, thank God. Maybe she was a reasonable female. "Well, there's no going back now."

She crossed her arms over her chest. "Meaning?"

"Meaning, I think we're on to something here. It'll be complicated, but it's worth it to me. Let's go get some dinner, and we can hammer out the details."

"Details?" she repeated slowly.

"Yeah. Our mutually beneficial arrangement. It'll need to be secret, for obvious reasons, but we can swing it. I'll take you to my condo. We'll order in. I'll show you how beneficial it can be."

She flipped the light switch on, unexpectedly. He blinked and took in the blazing fury on her face. It rocked him back on his heels.

"Not." She grabbed her purse, began shoving things into it.

He was perplexed. "Nell—"

"That's Ms. D'Onofrio to you, Burke," she said, scooping up the scattered stuff on the table and stuffing it into her purse. "You can take your mutually beneficial arrangement and shove it right up your ass."

She shrugged her purse over her shoulder and strode out. Her mane of black curls bounced with each brisk, angry step.

He lunged after her, grabbed her shoulder to spin her around.

"Don't touch me." She flinched away.

"You didn't complain about me touching you ten minutes ago. Are you fucking with me? Because we both know that was mutual."

"I am not fucking with you." She spat each word out. "It looks like we were fucking with each other, but we're done with that. Definitively."

He shook his head. "I don't get it. Just tell me if I need to call my lawyer."

She blew out an explosive breath. "No, Burke. I'm not setting you up for a lawsuit. I'm not an extortionist or a con woman. If you want me to sign and notarize a piece of paper saying I came six times, I'll—"

"Eight," he specified.

"Do not push me," she said, biting the words out. "The sex was great. You're amazing in bed. Actually, that's a misnomer. I'm sure you're amazing on the floor, in the shower, up against the wall. But the minute you zip up your pants and open your mouth, you're a rude, crass, graceless clod. So get out of my way."

She wrenched open the door of the office and flounced out.

He stared at the door as it shut in his face, running through every goddamn thing he'd said and done to her. He couldn't find any fault lines, any red flags, any horrible insults. What the hell had he said?

He felt like he'd been stripped naked and sucker-punched.

This was not over. He slapped the door open. The elevator down the hall was closing. He sprinted for it, but the doors pinged shut before he could wedge his fingers in. The other one was noodling up around the fiftieth floor. He dove for the stairwell.

Enough being baffled. Enough guessing games, enough bombs going off in his face. He was sick of it. She wasn't getting away from him until he knew exactly what he'd done to piss her off.

Fuck this stress-inducing bullshit.

Chapter
5

Nell stumbled out onto the street. Her knees wobbled with anger and everything that had preceded it.

She set out, wiping tears away with the back of her hands, leaving horrendous streaks. She must look like a Halloween horror.

Mutually beneficial arrangement, her ass. Hammer out the details? He might as well ask for a fee schedule. Like a sushi menu. A combination platter. Four pieces of sashimi, maki roll, and miso soup. How much for a mind-bending kiss, heart-pounding dry humping, amazing protracted cunnilingus, and a long, hard screw on the conference room table? Should she give a discount for all the orgasms?

Crass, arrogant asshole. Reducing it to that, after he'd laid her so bare. Her heart, her fears and hopes, her deepest self, all stripped down and raw. Live wires carrying a lethal charge. As he had discovered, to his cost. She'd overreacted, maybe, but it had been all she could do not to scream like a banshee and swing her purse at his head.

Or maybe that had been just one last lingering remnant of common sense. All she had to do was look at the guy to see that she would not fare well in any sort of physical confrontation with him.

Her legs shook as she stumbled down the sidewalk. Her crotch was wet, hot and flushed and glowing with pleasure. As if all the lights had been turned on, and left on. Every step, every clench of her thigh muscles felt . . . well, good.

Damn him. That had been so cold, so crude, so unnecessary. He should deal with professionals, not dumb-ass romantics like her, primed and programmed to fall like a ton of rock. Embarrassing themselves and everyone else in their immediate vicinity.

She bumped into people on the sidewalk and bounced off them muttering soggy, abbreviated apologies. The colored lights were a dizzying tear-blurred swirl. She stopped at a street corner and wiped the tears and mascara away with her sleeve. God knew, this dress would have to be cleaned anyway. She might never wear the thing again at all.

She peered up at the street sign. Broadway. Good. Busy at all hours. Even though a faraway, disconnected part of her mind reminded her of her promise to Nancy and Vivi. The Fiend. It wasn't safe.

But her wallet was so close to empty, she could not even afford a car service home, and her bank account was no better. She'd spent all of yesterday's tip money on that stupid haircut this morning, and today's tip money at the bank, on her break, paying down her hefty credit card minimum. And then the car service to Burke's building.

But fear not, right? Salvation was at hand. High-level call girls pulled in a thousand an hour or more, depending on the services they were asked to provide, the level of kink. Not that she could really boast of her sexual technique, as little effective practice as she had, but hey, she could wing it, she could fake it. She had it in her blood, after all.

All she had to do was whip up a stiff fee schedule for that ice-hearted bastard, and there was the cash she needed, for the cab fares, haircuts, dresses, rent. Hell, her tuition, too. If she wanted to spend that much time on her back. Or her knees.

All she had to do was kill something inside herself. Something shining and precious and delicate. Something she'd never even known she had until that moment of astonishing connection with him. *Hope.*

She was appalled at her own vapid stupidity. She'd actually been hoping for love. Real love. From him. And she hadn't let herself admit it.

She'd been walking for a long time. Her feet were aching. The busy, self-important city swirled around her. Wind swept down the street, cool against her tear-streaked face. She recognized a familiar sign. A big-chain bookstore where she loved to hang out when she had time. Standing for hours in the aisles, gobbling books she could not afford to buy. If any place on earth could offer comfort, it was that one.

Maybe she'd go in and buy something extravagant. Like the complete works of E. E. Cummings. She'd put it on her card.

And she'd stay in the place until they threw her out bodily.

Duncan dropped a few meters farther behind, keeping the pale flash of her dress in his field of vision. He'd charged out of there all fired up, with every intention of confronting her face on, right in the street, and demanding to know, exactly, in every particular, what her fucking problem was. Then he'd gotten close enough to see that she was crying.

And aw, shit. He'd lost his nerve. He might have known he was going to pay in blood for anything that good.

So he went into surveillance mode. Blank, emotions flatlined, attention focused on the target. Projecting a don't-see-me vibe, for camo. He was nobody important, just a faceless suit in a sea of suits. Though at this hour, there was no sea of suits on the streets. The suits were vegging in front of their TVs, or packed into bars managing their stress by consuming excessive amounts of alcohol. Not a problem, though. Nell wasn't noticing him. She was stumbling along the sidewalk, her hand over her mouth, clutching her purse. Attracting attention. A beautiful woman sobbing right out on the street. Christ.

That made his emotional flatline twitch, first with guilt and then with anger. What the fuck? Why? He hadn't intended any of this. The last thing he wanted to do was to hurt her feelings. All he'd done to the chick was give her multiple orgasms. So fucking shoot him, already. Of course, seducing her hadn't helped with her current off-the-charts stress level.

But he hadn't been able to stop himself. It just . . . happened.

Yeah, and now he was compounding his problems by stalking her. Nice. That was superintelligent. Yeah, that was razor sharp.

But his feet didn't hear the sarcasm, didn't get the message. His feet just kept carrying him along, keeping her a safe thirty meters or so ahead of him. Watching that mane of springy black ringlets sway and swirl with every gust of wind.

Then he felt it. Like the whispery brush of a cobweb breaking across his mind. Instinct that said, *Something's wrong with this picture.*

He looked closer. Since he'd snapped into surveillance mode, part of his mind had been tracking not just her, but everything around her. That gray sweatshirt had been around for a while. Too long. Behind, but not far. Gray sweatshirt, jeans. Long blond hair. Dirty white athletic shoes. Nell paused to wait for a light. The guy slowed and gazed into a cosmetics products shop window. Yeah, right. Like that skank could be interested in aromatherapy bath salts or orange blossom body butter.

Duncan got on line at a streetside bank machine, and watched out of the corner of his eye as the guy sauntered across the street, and continued on his way, in the same direction as Nell, parallel to her.

Duncan flash analyzed the data, which had been reliably gathering only since the moment he'd given up on the idea of confronting her. That guy had been in his field of vision that entire time, and might have been there since they'd walked out of the building. Lying in wait.

Thirty-five downtown blocks. Too far to walk voluntarily, to not take a subway or a cab, to not have some other business or detour along the way. Nell crossed the street again as well, and headed over toward the Astor Place subway stop. Gray Sweatshirt strolled after her.

Nell disappeared into a big, brightly lit chain bookstore. The guy stopped, muttered into his collar, and followed her in.

Fuck. A thread of ice congealed down his middle. The guy was wired. Reporting to someone, in real time. This wasn't some random sicko obsessed with Nell's tits. This was a team of random sickos. A team meant organization, financing, a serious agenda. What the *fuck*?

He eased to the back of the line for the bank machine again and waited, as intent and single-minded as a cat watching a mouse hole. Crunching data, speculating, presenting and rejecting hypotheses.

Time warped. People swirled by, like speeded-up film. He stood motionless in the middle of it, a laser-focused eye of contemplation.

Customers began coming out in numbers. He glanced at his watch. The store was about to close. His adrenaline started to rev as Nell came out of the store, swinging a plastic shopping bag in her hand. She looked around herself, as if trying to get her bearings, and took off in the direction of Astor Place.

Three seconds later, Gray Sweatshirt came out and followed.

Duncan forced himself to move in a casual stride. No sprinting, no primordial roars of rage. His heart thudded. Blood roared in his head. He had to pinch like a vise on the overwhelming urge to leap on that piece-of-shit dickhead and take him apart.

Nell turned onto Lafayette. Gray Sweatshirt muttered into his collar once again. Urgency began to prick at Duncan. Something was going down, and he was the only one around to stop it. He was only one guy.

So far. He pulled out his cell, and speed dialed Gant.

"What is it?" Gant snarled, in his usual bad humor. "You again? Got any more unreasonable demands to make, Dunc?"

"Yeah. Remember the chick who I'm obsessed with?"

"Yeah, the daughter of Lucia D'Onofrio. What about her?"

"I'm tailing her right now," he said. "Stalking her, you might say."

Gant hissed something viciously obscene in Pushtu. "And you are burdening me with this embarrassing, unwelcome, extremely personal information about yourself exactly why?"

"Because I'm not the only one who's doing it," he said.

Gant was gratifyingly speechless for a moment. "Come again?"

"She's under surveillance," he said patiently. "At least a two-man team. I'm about half a block behind the guy who's tailing her. We're on Lafayette. Just past the Public Theater."

"Holy fuck," Gant muttered. "I'll send someone."

"Do it fast. They're gearing up for something," Duncan said.

"Dunc? Do not engage with them." He paused. "Did you hear me?"

"I heard you," Duncan said, noncommittal.

Gant snarled yet another curse in Pushtu. "Are you armed?"

"No, but I'll be careful."

Gant hung up with no farewell, and Duncan hurried to catch up, having hung back to call Gant. He did not like Lafayette. It was darker than Broadway, more deserted, fewer storefronts, everything closed. He wished she'd stayed on crowded Broadway, where he could afford to be closer to her. As it was, it was a miracle that Gray Sweatshirt hadn't made him yet. The guy might be incompetent. That, however, did not make him any less dangerous to Nell.

The cobweb whisper of alarm tipped him off again. Gray Sweatshirt's demeanor had changed. He looked more focused. Was walking faster, as if he'd been released from some imperative, or given a new one. Beyond Nell coming toward them in the opposite direction was another pedestrian figure. A tall, rangy black man with a shaved head. They had her in a pair of tweezers. Then the car pulled up, driving slowly. Too slowly. It passed Duncan.

Its brake lights flickered, on and off, for no good reason.

It sped up. Gray Sweatshirt did, too. So did the guy coming on.

Duncan didn't remember starting to sprint. His legs pumped with frantic speed as he struggled to close the gap. The car door swung open. The guys grabbed Nell, started wrestling her into the car, headfirst. She struggled, screamed. Duncan flung himself at the closest of the two men, the tall black guy. The man hit the side of the car with a grunt of surprise. Gray Sweatshirt's head whipped around. "What the fuck—"

Duncan rammed a fist into Gray Sweatshirt's nose, knocking him against the car door. In that split-second opening, he grabbed Nell by the waist, yanked her out and away from the car, and flung her in the direction of the sidewalk. She hit the ground, rolled into the gutter.

He surged back as a boot whipped past the tip of his nose, blocked Gray Sweatshirt's swing with his forearm, rammed an elbow into the black guy's neck. He blocked a punch to the gut, spun to take Gray Sweatshirt's knee-jab to the groin on his thigh instead. An uppercut to the black guy's chin sent the man bouncing heavily against the car, and he whirled just in time to meet Gray Sweatshirt's renewed attack.

People had noticed. Yelling. A woman screamed nearby. Not Nell.

Block, duck, lunge, retreat. He caught Gray Sweatshirt's fist, whipped it up, over, around, sent the guy flying over the hood of the car. The black guy came at him again with a length of pipe. It whipped down. Duncan lurched to the side. The pipe whooshed past him, displacing air, and shattered the passenger-side window. Pebbles of glass flew.

Duncan darted in, grabbed the end of the pipe before it could work up to another swing and twisted the thing up, torquing the guy's arm and sending him bouncing over the hood of the car. The car surged forward, pitching the guy off and onto the street. He rolled, howling.

Tires shrieked as the car peeled around the corner and sped away. The black guy dragged himself up and fled, limping, the heavy, irregular slap of his rubber-soled shoes retreating into the distance.

Gray Sweatshirt came at him with a spinning back kick. In ducking back to avoid it, Duncan lost his center, stumbled back and went down onto his knees. *Fuck.* The guy leaped for him, eyes lit up.

Crack. Nell had swung her plastic shopping bag, and whatever was in it had connected with the guy's face. He let out a hoarse shout and stumbled back, hand over his nose, which streamed blood.

Duncan rolled up onto his feet, lunged to grapple—

Gun. He stopped, reeling. Fighting for balance. Hands up, open.

Gray Sweatshirt held a pistol on them, in a shaking, sideways two-handed grip he'd learned from watching bullshit action films. But at point-blank range, even the guy's compromised aim from the stupid grip wouldn't save them. That Glock 9mm would leave a big hole.

Duncan scooped Nell back behind him with his arm. "Easy," he soothed. "Easy."

"Fuck you, you fuck." The guy's trembling voice was thin and high, bubbling and phlegmy with the blood running down his throat. "Back off, or I'll shoot you like a fuckin' dog. And then I'll shoot the bitch." He backed away from them, gun wavering. He swung it in a wild arc around himself that sent all the looky-loos who'd gathered around into a screaming, scattering panic. Like a bunch of startled pigeons.

"You don't need to shoot," Duncan said quietly. "Who hired you?"

"Some stupid fuck. Shut up. Don't talk to me." The guy backed away farther. "Back off. Everybody. Get the fuck back." He turned, suddenly, and ran like a double-jointed cheetah, his legs a blur.

Nell sagged down onto the sidewalk. Duncan sank to his knees to break her fall, held her up. He fished his cell phone out of his pocket and realized, embarrassed, that his finger shook too much to punch in the number. Shit. He was getting soft. Going civilian.

It took a few tries, but he finally got Gant's phone ringing. Then the car pulled up, and Gant himself unfolded his long, lanky self from the seat, holding up the ringing phone. Duncan stopped the call and dropped the phone back into his pocket. The asshole was long gone, but he relayed the info with weary precision. "Three of them. One's rabbiting down Great Jones Street. Blond, six one, jeans, gray sweatshirt, goatee. Armed and dangerous. Glock 9mm. The other two are long gone. One was a black man, tall, thin. He ran, too. The car was a silver Jeep Cherokee. Busted front passenger window. Didn't get the plates. Didn't get a look at the driver."

Gant relayed the info his radio. He was a square-jawed guy, with cold blue eyes and sandy hair, buzzed off short. He looked down at Nell, still curled up on the sidewalk. "This is her?" he asked.

Duncan pulled Nell to her feet. "Nell, Lt. John Gant, of the NYPD."

She swallowed, coughed. "Ah, hi."

"You okay, miss?" Gant asked.

"Been better," she croaked. "I'll be fine. I think."

"Did he hit you? Hurt you?"

"She broke his nose," Duncan announced, in ringing tones. "She broke that pig-fucking son of a bitch's nose."

Gant blinked at the fierce pride in Duncan's voice. "Uh, wow. Hot damn. How'd you do that, miss?"

Nell held up the plastic shopping bag, and fished out a massive volume that she could not even hold in one hand alone. "The complete works of E. E. Cummings," she said. "Just picked it up at the Barnes & Noble. Ten percent member discount." She startled to giggle. "Oh, God. I had no idea what a good deal I was getting."

Her face crumpled, her hands covered her face. Duncan stared at

her in helpless dismay. Fuck. Again. Gant gave him the hairy eyeball, and jerked his hand toward Nell, snapping his fingers sharply.

"Hug her, you asshole!" he mouthed.

Duncan scowled at him and grabbed Nell, wrapping his arms
around her. She stiffened against him, but she didn't jerk away.

And her soft body felt amazingly good next to his. He was panting, raw and zinging with combat adrenaline, bruised and pounded
and scraped and generally fucked up, but still, she felt so goddamn
good.

His arms tightened. He inhaled the smell of her hair and then focused on the blood and imbedded grit and grime on his own filthy
knuckles. She shook in his arms. A fine, high-frequency vibration.

Don't get yourself all excited, butthead. She's traumatized.

Gant harrumphed. "Fucking cretin," he muttered. "Have to tell
you everything."

Duncan flipped his friend the bird behind Nell's back, and pressed
his nose into those perfumed curls again. Inhaling her.

The next couple of hours were long and hard, down at police
headquarters. She spent a long time on his cell phone, pouring her
heart out to her sisters, first one, then the other. Hashing the whole
thing out and filing the report took a tediously long time, and after a
while Duncan started eying Nell's pale, stiff face and staring eyes
and wondered uneasily if he'd been stupid not to insist that she get
medically evaluated. She'd said she was fine. Maybe a bruise or two.
But he hadn't considered psychological damage. He was as tough as
boot leather himself. Used to rough treatment. He'd forgotten what
a tooth-rattling shock violence was to normal human beings.

Her hand was icy cold. He rubbed it between his. "I need to get
some food and a good stiff drink into her," he said to Gant. "Can we
finish this up another time?"

Gant studied Nell with narrowed eyes. "Miss D'Onofrio, do you
have someone to stay with tonight?" He shot a keen glance at Duncan. "A family member, maybe?"

She looked lost, chewing on her soft, cushy lower lip. "Ah . . ."

"She's staying with me," Duncan blurted.

Nell blinked at him, startled. He stared back, willing her not to
fight it. It seemed so obvious to him, so inevitable. So right.

She let out a long breath, in short, jerky segments, and nodded. "With him," she murmured to Gant.

A jolt of hot triumph shook Duncan. Urgency, too. He wanted to get her home now. Trap her into his lair. Before she changed her mind.

He made sure the car service was waiting before he let her leave the building. Snipers could be after her, for all he knew. He bundled her hastily into the car and gave the driver his address.

"Wait," Nell said. "My place, first."

He rounded on her, ready for battle. She put her fingers over his mouth. "Shhh. Don't start. I need to touch base. I need fresh clothes."

"I'll buy you clothes."

"Not at one in the morning, you won't," she said. "And I need to check my answering machine. And pick up my laptop."

"Those guys know where you live," he growled. "I don't want to come across like I've got no balls, but I wouldn't mind avoiding any more mortal combat this evening. If it's not too fucking much to ask."

She tapped his lips again, gently. "Don't be sarcastic. I am very aware of your big balls. But I doubt very much they'll be lying in wait for me there tonight. We'll park right outside the door, we'll see if anyone's there, we'll only be inside for a few minutes. Please, Duncan."

He settled back against the seat, defeated but disapproving. Her hand was no longer on his mouth. He missed it. It was almost worth goading her, to see if she would try to silence him again.

Then another possibility occurred to him. He reached down and took her hand. A long and cautious minute later, her fingers curled around his. The city slipped by, but they were fixed in space. A hub, the unmoving center of the universe, and the rest of the world was a shifting illusion swirling around them. But she was so warm, soft. Real.

"Thank you," she said finally. "For saving my life."

"Anytime." He punctuated that statement by sliding his thumb into the warm recesses of her hand. He thought about the conference room table, and blood pounded in his ears. He fought it down. "I was, ah, wondering something."

Her fingers tightened around his. "Yes? What?"

"If that earns me enough points to cancel out whatever the hell it was that I did to piss you off before."

He braced himself, but she didn't freak out. She just made an impatient gesture with her free hand. "That's it, Duncan. That's exactly the problem. This idea that you have, that everything can be reduced to an economic exchange. Human emotions don't run on a point system."

He sighed. "It's a figure of speech, Nell," he ground out.

"No, it is not. Not with you." Her voice was soft but stubborn.

Aw, fuck. He drew comfort from the fact that she was still squeezing his hand. "It's been a really hard night," he said wearily. "This shit is complicated. Just show me some fucking mercy, already."

She grabbed him, gave him a quick, awkward hug. "Okay," she whispered. "I hereby grant you points. Lots of them. Happy now?"

"Very," he said. And he was. He was hard, too. Like a diamond. He wanted to roll her onto the cushy leather seat and just have at her.

"One question," she said. "How did you happen to conveniently be there when they attacked? Were you following me?"

Tension gripped him. Here was where he tiptoed over blown glass.

"Yeah, I was," he said. "I, uh, wanted to apologize. But I'm not great at it. And you were crying, and that intimidated me. And I didn't even know what the hell I was apologizing for. So I stalled."

"Until I got attacked," she said.

"You have to admit, it was a great opening," he offered. "Works like electroshock therapy. The woman forgets what she's mad about."

She snorted with laughter. "Uh, yeah. Right."

"No, really," he said. "If not for those guys, you'd still be pissed as hell, and I'd still be as confused as ever." He paused. "I'm still confused," he admitted. "And you're probably still pissed. But at least you're talking to me. That's progress."

She harrumphed. "Talk about looking on the bright side."

"I might as well," he observed.

The car stopped outside her door. He told the driver to wait and got out, peering around the street before he let her out. He blocked her body with his as she unlocked the metal warehouse door, and peered around every twist of the echoing stairwell before letting her proceed.

Her apartment was so full of books, there was barely space to move. The bathtub in the kitchen was covered with a wooden top. A mini water closet occupied the corner of the room. A half refrigerator was tucked under the sink. There was a two-burner gas range, a toaster oven. He'd never seen a place so miniature.

He peered at the photos on the wall while she hustled around, pulling a suitcase out of her closet. Most were pictures of two young women and a distinguished-looking elderly woman in varying combinations and settings. "This is your mother, and sisters?"

She glanced around from where she knelt in front of a small chest of drawers. "Yes."

He studied them. Pretty, like Nell, but in very different ways. "They don't look anything like you," he observed.

"We're all adopted," Nell said. "Lucia took us in as foster children when we were teenagers."

That teasing bit of info made him curious. About who had made her, what had forged her. How she'd gotten to be so smart and pretty and difficult. But not tonight. There would be other chances. He hoped.

She looked exhausted, staring down at two different T-shirts in her hands as if she couldn't decide which one to bring.

"Pack both," he advised. "You're not coming back for a while."

She shot him a narrow glance. He walked over to her, and knelt. She swayed back, her eyes going big and wary as he pulled her first drawer open. He grabbed a big fistful of silky stuff. All colors. Panties, stockings. Things made of lace, ribbons, silk. He dropped the tangled wad of stuff into the open suitcase. "Pack a lot," he repeated softly.

Her eyes dropped. Color rose in her face. Her nipples were tight, nubs poking against the stretchy fabric of her stained, rumpled dress.

That white-hot episode in the conference room hung between them in the silence, complete in every heart-thudding erotic detail. She was licking her lower lip until it gleamed, enticing him. The look in her eyes was cautious, but there was a smile hidden in it.

He scoped the room with his peripheral vision. The bed looked uncomfortable with those heaps of books, but the beanbag chair behind her had possibilities. He could wedge her into that and pin her down with his weight, juicily rocking and sliding. Her pussy doing that fluttering clutch around his cock every time she came. Yes.

He reached out, let his fingertips slide down her cheek, her soft throat. Over her breastbone. He spread out his whole hand, felt the quick, hard throb of her heart against his palm. He slid his other hand up her thigh, to the top of her stockings, gripping her where the fabric ended, and soft, hot skin began. The energy grew, swelling into something huge and inevitable. She bit her lower lip, breathing hard.

It happened again, as it had on the street. That feeling brushing by. A cobweb breaking across his mind, as his guard went down.

He froze, and his grip tightened on her thigh. He looked around the small apartment. Nothing moving. Nothing had changed. It was silent. Just the sounds of the street outside.

"What is it?" Nell asked.

"Shhh," he hushed her, feeling around with his subtlest senses.

Two steps brought him to a barred window that looked out on a blind courtyard full of garbage cans. Empty. Just a couple of rats on the scrounge. He looked for a reason for the feeling. There always was one. By now, he trusted it blind. He was being watched. His neck crawled.

His eyes fell on the smoke detector attached to the low ceiling. He reached up and carefully detached it.

"Duncan, what are you—"

"Shhh." He didn't want to talk, even to explain himself. Not with unfriendly eyes watching, unfriendly ears listening.

It was almost too easy. The tiny vidcam was taped to the side of the black smoke detector, virtually invisible. The device had been gutted of its usual contents, the space inside the shell used to house the wiring and battery and radiofrequency transmitter of the camera. He stared at it, wishing that he had not touched it. Fingerfucking the evidence. Gant would lecture him. His friend never wasted an opportunity to give him hell.

"What on earth is that thing?" Nell's voice was thin and high.

"A vidcam," he said. "Someone's been watching you."

She made a strangled sound. Put her hand over her mouth.

Shit-eating bastards. Violating her hard-earned private space. Watching while she undressed, bathed, ate, slept. Probably watching her now, being hurt and scared. That infuriated him.

He laid the thing down on her table. "Don't touch it," he said. "It might have prints." He looked around the room again, trying to imagine where he would plant spyware, if he were one of them.

She had an old-fashioned phone. He grabbed the horn, unscrewed the mouthpiece. Bingo. He shook the listening device onto the table without touching it, and answered the question in her eyes. "A drop-in bug," he said. "They've been monitoring your phone conversations."

Her eyes were huge. "I . . . but I talked to Vivi just this morning—"

"We'll discuss it later," he cut her off. "Not here. Let's just get the fuck out of this place. It's making my flesh creep."

"Ah, y-y-yes," she agreed, flustered. She looked around herself, wildly. "Um . . . what was I—"

"Laptop. And clothes," he reminded her. "Quickly."

It didn't take her long once he started helping, scooping stuff out of drawers at random. That perked her up. She shoved him away with an irritated sound and finished packing clothes, but then came the shoes, the toiletries bag: vials and bottles and tubes, packets of this and that. And then the books. Fuck a duck. She heaved eight of them into the huge suitcase. Big motherlovers, too. The trolley wheels were probably going to collapse.

He dragged her out the door after that, scanned the stairwell landing, and stuck his head back inside her door. He made an obscene gesture, for the benefit of any hidden cameras he hadn't found.

"You're not getting her," he told the bug that lay on the table. "Fuck off and die, shithead." He slammed the door, for emphasis.

Nell was alarmingly quiet in the car, staring ahead, throat bobbing. He knew the feeling. She was trying to swallow it. It wouldn't go down. But the silence was so heavy, it was making him twitch.

He reached for the first thing he could think of to break it. "Do you have a copy of that letter your sister found?" he asked.

"I have it scanned onto my computer," she said. "Why?"

He shrugged. "I'm just—"

"Interested. Yes. I've noticed." There was a touch of acid in her voice that silenced him again.

He stared out the window, wondering what his next move should be. He saw a Korean deli coming up on the corner, with banks of multicolored flowers on display. "Stop the car," he told the driver.

Nell looked startled, as the car braked and he flung the door open. "Don't worry," he assured her. "This'll just take a second."

He stared at the flowers, at a loss, and grabbed a bunch of the best-looking long-stemmed roses out of a bucket. He handed the boy sitting next to the flowers a couple of twenties, and got back into the car.

"Here." He handed her the flowers, realizing too late that the long, thorny stems were still dripping. He hadn't even had them tied, wrapped, trimmed, anything. But she was looking wide-eyed, charmed. She sniffed them. Smiled at him. It had worked. Praise God.

After a moment, she groped for his hand. "I'm sorry," she said. "I appreciate the fact that you're interested. I'm probably alive because of it. I just don't get it. Why is this happening? It's senseless."

"Money," Duncan said.

She looked over at him, blankly. "Huh?"

"Money is why this is happening," he repeated.

She looked doubtful. "Maybe you haven't noticed, Duncan, but I don't have very much of it. Practically none, to be honest."

He shook his head. "There's a short list of probable motivations for crimes like this. Insanity, revenge, or money. It doesn't look like you girls have pissed anyone off that badly—"

"We haven't," she cut in. "We're goody-goody pussycats."

"And there's the murdered jeweller and his whole family, too, so I'd strike personal revenge as a motive. We could consider revenge against your mother, but that falls pretty flat, since she's passed on. Insanity's a possibility, but there are the references in those letters, to maps, searches, keys, secrets. Whoever this dickhead is, he's invested time and money watching you, and probably your sisters, too. Whatever Lucia wanted you girls to find? It means big bucks. Very big. And they're not going to stop till they have it."

Nell hid her eyes and massaged her temples. "It's so ironic," she murmured. "If that's true. We don't need this money, wherever it comes from. We don't give a shit about money. None of us do. All we want is to live our lives in peace. Oh, God. There's so much to freak out about, I'm in tilt."

"Don't think about any of it," he suggested.

"Slick solution. Neat trick." There was a smile in her voice. "And just exactly how do you suggest I do that?"

It had been such a weird evening already, he decided one more crazy risk wouldn't change anything. He lifted her hand, and gave it a long, lingering kiss. "I've got a few good ideas," he said.

She laughed behind her hand, and the vibrations in her shoulders went on for so long, he got scared she was crying again.

"I had no idea I was so damn funny," he said. "Who knew."

Her shoulders shook harder. She threw her head back, and wiped her eyes. "It's not you. I just can't believe it. I felt safe, in my place, after I put the alarm in. The thing cost a fortune. And the whole while, they were watching me. God, it's disgusting. How did they get in there?"

"They probably wired the place before you put the alarm in." He handed her his phone. "Call your sister. If she's told you where she's going on that telephone, tell her to change her plans."

"Oh, God, you're right," she whispered. "Vivi."

She called, and he listened to her garbled, one-sided conversation for the rest of the drive to his Upper West Side condo. The driver pulled over at the lobby entrance. She was still talking as he paid the driver.

". . . can't stay with me there any longer, Viv. Haven't you been listening? They've been watching us all along! We can't go near the place until we fix this mess. Go to Liam and Nancy's . . . Yes, I know, but be a grown-up, Viv. Being a fifth wheel is better than being stuffed into the backseat of a car. . . . Oh, no, don't worry about me. I'm staying with a friend." Her eyes flicked to Duncan. Her voice got defensive. "No, you don't know him. . . . Yes, it is a him, okay? And so? What of it?"

Duncan heard a shrill, tinny burst of female verbosity from the telephone, and Nell rolled her eyes and snorted. "If you must know, he's the one who clobbered the kidnappers for me. . . . Of course I knew him before! He's my new boss." Another impassioned burst from the phone. "Look, Viv, I know it's crazy, but can we thrash this out another time? Come to the seisiun at Malloy's tomorrow night with Nancy and Liam, and we'll talk there, okay? . . . Of course. You be careful, too."

She ended the call and handed the phone back. "She's staying with an old art school friend she met at the fair by chance, so we never discussed it on the bugged phone. Thank God. The Fiend has no line on her there."

"Could you folks work this out once you're outside the vehicle?" the driver asked, his voice plaintive. "I got another call. I gotta go."

Duncan led her into his building, dragging her huge trolley behind him into the elevator. Up thirty-five floors, and he closed the door after her, engaged the chain, the dead bolts, the alarms.

He let out a long, relieved breath. Finally. He had her right where he wanted her.

Chapter
6

Nell looked around, impressed. His apartment was huge, almost empty. Austere to the point of chilliness. Blond wood on the wide expanse of gleaming floor. Three gray couches, grouped in a square around a low table with a vast plasma TV and entertainment console. A big, shadowy kitchen, back in a distant corner. Picture windows with stunning, brilliant cityscapes on two sides. A big terrace. A scattering of black-and-white photographs hung on otherwise blank walls.

"Wow," she murmured. "Is this place, uh, yours?"

He nodded.

Um. This apartment answered any questions a person might have about how lucrative the business of intelligent data analysis program design had been for him. It beat academia and poetry writing all to hell. Not that it mattered. She hadn't chosen to be a scholar for money.

He disappeared into the kitchen. Lights flipped on. She heard water running, clattering and clinking. When he came back out, he was holding out a big glass of wine, so densely red it was almost black.

"This stuff will knock you out on an empty stomach, so sip it slowly," he said. "I've got some water on to boil for some artichoke ravioli, and some red sauce. That work for you?"

She laid the flowers down on a table and accepted the glass gratefully. "That sounds like heaven."

She savored the complex, aromatic wine as she gazed at the photographs. They were stark, dynamic, full of high contrasts. One showed a young man diving off a cliff into a lake. He was still upright, his body starting to jackknife, his face a grimace of concentration.

She peered more closely and realized that it was Duncan's brother, Bruce.

She took a closer look at all of them. There was a young girl, curled up asleep, her mouth open. The same girl again, older, laughing, swinging on a rope swing, hair flying like a banner. She was pretty, with the same narrow face and uptilting eyebrows as Duncan. Then a photograph of a handsome older woman in profile, staring off a porch, smoking a cigarette. She looked like Bruce. Mother. Family.

There were landscapes, too. Deserts and mountains, barren and stark. Cruelly sharp contrasts of light and shadow made them almost like moonscapes. They were lonely, strange, aching. Very personal.

She called back to the kitchen. "Did you take the pictures?"

"Yeah."

"They're beautiful," she said. "Is there one of your father here?"

He came out of the kitchen and leaned against the entryway, sipping his wine. "No. He's long gone. Haven't seen him in years. Off in California, working on his fifth wife. She's welcome to him."

"Oh." She stared down into the cup of bloodred wine. "I think I can one-up you there. I doubt my father even knows of my existence."

"No? Your mom kept it a secret from him?"

"In a manner of speaking. Are these landscapes Afghanistan?"

His brow furrowed. "What do you know about Afghanistan?"

"Bruce told me you were stationed there. That you were a spy."

He grunted. "Bruce babbles about things he knows shit about."

"So? Did you take them there?" she prodded him, staring at a picture of jagged mountain peaks, the sun a blazing halo behind them.

"Yes, most of them," he said.

"Was that where you learned to fight like that?" she asked.

He hesitated. "More or less."

"Amazing photos," she offered. "I wouldn't have dreamed that you had an artistic side."

He looked uncomfortable. "I wouldn't call it that."

"Heaven forbid that you engage in something as frivolous as art."

He crossed his arms over his chest. "Are you busting my balls?"

"No. I just like your pictures. I like what they say about you."

He looked alarmed. "What do you mean? What do they say?"

"Relax," she soothed. "I couldn't tell you in words. I can't discuss visual art intelligently. I just . . . I like the way they make me feel."

A cautious smile started in his narrowed eyes. "Thank you."

Duncan slowly lifted his glass. She lifted her own in response. Toasting rare, delicate perfect moments of connection, the kind that got her worked up and longing for things she could not have. The tinkle of crystal was a chime, sweet and faint as a blown kiss. The sound of an unspoken pact, delicately sealed. *Stop it, D'Onofrio.* She had to stop projecting wishful fantasies onto every single interaction. It was stupid.

She'd been privately dubious about eating pasta at two in the morning after an evening like this, but when he set the plate loaded with plump ravioli, red sauce, and a generous dusting of savory pecorino, something inside her stood up and cheered. It smelled superb.

They ate in silence, every last bite, and afterward, he watched her finish her wine. His unwavering gaze made heat rise in her face.

"I expect you want a shower," he said.

She nodded, mutely.

"The best one is off my bedroom," he said. "Come this way."

Ah. Well, he could hardly be blamed for assuming, she thought wildly, as she followed him and her suitcase down the hall. Was this what she'd intended? And if not this, then what? *Get real. Calm down.*

He didn't join her in the shower. Part of her was disappointed. She stayed in the pounding hot water, pondering it.

Duncan Burke was wrong for her. She'd known it in the restaurant. His mind was wired in a way that was foreign to her. He would annoy, insult, and disillusion her. He already had. He would again. It was a sure thing. A death-and-taxes type of sure thing.

This was set against the fact that he aroused her to a screaming pitch of excitement, he was an incredibly gifted lover, and he'd saved her life tonight. He'd used his body as a shield when that guy was pointing a gun at her. He was a good guy, beneath his hard edges. Brave, valiant, self-sacrificing. Incompatible or not. Insensitive or not.

And she wanted him. Bad.

When she got out of the shower, her decision was irrevocable. She toweled off, let her hair out of its clip, and shook it loose.

She hung the towel carefully back on the rack, and looked at herself in the mirror, naked but for the little pendent with the *A* in tiny rubies that Lucia had given her. Hanging right between those rather large breasts that had always embarrassed her. She'd felt since she was twelve or so as if her curvy body were flaunting itself to the world against her will, demanding attention that she did not actually want.

But Duncan seemed to like it. Finally, those boobs were good for something. She reached up, touched them gently. They were much more sensitive than usual. Goose-bumped with delicious anticipation at the thought of what lay ahead. Her nipples tightened.

She walked out into his bedroom like that. He had showered, too, in another bathroom, and wore a terry cloth robe. He glanced over, did a double take. "Ah . . . holy God. You're . . . just look at you."

"Did I thank you for saving my life?" she demanded.

He looked alarmed. "Yeah, but you don't have to thank me by—"

"Shut up, Burke. Make love to me now, before I lose my nerve."

He blinked. "Ah, okay," he said hoarsely. He started toward her.

"I know this is a mistake," she announced.

He stopped, looking perplexed. "It is?"

"Yes," she told him. "But I don't care. I'll pay whatever price I have to pay. Life's too short. I figured that out when those guys shoved me into the car. It could all go away so quickly. And I want to feel this."

He touched his finger gently to her lips. "Shhh. Don't work yourself into a state," he soothed. "How much wine did you drink?"

"This is not about wine!" she yelled. "I know exactly what I'm saying and doing, Duncan Burke! Don't you dare condescend to me!"

"How could I?" he asked, dryly. "You're terrifying."

"Oh, yeah? Do I intimidate you?" She put her hands on her hips.

"Some of me." He tossed off his robe, displaying his naked body and his huge erection. "Other parts of me are fucking fearless."

She stared at him. He was so perfect. Tall, broad, those lean, defined, capable-looking muscles, just the right amount of hair, beautiful thighs and flanks, long, narrow feet. And his penis. Oh, boy.

She wanted to read him like braille. Lick him like a lollipop.

He tossed the comforter back and pushed her until she tumbled backward onto the silvery sheet. It was cool against her damp skin. She scrambled up, curling her knees beneath her.

He stood there, erection bobbing right before her eyes. He started to speak, and stopped himself. His face looked grim.

"What?" she demanded. "What is it? What's wrong?"

His throat bobbed. "I don't want to fuck this up again."

The raw, lost tone in his voice startled her into a rush of tenderness. She had been so overcome by her own reaction to him, it never occurred to her that he could feel vulnerable, too. The thought gave her a somewhat unwelcome sense of power. It reminded her of her mother. Elena had wielded power over men, whenever and however she could. And yet, she had died all alone. No one but Nell at her funeral.

She pushed the thought away. "You won't fuck up," she said. "You did fine in the conference room. You almost made my heart stop."

"As long as I kept my mouth shut," he said sourly. "I have an adrenaline hard-on that would drive nails. My hands are still shaking. I am not in control. At all. And I do not like it."

She hid her smile, sensing that he would not appreciate it. Instead, she ran her finger around the swollen tip of his cock. "Strange," she mused. "This ravenous, howling-at-the-moon beast managed to bring me to his fancy home, cook me a nice dinner, pour me wine, chat about art. Such savagery really chills the blood. Besides, I thought sex was all about losing control."

He shook his head. "Not when you're as big as me. I could hurt you." His voice was a shaking rasp. "I can't afford to make any wrong moves with you. You are a fucking minefield, Nell D'Onofrio."

She swirled her whole hand around him, making the tendons stand out on his throat. "Sorry I'm so difficult," she murmured.

He clambered onto the bed, dragging her close until their bodies touched. His heat was a sweet shock. The sheer mass of him, the crackling energy, his own male scent overlaid with perfumes of his soap and shampoo. He made her mouth water. She moistened her hand with the slick drops of pre-come, and began milking the long, broad stalk. "I think it would be exciting to make you lose control," she told him.

"We're not going there." He slid his hand between her legs, teasing her tender folds open, sighing when he found her already wet and slick.

"We're not?" She caressed him, two handed, long, tight, sliding strokes while his fingers delved. They stared into each other's eyes, fighting for breath. She squirmed around his fingers. "I'm not afraid of you," she said, breathlessly, for no reason she could understand.

And it was true. She'd changed. That was why the sex was so good. Apart from his very considerable talent, of course.

He reached down and trapped her hand at his cock, holding it motionless. "Do not provoke me. I'm walking a knife's edge, as it is."

She swirled her fingertip on the pre-come dripping off his penis. Then with the same finger, she gave his chest a tiny shove.

"What's that about?" he demanded. "You pushing me away?"

She smiled at him, mysteriously up through her lashes. "No," she murmured. "That's me, pushing you off your knife's edge."

He shoved her onto her back. "You asked for it."

"Sure did," she agreed. "Don't make me ask you twice."

She wiggled beneath his big body while he rolled the latex onto himself, lungs locked with excitement. He nudged against her, pushing until her body finally yielded, until she was gasping with the pressure of that broad bulb, caressing her sensitive inner flesh. She tried to move, but she could barely budge. He shoved deeper.

She was so primed, she came almost instantly, with a gasping shriek. Duncan stopped moving as she convulsed around him, his breath hissing. When the climax had widened out to a glowing ripple of residual pleasure, he hooked her legs up over his elbows and began.

He rode her hard, and she loved it. She gripped his arms, bracing herself against each jarring thrust. She was a hot shimmer melting for him. Long, sobbing spasms of delight rippled out into everywhere.

He got up some immeasurable time later, got rid of the condom. Then he slid back between the sheets and clutched her against his big, hot chest. She snuggled against him, suspended in a liquid dream.

Only a tiny, needle-thin part of her mind stayed apart, wondering how long the dream could possibly last.

Duncan was disoriented when he woke. He'd trained himself to wake at a quarter to five a.m. He was used to having his eyes open while the sky was dark, mind clear and sharp and already generating a streamlined plan of attack for the day's work.

The sky was not dark. The room was flooded with sunshine. And his mind was not sharp. It was drugged with a strange sensation of intense well-being. He was intoxicated with the scent of dark ringlets that tickled his nose. He was unbalanced by a rush of startled joy.

Nell. In his bed. He couldn't get over how soft she was. Her skin beneath his hands, as fine as a baby's. She slept, her back to him, her round, rosy ass pressed against his hips. With predictable consequence.

The urge to roll her onto her belly, mount up and slide into that hot grip of her luscious body took all his mental muscle to withstand. Too dangerous. He had no idea how she would feel when she woke.

Better that she not wake up with his cock already inside her.

He nuzzled her neck, instead. The graceful angle of bones and tendons under her soft skin, that little brown mole, the way the grain of her hair swirled in those wild vortices at her nape. The responsive skin there, perfumed and decorated with fine fuzz. The fine white-gold chain.

He scooted back, just far enough to let her roll onto her back, so he could properly admire her tits. God. World class. So full and soft, jiggling, the way they swelled out, the tight brown nipples. The glittering pendant lay on her collarbone, a bright point of light.

His self-control failed him. He cupped her tits in his hands and pressed his face against that soft bounty, and something snapped.

He went wild with hungry licking and suckling. That woke her up in a hurry. She stiffened, with a gasp that soon became a whimper. Her arms twined around his neck, her back arched. Offering her tits to him.

He'd rolled over so that he lay between her legs, and now she opened them wide, tilting her hips in instinctive invitation.

His body had no hope of refusing it. He grabbed his rigid cock, held it at the right angle until he got it wedged inside, and shoved.

So good. Hot. A slow, excruciatingly tight, naked slide. "Oh, fuck," he gasped. So much for eloquence. So much for poetry.

Her eyes popped open. She and Duncan froze. No need to speak. They both remembered the latex at the same moment. But it was too fucking good to resist. He rocked, sliding. So wet, so amazingly hot.

"I won't come inside you," he promised, his voice ragged.

"But I . . . we haven't even discussed—"

"I'm safe," he promised. "Tested negative for everything on my last physical. Never do it without condoms. Never. Only with you. I know it's stupid, but I can't . . . stop. You drive me out of my fucking mind."

She wiggled around him, her eyes big and dazed. "I'm safe, too, diseasewise. But I'm not on the pill, or anything."

He slid slowly deeper, until she hugged his whole length, and his cockhead pressed against the mouth of her womb. "I'll be careful," he begged. "I won't come. I'll be good. I swear."

She laughed, jerkily. "You're always good. That's not the issue."

"There is no issue. I just won't. Please, Nell."

She lifted herself against him in answer, and they were off at a wild, hard gallop. His body had an agenda all its own. He wanted to explode with each urgent stroke. The scalding liquid of her lube, the shocking immediacy of naked skin to skin, like nothing he'd ever dreamed, ever known. It revealed spaces in his mind that he'd never known were there. Sex had never taken him into other realms of consciousness before, much as he'd enjoyed it.

It was Nell who took him there. She was poetry, she was music, she was red hot, honeyed perfection. He lifted himself up so he could see every detail of their joining. The root of his cock, gleaming with her lube, her tender pink pussy lips stretched around it, kissing and caressing him as he plunged and surged, his body locked in motion. Her soft, shapely white thighs open for him, the lush curves, her tits jiggling with each hard thrust. The look in her huge eyes made something break open in his chest, but there was no time to be afraid of what he found in there, because his body was charging ahead, following the beacon of her impending orgasm. He drove her to the edge, over—

He wrenched his cock out just in time, spurted all over her belly, her breasts. He collapsed beside her, panting and shy. Hid his face against her neck. Felt the golden chain of her necklace against his lips.

"That was, um, crazy," she whispered finally, after a few minutes.

He lifted his head. "No. That was excellent," he replied forcefully.

She pulled away from him, and slid off the bed, mumbling something he could barely make out about taking a shower.

"I'll make you breakfast," he called after her disappearing back, just before the bathroom door clicked shut.

He was incapable of being disheartened by that, after such explosive sex, so he just yanked on a pair of sweatpants and got up. His eye slid over the small silver digital clock that sat on his dresser.

Nine thirty-seven. His jaw sagged. He was usually up at four-thirty. Out the door before five. Working out at the gym until six-forty. In the office by seven, maximum seven-ten. Granted, yesterday had been an unusual night. So had this morning been. So far.

Well, hell. Being the boss had to be good for something. Who knew? He might even get lucky again. That happy thought floated him right up off his feet and into the kitchen, to root around for breakfast for her. The phone rang as he was rummaging in the fridge. Nobody used this landline. Everyone else he knew called his cell. It could only be his mother. Of all times. Christ. He picked up the phone. "Yeah?"

"Duncan, honey! Thank goodness! I called the office, but you weren't there! What on earth?" She paused, significantly. "Are you sick? Is anything wrong? You never stay home from work!"

"I'm fine," he said brusquely. "Just taking a morning, working at home. What's going on?"

"It's Elinor. You will not believe what she's done!"

Duncan dutifully responded to his cue. "What about her?" Elinor was his sister, a sophomore at New York University.

"She's switched her major to theater arts! She dropped her business courses and signed up for theater history and dance! She wants to be an actress!" His mother's voice cracked with horror.

He stared at the scabbed-up scrapes on his knuckles, flexed them so they wouldn't stiffen. "So? It's her decision."

"It's madness to go into theater! You have to talk sense into her!"

He glanced toward the corridor, out of which his problematic sexy siren would issue. Check him out. No longer the poster boy for doing the sensible thing. Even so, he didn't want to get into it with his mother today. "I'll talk to her, if you want," he offered.

"Oh, thank you, darling. She'll listen to you. It's not too late to change her major back." His mother's voice was relieved.

"Okay, Mom." He hung up, and dove back into the fridge again.

Nell appeared in the doorway just as he was laying out French toast, grilled ham, and orange juice on the table. She looked damp and rosy and fragrant. She gazed at the food-laden table, her eyes big.

"Hope you're hungry," he said.

She sat down with a murmur of appreciation and tucked in a gratifying amount of what he'd cooked. After breakfast, they sipped their coffee and stared at each other across the table. Neither of them were able to hold the other's gaze for more than a few seconds without looking away, or laughing. Jesus. Look at him. Giggling. Touching her toes under the table, with his own bare feet. Acting like a goofy kid.

But it was getting on toward ten-thirty, and he had to get his shit together. "I have to get down to the office," he said reluctantly.

She glanced at the clock. "Me, too. I'm going to be late for the lunch prep, as it is." She let out a gasp when his hand shot out and grabbed her wrist. She stared at it.

He did not let go. "You are going where?"

Her eyes got big and wary. "Duncan. Let go of my arm."

"Just answer my question."

"Isn't it obvious? To work! At the Sunset Grill! Remember?" She yanked at her wrist again. "Hello! I work there six days a week!"

"After what happened to you last night, you think I'll let you walk out onto the streets? Just like that? Like nothing even happened?"

"Let me?" She straightened up. "You aren't going to 'let me' do anything. I do not have to ask your permission. For anything I do."

"Wrong," he said.

She stared at him, outraged. "Excuse me?"

"If I hadn't been there last night, you'd be dead, or God knows what else. I changed the course of things. That gives me responsibility. That gives me a say. So deal with me, Nell. You don't have any choice."

Her eyes were wide. "Let go of my arm. You're scaring me."

"Fine," he said. "You should be scared. It's about fucking time."

He slowly let go of her wrist. She rubbed it, avoiding his eyes. "You don't understand," she said. "I am flat broke. The Fiend situation ate up all my savings. I'm already a month behind on my rent. I don't even have money for cab fare if I don't get out there and go to work."

"I'll give you money, if you need some," he said.

Her face tightened. "That's not a solution, Duncan."

"No? And having you waltz out into the street, you call that a solution? They picked you up off a main thoroughfare, Nell. In downtown Manhattan, in front of multiple witnesses! By now, they know who I am, and where I live. They'll nail you down. Count on it."

She shut her eyes, looking exhausted and lost. "Duncan, I don't have any choice but to work. I have to pay my rent, and I—"

"Oh, yeah. You mean that place with the bugged phone, the compromised alarm, and the hostile vidcams?"

"I still have to pay for it, and find some other place to—"

"Here," he cut in rashly. "Stay here. With me."

She gazed at him for a few moments, blankly.

"There's plenty of room," he urged her. "The security's excellent."

Nell tossed up her hands. "Duncan," she said helplessly. "That's very sweet, but it's premature, and in any case, I still have to work."

"No, you don't. And it's not premature, after last night. Work on game texts, if you have to work on something." He stared at her back for a moment. "I don't need help with the rent or the groceries, Nell."

"I noticed that." Her voice was acid. "So what does this mean?"

He shrugged. "What does it sound like?"

She swiveled her head, fixed him with a piercing gaze. "It sounds to me like I'd be kept."

"It sounds to me like you'd be safe," he countered.

"Safe, and sexually available to you, twenty-four hours a day?"

That made him angry. "Would that be so terrible?" he demanded.

She shook his words away with an angry flip of her hand. "The sex is not the problem."

"Oh? Then what is your fucking problem, Nell? Is it money? Yeah, I've got a lot of it. Big fucking deal. I worked for it. You want to punish me for having it? Fuck that! That's not fair!"

"No," she snapped. "It's not that."

"Then why are you so uptight about accepting any help from me?" he snarled. "Because it is starting to mortally piss me off!"

She held her hand over her mouth for a moment and cleared her throat. "My mother was a prostitute," she said.

Of all the things she could have said, that was the very last one he expected. "Huh?" he floundered. "You don't mean . . . the lady who . . ."

"No. That was Lucia, my adoptive mother." Nell's voice was colorless. "I'm talking about my birth mother. Her name was Elena Pisani. She wasn't a streetwalking kind of prostitute. She was always kept in style by her lovers. Nice apartments, beautiful clothes, jewels, spas. But in the end, that part's just window dressing."

A heavy silence followed her words, and Duncan struggled for something intelligent to say. "Why are you telling me this?" he asked.

She fixed him with her blazing look, the one that took his breath away, scared him and aroused him, all at once. "I remember her hammering out the details of each new mutually beneficial arrangement. As soon as she was done, off I'd go to another boarding school. Until the guy got bored. Or she found a richer client."

He searched for a place to put this new and extremely dangerous information, but it wouldn't stick to anything. "Ah. Oh. I, uh, see."

"Do you?" She looked away. "It looked all right on the surface, I guess. She handpicked her lovers. They were always rich. She lived in beautiful places. But her whole existence was in function of her patrons. Their egos, their convenience, their tempers. She didn't have energy to spare for me. Being beautiful, charming, seductive, and entertaining is hard work. Doesn't leave much time for a kid."

"I . . . ah—" He floundered for something to say that was not either stupid or offensive, but he couldn't think of anything.

"I don't want that," she said. "I don't want a man to be in the center of my life, and me circling around him, anxiously scrambling to please him. Hell with that. I've got plans. I have ambitions of my own."

"I never meant to imply that," he said, helplessly.

"I'm sorry this embarrasses you," she said. "It embarrasses me. But I want you to know why I feel so strongly about this. I am not for sale. Not to anyone, for any reason. Not even for protection from the Fiend. Now, or ever. Because that mutually beneficial arrangement you were talking about last night? It's not a good bargain, whatever it might look like. Not even if the sex is great. It wouldn't benefit me. On the contrary. Eventually, I'd start to feel about two inches tall."

He pondered what she said for several moments. Then he walked slowly around her, pried her clasped hands apart, and held them tightly.

"You misunderstood," he said. "It was just semantics."

She stared into his eyes, trying to peer inside his brain. "Was it?"

"I would never dream that you were for sale." His fantasy of the sexy secret affair with the juvenile waitress flashed guiltily through his mind, but the point was moot, because Nell was not that girl.

Nell was infinitely more than that girl. More complicated, more fascinating, more trouble. And she never needed to know about his politically incorrect horn-dog fantasies. He lifted her hands to his lips. "What happened between us can't be bought," he said. "For any money."

She heard the raw, blunt sincerity in his words and blushed. "Thank you for saying that," she said softly.

He kissed her hands in answer, and couldn't stop kissing them. Those long, tapered fingers, those pink oval nails. Funny. He'd never noticed a woman's hands before.

"But I still have to go to work," she persisted. "Maybe if you could spot me the cab fare this morning, I'll pay you back from my tips."

He bit down on his frustration. "I will drive you," he ground out. "On one condition. You do not leave the restaurant until I come to pick you up and take you to my office. No errands, no breaks, no shopping, no bank machines, no Starbucks coffee, nothing. Is that clear?"

She sighed heavily. He cut her off before she could object again.

"Let me put it this way," he said. "Do it as a favor to me. Because I care. I'm scared for you. I've earned that much."

"Duncan—"

"Whoops! Sorry. Let me take that back, about earning anything. It's not about earning. No way. No economic metaphors here. No, sir."

She tried not to smile. "Don't make fun of me. This is serious."

"Christ, yes! That's what I've been trying to tell you!"

"But I have to go to that seisìun at Malloy's, too. I have a date to meet my sisters later this evening," she informed him. "I have to go."

"I'll take you to that, too. And then I'll take you home." He stared keenly into her eyes, and added, deliberately, "My home."

She cocked her head at him. "Surely you have better things to do than chauffeur me around the city and listen to Irish tunes in a pub."

"No. Just, you know, making money. But I've got enough of that to piss you off already, so I might as well slow down, right?"

Her eyes flashed. "Do not make fun of me."

"Sorry," he said meekly. "I would really like to meet your sisters."

That mollified her. "All right. But that's a dirty trick, you know."

He blinked up at her, all innocence. "Trick? What trick?"

"You get me softened up, and go into supercontrol mode."

He grunted. "Whatever works."

They stared at each other, and, like always, the oxygen in the air between them began to combust. But she darted back when he reached for her. "Uh-uh! We're late, remember?"

He headed for the shower, trying to breathe his spring-loaded, rock-hard boner down and concentrate on the task at hand. First, haul out his old SIG Sauer 229 and a full clip of ammo. Root around in his utilities drawers for the shoulder holster. Identify the suits in his closet that were tailored to accommodate it. Then bathe, dress. Pull it together. His heart pounded. His palms were damp.

Only the thought of her in his bed again tonight consoled him.

Chapter
7

Nell listened, guiltily, to the sound of the shower through the bathroom door. Thinking of his amazing, powerful naked body in there under the pounding stream, water and soapsuds cascading over his contoured muscles. So tempted to just peel off her clothes, and—

No. He was never quick. It would be long and wet and steaming and soapy and marvelous, and they would both forget all practical issues such as making money, safeguarding her self-respect, meeting her professional obligations. She was already missing the lunch prep. He'd completely disarmed her. Wrapped her around his little finger.

Or maybe she was wrapped around something more substantial.

She stared at the suit he'd slung upon the bed. She didn't know much about fashion, having remained deliberately ignorant, but she recognized the cut and fine finishing of costly men's clothing when she saw it. Thousands of dollars lay there on that rumpled bed, in those smooth, graceful silver gray garments. He looked so good in his clothes.

She went back out into the front room. The roses still lay where she'd forgotten them on the telephone table. They hadn't been put into water, what with one thing and another, and they were looking shabby.

Which was a shame. She grabbed the flowers, with the half-formed intention of looking for a vase in the kitchen. What a sweet thought, last night, for him to stop and get her roses. Some of the roses disintegrated, bruised petals scattering over the gleaming wood floor. She gathered them up, hesitated for a moment, and pulled a handful of silky petals off the wilting bouquet.

She carried them into his bedroom and slipped some into the pockets of his suit jacket with them.

He was all brusque practicality when he came out of the bedroom, clean-shaven and fragrant. Their cautious truce lasted all the way down to the Sunset Grill, but as she was getting out, he pulled her toward him and gave her a hard, possessive kiss. "One more thing, Nell."

"It's always one more thing," she grumbled. "Enough things."

"That's for me to decide," he said, with his usual breathtaking arrogance. He pulled a cell phone out of his pocket. An extravagant, eight-hundred-dollar one. "Take this. Keep it. No arguments."

She rolled her eyes. "I was going to buy one today anyhow."

"You can't," he said. "You swore a blood oath that you would not leave the restaurant until I came to get you. Remember?"

A shivery burst of laughter shook her. "A blood oath?"

"Fuck, yes. Take it. Don't fight me on this. Keep it until I have a chance to take you phone shopping. My number's programmed in."

He looked straight into her eyes, his fingers clamped around her wrist, and she realized that she could not win. He simply would not let her go unless she gave in, and for God's sake, why didn't she? She was fighting just on principle, just to be contrary. She couldn't afford this silliness.

She slipped the phone into her purse. "Thank you," she said.

"Keep it in your apron pocket at the restaurant, while you're working," he said. "I'll be calling, to check on you. And I'm going to give you holy hell if you're not reachable. Believe it."

She snorted at him. "I'm shaking in my boots."

The guy worked fast. Fucking her, already.

John chewed the inside of his own cheek until he tasted blood.

Antonella disappeared into the Sunset Grill, still smiling. Her face rosy red. Probably saddlesore from being fucked all night long. Slut.

Burke's silver Mercedes pulled out into Eighth Avenue traffic.

It made him angry, and he was already chronically angry, dealing with Haupt night and day. He was starting to consider recreational murder, just to unload, or he was going to start having panic attacks.

Amazing, that the guy was fucking her already. She'd been so celibate all those weeks that John had been watching her. Such a good little girl. Sleeping alone, with her piles of books, like a sexy, succulent little nun. Not anymore. Dirty whore, spoiling it. She would pay for that.

Not that John wasn't still going to enjoy his own turn when it came, as it inevitably would. But he would have to punish her severely for spreading her legs. Soiling herself with that rich prick. Just like her sister, cheating on him with that randy carpenter. Who was slated to die a slow and ugly death. Just as soon as it was convenient for John.

Maybe Burke would join the carpenter on John's special short list. He wondered idly if the youngest girl was as much of a slut as her sisters were. Probably more so, with that tattoo, her nose ring, her painted van. What the hell. He'd fuck them all. Punish them all. And punish them, and punish them. Thinking about it made him hard.

But speed dialing Haupt's number on his cell wilted him fast. He gritted his teeth, resigned to the scolding he was about to receive.

The stinking geezer picked up, with no salutation. He just waited for a report, line open. Telegraphing his disgust with silence.

"She's back at the restaurant," John said. "Burke brought her in his own car. Looks like he's fucking her."

"And upon what do you base this deduction?"

John's lip curled at the old fart's choice of words. "The way he stuck his tongue down her throat was my first clue."

"Tell me about Burke," the old guy challenged him.

John rifled through the documents he'd spent a long night collecting. "Bad news," he admitted. "Ex–undercover field agent from the NSA, turned successful businessman. Designs software for the NSA, the CIA, Homeland Security, and various others. Close connections with various law enforcement agencies. I had difficulty getting info on him. Most of it's top secret."

"Ah. You must be happy, John. Now you have a plausible justification for your incompetence, eh?"

John tapped the console of the SUV with his fingernails and considered various tasty options in killing this old shitbird. After he'd gotten paid, of course. In fact, he was starting to consider fucking the old goat out of the entire prize. It was the only thing that could make this constant, grinding humiliation worthwhile.

"It does make things more complicated," he said carefully.

"Yes, and the idiot carpenter with his violin complicated things for you too, eh? And he was no secret agent. Did Turturro have any luck with the younger sister?"

"No," he said, after a painful pause. "He combed that crafts fair for hours. Apparently she never showed up."

"Of course she did not. She is not an idiot, unlike others I could name. Stay on Antonella, John. Do not delegate. Do not lose her again. Your hired muscle so far has not failed to disappoint. Did she take anything with a listening device with her when she went to Burke's apartment?"

"Just the laptop. It has a short range, however."

"I'm no longer interested in excuses. Find a place to receive the frequency, no matter where she is. Failure is no longer an option."

Haupt hung up on him. John's teeth ground until his jaw ached.

He was going to need to kill something soon. And he had a feeling it was going to be that prick who was fucking Antonella. Yes, that would be good. John was still smarting from the man's brazen challenge.

You're not getting her. Fuck off and die, shithead. Yeah? His ass.

Burke would die for that. And Antonella would pay, and pay.

It was the strangest sensation. Duncan observed it curiously as he drove to the office, parked, and tipped the astonished garage attendant. Like a helium balloon in his midriff. The buoyancy floated him along. People were giving him strange looks.

He realized that he was grinning like a fucking idiot.

Jesus, it wasn't totally abnormal to be in a good mood, was it?

Then the middle-aged lady behind the coffee counter in the building lobby gave him a strange look when he told her he liked her as a redhead. It was the truth. She'd looked like hell as a blonde.

Strange. Like nobody'd ever seen a guy in a good mood before.

He headed up to the office, whistling. The grizzled divorce attorney in the elevator gave him a dark look. Duncan grinned back. The man harrumphed. Maybe dealing with divorce all day gave a guy gastritis.

He strode into the lobby. Derek was there, briskly collating something, dressed for Saturday in jeans and a T-shirt.

"Good morning, Derek," he said.

Derek looked at him as if he'd sprouted wings. "Uh, hi, boss."

"I appreciate you working Saturdays," Duncan told him.

Derek's eyes bulged even more than usual. "Uh, it's no problem."

Duncan clapped him on the shoulder as he passed Derek's desk. "You get paid extra for Saturdays, right?"

"I get time and a half for overtime." Derek's face was fearful.

"Good. I'll tack on a bonus. You deserve it. Keep it up, Derek."

Odd, Duncan mused as he nodded and smiled at the die-hard Saturday-morning types. Derek didn't blink an eye when Duncan snapped and barked, but a simple compliment scared him to death.

Come to think of it, all his employees were giving him that nervous look. Duncan glanced down to see if his shoes were mismatched, his fly unzipped. Nope. Everything was in order.

He shrugged, inwardly. Fuck it. He was having too much fun floating on his own private helium balloon to worry about it.

The phone began to ring the second he walked into his office. His private line. Nell, maybe, calling to tell him she was in as good a mood as he was. This daydream was quickly deflated by the recollection that she did not possess his private office number. Only his cell.

Answering the phone became suddenly a lot less appealing.

He sighed and grabbed the phone. "Burke here."

"So, you finally came into the office!" his mother said. "What on earth is going on?" She paused expectantly.

"Nothing," he said. "Business as usual."

"Whatever you say. If you don't tell me, I'll just have to find out some other way. Have you talked to Elinor?"

Duncan's good mood began to sink. "I haven't had time yet."

"Duncan, it's so important that she change her mind! She's determined to rebel. Please, you have to back me up on this—"

"I'll call her," he promised. "As soon as you get off the phone."

He extricated himself from the conversation and punched in Elinor's number. Her roommate, Mimi, picked up the phone. Loud, incoherent music pulsed in the background. "Who is it?" Mimi shrieked.

"Elinor's brother. May I speak to her?"

"Elinor's brother? Like, which one? The bodaciously cute one, or the uptight, stuffed-shirt one?"

"The stuffed-shirt one," he specified, with weary patience.

"Yo, Ellie!" Mimi screeched. Duncan winced and held the phone away from his ear. "It's your bro. The stuffed-shirt one." Mimi listened, and said, "She's coming. Hang on." There was a clunk. Duncan leaned back in his chair, started to shrug off his coat, and stopped. The SIG.

Shit. He had to keep it on, sweat and all. He stuck his hand in his pocket and gasped at the soft, silky texture that assaulted his hand.

Petals. He jerked his hand out, startled. Rose petals scattered all over the desk, his chair, his lap, the floor.

He laughed out loud, causing a graphic designer and a junior accountant to peer through his open door, eyes big. They probably thought he was losing it. Maybe he was, he thought, with delirious glee.

"Hello? Hello?"

He yanked his attention back to the telephone. "It's Duncan."

"Hi." Elinor sounded guarded. "Did Mother tell you to call?"

Duncan paused for a second. "Well—"

"Your job is to convince me to change my major back to econ. Consider my retirement plan, split-level suburban home, SUV, and cemetery plot, right? Not! Forget it. I'm going to follow my dreams!"

"I think that's great," Duncan said.

There was an uncertain pause. Elinor pressed on. "You can't make me change my mind. I've got what it takes to—"

"Of course you do," he agreed.

There was a confused silence from Elinor. "What?"

"You'll be great. Go for it. Give it your best shot."

Elinor was stupefied. " You're not being sarcastic, are you?"

Duncan sifted petals through his fingers. "Am I such an ogre?"

"I was just wondering if, you know, an alien took over your body."

"Hah." He buried his nose in the petals. Like Nell's skin.

"Mother's gonna kill you," Elinor predicted cheerfully.

"No doubt," he agreed. He said good-bye and hung up, staring at the crimson mass of rose petals. His helium balloon reinflated, floating him up off his chair. He was done being the official wet blanket of the family. He entered the number of the cell he'd given Nell, and fingered a petal while it rang, savoring the agony of anticipation.

"Hello?" came her sweet, musical voice.

"I found the petals," he announced.

In her pause, he could actually feel her smiling that secret little smile that drove him wild. "And? I hope they didn't embarrass you."

"Nothing could embarrass me today."

There was a shy silence. "Um, Duncan? I'm sort of in the middle of the lunch rush, so could we—"

"Do rose petals go bad, like vegetables, or do they dry out?"

"They dry out," Nell said. "Do you think I would have filled your pockets with something that turns to slime?"

He ignored that, grinning. "I can't wait for six o'clock."

"Me neither," Nell whispered. "Bye."

She broke the connection, and Duncan laid down the phone.

He tried to concentrate. He really did. But the urgent, pressing, serious business that grimly occupied him on any other normal day seemed so much less important today. So much less interesting. The only things that engaged him were conversations with Gant and his buddy Braxton, another ex-agent from the old days who had a security outfit. He arranged for Nell's apartment to be bug swept that day.

He called Nell so often, she started to snap at him and hang up, but always with laughter in her voice. He'd never been the type who had any luck making girls laugh before. He finally understood why guys worked so hard at it. It was irresistible. He would do any crazy thing to get that gurgle of laughter out of her.

Meetings, conference calls. Seconds ticked by, heavily, laboriously. His employees were acting strange. Whispering conversations, cut off when he walked by. Smothered bursts of laughter. Bruce had a shit-eating grin plastered on his face.

At ten to five p.m., he gave in to it. It was an hour early, but he wasn't getting diddly-shit done here. He might as well go to the Sunset, park his ass, and make damn sure she didn't leave the place alone.

She was scheduled to work three hours on the game texts with Bruce, from six until nine. Too much, with a long shift of waitressing behind her. She pushed herself too hard. He might insist that she cut out early. They could get dinner before they met her sisters at that pub.

He found a good parking spot not far from the Grill and went in, heart thudding. There she was, swathed in her orange apron, hair twisted up and corkscrewing around her face. She looked tired, harassed.

And freaking drop-dead beautiful.

She glanced over and ran into a table. He was with her in two steps, steadying her tray. She pulled back, spilling half a bowl of French onion soup. "Thanks, I can manage. What are you doing here?"

"It's a restaurant, right? Don't I have the right to come in here?"

"Yes, of course. Sorry," she said, biting her lower lip. "The tables are full. You can wait fifteen minutes, or you can sit at the counter."

Duncan seated himself at the counter. The place was hopping with late lunchers and early diners. Nell and a redheaded girl were the only waitresses, both running frantically. He watched Nell serve people, gracing them with her luminous smile, carrying trays that looked far too heavy for her. She sneaked an occasional glance at him. Some minutes later she made it back to him with the coffeepot. "Stop staring. It's making me nervous," she hissed into his ear, pouring him a cup.

"What's with you tonight?" he asked. "You're tense."

"Oh, nothing. Business as usual. Money problems. Credit card debt. A bugged apartment. Armed kidnappers shoving me into a car. Nights of wild monkey sex with a man who's practically a stranger to me. Then I get to work and discover that not only does Kendra have one of her weird illnesses, but Lee broke his toe, so we're short-staffed. And now you're here, staring at me like I've got two heads. Other than that, I'm fine. Let me take your order. Strip steak, I presume."

"Actually, I ordered out for lunch," he said.

Her eyebrow lifted. "Then why are you here?"

"I wanted to see you," he said simply. "I couldn't wait anymore."

She swallowed, a blush warming her cheeks. "We have a three-dollar minimum at night."

"More coffee," he said. "And bring my usual dessert."

She looked disapproving. "You should try something new." She marched away, chin high.

"So. You're the one, eh?" a gravelly female voice said.

He looked across the counter, into the clear gray eyes of a strong-jawed, wide-hipped lady of about sixty. "Excuse me?" he said.

The woman smartly dressed a tray of salads and passed it across the counter to the redheaded waitress. The waitress hung over Duncan's shoulder from behind, popped fragrant strawbery gum in his ear, and studied him as if he were some strange species of mold in a petri dish. "Not bad," she commented, her voice judicious.

"I'm Norma," the older woman said, examining him over the lenses of her glasses. "I own this joint. And you're Strip Steak."

Being defined and labeled in terms of his lunch choices was a new experience for him. "Duncan Burke, at your service," he said.

"So you're the one," Norma said again, wrapping silverware in napkins and stacking them on a tray with machinelike efficiency.

He sipped his coffee. "What one am I?" he asked guardedly.

"The one who's taking away my right-hand woman."

"Sorry, ma'am, but it's a dog-eat-dog world out there," he said.

"Don't I know it," Norma replied, her gray eyes steely. "In fact, I'd like to take this opportunity to tell you what a prize you've got in her."

Duncan's coffee cup froze halfway to his mouth.

Norma went on. "I heard about that kerfuffle last night. You, saving her from those guys on the street. That's good. Bravo. I like it that you can handle yourself in a tight situation. That's a good quality in a man. Useful. But that's not enough."

Duncan blinked. "It's not?"

"No. Not for Nell. She's special. Very sensitive, very romantic. She has more to give than you could imagine."

He started to feel hunted. "How do you know what I can imagine?"

"Any guy who orders the same lunch for six weeks in a row has imagination issues," Norma informed him, not without sympathy.

The redheaded waitress swooped by and leaned over his shoulder again. "But don't despair," she said, popping her gum in his ear again. "You can make up for a lot of that egghead intellectual imagination stuff in bed, if you treat her good. And I mean, like, good, buddy boy."

"Exactly my point," Norma agreed. "If you don't treat her like a goddess, you'll have me to answer to."

Duncan forced himself to close his slack, dangling mouth. He coughed to clear his throat. "Just what are you implying, ma'am?"

"That depends on you," Norma said crisply. "You see, unfortunately, our Nell is an orphan. There aren't any parents around to judge you and break your balls." She pointed at her chest. "But here's me, Strip Steak. Ready and willing to pick up the slack. Worse than the very worst mother-in-law could ever be. Just be aware."

"There's me, too. And Monica. And don't forget her sisters," the redhead piped in from behind as she swept by. "Mess with Nell, and Nancy and Vivi will rip you open and toss your entrails into the gutter."

"Ah." He pondered that memorable image for a moment. "You want me to declare that my intentions are honorable, you mean?"

Norma smiled approvingly. "That sounds like an excellent idea."

Nell appeared with a plate. "Here's your dessert. Carla, table five needs a slice of Black Forest and a Key Lime. They're in a rush, okay?"

Carla gave her gum a final loud pop, and sashayed away, ass twitching back and forth. Nell set down the dessert. It was not apple pie with vanilla ice cream. It was a fluffy confection. Lots of whipped cream.

"I decided you needed a change of pace," she said, a note of challenge in her voice. "This is a house specialty. Banana cream pie."

She stared at him, her soft mouth pressed flat. Norma stared, too, from behind the counter, her large, chubby arms crossed across her voluminous bosom. Seconds ticked by.

It irritated him, being jerked around, but this was not about pie. This was some sort of subtle test that he could not afford to fail.

Ah, what the fuck. It was only pie, after all. He forked up a bite.

"It's good," he said, automatically. Then he took another bite, and realized that it was true. It really was good. In fact, it was damn good.

Nell's face relaxed. Norma raised an eyebrow, harrumphed, and stumped away to serve a customer at the other end of the counter.

Nell leaned down. "What did they say?" she hissed in his ear.

Duncan felt an unexpected smile tug at his mouth, swiftly followed by a desire to laugh. "I was just informed that I should declare my intentions. And if I don't treat you like a goddess, I'll be sliced wide open, and my steaming viscera tossed out into the street."

"Oh, my God." Nell turned a delicate pink. "I'm going to kill them."

"No need." Suddenly, with no warning, he was laughing. Out loud. In public. People were looking. He didn't care.

It felt great.

Chapter
8

He kept catching her eye, giving her that wicked grin that scrambled her brain. The grin with the dimples that carved sexy lines into his cheeks. He'd done it in the restaurant and made her screw up the orders. He'd done it on the drive to his building. He was doing it now, from behind his desk in his office. She crossed her legs and tried to catch her breath. Bastard. It wasn't fair. It really wasn't.

"Nell? Earth to Nell? Do you have any of those finished?"

She jerked her gaze back to Bruce. "Uh, do I have what finished?"

Bruce rolled his eyes. "The manuscripts for the goblin caves! Did you get those done? I need to submit them to the graphic artists."

"Ah . . . um . . ." She winced. What with attackers and protracted bouts of incredible sex, she hadn't had a second to work on the game. In fact, she'd forgotten about its existence. "I'm so sorry, Bruce, but I—"

"She's been busy," Duncan said curtly, from behind his desk.

Bruce's eyes narrowed. He looked from Duncan to Nell. "Busy?"

Nell began to blush. "My life's been kind of crazy. If you want, I'll try to whip something up right now."

"Okay, fine, but I was hoping to brainstorm about the octagonal tower and the magic mirrors tonight. And how about the prophesies for the cursed tomb of the lost kings? Haven't done those, either, huh?"

She resisted the urge to excuse herself for slacking off. "Not yet, but I have some ideas," she said. "They'll need to be encrypted."

"I roughed out a Rosetta stone last night. Looks like we're going to be here till midnight if we want to have a chance in hell of finishing—"

"No," Duncan said. "She's been waitressing all day. She needs dinner, and a rest. Plus she has an appointment, in Queens, at nine."

Bruce stared at them, and started to grin. "Ah. I see. Does she need her beauty rest, then? So that's the way the wind blows."

"Shut up, Bruce," Duncan growled.

"Tired or not, we gotta get that material churned out by Monday," Bruce fretted. "I don't know how you expect us to—"

"Do it tomorrow," Duncan said.

Bruce slanted him a glance. "Tomorrow's Sunday, Dunc."

"So? Work doesn't care what day it gets done."

"I'm free tomorrow," Nell said quickly.

Duncan looked at his brother. "See? Problem solved. Get lost."

Bruce got up and backed toward the door. "I'll just go on home and slave away on my Rosetta stone while you two lovebirds—"

"Out, Bruce!" Duncan's voice was like the lash of a whip.

"I'll just, ah, engage this lock for you." Bruce flicked the lever, grinning, and ducked out the door. It snicked shut behind him.

"That was unnecessary!" Nell hissed. "I promised him that I'd get those goblin cave manuscripts—oh!" She squeaked as he pulled her up to her feet and dragged her around his desk. He yanked her onto his lap, so that she was straddling him. "Are you nuts?"

He stifled her protest with a hot, persuasive kiss. She grasped his wrists for balance. Wow. But this was his office, for God's sake.

"Just a kiss," he said, nuzzling her throat. "Every time I passed the conference room, my dick got hard. Don't worry. Door's locked."

"That makes it worse!" she protested. "Everyone is speculating!"

"What everyone? Everybody's gone home but Bruce, and he's already drawn his conclusions." He gripped her hips, dragging her closer. "I did a crazy thing today," he said, between ravenous kisses.

"Oh, really?" She laughed, breathlessly. "Crazier than usual?"

"Yeah. I was supposed to convince my sister Ellie to change her major from theater back to economics." His arms tightened, grinding his erection against the melting sweet spot. She could hardly breathe.

"So I called her," he continued, his voice silky. "I was about to do my spiel. And then I found your petals."

"Really?" Nell said. Her panties were a whisper-thin barrier between the scorching heat and hardness of his erection. "And?"

"And I told her to go for it." He sounded astonished at himself.

Nell was startled into lucidity. " Just like that?"

"There I was, rose petals all over me. I couldn't bring her down."

Nell's heart swelled. She cradled his face in her hands and kissed him. "Congratulations," she whispered. "You did a great thing."

He cupped his hand behind her head and deepened the kiss.

Her long sweater skirt was rucked up high on her thighs, over the same beige gartered stockings she'd worn the day before, and his erection pressed against the gusset of her panties, behind which was a melting, throbbing ache of rising desire. She pulled away, gasping for breath. "I'm going to give you a great big wet spot," she warned him.

"Only one thing to do about that." He lifted her up so she stood on her feet, cupping her bottom so she couldn't wiggle away. He wrenched his belt loose and his pants open. His cock sprang up, empurpled and huge. He slid his finger inside the crotch of her panties and into that hot, liquid well, swirling and stroking. A tug against her hip, fabric ripped, and he pulled her back down, fitting her over himself.

Forcing the thick club of his penis slowly, insistently, inside her.

She braced herself against his chest. "Hey! Hold on! I spoiled you this morning, but don't you dare start to think you can play dangerous games with me without protection whenever you feel like it!"

He slid relentlessly deeper. "I always feel like it with you."

"You're not the one who pays the price if there is a mishap!"

He stopped moving, and cupped her cheek, stared into her eyes with fierce intensity. "That's not true. I always take responsibility for what I do. I would never bail out on you, Nell."

Um. Nice sentiment, but Nell wasn't precisely sure of its practical applications, and she was afraid to ask. And her body was betraying her. She could barely speak, swaying on top of him, quivering around his cock, squeezing him convulsively inside herself. She coordinated her shaky voice. "How do you take responsibility for an irresponsible thing? It's contradictory!"

His fingers bit into her hips, dragging her against him. "That's way too deep for a guy like me," he said. "Especially when all the blood in my body's been diverted to my dick."

"That's a cheap excuse," she shot back, writhing helplessly.

"Just doing what I can," he said. "Your waitress friend told me I could make up for my intellectual shortcomings by being good in bed."

Her eyes popped open. "She didn't!"

"She did," Duncan said solemnly.

"Oh, my God." She covered her face with her hands, and began to laugh. "I can't believe them. I just can't believe it."

"I have to admit, I found it kind of comforting," he mused. "I figured, maybe there's hope, you know? Even for a meathead like me."

"Oh, you just shut up!"

"Good thing you like 'em big and stupid, right?"

She swatted at him. "Stop it! You're making it worse!"

"Oh, no. Not worse. Better," he said. "I won't stop. It feels fucking amazing. Those little fluttery clenches around my dick, every time you laugh. Laugh all you want. I'll keep you laughing as long as I can."

She pressed her hand to his mouth, chest hitching, eyes watering with shaky giggles. "Shhh. Really. Please, Duncan, damn it. I'm serious. Stop."

"Fuck, no." He pulled her hand down, grinning. "So this guy walks into this bar—"

"Shhh!" She stared into his eyes. "Just don't get me pregnant," she said. "Do. Not. Get it? I've got enough to feel scared about right now. Is that clear?"

He nodded, and kissed her palm. "I won't come inside you," he promised. "I won't even move. I'll sit like a statue. Your personal life-sized sex toy. You just squeeze me, ride me, do whatever you want with me until you come. Sound good?"

Oh, boy, did it ever. So good, it stole her breath, her voice.

She did as he offered, squeezing him inside her until her lower body flushed with pleasure, shaking with firecracker jolts.

He kept his promise, though she could tell that it cost him. It took a while to get there, with him so motionless. He trembled, holding her arms in a tight grip, staring at her face as she writhed and whimpered, too lost to pleasure to be self-conscious. It was a long, slow climb, but the outcome was inevitable. He caught her as she arched back and launched into free fall, his growl of satisfaction vibrating through her.

She collapsed over his shoulder, breathless and limp. Blushing and damp with sweat as the aftershocks rippled through her. She could feel his heartbeat in his cockhead, throbbing against her womb, he was wedged so deep inside her. A deep, steady, pulsing rhythm. So close.

She lifted her head and was startled by the look on his face. It was no longer that taut, tense mask of self-control that he'd worn while she was pleasuring herself with his body. It was soft. Almost wistful.

"What are you thinking?" she asked him.

He touched her eyebrow, then her cheekbone, then her lips. "I was just wondering what a baby of ours might look like."

The feeling that pierced her was indefinable. Joy, terror, fury. That bastard. How dare he. Playing with her emotions.

"You bastard. Don't say crazy things like that to me," she forced out, through shaking lips. "It's not fair. It's . . . irresponsible."

He shrugged. "You asked."

So she had. Her hands shook. They stared at each other. Both fully clothed, but she had never felt so naked.

She untangled her legs from his, set her feet on the ground, and lifted herself up. They sucked in air in unison at the sweet slide, the delicious friction as his cock caressed her sensitized inner flesh. The cold air that hit them when they were separated.

She stared down at his cock. It stood high and hopeful against his belly. Rigid, pulsing. Gleaming with her own juices.

She had no intention of sinking to her knees. It just happened. She grabbed his thick, pulsing handle, stroking smooth, hot skin, and licked him, tasting herself. It was a classic thousand-dollar-an-hour call-girl scenario. Riding the boss on his swivel chair in the high-rise corner office. On her knees under the desk giving him a blow job. It looked sordid, squalid. Even pornographic, from the outside.

But she wasn't on the outside. She was so far inside, she was in a new universe, where the rules had changed. She herself was different. Softer, more joyful, more sensual. Fearless. And shameless. Just this desperate desire to give to him flowing out of her, from her chest, her face, her throat, her crotch. All aglow.

Of course. She was miles in love with him.

She let that thought slide away. She didn't dare examine it, and besides, it took all her concentration to fellate a man as ridiculously well endowed as Duncan Burke. He was hung like the proverbial horse, and she was far from expert. But oh, so motivated.

She petted and stroked, swirled with her tongue around his cock-head, and tried to draw him deeper. Loving the sounds, the shaking grip of his hands in her hair, the shudders that went through him. She was just getting the hang of it and starting to hit her stride when his fingers tightened, and he let out a choked, desperate shout.

His come spurted into her mouth in hard, rhythmic jets.

She got to her feet after a few silent, shaking minutes, holding on to the desk for balance. She wiped her mouth, too shy to look at him.

He grabbed her and dragged her over between his legs, hugged her tightly around the waist, hid his face against her breasts.

Her chest melted, her shyness evaporated, leaving only tenderness. He felt vulnerable, too. And somehow, that made it okay.

They swayed in that clinch for a long time. Finally he looked up. "There's a private en suite bathroom with a shower, off my office."

She widened her eyes. "Holy cow, Burke. How luxurious and elitist of you. What, can't bear to pee with the hoi polloi?"

His teeth flashed in the deepening twilight. "Every now and then I pamper myself," he admitted. "I like to run to work. And I like to smell good. I keep fresh clothes here. So we can clean up. If you want."

"You ripped my panties," she lectured him. "Beast."

He gave her an exaggeratedly innocent look. "If I'd stopped to peel them all the way down your legs, you'd have wimped out on me." He caressed her buttocks through her skirt. "I'll buy you new ones. If we hurry, we have time for dinner before we meet your sisters in Queens."

"What about the texts that I have to write for the game? I have to have something ready for Bruce tomorrow!"

He shrugged. "You need to eat. Come on." He grabbed her hand, and dragged her through a door and into a small but luxurious bathroom.

"Hey! Wait," she said, laughing. "I thought we were in a hurry."

He flashed his devilish grin in answer, grabbed a fluffy white towel off a pile on a shelf, and dropped it in her arms. "Everything's relative."

He shrugged off his suit jacket, and she froze at the sight of the gun strapped onto his shoulder. "Um, Duncan?" she asked, in a small voice. "What on earth are you doing with that, uh, thing?"

He slanted her an "are you kidding" look. "Being careful," he said. "Those guys were armed. I wasn't. It was just blind luck and timing that they didn't kill me and take you, because I wouldn't have been able to stop them if they'd been better organized. They weren't expecting any resistance, but they will be the next time they go for you. Don't worry. I can handle myself with this thing." He unbuttoned her blouse, peeled her stretch lace chemise off over her head.

She gazed at him through the disarranged mess of curly hair that fell over her face. "Don't worry," she murmured. "I have absolutely no doubts about your ability to handle, um . . . just about anything."

He proceeded to live up to her faith in him. To the fullest.

*   *   *

Duncan looked around Malloy's. Too many people crowded together. Not safe. Good thing he'd had jeans and a polo to change into at the office, because he'd have felt like a fucking clown in his suit.

He'd never been in an Irish pub, and the loud, noodling melody of the Irish tunes played by the table of musicians made his brain pound.

But whatever. He'd follow Nell D'Onofrio to the bowels of hell. Complaining bitterly all the way, sure. But he'd be there.

His attention was weirdly divided into independently functioning units. One constantly scoped the scene for attackers. Another was anxious about meeting Nell's sisters, who might or might not want to toss his entrails into the gutter if he didn't adhere to some incomprehensible code of behavior. A third was intensely aware of the fact that Nell wore no panties. She looked decorous and ladylike, her tidy blouse stretching slightly across her tits, her long sweater skirt reaching to her ankles.

Paradoxically, that made it even worse. Her sexy secret. If he slipped his hand under that skirt and slid it up over her stockings, he'd find just hot, velvety skin between her legs. Warm fuzz. Damp ringlets. Tender, moist pink folds inside her pussy lips. That hot, tight, slick well.

Talk about distracting.

They were the last to arrive, since he'd insisted on tanking up at a good steak and burger joint that he knew near the Midtown Tunnel, to get some protein into her. When they walked into the bar, two women leaped up and went straight for Nell, sneaking fascinated peeks at him.

He was grateful for the noise level, so he didn't have to hear what they were whispering. Whatever it was made her blush furiously.

"Duncan, this is my sister Vivi," Nell spoke loudly into his ear, indicating the smaller of the two, a waiflike, slender girl with long red hair and big gray eyes. "And this is Nancy." She touched the shoulder of the other woman, a pale beauty with hazel eyes and long, curly auburn hair that reached her ass. "This is Duncan, my, ah, friend," she told them. "And that tall guy at the table playing the fiddle is Liam, Nancy's fiancé."

The tune finished with a flourish and a burst of hoots and hollers. The guy whom Nell had pointed at glanced over at them, laid his fiddle on the table, and excused himself, to unanimous cries of protest. He came toward them, sizing Duncan up with keen green eyes. He had a strong grip and a clear, unwavering gaze. Nell had told him the story of how Liam had defended her sister Nancy from the Fiend.

He was a good judge of men, after years as a field agent. This Liam seemed okay to him. A guy he'd want at his back. That was good.

The musicians launched into a new tune, louder than the one before. "Let's go sit at a table in the back!" Liam shouted over the din.

The back room was deserted. They sat down around a table and Duncan silently, stoically endured their collective scrutiny.

"So, Duncan," the sister named Vivi finally broke the silence. "I'll just start things off by saying thanks for saving Nell's ass for us."

"My pleasure," he replied.

"Yes, I'm grateful, too," Nancy said. "But that brings us to a very important issue. Nell, you and Vivi can't live in New York alone anymore. You should both leave the city. Go into hiding. I know it sounds dramatic, but so is getting jumped by three guys on Lafayette."

Sensible though that was, Duncan was instantly unhappy about the prospect of Nell leaving town. But no worries. Nell was shaking her head, true to form. As contrary with her sisters as she was with him.

"I am so close to getting my doctorate," she said, her voice rebellious. "It's taken me years having to work full-time while I do it, but I'm almost there. I'm not going to let this butthead take that from me."

"But where will you live? You could stay with me and Liam, but you'd be exposed every time you traveled back and forth—"

"She'll live with me," Duncan cut in.

All eyes cut to him. There was a flurry of silent signals, significant glances. Nell leaned over to him. "Duncan, do you mind?" she hissed. "This is not an issue for everyone to—"

"Wrong. It is now, babe," Vivi said sternly. "You're my sister, and

I don't want you snatched. How's the security in your building, Duncan?"

"Good," he replied. "Even better when I'm with her. Which I'll make a point of being, as much as possible. And if I can't, for any reason, I'll make arrangements for a professional bodyguard."

Nell glared at him. He stared back, unrepentant. The sisters and the future brother-in-law glanced exchanged nods of cautious approval.

"I'd like to be included in the decision-making process here," Nell snapped. "And who's going to pay for a bodyguard? They're expensive!"

"So Nell's covered," Liam went on, ignoring her. "That leaves you, Viv. You can stay with us. You shouldn't go back on the road. At least not unless you change your name."

Vivi looked forlorn. "You're sweet, Liam, but staying with you guys is not a long-term solution. I'm the only one of us with no pressing reason to stay in New York. But I can't do the crafts fair circuit if I don't use my own name, or else I'd be starting from zero all over again. I can't afford that now, after six years of working my ass off to build my brand."

Nancy looked worried. "I thought you wanted to quit the circuit!"

Her younger sister looked wistful. "Sure, when I've saved enough to buy a little house someplace beautiful. Someplace with lots of trees, where my dog can run around. Where I can have a big studio, do sculpture again, maybe open my own shop. But that's just fantasy. I lost thousands of bucks in registration fees when I came back for Lucia's funeral. Then I lost more after the Boston adventure, too. I'm playing catch-up now. With my credit card."

Duncan squinted at her, thinking hard. Trees, flowers, a big art studio, far from New York. He had an idea. A fucking awesome idea.

"I know a place you might be able to go," he said.

They all turned. "What might that place be?" Vivi asked slowly.

"I've got this friend. I met him in Afghanistan," he said. "We were on an intelligence-gathering task force. He got out of that line of work a few years ago and bought a place out in Oregon. He's into organic gardening, horticulture, that kind of thing. Grows flowers, I think. The guy he bought the land from was an artist who'd converted the barn into a studio, with a little apartment in a loft above it."

Liam and Nancy gave each other speculative glances.

"And why would this guy want to host me there?" asked Vivi.

Duncan shrugged. "He's not an artist, so he doesn't need the studio. He doesn't raise animals, so he doesn't need the barn. He built his own house, so he doesn't need the apartment. He likes dogs. Maybe he'd consider renting it to you. Want me to talk to him about it?"

Bully and guilt-trip him was more like it. Jack owed Duncan his life, like Gant. Actually, they all owed each other, but Duncan would bring out the big guns to help Nell's sister. And the best part was, Jack was a serious bad-ass. If anyone gave Vivi trouble, Jack could handle it.

That would comfort everyone. Which would earn Duncan big points. He'd take every opportunity to do that. No matter who he inconvenienced.

Vivi's shrug was casual, but he read signs of stress in her face, in the nervous movement of her hands, her mouth. The shadow in her eyes. She looked pinched. Like Nell's face had been, just a couple of days ago. But Nell was looking better now. Rosier, eyes sparkling.

So pretty. Jesus. It knocked him back. In fact, she was giving him a look of such shining, unmixed approval, he was almost disoriented.

She grabbed his hand under the table, and his brain went haywire at the contact. His fingers curled around hers, and for a moment, he completely lost the thread of the conversation.

". . . told us about the secret drawer," Nancy was saying when he tuned in again. "Like the many other things Lucia never told us about."

"Secret drawer?" Duncan asked. "In what?"

Nancy glanced at Nell, Nell gave her an eloquent nod, and Nancy proceeded. "Lucia had a priceless *intaglio* Renaissance writing table," she said. "It belonged to her family for the past four hundred years. It was smashed in the second B&E. You do know about our mother,

Lucia? What happened? The burglaries, and all the rest of it?" she probed delicately.

"Yes, Nell told me the story," he said. "So what's with the table?"

"Liam's been restoring it," she said. "And he found a secret drawer. You push one of the flowers carved into the back, and a drawer pops out. And it had a letter in it."

He waited for the punch line. "And? So? What's in the letter?"

Nancy smiled at his impatience. "We don't know," she said. "It's in Italian, and Nell's the only one of us who speaks Italian."

He looked at Nell. "You speak Italian?"

"And Spanish. And French. And Latin. And ancient Greek," Vivi piped up, intense pride in her voice. "Our Nell, the linguist."

Nell looked embarrassed. "My birth mother was Italian," she explained. "I learned it from her. And I was in a foster home for a while with a couple of Venezuelan girls. I learned their Spanish before they had a chance to learn English. French was an easy step after that. So it's not like it's any big accomplishment."

He grunted. "And the Latin and ancient Greek? Sure. No biggie."

"Can I see the letter please?" she asked primly.

Nancy pulled a sheet of lightweight airmail paper out of her purse and passed it to Nell, who scanned it briefly.

"It's dated three months ago," she said, and began to translate.

Dearest Lucia,

Perhaps you will refuse even to read this letter. It would be no more than I deserve. Be aware that my silence was not due to lack of sentiment. On the contrary.

I have given up the search. I accept that I will never find what I seek, and yet possession of the map is still a torment to me. I have no right to destroy it, as it is not mine, and your father paid the highest price a man could pay to keep the hiding place a secret. I wish only to be free of it now. It gives me no peace, and after fifty years of fruitless searching, peace is all I can hope for. Perhaps even that is too much to hope.

I wish to bring the map back to you. You are the rightful owner. Dispose of it as you think best. I beg you, take this burden from me. Your pure heart and lack of avidity make you its perfect guardian.

I have a flight reservation that will bring me to JFK Airport on May the 16th, if you will receive me. If you do not wish to see me, or you do not wish to take custody of the map, I will respect your wishes, and you will not hear from me again. I await news from you.

Marco Barbieri

Nell put her hand over her mouth. "May sixteenth. The day she died."

They all stared down at the letter, chilled. "So he brought this map that day," Liam said slowly. "And led them straight to Lucia. But they still didn't find what they were looking for."

"But Marco didn't bring Lucia the treasure itself. Just a map," Nell said. "The treasure's still lost. Marco couldn't find it, and it sounds like he looked really hard. And then he came here, and gets murdered, still unsatisfied. Poor guy."

Duncan looked at Liam. "Did you go over that whole table?"

"Centimeter by centimeter," the other man replied. "No other secret drawers that I could find. But there's still the safe. It's a big question mark. The bad guys haven't seen it. It was never found or forced, in either of the burglaries. I pulled the safe out and took it to my house."

Nancy held her hand up to her throat. "But we can't open it without all three of the necklaces, according to Lucia's letter. And the filthy rat-bastard Fiend took mine."

"Can't you force the safe?" Duncan asked.

Nancy and Liam shook their heads. "It's a trick design," Nancy said. "God knows where Lucia found the thing. There's a warning printed on the top. If you try to open the safe in any way other than the numerical combination, a tiny minibomb explodes and destroys whatever's inside. Damn good safeguard. Keeps everybody honest."

"So we'll go at it from another direction," Nell said briskly. "We find out more about Marco Barbieri and whatever he's been looking for these past fifty years. Maybe someone in Castiglione Sant'Angelo can tell us."

"So let's go to Italy. You can ask them," Duncan said, impulsively. Everyone stared at him, mouths agape.

"Um, Duncan?" Nell began. "You're going off the deep end."

"No, I'm not." The fantastic idea was taking hold in his mind, driving everything else out. Castles, frescos, fields of sunflowers, great pasta, thick slabs of Florentine steak, liters of kick-ass red wine. Walking with Nell on his arm through winding cobblestone streets. Her, dressed in a skimpy little sundress with lots of cleavage, getting a tan, eating gelato, getting relaxed. Having fun. Nell, naked in their rumpled hotel room bed, her eyes sultry, satiated. Yeah.

Nell snorted. "Please. Be reasonable. What about the game? And my summer school students? And your business?"

"The game will wait," he said. "The students will live. And I haven't taken a vacation since I started the business. It's hard to justify vacations when you're running your own operation."

"Tell me about it," Vivi said wearily.

"I cannot afford a trip to Italy," Nell said, her voice sharpening.

"So we'll divide the labor," he offered. "You do all the ordering in the restaurants, and I wave my credit card around. Sounds fair to me."

Vivi laughed with delight. "Sweet. I like your style, Duncan."

He shrugged. "It's a perfect way to get you out of their sights."

"Not really," Liam said quietly. "It's the first place they'd expect her to go. She'd be noticed there and watched."

Duncan was somewhat deflated by that acute observation, but even so, he couldn't let it go. He tracked with part of his mind, taking in data while they brainstormed about the letter, the safe, Marco, the attackers, the map. The rest of him played with the Italy fantasy, like a dog with a bone. Gnawing it, licking it, loving it.

Nell began rubbing her eyes at about one-thirty in the morning, and Duncan took her hand. "We should get back, get some sleep," he told her. "We promised Bruce you'd be at the office tomorrow."

She stifled a yawn and smiled her agreement.

"Give them your new cell phone number," he reminded her.

Nancy and Vivi looked at each other, mouths theatrically agape. "A cell phone? Nell? Do our ears deceive us?" Vivi breathed. "No!"

"Oh, shut up, Viv," Nell grumbled. "He bullied me into it."

"We've been trying to bully you for years!" Nancy said, aggrieved.

Nell scribbled the number twice on a cocktail napkin and ripped it into two pieces, handing one to each sister. Hugs and giggles, jokes and teasing admonitions followed among the three sisters, while Duncan and Liam eyed each other. Liam's face was grim.

"Stay sharp," he said. "Those fuckers are motivated."

Duncan nodded. "I'm on it."

"Good." Liam looked cautiously relieved. "Let us know what your friend in Oregon says. When Vivi's on the road, we don't sleep nights."

"I hear you." They shook hands and made their way out.

Duncan and Nell were silent on the way home. He was so heavy into his Italian-vacation-with-Nell fantasy, it took him by surprise him when she spoke.

"They liked you," she said.

That gave him a rush of pleasure. "How do you figure?"

"They said so," she said. "But even if they hadn't, I could tell, the way they talked about our private problems. Like it was a given that you were part of it. They would never have done that if they didn't like you."

"So I don't have to worry about being disemboweled?"

Nell stifled a giggle. "Not for the moment," she said. "You sure did throw your weight around, though. Your bank account, too."

He glanced at her profile. "I'm sorry if that was offensive to you."

"It seemed like you were trying to communicate to them that you've got money. I think they got the message loud and clear."

He took a few seconds to breathe down the surge of anger and frustration. "You're hung up on the money thing, Nell," he said. "I was communicating to them that I'm willing and able to protect you. Money is protection, too, whether you like it or not. And they know it. In fact, I didn't hear anyone objecting to it but you."

She was silent for a moment. "Sorry if I'm oversensitive," she said finally, her voice subdued. "And thanks for making that offer to Vivi, about your friend in Oregon. I hope that works out. She needs a break."

"I got that sense, too," he said. "I'll get right on it."

The silence that followed was an invisible wall between them.

She was lost in her thoughts behind it, hidden from him. It made him anxious and lonely. He wanted to break through, get inside.

He needed more info. More intel. She was so complex, so goddamn much going on in her head. He wanted her exact specs, a manual of her operating systems. He wanted to study her, absorb her. Master her, as if she were a math problem, an insanely complicated puzzle. And she'd have his ass barbecued if he ever said anything like that to her. He had to watch his metaphors with this woman.

"Talk to me," he blurted.

She looked at him, startled out of her reverie. "About what?"

"About yourself. I want to know more. You're incredible. Unique."

She harrumphed. "Yeah. I'm so unique, I'm practically extinct."

He ignored that. "Tell me about your childhood, your mother, your sisters," he urged. "Tell me anything. I don't care what."

Her big eyes were wary of the need she felt emanating from him, a vibration he could do nothing to hide. "Duncan . . ."

"You make me feel so alive. Just . . . please, Nell. Just tell me how it is to be the way you are."

His appeal touched her, and she gave him a tremulous smile. Something relaxed inside him. Excellent. By sheer chance he'd hit upon the exact trick to calm her down. Some judicious pity mongering, a small, tasteful glimpse of desperation, and she'd melted. He hadn't calculated that strategy, either. It had simply come to him. Instinct.

Maybe this convoluted emotional shit could be learned, after all.

Chapter
9

The look on his face, that note in his voice, it released the flood-gates. Nell talked so much, she embarrassed herself. She told him things she hadn't let herself think about in years, things she'd pretended to forget. The lonely boarding schools, the bad foster homes. Her mother's death. And that solitary afternoon in the funeral home, alone with her mother's coffin.

The endless, terrible afternoon that still haunted her.

She had no idea there was so much to say about her childhood, but it tumbled out, charged with raw emotion. She told him about Lucia finding her. About Nancy and Vivi, and discovering that she could have a family after all. She talked about stories, poetry. Her magical refuge.

Duncan had listened intently. His rapt attention was flattering, but the car clock said it was after three a.m., and she looked up at the street numbers and realized that he'd been driving in big, aimless circles around his neighborhood for the better part of an hour.

"Why aren't you going home?" she asked.

"I wanted to hear you talk."

"We could talk at your apartment," she pointed out.

"What I want when we get home doesn't involve much talking."

She crossed her legs with a shiver at the sensual promise in his voice. "Well. Be that as it may. I'm about talked out for now."

He turned the car at the next block and started back toward his condo. "This morning you told me that you've got plans for your life," he said. "Ambitions. Do those include a man? Or any room for one?"

She hesitated. There was a peculiar tone in his voice when he asked the loaded question. Something that made her vaguely nervous.

"You know, Duncan, I've babbled for over an hour, but you haven't volunteered one single thing about your own life," she said.

"You're evading my question."

"Why, what a coincidence. You're evading mine, too."

"I asked first," he said stubbornly. "And? So?"

She twisted her hands together. "Well, my plan is to finish my thesis, get my doctorate, and find a teaching job. At which point, I guess I will attempt to have a normal life. The Fiend permitting, and all that."

"Let me rephrase," he said softly. "By normal life, do you mean marriage, kids?"

Nell stared at him. Her heart had started to thud quickly, and her palms felt damp.

He simply waited.

Nell stared at the streetlights swooping by. "Of course I dream about love," she said quietly. "After all those novels and all that poetry, how could I not? But I know better than to take anything for granted. There are no guarantees. I'll do the best I can. Try to get over my baggage. Hope that I get lucky." *With you* was the real ending of that phrase, but her lips and throat trembled too much to say it.

He was quiet as he pulled into his parking garage and drove down two ramps to his own slot. He parked, killed the engine, and stared at the concrete wall in front of them.

"You're special, Nell," he said. "You should ask for more."

Warmth softened her chest. She touched his face with the palm of her hand, and stroked his cheek gently. "So should you, Duncan," she whispered. "So should you."

This was the moment. It could make or break them, if he said the right thing. He looked like he was poised to say it. He covered her hand with his own. She was poised to hear it. She couldn't move, or breathe.

Seconds ticked by, stretched to a minute. More. He didn't say it.

She turned her gaze away, blushing madly, feeling like an idiot. Here she went again, projecting her silly romantic fantasies onto the unsuspecting man. And him, just bumbling along. No freaking clue.

She tried to cover her embarrassment. "So? I answered your question. It's your turn to bare your soul. Let's hear it."

He looked alarmed. "I don't know how to do that."

"You just saw me do it," she said. "Watch and learn, Duncan."

"That's different." His voice was defensive. "You're . . . you're you."

"Right, and you're Duncan, and that's what I'm interested in. Why don't you start with parents? They're usually at the bottom of things."

He let out an impatient sigh, as if humoring a child. "My mom's great. She taught elementary school for thirty-five years before she retired. She raised us on her own. She's a general. Tries to run our lives, and mostly fails, but she's a pretty good sport about it. Usually."

"How did she feel about you being a spy?"

He grunted. "Hated it. She nagged and schemed."

"Is that why you quit?"

His grin flashed. "No. I know how to block and fake. I suit myself."

"I've noticed," she murmured. "And your father?"

His face changed, like a door slamming shut in her face. "I have nothing to say about him."

She flinched, took a deep breath, and tried again. "So tell me what there isn't, instead of what there is," she suggested.

He looked baffled. "What the hell are you talking about?"

"Silence is as revealing as words," she said softly. "But you already know that. I can see it in your photos."

"Don't go all poetic on me, Nell," he warned. "Or I'll devolve on you. Start to grunt and snort, and scratch my tufts."

"Stop being ridiculous, and just tell me about him," she snapped. "It can't be worse than my father story. At least you know his name."

He looked hunted, scowling down at the steering column. Finally started to speak, but his voice was very flat.

"He fell in love with a woman who worked for him," he said. "His accounts manager. Sylvia. She was younger than him and my mother. I was thirteen. Bruce was nine, and Ellie was a newborn. Ellie was Mom's last-ditch effort to tie Dad to her. Bad idea. Didn't work." He shook the memory away with a sharp wave of his hand.

"I'm sorry, Duncan," she whispered.

"He tried to explain it to me before he left. How love was this great force he couldn't resist. It was just his dick that he couldn't resist. But his family paid the price." Duncan shook his head. "He divorced Sylvia seven years later. Traded her in for a younger model. There you go. There's the power of love for you."

The bitter contempt in his voice chilled her. "That's not love," she said quietly. "I don't know what it is, but it's not love."

He made a low, harsh sound of negation. "Whatever it is, I don't want to talk about it anymore. It depresses me. Let's go upstairs."

He got out of the car. She flung the door open before he could come around and do it for her. She followed him into his building, miserably aware of having maneuvered him out of that wonderful, close place that they'd been before. She'd made him tense and defensive. Clumsy of her.

Well, hell. There were ways and ways to sweeten his mood. And she was not without her resources.

Duncan stood aside to let her in first, and flipped on a small row of track lights near the entry space, leaving the rest of the apartment in shadow but for the glittering cityscape outside. The delicious imminence of sex trapped her air in her lungs. She drifted over to the couches. They were big, oversized. Gray, velvety, plush. An odd choice, for him. She would have expected gleaming black leather, stainless steel, and glass. She sank into one with a sigh and stared at his perfectly proportioned black silhouette standing there. A hot sexual energy pulsed out of him, all the more potent for his silence, for how fiercely it was controlled.

It made her hot, shaky. Unstable inside. She could hardly wait.

"All evening, I've been thinking about your bare ass under that skirt," he said.

She grabbed handfuls of the knit fabric, and screwed up her courage. "Do you, um, want to see it?"

"Yes," he said. "Show me."

She took her time pulling her skirt up. She drew it out, gathering up folds of fabric inch by inch, until she had an armful of knitted jersey pressed against her belly, and the tops of her stockings showed. And a strip of pale thigh above them. A tuft of her dark, curly pubic hair.

But her legs were still clamped together.

Duncan sank to his knees in front of her. His hot hands settled on her knees, pushing them wide. She closed her eyes, her face hot.

He sighed. "Ah, God. I love the stockings," he muttered. "You are so fucking beautiful, Nell."

She felt more naked like this than she had when she hadn't worn a stitch with him. He grabbed her hand and pulled it down, arranging her fingers so that her clit was gently clasped in the V between her index and middle finger. "Touch yourself," he said. "I want to see how you do it. You know. Watch and learn."

She laughed silently, parting herself for him. Aroused by his intense attention. The feeling of exposure was transforming into something pleasurable. She slowly relaxed into it, like a cat sprawled in a patch of sunlight. "That's one area where you don't need any lessons."

"I'm gratified to know that I've got at least one piece of the puzzle in the bag," he muttered.

She ignored his sarcasm, and stroked the jut of his cheekbone with her finger. His skin was so hot and supple. "I fantasized about you, ever since you started eating lunch at the Grill," she confessed.

He pressed a hot, lingering kiss to the top of her thigh. "Is that a fact? What did I do to you in those fantasies?"

"Lovely things," she admitted.

He grinned, caressed the crease of her groin. "Such as?"

He waited, but she couldn't speak. Her lips were trembling too much. "My mouth is watering," he said, parting her labia tenderly, and slowly penetrating her. "Did I lick you in those fantasies?"

"Oh . . . yes," she said, jerkily.

"Was it good? Did I treat you right?"

"It was amazing. It was . . . it was superdeluxe."

He bent lower, and lapped the length of her labia voluptuously with his tongue. "And how do I measure up to myself?"

"You surpass yourself," she admitted. "There's more of you in real life. More of everything. More feelings, more orgasms. More problems."

He chuckled, silently, his lips tenderly holding her clit, his tongue fluttering expertly, swirl, flutter, swirl. "Never mind the problems," he suggested. "Let's just stop at the orgasms. And linger there."

"Okay," she agreed.

"Forever," he whispered.

It was the word that set her off. *Forever.* It made her pleasure rise to a crest and break in great, pulsing ripples of milky foam through the endless ocean of sensation. That sweet, hot swell of . . . hope.

After that, they went wild. A frenzied, feverish blur. No control, no need for it. His clothes came off, her blouse was ripped open, her bra unhooked. He produced a condom out of thin air, and he was inside her, pressing her down onto the couch. Folding her legs high. Hard, driving. Demanding and wonderful. They struggled, twining and writhing and pumping toward a violent, explosive shared orgasm.

His vital energy poured into her. She clung to him and felt its wonderful heat, transforming her, and a single, piercing thought formed in her mind. He lifted his face, and it popped out. "I love you," she said.

His eyelids went tight. His face, blank.

Fear stabbed through her like a blade of ice. She'd ruined it. Now he would take back his intense, passionate attention—never mind that it wasn't love—and she would proceed to shrivel up and die.

Then came anger. How humiliating, to be terrified just because she told a man she loved him. She had nothing to be ashamed of. He should be grateful. She should not have to beg for any man's love.

"Nell," he said, sounding pained.

"No. Forget I said it." Nell tried to wrench herself free, but his full weight was pinning her down into the squishy couch cushions.

He rolled off the couch, onto the floor. "Nell, I'm sorry if I—

"Shut up, Duncan. The worst thing you could do would be to apologize. It's the one thing I could never forgive you for."

"So what can I say?"

"Nothing," Nell whispered. There was a burning tightness in her chest. It felt like her heart was imploding. She collected her clothes and marched into the bedroom. He followed her in on bare, silent feet. Disappeared into the bathroom for a moment, to deal with the condom, and then appeared in the doorway again.

"Nell, don't," he said, his voice rough. "Don't do this to me."

Nell fought the tears. "Please, Duncan. Just give me some space. I'm too embarrassed to talk to you right now."

"Don't be. Please." He slipped his arms around her from behind, and squeezed. "Thank you for saying it. Thank you for giving yourself to me like you do. You're beautiful and special, and you make me feel awake and alive like nothing else. Please. Don't be embarrassed."

Nell covered her face. "You drive me crazy when you talk like that," she whispered. "You're schizo, Duncan. Don't confuse me."

"I'm just telling you how I feel. And being honest. Isn't that what women say they want from men?"

"What I want and what women in general want are two separate things," she said haughtily. "Do not generalize me."

"Never," he said, smoothly, fervently kissing her neck.

Nell sighed. "It's strange. All those things you say, about how you feel about me? That's exactly the same way I feel about you. I just interpret those feelings to mean that I'm in love with you."

Duncan's arms tightened. He buried his face in her hair.

"But we define those feelings in such different terms," she finished. "And that shouldn't be so important. But . . . but it is."

She squeezed her eyes shut. Tears overflowed. She let them slide down her cheeks.

He jerked as a tear splashed his forearm.

Nell stroked his arm, brushing the moisture away. "It's okay,

Duncan. I appreciate you telling the truth. Honesty is better than lies. I guess."

"I'm giving you everything I have to give."

Nell turned in his arms until she faced him, and rested her face against his chest. "Yes. And you give a lot," she admitted. "I just asked for the wrong thing, that's all. I love our time together. Don't worry."

It was confusing, maddening, but maybe she should just relax, and try not to put this experience in a marked box. After all, the feelings he described for her were more than most lovers had to brag about.

Dread lay heavy in Duncan's gut. Something precious was slipping away from him, and he didn't know how to stop it. He massaged the muscles in her shoulders and back, but she couldn't relax. He didn't blame her.

Duncan coaxed her over to his bed, stripping off what remained of her clothes, and turned off the light, dragging her close to him. She hid her face against his chest, and he cuddled her, stroking her back in long, soothing passes of his hand over the perfect fine texture of her skin, all the way down to the curve of her ass. His dick rose up, hot and hard, prodding her thigh, but he gritted his teeth and ignored its insistent, throbbing demands.

Patience. This time was all about Nell.

He slid his hand down the cleft of her bottom. She didn't recoil or stiffen up, just nuzzled her face to his chest with a wordless murmur, and parted her thighs, letting his hand slide lower, delve deeper.

He slowly, tirelessly apologized for what he didn't have to offer her by showing her what he did have. His other hand joined the action, caressing her clit from the front while he thrust two long fingers into her slick, hot little pussy from behind, petting and stroking in ways he knew she liked. Long and slow. No hurry. He drove her higher, until she was squirming, panting, thighs clenching, fingernails digging into him.

Finally, a little shriek, and her cunt pulsed greedily, hungrily around his hand. She flopped onto her back, limp.

He put on a condom he'd left on the bedside table, rolled on top of her, and filled her with a powerful, relentless thrust. He wanted to chase the pain and unease of their last conversation away. This was the only way he knew to do it, to lose himself in the heavy rhythm of his body jolting against hers, her gasping cries, his harsh breathing. Somehow he managed to wait for her climax again, and his own release followed a split second after, her hot pulsations prolonging his pleasure.

And then she burst into tears.

Duncan was appalled. She disentangled herself and curled up with her back to him, sobbing. He wrapped his arms around her from behind until her sobs quieted. She fell into an exhausted sleep.

He lay there with her for what felt like hours, until the pressure inside him built up to the boiling point. He crept from the bed, tucked the comforter around Nell, and got rid of the condom, then he slipped on some sweatpants and wandered into the living room. He felt scared, shell-shocked, and the ache of impending doom in his gut was growing. He went out onto the terrace and stared out into the endless skyscrapers while the chill made his hairs rise up on his naked skin. It was almost dawn. The city below would wake up soon. But chill or no chill, he just stood out there, staring. Thinking, and feeling.

He was losing her. He could feel it. He put his head into his hands, tried to think it through. The weirdness had started when he'd asked her that stupid, ill-considered question about marriage, kids.

Marriage. He examined the concept. Was that what she wanted? Because if it was, the more he thought about it, the more he realized that it wasn't such a terrifying idea. It wasn't actually so crazy, either.

He ticked off the positive aspects. Protection. He would have a God-given reason to stay stuck to her like glue, if they were newlyweds, and that was fine with him. Then there was work, too. If they were married, their relationship would not be fodder for rumor and scandal in the office. No one would have any right to judge or criticize them. He would have a further claim upon her undivided attention and expertise for his company. He could easily pay enough so she could quit her other work, and have more free time. Hell, he had plenty of money. How much he paid her wasn't necessarily relevant, once they were married.

She was so smart and imaginative, he would never get bored with her, as he had with other women he'd dated in the past. Sex was an important element of marriage, and they certainly had no problems in that area. And he would be faithful. No question about that. At all.

He would wake up every morning and find her there, beside him. That gave him a wonderful, spine-tingling sense of rightness.

Yes, marriage was the logical culmination of a partnership that worked. It was a win/win situation. So logical, he couldn't believe he hadn't thought of it before. He could hardly wait for Nell to wake up, so he could tell her what an excellent idea this was. He hoped it would make her feel better. That she would see that he was trying to meet her halfway, as far as he possibly could. And it was pretty damn far.

Marriage, for Christ's sake. How much further could a guy go?

The cold ache in his gut had entirely vanished at the idea. He went back inside, with the intention of creeping into the bedroom, lying down beside her, and watching as she slept. Then he saw the eerie blue glow of a computer monitor emanating from one of the couches.

Nell sat there cross-legged, wrapped in one of his bathrobes, tippity-tapping on her laptop. She must have felt the breeze from the door, but she did not look up. She just worked on, utterly absorbed.

He must have stared for ten minutes before she took notice of him. Her smile was wan. "Hi. I woke up. Couldn't get back to sleep."

He stepped in. "What are you doing?"

"I had an idea for the last level of the game," she said.

The freaking game was the last thing he wanted to talk about, but he wasn't sure of a smooth way to shift topics and get from here to there. And a proposal of marriage had to be a segue as smooth as oil.

He swallowed, closed the door, strolled across the room toward her. "What's the idea?"

Her voice was strangely businesslike. "As it is now, the player rescues the princess only if he garners sufficient points and collects all the magical weapons necessary to defeat the Sorcerer. If the player is clever and ruthless and forgets nothing, he gets the princess. It's a very simple, banal, mercantile sort of exchange. It's cold."

The tension was back in his gut again. This was one of those dangerous conversations with undercurrents, where a phrase like "pass the butter" could blow up in his face and kill him. "Hardly simple," he muttered. "You have to sweat blood to make it through all those levels."

"I propose something different," she went on. "These tricks should get the player through the Sorcerer's defenses and to the door of the enchanted tower, but no farther. I propose one last barrier. To win the game, the player must make a leap of blind faith. Go against everything his senses and past experience tell him. To break the last spell, he has to leave his weapons and spells behind, and do something crazy. Dive headfirst into a pit of snakes. Jump into the mouth of a dragon. Walk into a wall of flames. He has to . . . to sacrifice himself for love."

Duncan's fingers bit into the top of the couch. She was still pissed. And fucking with his head. Brutally. He fought with his anger.

"I've been playing with a short text that could be inserted," she went on. "Something like 'only empty hands and a full heart shall pass through the wall of flames unburned'. This way, it's not just cleverness that wins the game. It's faith, and courage. And love."

"It would make the game impossible to win," Duncan said.

"That's not true for everyone," Nell replied. "Just for you."

A muscle pulsed in Duncan's jaw. "What are you saying, Nell? No symbolism, no bullshit. Could I have it in plain English, just this once?"

Nell wrapped her arms around herself, shivering. "I think we understand each other perfectly," she said quietly.

He circled the couch and sat down next to her. This was probably futile, given her unapproachable mood, but he had to get it off his chest. "You're cold," he said, grabbing the afghan off the couch. He wrapped it around her. "I don't want to talk about the game right now. We need to talk about us. I've been thinking."

"Me, too," Nell said quietly.

"I've decided that the best thing would be for us to get married."

Dead silence greeted that statement. Her eyes were huge and startled. "What?" she squeaked.

Duncan cracked his knuckles uneasily. "I was thinking about the situation after you went to sleep. And I decided that—"

"You *decided*?" Her voice was deceptively calm.

Duncan paused, sensing a pitfall. "Well, uh, of course your agreement is crucial to the plan," he said cautiously.

"So I should hope," Nell murmured.

"After I explain my reasoning to you, you'll see that it would be the best thing for both of us."

"Oh, really."

Nell's voice sounded strange, almost strangled.

"Yes. Let me explain." He presented his analysis, during which Nell was ominously silent. The chill in his gut was a lump of ice by the time he concluded his well-balanced, watertight, foolproof argument.

Nell tugged the afghan around herself and looked into his eyes. "Do you love me, Duncan?"

He closed his eyes, sighing. Aw, fuck. She had to say it. She just had to insist. "Goddamn it, Nell," he snapped, "that's not the point."

Nell shook her head. "I think it is the point," she replied. "In fact, I think it's the only point."

"Marriage is about partnership. Trust. The long haul. Not a bunch of stupid platitudes that don't mean a goddamn thing! If I had you on staff full-time, we could—"

"Duncan, I've studied for years for my advanced degree. I want to teach literature," Nell said quietly. "It's what I've always wanted."

Duncan threw up his hands in disgust. "You're being deliberately difficult. Tell me what you'd make as a professor. I'll top it."

"If I wanted money, I would've gone to business school."

"We're straying from the issue," he ground out. "We're good together. If you would let go of your lofty romantic ideas—"

"Marriage is not a merger. Love is not a stupid platitude. If I was as detached and cool as you are, it might work. But I'm not." Her voice faltered for a moment. "I'm in love with you," she finished, softly.

Love. Jesus, all he wanted was to be honest with her, to be fair. Not to lie or manipulate her with falsehoods. And this was what he got. His chest felt like it was in a trash compactor. Getting squished, smaller and smaller, into something as cold and hard as a diamond.

Nell rewrapped the afghan around herself. "And the worst part of this is that I think you love me, too, but you can't or won't see it."

"Don't tell me how I feel. I'm not talking about feelings. I'm talking about real things, concrete things. Commitment, fidelity, protection, everything I have. And children, too, if you want them. I thought that if you cared for me at all, you'd be pleased."

It took her a while to respond to that. "I don't 'care for you,' Duncan," she said, her voice small. "I love you. Greedy Nell. Always asking for more. And besides, feelings are real. Mine certainly are. What would it cost you to admit that you love me? Is it just a control thing? You have to have the upper hand? You can't give in to a strong feeling?"

"They're not necessary," he retorted. "None of this drama is necessary."

"This is about your father, right? You hated him for calling what he did love. You have to be his opposite. No matter what."

That deep-froze him. "Don't talk about my father," he said.

The tone in his voice made her lean back, her eyes big.

"Sorry," she whispered. "I can't marry you. Not on these terms."

"I figured that out by myself, by context and inference," he said. "I'm not as intellectually stunted and backward as you seem to think."

"Don't be sarcastic," Nell snapped, dashing away tears. "It's one thing to wait around for a lover to admit to loving you. It's entirely another to wait around for a husband to do it."

Duncan stared at her. "You would have waited a long time," he said. "I've offered you more than I've ever dreamed of offering anyone. If it's not enough, then there's nothing more to be said."

Nell straightened up, stiff and dignified. "I understand."

A phone began to ring somewhere. He recognized the muffled

ringtone of the cell he'd given to Nell. It was in her purse, which she'd left on the floor next to the couch. She made no move to get it.

He leaned over, fished it out, and checked the display. "Upstate area code," he said, handing it to her. "Maybe one of your sisters."

She stared down at the ringing phone in her hand, a perplexed frown between her brows, as if she wasn't quite sure what to do with it.

That was his cue to get the hell out of the room. He walked back out onto the terrace, and pulled the sliding door firmly shut behind him. Letting her take her goddamn phone call in privacy.

Since her affairs were no longer any of his fucking business.

Chapter
10

It took a ridiculously long time to find the right effing button to push, since Nell could barely see, her eyes were so blurred with tears.

She finally got it, and held the phone to her ear. "Yes?"

"Nell? Finally! It's Nancy. Sorry I'm calling so early, but I couldn't stand to wait. I hope I'm not interrupting anything, you know, delicious?"

"No," Nell forced out, after a pained little pause. "You're not."

Nancy was silent for a moment. "Um . . . is everything okay?"

"Fine." Nell forced false brightness into her tone. "So what's up?"

"I just got off the phone with Elsie."

Elsie was Lucia's sweet, kind, nosy next-door neighbor since decades before any of the sisters had come to live there. Nell was surprised to hear her name spoken. "But I thought Elsie went down to the Jersey Shore to live with her daughter after the burglaries!"

"She did. She just spent a full half hour telling me the horrors of sharing a bathroom with her teenage granddaughters. Alison brought her home last night. Elsie had the key Lucia had given her years ago, so this morning she decided to go over and check the place out for us."

Nell sucked in a breath. "Yikes. Did you ask her to do that?"

"Hell no! I told her not to do it again. Could be dangerous. But you know how she is. Anyhow, she found a letter under the mail slot, from Elisabetta Barbieri, in Castiglione Sant'Angelo. Elsie opened it—"

"Good God," Nell muttered.

"I know, but I wasn't inclined to criticize, and besides, it didn't matter because it's in Italian, and Elsie's Polish. So she called me."

"I'll go up there right away and get it," Nell said.

Nancy made a suspicious sound. "With Duncan, right?"

Nell squirmed, pressing against the ache in her middle. "We'll see," she hedged.

"You be careful," Nancy scolded. "Are you sure you're okay?"

"I'm fine," she lied. She closed the call, trying to sound cheerful, and stared through the glass doors at him, leaning over the railing.

He'd asked her to marry him. She'd said no. She was nuts.

Could she risk it? She knew he had feelings for her. He just couldn't admit them or articulate them. Could she accept a cool, practical "partnership"? With protection and money and lots of hot, excellent sex? Just hoping that someday he'd finally recognize his feelings for her as love?

No. She wasn't made that way. Maybe she would always be alone. Maybe she was unrealistic. Or just plain dumb. Letting her one chance at true love and passion go by. For the sake of stupid semantics.

But she wanted her man to love her. With an open heart. That was not too goddamn much to ask.

She opened the door, and stepped out onto the terrace. A gust of wind blew the terry cloth bathrobe open over her legs. She yanked it closed. She was nude underneath. Nudity that had abruptly become inappropriate. In fact, it had become an agony of embarrassment.

"I, um, have to go," she quavered to his rigid, muscular back.

"Why am I not surprised," he said, without turning.

She told him the story of Elsie and the letter. Duncan stared out at the city. "I'll take you up there," he said, his voice stony.

"No," she whispered.

"No?" He turned, and the fury in his eyes knocked her backward, like a punch. "What the fuck am I supposed to do? Nothing has changed. You've still got criminals prowling the city waiting for your guard to go down. Am I supposed to cut you loose? Let you get wasted?"

She shook her head, helplessly. "It's not your responsibility any-more, Duncan," she said. "It never really was."

"What a crock of high-minded horseshit," he snarled. "I get the message, Nell. You can't stand to be with me—"

"That's not it!"

"—so fine, I'll arrange for a car service and a professional armed escort to accompany you. When you get back with your letter, you'll check into a suite at the Hilton. Twenty-four-hour bodyguard cover-age. No more Sunset Grill shifts. Just your university work."

Her mouth dangled, and her head shook helplessly back and forth. "Duncan. But . . . but that's insane."

"I'll finance it until you've written your fucking thesis and gotten your precious Ph.D. At which point, we'll reassess the situation."

"But I—"

"Consider my position, Nell. Cold and detached as you think I am, I don't want you to die. Even if you're blowing me off, even if I'm not fucking you, I don't want you to get hurt. If you got hurt, or dead, that would suck. Is that clear? Are we on the same page here?"

She scrubbed her eyes with the back of her hands, and nodded.

"Good. Then stop arguing. I am sick of it. And I no longer need to bother trying not to piss you off. What a fucking load off my mind."

Cold. Hah. He was anything but cold, standing there like some sort of raging, thunderous pagan god in the chill morning air, the towering cityscape as his backdrop. His face was rigid with fury.

He made a sharp gesture for her to precede him inside. "I'll make the calls. Come on, let's get this thing moving," he said. "This shit is killing me. Go get dressed and packed. Fast."

She scrambled to do so and dragged her suitcase out of his room into the living room. She overheard snippets of Duncan's conversa-tion with someone named Braxton as he arranged for the bodyguard. He turned, frowning. "What's the address of this neighbor?"

"Twenty-one thirty-one Fairham Lane, in Hempton," she said.

He repeated the address to Braxton. "Put this one on my personal account, not the corporate account," he said into the phone.

His personal account? She'd be in debt to this guy for the rest of time. Well, hell. In essence, she already was. For her life.

Duncan escorted Nell down to the parking garage, where the car service was waiting, and bundled her into the vehicle. He lectured the bodyguard, a burly guy with long arms and a low, bulging forehead, about the mortal danger Nell was in for about fifteen minutes before he let the guy get into the car, still rolling his eyes. Fucking jerk-off.

He watched the car pull out of the garage, turn, and disappear.

It felt wrong. He wanted to run after the car, screaming and waving his arms. Something had been wrenched out of him. It left a bleeding hole.

He stumbled upstairs like a zombie, dropped onto the couch.

The sun got higher. His landline phone rang. His mother, for sure. Calling to give him hell about Ellie. The machine got it. His mother talked for five minutes onto the machine, her voice shrill. Not a word of it sank in. The square of sun on the floorboards inched along.

His cell rang. He checked the display. Bruce, wondering what the hell was going on. Nell had stood him up. He tossed the thing back down onto the couch, still ringing. Later for Bruce.

The only reason he didn't turn it off altogether was because Nell was out there in the world without him. With just some jerk-off clown bodyguard to protect her. That phone was his last and only link.

Some time later, the phone rang again. This time it was Braxton. He pushed "talk." "What happened?" he barked. "Is she okay?"

Braxton was taken aback. "Ah, yes. As far as I know," he said carefully. "I haven't heard from Wesley, so I assume things are fine."

Duncan's lungs released, allowing him to inhale. He felt stupid and hysterical. "Oh. Good. So, uh, what's up?"

"Just letting you know that Teiko and Sam just presented their report about the apartment they bug-swept yesterday."

"Yeah? What about it?"

"It was riddled," Braxton said. "High quality, foreign made. Amazing stuff. There were cameras behind both air vents, and bugs and traces everywhere. Teiko's convinced that they didn't find everything."

"Did you have them deliver the material to Gant for the evidence techs to look over?"

"As promised. One question. Did she bring any stuff with her when she came to your place? Suitcases, electronics?"

"Who told you she was at my place?" he snapped.

"Word gets around," Braxton said patiently. "So? Did she?"

"She brought a suitcase," he said. "But she took it away with her again. It's in the car, with her and Wesley." A cold chill began to prickle up his back. "Oh, my God. Oh, shit."

"Probably tagged," Braxton said. "So they know where she is."

His eyes fell on her laptop, which lay where she'd forgotten it on the couch. The chill transformed into an icy cramp, squeezing his guts. "Fuck me," he whispered, his voice a thread. "Her laptop. It's still here."

"Check it," Braxton said.

He grabbed it. It was a big, clunky dinosaur of a thing, at least eight years old. He found a screwdriver and pried the case open.

There it was. A listening device. It had its own battery and a powerful microphone. It was transmitting in real time, as he watched. Everything they had said had been heard, clear as a bell. Including the address where Nell was headed right now.

Where she might have already arrived. It had been over an hour.

He yanked the thing out, detached its power source with a brutal yank. "Bugged," he said. "They know where she went."

"I just tried Wesley." Braxton's voice was grim. "He didn't answer."

"Fuck," he hissed. "Call the cops for me, right now. The local ones. Have them check the place out. I'm on my way."

"Wait! Dunc, don't go alone. I'll organize a—"

He clicked "stop." No time. He shoved the phone into his pocket, sprinted for the bedroom. Tossed on a T-shirt, a pair of army-issue pants, shoes. Shoved his gun into the back of his pants, buckled on his ankle sheath and knife. Dug out the drug-treated throwing stars from his weapons stash, filled his side pants pockets with them.

Grabbed the laptop with the software to triangulate the GPS signal implanted in the cell phone he'd given her.

And ran like holy hell on wheels.

Nell kept her face averted in the car, so she didn't have to see the bodyguard Wesley's sympathetic glances. Her stores of dignity and restraint had been exhausted by the last scene in Duncan's apartment. Now all she wanted was to crawl into a hole and stay there.

Funny. That was exactly the scenario she had in store for her, once she collected this letter, if she accepted Duncan's help. Huddled in a hole. Cloistered in a hotel suite with the blinds drawn. She supposed she should be tough and brave and loftily refuse to do it, but that would mean fleeing New York, starting over. Abandoning everything she'd worked so hard for in the last decade.

But once she got her degree, what could she do with it, if the Fiend was abroad? Even if she changed her name and ran, she would still be barred from teaching literature. Colleges and universities would be the first place any fool would look for her. The Fiend was no fool.

No, it would be waitressing for her, with her new Social Security number, or being a cashier or an office temp. She'd survive, of course. She had so far. But oh, God. All those years of study. All that work.

Nell snorkled back her tears. She had to be practical. Break this problem into pieces, and tackle the pieces one at a time. She could not control the future, but she could do something useful right now.

Finishing her thesis, now. That was within her power. Maybe this awful mess could be an inspiration. After all, the poets she studied were all heart hungry, lovelorn. Bleak despair was the very stuff of creativity. Look at Emily Dickinson, the Brontës. There was a long, noble literary tradition of hunger for love and sex being sublimated into deathless art.

Perhaps, like them, she could salvage something from the wreckage. Transmute pain into useful activity. She was unemployed, homeless, rudderless. Too scared to walk out on the street by herself. Her days would be long, silent, boring. What excuse did she have now not to hunker down and write a kick-ass thesis?

She grabbed her big black shoulder bag and unzipped the central pocket where she kept her laptop. It was not there. She'd forgotten it.

Shit, shit, shit. She blew out a shuddering breath through trembling lips at the idea of having to face Duncan's rigid face and blazing eyes and cutting remarks again in order to retrieve it.

Maybe she could have it sent over by courier. Uh-huh. With what cash? The cost of that courier would go right onto Duncan's personal account. Ka-ching, ka-ching. And her debt to him was already crushing her.

Her laptop was gone, but the cell phone he'd given her was there. She picked it up, turned it off. He wasn't going to call her on it. She slid it into the side pocket of her pants.

Onward. She dragged out the folder where she kept her tattered notes, outlines, and ideas. She pulled a fresh sheet out of her notebook and dug out a pen. She could just scribble. The old-fashioned way.

By the time they pulled up in front of Elsie's house, she'd roughed out a pretty acceptable main thesis paragraph for *"Sex, Desperation, Despair, and Death in Nineteenth-Century Women Poets."* She was even feeling a little bit better, after some useful activity. Hey. If she had to have a broken heart, at least let it be broken to good purpose.

Wesley got out and opened the door for her, peering around the deserted block. Nothing moved on the narrow lane. They climbed up Elsie's stoop, which was identical in every particular to Lucia's. She rang the bell, and waited. And waited. She rang again, and then knocked. "Elsie?" she called. "Are you in there? It's me! Nell!"

Still no answer. Wesley muscled her behind himself, holding up a very large and businesslike-looking pistol.

"Nell?" It was Elsie, all right, though her voice was muffled behind the door. It sounded higher and thinner than usual.

"Elsie?" Nell knocked again. "Is everything okay?"

"Ah . . . yes, honey, everything's fine," Elsie quavered. "Come on . . . come on in. The door's unlocked."

Nell reached for the door handle, but Wesley gently pushed her hand away and pushed the door open himself. She stood on her tip-toes and looked over his bulky shoulder as he peered into the dim interior, through the foyer.

Elsie stood across the room, in the entryway to the kitchen. Wesley started inside just as Nell registered the look on the old lady's face. The pallor. The stiff, frozen expression. The staring eyes.

She knew that look. She knew that vibe. Oh, God. Oh, no.

"Wait!" She lunged after Wesley's coat, trying to yank him back—

Thhhpt, the thud of a silenced gun, and Wesley grunted, spun, and crashed heavily to the ground.

The room boiled with black-clad masked men, leaping for her. A burlap bag whipped down over her head. She struggled and screamed in airless darkness that stank of mold and rot, arms and legs flailing—

A sting like an insect bite in her arm, a sickening weakness sweeping through her with horrible quickness—

And it all went away.

Chapter
11

Duncan kept the car between 95 and 105, depending on the sharpness of the curves. He was glad that the road leading away from the city was clear. It was the opposite direction that was clogged with rush-hour traffic. The laptop was open on the passenger seat, GPS program running. The signal was stationary, fixed at Elsie's address in Hempton. He wanted desperately to call, but the fact that Wesley no longer answered was reason enough to be terrified. Maybe they'd already discovered the phone and left it behind, since GPS traces in phones were so common. But maybe they hadn't. If not, he didn't want it to ring and give her away. That trace was his only hope.

Then the signal began to move.

The wave of fear made him want to retch. The signal moved along the main drag in Hempton and took a highway heading north and east. He had to change routes if he wanted to intercept them.

It was like walking a tightrope, driving at that speed while monitoring the computer and calculating possible shortcuts. A minute later, his cell rang, to add another ball and hoop to his balancing act.

Fortunately, he had his earpiece. "Yeah," he barked.

"The cops are there," Braxton said. "It's bad. The old lady was tied up on the ground. Wesley's shot. No sign of your lady friend."

His gut cramped. "Her signal's heading northeast," he said. "Keep me informed. Later."

"Wait. Dunc. I'm sorry about this, man. I let you down."

"Not your fault," he said curtly. "I miscalculated. She should have had a team. She shouldn't have been let out at all. Gotta go. Later."

"Gotcha." Braxton hung up.

He pressed the accelerator harder, glancing over at the map on the screen. He had to close that gap. More speed. He let the powerful motor open up and breathe, humming at 115 mph.

Play it cool. Like a glacier. After all. As long as she was moving, they probably weren't hurting her.

But when that signal stopped once again, man, he could fucking forget about playing it cool. He was going to be twisting in the flames of hell.

Stabbing pains in Nell's head woke her. She was confused, terrified. It was horrifically dark. She couldn't get any air. She was buried alive, dirt and rot in her nose. Air. God, she needed air.

She started struggling. Her arms were wrenched back, wrists bound. She was curled in the fetal position. She couldn't move. Her own weight made her hyperextended shoulders burn and throb. The vibration confused her. A bump slammed her head against the floor.

Ah. Yes. She was folded up in the trunk of a car.

Panic would not help. She tried to relax, took the slowest, shallowest breaths she could. Lack of oxygen explained the headache. Or carbon monoxide, maybe. Or both.

The car began to rattle and bump. They'd left the asphalt and gotten onto a rutted dirt road. It stopped. A murmur of male voices. Car doors popped open. The vehicle shifted as men got out. She tried to remember how many she'd seen at Elsie's. Four, maybe.

Elsie. A fresh wave of emotion jolted her. Oh, God, poor Elsie. And Wesley, too. They'd shot him.

The trunk opened with a hollow *pop*. Daylight filtered through the filthy, stinking burlap that shrouded her. Rough arms grabbed her under the armpits, giving her shoulders an agonizing jolt. She was jerked out, legs bumping over the lip of the trunk. The ground whipped up and smacked her a blow that loosened every sinew.

"Take her into the building," said the harsh, cracked voice with a thick German accent. "And tie her to a chair."

She was hoisted up and dragged, feet bouncing over rough ground, into an enclosed structure. The sunlight she'd felt outside did not penetrate here. It was humid, chill, as if she were in a cave.

The man dragging her dropped her onto a straight-backed chair. Her arms were jerked tighter, fastened to her ankles, twisting her into an agonized pretzel around the chair back. She gasped with the pain.

"The rest of you, out. Go keep watch," the German-sounding man ordered. There were mutters, tramping feet, and a large door creaked, banged shut. The light filtering through the burlap diminished sharply.

A latch fell into place. *Clunk.*

Silence. Her teeth chattered. She shook, with huge seismic shudders, as if she were freezing to death. She trembled so hard, the chair vibrated against the floor. The two remaining men stood there, watching her. She could sense their enjoyment. Feel their smiles.

"Take off the bag, John." The German-sounding man's voice oozed satisfaction.

The bag was wrenched off, whipping her head forward against the brutal pull of her tied arms. She coughed, dragging in big gulps of air.

Her hair was over her eyes. She tried to shake it back, but the slightest movement made her head throb. She just stared through the veil of tangled hair, like a captured prehistoric cavewoman, face dirtied, mouth open, eyes staring and wild.

It was not bright inside that room, but it still took a moment before her eyes readjusted. By some miracle, her glasses were still clinging to her face.

Two men. One old and collapsed in on himself, with a flabby, jowly face. Watery blue eyes peered out from puffy bags of unwholesome flesh. His lips were an unhealthy purple. He leered at her.

So did the other man, who fit Nancy's description of the Fiend. Burly, with piggish, deep-set eyes glittering in the flushed, tightly packed fat of his heavy face. His lips were wet from being compulsively licked.

Both were loathsome. Neither seemed concerned about her seeing their faces. They didn't expect her to ever be able to identify them.

She shoved that unwelcome thought out of her head.

The old man stumped forward, and tipped up her chin. "Antonella," he crooned. "In the flesh. And such lovely flesh." His hand crept down her chest, groping. He found her nipple and pinched.

She did not allow herself to scream. "Who are you?"

"My name is Ulf, my dear. Ulf Haupt. And this is my assistant, John. But I am the one who will ask questions today. Not you."

"Wh-what do you want from me?"

The light in his eyes was evil, insane. "Information, of course."

Her stomach plummeted. That was a commodity of which she had so little. The other man, whom Ulf Haupt had called John, rummaged in her blouse, groping her boobs until he got his fist around her pendant.

He wrenched it until the chain broke. "We'll add this to our growing collection," he said.

"John's been eager to question you," Haupt said.

"Yeah, since this morning," John agreed. "When you broke up with the prick." He waited for a reaction, laughing at Nell's shocked expression. "I heard it all," he taunted. "I bugged your computer, you stupid cunt. You wanted him to declare his love, huh? You wanted him to grovel, suck your toes? I almost found it in my heart to pity the guy. If I hadn't had to listen to him fucking you for the last two days."

She recoiled. He leaned forward, until his face was inches from hers. "I heard it all. You dirty little slut. Heard you screaming and begging and coming." He slapped her, rocking the chair so hard it teetered on two legs. "You love it, don't you? Filthy whore—"

"Enough, John!" The old man's voice was sharp. "Do not get carried away. She must not lose consciousness before we get the information we need. You can play later."

John subsided, muttering something vicious under his breath about cunts, sluts. His fists were clenched, and his mouth was open and wet, breath rasping fast. Irrational hate shone in his eyes. God help her. She was tied to a chair in front of a pair of raving madmen.

Haupt patted the cheek that John had slapped, as if she were a little girl and he was some hideous parody of a benevolent grandfather. "So, my dear. Tell us what you know about the sketches."

Sketches? She seesawed frantically, wondering what would get her killed the fastest—admitting ignorance or feigning knowledge. Either option looked bleak. "I don't know anything about any sketches."

Haupt's eyes hardened, and his fingers tightened on her cheek, pinching. "Do not lie. We read the Contessa's letter, stupid girl. She said the three of you could solve the puzzle, so you must know something!"

"But I'm alone. I'm not with them." Nell shook her head to clear it, blowing hair up and out of her eyes. "And you took the letter, so we never got a chance to read it. And Lucia never had a chance to—"

Another vicious slap. Her head rang. Tears sprang into her eyes.

"So the Contessa never told you how her father died?"

Nell shook her head, gulping. "No," she whispered.

"You want to hear the tale?" Haupt sounded eager to talk. "My father knew the old Conte deLuca, you see, back in their youth. In the thirties, before the war. They attended the art academy together in Rome, for a time. They became friends. Such good friends, the Conte even invited my father to visit his ancestral home. To show off the family's art treasures."

"Ah. I, um, see," said Nell, although she didn't.

"And then, the war. And the Reich," Haupt went on. "My father was a high-ranking officer in the SS. He arranged to be headquartered in deLuca's palazzo during the occupation. One of his duties was to appropriate the cream of the art pieces, for the glory of the Reich. But the Conte deLuca was greedy. He kept aside his greatest treasures. He hid them, but he wrote a map describing where to find them."

Nell held her breath, hypnotized by the pale, mad eyes of the ruined old man. Spittle landed in her face as he talked. She silently begged him to go on and on. Keep on talking, all day, all night.

As long as he was talking, they would not tear her to pieces.

"The war ended," Haupt went on. "My father fled to Argentina after the war, but he never forgot. He paid deLuca a visit fifteen years later, but the sketches were still hidden. Would you like to know what my father did to the Conte? In his efforts to convince him to reveal the hiding place?"

"N-n-no," Nell quavered. "Thanks, but no."

"Do not be insolent!" Haupt shrieked. "Perhaps if I tell you that you will share his exact same fate, it will spark your curiosity, hmm?" He slid his cold, puffy hand down over her arm, her breasts. "All that smooth, flawless skin. So pale, and soft and perfect. A pity, really."

Delay, delay. "And, ah, wh-what about M-m-marco?"

"So you know about the Marchese Barbieri? Worthless old turd. He was the one with the map, little good it did him. My father and then I myself stationed domestic spies in the Palazzo deLuca for decades, watching him search, but he never found the sketches. And then, one fine day, he climbs on a plane! And flies to America! What a curious thing, eh?" He rubbed his hands together. "John was there to meet the old Marchese. That was how we finally located the elusive Contessa. But John has an impulse control problem. I call it, 'kill now, ask questions later.'" Haupt shot a poisonous glance at John. "The Marchese and Contessa were dead before we could find out what he brought, or where he hid it. So be a good girl, Antonella. And maybe John won't be so harsh with you, eh?"

She swallowed. "I will cooperate. As much as I can." Which wasn't very goddamn much. As they would discover, soon enough.

Haupt held up the necklaces. They swung and glittered in the dim light filtering through the dirty, cobwebby windows, the sapphire *N*, her ruby *A*. "Tell me the secret of the necklaces," he commanded.

She winced. "I don't know. I only saw an incomplete draft of the letter you took, and it said that only the three of us working together, using our love of art, could open some sort of key, but we never figured out exactly to what. I'm sure she meant to tell us more before she—"

Crack, another slap. Her nose was dripping blood.

"Do not lie!" Haupt screamed. "I know you know more! We have researched you, Antonella. The bitch Contessa had you study Italian and Latin. You were being groomed to take over the search! Admit it! Why else would you study a dead language? Have you seen the map? Have you read it? What does it say?"

"No! I-I-I haven't s-s-seen . . ." She floundered, stammering. Her imagination was failing her, utterly. How could she describe a passion for language and literature for its own sake to subhuman monsters? They wouldn't understand it. They didn't even know what beauty was.

John stepped up, with a businesslike air. His next blow knocked her chair off balance. It teetered on one leg, tipped. The room swirled as she tumbled backward, onto her tied hands. *Crunch*, wood splintered beneath her, and oh, shit, oh, dear God, her hands, oh, that *hurt*—

A long broken shard of wood from a piece of junked furniture had stabbed into the pad of her thumb. She wrenched her thumb loose from the shard, again, groping with her fingers feeling blood flow, slippery and hot. Felt for the shard. There it was. Her hand closed around it, and clenched.

Snap. She broke off the tip. Small, but hers. Hidden in her fingers.

John hooked the back of her chair and heaved her upright. "Let's try that question again, Antonella." He leaned down, the whites of his eyes showing all around his irises, and slid the point of his knife under her blouse. A few sharp jerks, and the fabric gave, gaped. Buttons flew, skittering on concrete.

He dug the knife tip under the crossed silk cord that held her bra cups together, flicked the knife. This time, he nicked her skin. Blood welled up, trickled down her belly. Blood dripped from her wounded hand, as well. She clutched the splinter, hard enough to hurt, to ward off the squirming nausea, the waves of shimmering dark faintness.

The knife gleamed in front of her wide, hypnotized eyes.

"Now, Antonella," he said, companionably. "Let's talk about art."

"Right on Connemara Drive, four point two miles. Hard left onto a dirt road, half a mile after you cross a creek. Her signal's three hundred meters ahead of me, perpendicular to the main road and ten degrees to the right. I'm leaving the car. Tell the cavalry to hurry the fuck up."

"Dunc! Hold on! Don't just—"

He killed the phone and took off running. Glad for whatever instinct had prompted him to put on brown and olive drab. Her signal had been stationary for twenty minutes. Plenty of time to hurt her, if that was their intent.

He felt cold, his emotions flat-lined. A virtual figure in a video game, sent out to earn points, defeat goblins, gargoyles, basilisks, defeat the evil sorcerer. If he scored enough points, and made no wrong moves. But in the vid game, the player's life wouldn't be gutted if he fucked up. There would be no "game over" flashing on the screen. No invitation to try his luck again.

One chance. One.

He ran onward, darting from bush to tree, until the building came into view, and then the car. He hoped there were no infrared alarms. He doubted it. This was an improvised, last-minute snatch. This place wasn't their turf. He hoped.

The building looked like an abandoned, crumbling barn. He spotted the first sentry, and sank down into the bushes. He recognized the tall black guy from Lafayette. Duncan dropped to his belly and slithered around the guy, keeping beneath his line of vision. When he spiraled in closer, the guy was turned, pissing against a tree. Good.

Duncan leaped up behind him. The guy spun around, mouth dangling, dick still in his hand. He sucked in air to yell, and took the heel of Duncan's boot to the point of his chin. *Crunch.*

He toppled, eyes rolled back. Hit the tree, slid to the ground on his ass, slumped. Penis still drooping out of his opened pants.

Voices. He followed them, slithering toward the hushed murmur in the clearing around the barn. It was the blond dickhead from Lafayette, smoking a cigarette and talking to a stocky shorter guy. The blond guy had bruises beneath both eyes. Duncan crept closer, recognizing his reedy, whining tone before he could make out the words. He pulled out a couple of drugged throwing stars.

". . . with this kind of shit! It ain't worth the fuckin' money to get treated like fuckin' dogshit," he bitched. "All I say is, they better let me take my turn with the bitch after John works her over, because I mean to teach that cunt nobody messes with Curtis, man—ay!"

His monologue choked off to a shriek. He pawed at his buttock, and held up the throwing star Duncan had lobbed. "What the fuck?"

The second guy howled. A star protruded from his shoulder.

Curtis spun, and sprayed the woods with bullets from his Uzi. "Who the fuck are you, you fuck?!" he shrieked. "I'll waste your ass!"

So much for stealth. Curtis was wavering, toppling. The other guy went down even faster. The points of the stars were treated with a high-power, quick-acting sedative. He waited for some reaction from the barn. Sure enough. The door opened. A man poked his head out.

"What the fuck is going on?" he snarled. He saw the unconscious men collapsed on the ground, and his face twisted with disgust. "Fucking jerk-offs," he muttered, and lifted his automatic pistol.

He pumped a short burst of bullets into them both. The sprawled bodies jittered on the ground and then lay still.

Duncan stared through the foliage. The men were torn apart, lying in pools of blood. The Fiend lifted his gun and sprayed the woods in a wide arc. Bullets sliced through grass and leaves, right above Duncan's head. Splinters of bark and earth flew, bullets thudded into the ground.

The Fiend laughed, hysterically. "Fuck off and die, shithead!" he howled. "It's your turn, now! I got her! Go fuck yourself!" Another spray of bullets punched into the forest, *rat-tat-tat-tat.*

The guy ducked back inside. In the distance, police sirens started to wail. Duncan flew like a bolt from a crossbow across the carnage in the clearing and flung himself at the door. "Nell!" he bellowed.

"Duncan?" she called back, just as bullets pumped through the door.

One of them grazed Duncan's hip like a lick of flame. Another caught his pocket above his knee, ripping the fabric. She screamed, a wrenching cry that curdled his blood.

He sprinted around the building.

"They're coming," John said to Haupt. "We have to cut loose. Curtis and Turturro are meat. Didn't see Gerard. Probably dead, too."

"They're coming? Who is coming? How did they know where to come? How is it possible?" The man's voice rose to a shrill, querulous squawk. "You stupid, incompetent—"

"You want to berate me on our way to jail, or save it for later?" John snarled back. "Move it!"

He slashed the ropes that bound Nell's arms. Her arms fell free, numb and tingling. John yanked a handful of her hair, jerking until she cried out. "Be good, bitch," he hissed. "Or I'll gut you like a steer."

He hoisted her up and flung her over his shoulder, letting her head and arms dangle down over his back.

Something banged against the door. "Nell!"

Duncan. Oh, God. Oh, God. "Duncan?!" she yelled.

"I said, shut up, bitch!" John swung up his gun, riddled the door with bullets. Light shone through the pattern of holes. She screamed again, in horror and despair, but John was running now, and her voice was jolting in her throat, her torso bouncing and thudding against his back.

They burst out of the back of the barn. She could not see where they were going, just green leaves, the ground behind John's pounding heels, the fact that John's belt was loose, his T-shirt riding up, showing acne-spotted rolls of flab hanging over the waistband of his jeans.

The sound of his footsteps changed. A hollow thud, on wooden planks. Haupt hurried along beside them, huffing and puffing.

A bridge. She heard hollow footsteps on wood, saw weathered planks below John's booted feet. Water murmured below. John swung around, started shooting, a deafening barrage of bullets. Her whole body shook and jiggled with the jackhammer explosions.

Her blood-slicked hand tightened around her splinter. She worked it down in her hand until the sharp part protruded a couple of inches, and the blunt part was clutched in her fist. The point was wickedly sharp. She gathered her nerve for the blow. Everything she had to give: her passion for Duncan, her love for her sisters, for Lucia. Even for Elena. Her reverence for beauty, fineness, love. Her respect for effort and honest sweat. For things that could not be bought. Not for any money.

John turned. The gun rose up. *No*. Because he had no right to hurt her, or Duncan, or anyone.

He had . . . no . . . *right!*

She stabbed down, driving the splinter deep into the meat and fat that covered his kidney. He squealed. His shots went wild.

Bam, Duncan's bullet blew John's gun out of his hand. It flew up, curling and turning in the air. John lunged to catch it one-handed, but it danced off his fingers and down. An eternity later, it splashed into the river.

"Put her down." It was Duncan's voice, incredibly cool and even.

John stared back, panting. He laughed. "Sure thing, shitbird."

He heaved her over the bridge railing.

She flew, fell, down, turning, spinning. Cold green water closed over her head.

Duncan sprinted to the middle of the bridge and pitched himself over the side. The current was strong when he came boiling up for air, the river swollen with the recent rains.

Nell bobbed to the surface, face plastered with hair, gasping for breath. He fought his way over to her, clasped her to him.

When he finally got them over to the shore, he scooped her out into his arms. Her cheek was swollen, her lips split. There was blood crusted in her nostrils. They'd been hitting her. Rage clawed at him, but the fuckers were long gone. No one to catch and punish. Not yet.

Her eyes fluttered open and fastened onto his. Her lips chattered so hard, it took a long time for her to speak.

"Y-y-you c-c-came back for m-me," she said.

She dropped her face against his chest and shut down. Shock. Her face was so pale. He struggled up the steep creek bank and launched into a heavy, stumbling run through the forest.

Hoping to God that whoever was blowing those police sirens had the presence of mind to bring a goddamn ambulance along.

Chapter
12

Duncan stared at himself in the hospital bathroom mirror. He stank of that foul, bitter antiseptic foam soap in the squeeze bottle over the sink, with which he'd attempted to clean himself up. He supposed it beat out the stench of river mud. But the blend was pretty nasty.

Nancy and Liam had brought him a change of clothes. Liam's stuff fit well enough, although the shirt was tight around the shoulders. His own clothing lay in a clammy, mud-slimed snarl on the bathroom floor. He shoved the gun back into his jeans, covered it with the shirttail. He was crashing. He felt icy cold inside, and his hands couldn't stop shaking. His face was a rigid, staring mask.

The doctors and nurses had forced him out of Nell's room to get her examined, and all the various tubes, needles, and machines hooked up. He'd waited outside the door like a wet, patient hound shivering on the doorstep until they took pity on him and let him in again.

She looked so fragile. So pale. Only her hair had vitality, lying in great curling snarls all over the pillow.

He was so scared, he could hardly breathe. Wondering if he'd earned enough points with this stunt to get another chance with her.

He'd seen the world without her in it. He'd felt that reality to the fullest during that hellacious race against time. Gut-wrenching fear that never eased. The ache of loss. Emptiness, silence. Sick regret.

He couldn't face it. He'd say any words she wanted to hear. He didn't give a fuck whether they were true or not, realistic or not. He no longer cared about honesty, dealing straight, any of that meaningless bullshit. She could write out a script for him, if she wanted, and he'd parrot it back to her, get it signed and witnessed and notarized. He wasn't even ashamed of it. He didn't have the energy for shame. He knew when he was whipped.

The only reason he'd left her bedside at all was because Liam and Nell's sisters were there, talking in hushed tones, giving him those worried looks. Vivi had brought him coffee and a sandwich at the lunch stand in the lobby. He hadn't been able to eat it. His insides felt like they were turned to cold stone.

He kicked his stuff into the corner of the bathroom and walked out, braving the sympathetic glances. Vivi vacated the chair near the head of Nell's bed. He jerked his chin at it, indicating that she should sit again.

"As fucking if. Sit." She grabbed his shoulders and pushed him into the chair. "You're the one who's been out there being heroic."

He slumped into the chair, and took up Nell's hand again. The one that wasn't torn up, bandaged into a puffy white ball. Her hand was so cold. But so was his. Clammy with fear. He had no heat to give her.

Vivi put her hand on his shoulder, leaned over, and kissed the top of his head. "Hey. Duncan," she said softly. "You did good. It's going to be fine. Try to relax, okay? You're scaring us."

He jerked his head and hunched lower over Nell's hand.

Some time later, her fingers twitched inside his. His heart jumped up into his throat. Her eyes were fluttering open. Dazed.

Nancy and Vivi got up and came over to the other side of the bed.

"Hey, sweetie," Nancy said, her voice thick with tears.

Nell gave them a tiny smile, as if the corners of her lips were too heavy to lift. Her eyes flicked over to Duncan's. He stared back, mute. A silence took over the room. An electrical charge that grew. And grew.

"Ah, maybe the three of us can just go take a little coffee break," Vivi suggested, her voice brisk. "Come on, you guys. Let's, ah go."

They trooped out the door, leaving the two of them finally alone.

* * *

Nell gazed up, so happy he was there. Both of them, still alive. How marvelous and improbable was that?

Her heart was swelling, so soft and full, it felt like a supernova inside her chest. She was exhausted, limp. And so soft. A fuzzy glow of light lying in the bed. Probably it was whatever they'd drugged her with. Nice stuff.

Duncan lifted her hand and leaned forward, elbows on the bed. Rubbing her knuckles against his cheek. His beard stubble was a delicious cat's-tongue rasp of pleasurable friction against her skin.

He didn't look good. His eyes were shadowed, and his mouth was grim.

She tried to speak to him, but her muscles wouldn't respond.

"Don't talk," he ordered, frowning. "Rest."

She finally got words out, letting them ride on the outbreath. "Did I thank you for saving my life?"

A smile softened the grim cast of his face. "Not too recently," he admitted. "Not in the last thirty-six hours, at least."

"Ah. Well." She squeezed his hand. "For the record."

There was so much to say to him, it was bottlenecked inside her. Then, suddenly her memories coalesced. And with them, a clutch of fear. "Elsie?" she asked. "And Wesley?"

"They're okay," he assured her. "Elsie was treated for shock and contusions, your sisters told me, but she's already getting off on being a local celebrity. She's in hog heaven, giving interviews to the local paper from her hospital bed. Wesley's pretty bad, but he's in stable condition now. Bullet to the shoulder, lost a lot of blood. But he should be okay."

"Thank God," she murmured. Her eyes drifted closed again. She felt like a radio, tuning in and out of the frequency of consciousness, but Duncan was always there, like a rock coming in and out of view in the mist. So comforting. Another factoid popped to the top of her mind.

"They're looking for sketches," she said.

He frowned. "Huh? Who is looking for what?"

"John and Haupt. The bad guys. Lucia's treasure. They're after sketches of some kind. Haupt told me his name and a bunch of other stuff, just for the fun of it. To taunt me. Hah. Funny, isn't it?"

His eyebrows furrowed. "Don't know if funny's the word I'd use."

"The Conte deLuca, Lucia's father, hid these sketches from the Nazis during the Second World War," she went on. "And they're still hidden. Wild stuff. How did you know to come after me?"

"Found a bug in your laptop. Followed the GPS in your cell."

"No way," she whispered. "Saved by a cell phone. The irony of it."

He pressed his face to her hand. "I couldn't let them hurt you."

She stroked his jaw. "You're cold," she fretted softly. "Why are you cold? You're usually so hot."

"I'm scared shitless," he blurted out.

Her eyes widened, shocked. "Huh? You? Why?"

"I thought I'd lost you." The words rushed out as if they were under pressure. "Nothing's worth shit without you, Nell. If they hurt you, that would be it for me. I'd be finished. Dead meat. Worm food."

She petted his cheek, trying to soothe him. "Duncan. Don't—"

"I have to have you in my life," he said. "Have to. I don't give a shit anymore about all that crap we argued about. You want me to make a formal declaration of love, fine. I'll do it. You want me to memorize poetry and recite it to you naked and standing on my head, I'll do it. Any fucking song or dance routine you want—"

"No," she said softly.

He cut off the stream of words, alarmed. "Uh, no in what sense?"

"No in the sense of no, it's not necessary. You don't have to stand on your head or do any routine. You don't even have to tell me that you love me. Because you already did."

He blinked. "I did? How do you figure? When?"

"Just now," she told him, smiling. "And not only that. You get big points for being really poetic and original about it."

His face cleared, but he still looked perplexed. "Great," he said doubtfully. "Hold on, here. Points? What's this I hear about points? I thought points pissed you off."

She laughed, softly, petting his cheek again. She couldn't bear to stop. "There's something about staring death in the face that helps a girl get over her pet peeves."

"Ah. Well, hell, I didn't even know I was being poetic," he said. "Don't I have to tell you your eyes are like stars and your skin like lily petals? And your ass is like a ripe, juicy peach?"

She shook her head. "Stars, lilies, peaches, pah. Overdone. Having a guy charge in to save you from a horrible death at the hands of psychopathic sadists? Now, *that's* poetry."

He lay his head on her chest. His shoulders shook. She petted them and ran her fingers through his hair, again and again. She didn't want to break their physical contact for a single second. She wanted to cling to him. Just stay eternally fused.

"So we're getting married?" His muffled voice had a challenging tone. "Soon? Like, now?"

She smiled up at the ceiling, euphoric. She was going to float up there, get stuck on the ceiling. "As soon as you like," she said.

He raised his head and fixed her with a narrow gaze, as if daring her to contradict him. "And we're having our honeymoon in Italy."

"Sounds amazing," she said.

He hugged her tighter. "You are so beautiful," he muttered. "And by the way. Your ass really is like a ripe, juicy peach."

"Thank you," she said softly. "That's a lovely sentiment."

"I know I'm stubborn," he went on. "And resistant to change, and I always order the same thing in restaurants. But the flip side is, I know what I like. Once I make up my mind, I don't change it. I'm talking about to the end of time, Nell."

"That's wonderful," she whispered. "To the ends of being, and ideal grace. Lovely. I'm melting. Keep going."

He looked worried. "Keep going? Oh, God. This is the hard part, right? I have to keep being poetic? For the rest of my life? Fuck me!"

She giggled. "So the part that came before was easy, for you, then? The gunfights and the car chases and the mortal combat?"

"Oh, that stuff's more or less straightforward," he said gruffly. "You either get killed or you don't. But love, man. That shit's complicated. I don't understand why it works now, but it didn't before."

She traced his mouth with a fascinated finger. "Because we met halfway," she said softly. "You're so beautiful, Duncan."

"Uh, thanks," he said. "So this is the halfway point, then?"

She pulled his face down, kissed him. "Yeah. Nice, isn't it?"

"I love our halfway point." He touched his lips to hers, as gently as if she were a newly opened flower. "Let's live there forever."

"Sounds great to me," she replied.

Ready
or Not

Chapter
1

The van was stuck in the mud. Nothing could be served by denying that fact any longer. She had to face it. And eat it.

Vivi D'Onofrio killed the engine, shoved her hair back behind her ears, and pounded the steering wheel. The world outside the windshield was a wavering blur of green. Lightning flashed, and she braced herself for the crash. Edna yelped, and scrambled into her lap. Vivi petted the quivering dog. "Easy girl," she crooned. "It'll be over soon."

It had seemed like a good idea late last night, just push on, rain and all.

The real truth was, she'd been scared to stop, with all the weird shit that had been happening. It was hard to argue with stomach-turning fear when she was all alone, with no one to act tough for. She hadn't been able to face a roadside motel with a single door lock against the night, which was all she could afford. She was the only D'Onofrio chick without a big, vigilant, protective guy giving the hairy eyeball to everyone within shouting range of his new lady. The obvious soft target.

Nope, Vivi was on her own, as usual. Not that she begrudged her sisters their good fortune. They both deserved to have a foxy guy worshipping at their shrines. In fact, those men still didn't know how lucky they were. They would be discovering it for the rest of their lives.

Thank God, her sisters were as safe with Duncan and Liam as they could possibly be in these strange days. But she was feeling very unworshipped these days. Truth to tell, she'd been feeling that way even before Ulf Haupt and John the Fiend started attacking the D'Onofrio women.

Both her sisters and their men had tried to persuade her to stay with them, but that struck her as nonproductive and embarrassing. How long could a woman realistically sit around like a bump on a log in someone's home, bored out of her mind, not working, being a financial drain and a big fat fifth wheel? And besides, she really missed her dog.

Nah, she just had to muddle on with her life. Fiend and all.

Vivi stroked Edna's floppy, velvety soft ears and tried to avoid the hot cloud of dog breath from Edna's panting mouth. She looked up at the heavy, swollen gray sky. She could call her new landlord, but how embarrassing was that? She checked her phone. Ah. No coverage anyway. She was in the ass end of nowhere. That was the idea. To hide out where the Fiend would never find her.

She'd made it to the town of Silverfish around two in the afternoon, if one could call it a town. Through the torrents of rain, all she had seen was a convenience store, a gas pump, and a boarded-up Dairy Queen. She had followed the directions to progressively smaller roads, arriving at a dirt track with a hand-painted sign that read MOFFAT'S WAY. The last detail scribbled on the envelope.

But Moffat's Way wasn't a driveway, but an old logging road, deeply rutted and steep. By the time she realized how rough the road was, the ruts were streams, no place wide enough to turn around. She made a turn into a puddle, sank into the mud, and that was that.

Vivi leaned her hot cheek against the cool window. Edna stuck her nose into Vivi's hand and gave it a comforting lick. Who knew how much farther this road went on before it came to Jack Kendrick's land? She hadn't bothered to inform herself about the nitpicky details.

She spun the tires, just to torture herself, and pondered her options. Time for action. Self-sufficient, proactive Vivi D'Onofrio rises to any occasion, she affirmed bracingly to herself. Psychopathic kid-nappers assholes? Bring 'em on.

A long shudder racked her body. Um, maybe not.

She flung open the door of the van, looked in vain for a solid place to put her feet. Edna crawled over her lap, and Vivi clutched the dog's collar. "Oh, no! That's all I need," she said. "Get back in. *In!*"

Edna shrank back, looking reproachful. Vivi rolled her pants up, looked at her cheerful, bright-green high-tops regretfully, and jumped out.

Cold, sucking mud swallowed her feet. She slogged around the van. The tires were half buried. Chilly rain plastered her hair to her scalp and the green T-shirt to her body. She let loose with a stream of explicit profanity, the kind she'd learned in the Bronx as a child, and punctuated it by kicking a slimy tire. Pain shot up her leg.

That's right, she thought. *Very impressive, Viv. Very mature.*

Farther back, she'd seen what looked like a collapsed shack. Maybe planks laid down in front of the tires would give them purchase to get out of the muck. Beyond the puddle, the road looked driveable.

She'd exhaust every possibility before limping to Jack Kendrick's house on foot like a cat left out in the rain. Fine first impression that would be, she fumed. She knew only what Duncan had told her. Kendrick was some sort of ex-spy commando who'd been on some top-secret intelligence gathering task force with Duncan years ago. Now, unaccountably, he grew flowers. Duncan had been somewhat vague about the details of that career change, his brain being deep-fried from being insanely in love with Nell.

So this mysterious Kendrick lived in the woods, had an apartment in his barn, and was willing to let her huddle in his flowery bower and hide like a quivering, nose-twitching bunny until they all fig-ured out what the hell to do about these art-hungry psychopaths. Nice of him.

Seriously, though. She was still waiting for the other shoe to drop. Duncan assured her that Kendrick knew the score, had agreed to the plan. It had sounded perfect, back in NYC. Too perfect, actually.

Finally. There it was, a stack of gray, weathered planks, rusty nails sticking through them at crazy angles. She wrestled and yanked until she'd extricated a few boards, along with some ugly splinters. Negotiated the slippery boards through the fir thickets. Arrived at the van, soggy, scratched, and panting, issuing a stream of profanity. She hauled out her toolbox, hammered the nails flat, and got down to wrestle them into place. Mud oozed over the tops of the boards, and she was slimed from chest to feet, when she heard the deep voice from behind her.

"I don't think that's going to work."

She started violently, knocking her head on the bumper. "Who is that?" She scrambled to her feet. There was no one there that she could see.

Vivi scanned the trees and reached for the tire iron stowed under the seat, groping until her fingers closed over cold, hard metal. "Where are you?" she called out. She was starting to shake.

"Over here."

She spun, brandishing the tire iron. A tall man, stood there, half hidden in the trees. He was shrouded in a dull-green hooded rain poncho, dripping with rain. She would never have seen him if he had not spoken. Adrenaline zinged through her. She gave the tire iron an experimental heft.

"What do you think you're doing, sneaking up on me like that?"

He took a step forward. She raised the tire iron. He stopped. Edna whined.

"Stay, Edna," she snapped. "Who are you?"

"I'm not going to attack you," he said, pushing back his hood.

Light, silver-gray eyes, cool and unreadable. His face was brown, lean. High cheekbones, a hooked nose. A scar on one temple slashed down into one of his straight, dark eyebrows, leaving a white line. He had a short beard, or maybe long beard stubble. Dark hair, long and shaggy. He regarded her steadily. Drops of rain beaded his face. He did not look like the Fiend, as Nancy and Nell had described him. This guy was not loathsome, pig eyed, or malodorous.

By no means. This guy was oh-my-God fine looking. She tried to breathe. Her terror was transmuting itself into utter embarrassment.

"Put it down." A small smile crinkled up the skin around his eyes.

"What?" She realized that her mouth was hanging open.

"The tire iron." He glanced at her white-knuckled hand.

"Oh." She felt foolish, panicked. Acutely conscious of the mud on her clothes, the hair stuck to her face, of the way her wet, muddy shirt clung to her tits. Of how incredibly tall he was. Even if he wasn't the Fiend, he was a complete stranger, and there was nobody around here for miles. Just her. And Edna, the world's friendliest dog. She looked at the hand that clutched the tire iron. It was shaking.

"The boards won't work," he said gently. "It was a good idea, but the mud is too wet and deep." He took a step closer. She backed away.

He sighed, silently, and picked up a stick, walking away from her around the back of the van, prodding the mud.

Released from the spell of his eyes, she finally managed to exhale. *Get a grip.* He was not going to leap on her like a mad dog. He didn't look like a killer. Try to be civil. Her face felt so hot, raindrops should be skittering on it like water on a griddle. Insane. She never blushed. "I asked what you were doing here," she said, trying to sound authoritative.

"This is my land," he said.

"Oh." She dropped her gaze, before his bright eyes could catch it and nail it down again. "Do you always walk around in thunderstorms?"

"I like the rain," he said. "I like the way it smells. And I wish you'd put that thing down."

"I'll put it down when I'm ready to put it down," she said shakily.

He tossed down his stick. "Whatever. Just don't hit me with it."

"Not without provocation," she said.

His mouth twitched. "Would you just chill the fuck out?"

She felt ridiculous, and threw the tire iron back into the van in disgust.

"You travel alone?" he asked.

"No. I travel with my dog," Vivi replied.

Edna bounded out when her existence was mentioned, landing in the mud with a wet plop. She shook herself, trotted over to the stranger, and gave his large brown hand a sniff. She yelped her approval and leaped up on him.

"Down, Edna," Vivi ordered, startled. Edna had never cozied up to strangers. It made her feel vaguely betrayed. "Get back in here!"

The dog trotted back, panting into Vivi's face. "Sorry about that," she told him.

"No problem." A brief smile lit his face. "Nice dog."

"Too nice," Vivi muttered. She started to push back the tangled hair that clung to her face, but stopped. Mud on her hands.

He gazed at her, with that supernatural calm. Maybe hanging out in nature for too long did that to a guy. Look at him, walking through the pouring rain because he liked the way it smelled. Give her a break.

It made her feel frantic, citified, stressed out. A shallow little squeaking hamster racing on the wheel. And the hungry fanged kitties lurking, licking their chops. Waiting for their lunch.

Oh, Christ, she needed a vacation. A night's sleep. Something.

"You're stuck," he remarked.

She suppressed a sarcastic comment about stating the glaringly obvious, and concentrated on wiping her hands on her drenched T-shirt. Good grief. He could see everything through that shirt. She hadn't worn a bra. She wasn't wearing a jacket. She was blushing. Again.

"I noticed that actually," she said. "Can you tell me how might I get a tow around here?"

He prodded the mud with his stick once again, looked up at the lowering clouds. "No," he said. "See how steep that hill is? No one can pull you out until this dries up." He stroked Edna's head. "So why did you bring this piece of junk out onto the worst road in the county in the middle of a thunderstorm?"

"This van is not junk," Vivi flared. "It's been my home for years, and it's perfectly fine. It's the road that's the problem, not my van!"

He looked incredulous. "You live in this thing?"

"I'm a craftswoman," she informed him. "I work the craft fair circuit, so I live on the road. Up till now, that is."

"Interesting, but it doesn't explain what you're doing on my land."

Why, that arrogant putz. "None of your business," she snapped.

"It is now," he said. "This thing is blocking my road."

Vivi lifted her chin. "Didn't you just say that nobody's going to be driving on it until it's dry?"

His eyes caught hers, held them fast. "True enough," he said. "But it's still my land." He gazed at her thoughtfully. Not ogling her, but her body still shivered, as if he were checking her out inch by inch.

She suppressed an urge to cross her arms across her breasts. She would remain nonchalant, or die in the attempt. "Besides, I'm not trespassing. I'm going to my new place. How far is it to Kendrick's?"

The man's face went blank for a second. Then his brow furrowed. He stared at her, then at the mud-splattered, fantastical painting on the side of her van. "Don't tell me you're Vivien D'Onofrio."

Tension started to tighten, in her belly, her neck. "And just why shouldn't I tell you that?"

"You're not what I expected," he said. "I have to talk to Duncan."

"Oh, my God. You mean, you're Jack Kendrick?" She stared at him, speechless. She'd been expecting a stolid jarhead type, older, thicker, with graying hair buzzed off.

Not a silver-eyed sex god who loved to walk in the rain.

"You're early," he said, an accusing note in his voice. "Duncan sent me an e-mail last night saying you were still in Idaho yesterday. I expected you this evening, or tomorrow. What, did you drive all night?"

"Uh, yes." He didn't need to know what a cowering scaredy-cat she was, so she skipped the explanations, while running their entire conversation through her mind, trying to assess how rude she'd been.

Hmmph. Pretty bad. No ruder than he deserved, but still. She had to make an effort. He was doing her a big, fat favor, after all. "Um. Seems like we got off to a bad start," she said, trying to sound conciliatory.

"Yeah, it does." He no longer looked Zen mellow. He looked pissed.

Vivi asked carefully. "What do you mean, not what you expected? she asked. "What were you expecting?"

"Duncan told me you were a professional designer with a stalker problem who needed to drop out of sight for a while. He did not tell me that you were a tattooed, itinerant teenager sexpot neo-hippie."

Vivi's jaw dropped. Teenager? Neo-hippie? *Sexpot*, for God's sake? All thoughts of conciliation vanished. "You rude son of a bitch!" she hissed. "I *am* a professional! You owe me an apology!"

"We'll see." Jack's face was blatantly unapologetic.

Sexpot? Her brain stuck on that like a hook. God knew, it was not how she'd describe her muddy, strung-out, sleep-deprived, what-the-cat-dragged-in self, but holy cow! Who did the guy think he was?

So he was that insufferable type of man who made snap judgments based on a nose ring and a tie-dye T-shirt. Truth to tell, she'd been meaning to take the nose ring out before meeting him, just to suss him out first. She'd meant to stop at a place with a bathroom, put on some decent clothes, brush her hair, maybe even put on some makeup.

So much for that brilliant plan. Add another mistake to the list.

She held up her arm, displaying the tattoo of coiled barbed wire that circled her narrow wrist. "You've got a problem with me, Kendrick?"

"Yes," Jack said flatly.

Vivi was blushing again. Smarting, from being judged by him. She bit back a babbling flood of explanations that were none of his business. Explanations that she owed to nobody. In truth, that tattoo wasn't one she'd chosen. Her mom's boyfriend had taken her to his buddy's skeevy tattoo parlor when she was ten, to spite Vivi's mom. As an attention-getting technique, it had bombed, big-time. Vivi's mom had been too focused organizing her next heroin fix to notice. Vivi figured she was probably lucky the guy hadn't put the tattoo on her face. Talk about an alternative look.

But she didn't enjoy playing the victim, so she'd flaunted the tattoo. And nobody had forced her to get the mandala tattoo over the crack of her ass, or the crescent moon and star on the top of her foot, or the smiling gothic sun face that adorned her shoulder blade, or the flower over her left breast. And Kendrick couldn't even see those.

She'd never felt embarrassed about her funky, alternative look before. Usually, she enjoyed getting in the face of uptight people. It was good for their health, to have their assumptions challenged. But for some reason, the self-appointed task of challenging assumptions was no fun for her today. She didn't have the juice for it. Not with this guy.

"Would you mind answering my original question?" she asked, her voice tight. "How far is it to your place?"

"By this road, two and a half miles. Cross-country, a little over a mile and a half. Why didn't you take the other road?"

"What other road?"

"I just put in another road, from the other side of the property. It's much shorter, and better kept. I e-mailed the directions to Duncan. He should have passed them on to you."

Vivi shoved back her hair and wondered uncomfortably if she'd left mud across her cheek. "These were the directions he gave me last week, before I took off. He must have forgotten. I wouldn't be surprised. He's been distracted lately. Love, and all."

"I see," he said.

"But just for the record, I'm not a teenager. I'm almost twenty-eight. Nor am I a neo-hippie. Nor am I flaky, in any way." She crossed her arms over her chest, and glared at him. She couldn't deny the itinerant or tattooed parts. She wasn't sure if she wanted to deny the sexpot part. That was a matter of context, mood. Inclination.

He raised an eyebrow. She willed herself not to drop her gaze. A raindrop rolled down the sculpted contours of his jaw. She watched it, breathless.

"You don't look twenty-eight," he observed.

She shook herself loose of the hypnosis, and steeled herself to do the grown-up, dignified thing. "Well, I am. If you've drawn your conclusions about my intrinsic value as a person after two minutes of conversation, there's nothing left to be said. I'll just hike back to town and find a motel and someone who can help me pull my van out."

He frowned. "Don't be silly. We'll talk about it later. Get what you need out of your van for the time being. You can't walk back to town."

She drew herself up to her full height, which was about five three, unfortunately. "I can do what I goddamn well please. I don't need your help, and I don't need your attitude. I'll just pack my bags, if you don't mind, and Edna and I will be on our way."

"You can't—" He cut himself off, looking irritated. "This rain isn't stopping. It's six miles back to town. You aren't going to find anybody to help you with that van today. Get your stuff." He stared at her stiff, stony face, sighed, and said, "Okay. I apologize, already. Let me rephrase. Please, get your stuff."

Vivi was cautiously mollified. She climbed into the van and shoved clothes into her duffel, too nervous to be methodical. She tossed cans of dog food into her backpack, attached her sleeping bag, and jumped out with both bags. He was examining the lurid fantasy mural on the van while he waited. "What's this, a dragon?"

"No, it's a serpent," she informed him, ridiculously defensive.

He harrumphed. "Is that your work?"

She snorted. As fucking if. "No," she said crisply. "That's not my style. Actually, I don't paint. I'm a sculptor. An old friend of mine named Rafael painted that. I bought the van from him years ago."

"Hmmm. Whatever. Let's go, if you're ready." He grabbed the heavy duffel from her shoulder, flung it onto his back, and headed straight into the thickest-looking part of the forest.

She struggled after him with her backpack as he wove and ducked through evergreens, brambles, and clinging foliage and festoons of lichen with supernatural grace and ease. She felt clumsy and heavy with every step, dragging her mud-covered high-tops out of the ground with a wet, squelching sound. Fir boughs slapped her face, snagged her hair.

Kendrick glanced back to make sure she was following and started up a steep incline. The soft mud was very slippery. She climbed the hill, half-crawling, grabbing trunks of little sapling firs for balance. She started sliding downhill, and tried to steady herself by reaching for a clump of innocent-looking broad-leafed plants. Their tough, leathery stems proved to be covered with thorns. She lost her footing, and fell into the sloppy mud. Painfully.

"Need a hand?"

Jack Kendrick was looming over her, though to be fair, it wasn't his fault. He was standing above her on the slope, after all, and the guy was ridiculously tall to start with. His silvery eyes examined her narrowed thoughtfully. "Are you hurt?"

She pointed at the plant, and struggled to rise, cradling the stinging hand. He helped her to her feet, his hand under her elbow.

"Let me see." He turned her hand over, examined it, and began pulling out the tiny thorns embedded in her palm.

Vivi's breath stopped. Her senses were swamped with close-up sensory details. His head bent over hers, rain dripping from the ends of his shaggy, dark hair. Every detail of him etched itself into her brain. The way the hair grew back from his forehead, the white streak on his temple where the scar disappeared into his hairline. His sensual mouth. Very sensual, when it was relaxed. His lower lip, so cushiony and pink. It looked like it would be hot, soft. Kissable.

She was close enough to smell him. Soap, pine trees, wood smoke. Coffee. She wanted to touch his face, smooth the rain-drenched strands of hair that clung to his forehead.

She recoiled, alarmed at her own impulses. "Let's go on."

"Give me this," he said, pulling her backpack off her shoulders.

She was irritated at the implication that she couldn't handle it. She was small, yes, but no weakling. "I'm fine!" She tugged it back.

He plucked it from her hand with an impatient jerk and slung it over his shoulder, along with her duffel. He started back up the hill, and she scrambled after, knees wobbling. "A little farther, and the hard part's over," he said over his shoulder.

"And I'm not helpless! I was doing fine!" she shouted after him.

Her words seemed to bounce off his back. His lack of response made her sound foolish and ineffectual. She hated that. Dirty trick.

Over the crest of the hill, the forest opened into a broad sweep of gentle downhill slope. The trees here were taller, with more space between them. Edna pranced around, sniffing at the fallen tree trunks. The rain had slackened. The air was luminous and heavy with fog.

The silent grandeur of the forest worked magic on her jangled nerves as they padded along. It was beauty that sobered her, calmed her. Luminous, magic. The pattering rain, the feathery delicacy of pine boughs, the paler green festoons of moss, and tiny star-shaped white flowers floating ethereally in shiny green clumps of ground cover. It was so beautiful, she forgot her stinging hand, slimed shoes, and outraged sensibilities.

About a half hour later, he led her through a waist-high tangle of blooming wild roses. And then she saw the house.

He watched as she caught sight of the house, and felt ridiculously gratified at the smile that lit up her face. *Yeah, of course she likes it, Kendrick.* What wasn't to like? He'd worked his ass off on that place.

Still, it pleased him that she appreciated the grace of the old-fashioned house under the enormous pines. The comfortable porch. The huge flower and herb garden that he'd meticulously landscaped. He was proud of it. After all that work, she damn well ought to appreciate it.

That, however, did not mean that he would let some wandering wild child whose body made him break out in a fever sweat park her lurid van in his driveway and disrupt his peace of mind. He hadn't signed up for that.

He'd known, in his bones, that something was up. The tone in Duncan's voice, that hidden smile. He knew that sneaky bastard. He'd been keeping something back, and there it was, in the flesh. His job was to babysit a doe-eyed, wet-T-shirt-clad mini-sex-bomblet and keep her out of trouble. Served him right, for letting Duncan jerk him around. It was true that he owed Dunc, but, God. This kind of trouble he did not need.

Duncan had said that the chick was in danger. Some muddled, improbable tale about evil Nazis, treasure maps, lost art. Christ on a crutch. He'd given up on drama. He wanted peace and quiet. Simplicity.

Still, he disliked the idea of Vivi D'Onofrio in danger. She was so small and delicate. Her skin, so pale against that red hair. He wondered if the color was fake. Its brilliance seemed exaggerated.

There was one quick, surefire way to find out, he thought suddenly, and he tried to squelch the thought in his mind before his dick could swell to maximum capacity again. Thank God for the rain poncho. Every detail of her figure had been visible in the damp tie-dye T-shirt. Those high, perfect tits, the kind that fit into a champagne cup. The classic, tender mouthful. He cursed under his breath.

"You said something?" she asked.

He shook his head, not trusting himself to speak.

"Did you build this yourself?" she persisted, waiting for his nod.

"Wow." Vivi's voice was reverent. They passed through riotous array of spring flowers, blooming lilac bushes, lush borders of aromatic herbs, flowers of every type and color. "Is, ah, someone in your family a gardener?" she asked delicately.

"I'm the only one who lives here," he said. "The barn is around the back." He led her around the building, beyond which stood a large, freshly remodeled and painted barn. The apartment was on the top.

He'd lived in it himself for the time it took him to build his house. He'd been using the bottom floor for a garage and the apartment above it for storage lately, but last week, after Duncan's bullying sessions, he'd dutifully moved his boxes out and into the attic to make room for Duncan's future sister-in-law. He'd pictured some uptight New York artistic type, all in black. Hah. He'd never seen anyone as colorful as Vivi D'Onofrio. The chick glowed, like neon. He needed fucking sunglasses.

He led her up the stairs, which were on the outside of the building, and onto the deck. He slid open the sliding glass doors and stood back to let her enter first. The place was plain, but freshly painted and nicely finished. She gazed at the living room that opened onto the deck, with the view of the river and the house.

She slowly walked into the big bedroom that looked out over the garden. She strode into the bathroom, surveyed the deep sink, the old claw-foot Victorian tub that he'd found at an auction years ago. It had a transparent shower curtain with old-style botanical illustrations of flowers, complete with their Latin names, splashed all over it.

She sidled out the bathroom door past him, careful not to touch him, and walked into the spacious kitchen. She opened the freezer, sighing when she saw the automatic ice maker. She pushed the lever, grabbed a handful of ice, held it to her pink cheek. "It's perfect," she announced.

She folded her arms in front of her chest, and waited for him to contradict her. Her face was battle ready. There was a streak of mud across one high cheekbone.

"Well?" she asked impatiently. "Spit it out, Kendrick."

"Well, what?" he snapped back. "Spit what out?"

Her hair was drying, fluffing up into a fiery mane. "The bottom line," she said. "Have we got a deal? You sounded like you weren't sure, back there. Sounded like my tattoos and nose ring scared you. Have you dug your courage back out from under that rock it was shivering under?"

Jack refused to rise to the bait. "I have to talk to Duncan," he temporized. "He gave me a false impression."

"No, maybe you just made some stupid assumptions. And you're still making them." She smiled brightly. "If you'll excuse me, I'm cold, and I really need a shower. Thanks for carrying my stuff. Buh-bye."

She gestured toward the door with a dismissive smile.

Once back in his own kitchen, Jack tried not to visualize Vivi's body naked in the tub, hot water streaming down her legs, her high breasts. Tried and failed. He felt flustered, sweaty. Stupid. He hadn't felt so unsure of himself since he was a teenager.

He was usually good at dealing with the unexpected. Being flex, turning surprises to his advantage. The trick was to stay calm in his center. That had helped him during those years on the task force with Dunc in Afghanistan. And before, in the military, in Iraq, in Africa. It had helped him negotiate his childhood and manage the characters who had peopled it. It had helped him those bleak months that he'd spent on the streets of North Portland, as a teenager.

He knew nothing lasted forever. That some people couldn't stay in one place for long. No need to blame or judge, it was just a fact. Getting upset or uptight about it was like blaming a leaf for being green.

He put on a pot of coffee, just to do something with his hands. People like Vivi D'Onofrio were liable to climb into their truck, or motorcycle, or van and disappear in a cloud of dust. No hard feelings.

That was not the kind of woman he wanted to be attracted to. He knew how that story ended before it began. He was not going to do that to himself. He would not be so blind, so stupid. No fucking way.

He did not feel calm in his center when he looked at her. He wouldn't be able to stay cool, detached. He'd get wound up, tied in knots. He'd fuck himself up. Royally. He knew it. For a goddamn fact.

But still, he pictured water streaming down over her body, and wondered. Curly ringlets, or straight swatches? Red pubic hair, or dark? Tightly furled, involuted, secretive pale pink pussy lips, or did she have a bright crimson one that burst proudly out of her slit like some sort of exotic flower? Shaved? Pierced, even? And her flavor?

Whoa. That gave him a head rush. He dangled his head between his knees. Trying not to imagine her flavor.

Chapter
2

Vivi tried to relax in the shower. She was so angry at herself for not stopping to bathe and dress before meeting Kendrick. How freaking irresponsible of her. First impressions were so hard to shake. And getting all snotty in his face—what had possessed her? Idiot. She'd always been impulsive, hotheaded. Lucia had lectured and scolded for years, trying to turn her into a lady.

With limited success. But it had been a noble effort.

She turned off the faucet and grabbed one of the big, fluffy towels she'd found on the shelf. She'd found some soap and shampoo over the tub, too, and thank God for it, since she hadn't remembered to pack bath stuff into her duffel.

She sorted through her bag, hair dripping, taking inventory. Kendrick's brooding presence outside the van had addled her wits. She'd remembered dog food, for instance, but had forgotten the can opener. She was usually extremely organized. Maniacally so. It was an essential survival skill when one lived in a camper van.

She dragged out bits and pieces from the pockets of her purse and duffel. Matches, pocketknife, flashlight. Strange guy, that Jack Kendrick. He seemed so mellow and quiet, soft-spoken, and then suddenly he was provocative and rude. She hauled out a handful of candles, a pack of her favorite incense. No pans, dishes, or human food. She had to hike back to the van if she wanted to eat.

A bleak, exhausting prospect. Her stomach rumbled.

First things first, though. Edna was waiting patiently, gazing through the glass door from the deck outside in limpid reproach. The pocket-knife would not open a can of dog food. She would have to face the man and beg a can opener off him. No avoiding this necessity.

A few careful, anxious primping minutes later, she walked down the stairs, wishing she had a blow-dryer. She needed to fluff herself up, get some volume. With wet hair, she looked even smaller and more insignificant than she already was. Like a wet Persian cat.

She was angry at her silly self for being so nervous. This man had no power over her. He was nothing to her. He just happened to be good-looking and charismatic, that was all. No biggie. She was a normal hetero female. She noticed a good-looking man when one came into her field of vision.

Although she certainly hadn't thrown out any come-hither glances since the Brian Wilder debacle. That bitter taste in her mouth still lingered, after six years. Six years of celibacy. She could hardly believe it herself, but there it was.

And this falling away, weak-in-the-knees feeling was absurd. Being afraid of what Kendrick thought of her. Wanting his approval. Yikes.

She could not afford to feel so vulnerable.

She'd spent too much energy fighting other people's opinions and efforts to control her. Like she had with Brian. Just thinking about Brian made her angry, exhausted. Sickened.

She'd worked so hard, given up so much, to be free to do as she damn well pleased. She'd sacrificed a brilliant, lucrative career as a sculptor for that precious freedom and independence. That was why she'd been on the road so long, making the best of the hard choices she'd made. And working her ass off, too, incidentally, which was nothing to be ashamed of. She'd be damned if she'd let some pin-headed, muscle-bound doofus make her feel small, no matter how hot he was.

Her sense of self was too hard-won.

She walked across the luxuriant lawn, up the porch steps, admiring the thickness and variety of the flowers bordering the house and the flagstone walkway. The garden was over-the-top beautiful.

At the front door, she raised her hand to knock, and her hand stopped in midair as her chest constricted. Oh, please. Enough of this crap. She forced herself to rap boldly. Bam-bam, here I am.

The door opened after a moment, and there he was. He seemed even bigger than before, framed by the door. No poncho. She could finally check out all his assets. Wow.

She was absurdly glad that she'd changed into the green rayon dress. She'd even considered taking out the nose ring. Then she'd concluded that the damage was done. Taking it out now revealed more about her fears and insecurities than leaving it in did. And as if that wasn't enough to make her feel self-conscious, the dress she'd shoved into the duffel was the very one that dipped down in the front and the back, showing off the little flower tattoo over her breast and the sun tattoo on her shoulder.

Just as well. It kept her honest. She'd flaunt 'em. He'd just have to deal with the tattooed, itinerant sexpot that she was. Nyah, nyah.

Other than that particular, the dress was quite modest and feminine and pretty. It was ankle length, just skimming her curves, and it looked great with the little gold and emerald V pendant that Lucia had given her. If her hair had only been dry, it would have covered both tattoos, being more than long and thick enough. But not when wet.

His eyes swept over her, and she suffered a burst of agonizing self-consciousness. She hadn't packed a bra into her duffel. Her brights were on, big-time, and not just because of the cold, either. She'd put on a little bit of makeup, too, just because, and he was noticing it. Maybe he would think she was trying to impress him. Allure him. God forbid.

He was still in his mud-spattered jeans. Without the poncho, she could see how barrel-chested he was. The T-shirt revealed the muscular breadth of his shoulders. The faded jeans affectionately hugged his powerful thighs. *Talk to the man, Viv*, her frozen brain pleaded. *Say something. Anything. Don't just stand there gawking at the guy's pecs.*

"Sorry to bother you," she said, kicking herself for the breathless, kittenish tone. None of that fluttery shit. She had to be an Amazon. A tough broad.

"No bother. Come on in. I made coffee."

Vivi followed him into a big room with an open kitchen on one side, banks of windows on all sides, paneled in rosy, fragrant cedar. An old-fashioned woodstove had a couple of soft, battered-looking couches grouped around it, and a stack of cut wood tucked into a recessed space in the wall. There was an old-fashioned braided rug, in deep, brilliant colors, on the wood-plank floor. Plants were everywhere: ferns, jades, spider plants, begonias, scores of others she couldn't begin to identify. The deep windowsills were all lined with clay boxes filled with pale sprouts and tender seedlings. It was warm, cheerful, welcoming. Beautiful.

Jack gestured toward an old trestle table in the kitchen area. "Have a seat. How do you like your coffee?"

"Milk, if you have it, and sugar, please."

He poured coffee into a huge earthenware mug, reached into his refrigerator, and held up a carton of half-and-half. "This do?"

"Oh, yeah! How luxurious. Nobody I know uses half-and-half anymore. It's always one percent, or skim. Or that foul nondairy stuff."

He grunted. "I eat what I like."

A sudden memory of Brian, who had a precision scale in his kitchen and counted every gram of fat he ate, rose up in her mind. She fought back a silly impulse to giggle and concentrated on stirring a spoonful of glistening, sticky brown sugar into her coffee. She tried not to stare at the way his biceps distended the short sleeves of his shirt.

He sat down across from her. She took a cautious sip. The coffee was delicious. "Great coffee," she offered, feeling idiotic.

He nodded. Vivi tried to relax, studying the plants, and then noticed that he was staring fixedly at the neckline of her dress. She glanced down, terrified that it was gaping scandalously over her nipple, or something, but no. Nothing was out of the ordinary.

"Sorry," he said, looking down. "I, um, was just looking at your *eranthis hyemalis.*"

She blinked. "My . . . ah, my *what?*"

He looked embarrassed. "The flower. On your chest. I thought at first that it was *Ranunculus acris,* but then—"

"A *what?*"

He let out an impatient sigh. "A buttercup. But then I saw the leaves. Definitely *Eranthis hyemalis*. Winter Aconite, I mean."

She looked down at her tattoo. "Oh. Yeah. I like this flower. I noticed it in a friend's garden, blooming in the snow. That impressed me. The perfect combination of toughness and a good attitude."

"Yeah, they're great flowers." He tore his gaze from her body and stared down into his coffee cup as if there were something really interesting at the bottom of it.

Vivi shoved her damp hair behind her ears. "I came down to ask you a favor." She took another sip of the bracing coffee. "I forgot some key things when I left the van. Most I can do without, but the most important is a can opener, so I can feed Edna."

He reached around, pulled open a drawer, and handed her one.

"And some sort of bowl? I forgot her dish, too," she admitted.

He rummaged in a cupboard for a plastic dish. "Anything else?"

"If I could borrow your broom to sweep out the mud?"

He gestured behind himself, to a corner where a broom and dustpan were tucked. "Help yourself."

"Thank you. Edna thanks you, too. As only a Labrador retriever can." Viv took a final sip of coffee and scooped up the bowl and can opener. "I'll just head on back up to my apartment, then." She grabbed the broom and dustpan, and pointed herself toward the door. She'd managed not to giggle or simper. Now, if she could get out the door without tripping over the rug, she was home free.

"Wait. Do you have anything to eat tonight?" he demanded.

"No, but Edna and I might just hike back to the van and grab some stuff. It's no big deal."

"I'll take you into town to do some shopping."

"No, really," she said hastily. "You've gone to enough trouble."

"No trouble. I need groceries anyway. There's just the convenience store here in Silverfish, so I'll take you to the Safeway in Pebble River."

She was still shaking her head. "I don't want to put you to—"

"Look," he said, impatiently. "I won't be able to eat tonight if I know you've got no food up there."

"Well. That's, uh, sweet of you," she said, flustered.

"No, just practical. If you fast, I have to fast. And fasting makes me crabby."

That was a new concept for her, and she didn't know what to do with it. He took her baffled silence as assent, scooped up her coffee cup, and took it to the sink. "Be ready in half an hour," he said.

She opened her mouth to argue but stopped when her stomach rumbled. It was thunderously loud. He glanced over his shoulder, gave her a smile that dazzled her.

And oh, for God's sake. Whatever.

"Thanks." With all the dignity she could muster, she still managed to trip over the rug as she left.

To shave or not to shave. It took him ten minutes to work out that philosophical conundrum. He'd been letting his beard grow, figuring what the hell, but after assessing himself in the bathroom mirror, he decided he looked scruffy. He couldn't go into town with her looking like a bum. Not if she was going to wear that green thing.

He should take her out to dinner, he thought, lathering his face. The thought made him nervous. Like he was a teenager, asking a hot girl out to a dance. What the fuck was he going to do with her now?

His dick had some very good ideas, but they weren't practical.

The way she'd talked about the flower she'd seen in the winter garden surprised him. That combination of toughness and a good attitude in the Winter Aconite. She'd seen it. That was rare. Most people saw plants as a commodity, a decoration, a means to an end, if they saw them at all. Not many saw them as entities in their own right.

Yeah, and she was probably a woo-woo earth mama type who would commune naked with nature spirits, or something terrifying like that. Jesus. He had to stop shaving for a minute to process that concept, or else risk nicking an artery. Pathetic, sex-starved mountain man that he was.

It had been so long for him, he didn't even want to do the math.

Maybe he could make the situation go away by pissing her off until she left in a huff. She was proud, prickly. Shouldn't be too hard.

He wiped off shaving cream as he pondered that option. Maybe he could make crude sexual advances. Infuriate her into leaving. Duncan would kick his ass, but hey. A man had his limits.

But excitement flooded him at the thought of touching her. Stiff dick, red face, pounding heart. He gripped the sink with both hands, and thought it through.

Bad idea. Too volatile. She might press charges against him for sexual harassment, which would be embarrassing and stupid.

Worse yet, who knew? Maybe she'd reciprocate. God help him then. And there was the danger issue, too. Entirely aside from the evil Nazi art freaks, it was flat-out insane for a tiny woman like that to wander around alone in a fucking van, flaunting her sexy little body right and left. Any ignorant redneck dickhead who saw tattoos and a nose ring would instantly draw his conclusions and make a pass.

Repeat after me, he told himself grimly. *Not. Your. Problem.*

That would be the mantra for the day.

Vivi opened to Jack's knock. He'd shaved, and combed his wet hair back off his face. His face was even more striking now that she could see the stark, lean angles of his jaw, his chin.

She suddenly wondered how long she'd been staring.

At the grocery checkout stand in Pebble River, they eyed each other's choices with open curiosity. She went for fruit, veggies, stuff from the health food section. He was classic in his tastes, and definitely a carnivore, but most of his groceries were real food, not empty junk. Which did not surprise her, when he looked at his body.

Which she did, at absolutely every opportunity. Unreal. So hot.

In the parking lot, he turned to her as soon as he started up the engine. "Let's get food," he said.

"Didn't we just?"

"I mean a restaurant. You like Mexican?"

"Uh, yes," she admitted. The idea of a plate of steaming, cheese-smothered enchiladas took her by storm.

The meal went smoothly enough, at first. He started by asking her for a rundown of the security situation, so she munched freshly fried tortilla chips with fabulous fresh salsa and regaled him with the long and harrowing tale of Lucia's death, the necklaces, the abductions of her two sisters, and the evil Ulf Haupt and his nasty, piglike minion, John, both of whom were convinced that the D'Onofrio sisters could reveal the whereabouts of these mysterious lost sketches if sufficiently terrified or tortured. She showed him her necklace, with its emerald *V*, the last of the trio that Lucia had given them. He squinted at it for a while, from every angle, and handed it back, shaking his head.

"Un-fucking-believable," was his laconic comment.

"Tell me about it," she agreed, fervently.

Then he started asking questions about herself. She told him about studying art in New York, and her brief, dizzying burst of artistic success when she signed the contract with Brian's gallery. She did not mention her personal relationship with Brian, or why she'd broken the contract and run. In fact, she started glossing over more and more details. It was that cool, assessing look in Jack's eye that shut her up. It bugged her. Like he knew something about her. Or rather, like he'd already made up his mind.

"So, you just left everything you built when it was all going so well, and ran off into the sunset to find yourself?" he asked.

She bristled. "I suppose you could say that, if you were being unkind. I didn't like the way the gallery management was pushing me around. I decided I'd do better on the road, on the crafts fair circuit, developing my own designs. With nobody breathing down my neck."

"I guess you must hate that more than anything," he said.

She frowned, unnerved. "Hate what?"

"Having someone breathing down your neck."

She frowned at him, pondering that. "Depends on the person," she said slowly. "And it depends on what they want from me."

"Doesn't it always. Did you break any hearts when you ran?"

Vivi's eyes narrowed. His hidden agenda was rearing its horned, fanged head, big-time. "That sounds like a trick question," she said. "Personal, too."

"Just wondering."

She stared down at her half-eaten enchiladas. Her appetite was fading.

"So you did leave someone," he said.

Her teeth clenched. "I broke up with the man I was seeing be- fore I left, but I had damn good reason," she said.

"Yeah? What?"

Well, actually, I found out that he was the devil, she wanted to say, but didn't, it being none of his damn business. "You have no right to judge me," she told him.

From there, the conversation went sharply downhill. She did her part, but his responses were terse monosyllables. And his shuttered, glittering stare was starting to unnerve her.

She took a swallow of her margarita, and stared him in the eye. "Look, Mr. Kendrick—"

"Call me Jack."

"Okay, Jack. Just tell me what's on your mind, okay?"

His eyebrow tilted up at the corner. "What do you mean?"

Vivi shoved her hair back. "I mean, how you judge me for things you know nothing about. I mean, how uncomfortable you are with me."

"Is that all?"

She shook her head. "What else would I be talking about?"

"I thought you might be talking about the fact that I'm attracted to you," he said. "I figured you might have noticed that. It's kind of hard to miss."

Vivi's fork clattered loudly down onto her plate. "Ah . . ."

"But since you brought it up," he continued, "I might as well just be honest. You're right. I'm uncomfortable, for two reasons. The fact that I'm attracted to you is one reason. And the other reason— and I'm sorry if I hurt your feelings—is that you are not the type of woman whom I want to be attracted to. That puts me in a bad place."

Her mouth dropped. "My . . . type?" she repeated. "And what type is that? Are you one of those meatheads who think that girls with nose rings and tattoos are automatically promiscuous?"

He waved that impatiently away. "No, that's not the issue. I'm talking about living in a van, moving around all the time, getting bored easily, and leaving things half done. I don't want to get in- volved with someone who's just passing through. It's a big waste of time."

Anger burned in Vivi's stomach. "Hold on, here. Did I invite you to get sexually involved with me without me noticing it? Or did you just assume that my type is sexually available to everyone?"

Jack took a swallow of beer. "No. You didn't. And I didn't."

"Let me get this straight. You want to nail me, but you think I'm scum, and you don't want me around lowering your property value."

He frowned. "Don't put words in my mouth. I didn't say 'scum.'"

"I call it how I see it," she shot back. "You want me to get so pissed off, I just pack up and leave, right? Is that your plan?"

He forked up a bite of his steak fajita and stared at it. "That would be my plan, if it weren't for this danger issue," he said, reluctantly. "It does sound like you've got one hell of a security problem. But I don't—"

"Then let me make a revolutionary suggestion," she announced. "Get this, Kendrick. I know this idea might shock you to your toes, but how about if we just don't have sex?"

He smothered a laugh, covering his mouth with his napkin, his eyes darting around the restaurant. "Uh—"

"It's the perfect solution," she went on, with false cheerfulness. "Amazing in its streamlined simplicity. You don't have to fuck me, if it would be so upsetting to you. Aren't you relieved? Isn't that just an incredible load off your mind? Just ignore me, okay? It's easy. I'll just stay out of your way and do my own thing."

He looked alarmed. "And what exactly is your thing?"

She shrugged. "Living my life. Making my art. Duncan mentioned that you have a studio in the barn, but I'll understand if you don't want me to use the space. The apartment will do nicely for now."

Jack rose, bumping the table and knocking over the beer bottle. A fork fell to the floor. The restaurant went dead silent, and a waitress froze in position, holding her trays of food. Jack cursed softly. "Let's get out of here."

"Fine." She got up, and began digging for her wallet.

"I've got the check," he said.

She swept past him, elbowing him out of her way at the cash register. "I'd rather die than let you pay for my meal."

* * *

Vivi sat as far from Jack as possible in the truck. After he pulled into the driveway, she climbed out without a word, slammed the door, and reached for her groceries.

He tried to take the bags from her. She jerked them away. He yanked them back. "Don't be stupid," he growled.

She followed the crunch of his boots on the gravel through the darkness and followed him up the stairs, still fuming.

He opened her door with his own key, flipped on the light, and set her bags on the kitchen counter. They stared at each other as Edna leaped and danced and wagged her enthusiastic greeting.

"Good night," Vivi said, pointedly.

"Where are you going to sleep?" he asked.

She opened and closed her mouth. "Wha—what?" she forced out.

"There's no bed here. Where are you going to sleep?"

"Ah," she murmured, blushing.

There was a faint, fleeting hint of a smile in his eyes. "I wasn't suggesting my own bed."

"I didn't think you were," she lied, her blush deepening. "I'm sleeping in my sleeping bag. It was hooked to my backpack. See?"

"Just a sleeping bag? On the bare floor?" He sounded shocked.

"I'm used to roughing it," she said coolly.

He frowned, ruffling Edna's ears. "No one sleeps on a bare floor in my place," he said. "I don't care what you're used to."

"Well, I appreciate the sentiment, but strictly speaking, it's not your place. I'll be paying rent. So don't treat me like a guest."

He turned and stalked out the door, disappearing into the dense darkness. Vivi shut the door behind him, breathing out a sigh of relief.

Her battle tension dissipated, leaving her exhausted. She opened the sliding doors and let the fragrant night air into the room. Then, slowly and systematically, she put away her groceries in the big, clean kitchen. So much space, for everything. It felt strange, after the van and her sisters' microscopic apartments.

Then she lit her scented candles and some sandalwood incense, turned out the overhead light, and sat down cross-legged on her sleeping bag. The graceful, empty room flickering with candlelight soothed her. It felt strange and lovely, to have the door open to the night. To let her senses open and soften, to listen to frogs and insects singing their sweet night songs. She'd been so paranoid and closed up tight these last few weeks. But here, oddly, she felt . . . safe.

From the Fiend, anyway. If not her own sex-starved stupidity.

It was more a sense of his presence rather than any noise he made that made her nerves jolt into a state of alert. She jumped to her feet as he pushed open the mosquito screen with his boot and stepped through the sliding glass doors. He carried a rolled-up futon without apparent effort, a feather pillow wedged beneath his muscular arm.

"Knock next time," she said. "I'd appreciate it."

He gazed over the futon, looking aggrieved. "My hands were full." He unfolded it onto the floor, tossed the pillow on top.

"For the record," she persisted, "in the future, I prefer that you not barge in on me like that. Whether your arms are full or not."

That condescending, dismissive movement he made with his shoulders was making her tense. "You're not taking me seriously," she said tightly.

"Don't worry, I heard you." His eyes swept the room until they found her sleeping bag. "Will that keep you warm enough?"

"It always has before," she said. "The futon wasn't necessary, but thanks, anyway."

"The incense smells good." His eyes followed the thin stream of smoke that undulated sensuously from the tiny bronze censer.

"Yes, it does. It's my favorite."

A heavy silence fell. "Ah . . . thanks for the futon," she said. She'd intended the words to be a dismissal, but they emerged so husky and low and tentative, they sounded almost inviting.

Vivi tried to think of something else to say, but after a couple minutes of struggling, she abandoned the effort. She was too tired. It felt false. And this guy wasn't interested in social chatter. He just stood there like a mountain in her bedroom. As dense as granite. An unidentifiable emotion burning from his shadowed eyes. He wasn't leaving until he was ready.

So Vivi waited. She quietly bore the weight of the silence that spread ever wider in the flickering dimness, until it became something more than silence. Anticipation, taut with things that were longing to be said. Waiting. A breeze wafted through the door and put out a candle, casting the room into deeper shadow.

Vivi took matches from her pocket, and turned to relight it.

She started to turn, and froze. He was right behind her.

"Just looking at this." He pushed aside the hair hanging over her back with his fingertip, barely touching her sun tattoo. "I caught a glimpse of it while you were paying for your dinner, but I couldn't tell what it was, under your hair." He traced the small circle with radiating lines. "A sun. Does it have some special meaning? Like the flower?"

"Yes," she said quietly. "It's in memorium. For a friend I lost."

His hand dropped. "I'm sorry."

She nodded and turned to face him again. It took all her nerve to raise her eyes to his. When she did, the smoldering hunger in his gaze stole her breath.

"Do you have any other tattoos?" he finally asked.

She lifted her chin, straightened her spine. He had no right to do this, when she was all alone in the dark. Throwing those hot, intense sexual vibes at her, when she was feeling so vulnerable. "That's for me to know, and for you to wonder about." She aimed for a crisp, dismissive tone of voice. Insofar as she could, with no breath to back it up.

The breathlessness made it sound like . . . flirting. God help her.

Sure enough. He didn't look dismissed. He looked like he was wondering, as she'd just invited him to do. And who could blame him?

He was wondering so hard, she could feel it against her skin.

If he made a move on her now, she wouldn't have the force of will to push him away. She was gooey to the core. Sopping wet for him. One featherlight push, and down she'd fall, right onto her back. *Take me.*

After all her uppity pronouncements. All her fighting words.

"Good night." He turned, and headed out the door.

Vivi stood for a moment, looking at the black rectangle, open to the fragrant, noisy night. The candlelit room seemed blank and empty.

Chapter
3

Jack paced the length of his living room, hands clenched, stopping at each end like a caged beast.

He'd just spent hours on the Internet, researching Vivi D'Onofrio. Browsing around on her commercial website, looking at her jewelry designs. Necklaces, rings, brooches, earrings, nose rings. Perfume bottles, Christmas tree ornaments, mobiles, jewelry boxes. Made of glass, beads, metal, wood, homemade paper, found materials. The stuff was weirdly beautiful. Unusual. He couldn't put his finger on what it was exactly that he liked about it, but he liked it.

He wondered how she dealt with her mail-order business. If he were one of the bad guys, the first thing he'd do would be to order a pair of earrings from her site, go to the address they were sent from, and start pushing whoever he found there. Dangerous for everyone involved.

There were also a lot of references regarding a big-shot art gallery in New York City, run by a guy named Brian Wilder. There was a picture of him, one of those stiff, mannered shots, where the guy tried to look smart by holding on to his chin with a hooked finger as if hiding a zit. The guy's photo triggered instant dislike. Made Jack's prick-o-meter register way off the chart.

Then he'd studied shots of Vivi's artwork from the archived catalogs of the Wilder Gallery, from five, six years ago. The same vibe as the pieces on her website, but they were bigger, bolder more ambitious. And the prices staggered him. Jesus wept. Even if the gallery took a huge cut, she could have gotten rich, if she'd stayed with it.

But for some people, freedom was more important than wealth.

That was the thought that had propelled him to this frantic pacing. The situation was fucked. He could hardly breathe, he was so tense. Wound up, turned on. The way things were going, he wasn't going to be able to stop himself from tossing her down and having at her, like a beast in rut. And his instincts were telling him that angry and proud or not, she wasn't going to stop him.

No checks or balances. Nothing to hold him back but his own fast eroding self-control. Everything about her pulled him. He was strung out on the fruity, sweet smell of her hair. The outrageous vivid color of it. He couldn't get over those big, brilliant eyes, the exotic shape of them. Her delicate, pointed chin. Her pink, full mouth.

He wondered, uncomfortably, who that friend was, the one she'd lost and gotten the memorial tattoo for. He wondered if it was her lover who had died. Wondered if she still missed the guy. Or grieved for him.

Can of worms. None of his business.

Her shoulder was so thin and delicate, decorated with that tiny, stylized sun image. Her skin so smooth, her muscles sinuous and strong, despite how slender her small frame was. Small and perfect.

He looked up at the clock, and did the math. It was six-thirty a.m. in Italy, where Duncan was currently wallowing in romantic bliss, in some picturesque B&B in Tuscany. He'd be unthrilled to be dragged out of the clasp of his new lady's silken limbs. Served the bastard right for getting him into this. Duncan's satellite phone rang and rang.

Eight times, nine, ten, eleven. Jack waited, grimly.

Duncan finally picked up. "Jack? Huh? What the fuck?" His voice was thick with sleep.

"I think that's my line," Jack said.

"Is Viv okay?" his friend demanded.

"She's fine," he said.

"So? What's the problem?"

"Think about it," Jack snarled. "Figure it out, Dunc."

A soft, feminine murmur in the background. A questioning tone.

"Nah, just Jack," Duncan replied. Another questioning murmur. "He says Viv's fine. I'll go talk in the other room. Go on back to sleep."

Jack heard the sound of a door clicking shut, and Duncan's voice got harder. "You woke Nell, numbnuts. She needs her sleep. She's been through hell. Do you have any idea what time it is?"

"You never hesitate to call in the middle of the night when the urge takes you. Besides, the sun should be up where you are. Why didn't you tell me what to expect?"

Duncan paused, baffled. "I did," he said. I told you all about those sadistic motherfuckers who are after my fiancée and my soon-to-be sisters-in-law. What else do you need to know about the—"

"No. Not about them. I mean, about her."

"Ah . . ." Duncan's voice trailed off. "Oh. I see. You mean, why didn't I tell you how cute she was? You're mad because I didn't fill you in about the long red hair, the big gray eyes, the slender limbs, the rosy lips?"

"Goddamn it, Dunc—"

"You're a sad case when you need to be warned about shit like that. Did she knock you backward a couple of paces? Figured she might."

"You didn't tell me she was a tattooed flower child with a fucking dragon painted on her camper van." Jack felt frustrated, and stupid. He couldn't express why he felt so misled, jerked around.

"So it's the tattoos that bug you." Duncan clucked his tongue. "Did you see the one she has right over the crack of her ass?"

Jack sat straight upright, as if he'd been stung by a bug. "How the *fuck* do you know that?"

"Saw her in low-rise jeans and a halter top once," Dunc said laconically. "Sweet."

"You stinking bucket of festering slime! Aren't you supposed to be in love with her sister?"

"Whoo-hah, aren't we passionate," Duncan murmured. "I *am* in love with the sister. I'm marrying the sister. I'm having fifteen kids with the sister. I'm all over that sister twenty-four seven, like white on rice. But I still notice a mandolin-shaped ass when I see one. So shoot me for sending it your way. God knows, you need something to get you going. Vivi's good for giving jolts. Chick's a walking firecracker."

"So you admit it, then? You set me up?" Jack demanded.

Duncan was silent for a moment. "You're thinking this is all about you and your deep-frozen dick, aren't you?" he said slowly. "Well, it's not, man. Did she tell you what they did to Nell when they took her?"

Jack rubbed his aching forehead. "Dunc, that's not what I'm—"

"They drugged her. Shoved her into the trunk of a car. Tied her to a chair. They beat her. They would have cut and raped and killed her, if I hadn't gotten there in time. These are the guys who are after Viv. That's what they'll do to her. Think about it, butthead. You paying attention?"

Jack let a fierce sigh hiss between clenched teeth. "Yes."

"The reason I'm breaking your balls about this is because it's the only way I could think of to keep her relatively safe short of tying her, gagging her, and locking her in a fucking closet. She is not the most reasonable of females. In fact, she's, ah, real independent minded."

"I've noticed that," he said sourly.

"Family trait," Duncan confided cheerfully. "It'll drive you bugfuck, buddy."

"You need to resolve this thing before that happens," Jack said tightly. "Got any leads?"

"Not much. Nell and I are renting a car tomorrow, to drive down to Castiglione Sant'Angelo and ask some questions. Nell speaks fluent Italian, you see."

The fatuous pride in the guy's voice set Jack's teeth on edge. "Well. How nice for you," he said sourly. "Eat a pizza for me. Isn't that a great excuse to run off and leave me holding the bag."

"Dude." Duncan's voice dropped thirty degrees. "That's no bag you've got there. That's Nell's precious little sister. You don't get any further from a bag than that."

Jack gritted his teeth. "I didn't mean to imply that she was a—"

"Stop being such a contrary dickhead. I send a hot, sexy little redheaded thing to liven up your monotonous existence, and you complain? Jesus, Jack! Get the fuck over it!"

"Oh, shut up," Jack growled.

"Hah! You're the one who woke us out of a sound sleep at six-thirty in the morning. Just stay on your toes, man. Because those bastards are looking hard for her, and if they find her, she's meat. And so am I, incidentally, if Vivi doesn't stay okay. So make her lay low."

"Yeah, right," Jack scoffed. "Like I can 'make her' do anything."

"Sweeten her up," Duncan said impatiently. "Take her to bed. You're suffering from testosterone poisoning anyway, man. Unload some of that energy before you hurt yourself. Use your dick, use your tongue. Melt her brain. Do what you have to do. Find a way. Keep her safe. Or else."

Jack hung up on him. He slumped in his chair, dropped his throbbing head into his hands, shifted uncomfortably in his jeans. He was going to rip out his seams if this shit went on much longer.

Sweeten her up. Take her to bed. Use your tongue. Melt her brain.

Right. Duncan's helpful suggestions contained a small but problematic snag.

The brain in question that was melting was Jack's own.

John did a drive-by of the Jersey City address stamped on the outside of the mailer. The one with the Vivi D'Onofrio art box in it. Excitement pulsed through him. Finally, a new lead, after these weeks of waiting, listening to Haupt's shrill lectures. Two weeks ago, he'd ordered the gift box from Vivi D'Onofrio's website, for the modest price of $115. Today, it had arrived. Finally, a chunk of meat to throw to the old bastard. Finally, something to fucking *do*.

He was trembling with sexual anticipation. Vivien was a skinny little thing compared to her older sisters, with no tits to speak of, but her ass was nice and round, and he liked the fiery hair and the full, pink lips.

He bet she was excellent at sucking cock. She'd have ample opportunity to demonstrate her skill. Girls tried so hard to please when they were motivated. And bad-boy Johnny knew just how to motivate them. Oh, boy, did he ever.

He no longer even bothered to ask himself why he hung around to take the abuse from Haupt. John was a skilled professional, at the top of his game, very highly thought of, in certain select circles. He didn't need the money, God knew. He could retire right now if he wanted to.

But he wouldn't. He'd gladly kill for free, for the fun of it, but he didn't advertise that fact. Bad for business. And besides, he liked money just fine, too. But this job had gone down the tubes weeks ago. It was like he was cursed. It had gotten under his skin. He'd lost his professional detachment, gotten personally invested in the outcome. That was dangerous. A man had to be able to walk when he reached a point of diminishing returns.

His returns on this job had been diminishing almost from the start, but here he still was. Taking it, right up the ass. Day after day.

He couldn't help himself. He'd been insulted, thwarted, shot at. Stabbed, for God's sake. That sneaky bitch Antonella had practically punctured a kidney. He'd needed internal and external stitches to fix the damage. He was still on antibiotics. It was still bruised. It still hurt.

Those girls were his now. All three of them. He wanted to feel their hot blood pumping over his hands. Wanted to feel each of them in turn flailing desperately in his grip. Hear them shriek and beg.

Vivien was the obvious one to target. Security was too tight around the other two, at least for now. When the dickheads currently fucking Nell and Nancy were put down like rabid dogs, the situation would be different. Then the way would be clear. Much simpler.

But Vivien had not cooperated with his plan. She'd dropped out of sight. She could no longer be found on the crafts fair circuit. Nor had she been spotted, on vid or in real time, outside her sisters' residences.

Maybe she was hiding here. In any case, whoever lived at this Jersey City address was going to get a long, chatty visit from John about that mail-order business, and where its owner could be found.

A car stopped outside. John slumped, watching. Four large, burly men in dark suits got out and trotted up the steps of the place.

They entered without knocking. The subtle bulges under their jackets were immediately recognizable to a trained eye. Oh. *Shit.*

John's teeth began to grind, and he clicked open his laptop, typed the street address into a search engine, scanned the hits. *Fuck.* Braxton Security? He knew the name. It was the security firm that rich prick Burke, Antonella's boy toy, was affiliated with. She'd based her fucking mail-order company out of a goddamn security firm. Swarming with ex-military types, mercenaries, spies, techs.

John was not going to have stimulating chats with anyone today.

Probably cutthroat computer geeks were analyzing all e-mails that arrived at her site. And the addresses to which her merchandise was sent. He accelerated out into the street and peeled away, infuriated.

Fortunately, he was smarter than that. The addresses he'd used were untraceable. The address at which the package had arrived was a busy post office in Queens. He was confident he had not been observed.

But even so. How dare she. Challenging him. Flipping him the finger. He drove for a while, until he came to a large chain store with a vast parking lot and pulled into it. His laptop was still open, so he put it on his lap and pulled up his short list of Vivi D'Onofrio favorites.

One was Brian Wilder's art gallery. Her work hadn't been in the Wilder catalog for years, but John was confident Wilder would remember her. Any guy who had sold pieces of art for twelve, fifteen, even eighteen K, would remember the artist who had produced them.

He called up Vivi D'Onofrio's own commercial website. Clicked on her bio for the photos. She smiled in the sunshine, hair blowing free, wearing a diaphanous white blouse. In another photo, she was decked out like some pagan bride from the Bronze Age in her own jewelry designs. Necklaces, bracelets, earrings, armlets, chokers, even a headdress.

Smiling that mischievous angel smile into the camera. He rubbed his tingling dick as he stared into those gray eyes.

Slut. Laughing at him, from the computer screen. That full, pink mouth wide with mirth. *You idiot,* those eyes said. *You dumb fuck. You just can't get us. You can't get close enough. You're not smart enough.*

He could actually hear her shrill, mocking laughter in his mind.

The white mailing box sat on the seat next to him. He wrenched it open and pulled out the gift box. Imagining how her hands had touched it, rubbed it, caressed it. His erection was painfully hard.

The box was made of variously sized chunks of translucent, sand-smoothed bottle glass, both brown and green. Edges lined with strips of copper foil. Soldered together by a webwork of fine silver wire. Her business card was tucked into the bottom of it.

His hand closed over the box in a tight, shaking fist, crushing it. Pieces of glass cracked. Pain stabbed into his hand. Blood dripped out between his fingers. He forced them to open.

The box was mangled, shapeless, poised on his bloody, shaking claw. The business card with Vivien D'Onofrio's name was crumpled, bloodstained. He liked the effect.

He stared at the chunk of garbage and began to laugh.

Uppity bitch. She thought she'd won. Thought she was smarter. But she'd see who was boss, in the end. Oh, yes, she'd see.

Vivi woke up slowly, in a bright patch of morning sunshine that streamed through the curtainless window, straight into her eyes.

She rolled over and found Edna panting right into her face. She stroked the dog's velvety ears. Wow. She felt so comfortable. The futon was so much softer than the little mattress in her van. Ah.

And she had to find another bed, fast. She could not be obligated to Kendrick for something so intimate as a bed.

She pulled clothes on, fed Edna, and munched on some yogurt and granola. The weather was gorgeous. A great day to hike back to the van, locate someone with a tractor, and stay out of Jack Kendrick's way. But first, she needed to touch base with her sisters and check her e-mail.

The cell phone had no coverage. She looked around the apartment for a phone jack, and found one next to the back door in the kitchen, but there was no phone attached. She needed a vehicle to buy herself a phone. But it was probably the same phone line as the one in his house. Which meant she would have to ask permission to use it.

That thought turned her legs rubbery with anticipation.

She marched out—and a spasm of doubt stopped her on the steps. Maybe just a casual peek in the bathroom mirror, to wash the crumbs out of her eyes. She hustled inside and did the facial-cleansing routine. With toner. And moisturizer. And brushing her hair would be good. And that sweatshirt with the sleeves ripped out was terribly shabby. She rummaged through the duffel. Maybe the green tank—no. Too revealing. The red jersey. A belt, with a big, intimidating buckle. A hint of mascara. And a tiny swipe of gloss for her lips. Barely any.

One last look into the mirror sent her back to her purse to pull out a pair of silver and carnelian drop earrings. She posed for Edna, who wagged her approval, and out they stepped into the cool morning.

The fragrance was overwhelming: earth, flowers, pine needles, dew, rain. The air itself seemed to sparkle as it went into her lungs. Birds warbled. Pale sunlight sifted through pine needles, in a fluttering, swaying pattern. She looked around, openmouthed.

She hesitated before his door. It was seven-thirty, after all. Maybe he was a late sleeper. She'd decided to come back later when an unfamiliar voice called from across the yard. "Hello, there, missy!"

Vivi whirled around. A small, elderly lady with bluish hair, dressed in a rose-spattered dress and carrying a paper bag, was making her way up the path with the help of a cane. "Good morning," she replied, smiling at the welcome that creased the old lady's wrinkled face.

"And what's your name, young lady?"

"Vivi D'Onofrio. Pleased to meet you." She extended her hand.

The old lady set down the paper bag and took Vivi's proffered hand, squeezing it gently. "My name is Margaret Moffat O'Keefe, but you can call me Margaret. So! My Jack has been a naughty fellow, hmm?"

Vivi was nonplussed for a moment, until she understood the twinkle in the old lady's eyes. "Oh, no! Um, not with me! I barely know him. I'm just a friend of a friend, staying here for a while. In the apartment. Up there." She pointed to the barn. "I was just looking for him. I was afraid he might be sleeping, so I didn't want to—"

"Oh, good heavens, no. Jack's no slug-a-bed." Margaret's faded eyes took on a speculative gleam as she stumped up the porch steps. She rapped smartly with the head of her cane on the front door.

"Jack, dear?" she called. "Are you home?"

There was no response. "Well, his truck is here, so he's probably just gone down to see to his flowers," Margaret said. "Have you seen his flowers?" Vivi shook her head, and Margaret clucked her disapproval. "Young Jack must show you his flowers! They are a sight."

"Not these, you mean?" Vivi indicated the flower beds in the yard.

"Oh, no. I mean down by the river. I think he has columbines and lamb's ears and Sweet William coming in now. And bachelor buttons, of course, and heaven only knows what else."

Vivi smiled at the beaming old lady. "It sounds magical."

"I'd take you down myself, but this arthritis has slowed me down some. You just sit down on the porch and have a cookie, and Jack will be along. I baked some molasses crinkles for Jack. He loves cookies."

"Is he related to you?" Vivi asked.

"Not technically, but I think of Jack as my honorary grandson, since he came here to live with me some twenty-five ago, or so. In fact, he bought this property from me some years back. Dear boy."

Vivi had to stifle a giggle at the thought of that big block of seasoned manhood being referred to as a "dear boy."

"Well, I'll be running along. Come have a cup of tea with me one of these mornings when you're settled in. And say hello to Jack for me." She held out the bag. It was heavy and fragrant. "And you tell Jack to show you the hot springs," Margaret added, a gleam in her eye.

"Hot springs?" Vivi was intrigued.

"Oh, yes, dearie. There are some natural hot pools a couple of miles upriver. Very private. Just beautiful. Something tells me you would like them, bless your heart." She patted Vivi's shoulder.

"Something told you right," Vivi said, with relish. Wow. Cookies.

Flowers. Hot springs. She'd hit the mother lode. This place was paradise on earth.

Vivi gazed after the old lady as she made her slow, careful way down the walk. How incredibly sweet of her. An intoxicating buttery-sweet fragrance rose from the bag. She peeked inside. Molasses cookies, warm and fresh. She sat down on the porch steps and reached for one.

Predictably enough, her hand was in the bag when Jack strode around the house, carrying an armful of what looked like columbines, though they were much bigger than any columbines she'd ever seen. She yanked her hand out guiltily, licking her fingers with embarrassed bravado. He stopped in front of her, and nodded in silent greeting.

"Hi. I, uh, just met Margaret." Vivi closed the bag and folded down the top. "She brought you cookies."

"So I see," he said.

"She said I could have some," Vivi said, before she could stop herself, and blushed furiously as he began to smile. The lines crinkling up around his eyes sparked a warm glow somewhere in the vicinity of her navel. It crept inexorably downward.

"Eat all you want," he said. "What kind are they this time?"

"Molasses," Vivi informed him. She wrenched her gaze away now from the smile that had now become a grin, complete with shockingly white, beautiful teeth, and focused on his long, work-hardened hands, gently holding those long flowers. Whew. That grin. This guy had a whole store of secret weapons. Every one calculated to lay her low.

She struggled to remember what she'd come down to ask him.

"Ah, I need to make some phone calls, and get on the Internet, too, to check my mail orders. And, ah, my cell has no coverage here," she said. "So I was just wondering—"

"Of course. There's a jack in your kitchen, but it's my phone line. I assumed, considering your security problem, you weren't going to want to list a number right now. You mind sharing a line with me? I don't spend much time hanging on the phone."

"Me neither," she said. "That's fine with me, if it's okay with you."

"If you want to use your cell, hike up to the top of that rise," he said. "See that stand of spruce? You'll get some coverage up there. But for now, use my phone. Hook your computer up in the kitchen."

"Thanks," she murmured.

"I meant to get you a phone. You weren't supposed to arrive so soon." He gazed at her accusingly through the stalks of columbine.

"Yeah, right," she mumbled. "Don't you want to go and put those down somewhere?"

"Yeah, and then I'm, going to make coffee. Come and have a cup."

She watched, fascinated, as he walked across the yard toward a small outbuilding. Oh, boy. The back view of his jeans was as appealing as the front. She leaned her head on her hands and exhaled, slowly.

Inside his cozy kitchen once again, she gazed at trays of seedlings while he put on the coffee. When she felt his big, silent presence drawing near her again, she gave in to her curiosity. "Margaret and Duncan said you grow flowers," she ventured

Jack stroked the bottom of a delicate leaf in one of the trays. It trembled above the forest of thin, delicate pale stems, as if floating there. "Yes. I've got some *Aquilegia flavescens*, and *Delphinium exaltatum*, and *Dianthus barbatus* coming in right now. I'm taking a load into Portland today."

"What's that in English?"

"Columbines, larkspurs, and sweet william," he clarified.

She sneaked a quick peek at his somber profile. "Why do you use Latin names?"

"I like how specific it is. There are hundreds of subgroups for common flower names. Each one has its own totally different personality."

"Wow," she murmured, impressed.

He looked self-conscious. "I don't mean to be a nerd. I got off on studying them when I was in the military. Nothing like staring at flowers when you're sweating in the desert with sand rasping in every crack under your body armor." He paused, and looked at her chest. "Like dreaming of water while you're dying of thirst," he finished.

He was standing so close, she could smell the loamy scent of plants and earth on him, although his hands smelled like lemon dish soap. "You're, um, staring at my *Eranthis hylematis*, Jack," she said. "It's making me nervous."

"Sorry," he said. "And it's *Eranthis hyemalis*, not *hylematis*."

Whoa. That hot, dangerous flirtatious energy was starting to stretch and twist between them, muscular and dangerous and unpredictable.

She had to distract them, before things got weird. "How'd you get into this business?" she asked.

"I like plants," he said. "My uncle Freddie was into organic gardening when I was a kid. I studied plant biology on the Internet when I was in the service, and afterward, when I worked overseas."

"In Afghanistan? On that task force with Duncan, right?"

"Right. I've done some landscaping work for the parks department in Portland and Vancouver, too. Ornamental horticulture, stuff like that. But I prefer to live out here. I've built up a good business. The land down by the river's good for rare specialty stuff, and I know florists who are happy to buy local and get stock that's days fresher than the flowers they fly in over the pole from Holland. I've got a refrigerated truck and a twelve-by-twelve walk-in cooler. I harvest and deliver them myself. Simple and direct. Works out well for everybody."

"What an awesome way to make a living," she said.

"It's hard work," he said. "But I like the flowers." He turned his silver-gray gaze on her face, and she realized what his eyes reminded her of. They had the same glowing depths that she'd seen in the eyes of a timber wolf.

"Did you sleep well on the futon?" he asked.

"Yes, wonderfully. Thank you."

The coffee began to gurgle. He went to the stove, leaving her free to normalize her breathing and get herself in hand.

The coffee tasted wonderful with Margaret's cookies. Jack finished his cup, got up, and rinsed it briskly. "I'd better get going," he said. "You going to be okay by yourself here, with no wheels?"

"I'll be fine," she said. "I've got Edna. We're set."

"Help yourself to anything you might need, in my cupboards, or the fridge," he said. "There's the phone, as you see. Oh, and I called Dwayne Pritchett about your van. He'll be coming over with his tractor as soon as it dries up, but he doesn't want to risk it for a few days yet."

"Great. I appreciate that," she said. "Also, could you tell me how to find the hot springs? Maybe Edna and I will hike up and take a look."

He spun around. "Hot springs?" His eyes had gone cold.

She shrank back, apprehensive. "Uh, Margaret said there were some natural hot springs upriver a couple of miles. Something wrong?"

He scowled down into the sink. "Shit."

"What's the matter?" Vivi demanded. "Are you pissed at me?"

"Not at you. I'm irritated with Margaret. We have an agreement to keep the springs secret. Nobody wants hikers trespassing on our land. Now Margaret decides to tell a stranger."

"I'm hardly a trespassing hiker," Vivi pointed out, insulted.

"No. But it's not as if you're a long-term resident, either."

"Does that mean you'll be kicking me out soon?" She sprang to her feet. "Please be clear about that, Kendrick. Before I start ordering furniture."

"Don't take it personally. Margaret should've discussed it with me, that's all. And don't call me Kendrick. It makes me feel like I'm back in boot camp. I'll take you to the springs when I get back from Portland."

Vivi counted to ten, lips pressed flat. "Please, don't trouble yourself." She wished she hadn't asked. She could probably find it on her own. A couple of miles upriver. How hard could it be?

He read her mind, and fixed her with a stern glare. "Do not go without me," he said forcefully. "The cliffs are dangerous, and the path is washed out."

"Fine." Vivi deposited her coffee cup in the sink.

"I'll be back around four, if you want to go then," he added.

"Like I said, don't go to any trouble."

"It's no trouble. I meant what I said about not going alone."

"I heard you the first time." She let his door slam shut.

Oh, ouch. She'd done it to herself again. Whenever she let down her guard, zing, pow, he insulted her again. The second she heard his truck pull out, she went downstairs and into Jack's kitchen and dialed Nell's new cell.

Her sister picked up promptly. "Hey, you. Everything okay?"

"Hey, yourself," Vivi replied. "How's Italy?"

"Amazing," Nell replied. "We were just finishing up a late lunch. Fabulous, of course. So how's the flower farm?"

"Hmmph." Vivi recounted the debacle in the rain and mud, and Nell expressed the appropriate horrified sympathy.

"Anyway," Vivi concluded. "Here I am, stuck like a bug on flypaper. But that, I kid you not, is the least of my problems."

"Oh, really? What's going on?" Nell prompted.

Vivi paused, suspicious of the cheerful curiosity in her sister's voice. "Jack Kendrick is my problem, as I am sure you know."

"Oh? In what sense?" Nell asked, all innocence.

"Nell, what exactly do you know about the guy?"

Nell hemmed and hawed. "Um, exactly what Duncan told you," she said. "There's a photograph on Duncan's wall of Jack climbing a sheer rock face. So I knew he was big, with dark hair, nerves of steel, and lots of thick, sinewy muscle. But that's about it."

"He despises me," Vivi announced. "He thinks I'm a piece of insignificant fluff. A rootless, brainless tattooed bimbo incapable of making commitments or seeing anything through to the end. And he hates my van."

"Wow." Nell sounded impressed. "That sounds deep, Viv. Fear of commitment issues, after one evening's acquaintance?"

"It wasn't my fault!" Vivi wailed.

"I never said it was, honey," Nell soothed. "What's the place like?"

"Out of my wildest dreams," Vivi admitted, staring out the window. "The place is covered with flowers. Edna's having the time of her life chasing something across the field. I hope it's not a skunk."

"So? What's the problem?"

"What do you mean, what's the problem? I told you! The man doesn't want me here! He thinks I'm trash! This is a big, big problem!"

"But the van is stuck, right?" Nell prodded.

"Yes, at least until—"

"Well, good, then." Nell sounded satisfied.

"Good?" Vivi's voice rose to a squawk. "What do you mean, good?"

"I mean that, at least until your fucking van gets unstuck, I, your sister, and Nancy, too, will be able to breathe easy and sleep at night because for once in your goddamn life, somebody is looking after you!"

The violence in her sister's voice startled Vivi. "Um, okay," she whispered.

"I know what these guys are capable of." Nell's voice quivered. "You don't. You have no clue, Viv. And you don't want to. Trust me."

"I do trust you," Vivi assured her. "And I promise. I'll be careful."

"You know what we did this morning?" Nell asked.

Vivi hesitated. The tone in Nell's voice made her wary. "Ah, what?"

"We talked to the domestic staff at the Palazzo de Luca. There was a lady there in her seventies, the daughter of the previous housekeeper. She remembers when Lucia left. And why."

Vivi swallowed, hard. "And? Stop teasing."

"It was after finding her father's dead body," Nell said. "In his study, under his writing table. The table we still have. He'd been tortured to death. Cut to pieces. Slowly. Like they threatened to do to me. Like they would have done to Nancy. Or to you, if they get you. Keep it in mind."

Vivi flinched. It wasn't like it was a big surprise, but still. This evil had deep roots.

"So be careful, okay?" Nell begged. "Just be very, very careful."

"I will," Vivi soothed. "I promise."

Nell sniffled. "Right. At least, you're finally attracted to somebody again. Thank goodness for that, at least. It's about freaking time."

Vivi felt strangely cornered. "You don't get it, Nell. Whether I'm attracted or not, it's a bad scene. He despises me. He sees me as a type, not a person. It's just like when Brian—"

"Viv, stop it," Nell cut in. "It's been years since that dumb putz messed with you! Get over it! Stop living like a wandering nun!"

"I'm feeling manipulated," Vivi said tightly.

"Manipulated?" Nell snorted. "Poor Vivi. Trapped in a flowering wilderness paradise with a gorgeous, eligible hunk sworn to protect you from the evil villains. How cruel of us, for doing this to you."

"I'm hanging up," Vivi said. "I'm too pissed to talk anymore, but I love you anyway. Later, bye." She hung up, her face hot. The mention of Brian's name made her squirm with anger. After six years.

She was twenty-one when she met Brian Wilder, at her student art show. It was during her rebellious period. Wilder was a suave gallery director out scouting for hot new talent. His gallery was affiliated with an art museum specializing in works by emerging artists. He expressed an interest in her work. Soon after, he expressed an interest in her personally. He was handsome, intelligent. She'd been dazzled. At first.

Everyone had been thrilled for her when Brian offered her a contract with his gallery. She remembered the fateful day as clearly as if it had just happened. They were sitting in a coffee bar on Bleecker Street. She drank espresso. Brian was sipping a decaf soy milk latte.

"What do you think?" Brian asked, flicking hair out of her eyes.

"I-I don't know," Vivi stammered. "I'm not sure yet what it entails."

"Let me explain," Brian said, in a patronizing voice. "I see huge potential in your work. Energy, anger, power. But it lacks discipline."

"Um." Vivi sipped her espresso, pondering that.

"Just like you," Brian observed. His eyes flicked down, checking her out. "That skirt and boots you're wearing, for instance." His thin lips twitched. "You have to polish up your image."

Vivi tugged down her purple velvet miniskirt to cover another couple of inches of thigh, wishing she hadn't worn torn-up fishnet stockings. She stared down at her thigh-high lace-up black leather boots.

Brian flicked another lock of her hair back, and look her up and down. "We'll start with a haircut and a new wardrobe."

"I can dress myself," Vivi said.

"Yes? Well. If this is the result . . ." His voice trailed off, and his eyes took on a weird, hot glow. He chucked her under the chin. "I've never gotten intimate with your type before."

Vivi wrenched her chin away from his pinching fingers. "What do you mean, my 'type'?" she demanded, irritated. "What type is that?"

"You know. The bad girl with the innocent eyes. The lost waif.

You're like something out of a Japanese anime film. All eyes, and that wild mop of hair. It's . . . mmm. Stimulating." He tilted her chin up again. "About the contract. What do you say?"

It was an incredible opportunity. Any of Vivi's struggling artist friends would have cheerfully killed for it. And her jaw was aching with tension. Vivi pulled her face away from his fingers again. She gulped the rest of her bitter coffee, wondering why she wasn't feeling happier.

"If you sign the contract, it will be with the understanding that you'll accept me as an artistic mentor," Brian said sternly. "And I'll expect you to produce. I can make you successful, Viv. That's what you want, isn't it?" Brian turned the full force of his cold gray eyes on her.

Her doubts felt vague and foolish. Destiny called.

"Yes," she said.

She'd signed. Agreed to let Brian groom her into an artistic sensation. The stupidest move of her life. So far.

Vivi stared at the luxuriant spider plants that hung in Jack Kendrick's kitchen, thinking grimly about the way one's worst mistakes tended to repeat themselves, again and again. They dressed themselves in slightly different outfits, but the basic content was always the same.

Here was another man who saw just a type when he looked at her. Another man who made her feel inadequate and embarrassed, just for being what she intrinsically was. Except that this time, it was worse. Maybe because her desire for Jack Kendrick's good opinion was so irrationally strong. And her chance of getting it so small.

It was odd. She'd always considered Brian handsome, in his cold, austere way. But compared to Jack Kendrick, Brian seemed effete. Dried up and stringy, even. Maybe it was that empty, no-calorie crap he ate. But Kendrick, whew. A girl could just sink her teeth into that one. She would never wear that guy out. Never use him up.

But there was no excuse for making the same mistake twice. She grabbed a handful of cookies and marched out of the kitchen, munching them defiantly. *Compensate, Viv, compensate.*

Celibacy wouldn't kill her. At least, it hadn't killed her yet.

Chapter
4

Tap, *tap, tap* on the office door. Interrupted again, Brian Wilder whipped the herbal face pack off his face and waved away the masseuse doing his foot reflexology treatment.

"What the fuck is it this time?" he rapped out.

The door to his office cracked open. Damiana, his current assistant, peeked in. Her huge, dark eyes were big in her kittenish face.

"There is a client outside who needs to speak to you," she said, with her faint Italian accent that utterly failed to charm him today.

"Can't you help him? What the hell have I trained you for?"

Damiana shrugged, helplessly. "He says just you. He says it cannot wait. I do not know what to do with him. He is a strange type."

Brian gestured for Coco to wipe off the Ayurvedic oils that were dripping off his feet and to collect crystals and stones from his body. Looked like his fucking chakras would have to get tuned another time. Another swollen ego to wank.

He shot Damiana an unfriendly look. What was the point of hiring pretty fluff from the local art school if not to have her do the ego wanking? Damiana should be down there, making the guy come in his pants while Brian was left unencumbered to rake in dough. But no. He could not seem to delegate. The ego wanking always fell to him.

Coco and Damiana exchanged commiserating looks as Brian threw on his linen trousers and shirt. He shoved past them, jostling more roughly than he needed to. Punishing them in advance for the whiny cat bitching they were going to do behind his back, on his time, on his payroll, as soon as he was out of earshot. Treacherous twats.

He headed out onto the second level of the gallery, a broad balcony all the way around the room. He took the opportunity to look down and check the guy out. He was currently staring at the Waylan Winthrop bronze that Brian had just placed on display in the center of the gallery. A strong piece, entitled *Teeth*. Price, a modest $38,000. The jaws of the beast reared toward the heaven in a wordless shriek of inchoate rage, its snarl of teeth pointing straight up, like spikes.

The guy looked baffled at the spectacle, but maybe that was the default expression on his thick face. Brian sized him up as he headed toward the stairs. A behemoth. Six four, but an extra eighty pounds on him. Brian brushed his hand over his own washboard abs as he trotted down the stairs. He had only contempt for such a lack of discipline. His own body was buff and toned. Seven days a week in the gym. He watched every bite he ate, made sure it was pure, organic, and calibrated to fine-tune his health and well-being. His body was his prized possession. He honed it.

This guy did not. Brian analyzed the guy's wardrobe, pricing every stitch, as Damiana should have done. Off the rack, bargain basement. Not even particularly clean. And his breath, God. He was going to have to send Damiana around with a lemon essential oil spritz bottle. The stench of the man's halitosis was sucking all the prana out of the room.

He extended his hand and smiled. "My assistant said you're looking for me?"

"You're Brian Wilder?"

The man's voice and manner were not cultured. He sounded like he'd come from the wrong side of the tracks in some depressed industrial town upstate. This guy was not walking money. Brian retracted his outstretched hand and gave him another smile, carefully dosed this time. Briefer, thinner. "That would be me. And you are?"

"My name is Craig Wilcox," the man said. "I was told you once handled the work of an artist my client is interested in acquiring."

Brian stuck his fingers into his pockets. "And your client is?"

"My client prefers to stay nameless at this time."

Brian waited. "And the artist? He or she will stay nameless, too?" The guy's eyes squinched in the puffy fat of his eyelids, not appreciating Brian's quip. His black hair was the wrong color and texture for his face, Brian thought. Wig, or dye job. Strange.

"The artist is Vivien D'Onofrio," the man said.

If Brian had needed anything to convince him that his time was being wasted, hearing that woman's name was it. "I no longer handle D'Onofrio's work. In fact, I make a point of seeing that none of my professional colleagues handle her work, either. I don't even think she's a working artist anymore. For her sake, I hope not."

The guy blinked, stared with those strange dark gray eyes. Flat, opaque, and metallic, like hematite. "Why?"

"She's unreliable and unprofessional," Brian announced, as he did to anyone who would listen. "And her work is uneven and derivative. Let me suggest some far better investments for your client. There's a new artist I've just taken on who's created a stunning series of—"

"My client's only interested in D'Onofrio's work," the man said.

"I'm the last person you should ask about her," Brian informed him. "I'm not in touch with her, and have no plans to be in the future."

"That's a terrible shame," the man said blandly.

Brian was about to tell the buffoon to stop wasting his time and leave when he caught the man's eyes. Brian's eyes stuck there. As if those hematite eyes were magnets. Sucking at his vital energy, like a vampire.

The fleeting thought gave him an irrational stab of fear. He shook it away. "It's not my problem," he said.

"That's an unhelpful attitude, Mr. Wilder," the man chided. "My client hates to be denied. Price is no object. He likes to indulge himself, especially when things are forbidden. Surely you can relate to that? Can't you, Mr. Wilder? I think . . . maybe . . . you can. Hmm?"

Fear stabbed, deeper. "What do you mean?"

The other man lifted his shoulders, in a casual shrug. "I make it my business to inform myself about people. I've heard about your late-night assignations from the escort agencies. You like them young, right? No more than fourteen? Slim, small breasts to none, big eyes, no makeup? A different one every time? Perv."

Not possible. Brian stared, transfixed. The man began to smile. He stepped closer, words coming fast like a concentrated venom. "You like those little lost waifs, hmm? Poor vulnerable creatures, no big strong daddy to protect them. What do you do to them, Wilder? Do you like to make them cry?" He studied Brian's face and let out a muffled crack of laughter. "You do! You sick, sick fuck."

"G-get out of here," Brian quavered. "Are you threatening me?"

Wilcox laughed. "Threatening? God, no. My client has so much money, he has no need to threaten."

"Then why . . . why—"

"Let me reiterate. D'Onofrio is the one my client wants. If you want someone else to sell her pieces to my client, and let that person enjoy my client's good opinion and all that it entails, that would be a big shame—for you. Think about that, Mr. Wilder. And think fast."

"I don't know where she is," he repeated. Fear loosened his bowels. He struggled to control his physiological functions.

The guy's grin looked discolored. "I bet you could run her down. The art world is small. It's worth getting over your differences."

Brian needed to sprint for the bathroom, but he didn't have the nerve to just walk away from Wilcox. "I, um . . ."

"Take this." The guy handed him a card, with a cell phone number scribbled on it. "I'll be back to see you, if I don't hear from you first. I know some people are shy about calling. Don't be shy, Wilder."

Wilcox walked out. Brian made his way up the stairs, clenching the banister and his sphincter muscle with the same desperation.

Damiana came out of his office, eyes big with curiosity. "So what did he want? I am so sorry, but he kind of creeped me out, so I—"

"Go get my electronic organizer. Get on the Internet," he snapped. "I want you to find Vivien D'Onofrio for me. Now."

"Her? But I thought you . . . I thought she—"

"Do it!" he bellowed, and she darted away, heels clicking.

He lurched into his office, dismayed to see Coco taking her own sweet time putting away all her oils and colored crystals. "Get out!"

She shoved her stuff into her case and scurried.

He got to the bathroom just in time to avoid the unthinkable. He sat there so long, his ass fell asleep on the cold ring of porcelain.

How had that man known? No one in his life knew. He kept his dirty little thing so fucking secret, it was practically secret from himself.

He had many lovers. This had nothing to do with his love life. This was a private thing. Deep in the night, he got that secret, nasty itch. To play with a fantasy that had started with his affair with Vivi D'Onofrio.

So small, so slender. A lost kitten. So young. She'd been twenty-one when he met her, but she could've easily passed for fifteen. And so talented. He had secretly hated her for that. All that talent, coming out her fucking pores, and she didn't even know it. So goddamn innocent.

The talent was wasted on her. It had driven him mad with envy.

The next best thing to having talent was controlling talent. And he had tried. God, how he had tried. But she was like an unbroken horse. Ungrateful, whining bitch, biting the hand that fed her. They'd have made money hand over fist, if she'd just done as he told her. But no.

He'd wanted to play her, like an instrument. Wanted it so bad, he lay awake in the dark of the night, grinding his teeth, milking his dick.

After she left, he'd held his nose and done a little digging into the seamy underworld of the New York sex industry and commenced a brand-new secret indulgence. Re-creating a scenario calculated to make himself feel exactly the way he needed to feel. To get off. Explosively.

He didn't do it often. Every couple of months or so. A slender big-eyed girl in a hotel room, lost and scared. Him, controlling her. Using her. Punishing her for what Vivi had done to him. Making her cry.

His heart rate kicked up, hot and jagged, just thinking of it.

This situation was probably Viv's own fault. She'd behaved badly, got on the wrong side of some criminal badass. The badass was out for payback. Brian was an innocent bystander. Caught in the cross-fire.

Fuck that. He was rolling over on her, the minute he got the chance. He owed Viv D'Onofrio nothing. She'd stiffed him in every way.

Let her pay the price for her own fuckups.

He was already imagining how he'd respond when the news of her violent, untimely end came to him. He would be shocked and sad but not surprised. What a waste, he'd say, his face pale and grave. Shaking his head at the tragedy of it. But he'd seen it coming. Oh, yes, he had.

It was just the law of karma in action.

Vivi was deeply absorbed in making a list of all the furniture she wanted. Bed, couch, coffee table, bookcase. A nice rug. A dresser, a floor lamp. A spice rack, even, by God. Such a luxury, to hang clothes in a closet. To tape a favorite photo onto the fridge.

The knock on the door made her jump. "Who is it?" she called.

"It's me." His deep voice made the entire surface of her skin tingle madly. She braced herself as she opened the door.

Jack stood there, holding a tray of tiny, feathery green seedlings. She stared, confused. He handed the tray to her. "These are for you."

"For me?" she repeated stupidly.

"*Eranthis hyemalis*," he said. "Winter Aconite. I saw some, at the nursery. I thought of you. They're not blooming now, of course, and it's late to plant them in the green, but what the hell. We can give it a try. They like well-drained soil, and lots of shade. We can set them out beneath those big oaks over at the far side of the lawn. If you want."

She closed her open mouth. "Ah . . . wow. I, uh—"

"If we get lucky, they'll multiply. Make a floral carpet."

She was so charmed, she felt her face heat up and her throat clutch. "That is so sweet of you," she whispered.

He shrugged. "I'm sorry. I was a jerk, today. And last night."

The heat in her face and her throat spread, a soft, warm glow.

He stepped in the door as she laid the seedlings on the kitchen counter. "Do you want to go to the hot springs now?"

Nothing had changed, even if he had apologized, Vivi reminded herself. Going to a beautiful remote place to sit in a pool of hot water all alone with this man was a dumb idea. And the fact that he was acting sweet was all the more reason to stay away. "I don't know much about plants," she stalled, stroking a tender frond.

"Don't worry about it. I'll show you," he said. "So? You coming?"

"Yes," she heard herself say. Sealing her own doom.

"Let's go." He started down the stairs, Edna scrambling after.

"You mean, right now? This minute? Don't we need towels, bathing suits? Anything?"

"Bring what you want, but wear jeans. The poison oak is thick."

"One minute." Vivi closed the door, shucked her clothes, and pulled on her old one-piece. She yanked her clothes on, tossed a towel over her shoulder. About to do the stupidest thing she'd ever deliberately done, and she couldn't even breathe, she was so excited.

The path was difficult. They hopped boulders by the rushing river for a mile or so, until sheer cliffs rose up from the swift, green glacial water. She followed Jack into a thicket of dense bushes, clambering up one steep hill and down another, through a narrow cleft between two towering boulders, and under the draped fronds of a blackberry bush.

A tendril snarled in her hair. She was struggling to untangle it when he appeared beside her. He took the long, thorny vine in his hand. Vivi stared at the hollow at the base of his throat. He was so warm. He smelled so good. Her body ached to know how it would feel to lean against that solid chest. What would she do if he kissed her?

Oh, please. Duh. She'd jump all over him. Eat him for lunch.

He let go of the lock of hair, laying it over her shoulder. He turned without saying a word and started to climb. Vivi scrambled after him, relief warring with disappointment.

The path merged with a smaller streamed from the hillside above that had carved a gully leading down to the river. The walls of the gully were steep, the rocks covered with moss, thick with wild mint and luxuriant, spotted yellow flowers with heavy heads like snapdragons, and tufts of fragrant wild mint. Vivi picked her way from boulder to boulder, Edna splashing ahead of her. At the mouth of the spring, Jack pointed upriver. "Look there, past that tall rock."

Her eyes followed his hand. There were several pools, sunken into the huge, flat gray rocks of the riverbank. They were surrounded by the nodding yellow flowers and mint. The last rays of sun that still managed to slant into the river canyon lit up the water, the multicolored pebbles, and the glittering sand. Faint curls of steam rose from the water. The river rushed noisily by a few yards away.

He watched her face, intently. "Like it?"

She looked around, enchanted. "Oh, my God. It's superb."

Her delight was shattered when she realized that Jack had stripped off his shirt and was unbuckling his belt. Oh, God. Jack Kendrick fully clothed was already too much voltage for her circuits to handle. Jack Kendrick naked would blow her fuses to hell and gone.

"Hey, you! Just wait a damn second!" she said sharply.

His hands stopped on his waistband. "Yeah?"

"Are you wearing swimming trunks?" she demanded.

"No." He waited patiently as she processed this.

"I'm not comfortable with that," she said. "Things are already funny between us. I'd rather not, uh . . ."

"See me stark naked," he finished.

She blew out a sharp, nervous sigh. "Right on, buddy."

"Do you want me to leave? Can you find your way back alone?"

Ow. That would be so flat. So blah. She did not want him to leave.

Damn, she didn't know what she wanted. She wanted the world to be different. She wanted him to be different. She wanted . . . aw, shit.

She just wanted him to want her. Her, Vivi D'Onofrio. The whole damn tattooed, itinerant, sexpot, complicated, prickly package.

That was too extravagant a thing to hope for. Besides being way too soon. For Pete's sake, she'd just met the guy the day before. She just had so much intense, scary emotion about sex backed up in her system. After six years of celibacy anyone would be climbing the freaking walls. She had Brian Wilder to thank for that, too. The jerk.

"No, don't leave," she murmured, abashed. "Can't you just, um, keep your underwear on?"

His lips twitched, making her feel foolish and prissy. "Yeah, whatever," he said. "If it really bothers you."

He pulled off his jeans. He was wearing white briefs. The muscles in his torso were finger-licking delicious. Luxurious curling dark hair tapered down to his belly and turned into a furry mat that disappeared into those briefs. Narrow hips, powerful thighs. She might not survive this visual sensory experience even if he did keep his briefs on.

He stepped into the water, descending until he sat in the pool cross-legged, clouds of glittering sand wafting up from the bottom to swirl and turn in the water, glinting in the sunlight. The water reached to his collarbone. He leaned against the rim of the pool and closed his eyes. A nice show of delicacy, while she undressed. He was in perfect gentleman mode now—but she knew his tricks. If she relaxed and let down her guard for one instant, he'd turn on her for sure.

She pulled off her jeans and T-shirt, wishing her bathing suit were less thin and worn, and stepped into the water. Deliciously hot. Like an enormous, full-body kiss. A sprig of mint dangled over her shoulder, brushing her cheek. She was blushing furiously.

"Why are you blushing?" His voice was silky, amused.

"The water is hot," she snapped. "And how did you know that with your eyes closed, anyway? That's sneaky."

He smiled briefly and made no reply.

They sat there, listening to the river rushing by, for a very long time. He kept his eyes closed, until it felt as if he were hiding from her.

She wanted to make him reveal something about himself. She'd bared her soul in the restaurant the night before. He owed her some freaking personal history, too. "So. Nudity doesn't embarrass you?"

"I grew up around people who weren't embarrassed about it," he said. "The sexual revolution. Let it all hang out."

Interesting factoid, that. Vivi pinched off a mint leaf and chewed it, letting the fresh, clean flavor clear her head. Jack dunked his head under the water and smoothed his hair back from his square forehead, and she noticed once again the white streak of the scar that disappeared into his hairline. "How'd you get that scar?"

He didn't open his eyes. "Long story."

"I'm not in a hurry," she said.

His forehead contracted, and then he wiped his face clean of expression once again. "Another time."

She plucked another mint sprig. "Sorry. Didn't mean to pry."

"It's okay. Talk all you want. Just don't expect me to be scintillating when I respond. Or even coherent."

"Why? Is something wrong?"

He opened his eyes, and looked at her, with that bright, clear timber wolf gaze that made shivers of delicious terror race through her.

"I can't concentrate," he said. "I can barely hear you talk. All I can hear is my own heart pounding."

The flat statement hung between them. The force of his gaze burned against her face. She closed her eyes, counted to ten.

She opened them, and gazed at him. A lock of hair was clinging to his forehead. A drop of water rolled down his cheek. Vivi leaned forward and touched it with her fingertip. His face was so hot, his skin so resiliant, velvety.

He caught her wrist in his hand and pulled. She floated effortlessly, inevitably closer to him. For a few breathless moments, they were face-to-face, staring at each other. Her breasts brushed his chest. He touched her lips. Slid his finger into her hair. Kissed her, hungrily.

She went nuts in his arms. An explosion of emotions, sensations, bursting into being from deep inside. Achingly sweet, and tinged with desperation, and something fierce, like anger, but brighter, hungrier. Twisting, twining, growing. She wound her arms around his neck and hung on, digging her fingers into those thick muscles.

He drew back for a moment, his eyes dilated and full of wonder. "You taste like mint," he said huskily, and then that huge vortex sucked them right back into another desperate, twining kiss.

Oh, wow. He was outrageously beautiful close up. His eyes, the incredible length of his wet black eyelashes. Water drops trickling along the crest of the graceful, angled sweep of his eyebrows.

His lips were hot and soft, as wonderful and kissable as she had imagined, and his breath tasted so sweet. His skin was so supple and beautiful, with that delicate rasp of new beard shadow over strong, graceful bones, over chiseled manly angles. God. So fine.

She was charged with emotion. She explored his muscular back with her fingers, wound her arms around his neck, and opened to his kiss. An opening from somewhere deep inside her, someplace vast and beautiful. A universe of bright, open space.

She barely noticed the shoulder straps of her bathing suit being peeled down. She arched back, abandoning herself to his strong grasp, letting her head fall back and her hair float out in the water like a lily pad. She cried out with pleasure as he hungrily suckled her breasts.

So sweet, so shivering melting hot for him. Her nipples felt like points of glowing light. Her breasts had always felt so deplorably small, insignificant even, but under his hot mouth, they felt plumper, bigger. Swollen with eagerness, alive to pleasure. Her whole chest was melting and soft, as if he drank some magic elixir from her body as he licked her, and the more he took, the more she had to give.

And the breathless aching pull of want between her legs grew keener every moment.

Jack pulled her down onto his lap and slipped his finger under her bottom and into the stretchy fabric of her bathing suit, dragging in a sharp breath to find her slick and hot. He slid the tip of his finger slowly inside her. She squirmed, clenched around him, making a keening sound almost too high for herself to hear.

"Oh, wow," he muttered. "You're . . ."

"Yes," she said. "No hair. I do a Brazilian wax whenever I get the chance. I like the way it feels."

"Me, too," he rasped.

She hid her face against his neck, her breath jerking in and out in short, hard sobs. Her bathing suit was floating away, forgotten. She had to slow this down. "Um, Jack? Wait."

"Why? You're ready. I've never seen anyone so ready in my life." He bent his head to her chest again, pulling her nipple into a wet, silken vortex of sensation, his hot tongue rasping, swirling.

"But I . . . b-b-but I can't—"

"Shhhh." He thrust a finger inside her slick pussy, penetrating, pressing and swirling deep inside as he licked and lapped, and *ah* . . .

She cried out, arching back in his grasp as a totally unexpected climax pumped violently through her.

When she opened her eyes, she was floating in his arms, staring up into the bright blue sky. Her eyes were awash with tears.

Jack rose to his feet. Water sloshed and slopped as he hoisted her up and set her on the edge of the pool. The cool air felt delicious on her pink, overheated flesh. Heat steamed off her wet body. She felt poppy red, feverish, weak in the knees. Terribly exposed.

He pressed her legs apart, and stared down at her. "Oh, yeah," he whispered. "I knew it."

"Knew what?"

He pushed her gently back, until her back was pressed to the flat rock, her legs wide. Laid out like a sacrifice on the altar of sexual misbehavior. Open to the sky. A warning to foolish, unwary girls.

But she wasn't choking up, she wasn't panicking, like usual. It was magic. She couldn't stop. At least not yet. It was too wonderful.

"I knew that your pussy would be like this." He knelt down in the pool to get closer, and kissed the inside of her thigh. "Those dark red folds, bursting out of your slit like some hothouse flower. Exotic."

She laughed, shakily. "You've got flowers on the brain, Jack."

"No." His teeth flashed, in one of his rare, gorgeous grins. "I've got your pussy on the brain." He nuzzled her labia, light kisses that promised and teased. "I was half expecting your clit to be pierced."

She jerked up onto her elbows. "Hah! You won't catch me sticking a metal pin through the most nerve-dense part of my entire body!" She peered at him, eyes narrowed. "I bet you're disappointed, right? I'm not quite as wild as you'd fantasized?"

He played with her inner pussy lips, spreading them tenderly wide like butterfly wings, and the tickling caresses were driving her mad.

"Actually, no," he said. "I'm relieved, to tell the truth. We're on the same page about how we like to treat those nerve-dense parts of our bodies. That bodes well."

"Yeah? For what?"

"Orgasms," he said, and leaned down, pressed his lips against her clit. Swirled his tongue. Oh, God. He was so . . . *good*.

She jerked helplessly against his face. She wasn't ready. It was too intense. She was scared to death. She pushed his face away.

He rose up, kissing his way up over her mons, the tiny swatch of decorative red pubic hair, over her clit hood. Then over her belly, her rib cage, her breasts.

"Get comfortable with it," he said, resolutely. "I'm going to lick your pussy until you're a lake of lube."

"Jack." She grabbed his hair to hold him there, licked her lips, and dragged in a jerky breath. "I don't know if this is such a good—"

"I have to." He unwound her hands, sank down. "It's going to be a really tight fit." He slid his tongue boldly between her pussy lips.

The rasp of his plunging tongue, his matter-of-fact words, the thought of him inside her, it kicked her over the top and into a powerful orgasm. Her pussy pulsed around his thrusting fingers, throbbed against his swirling tongue. Long, sweet, echoing ripples went on and on.

He pulled her back down into the pool after the spasms had moved through her, and she sank into his arms as if she had no bones. He held her so she floated right over the thick, prominent jut of his erect cock against her thigh. In silent pleading.

She draped herself over his shoulder. Trying to catch her breath.

"Jack. Um, I hate to say it, but we can't have sex," she whispered.

He stiffened, nuzzling her shoulder. "No?"

"We have no latex," she pointed out. "I certainly didn't bring any."

Breath hissed in sharply, between his teeth. "Ah, yes. That."

"A small detail, but an important one. I don't have contraception, either. And we haven't even discussed our sexual histories yet. I'm sorry. I don't know how I let things go so far." She couldn't stop herself from apologizing, even though the situation was only half her fault. "Just for the record. I'm, ah, fine," she offered. "No STDs of any kind."

"Me neither," he said.

"No lovers, either. For a really long time," she added.

"I noticed that," he replied. "You're tiny. Like a virgin."

"But I'm not, ah . . . I'm not babyproof," she said.

He stared at the river. Wiped water off his face, expressionless. "Forget it." His voice was remote. "I'm disappointed, but I'll live."

His cool tone made her feel punished, and frustrated. "Besides, it's just too soon for going all the way," she rattled on. "Call me silly and old-fashioned if you want, but I barely know you, and things are really weird between us anyway, and I just don't want to give it all up to you if you just want to . . . ah, I mean, if the relationship has no future."

His eyes narrowed. "I should think you would be good at those."

She stiffened, suspicious. "At what?"

"Relationships with no future. What other kind could your type possibly have?"

She shoved away from him, her boneless languor gone. A wave of hot water splashed up into Jack's chest and face.

"Screw you, Kendrick," she said savagely, leaping up.

"I'm sorry," he said. "I didn't mean to insult you."

"Oh? You want to know a secret? A couple of minutes ago, I truly, sincerely wanted to suck your dick. You want to know something else? I don't want to suck your dick anymore." She yanked her jeans up over her bare ass. She couldn't seem to make her trembling fingers work. He got out of the pool and moved toward her. She kept her face averted. "Don't touch me," she snarled.

"Aw, shit," he muttered. "What a mess."

"Yes. My feelings, exactly. I've known you for about one day, and every time you see me, you insult me. Big, nasty, mortal insults. And it's ten times worse when you seduce me first. Freaking sadist."

"I didn't mean to insult you. Nor did I succeed in seducing you, evidently." He got up out of the pool, and she whipped her gaze away.

"Keep your back turned," he said. "I want to take this wet underwear off before I put on my jeans."

"Do as you like. I'm leaving."

Vivi made her way up the flower-lined, moss-choked streambed. She could barely see where she was going. Slowly, the path came back into focus. The cleft of rock she had to clamber past. The thicket of posion oak. The tunnel of blackberry brambles to slither through. Then back down to the riverbed, for the rock hopping.

She was mortified. He melted her down. Turned her into hot goop. And then made her feel cheap and easy for giving in to it.

Hell with him. It was a mistake she would not make again.

Her knee-jerk instinct was to gather up her stuff and her dog and get the hell out of there, but her van was still stuck, and the Fiend was still out there, and she had no place to go, except back to New York, to park on her sisters' lives. Once she'd started planning her hideout in the flower bower, she'd ceased to send in registration fees for upcoming crafts fairs, or to churn out new stock. So she couldn't even do the circuit, at least not for a while. Working the crafts fairs took a certain amount of lead time and advance planning.

So even if her van were unstuck, if she left now it would just be for aimless, money-draining, gas-guzzling wandering the road. And she would be too scared to stop. The gas would run out when the money did. And it wouldn't take very long.

And there she'd be, a sitting duck.

No. She was a grown-up. She'd been through hell in her life, and come out battered, but okay. She would not be chased away like a stray cat. Her safety was more important than her hurt feelings.

But neither would she play the nymphet sex toy for that arrogant prick. Thank God she hadn't gone down on him. She'd be feeling ten times worse about it all if she had the taste of his come in her mouth.

And she'd come so close, too. Her mouth had been watering. Bad enough that he'd spent all that time with his face between her legs.

That took the strength out of her wobbly legs. She sat down heavily on a rock. Clenching her thighs around pulses of remembered pleasure.

Only the thought of him finding her there on his way back was scary enough to nudge her up off her ass and get her stumbling home.

Chapter
5

"So. Your own store, hmm? What a lovely idea. Jewelry, pottery, art objects, gift items? Pebble River is just right for a place like that, now that the windsurfers found it. Lots of tourism. Windsurfers have money, you see." Margaret poured Vivi another cup of tea out of a rose-spattered teapot and nudged the plate of pecan puffs toward her. "Come on, dearie! Indulge! Heaven knows, you can afford the calories!"

"Margaret, I've eaten five already, and they're not small." Vivi gazed appreciatively at the heap of sugar-glazed cookies.

"I could help you find a place, you know," Margaret offered. "I ran a cross-stitch shop in Pebble River for thirty-five years. We can get started right away."

"I would, but my van's still stuck," Vivi explained. "Dwayne keeps putting me off because of the rain, but it's been sunny for days, so—"

"Well, now! Speak of the devil. Look what's coming up the road!"

Vivi peered through the floral print swags of Margaret's window. A tractor chugged up the road. A big, round man with a cowboy hat was behind the wheel. "Is that Dwayne?"

Margaret hobbled to the window and lifted her spectacles. "It is. I told him all about you. He runs the gas station at the exit for Pebble River. Put some cookies in a napkin for him, would you, dear?"

Vivi soon found herself on the road, shaking the hand of a smiling guy with several chins. "You're the artist? Good to meet you."

"Same here." She handed him the cookies with a smile.

"I thought you might be coming by, Dwayne, so I baked your favorite," Margaret said. "Vivi, let me know when you want to go to Pebble River. Maybe we should all go together."

"All? All meaning who?" Vivi asked.

"You, me, and Jack," Margaret said brightly. "I'm sure Jack will have wonderful ideas."

"Oh, no. I don't want to bother Jack," Vivi said hastily.

"Bother me about what?"

Her heart jumped up, to her throat. She turned. Oh, boy.

She'd managed to avoid him since the hot springs incident, and she'd been fondly imagining that her feelings were back under control. Nope. Vivid images of the hot springs incident blazed through her body.

Her face turned pink. No. Her whole body was turning pink.

"Hi." Jack nodded to Dwayne and Margaret. "Heard the tractor."

"I figured it was dry enough by now," Dwayne said.

"I'll walk down with you," Jack said.

Oh, God. All she needed. Vivi swallowed her dismay. "Okay."

Fortunately, the rumble of the tractor chugging ahead of them made their silence less embarrassing on the walk. Vivi had been using the quiet days while the weather dried up to hang pictures, write down goals, make shopping wish lists for some future when she had money to spend. She'd set up her portable studio on the floor, and had made several trips back and forth to the van to haul back her work supplies.

It was a new artistic era. She had to beef up her stock, dream up new designs. Scrounge for pretty rubbish. She liked to incorporate what people thought of as garbage into her work. Part of her artistic philosophy. Making garbage beautiful. All in the attitude.

Her first investment would be a big worktable. Then some metalworking equipment. Big pieces of stained glass to play with. She was eager to spread out. Everything in her life for the past six years had been miniature; from her income to her camper-van home all the way to her artistic ambitions. She was sick of being miniature. She wanted to sprawl. Take up space. Breathe big breaths.

Not that she regretted the choices she'd made. Her back straightened up at the thought. The traveling jewelry business had been good to her. Her jewelry sideline had started one day when Nancy admired a sculpture Vivi was making out of beads, wire, and glass.

"This is beautiful," Nancy had said. "If it were jewelry, I would wear it."

The comment had given her an idea, and for each of her sisters' and Lucia's next birthdays, she'd made personalized earrings. Then necklaces to match. Then she'd tried a couple of brooches. It was fun. Ideas for designs flowed easily.

Her art school buddy Rafael had persuaded her to try selling them in his booth at the open-air market down on Sixth Avenue. She had sold several, to her surprise and Rafael's glee. The profit had almost paid her rent that month.

Brian had been disdainful of her "craftsy hobby," and resentful of the time it took from the work he demanded from her, but she'd kept quietly on with her sideline. And after things exploded with Brian, the jewelry gave her something to fall back on. Not what she'd dreamed of, but it was creative, and it paid for her gas, her car insurance, her food.

She'd been trying to use some of these long, silent days to churn out some more work, but she'd had no luck. She'd chalked it up to exhaustion, worry, and unsatisfied lust. And Haupt, and John the Fiend, of course. That zesty pinch of mortal dread, just to liven things up.

She hoped it wasn't artist's block. She'd experienced a bad period of that some time after she'd signed the contract with Brian's gallery.

Working with Brian had been great, at first. He sold a bunch of her pieces, the wilder, angrier ones. Money started coming in, and she'd quit her cocktail-waitressing job and basked in the thrill of being the hot new thing on the art scene. She spent a lot of the money she made on clothes, preapproved by Brian, of course. Then she started experimenting with another style. Brian didn't like the new pieces. He demanded that she make more of the old series that sold so well.

"But I'm bored with them," Vivi protested. "They're so angry and negative. I'm not as pissed off now as I was a year ago."

"They sell, babe. The new ones aren't right for our catalog, and they're not right for our clients. I need more pieces like *Scream* and *Howling Skeleton*. You're making your name. Ride the market trend."

Vivi chose her words carefully, already afraid of making him angry. "But inspiration doesn't depend on market trends. It—"

Slam. Brian's hand slapped down into his desk. "Don't even start," he snarled. "I'm already bored."

She jumped back. An ebony goddess figurine teetered and almost fell on her substantial behind. He stared at her, his gaze menacing. "Don't be an idiot," he said. "You'd better fulfil your contractual obligations to me. Or else."

She was shocked by his ugly tone. "But . . . but I just—"

"You signed that contract, Viv. Don't forget. Your future as an artist depends on it."

She gaped at him. Brian leaned back in his chair and leafed casually through a big glossy catalog of Wilder Gallery artwork.

"What do you mean?" she finally managed to force out.

His smile did not reach his eyes. "We discussed this, remember? Before you signed. You agreed not to play the diva."

"Yes, but I didn't mean that I would be a—"

"I need more pieces like the old series. End of discussion." He slapped the catalog shut. "Another thing. Our date tonight. I can't make it. Something's come up. Since you have the evening free, I suggest you get to work. I have clients asking for your work. I mean to satisfy them."

He got up and stood in front of his desk, hands twitching in the pockets of his tailored suit. He sighed and tilted her face up to his. His cold, hard lips brushed hers. She flinched from his touch. "I know you're upset, but it will have to wait," he said, sounding bored. "I'm busy today."

She'd done as she was told. Trotted to her studio, tried to make pieces that would please him. Vivi cringed at the memory of how hard she'd tried to satisfy his demands. How pointless her efforts had been.

She'd run dry immediately. She'd cranked out a few things, but they were obviously bad, flat. Her output ground to a total halt.

Brian had been furious. He was convinced that she was doing it on purpose, to spite him. That was when sex with him started to go from tense and problematic to outright scary. Brian used sex to punish.

The only thing she'd still been able to work on was the jewelry. It was the one thing that Brian had never tried to control, so she'd gone with it. Thrown herself into it, heart and soul. What else could she do?

She cast a covert sideways glance at Jack, walking silently beside her, trying not to think about how he looked soaking wet. How he tasted. The solidity of his shoulders when she sank her nails into him.

Brian might have derailed her artistic career and given her a closetful of stupid sexual complexes. But he had never driven her out of her mind with breath-stealing, toe-curling lust.

The tractor chugged on until the van came into view. Dwayne and Jack attached the chain, and Vivi got in the van and started the engine.

They pulled and pulled. The van shuddered and strained. Dwayne whooped in triumph when it rolled out of the deep ruts.

Vivi felt like cheering herself when she felt those wheels turning, bumping over the ruts. She got out and strode over to the tractor with a huge smile of relief. "Thanks so much, Dwayne. How much do I owe you?"

"Ah, nah," Dwayne said bashfully. "Just being neighborly."

He pushed away the banknotes she held out, so she folded them back into her wallet, peeking to make sure he had a wedding ring.

"Well, bring your wife over one of these days to pick out a necklace or a pair of earrings," she offered. "I'd love to meet her."

Dwayne agreed to that plan cheerfully, and Vivi and Jack watched the tractor chug up the road and disappear around the bend.

Vivi got into the driver's seat. Jack climbed in. They sat in silence. "So?" she said finally. "Where do we stand? I'm mobile again. Do I need to get lost? I could be out of here in ten minutes. Just say the word."

"Please don't be so defensive," Jack said.

Vivi put the van in gear. It lurched forward, bumping over ruts, and crawled gamely up the hill. "That's hard, under the circumstances."

"I have an understanding with Duncan. You're welcome to stay for as long as you have this security problem," he said. "If you can stand it, that is. I doubt you'll be staying that long anyway."

"And why is that?"

"Your kind never do," he said calmly.

The van crested the hill. Vivi stared out the windshield with hot eyes. "My 'kind'?" she repeated.

"I don't mean that the way you're taking it. But I can see from the kind of person you are that you won't settle in one place for long."

"Ah." The van lurched violently over the deep ruts, making her teeth jar painfully in her head. "Indeed."

"It's a valid lifestyle choice," he went on. "I'm not judging you."

"The hell you're not." They crawled slowly up another steep hill. "I'm going in to Pebble River after lunch," she announced. "I'm going to a furniture store. I'm buying a bed. A table. A bookcase. And I'm going start looking for a place to open my shop."

"Shop?" He turned to her, frowning. "What's this about a shop?"

"I mean to open a shop. Pebble River is a perfect place for the kind of business I have in mind—"

"Hold on, here. Wait a fucking minute. I thought you were in hiding. I thought these bastards were trying to kill you. I thought that was the whole point of being here. Now you're talking about opening a shop? Public records, databases, the Internet? What the fuck are you thinking? You're out of your mind!"

She blew out a long breath. She'd been going back and forth about this issue into the wee hours every night. "How long can I huddle in a hole and shiver?" she exploded. "I can't afford this! I have to support myself somehow, and this is the—"

"Are you doing this to prove something to me?"

"Don't flatter yourself, you self-absorbed jerk!" she yelled at him. "This isn't about you! I'm just going about my business!"

They arrived at the house. Vivi pulled in next to Jack's truck, got out, and slapped the door shut. Her eyes glanced over the painting on the side and winced away. Jack was looking at it. And judging her for it, too.

She'd always been ambivalent about that painting, but Rafael would have been so hurt if she'd painted over his masterpiece. And he'd been so sweet and supportive after the Brian debacle, sharing his booth, showing her the crafts fair ropes. The writhing serpent and muscle-bound warrior on her van was a small price to pay.

Jack was following her up the stairs. She glared over her shoulder. "Excuse me? Where do you think you're going?"

"I just want to see what you've done with the place," he said.

"I haven't done much of anything. It looks about the same," she said. "Please excuse me. I want to make myself lunch."

Jack raised an eyebrow and waited. Vivi sighed, and fitted the key in the lock. "Whatever. Come on in. I imagine you want lunch, too?"

"Lunch would be nice," he said, blandly.

The first thing he did was check the seedlings. She'd been watering them, afraid to kill them by planting them incorrectly, but even more afraid of asking for help. But he just stroked the little plants with his fingertip. "We should set these out today," he said.

"Fine." She got to work making the grilled cheese sandwiches, so she could have an excuse to keep her back to him.

He walked into the living room. She'd been doing inventory, and her current stock was spread across the green velvet drape on the floor: earrings; pendants; brooches; her compartmentalized boxes of beads; her stash of chunks of broken hand-blown glass, coils of silver and gold wire, hooks and clasps; her boxes of fun and colorful collected junk. The walls were decorated with hangings, paintings, drawings.

"Did you do these pictures?" Jack asked.

"No," Vivi said. "I've met lots of artists in the past few years. I collected my favorite pieces. The ones I could afford, anyway. This is the first chance I've ever had to hang them up and look at them properly."

Jack walked slowly around the room. "And your stuff?"

"There's not a lot of my work here," Vivi said, feeling defensive. "Just what's on the floor. My favorite meda are bronze and blown glass, but you can't do that in a camper van. I got sidetracked by my jewelry sideline, but I'm tired of it. I want to get back to sculpture." Jack leaned over the cloth and picked up a fine lacework of antique beads and colored glass. "You sit on the floor to work?"

"I can't wait to buy a table," Vivi said.

He frowned. "I could have found you something." He picked up a green bottle adorned with onyx beads and a filigree of silver foil. "These are beautiful. Unique."

"Thank you." She was uncommonly flustered by the compliment.

"You're tired of making jewelry? That's too bad. You must get tired of things quickly," Jack said.

There he went again, poking his stick between the bars of her cage. Vivi suppressed a flare of savage irritation. "No," she said tightly. "I love designing jewelry. What I'm sick of is mass-producing for the crafts fairs. That's just assembly-line work."

"Ah," he murmured. "I see."

"I have a good feel for what will sell," she went on. "I study the colors and styles in the women's magazines, make pieces to match, and they go like hotcakes. It was fine for a while, but I'm burnt out."

"Remember, you don't have to prove anything to me," he said.

"Then stop jabbing at me!" she flared. "You're pissing me off!"

He put the bottle down. "Sorry," he murmured. "So if you're not a jewelry designer anymore, what exactly are you?"

"I think I'm a sculptor, but ask me again in six months."

"But who knows where you'll be in six months?" He held a pair of malachite earrings up to the light, letting them dangle from his fingers.

Vivi did not dignify that with a reply. She stalked back into the kitchen.

She stuck her head around the door when the sandwiches were sizzling. "Lunch is on. Come get it while the cheese is gooey."

Jack sat opposite her on the kitchen floor. They ate their sandwiches, and the usual tense, charged silence fell upon them after.

Vivi stared at the crumbs on her paper plate. "Would you like a cup of tea?" she asked, with rigid politeness.

"No, thanks," he said.

"Then excuse me while I make one for myself." She put the kettle on and stuffed napkins and paper plates into the garbage.

"You've been talking to Margaret?" he asked.

"That's right. She's got some good ideas for possible locations for me."

"For your shop," he said. "To sell your own designs?"

"Among other things. I know lots of excellent artisans, after all those years on the circuit. And there's money around here, to support a business like mine. A gallery of wearable, usable art."

"And aside from the danger issue, you think that's a good idea?"

"Why wouldn't it be?" Vivi stuck out her chin.

"It's a big layout of money," he said. "A big risk."

"Yeah? So?"

"I hope you're not being unrealistic. To say nothing of stupid."

She decided to let the "stupid" comment slide. "Why? Lots of people start businesses. Sure, it's risky. Life is risky. Why do you think it's unrealistic for me?"

She had to ask, even though she was afraid of the answer.

He was silent for a moment. "I think you'll regret it," he said. "That kind of investment requires a huge time commitment. And a serious attention span."

Vivi counted to ten. "I'm not going to play this game anymore."

"Any woman who sleeps in a sleeping bag, eats off paper plates on the floor, and cooks with aluminum campware doesn't impress me with her readiness to put down roots."

Vivi grabbed up the last plate and stuffed it into the garbage. "I've been stranded here for five days with no vehicle," she snapped.

The teakettle began to hiss. Vivi turned it off. She reached in the cupboard for a mug and pulled out a plastic travel mug with a sip lid and adhesive plastic on the bottom for sticking to the dashboard of a car. She stared at it, jaw clenched. Threw in the tea bag, poured the water. Everything she looked at felt like a slap, a reproach.

"Think what you like," she said. She grabbed the broom and dustpan and began to sweep up crumbs. "It makes absolutely no difference to me. I'm just going to keep doing my thing."

"Yes, I'm sure your intentions are good."

The detached tone of his voice maddened her. "I can make my business work. I know I can." She grabbed a dishcloth from the sink. "Whatever."

She blocked the bad language that wanted to burst out. Lucia had taught her that much. She shook the swept-up crumbs into the garbage and rinsed off her hands at the sink. His sudden presence behind her made her gasp.

"I can't seem to stop making you angry," he said. "I'm sorry."

"You're making me crazy." She closed her eyes. "You say, don't go, stay safe. Then you insult me and try to drive me away. Then you flirt with me, mess with me, seduce me. What am I supposed to think?"

"I'm sorr—"

"Stop! Shut up." She twisted around. "Not one more word. You'll just piss me off worse."

He drew in a breath, opened his mouth. She put her finger on it, but when she started to lift her hand away, he trapped it there, pressing it against his hot, soft lips. His breath tickled her palm.

She snatched her hand away and turned her back again. "Don't. You're making it worse."

The proximity of his body transformed into the pressure of the lightest touch against her back. His lips pressed against her nape. Exquisitely soft. A point of warmth, of silent tenderness that spread and grew. Like the sunrise, slowly turning snowy mountains pink.

This was as bad an idea now as it had ever been, she told herself.

But she felt so pink and soft inside. So hungry for the feelings he triggered. For what happened to her body when he touched her.

Like a junkie. Craving the poison that was destroying her. She'd watched that drama play out when she was a kid. She'd never touched drugs, but look at her now. Doomed to repeat that nightmarish trap in a different form. People got sucked into their ancient bullshit all the time, in spite of their convictions, their best intentions. They were imprinted. There was no escape.

And she couldn't stop. She could not push his hands away.

He stroked her breast, brushing the tight nipple that poked

through her tank top against his palm. He slid his other hand down her spine, his fingers tracing every bump of her backbone until it hit warm skin under the hem of the top—into the waistband of her gauze skirt.

It was hanging a bit loose these days. Ever since the Fiend had started circling around, stealing her appetite and shrinking her ass. He slowly, tenderly petted her ass cheeks.

"Why?" she whispered. "Why torture me like this, if you think so little of me? Why not just kick me out? It would be kinder."

"I don't think little of you. On the contrary." He kissed her bare shoulder, lips moving in a caress that left shimmering warmth in its slow wake. "I think you're amazing. Talented, beautiful, fascinating. So amazing, I can't do anything except speak the truth to you. Even when you don't want to hear it. That's respect, Viv. That's the real thing."

"Your truth," she said.

He shrugged. "Only one I've got."

"But it's not the only one there is," she informed him.

Silence was his response to that. Slowly, he lifted his lips from her shoulder. "I know you're scared to leave because of what's happening in your life. But I also know that once that situation resolves—"

"If it ever resolves," she broke in, her voice bitter.

"Once it is resolved, you'll pack up your van and drive away. As soon as it really sinks in."

She twisted around to stare at him. "What sinks in?"

"What it means to look at the same damn place, day in and day out. Or the same person." His voice was quiet but utterly convinced. His hand stopped, barely touching the quivering, hot fulcrum of excitement between her legs.

"And I can't convince you any different?" she whispered.

He paused for a moment, motionless, and said, "No."

Her laugh felt more like a sob. "But you still want to fuck me."

"I still want to be your lover," he corrected. "And I want it respectfully." He pressed his hot face against her shoulder, his hands delving deeper, making her squirm. "I ask it . . . respectfully."

She clamped her thighs around his hand. "You call that respect?"

"I love to make you feel good," he offered. "That's not dis-respect."

She could hardly breathe. She tried to hold his hand motionless with her thighs, but he kept caressing her, and it felt . . . so . . . *good.*

"I don't want to get hurt," she blurted.

"I don't see any way to avoid that." His voice was muffled against her hair. "It already hurts. It'll hurt no matter what we do."

"So we might as well make the best of it?"

He pulled her against him, tightly. "I will make it the best."

"One question. What happens if I just don't leave? Is there a statute of limitations on this notion that I'll run? If I'm still here in five years, ten years, what then? Would you be glad? Disappointed? What?"

He declined to reply, but she could see his answer in his eyes. That door in his mind was closed, locked, barred. Nailed shut.

He would never give himself up to her completely.

And still, she wanted what he offered. No matter what was held back. She wanted every last fragment. Every tiny crumb she could get.

"Yes," she said. "I want you."

Chapter
6

Jack's eyes flashed, and his fingers tightened on Vivi's ass cheeks. She waited until she got impatient. "So? Jack? Did you hear me?"

"Yes, I heard you."

"So? What now?" She clamped down on the giggles before they could turn to tears. "Do we just, ah . . . do it?"

His grin flashed, but his face was wary. "Sounds good to me."

She groped for a tissue in her skirt pocket, and blew her nose. "I'm so embarrassed. It's been so long. I don't even know where to start."

"I do," he said baldly.

She covered her face with her hands. "So? What's the plan?"

He sank promptly to his knees in front of her and pressed his face against her mound through the thin fabric of her gauze skirt.

"Oh, God," she said weakly. "That, again? You're obsessed!"

He lifted up the yards of fabric, seeking his prize. "God, yes. Your pussy is so pink and salty sweet. I want to make it puffy and slick. I want to lick you like candy, till you melt into hot woman juice."

She could barely speak. He shoved the wad of skirt into her hands and murmured with approval at the skimpy white lace thong. "On my knees," he continued, flashing her a mischievous grin. "Have pity on a desperate supplicant."

"Oh, stop it." She shook with a new attack of giggles.

He pulled aside the gusset of her panties and tucked it to the side. Her legs buckled when he pressed his mouth to her naked flesh.

"I can't handle it," she whispered. She had no experience with oral sex. Brian had been uninterested in it. In performing it, at least. He'd been happy to receive it. Had considered it his God-given right, in fact.

The fierce glow in Jack's eyes transfixed her. "You're small," he said. "Relax. I'm going to take my sweet time with you."

Her legs trembled. Jack looked around for a chair, saw none, and hoisted her up onto the kitchen counter. He tugged the tiny wisp of stretch-lace thong off her legs, tossed it away. She balanced there, clutching his head and trembling, skirt wadded against her chest. So aroused, the feeling bordered on terror.

"I love your taste," he murmured. "I could lick you for hours."

"I wouldn't survive it," she quavered, and he laughed, pleased.

He knew instinctively just how to touch her, how deep, how hard, how soft. Voluptuous thrusts of his tongue, lapping up and down, plunging deep. His long fingers opening, stroking, while he suckled, insisted, pushing her to that screaming point of no return . . . and *oh*.

Pleasure flooded through her, deeper and wider and sweeter every time. She floated back, and found herself draped over him. He'd caught her, held her as she came.

He lifted her up so that she straddled him, and braced her against the wall, reaching down to fumble with his belt—

And her shimmering pink warmth flash-froze. Her heart skipped, bumped. Panic flashed through her. Faintness, suffocation. It was happening again.

The sickening black fog rising. Those last awful times, with Brian.

Brian had liked that position, especially when he was snorting coke. On his feet, pinning her to the wall. Or else holding her down, immobilized. His face, a taut, stiff mask of lust. Eyes fixed, staring. A million miles away. Not listening when she told him that it hurt. Not caring.

She hadn't been able to be intimate with a man since. She'd tried a few times, but nothing but nothing wrecked the mood faster than a stress flashback. Finally she'd let it go. Learned to do without intimacy.

But goddammit, she wasn't going to do without this.

She grabbed his shoulders. "Just a minute," she said, gasping for breath. "Just . . . let me get myself together. Don't go away."

She could hear him talking, from far away. His tone was urgent, anxious, but she couldn't make out the words over the frantic, deafening trip of her heart.

Breathe, silly. It's now, not then. It's Jack, not Brian. Get a grip.

". . . okay? Jesus, Viv! What did I do?"

"It wasn't you," she forced out, through shaking lips. "I'm sorry."

"What the fuck? What happened to you?" he demanded.

"It's just . . . it was that position," she said. "It just triggered some bad memories, that's all. No big deal. I'm okay now. Really."

"What do you mean, that's all?" His face was pale with alarm.

Crap. So close to getting through this stone wall in her head, and she had to have a meltdown right when she got to the good part. So freaking typical.

". . . memories? Can you talk about it?"

The look on his face told her that he wasn't going to let this slide. She sighed, and gave in to the inevitable. "It was a bad boyfriend I had once, years ago," she explained. "The relationship went sour. So did the sex. It took a while for me to pry myself out of the situation, and in the meantime, well. It left me hung up. He was heavy into control."

She was afraid to look at Jack's face. Pity would make her cringe.

But when she finally looked, it wasn't pity she saw. It was a blaze of fury that made her heart do a weird galloping skip of primitive fear.

"Tell me his name, and where he lives," Jack said. "I'll rip that filthy piece of shit to pieces and grind him into the fucking dirt for you."

She blinked at him, stupidly. "Ah, well. Um, thank you," she said, flustered. "That's a very kind offer, but I'm okay with it now."

"You didn't look okay two minutes ago," he said grimly.

"I'm sorry I—"

"Stop apologizing!"

The harshness of his voice startled her. He looked away, shaking his head. "Fuck," he muttered. "Sorry. I didn't mean to yell at you."

"We can't seem to stop apologizing to each other." She kept her nails dug into the muscle of his shoulder, as if afraid he would run away, but he didn't. Not at all. His hands crept up, crossing his chest, to cover hers. Enveloping hers. Flooding her body with reassurance.

"Do you want to, uh, just leave it for now?" he suggested.

"No!" she yelled. "I want this! I will not let him fuck this up for me, too! He has taken enough from me already, goddammit!"

Jack started to grin. "You don't know how happy I am to hear you say that. Just tell me what I need to do. Or, uh, not do."

"It's not that complicated. Just do what you do. You're fabulous. Just not . . . shoved up against the wall. And don't pin down my hands. Or my throat. And we'll be fine. I think."

That tightly leashed fury flashed again in his bright wolf eyes. "That sick, filthy fuckhead," he said.

"Yeah, maybe, but now he leaves the scene," Vivi said sternly. "No more airtime for the sick, filthy fuckhead. It's just us now. Just Jack and Vivi, *capisci*? Because I don't want any more company."

He nodded. The silence grew so long, they both started to laugh.

"I feel really shy, now," Jack admitted. "I think you're going to have to choreograph this one. I'll just follow your lead."

"But I don't know where I'm going," she protested. "That is to say, I have a rough idea, but I might drive us into the swamp, you know?"

"I'll give you a tip. Take my hand and lead me into the bedroom."

She lifted her hands from his shoulders and grabbed his hand, pulling him into the adjoining room. It was practically empty but for the futon with her sleeping bag and her suitcase tucked in the corner.

The walls were alive with shifting green shadows from sunlight sifting through oak and maple leaves. She longed for the cover of dusk, or night, but no. It was all going to be so visible. So terribly deliberate.

She gave him a questioning look. "Next tip?"

"Take off your clothes," he said.

She giggled nervously as she began, but she put her brave and brazen all into it. Kicking off her sandals. Peeling off her top. She stretched and preened as she pulled pins out of her hair and tossed them to the floor. The tinkle as they fell was loud in the green, flickering silence.

He watched her uncoil the long, twisted tail of red hair, shake it down into loose waves over her shoulder, her breasts. She began to circle him, and he followed her with his eyes. The movement felt ancient. A ceremony, a spiral dance, an invitation. Entwining their male and female energies into pure magic.

"The skirt," he reminded her. "Lose the skirt."

She loosened the drawstring and let the skirt drop. Naked, but for Lucia's little necklace with the emerald V that she never took off.

She scooped her hair up over her head, arching her back, tossing her hair. Turning, in front of the raw hunger in his beautiful silver eyes. Not a nervous thought for her itty-bitty boobs, or her not-so-little ass, or her in-your-face tattoos. Flaunting herself. Sure that she would please him.

"Now my clothes," he told her, kicking off his sandals.

Wow. Even his feet were sexy, and she'd never given a thought to feet before, as long as they smelled okay. His were beautiful; long and brown, with graceful toes, square nails, elegant bones.

She attacked his clothes. A goofy grin wasn't the right heavy-eyed, sensual temptress expression she'd wanted to assume for the occassion, but she was having too much fun to pretend to act serious.

She peeled his T-shirt off inch by inch, taking the opportunity to explore his torso with her fingertips. Feeling the grain of his hair, those lean, cut muscles. Every detail sumptuously lickable.

She flung the shirt away and attacked his belt, but as she started to shove his jeans down, he stilled her hand, dug into his pocket, and fished out a string of condoms. A long string. He flung them onto the futon.

Ah. Well and good that he was prepared, but the calculated gesture struck her as a provocation. He shoved his jeans and briefs down and stepped out of them, naked, kicking them away.

He was perfect. His huge cock thrust out, thick and high, bobbing with its own swollen weight. "Touch me," he ordered.

Her hands rejoiced as they closed around that velvety supple skin, vital pulsing heat, steely hardness. More than filling her hand.

She loved his gasps as she stroked, pulled him. It made her feel like a goddess for real, like she was handling storm clouds, thunderbolts. Fearlessly playing with devastating power as if it were her own personal toy.

"I know this thing of me leading started out as a precaution to keep me from freaking out on you," she commented, breathlessly. "But it's changed. It's turned into a kinky power game."

"Maybe," he admitted. "But if a woman as proud and strong as you plays along with my kinky power game without telling me to fuck off, it means she really wants me, right?"

She swirled her hands around his cockhead, making him gasp. "It turns you on," she challenged. "Telling me what to do. Admit it."

He grinned, busted. "Everything about you turns me on."

"You think you're so smart, huh?" she teased him.

He gave her a quick, rueful smile. "Not at the moment."

"I know your tricks," she said breathlessly. "You're showing how completely you're in control of the situation, right?"

His eyes went thoughtful. "No," he corrected. "I'm showing you how completely I'm in control of myself. I think you need to be reminded." He gathered up a hank of her hair, bent low and kissed it, with that lovely, secret smile glowing in his eyes.

He was so sweet, it made tears well up in her eyes, for no reason that she could understand. "I don't know how you do it," she said, her voice wondering. "You have a split personality, Jack. Either you say the exact wrong thing that makes me want to smack you, or you say the exact right thing."

"Yeah?" he prompted. "Which makes you want to . . . ?"

"Um, grab you," she said primly.

His grin flashed. "Go for it. I love how you grab me."

She took him at his word, caressing him with slow, sensual pulls. His hands clenched, flexed, trembled. "So I never say anything simple and neutral, like please pass the peas?"

"We haven't gotten that far in our relationship," she told him. *And we never will. According to you.*

She shoved the bleak thought away. She would not let anything screw this up. Not her fears, not Brian fallout. Not even the plain truth.

To hell with the plain truth. Who needed it. Live the fantasy.

She decided it was time to change the vibe, distract them both. She knelt down and unzipped her bright purple down sleeping bag with the lavender nylon lining, spread it out over the futon mattress.

She curled up, tits stuck out, hair wild and frowsy, and looked up seductively through her eyelashes at him. "So?"

He sank down, his face still cautious. "Do you need to be on top?"

She thought about it for a moment. "I'm shaking too hard," she confessed. "I don't think I'd even be able to stay upright. I'm melting."

He looked worried. "But I'm big. I wouldn't want you to—"

"Uh-uh," she said, shaking her finger at him. "Don't worry. I won't flip out on you. I know where I am, and whom I'm with."

He smiled, cautiously relieved. "You're sure?"

"Oh, God, yes," she assured him. "And I love it that you're big. Bring it on." She swirled her hand over his cockhead.

His face and neck went rigid. "Oh, God," he muttered. "You're laying all the responsibility on me, huh?"

"You can take it," she informed him cheerfully. "I have faith."

He put his hand on her belly, stroking her with a light hand. As if she were some delicate, exotic creature that he didn't want to frighten.

She stared at his hand, blinking at another rush of tears. Moved by how worried he was. How tender and gentle. Why, that big, yummy, succulent sweetheart. And he needed to get on with it. Like, *now.*

She grabbed his hand that petted her and gave it a yank. "Get down here," she ordered him. "I want to feel you. On top. All over me."

He allowed himself to be dragged down on top of her. Vivi opened her legs and tried to jerk him closer, but he pulled away.

"Hold on," He groped for the condoms. "Let me deal with practical details before I lose my mind."

He fumbled the latex on one-handed, and finally, she managed to pull him down on top of her. She twined her arms and legs around him and squeezed. The sweet shock of his hot body against hers opened the leaky tear faucet again, and off she went.

Jack looked into her wet eyes, alarmed. "Viv? Are you okay?"

"Fine, great, fabulous," she assured him. "You just feel wonderful. It makes me weepy, but don't worry about it. It's all good."

He stared into her face, speechless, his eyes soft, and kissed the tears away from her cheekbones her temples. Oh, Lord. He felt so good. Her hands were going crazy with so much to choose from: his thick shoulders; his powerful back; his taut, muscular ass; that dark, shaggy mane of silky hair tickling her neck. The urgent prod of his cock against her thigh. He wasn't hurrying her, but she could feel it, throbbing there, hopeful and eager, while he kissed her neck, her breasts. Caressing her between her legs, spreading her lube all around to ease his way. The wild fluttering anticipation kept rising. This was really happening. Now.

He lifted his head, unexpectedly and gave her his now familiar master-and-commander stare. "Tell me what you want me to do."

She tried not to giggle. It was too frivolous. "Isn't it obvious?"

"I want to hear the words."

She reached down and gripped his cock, squeezing it through the thin barrier of latex. "This is another kinky power game, right?"

"Yes," he said baldly.

She writhed beneath his weight, arching until she could press the thick bulb of his penis against her own slick opening, and with some breathless wiggling, forced him inside, until her inner lips clasped him. He felt huge. "Please," she whispered. "Put your cock into me."

He stared into her eyes, shifted his weight, pressed deeper.

She gasped, bit her lip. "Oh, boy. You really are enormous."

"Relax," he murmured, his voice low, strangled. "I'll go slow."

He did. She'd braced herself for pain, but he barely moved, just hovered over her, rocking gently, kissing her with all his incredible skill, melting her. Caressing her clit with his thumb.

His kisses were a language some deep part of her understood. Something deep inside him, pleading and coaxing at something inside her. Begging her to soften, bend, and melt for him. Demanding.

He made her come again, deep and hard and wrenching, and

when she opened her eyes and remembered who she was, his cock was seated deep inside her. Huge and throbbing. She could barely move.

Even then, he was in no hurry. He rolled her onto her side, draping her leg over his, and they kissed, embraced, hips pulsing together. Slowly, lazily rocking. Time stretched, warped, and created a magic universe around them. The room with its flickering leaf shadow was a verdant bower. Colors unnaturally strong. The sleeping bag was the splayed petals of some voluptuous, sexual flower, and the two of them writhed and undulated inside its glowing, silky depths. Lost.

At some point, she realized with some surprise that she was not uncomfortable at all anymore. Her body had re-formed itself around him. He was easing in and out of her, in slow, maddening thrusts, with a skillful swivel and slide that stroked every wonderful throbbing hot spot inside her. She jerked and shuddered with each plunge.

He was so attentive, so sensitive. Feeling his way. His passionate attention unlocked every closed, fearful place inside her and sparked an endless string of delicious explosions. They were fused, a single moving, surging glow. She could not stop the shimmer of tears in her eyes, slipping out, tickling her face. He kept tirelessly kissing them away.

It took her a lazily long and delicious forever to convince him to let himself come, too. To persuade him that he would not hurt her or scare her if he picked up the pace. She finally clawed him into action, inciting, demanding. Sinking her nails into his butt, pulling him deeper.

He finally gathered her up tightly against him, and gave it to her harder than she would ever have dreamed she would want it, but she did want it. She was transformed. No walls inside her to painfully slam against. He'd gotten past her walls. She was all softness, eagerness.

He could do as he wanted with her. She loved it all, his fierceness, his strength, his vigor, his size, jarring her, ramming into her, energy gathering, and his hoarse shout, that hot blaze of energy, pumping . . .

She loved . . . *him.*

The terrifying thought reverberated through her as the blast wave of their mutual climax wiped them out. When she opened her eyes, they lay side by side, limp and damp and spent. Arms and legs entwined.

He gazed into her face, touched her cheek with the tip of his finger. "I can't believe how soft your skin is," he said quietly.

She grabbed his hand, and kissed it impulsively, her realization shining inside her. Part pleasure, part a keen, stabbing pain.

It wanted so badly to be shared. But she couldn't.

She snuggled up to him, hiding her face against his chest, and they stayed that way until the rays of the afternoon sun began to lengthen and turn warm gold. Finally, he brushed her hair off her face.

"Want to go and plant that *Eranthis hyemalis* with me?" he asked.

She was taken aback. "Right now?"

"I don't know how much of a chance they have to root now, but we could give it a shot," he said. "What the hell, right? I'd hate to see them just wither away without even giving it a try. Doesn't seem right."

She thought about that for a moment. What an ironic choice of words. And he had no clue. She could tell from his face. He was just talking about flowers. His mind was hardwired that way. Completely straightforward. Calling a flower a flower.

She didn't know how much of a chance the two of them had to root. Not much, maybe. But she was going to give it a shot, by God.

She sat up. "Yes," she said, reaching for her skirt. "Let's go plant those little guys right this very minute. They deserve a shot."

This thing of theirs was not going to wither away for lack of trying. It was just too damn beautiful and rare for such a sad and stupid end.

Chapter
7

Jack patted the earth down after setting out the last seedling and rose to his feet. "There you go," he said. "Now we just watch, and hope."

Vivi's smile made him feel so strange and good. Charged with energy that crackled and glowed like a bonfire.

"Would you show me your other flowers?" she asked, hesitantly. "Margaret told me they were beautiful."

"Sure." He brushed earth off his hands, looked at them. He wanted to hold her hand, but it didn't seem right, with all that dirt.

She resolved his dilemma by grabbing his hand herself.

They set out toward the river, through a clearing on the hillside that glowed with wildflowers lit from the side by the setting sun so that they glowed, dancing and flickering like flames. She hardly seemed real, wafting next to him, in that floating skirt. Something from a dream. So pretty, she hurt his eyes, bright hair streaming, cheeks so pink, lips so red. Eyes that glowing gray. Already, he felt the hot tingle of a brand-new boner coming on.

They hadn't bothered to shower, just pulled on the minimum of clothing. Vivi seemed urgent about planting, as if something bad would happen if they lost any time. He'd seen no reason not to indulge her.

He kept looking at her, ogling, marveling. It was official. His brain had melted. He'd never even dreamed of sex like that.

After they'd gotten past the scary stuff, of course. His free hand clenched at the thought of her evil ex. How a man could hurt any woman was beyond him, let alone one like Vivi. So beautiful and scrappy and strong. She'd probably scared the shit out of the bastard. Given him a huge inferiority complex so that the dickhead felt compelled to use the one pathetic advantage he had—his greater size. Classic. Not that it was an excuse. He would pay. Jack intended to see to the matter personally.

Vivi stared up at the trees, the rays of sunlight slanting through them. Jack gazed at the perfect curve of her arched neck, the angle of her jaw. Then they stepped out of the pine thicket, into another world.

The floor of the little valley was covered with spires, buds, blossoms of wildly contrasting colors. Edna yelped and readied herself to plunge into a bank of *Kniphofia*. Vivi caught her collar and held her fast. "No, girl. You stay right here. Sit!"

A branch snapped in the forest, and Edna twisted out of Vivi's grasp and bounded off into the woods to investigate.

"Come out into the field," he offered. "I'll show you around."

He led her out into the field, between the beds, and pointed. "These are *Kniphofia*, otherwise known as red hot pokers. The *Lilium auratum* on the other side are almost ready. Down there are Oriental poppies, and *Anthoxanthum odoratum*, which is a type of ornamental grass. There's some *Centaurea cyanus* and *Stachys byzantina* on that rise over there. Bachelor's buttons and lamb's ears, in common English. And see those white and blue ones? *Campanula aurita*. Bellflowers. And columbine, at the far end."

She looked enchanted. "Who taught you to grow flowers?"

He hesitated. "My uncle Freddy," he admitted. "I lived with him for a while. Until I was fourteen. He was heavy into organic gardening."

"He grew flowers, too?"

"You could say that," he answered.

She lifted an eyebrow. "What do you mean? He did or he didn't."

"Uncle Freddy specialized in cannabis. Various strains of specialty marijuana. Very profitable for him, for a while. It was a different era."

"Oh," Vivi said. She looked startled, but not unduly so.

"The principles are the same," he said. "He loved plants. He knew how to give them what they needed."

"Oh," she said again.

"I prefer flowers," he went on, blandly. "More color. Less stress."

"Is your uncle still . . . um, never mind."

"It's okay. I doubt if he's still in business. It's more dangerous these days. And he had to leave the country one night twenty-some years ago. Haven't seen him since. Don't even know if he's still alive. He'd be pushing seventy by now." He kept his gaze averted and stroked a *Campanula aurita* bud. They were gearing up to bloom at any minute.

"That was when you were fourteen, you say?"

"I'm thirty-seven now. That would make it twenty-three years ago."

"Were you there when he ran away? Was it a drug bust?"

His discomfort surged up, turning into irritation. "Yeah."

"How awful," she said. "What happened to you?"

He walked into the fluttering poppies. "Nothing happened to me."

"Did he just vanish?" she persisted, following him.

"I'm fine now," he said tightly. "Let's leave it."

"Excuse me," she said. "It's none of my business."

Fuck. He felt like shit, but he did not want to talk about it. He was a dick-for-brains for bringing it up. Ruining their excellent mood.

A distressed yelping came from the trees. Vivi picked her way hastily through the flower beds toward the pine thicket. He caught up with her as she plunged into the trees. Her dog was whining and pawing at her muzzle.

Vivi grabbed her collar and knelt down, holding the trembling dog still. "Easy, girl," she soothed. "Oh, God."

Porcupine quills stuck out of Edna's nose and jaw, like long, crazy whiskers. Jack crouched down and took the dog's shivering head in his hands, examining it. "Only twelve," he said. "I've seen worse."

Vivi bit her lip, searching through Edna's coat for more quills.

"Let's go to the house," he suggested. "I've got scissors. Pliers."

"I don't want to bother you with this," she murmured, not meeting his eyes. "I've got pliers in my jewelry toolbox. I'll deal with it."

He gave her a look. "Get real."

Edna slunk between them, tail down, through the woods. Their camaraderie, that perfect elusive glow of joy, gone. Such a fucking mystery. He wished he knew how to hang on to it.

When they got back to the house, he led her and her dog into his front room, and got the scissors and the pliers out. He knelt down beside them on the floor. "Hold her," he said.

Vivi held her dog firmly as he snipped off the ends of the quills. Edna made high-pitched whining noises in the back of her throat.

"Why are you doing that?" she asked.

"I've been told that if you trim the end of the quills, the vacuum inside collapses and the barbs should let go more easily," he explained. "Theoretically."

Vivi blinked, and swallowed, hard. "Oh," she whispered.

They clenched their teeth and powered through the unpleasant job. It didn't take all that long to pull out the quills, but it felt like forever. Vivi winced with each shrill yelp and jerk, although her low voice never stopped murmuring low encouragement.

Jack tried to be brisk, but by the time he was done, Jesus. He sagged back against the side of his sofa, limp as a wet rag. Inflicting pain on an innocent animal was fucking horrible, whether it was for the animal's own good or not. Thank God he worked with plants.

Edna curled up in Vivi's lap, still trembling. Vivi was bent over her, her face hidden against the dog's silky golden shoulder.

Leaving him all alone, with memories that were coming back, weirdly sharp and clear. Taking over his whole goddamn mind.

That June night when a wild-eyed Uncle Freddy had slapped him on the shoulder. "Sorry, kid. I've got to run. They got Pete, and Pete's such an airhead, he'll give me up for sure. I gotta leave the country."

Jack's stomach heaved. "Where are you going?"

"I'm not going to tell you where. It's safer that way. Here." He thrust a handful of limp, grimy bills into Jack's nerveless hand. "Take this. I wish it was more, but it's all I can spare."

"Can't I come with you?"

"I wish you could, Jackie, but you don't have a passport. Shit, I don't even think you have a birth certificate. I'll be an outlaw, see? I can't have a kid. Keep your head low and your mouth shut, okay?"

"Sure," he said bitterly, pocketing the money.

"We shoulda drilled for this, but it was going so well. I got sloppy." Freddy gripped Jack's skinny shoulders in his big, work-stained hands. "Lemme give you some advice. Don't mix it up with the police, the social workers. Hit the road, go out and seek your fortune. You can do better for yourself outside the system."

"Like you did?" Jack muttered.

"Hey, don't hold this against me. Come on, chin up. You're, what, sixteen? Seventeen? You'll be fine. You'll land on your feet."

"Fourteen," Jack corrected, in a toneless voice.

"Fourteen? Jeez, kid. I thought you were older." Freddy tugged on his beard, looking annoyed that Jack was not older. "Tavia's number is on the fridge. And your mom—where is your mom, anyway?"

"The ashram. In India," Jack reminded him.

"Oh, yeah. The ashram. Damn. I guess Tavia is your best bet, kid. Oh, hey. You could always call Mrs. Margaret Moffat. Your mom and Tavia and I stayed with her one summer when we were kids, in Silverfish. Dad was working the carnival, and Mom had to go into the TB hospital, so she took us in for a couple of months. Nice lady. Baked great cookies. Call her, if you get in a tight spot. But try Tavia first."

Jack stared at his feet, mouth trembling. Uncle Freddy tousled his hair. "Sorry, Jackie. But you know how it is."

"Yeah," Jack said. He knew how it was. Better than anyone.

And after a flurry of packing and a rough, sweaty hug, Jack stood in the driveway and watched Freddy's taillights disappear into the dark.

He tried calling Aunt Tavia in L.A. A guy answered, and said she hadn't lived there in four months, and no, he didn't know where she was. He'd heard somebody say she'd gone to Baja. But it might have been Boulder. Or Bali. Then the guy told Jack that he seemed stressed, and should practice "letting go." "Hanging on" caused all the suffering in life. In fact, if Jack would tell him the date and hour of his birth, he would be happy to provide Jack, for a small fee, with a mantra calibrated to attain the serenity of nonattachment, and also—

Jack hung up on him. He took the tattered envelope off the fridge, and dialed the long string of numbers written on it for the ashram.

The guy who answered spoke only Hindi, and maybe German. Jack struggled with that for a while, and then hung up on that guy, too.

He stared dully at the phone. Finally, he picked up the receiver, dialed information for Silverfish, and asked for Margaret Moffat.

"I have an M. Moffat in Silverfish. Do you want the number?"

"Sure." He wrote it down, folded it, stuck it in his jeans.

He had no idea what to do next. He wandered around the empty house. Night deepened. The quiet terrified him. He wondered when the police would come. What would happen to him if they found him there?

At dawn, he filled his knapsack with as much stuff as he could carry, tied a rolled blanket onto the top, and headed out into the woods.

". . . okay?" He jolted out of his memories. Vivi's face was close to his, her gray eyes wide with worry. She patted his shoulder.

She tried again, louder. "Are you okay, Jack?"

He focused on the faint pattern of freckles on her perfect, narrow little nose. Like a constellation of stars. "Uh, yeah," he said dully. "Sorry. I was someplace else for a while."

She touched his cheek with her knuckles, a shy, tender stroke. "Noplace good. You had that look on your face."

He shook himself to alertness, embarrassed. "What look?"

"Sad," she said simply. "Can I make you some tea?"

"Coffee," he said, rousing himself. "Tea doesn't do it for me. Sit down. Stay with your dog. I'll make it."

"No, I'll do it." She pushed him back down. "The least I can do. Thanks for helping. It would have been that much more awful alone."

"It's nothing," he muttered.

"Not to me and Edna it's not." Her smile was so warm and bright.

He wanted to curl himself up around it. He followed her into the kitchen, just to stay close to her. Taking every sneaky opportunity to touch her, brush against her, sniff her scent as they put the coffee on together.

When it was done and poured, they sat across the table from each other. Jack reached out and grabbed her hand. They'd hit another smooth patch, and he was going to ride it for as long as he could. "I'm sorry for what I said in the—"

"Don't," Vivi broke in. "You apologized the last time you insulted me, and the time before that. Every time, I let down my guard and let you do it again. Let's establish a rule. No insults. No apologies. Okay?"

"You misunderstood. I never insulted you," he said.

"No? Me, the itinerant sexpot neo-hippie?"

He narrowly avoided spluttering his coffee. "That doesn't count," he protested. "You took me by surprise. In a wet T-shirt, no less."

"Oh?" She gazed at him over the rim of her mug, eyes sparkling.

"Give me a fucking break! There you were, soaking wet in the forest, nipples poking through your shirt, looking like something out of a *Penthouse* centerfold—"

"It's not my fault it was raining! I looked like a freaking mudslide!"

"Yeah, and it's not my fault all the blood in my body got instantly rerouted to my dick! You expect me to be rational when a gorgeous woman tricked out like that waves a tire iron at me?"

Her eyebrows went up. "Did the tire iron turn you on, Jack?"

"I'll tell you what turns me on. A proud, beautiful, self-reliant woman who takes no shit off of anybody. That turns me on."

Her eyes fell, but she was smiling. "I never insulted you," he went on. "I made a rational assessment of the situation based on the information I gathered. You read it as an insult, but I was not judging you."

"Wrong," Vivi said. "Your assessment is faulty."

"I don't think so," he said. "I've had lots of practice."

"Whoever you've been practicing on isn't me. But let's not talk about it, or we'll just crash and burn all over again."

She tried to tug her hand back, but he hung on to it. "That wasn't what I was apologizing for," he confessed. "I meant when we were out in the field. You asked about my uncle. I got all uptight. Closed you off." He blew out a careful, measured sigh, trying to relax his tense belly.

Her eyes softened. She set down her coffee and reached across the table. "There's a reason I was asking those questions about the bust."

"Yeah?" he asked warily. "What?"

"I wondered if it was something we had in common," she said. "I was in the middle in a big drug bust once, too. When I was a kid."

He stared at her, mouth stupidly open. "Huh? You?"

"Me," she said. "It sucked. As you are highly qualified to agree."

"But aren't you . . . didn't you . . ." He racked his brains for the details Duncan had given him about her background. Italian nobility? Priceless art? Drug busts? What the fuck? This did not compute.

"My two sisters and I were all adopted," she said, answering his silent confusion. "Lucia took us in as foster kids. I went to her when I was eleven. I got lucky. Nancy and Nell had to plow through years of bad ones before they found Lucia. I hit pay dirt right off, on my first placement. Lucia was amazing. And I got two kick-ass, ready-made sisters in the bargain. They were the best."

"And before?" he prompted.

Her face clouded. "Ah. Before. Well, my mom was a junkie. And the men she took up with were all dealers."

"Jesus," he muttered.

"I got used as a sentry," she said. "Deliveries, sometimes, too."

"No fucking shit!" He was aghast. "How old were you?"

She shrugged. "Eight, nine. Red pigtails, freckles, ruffles. Who would suspect what was in my Winnie the Pooh knapsack? I liked it, at the time. It made me feel important, grown up. Useful."

"Used," he corrected, harshly. "Anything could have happened to you! A little kid, for drug deliveries? That's fucking insane!"

She made a dismissive gesture. "Duh. But anyway, the shit came down. There was a shoot-out. My mom's boyfriend, Randy, got killed in the bust. And my mom went to prison."

He winced. "Tell me you weren't there when it happened."

"I wasn't," she assured him. "I was at school. And I didn't cry for Randy. He was a real zero. I have him to thank for this." She held up her wrist, with its barbed-wire tattoo. "This was his idea of a joke."

He stared at the fuzzy, faded tattoo, anger simmering inside him. "All I can say is, the list of people whom I want to dismember and grind into the dirt on your behalf is growing," he said.

"Thank you, but it's ancient history. So, how did the bust shake out for you? Did you end up with Child Protective Services, too?"

He shook his head. "No. I just took off."

Her eyes widened. "Alone? At fourteen? How did you live?"

He hesitated for a moment before replying. "Barely," he said. "So what about your mom? Is she out of prison?"

Vivi shook her head. "No," she said. "She OD'd in prison. About eight months after she went inside."

He flinched, sucker punched. That was what he got for trying to distract her from his own story. "I'm sorry," he said, helplessly.

She gazed intently into her coffee mug. "It was a long time ago," she said. "And I was as lucky with my second family as I was unlucky with my first. So I'm okay. You can relax, Jack."

They listened to the wind in the trees outside. He reached out until he touched the flower tattooed on her chest. "That perfect combination of toughness and a good attitude," he said quietly.

She blushed. "You're doing it again, Jack. Saying all the right things."

"Is it working? You want to grab me again?"

Her devastating secret smile turned dazzling. She got up, came around the table, sat down on his lap, and hugged him.

His arms encircled her. He was speechless. His dick was stone hard against the pressure of her ass, but it wasn't just that. He just couldn't believe she was there, draping herself over him, holding him. She was so beautiful, so special, so shining. Like a unicorn, laying its head in his lap, and him breathless with the wonder of it. And so turned on, he could barely suck in a lungful of air.

She gasped as he stood up and swept her into his arms, heading up the stairs. "Jack! What the hell do you think you're doing?"

"Being masterful," he said. "Stop giggling. Get into the vibe."

"Hail, O conquering hero," she gasped out, between giggles. "Do with me as you will, my wild warrior lover. How's that?"

"Works for me." He shoved open the door to his bedroom with his foot and set her on her feet. They faced off, breathing hard. Her color was high, her eyes were shining. He tossed off his shirt. Vivi whipped off her tank. Call and response. He jerked open his belt, popped his jeans buttons. She yanked loose the drawstring of her skirt, let the garment puddle around her ankles. So beautiful. It unraveled him.

"Turn around," he said hoarsely. "Let me see your ass."

She obliged him. He came up behind her and knelt, his hands sliding down over her ribs, her waist, and clasping her hips.

He pressed his lips against the swirling mandala tattoo at the small of her back. "So what's the story with this one?"

"Oh." She shivered as he licked her there, his hand sliding up between her legs. "That was a celebratory tattoo. To mark the occasion of getting away from Bri—from the crappy ex that I mentioned before. I called my buddy Rafael on the day that the shit definitely hit the fan, and he whisked me away in his van, which is now my van. Drove me to my first crafts fair, in upstate New York. I had a good day, sold a bunch of stuff. After, we celebrated with buffalo wings and beer and a tattoo. Rafael got a dragon tattooed on his butt that night, if I remember correctly. I was a little more conservative."

He turned her to face him, his eyes level with the contours and involutions of her groin. Breathing in the hot, heady smell of sex. His cock ached with eagerness. He placed her hand on his shoulder to steady her and lifted her delicate foot. She teetered, giggling, as he touched the tattooed images of the crescent moon and star on top of her foot. "And this one?"

"No story with that," she admitted. "I just thought it was pretty."

"It is," he said. All of them were. Fit embellishments for her vivid beauty. Even the barbed wire around her wrist had its own poignant grace.

He gazed up at her pink face, her dilated eyes, the whole perfect length of her sweet body. Her pussy, still shiny and flushed, poking proudly out of her labia. "What an incredible view," he muttered.

He rose to his feet, moving behind her, his cock prodding the back of her thighs, and slid his hands around her. Clasping her waist, sliding his hand down between her legs. The damp seam of her pussy beneath his fingers.

"I want to take you from behind," he said. "Is that a problem?"

A fine tremor went through her, but he couldn't tell if it was fear or desire. He nuzzled and petted. Waiting until she gave him a plainer answer. Several breathless minutes went by. She began to writhe and make keening sounds in her throat. His hands grew bolder.

"It's okay," she whispered, finally.

He let go of her, stepped back. "Show me, then."

She shot a puzzled look over her shoulder. "Show you what?"

"That it's okay," he said. And waited.

It worked again, as it had before. She thought about it for a moment, her full, rosy lip caught seductively between her teeth.

Then she straightened her spine, tossed her hair back, and sauntered over to his bed. Taking her time. She climbed on, positioning herself on her hands and knees, presenting her perfect ass. She looked back, with that secret smile, and parted her thighs, undulating. "Convinced?" she purred.

He didn't bother to reply. Seconds later, he was in position, condom in place. His fingers rejoiced at her flawless skin, her lithe muscles, her sweet curves. He teased the secret shadows of her pussy while he kissed the mandala tattoo, playing her quivering clit.

She squirmed and moaned, wet and hot, but he took his time easing inside. The tight, hot clutch of her was sweet torture on his cock. She clung to him, her pussy flushed and full, like a juicy, suckling kiss. He let her rock back to take him in, a little more each time, until he was buried deep. Then some gasping, panting minutes of stroking and petting, licking her back, working her clit, and she started to make catlike sounds, pressing back. Demanding that he move.

Yes. Now she was ready to ride.

He thrust, hypnotized by the sight of the shiny pink lips of her sex clinging to his shaft. He withdrew, gleaming. Drove in again, again, seeking the strokes that made her soften and yield, using that subtle, inner awareness he'd never known existed until he'd made love to her. Now that he'd discovered it, he was strung out on it. Life was going to be so flat, so flavorless, without her.

That realization stabbed in like a blade. His hands tightened on her hips. And something in him cracked wide open.

He lost control. Rammed into her with the energy of a lifetime of unsatisfied need, seeking that blinding moment where he wouldn't have to think, or feel. Or fear.

It hit. He exploded into nothingness.

When he finally surfaced, she was wiggling beneath him on the quilt, kicking at his ankles. "Roll over," she said tartly. "I can't breathe."

He rolled over, and she pulled away, sitting up. Her eyes were wide. "That was, um, intense," she said, her voice small.

"I'm sorry," he said. "Did I hurt you?"

"A little. It was exciting. I came, of course. You always make me come. But you weren't with me anymore. At the end. I felt . . . alone."

He didn't know what to say. He felt her withdrawal like a cold wind. He reached out, but she shrank back, and he let his hand drop.

"I'm sorry," he said, feeling helpless. "Get in bed," he pleaded. "Wait for me while I go take this thing off."

"Okay." She didn't move. He waited, until she rolled her eyes, wiggled across the bed, and slid between the sheets.

"You won't go?" he demanded. "Promise?"

"No," she said softly. "I promise."

He smoothed the quilt over her, his face reddening. He was afraid she would disappear. He was a goner.

"The sooner you go, the sooner you'll come back," she said.

He stared at himself in the bathroom mirror, clutching the sink. He turned on the cold water, splashed his face, tried to think clearly. Abandoned the effort, after about five seconds. Useless.

All he wanted in the world was to fuck her again. Hold her again. Wrap himself around her in a grip that she could not break.

He wiped off his face and grabbed the little wastebasket from under the sink. Stupid to run back and forth every time.

She was still there when he got back. Holding the covers open for him. He slid into bed and grabbed her.

Her face softened into a smile. Something tight in his chest uncoiled. He resisted the sensation, automatically, and then yielded to it, with a shudder of backed-up emotion.

He arranged her so that her head was cradled on his shoulder, her arm resting on his chest, her leg flung over his. He stroked her back, and felt her heart beating under his hand, until she fell asleep.

So soft. He stared at the swirls of red hair tickling his nose, his chin. Her slender shoulder. He loved her scent, the soft moist bloom of warmth of her breath against his shoulder. He memorized the curve of her spine. If he concentrated on these details, and thought of nothing, he could cling to this emotion that was vibrating inside him, like a tightly strung instrument. Part of him wanted to shove it back into the darkness, but the feeling sang on, a fragile, stubborn thread. He clung to it, counting the rise and fall of her breath. Keeping the rest at bay.

Late afternoon eased with the smoothness of a sigh into twilight. He barely noticed. He could lie there forever, feeling her ribs rise and fall. Letting that strange feeling vibrate inside him.

Contentment? No. He rejected the word. He was familiar with contentment. He was contented with his house, his work. Lucky, to spend his days with the smell of the earth and rain, the sun, the flowers. That was contentment. This feeling was new. It was a long, quiet hour before he dared to put a name to it. It felt like happiness.

Behind that word were doors in his mind that had been locked for years. Like when Randy left, when he was eight. Deborah, who always insisted that he call her Deborah instead of Mom, told him that Randy had to go and find himself. "I gotta have space," Jack remembered him saying, very loudly. Jack remembered thinking that was dumb. It was the Oregon desert. There was so much space, it gave him the willies.

But Randy needed more. He took down his teepee, threw it in his truck, and drove away. Jack remembered standing there, bewildered, while Randy's truck got smaller. Jack wondered sometimes if Randy was his father, but Deborah was somewhat vague on that point.

Then they'd stayed with Jim and Consuela, in the Yakima Valley, until Deborah met Manuel. They moved into Manuel's trailer in the peach orchards. Manuel taught him Spanish, how to fight, how to change the oil in a car. Then Manuel got in trouble because he didn't have a green card, and had to go back to Mexico. After a while, Deborah decided she had to follow her heart and go to Mexico, too.

"You'll stay with Tavia," she told the totally freaked-out Jack.

"But why can't I come?"

"Oh, it's complicated, baby. But I'll write you letters, and I'll send for you real soon. You'll love it with Aunt Tavia. Her commune has lots of kids, and a swimming hole, and a tree house and everything."

Off he went, to Tavia's commune, near Olympia. He got letters, but they came less and less frequently. He was just getting used to it when Tavia fell in love with Mick, a guy from Oakland, and decided to move to California with him. Mick didn't want Jack to come. "The family thing is just not my scene," Mick said firmly.

So he went to Uncle Freddy's place in southern Oregon. In the meantime, Deborah broke up with Manuel, who was "too enmeshed in his culture," the letter said. She decided to go to India to study yoga with a guru, "to get her head straightened out and recover her sense of self." Shortly after that, Tavia broke up with Mick, left Oakland, and moved to Los Angeles with a guy named Mike.

Jack had trouble keeping it all straight. But he liked the mellow, benevolent Uncle Freddy. He liked the garden, the farm, the mountains. He had almost begun to allow himself to think of the place as home when the bust happened. The time he most hated to remember. He hadn't thought of it in years. He stared at the barbed-wire tattoo around Vivi's slender wrist. Tracing it. And realized that her eyes were open. Studying him.

She scrambled on top of him, folding her arms over his chest. Questions in her eyes. She wanted to talk. It terrified him. Too much reality would chase away that feeling. But even so, he wanted to know her. Her history, her dreams, her hopes, her plans.

No, on second thought, maybe he didn't want to know her plans.

Chapter
8

Vivi felt so relaxed, sprawled on Jack. Her body just couldn't get enough contact with him.

"So?" she prompted him. "Shouldn't we talk?"

"Probably," he said cautiously. "I'm not feeling very articulate."

"Hmm." She shifted, breasts brushing his chest, her crotch rubbing against his thigh. He hardened beneath her. Ready for more. The man was tireless.

"You just wait a minute," she said. "We should talk before we make love again. This is too easy!"

"What's wrong with easy?" He groped for a condom and ripped the package open. "We can talk if I'm inside you, can't we? Nothing's stopping us."

"Like I'm supposed to chitchat while a two-hundred-and-thirty-pound sex god is nailing me to his bed with his enormous thing, giving me multiple orgasms? Puh-leeze."

"Consider it a challenge," he suggested, rolling the condom over his cock. "I won't move. I just want to be inside you. Please?"

He nudged himself inside and stared into her eyes for the whole, long, tight slide to his balls. She fit over his pulsing shaft like a skin-tight glove. She blushed, from her chest on up. She was the one who started to move. She couldn't help herself. Manipulative bastard. He knew she couldn't get enough of him.

She'd have felt embarrassed, if she weren't so busy working herself up to another climax. She flung the covers back and rode him, chest heaving, back arched. He touched her breasts, held her, played with her clit until she collapsed over him in spasms of pleasure.

After, she lifted herself up onto her elbows, hazy with residual pleasure, and realized that he was still hot and huge and hard inside her, staring into her eyes. "Ah, Jack?" she ventured. "What about you?"

"What about me?" he said. "I'm fine. Didn't you want to talk?"

"But, ah . . . don't you need to come?"

He gave her a swift grin. "It'll wait. No hurry. I want to hang out, miles inside you. My dick is in heaven. It wants to take up residence."

She buried her laughter against his silky mat of dark chest hair. "If you say so." She pulsed her stretched, quivering vaginal muscles around him and tried to compose herself. Here went nothing.

"I was wondering . . . if you'd go with me into Pebble River, like Margaret suggested," she said. "To look at rentals. For my shop."

His face stiffened. "You know what I think of that idea."

"It's what I plan to do," she told him. "I know you think I'm married to the road, but I took that path by necessity. Not by choice."

"Please. Don't make promises you can't keep."

She sighed, in frustration. "They're not promises. I'm just telling you my plans. Why won't you listen to me, Jack?"

He shook his head. "Duncan will kill me if I let you do this."

She jerked up onto her elbows. "Duncan does not make my decisions for me! I am almost broke, Jack! And I cannot hide forever!"

He let out a heavy sigh. "I see that."

She took another chance. "And you can't say there's nothing between us," she said, resolutely. "Not anymore."

"I'm not saying that. But let's just stay in the moment. Let's not look at it too closely. If we do . . ." His voice trailed off.

"It'll disappear?" she finished.

His silence was her answer. She drooped down onto his chest, feeling him shifting and pulsing. Reminding her of his presence inside her.

"So we can't talk about the future," she said. "What can we talk about?"

"The past," he said. "Tell me about your past."

She blew a wisp of hair out of her eyes. "Big topic. Want to break it down a little for me?"

"Tell me how you became an artist," he suggested.

"Ah. Well, it was a challenge. Lucia sweated for years, trying to turn me into a civilized human. I was a wild animal, even though I loved her to pieces from the start. Hyperactive, hot tempered, foul-mouthed. I got bad grades. I had impulse control issues. I got into fights."

"I'm not surprised."

She ignored that. "Lucia was determined to make me respectable. She wanted me to study something that would make me good money, turn me into a pillar of the community. She loved art, but she liked classics. She didn't understand wild experimental art. We had a hell of a time, fighting it out."

"And you won?" He twirled her hair around his finger.

"Not at first. I compromised. I agreed to study graphic design. I tried, I really did, but I was miserable, and my grades sucked, and I ended up losing my scholarship. Lucia was furious with me."

"And? What did you do then?"

She shrugged. "I waitressed, I tended bar. Was a bike messenger for a while. Saved enough to reenroll in art school, one semester at a time. And I survived on art show openings for a couple of years."

He looked puzzled. "How's that?"

"You know those wine-and-cheese receptions at art galleries when a new exhibit opens? You can find one every night in New York, if you inform yourself. Cheese, crackers, grapes, strawberries, mini-quiches, puff pastries. If you're too broke to buy groceries, they're great."

He stirred uncomfortably. "You were that desperate?"

"Oh, it wasn't so bad. I saw a lot of art. It did me good. And then I met this gallery owner, Brian. I signed a contract with him. And he started to sell some of my stuff. My brief artistic golden age."

He lifted his head. "Brian? He's the filthy fuckhead ex, isn't he?"

Vivi went very still on top of him. "Ah . . . what if he is?"

"Brian Wilder, right?" he said slowly. "Wilder Galleries. In Soho."

She was shocked. "How in the holy *hell* do you know that?"

"It's the age of information," he said, innocently. "Shouldn't be hard to find out where the prick lives."

"You wouldn't!" She felt panicked, as if that poisonous toxic waste from her past could contaminate this delicate, shining thing she had with Jack. "Don't you dare! Leave him alone! Promise me!"

He stroked her back. "Shhh. Don't worry about it."

She hissed at him, anything but reassured. "If you mess with Brian, I'll take you apart! I will deconstruct you and sell you for scrap!"

He pressed her ass, pulsing his cock inside her. Reminding her he was the man, no doubt. Hah. "I hear you," he soothed. "So the fuckhead started selling your work, and then? What kind of work was it?"

"I met him during my barbed-wire and broken-beer-bottle period."

His eyes widened. "Your *what?*"

"I was rebellious, at the time," she explained. "I felt put upon because of my tragic childhood, I was mad at my birth mother for going to jail and killing herself, mad at Lucia for trying to control me, et cetera, et cetera. And I was drinking way too much espresso. I put it all into my work."

"I see." His voice was guarded.

"Anyway, Brian discovered me, you might say," she went on. "Decided to clean me up, make me marketable."

"And you got involved?" He cupped her breast in his hands.

"Yes," she said, her voice catching breathlessly. "It was a disaster. On every level, not just a personal one."

"What happened?" He began to rock his pelvis up against her, pressing his pubic bone against her clit in a slow, circular movement.

She pushed against his chest until she was upright, glaring down at him. "Don't distract me," she lectured. "You're cheating!"

His pelvis surged, making her undulate on top of him. "Sorry. You're so sexy. I forgot myself," he murmured. "And then?"

"What happened was that he turned out to be an art vampire, in addition to being an evil fuckhead. All he wanted was to make me into his money-grubbing zombie slave."

"I see," he said.

"And . . . well, I couldn't. I tried to be a zombie slave, but nothing came out. And he got really angry. And . . . well, you know the rest."

"Yeah," he said. "I do."

He stared up into her flushed face. The deep rocking slide of his cock inside her was impossible to resist. He held her firmly, thrusting up, stirring her around, making her gasp and bite her lip.

"I . . . I destroyed his office," she said, breathlessly. "After the last time that he . . . well, you know. I was so angry. Freaked out. Out of my head. I think I smashed probably fifty thousand dollars' worth of art."

"Good." He thrust harder, jarring a whimper from her throat. "Did he say, 'You'll never work in this town again,' et cetera?"

"Yes," she said, bleakly.

"And you believed him?"

She braced herself against his chest. "Of course I believed him! It was true! He blacklisted me, Jack! The guy has clout!"

He stopped moving, petted her hair. "Okay," he murmured. "Sorry."

"I thought I was finished," she went on. "Then Rafael stepped in."

"Who's this Rafael, anyhow?" Jack frowned. "Another boyfriend?"

"Rafael? Good God, no. Rafael's just my buddy, and besides, he likes boys."

"So you drove off with Rafael, and left the whole mess behind you."

The flat finality of his voice made tension grip her chest. "Hey. Don't you dare blame me for—"

"I'm not blaming you," he said quietly. "You did the right thing."

She was dumbfounded. "You think so?"

He pulled her back down on top of him. "Yeah. I do."

Vivi relaxed against his solid warmth. His quiet statement soothed something deep inside her. "I think you're the only person who's ever said that, except for Rafael," she said. "Lucia thought I was giving up. My sisters, too. It's hard to go against everyone's advice."

He stroked her back without replying, warm and comforting.

"Poor Lucia," she murmured. "I was a heartbreak to her. I defied her in every way. From my clothes to all of my ill-fated career choices."

"Were you one of those girls with spiked hair and safety pins?"

She snorted. "Not quite. I did have thigh-high lace-up black leather boots, though."

"Wow," he commented, eyes wide.

"They were the centerpiece of my wardrobe. I wore them with ripped fishnet stockings and a purple velvet miniskirt."

"My God," he said, with feeling. He reached down to slide his thumb tenderly into the top of her labia, circling around her clit.

"Do you still have them?" he asked.

She writhed against him, eyes shut. "Have what?"

"The boots."

Her eyes popped open, and she started to laugh. "I don't think so," she said. "Maybe in a box, in Lucia's attic. It was a long time ago."

"Oh." He sounded disappointed. She giggled harder. He frowned at her. "What's so funny?"

"You," she said. "I thought you would disapprove of my slutty boots. Brian hated them. You surprise me, that's all."

"Brian was a sick, evil fuckhead. Don't compare me to him. Of course I want to see you in those boots. I'm a normal guy, okay?"

"You're not a normal guy, Jack."

He kissed her fiercely into silence, and lifted his head some time later, when she was dazzled with lust. "Besides. You're a fine one to talk about normal. Barbed wire and broken beer bottles, for God's sake."

"Oh, shut up," she murmured, and kissed him back hungrily.

A moment later, she pried herself up and touched his cheek. "Jack?" she asked, tentatively. "Would you do something for me?"

He froze, eyes guarded. "If I can," he hedged.

"I want to try something," she said hesitantly. "I want, um . . . I want to roll over. And for you to, ah . . . hold my hands down."

His face went blank, and he jerked up onto his elbows, rocking her back. His body was rigid. "Why, for fuck's sake? That's sick, Viv, after what he . . . why would you do that to yourself? Or me?"

"Shhh," she soothed. "Nothing sick about it. I think that it would be okay, with you. Sexy, even. But I can't know until I try."

"But I'm the one who feels like dogshit if it doesn't work out!"

"Please, don't get mad," she pleaded. "I just thought . . . I don't want all these dead zones and 'danger, keep out' signs in my head. I want to feel free. And if anyone in the world could do that for me, it would be you. Believe me. I would never ask such a thing of you if I didn't trust you."

Even though you don't trust me back. She held the thought at bay with difficulty.

He stared into her face for a long time, as if trying to read her mind. "You're sure about this," he said, carefully.

She nodded, swallowing hard, and smiled at him.

"And you won't blame me if—"

"God, no," she assured him. "Not in the least. I swear."

In one swift surge, he rolled them both over, pinning her beneath his weight. He folded her legs up high, hooking them over his shoulders, and then grabbed her hands, pinning them beside her head.

He waited, staring fiercely into her face.

She gave him a tremulous smile. "I'm okay," she whispered.

He leaned down and kissed her deeply, possessively. His tongue thrusting and twining boldly with hers. "Look into my eyes," he said. "The entire goddamn time. Or else. Got it?"

She nodded. Speechless. Her throat was quivering, and her heart felt full, as she stared into his face, but she wasn't panicking. No stabs of fear, no numbing black fog. Her heart pounded from excitement, not fear.

He was not gentle. She had not wanted him to be. He took her hard, his body challenging hers, and his face looked angry as he did it; eyes burning, mouth grim. Except that she knew him now. She could feel his concern for her, his tension, his need. His awareness of her.

And she was aware of him, too, on levels she'd never imagined. She sensed that the conquering hero pose excited him, and his excitement fed hers, in a confused feedback loop of emotion, sensation. No playacting. Her surrender was as real as his conquest.

She gasped for breath, jerking up to meet his hard thrusts. Staring with wide, tear-blinded eyes into his face. Struggling voluptuously against the implacable strength of his beautiful body, his steely arms, his gripping hands.

She could go there with him. She could go anyplace she wanted with him, as far as she could dream of going, and know that he would carry her back, completely safe, all in one happy, sated piece.

Afterward, they lay tangled together, limp and damp. They roused themselves at last to take a long, lazy shower, washing each other. Jack's tireless cock rose to full salute, but Vivi laughed at him.

"Dream on, big boy," she said. "I'm done for the night."

He toweled her off, with his usual passionate attention to detail and herded her toward the stairs. "Food, then," he said, resigned.

They made sandwiches in his kitchen. Devoured the rest of Margaret's latest batch of cookies. And when they could find nothing else that was quick and easy to eat, they went back up the stairs, and into Jack's bed, to twine their naked bodies as closely together as they could.

They talked, carefully. Tentative, groping conversations about their pasts, their histories. Circling around forbidden topics.

But she didn't want dead zones and "danger keep out" signs in their conversations, either. Vivi sat up, pushing his hands away when he reached to pull her close again. "I have a question, Jack."

"Ask away," he said, his face hidden in the shadows.

"What happened after the bust?" She let her hair curtain her face.

He took her hand. "We're having a beautiful time," he said, his voice halting. "Don't ruin it by asking me questions like that."

"I'm not picking a fight," she said gently. "I just need to know. Did you go to one of your other family members?"

He shook his head. "I couldn't reach any of them. My mother was in India, meditating with some guru. My aunt had moved on, to some other boyfriend. They hadn't stayed in touch."

"So you just took off, all alone?"

"It wasn't so bad at first. It was summer, and there was fruit and corn to steal. I ate a lot of hot dogs. Became an excellent shoplifter."

She laughed, incredulous. "You?"

"I was unbeatable. I told you, remember? Fasting makes me crabby."

He fell silent, then, and she reached out to stroke his shoulder. It was rigid. "And then?"

"I lasted about eight months," he said. "I found the places where the runaways crashed. But the winter got cold. One night, I was in this flophouse in North Portland. Some guys picked a fight with me.

It ended badly." He touched the scar on his forehead. "That's where I got this."

She leaned down, and kissed his eyebrow, his forehead.

"That was it, for me. I found a phone. Called Margaret, collect."

"Margaret? You mean, you knew her then?"

"Freddy knew her," he corrected. "From when he was a kid. He'd told me about her. So I gave her a try. The operator asked if she'd take a call from Freddy Kendrick's nephew. And she accepted the charges."

"Wow," she whispered. "So you went to live with her?"

"For a while," he said. "She was good to me. I joined the military as soon as I was old enough. Didn't want to be a burden to her."

She ran her fingers through the sable texture of his hair, and thought about it all. "You think I'm going to be like them, right?" she said. "Like your family? Running out on you?"

He rolled over, clapping his hand over his eyes. "Oh, fuck, Viv. Don't do this." He sounded exhausted. "It's so beautiful. Don't wreck it for me. Just let it be what it is. Please."

"But I just want you to—"

"Let me have this, okay?" He sounded angry again. "For however long as it lasts. Can't we just stay in the moment?"

She hid from the revealing shaft of moonlight that illuminated the quilt as she considered it. There was something to be said for staying in the moment, hard though it was. She was a normal, flesh-and-blood woman. She craved the usual reassurances, promises, declarations of trust, faith. Love. She wasn't going to get them from him. Period.

But so what? That did not mean that what he gave her instead was not precious. Or that she shouldn't cherish it anyway.

After all. Suppose they stayed in the moment, for, say, thirty years? Forty? Fifty? Maybe when he was a grizzled old man, he would give in, laugh at himself. Finally admit that it had been love all along.

She slipped back between the sheets and into his hot embrace.

The image made her smile, but her eyes were wet.

Chapter
9

Vivi stepped back from the wall she was painting and surveyed the warm ivory tone with satisfaction. She adjusted an elegant earthenware vase on its stand with her pinkie finger, the only finger with no paint on it, and stood back to admire the effect. Classy.

Her store was shaping up. Her friends were coming in from all over the West Coast to bring her consignments. Stock was pouring in. Just that morning, Betty and Nanette had left an assortment of handblown bottles and stemware. Yesterday, Rockerick brought leatherwork. Brigid left a pile of jewel-toned handwoven silk shawls and throws. Miraben brought teapots, vases, jugs, dishes. With her own stuff, the shop would be a gallery of wearable, usable art.

The bells over the door tinkled. Jack walked in. A smile spread over her face. His answering grin made her toes curl.

He looked around with his usual reservation. He disapproved of her decision to open the shop. Vociferously

"Looking good," he said, grudgingly.

Well, my. Unusually positive, for him. She gazed at him, savoring the glow of sensual energy that hummed between them.

"You look incredible," he said, leaning toward her.

Vivi pulled back. "Let me wash my hands. Paint cramps my style."

"Hurry," he said.

Vivi ran to the bathroom and scrubbed paint off her hands. She stripped off her T-shirt and cutoffs, threw her green dress over her head, shook her hair down. They had been lovers for weeks now, and she still got swirling flutters in her stomach when she saw him.

Jack gazed at the snowy bulk of Mount Adams when she emerged. "Great view," he commented, as she stood on tiptoe to kiss him.

"It's a great location," she said. "Ten days, and I'll be ready for my grand opening. So what brings you here, Jack? I thought you were taking those larkspurs and veronica into Portland today."

"I did. The truck overheated on the way back. It has a broken fan belt. I left it at the shop."

"So you're bumming a ride home? You're sure you can endure being seen in public in my disreputable van?"

"I'll wear a Lone Ranger mask," he said. "There's a blues concert tonight, at the riverfront park. Want to go dancing?"

"Dancing? Wow! Yes!"

He cupped her head in his hand, kissed her again, and was maneuvering her toward the privacy of the little office in the back. She giggled, and pulled away. They'd gotten up to hours of juicy, delicious mischief back there on her secondhand desk, every time he came to her shop. But not today. "Don't get any ideas," she protested. "I have a lot to do before I can fling myself into the abyss of rampant sensuality."

"I'll be back in a couple of hours, then." A dazzling smile, and the bells tinkled as he walked out.

Breath escaped slowly from Vivi's lungs. She was terrified at how happy she was, but the feeling was marred by a keen edge of uncertainty. She was trying to get used to uncertainty, but it still rattled her.

The last few weeks were like a dream. The two of them spent every waking moment that they weren't working together. She was sleeping in his bed, eating with him, living in his house. The apartment in the barn had turned into her studio, when she worked at all. She'd never been so distracted, so knocked off track. She was drinking too much of his powerful coffee, soaking in his big tub, eating his excellent cooking, wearing his huge shirts around.

Their hungry, intense lovemaking left her drained, shivering, empty of thought. When she was in that condition, she could stay in the moment, as he'd begged her to do. And she was in that condition a lot.

She'd gone on with her plan of opening a shop, in spite of Jack's anger and protests, and the objections of her sisters. If she wanted to put down roots, she had to get on with it.

She tried to protect herself emotionally, the way Jack shielded himself from her, but he was intensely sensitive to her moods. When he sensed her withdrawing, he promptly seduced her and rendered her mindless and whimpering. But he never let down his own guard.

Patience. They belonged together. They couldn't keep their hands off each other. They'd made progress. For God's sake, they were going dancing tonight. How very normal of them. That was progress.

Everything else was perfect. The trendy location she'd found for her shop in Pebble River was ideal. A local woodworking shop was making a carved hanging sign that read "Vivi's Treasure Box." Glass-fronted cabinets were ordered and on their way. She'd organized wholesale accounts with the most talented artists she knew. Her credit was maxed to the limit, but hey. Life was risk. She could stand it. All she had to do was persuade Jack that they had a future together. The biggest risk she'd ever taken. The highest stakes. All or nothing.

But she had no idea what she would do with herself if she lost.

The breeze was warm at the riverfront park. The sensual blues tunes of the band from Portland pulsed through the evening air. A slow romantic song began, and Vivi and Jack merged without a word, swaying like a single body.

It was really happening for her, Vivi thought, in a haze of unbelieving happiness. They were going to let their fears and hesitations go. Together, they formed something greater than the sum of their parts. The music throbbed around them, and his body was the core of her spinning universe. She would never find another man so right for her, who moved her so deeply, and now was the moment to tell him. He was ready to listen. She could feel it.

She was so enthralled as she stretched up to whisper in his ear, she barely noticed the large hand tapping on her shoulder.

A big, booming voice intruded on her consciousness. "Vivi? Viv D'Onofrio? Sweet thing, is it really you?"

Vivi turned. A stocky blond man with a goatee, a waxed moustache, and a purple silk shirt stood smiling at her. A narrow tie dotted with suns and moons adorned his shirt. Vivi tried to place him, and he grinned widely, revealing his trademark golden eyeteeth.

"Rafael!" she cried out, as he enveloped her in a bear hug. "Is it you? What happened to the beard, the dreadlocks, the tie-dye?"

"And this is my disheveled pixie Vivi? You look stunning. That long, long hair! I could eat you up with a spoon! Give me another hug!"

"Put her down." Jack's voice was quiet, but authoritative.

Rafael swiveled his head, leaving Vivi's feet dangling a foot off the ground. He took one look at Jack. She thudded heavily to the ground.

Rafael's widened eyes traveled the length and breadth of Jack's body. "Viv!" he exclaimed. "You devil, you! Where did you find this one?"

"Jack, this is Rafael, my buddy from art school, the guy I told you about. Rafael, this is Jack Kendrick. My van got stuck in his mud."

"How provocative," Rafael murmured. "The van clued me in that you were here. I saw it in the parking lot, and I've been prowling the grounds looking for you. And what does this Jack Kendrick do?"

Jack blinked at him, quizzically. "Uh . . ."

"He grows flowers," Vivi supplied.

"How picturesque. I love it." Rafael's golden teeth flashed. "What are you doing in these parts, angel? Apart from, ah . . . the obvious." His gaze flashed toward Jack, eyebrows waggling wildly.

"I'm starting a business in Pebble River," she said.

Rafael's eyebrows shot up. "Putting down roots?"

God, she hoped. "I'm burnt on the crafts fairs. But enough about me. Tell me about your transformation. Are you respectable now?"

"Prosperous, my dear. Different from respectable," he said, fingering a diamond that glinted discreetly in his ear. "Remember Rudolfo, the promoter of the show we did in Monterey? He made me his site manager, and one thing led to another, and now I'm a promoter!"

"That's great, Rafael! I'm so happy for you!"

Rafael twirled a diamond solitaire ring on his finger, batting his eyes. "Thank you. I was so ready to change my image. You should see me in full regalia! Armani, Prada. I look like a million bucks."

She tugged his tie affectionately. "What brings you here?"

"Business. I was in San Francisco, setting up a gallery show. And I'm heading back to New York tomorrow, because some clients are flying in from London on Saturday—"

"Whoa, you're riding high!" she said, impressed. "The last time I saw you, we were roasting hot dogs around a campfire!"

"Life marches on! The art in my New York gallery can be seen by appointment only, I'll have you know," Rafael said proudly. "Artists would kill to show me their work. I act disgustingly self-important. You'd laugh your head off if you saw. Anyway, this band is a fave of mine, so I popped over from Portland to see the concert before I fly back to New York, and am I glad! I've been desperate to get in touch with you! I have the perfect job for you, love. Mine!"

Vivi squinted at him, confused. "What? Yours? How?"

"You heard me. My clientele is growing, and I'm putting together high-end shows that travel, but with my gallery in New York, I can't always be on the move. I need a curator and site manager. You could do for me what I did for Rudolfo. I'm talking invitational shows, where you handpick the artists, jury the art, curate the show, plan the tour, choose galleries, lofts, ballrooms, hotels. The money is extremely good. And a canny career move for a developing artist, if I may advise you."

"Wow," she said thoughtfully. "It's a very generous offer, but—"

"Don't make snap decisions!" Rafael admonished. "This job has been good to me. I want to pass on the good fortune! Think about it!"

"I'm speechless," Vivi said, touched. "It's kind of you to think of me, but the truth is, my life is complicated right now. And I'm kind of in the midst of something here."

"I can see that!" Rafael eyed Jack with blatant approval. "But let me just explain how perfect my job is for you."

Vivi abruptly became aware of the quality of Jack's fierce, silent attention. "Um, Rafael, do you suppose we could meet for coffee and talk about this tomorrow? Now is not the best time for—"

"What better time? We arranged this time in the astral plane! I have to catch a plane tomorrow. Seize the moment!" Rafael took her arm and led her away from the crowd. Vivi glanced uncomfortably back at Jack. He followed closely, his face unreadable.

"Listen carefully," Rafael began earnestly. "A sample month in the life of Vivi D'Onofrio, art promoter. One week in San Francisco, eating sushi and going to the opera. The next week in Berkeley, taking in wild experimental theater. A tour of the wine country in between. On to Los Angeles, San Diego, Santa Fe, always a different view. No fleabag motels, no moldy campground showers. You eat in award-winning restaurants, you sleep in five-star hotels. You deal in outrageously expensive art. It's fun, stimulating, challenging. What do you say?"

"You know money has never been a big priority for me—"

"Oh, I know." Rafael patted her shoulder. "But just try making lots of money for a while, and see how fast you get used to it."

"The real reason is not the money," she plodded on. "I'm—"

"This job is your way back into the high-end art world! Everything that bastard Wilder took from you, you can have again! I'm not suggesting you be a site manager or curator forever. I'm thinking about your long-term artistic career! If you go this road, with the contacts you develop, you can write your own ticket!"

"But my shop is already organized, and I—"

"A little shop in a little town has its charm, but think about it. Work with me for a while, and that scumbag Wilder will be eating your exhaust. Just imagine the satisfaction."

Vivi imagined it. She twisted gently out of Rafael's grip and wrapped her arms across her chest. Shivering, although the night was warm. The crowd swirled around them, but the music faded to the background of her mind as she pondered the images.

The big-time art world. Success, fame, money. The life she'd dreamed of as a struggling young artist. It didn't make her heartbeat quicken anymore. She lifted her gaze past her friend's expectant face, to where Jack stood, behind him. His stance rigid. Eyes fixed on her.

That life didn't include Jack. The finality of that fact sent a stab of nervous panic through her. "Ah . . . ah, it's tempting, but—"

"And you could play fairy godmother to your artist friends! You'd have the power to bring their stuff to the attention of the high-end buyers! You could change their lives! Wouldn't that be grand?"

Vivi took a slow breath. "It sounds great, but I found a perfect location for my shop. I'm content with that. I'm staying put."

She twisted to see if Jack was still listening. He was close behind, but when she tried to meet his eyes, he looked straight ahead.

Rafael's gaze shifted, from Vivi to Jack, back again. "Ah. I understand, angel. You just think about it. I won't push."

Vivi turned to Jack and reached out to take his hand. "The band is starting another song. Let's go back near the stage, okay?"

Jack's hand was stiff, unresponsive. "I'm ready to leave," he said.

Rafael's smile faded. He looked at Jack fingering the waxed ends of his moustache. "I hope I haven't put you in a tight place, love," he said. "Will you think about it?"

"Certainly, I'll think about it," Vivi said quietly. "And thank you. It's a beautiful offer, and you're a wonderful friend."

Rafael gave her an impulsive hug. "Give me your cell number. Promise me you'll give it some serious thought. I'll walk you out to the van."

She pulled out her phone. "I don't get much mobile coverage out where I live," she told him. "I'll give you the landline number at my shop, and at Jack's house, too."

They exchanged various numbers as they strolled. Rafael's eyes grew nostalgic as they stopped at the van. He turned to Jack. "Did Viv tell you that I—"

"Yeah, she told me," Jack said dourly. "You painted the serpent."

Rafael's eyes turned dreamy. "This was my best van painting. I'd be more than willing to paint the other side for you, love. How about a portrait of the two of you? Chain-mail bathing suits, shreds of fur, a flaming sword? You can be hugging his leg. I love it when the girl hugs the guy's leg." His gaze flicked to Jack's muscular thigh. "Mmmm."

"Oh, no, that's okay," Vivi said quickly. "I like just having the one."

"I had such wild times in that van," Rafael reminisced. "One night Billy and Ronnie and I got some tequila and limes and salt, and we—"

"You told me that story," Vivi interrupted hastily.

"I painted that scene after I broke up with Ronnie," Rafael said, wistfully. "That was my 'man-alone-battling-his-demons' period."

"Yeah, that about sums up the last few years of my life, too," Vivi said ruefully. She dug her keys out of her purse and gave Rafael a hug. "It was great to see you, Rafael. I'm happy to see you doing so well."

"Thank you, angel. Let me know what you decide. Contact me on the astral plane, by all means, but call my cell phone, too, okay?"

"I'll do that. Thanks."

Jack climbed into the van and slammed his door shut. Rafael waved exuberantly as she backed out of the parking spot.

The silence was unbearable in the van. Jack sat like a graven image in the dark, not responding to her attempts to speak. They got to the toll bridge, and she scrabbled in the dark for quarters. He handed her the change. The small contact gave her courage.

She flung them into the basket. "Jack," she began.

"Don't start," he said, in the cool, detached voice she had not heard for weeks. Not since before they had become lovers.

"But you have the wrong idea. Rafael is a good friend, but he talks too much, and he has no idea where my head is right now—"

"Shut up and drive, Vivi," he said.

She closed her mouth with a snap. When she pulled into the driveway at home and killed the engine, he got out without a word and headed toward the house.

Vivi stared after him, wondering if she was still welcome in there.

Edna leaped and bounded at his heels, licking at his hand as he unlocked the front door, shoving her way in when the door opened. In any case, she had to retrieve her rambunctious dog. She walked slowly up onto the porch and stepped inside, shutting the door. It was dark inside the big room, but he had not turned on any lights, and she didn't either. The dark made it easier.

"I don't want Rafael's job, if that's what you're thinking," she told him. "It's a fabulous offer, but it's not for me."

"That's not how it looked." Jack's voice was bleak. "You looked tempted. And you should be. That job's a road back to the career you always wanted. All your hopes and dreams and training. Do what you have to do. Don't let me hold you back."

She shook her head in helpless dismay. "But I have everything I need, right here! Rafael was trying to help me, but I don't need any help! His timing just sucked, that's all!"

"No, his timing was perfect," Jack said. "I was starting to delude myself. I owe him for bringing me back to earth."

That drove her right over the top. She ran over to him, and whacked at his chest with the heels of her hands. "You were not de-luding yourself!" she yelled. "You were starting to trust me, and I deserve to be trusted! We have something special!" She whacked him, trying to shove him back toward the couch. "Thick-brained lug! Would you just take a goddamn chance on me?"

He trapped both her wrists in one hand. "Don't get in a wresting match with me, Viv."

"Why the hell not?" she shot back. "Why try to be good? What's the point of controlling myself? Why even bother?"

"Because I'll win." He dragged her close and cupped her ass so she could feel his erection. "Is that what you want? I'll give it to you like that, if it is. I'll give it to you right now."

They stared at each other, grim and furious. Angry as she was, he still aroused her. Her heart pounded when he tossed her onto the couch and shoved up her skirt. His fingers parted her folds, slid in-side her, found her wet and yielding.

She clenched around his delving fingers. Ashamed, to make it so goddamn easy for him. It wasn't right. She shoved at his chest, but without much strength. She was trembling, melting down.

And wondering, too, with what small measure of wit she had left, if sex might make him more mellow and receptive.

"You love it like this." He wrenched open his belt. "I can feel it."

"And? What if I do?" she responded, her voice shaking. "And besides. It's not 'it' that I love. It's you! Get it through your thick head!"

"Shut up, and let me work on the one thing we've got going for us," he muttered, sliding the thick bulb of his cockhead up and down her slit.

"Don't shush me, you son of a bitch—" Her protests were cut off as he kissed her. His kiss was angry and fierce, but so was she. She clawed at him, clutched him, cursed at him. Wound her fingers into his hair and kissed him as he spread her legs and nudged himself inside.

He thrust hard, driving inside all at once. It hurt, excited though she was. She cried out, and he stopped, lifting his panting mouth from hers. Staring into her shadowy eyes.

She jerked him closer with a furious yank. Ashamed to be sucked into that vortex of craving so instantly, but she was in it now, and there was nothing to do but ride it out to the end. Every plunging stroke of his cock was a licking lash of guilty delight. His hands on her breasts, his hot mouth, madly kissing her, his big body, pumping hard . . . *yes*.

She came, shuddering and wailing. He was still driving hard toward his own pleasure when she realized that he hadn't used latex, but she couldn't stop or even speak. Just whimper, at each wet slap of contact. His breath hissed with each jolt, gaining momentum, straining, jerking . . . and he flung back his head and came. And came, and came. Hot jets spurted inside her. He collapsed over her, panting.

Vivi stared up at the dark ceiling, pushed far beyond any recognizable emotion. Her fingers still wound into his hair, as if she could hold on to him. But no. He was slipping away. Receding into the distance.

And there wasn't a goddamn thing she could do about it.

The sweat on their bodies was cool before either of them dared to move. He lifted his head, cleared his throat. "I, ah . . . I didn't, um . . ."

"Yes," she said. "I noticed that."

He pulled himself out, stuffed himself back into his jeans, keeping his back turned to her. "Is it a dangerous time?" he asked.

"So-so," she said. "I'm not too regular. Hard to say." She got up, smoothed her skirt down. His sperm trickled hotly down her leg. "I wish I knew what you were trying to prove with this demonstration. That I'm a weak slut who can't say no? That you're stronger than me? What's the message, Jack?"

"No message," he said. "I just couldn't stop. It's that simple."

She laughed, bitterly, and pressed her hand to her leaky nose, longing for a tissue. "Simple, my ass. You're anything but simple."

He sighed. "Jesus, Viv. This is hell. What do you want from me?"

"I want you to believe me when I say I love you," she said.

He was silent for a moment. "Fine," he said. "Marry me, then."

She stared at him, dumbfounded. "Ah . . . what?"

"You heard me."

She stared at his inscrutable silhouette, then got up and turned on the lamp on the table by the couch. His face was hard, as if he were bracing himself for a blow. She exhaled, slowly. "Jack," she said.

"We're already working on making a baby, right? So let's go all the way. Tomorrow, we go to town. We'll get our documents in order."

"You bastard," she whispered.

"Yes or no, Vivi," he said. "It's a simple question."

Vivi chose her words carefully. "It's not a simple question. It's not a real marriage proposal. It's a rocket grenade attack. You're setting me up. And jerking me around."

He grunted. "That sounds suspiciously like a no."

"That sounds like an it depends," she said. "If I said yes now, you wouldn't believe me anyway. Not in the state you're in."

She put her hand against his chest. He stepped back. Her hand dropped. "But since you haven't said yes, we'll never know, will we?"

Dread twisted in Vivi's stomach. "I need for you to believe me," she said. "I can't keep trying to convince you. You're exhausting me."

"So get it over with. Dump me, Viv. I can't stand the suspense."

Vivi pressed her hand against her trembling mouth. "Dump you? How can I? That would imply that we were involved in a relationship. But we never were, according to you. You never let me get that close. You just wanted to fuck me, remember? And stay in the moment. So that's where I've been living, Jack. For weeks, now. The moment."

He was silent for a moment. "The moment's over."

"Yeah. I see." She mopped angrily at her eyes with the backs of her hands. "Party's over, huh? Everybody out of the pool."

"Time for you to move on to the next big adventure. No regrets."

Vivi put both hands over her face to block out the sight of him.

"You can stay up in the apartment for as long as you need to, of course," he added, stiffly. "I'm not throwing you out to the wolves."

A derisive laugh jerked out of her. "As if I would. Don't worry. I'm convinced. I'll be gone as soon as I can pack."

She wiped her hands on her skirt and started to walk past him toward the door. As if she were walking the plank.

One sign from him, the slightest softening, and she'd fall over backward. Marry him. Have his children. Weld herself to him. She stopped moving when she passed in front of him. Waited. Hoping.

"Better sooner than later," was all he had to say.

Well, then. She walked on outside, as stiff as an automaton.

She went up to the apartment, began to pack. She hadn't bought much stuff since she'd been there, just a set of Miraben's plates. She'd been sprawled all over Jack's life. Eating off his dishes, using his soap, sleeping in his bed. Too busy madly boinking to think of how she was going to feel when it all came crashing down on her head.

As she'd known it would. Goddamn it, she'd *known*. She was so pissed at herself.

She filled her arms with shopping bags, and staggered to the van. *Soldier on*, she told herself. *You've been through worse.*

But she didn't feel strong. Why bother soldiering on? To where? She was going nowhere. Her life sucked. The Fiend was welcome to it.

Well, then again. Maybe she wouldn't go quite that far.

Several of her new Miraben dishes broke as she tossed the box down onto the floor of the van. She didn't bother to check how many.

Chapter
10

John waited until the last few people came out of the Wilder Gallery. An hour or so ago there had been an exodus of well-dressed buttheads flooding out of the big opening for some hotshot new artist. The ones trickling out now were the employees of the gallery itself.

He shrank back into the shadows behind a Dumpster as the skinny foreign slut came out. Her tits were shoved up into a glittering silver tube dress, her lips shiny with hot-red lipstick, and her black hair was freshly bobbed with cruelly short bangs, like a dominatrix. Wilder's assistant, Damiana.

She was usually the last one to go, apart from Wilder himself. Probably stayed behind to suck the boss's dick.

And there was Wilder, a few minutes later, stepping out the door. Last one to go. Bastard didn't trust anyone else to close for him. First he armed the alarm with his remote, punching in a code. Then he got to work on all the locks and bolts. After came the rolldown metal door.

John sauntered over while he was still working on the locks. "Evening, Mr. Wilder."

The guy jerked back, hit the door, and dropped his keys. "What?"

John smiled, toothily. "Good evening," he repeated.

"What are you doing here?" Wilder's forehead was already shiny.

"I'm here to discuss the phone call we had a couple of hours ago."

"What's there to discuss? I already told you everything I managed to learn. Rafael Siebling was here tonight at the opening. He ran into D'Onofrio yesterday, in Oregon. Some place called Pebble River. She's opening a shop there. That's what I was told, and that's absolutely all I know. I did not speak with her, or get her number. I cannot help you any more than that, so . . . so, uh, good night."

Wilder gave him a smile that said, *Alrighty, then, you big inconvenient asshole, you're dismissed.* John waited until that smile started to quiver, and unravel itself. Into the raw components of fear.

"How about Rafael Siebling's address?" John asked softly.

"I'm sorry, I don't have it. It really shouldn't be all that hard to find. His gallery is very 'in' these days, though I can't imagine why. He has no taste. All flash, no content. I don't have his number in my cell phone because he's the last person I would ever call. I don't even know why he came in here tonight. To gloat, I suppose."

"Gloat?" John cut off the guy's babbling. "Why would he gloat?"

Wilder made an impatient sound. "Oh, he and Viv are old friends," he said. "I think he wanted to rub it in about her new boyfriend. As if I gave a shit who she fucks. She could do dogs and pigs for all I care."

New boyfriend? A hot, red glow began to obscure John's vision. His hands clenched. Boyfriend. So, it was true. Vivien, too. A slut, just like her slut sisters. He pictured her writhing and begging, taking it in every hole. And, all the while, laughing at him. Mocking at him.

Brian had shrunk back against the door, hands up, and his voice was a constant breathless babble that John cut off.

"What's the name of the new boyfriend?"

"Like I care," Wilder said. "Some big redneck farmer clod."

John immediately pictured the raw-boned, thick-necked guy, naked but for a John Deere cap, fucking Vivien from behind. She was bent over a bale of hay, squealing with delight at each poke, and looking up at John, that pink mouth open and panting, eyes bright with lust and malicious glee. Calling John a tub of lard. A big, dumb fuck.

Punish. He had to punish someone. Had to calm the screaming inside him. The wild hurricane wind. It wanted something. Tidal waves, atom bombs rigged to blow, hammers crushing. Had to be appeased.

Punish. *Now.*

"You must have Siebling's number in your office files," he said.

Wilder looked blank. "I don't think so."

"But you're not sure, hmm?" John picked up the bunch of keys, and shoved them into Wilder's limp hand. "Let's go check."

"I really . . . uh . . . I don't think that would be a good—"

"Let's . . . go . . . *check.*" John hissed the last word, a sharp, silibant punch that made Wilder cringe against the door.

"Ah, um, whatever," he muttered. He unlocked the door with hands that shook. "But I'm sure it's useless."

"We'll see," John said. Blood roared in his ears.

The place was dark, but Wilder flipped an all the big hanging banks of lights that hung from the high ceiling. He muttered as John followed him through the main gallery. They passed tables, one of which had several bottles half full of white and red wine, and trays of food with silver brocade cloth napkins flung over them.

Wilder's nervous prattle came briefly into focus, like a radio tuning into an elusive frequency. ". . . useless cunt didn't even finish cleaning up the food," he said. "I'm kicking her scrawny little Italian ass tomorrow. If we get rats, it's her fault."

He started up the staircase, shooting nervous little looks over his shoulder. As if he thought John was going to play grab-ass with him.

But Wilder's ass did not appeal to him. And it would take a lot more than that to calm the screaming, the pounding inside him.

He followed Wilder all the way around the upper balcony level of the gallery, to the lavish office in the back. Wilder unlocked the door, and pushed it open, blocking the door with his body. "Ah, one moment," he said. "Wait here. I'll check that address for you."

Not in this universe, you little squeaking shitbird. John smiled and followed him in. Wilder rolled his eyes and scurried to his desk. He powered up the laptop and thumbed through his desk Rolodex. He clicked and tapped on the laptop, and shook his head.

"Sorry, no Rafael Siebling here," he sang out. "Can't help you."

"Then why don't you just do a search for me, on your computer?"

The guy looked miffed. As if he were way too important to perform such a basic, simple favor for John. As if he were better than John.

Giving him that look. The look that said, "You big, dumb fuck."

John began walking toward the desk. Wilder turned gray, and scrambled to punch Siebling's name into the search engine.

"Hey!" His voice was passionately relieved. "Here's his gallery's home site. I'll just print out this page for you." The printer's buttons lit up. It hummed, and spat out a sheet of paper. Wilder grabbed it and handed it to John with a big, fake smile. "See? Address, phone number, e-mail, and website address. So glad to help. And now, if you'll excuse me, I have another appointment that I'm already late for."

John glanced at his watch. 2:39 A.M. "At this hour?"

Wilder yanked the door open. "Don't want to keep her waiting. You know. Women." That genial tone, that world weary-smile irritated the shit out of John. Condescending to him. *You big, dumb fuck.*

The mocking words echoed in his head as he followed Brian out the door onto the gallery walkway. Wilder began walking faster. John lengthened his stride, closed the gap. Wilder began to trot.

Enough. John leaped, took him down. Wilder's shoulder hit, with a brutal crunch, against the iron balcony rail. Wilder started to scream.

It hurt John's head. There was already too much screaming inside, that constant screaming, driving him crazy. He grabbed the guy by his collar and his belt, lifted, swung, heaved him over the rail. . . .

The screaming stopped.

Ah. He could breathe again, in the sweet, calm silence. John panted there for a moment, enjoying a sensation of intense relief, and began to stroll the entire perimeter of the balcony. It gave him an opportunity to enjoy the effect of his handiwork from every angle.

He was feeling much better. His vision had cleared, his breathing deepened, his heartbeat normalized. He was even feeling . . . nibblish.

He stopped at the table next to the enormous Waylan Winthrop bronze that held pride of place in the center of the gallery. The one he'd been so fascinated with a few weeks before. The one entitled *Teeth.*

He grabbed one of the napkins, and loaded it up with water crackers, mini caviar sandwiches, chunks of cheese, artichoke tarts.

And a couple of juicy pineapple chunks from the remains of the fruit bowl. He'd be wise to tank up on food. There would be no time for a meal. He'd need to race to whatever airport had the earliest flight to Portland, Oregon. That old turd Haupt would insist on going, too, but at least John had finally gotten a lead. Maybe it would earn a break from the scolding. Lucky, that he'd been able to unload some bad energy.

He stuffed his face with tasty tidbits as he gazed up at the new, revised version of *Teeth*. Dark drops of blood plopped heavily down, dangerously close to his shoes. He moved his feet out of range and ate another couple of juicy chunks of pineapple as he gazed up, admiring the effect. He dug out his cell, framed the shot, snapped a few pictures.

He'd gotten a feeling, weeks ago, when he first saw those sharp, spiky teeth pointing straight up into the air, that the sculpture was missing something. It lacked that extra little thing, some color, some interest, that would really make it pop.

It was perfect, now.

The gophers were eating the Asiatic lilies again. He was going to have to rotate the bulbs to another field. The idea exhausted him.

Jack rocked back on his heels and stared at the big, spotted orange lilies, struggling to remember what the fuck he was doing. Bucket. Lilies. Clippers, in his hand. Yes, it would seem that he was cutting them. Then, haul them to the cooler. Before dawn, he had to drive them into Portland.

He grabbed the bucket, pushed his way listlessly through the towering stalks of *Aconitum columbianum*. The royal blue blossoms were about to open. The vivid pink of the *Campanula medium* hurt his eyes. The *Penstemon azureus* was about ready. And the *Crocosmia 'Lucifer.'* The gladioli, too. He was behind. Slacking off. He'd been too busy rolling around in bed to keep up with his flowers. He was going to lose money if he didn't haul ass. That idea exhausted him even more.

He hauled the bucket across the field and squatted in front of the *Physostegia*, staring stupidly at the white blossoms. Snip. Put the cut stalk upright into the bucket. Mind on what he was doing. Second by second. Better to get used to it all at once. Much better than to get attached just to have it ripped away again. He'd be okay. He always was.

But she was everywhere. The cosmos flower reminded him of her posture. Colored yarrow, crimson bee balm made him think of her hair, her lips. His bed seemed as wide as a football field without her curled up in it. And her freckles. Faint constellations on her shoulders and throat. He knew them the way an astronomer knew the night sky.

He stared at a ladybug that was clambering into the glowing white cavity of a half-open *Physostegia* blossom, and thought of her skin, her throat. Her red hair, vivid against his pillows.

He'd never even told her he loved her. Didn't want to confuse things, complicate things.

It was raining. He'd hunkered on his haunches so long, his feet had fallen asleep. He staggered to a tree and leaned against it, waiting for the pins and needles to die down. Rain pattering on the pine needles reminded him of the first time he'd seen her. The way her shirt clung.

He picked up the bucket and slogged toward the house, with the vague notion of making coffee, maybe some lunch, though it was late for lunch. He hadn't eaten any breakfast. He'd have coffee. See if there was anything edible in the fridge. Didn't really care if there wasn't.

In his kitchen, he was as confused and slow as he had been in the field. Coffee. He unscrewed the pot, moving like an arthritic old man. Grabbed the half-and-half out of the fridge. The carton was empty.

He stared at it, wondering what he must have been thinking, putting an empty carton back into the fridge. So, he'd drink it black.

It took a long time to realize that the phone was ringing. Even longer to decide whether or not he cared enough to answer it. Whoever was calling was stubborn to the point of insanity. His brain kept count. Twenty-two rings, twenty-three, twenty-four.

Blessed silence. He'd just breathed a sigh of relief and slumped back down again when the fucking thing began to ring again. Jack jerked to his feet with a filthy epithet, and grabbed the thing off the wall. "Yeah! Who the hell is this?"

There was a nervous pause. "Uh, this is Rafael Siebling. Is Vivi there? Because I really need to—"

"No, she's not here, and she's not going to be in the future. Delete this number from your phone, and call her fucking cell."

He slammed the phone down, suppressing a twinge of guilt at having been needlessly rude. The guilt evaporated in an instant when the phone rang again. He snatched it up. "What?" he bellowed.

"I will overlook what an asshole you are because this is so important," Rafael said, his voice frigid. "I have to talk to Vivi, and I—"

"I told you! She's moved out! Call her cell!"

"I did, you cretin!" Rafael yelled back. "Her cell's not working! And I have to get in touch with her, like, now! It's a matter of life or death!"

Jack finally registered the fear in the man's voice. Life or death? A chill gripped him. "What's going on?" he asked.

"Well, since you're so monumentally uninterested in anything having to do with Vivi, I won't bore you with—"

"Cut the shit." Jack's voice slashed across the other man's nervous bitching. "Just tell me."

"It's a creepy coincidence." The other man's voice shook. "I went to an opening at Brian Wilder's gallery last night. The man is evil incarnate, but I thought it would be fun to do a little networking at Wilder's expense and let that nasty dickhead know that Vivi's happy and thriving, since he tried so hard to destroy her. But of course he didn't succeed, because she's a goddess with more talent in her pinkie than—"

"And the creepy coincidence?" Jack's guts twisted nastily.

"It's horrible." Rafael's voice rose in pitch. "The prick deserved it, if anyone ever could, but even so, it gives me the shudders that I was actually talking to him just hours before it happened, and he just—"

"What happened to him?" Jack bellowed.

"He . . . well, his assistant found him this morning. Impaled on the spikes of a big Waylan Winthrop bronze sculpture, like a hot dog on a stick. They say the sculpture was completely drenched with blood. Wilder's assistant is in the hospital, having a total breakdown."

Jack's body was electrified with fear. Thrumming with the excess voltage. "And Vivi won't answer her cell?"

"I've been calling for over an hour. As soon as I found out."

Jack ran it through his head. "Did you tell Wilder where Viv was?"

"I did mention that I saw her at a concert in Pebble River night before last," Rafael faltered. "And . . . but why should that . . ." His voice choked off for a moment. He gasped. "Oh, my God," he whispered. "Oh, my sweet God. What the fuck is going on?"

"Are you at home now?" Jack demanded.

"No, actually. I left this morning to meet a friend up in East Hampton. Why?"

"Don't go home," Jack said. "Under any circumstances."

"Oh, Jesus," Rafael moaned. "What have I done? What in holy hell is she mixed up in?"

"It's bad," Jack said. "But it's not her fault. And you're mixed up in it, too, so watch yourself. I have to go."

"But I . . . but no! Wait! Tell me what this is all—"

"I have to go find Viv. If they knew where she was late last night, they could be here by now. Or they could call someone in the area. Call this number." He rattled off Duncan's cell to the other man. "That's Viv's future brother-in-law. He knows everything. He'll tell you what to do. Do not go home. You got that straight?"

"Got it," Rafael echoed faintly.

"Good." Jack hung up on him and dialed Vivi's cell from his landline. The recording told him it was turned off or out of area.

The stench of burning rubber assailed his nose as he sprinted through the room. The coffee had all boiled away, and the heat had melted the rubber ring while he was on the phone.

He flipped off the gas, on the fly, and bolted toward his gun safe.

Vivi locked up her shop and headed toward her van. She'd finished painting the place, finally, and she was a rumpled, snarled, ivory-spattered mess. She caught sight of herself in the mirror as she started up the ignition, and winced. Yikes. Eyes red and puffy, face paper white, mouth blurry-looking. But who cared how she looked?

She pointed the van in the direction of Evergreen Acres. She'd asked around yesterday, and that was the one place she could afford that would accept her dog. It also bordered on a creek and had a little forested area nearby for Edna to run and catch sticks and do her doggie business. The downside was, it was a pathetic dump. It was clear that the creek had overflowed its bounds and flooded the rental units more than once. The number of discolored waterlines and the rotting carpet were her clues. And the overwhelming stench of mold, of course.

The cinder-block cube they'd assigned to her was the last in the row. Tiny and cramped, and it stank of cigarettes, damp, and, faintly, of urine. The ceiling was so splotchy, it looked like it would fall down right on top of her. The curtains were full of cigarette holes.

She pulled into the Acres, parked her van next to her wretched little abode, and stared at it, dispirited. Back to roughing it. Making do.

Well, then. Chin up. Feeling sorry for herself would not help. She'd learned that lesson so many times, in so many ways in her life, it still amazed her when the "poor-little-me's" took her by storm.

She let Edna out of the van, and they headed down to the creek, so Edna could stretch her legs. After that, she would clean up, change, organize her stuff, and get motivated for some tight-assed, one-dollar-a-day grocery shopping. Not that she had any appetite, but still. Starving herself would not help matters. She had to be a grown-up.

She flung the stick for Edna until her arm felt like it was about to fall off, and decided to stop procrastinating. She walked back to the cabin. Staring at the flimsy door with the knob lock that a credit card could swipe open in one pass. At the single-paned windows with the warped, swollen wood sills that she was not able to wrench closed.

She hadn't known how safe Jack's infrared alarm and his tough, stalwart presence at her side had made her feel until now. She'd been so relaxed, soft and open inside, for weeks. Now that it was taken away, she felt like a snail with no shell. With fear her constant backdrop.

She shoved the key into the lock. Edna stopped at the threshhold and shrank back, whining, but Vivi was trying so hard to be tough and grown up, and not cringe at the stinky little room, she didn't register the dog's gesture until she'd stepped in, flipped on the light—

And found the two men lurking in the dark on either side of the door. Their pistols pointed straight at her.

Jack drove by the highway interchange for the third time, scoping out the parking lots of the budget hotels clustered there, scanning for her van. Her shop was locked up, at four p.m. Usually, she stayed there working until dark or later.

He could hardly breathe, he was so fucking scared. And furious at himself. So wound up in his self-pitying bullshit, he'd lost sight of the danger. He should have known a guy like Rafael would spew Vivi's location to the four winds. He should have taken steps, been thinking clearly. About her. Not himself. Dick-brained *asshole*.

He pointed his truck back up the hill to Pebble River Heights, where the commercial district and Vivi's shop were located, hoping this was just a paranoid freak-out. But the image of Wilder spitted like a hot dog on a stick jangled his nerves. Could be the fuckhead had other enemies, of course. But an enemy like that was rare and special.

He jerked the truck to a stop in front of her store, deciding to make the rounds of all the shops. He got lucky on his eighth stop, at the Bakitchen lunch counter. Myra, the proprietor, gave him a smile.

"Hi, Jack. Coffee?"

"Not now. Quick question, Myra. Do you know where Vivi D'Onofrio is staying?"

"Thought she was staying with you, honey. Had a fight?"

Jack clenched his jaw. The older woman crossed her arms over her chest. "Well, she was in here yesterday morning," Myra conceded. "Asking about an inexpensive place that would let her keep her dog. The only thing I could think of off the top of my head was Evergreen Acres, but it's such a dive. It should be condemned. Hope she didn't go there."

He tensed. Evergreen Acres? He hadn't even checked there, it was so unthinkable to him that Vivi be in a place like that. The Acres was an end-of-the-line place, frequented by bums, drunks, addicts, down-and-outs, prostitutes and their clients. Visited often by police cars in the middle of the night. Jesus. Of all places.

"Love problems. That would explain why she looked like she was coming down with the flu," Myra said knowingly. "Come to think of it, you don't look so hot yourself. Hope you work it out."

He barely heard her words. "Later, Myra." He turned for the door.

"Nice girl, Vivi. Sweet little shop she's got. Sure is popular today. You're the second one come in asking for her in the last two hours."

He spun on his heels. "Who? Who was looking for her?"

Myra smiled, archly. "A man. Not surprising. She's a hottie. If you're not careful, some other guy's going to snatch her right up and—"

"What guy?!" he bellowed. "What does he look like?"

Myra looked affronted. "Do not yell at me, Jack Kendrick!"

His teeth ground. "Sorry. Please. It's important."

Myra grunted. "Well, he was no good-looker, I'll tell you that much," she said. "Big, heavy guy with squinchy little eyes. He said he'd heard she was opening a shop, and would I tell him where it was."

"And did you?"

"Of course I told him! She can't afford to lose any business. She's just starting out."

Panic swept up, threatening to engulf him. "Myra, do something for me." He struggled to control the shake in his voice. "Call the cops. Send them down to Evergreen Acres." He bolted out the door.

"But why?" Myra shouted after him. "What do I tell them?"

He leaped into the truck, started the engine. "Whatever the fuck you want!" he yelled back. "Just tell them quick!"

His truck surged forward with a roar. The urgency inside him was building so fast, he felt like his chest was going to explode.

Vivi felt strangely calm. Numb, even.

Finally, the other shoe had dropped. There was a sense of colossal inevitability to it all. Like continental drift, this moment had been coming her way all her life. All the anxious scrambling and scurrying in the world could not have stopped it.

"I was wondering when you two gentlemen were going to pay me a visit," she said. "I was starting to feel left out."

She was proud of how her voice did not shake. Not yet, at least.

Edna was growling, fangs bared, head down. What a strange spectacle. Vivi had never seen her bouncy retriever in defensive mode.

"Take the animal. Put it in the bathroom," said the old guy with the accent. Ulf Haupt, she presumed. Just as Nell had described him.

She hesitated, and the other, younger guy pointed his gun at Edna. "Now," he snarled. "Or I shoot it."

That broke Vivi's paralysis. She gripped Edna's collar and dragged the growling, barking dog toward the tiny bathroom in the corner.

She closed the door. Edna whined and pawed at the door.

"Come back to the center of the room," Haupt ordered.

Vivi did as she was told. "How did you find me?" she asked.

"With difficulty. But we prevailed at last." John gave her a wide, manic grin. "We found the shop through your old boyfriend, Wilder."

"Brian?" She was astonished. "But how did Brian—"

"Your friend, Siebling," John taunted. "He went to Wilder's gallery. Told him all about this big, randy stud who's been servicing you. That you were all pink and juicy, getting it left, right, and sideways ten times a day, huh? Filthy slut. Dirty little cocksucking whore—"

"Enough!" Haupt's voice was shrill. "Do not get distracted. Please excuse him, my dear. John is a bit single-minded when he gets worked up. I have to constantly remind him, work before play, no? Vivien, your cell phone is in your purse? Give it to John."

She picked up her purse from where it had fallen and passed it over. She'd turned the thing off the previous day, not wanting to deal with any calls from her sisters. She was too raw to face even them.

John cracked open the shell and ripped the various components apart. He dropped the pieces, and crushed them beneath his boot heel.

"Rafael?" she whispered. "You hurt Rafael?"

"We have someone on it," John told her. "We've hired an army for the endgame. Men are waiting in his condo. I can arrange for them to film the event. Popcorn, beer, arterial gouts, and detached body parts."

She fought a wave of faintness.

"Wilder's dead, too" he went on. "You should've seen him when I was through. A work of art, quite literally. I took pictures. Want to see?"

John held out the cell. She flinched away in revulsion.

"Focus, John," Haupt reminded him sternly. The old man stumped heavily over to her, his watery, pink-rimmed eyes shiny with mad cheerfulness. "I think she's my favorite of the sisters."

"Her tits are too small, but other than that, yeah." John licked his lips, his eyes hot. "I like the ones who spit and squirm."

"I am seldom tempted at my age," the shambling old horror whispered. He lifted the silenced barrel of his pistol, petted Vivi's cheek with it. "But you inspire me. Perhaps I will indulge, as well. In my own special way." He used the silencer to tug down the neckline of Vivi's shirt, revealing the tattoo. "How pretty," he commented. "A buttercup."

"No, actually." She cleared her throat. "It's *Eranthis hyemalis*."

The gun jabbed her breastbone. "Are you contradicting me?"

Fear was poking through the numbness, big-time. "Um, no."

He petted the flower tattoo with the gun. "I've heard you have tattoos. My father kept a collection of tattoos. He gathered them during the war. I inherited his secret album when he died. There must be fifteen, twenty. Papa did love his trophies, but he had so few people to share them with. People are squeamish, you see. But not me. I treasure it." He chuckled. "Perhaps I'll follow Papa's example. Take your tattoos for mementos. I can start my own album. Never too late, hmm?"

Vivi was shuddering violently. "What do you want from me?"

Haupt sighed. "The usual, my dear. For you to tell me something I don't know about the Conte deLuca's hidden treasure."

Vivi bit her lip, squeezed her eyes shut. "Oh, shit," she whispered.

"I understand. You're as ignorant as your sisters. But the Contessa's letter suggests that the three of you together have a chance.

If Lucia deLuca was convinced of this, then I continue to be optimistic."

"You'll never get my sisters," she said, with quiet conviction.

"No? I'm already planning the hits on your inconvenient future brothers-in-law. As soon as they're out of the way, we'll have no problem with your sisters. Particularly after we send them the DVD of John having his naughty fun with you. That will flush them out." He leaned closer, so she could not avoid his sour smell, and pushed her chin up with the gun. He twisted his hand around her pendant until the chain snapped, and stared at it intently. "Just like the other two. Worthless bauble."

He opened a briefcase and flung it inside. Vivi saw the gleam of gold, a snarl of chains. Nell's and Nancy's necklaces were there, too.

Haupt jerked her chin back up. "Last chance, Vivien. Do you wish to spare yourself pain and disfigurement? We can be reasonable."

"Of course," she choked out.

"So tell me something interesting. Make our lives easier." His tone was coaxing, as if she were being tiresome, refusing to cooperate.

Tears of frustration leaked from her eyes. "I don't know anything," she said bleakly. "Believe me. I would tell you if I did."

Haupt let out a sharp, annoyed sigh. "Well, John, your dream has come true. We have to play out the whole noisy drama here and now. Set up the video. Aim it at the bed. You brought in the tripod?"

John set up the scene as Haupt held the gun and barked orders. The barrel was against her jugular. She felt the quick throb of her heart against the pressure of the metal. Beating stubbornly on. For a little longer, at least.

"How will you get all of us together if you kill me?" she asked.

"We won't kill you. Not yet. John promised he will be careful. He's a specialist, you see. He can inflict excruciating pain without causing mortal injury, particularly if the subject is healthy and strong willed. As I can see that you are." He chortled, and chucked her under the chin with the gun. "You may not be that pretty by the time your sisters join you, but never fear. You'll be able to contribute to the brainstorming."

"Another thing," John said, fiddling with the camera. "This guy you're fucking. I don't want surprises. Who is he? And where is he?"

Vivi swallowed hard. "He's no one. And nowhere."

John applauded, slowly and sarcastically. "Brave words. But we'll get it out of you. Or Siebling. Whoever cracks first."

"John, go do a final check," Haupt directed. "We were going to take you to a different location, but this atmospheric place is even better for our purposes. I doubt the inhabitants of this establishment will call the police even if they do hear you screaming. Chances are, they've got problems of their own." He stroked her hair. "Amazing color. Perhaps I'll keep the hair, too. . . ." He shook himself out of his reverie. "Well, then," he said briskly. "Let's get on with it. John, tie her."

Chapter
11

Jack's heart beat like a jackhammer when he saw the van parked at the end of the Evergreen Acres complex. He killed the engine and let the truck roll silently down the downward grade toward the parking lot. A black SUV with tinted windows was parked a few units up from the battered van. Shiny and new. Glaringly out of place.

He pulled up the emergency brake, wondered for a split second if it would be smarter to wait for reinforcements or just dive in.

Hah. A no-brainer. Waiting was not an option. His mind would snap under the strain. He left the door open and slunk along the row of dingy, scarred doors in the long, white-painted cinder-block complex.

He came to the last window. Edna was barking shrilly and desperately inside. He heard men talking. A man laughed, nastily. There was a smack, a feminine cry of pain, bravely choked off. *Vivi.*

He had years of experience, of training. He knew better than to let rage control him, but the force that moved him was like demonic possession. He whipped up his H&K, squeezed off a shot through the window toward the ceiling. Shattering glass, shouts, frantic yelling. He flung himself at the door, took the fucker off its hinges. He swung the gun around wildly as his eyes adjusted to the dim interior.

The *thunk* of a silenced pistol, and a bullet rustled his hair, punching into the cement blocks. Dust and debris flew. He returned fire. The bearded hulk of a guy dove behind the bed, where Vivi lay hogtied, twisted into a knot on her side. Her eyes on him, wide and terrified. The muzzle of the silenced gun rested on her ribs.

The guy peeked up over her body. The gun spat. Jack dropped, noticing with eerie clarity how the carpet was crumbling into stinking chunks. He peered beneath the bed. Squeezed off a shot from below.

A squeal, like a stuck pig. A hit. *Yes.* Jack scrambled to his knees, waiting for the big scowling guy to peep up over Vivi's body. The guy crawled out, clutching his bloody right arm, howling something unintelligible. He took aim from the floor. Bullets sang by Jack's shoulder, punched into the easy chair. Stuffing flew. One slammed into a plasterboard armoire, splintering it.

Jack pitched into a forward roll, leaped to his feet, and whipped his leg up, knocking the gun out of the man's hands. It hit the wall, fell to the floor. His own gun swung up, took aim—

"One more move, and her head explodes," a cracked voice rasped.

Jack's head jerked around. A hideous gnome clutched Vivi's trussed body against his. His pistol was shoved under her chin. Her breath hitched. Her bright eyes were fixed on Jack's. They were wide and desperate.

The old goblin giggled shrilly. "Drop the gun. Or I'll kill her."

Jack doubted that was true. Whatever their kinky plans were, they involved live D'Onofrio women, not dead ones. But he could be wrong. And his whole universe hung on that yes-or-no question.

He would far rather die than get it wrong.

The old guy edged along the wall, dragging Vivi's slight body for a shield. "Drop the gun!" he shrilled. "I will kill her!" He jabbed the barrel against Vivi's soft, white throat. She made a desperate, choking sound.

Jack's hands opened. The H&K dropped to the floor.

"Cut her hands and feet free," the old guy ordered curtly.

The younger man gave him a stupid, confused look. "Huh?"

"She must drive the van, you moron!" the old man shrieked.

Jack watched, paralyzed as the man sliced the ropes near Vivi's wrists. She winced. He slashed between her ankles.

"Kick the gun to me," the young guy growled.

In the seconds that followed, every detail was printed and burned into Jack's memory. He stared into Vivi's eyes, tried to scream through the silent realms of eternity that he loved her. Hoping she'd hear.

And suddenly, she wrenched out of the old guy's grip and head-butted the bastard.

The old man screamed, stumbled back. The big guy swung a savage backhand blow that knocked her sprawling. The old man squeezed off a shot at him, then another. Both went wild. The guy didn't have the strength to aim the thing accurately. But he didn't need to, to kill Vivi. Not at that range.

Jack was in motion, kicking his gun to the corner. His boot whipped up to crack into the big guy's jaw. The old man scooped the dazed Vivi up, arms locked under her armpits, gun shoved in the hollow of her cheek. "Deal with him!" he yelled. "Meet at the rendezvous point!"

The big guy lunged with a knife. Part of Jack's brain dealt with weaving and dancing to avoid the blade, while the old man herded the stumbling Vivi to the passenger's side of the van, bullied her into the driver's side, and climbed in behind, jabbing the gun into her ear. He could hear the man's shrill, scolding voice from in here.

The van's engine roared, the lights flicked on. It squealed backward, and accelerated out of his line of vision. Gone. Nothing to concentrate on except not getting cut. And keeping that berserker son of a bitch too busy to get near the guns on the floor. He arched back to let a huge boot whoosh through the space where his face would have been, then spun to the side to avoid a knee to the gut. He took an uppercut to the nose that sent him spinning into a rib-crunching whack against the cement-block wall.

Pain and lost breath cost him a precious fraction of a second. The blade whipped down. Jack jerked to the side. The tip hit cement, bounced, skittered, stung the top of his shoulder. His knee jabbed up into the guy's balls. The man lurched back, bellowing.

They circled each other, breath rasping. The other man lunged, and Jack saw the movement broken down to infinite increments. Parry with his forearm, spin until he was side to side, seize the knife hand between scissored wrists, torque until the guy screamed, doubling over. The knife clattered to the ground. Jack applied more pressure, whipped a vicious side kick into the side of the knee, guided the top of his head toward the wall—and swung him, hard, like a battering ram.

His opponent thudded to the ground, the crown of his head wet with blood. A red, bloody smear on the wall. Jack stared down, breath jerking in and out, every limb trembling. Trying to think. Hard, with combat hormones flooding his system. Sirens wailed, far away. Myra had called the cops. Good, but he could not stay to talk to them. Every second that passed widened the space between himself and Vivi. He touched the big guy's carotid artery. Alive. He was tempted to kill him, just to have one more player off the board. But he would have to change into a different person to kill an unconscious man.

He didn't want to be that person. He couldn't bring himself to do it.

Let the cops take care of him. He scooped up the guns and leaped over the bulk of the fallen man to jerk open the bathroom door.

Edna leaped into his arms, shaking and whining. Jack ran for the truck, tossed the dog through the door. He burned rubber, turning out of the lot just as sirens approached from the opposite direction.

He jerked the wheel around, fishtailing to a shuddering stop at Dwayne Pritchett's gas station, at Pebble River's exit from the highway.

Dwayne jogged forward, his big, ruddy face alarmed. "Jesus, what the fuck? Were you in a car accident?"

Jack realized abruptly that his nose was streaming blood, all the way down over his chin. His shoulder was wet with blood as well, from the knife wound. "I'm fine," he said tersely. "Did you see Vivi's van?"

"Yeah, I seen it come by here. Going hell for leather. Didn't stop at the sign. Took the turn on two wheels. Big fuckin' hurry. Did Vivi do that damage to you? Jesus, she must have been pissed as hell. Wadja do to her, for Chrissakes? You want to come in and clean up that—"

"Which way did she go?" Jack roared.

Dwayne nodded toward the northbound road. "Thataway."

Jack gathered up the shivering golden dog, pushed his door open, and shoved the animal into Dwayne's arms. "Vivi's dog. Look after her."

"But . . . but I . . . but you—"

"Later!" The truck leaped forward, squealing toward the exit.

"Faster!" Haupt shrieked. "Drive faster, you stupid bitch!"

Vivi pushed down on the accelerator. Not much point telling the guy that her decrepit van was already making a valiant effort, and didn't have any more speed in her. The frame of the vehicle shuddered scarily, as it was. Or maybe the shuddering came from inside her own self.

They were on the northbound Kaneset Highway, which looped alongside the steep-banked, meandering Kaneset River. Haupt rolled down his window, stuck his empurpled face out to drag in air.

She was in conflict. A quick, fiery death after a few seconds of falling through midair was a far better death than the one Haupt had described for her. But what about Jack? He'd come back for her.

In back of the panic and terror was a thread of music in her head, sweet and poignant. She hung on to it, and with it, to her sanity.

He'd come for her. How had he found her? How had he known? It made the prospect of driving off a cliff oh, so much harder to accept.

She tried to concentrate on high-speed driving. No future, no past. Just this breath, into her lungs. Just this heartbeat, then the next, and she was grateful for every one of them, even with a gun to her head. She hoped he was okay. *Please.* He'd come back for her.

"What are you smiling at, you insolent slut?" Haupt shrilled. "Are you laughing at me?" He jabbed the gun into her ear.

The van lurched and wove. "No! I wasn't, I wasn't!"

She reached down with her left hand to touch the tire iron. The road ahead did a hairpin and started to gain altitude. Farther on, the road was high over the canyon. Any further attempt to drive off the road once she drove higher would result in certain death. This turn coming up was her last chance at a slightly more favorable compromise with certain death. Right . . . *now.*

She widened the turn, wrenched the wheel, and braked, violently. Haupt lurched forward, holding out his arms to brace himself. Vivi whipped the tire iron down over his forearms. *Crack.*

He screamed. The gun dropped. She spun the tires in the gravel, accelerating, gaining the crest . . . tipping over the top. They were sliding and bouncing down the other side, tipping crazily, and Haupt screamed, scrambling for the gun, but the van bounced wildly in every direction as it rattled down the steep slope of rock and shale—

It hit a large rock at the river's edge, knocking them forward. The van teetered, tipped, hung on two wheels for what felt like eternity. . . .

And flopped onto its side into the river, Haupt's side down. She slid down on top of him. Icy water flooded from the open window into the van. They were a screaming, struggling knot, fighting, clawing. She couldn't let him find that gun. His strangling grip was like the gigantic kraken of the abyss. The water bubbled in, swirling, getting higher.

She struggled up, yanking the steering wheel, trying to trample him down beneath her feet. The van was tipping, moving. If water covered the top of her side, she'd never get the door open. She shoved the door above her, expecting a bullet to punch into her at any second from below.

Haupt still struggled, but his head was below the water level. The water was up to her chest now, gurgling and swirling.

Haupt seized her ankle and chomped. She screamed, struggled. He looked up from beneath the water, a blaze of mad hatred in his eyes. Bubbles rose from his mouth. The water gurgled higher.

She thought about the tattoos he was going to keep for his album. Her hair, which he wanted for a trophy. She put her feet on his shoulders, holding him down as she shoved herself up, and pushed the van door completely open. The van was moving with the current. She saw Haupt's briefcase, bobbing on the surface next to the steering wheel, and grabbed for it. His hand still clung to it.

She yanked. He gave her one last hateful look before his eyes went blank. He was dead, floating in the water.

Vivi clambered out and pitched herself into the river, shocked by the violence of the current. It tossed her like a twig. She couldn't swim in any direction. All she could do was try to stay afloat as she zipped along, fighting her way toward the rocky shore. She almost let the briefcase go, but they had suffered so much for those necklaces. She stuck the handle in her chattering teeth and struggled vainly with the current.

The van floated behind her for a while, until the last air bubble inside disgorged itself. A half mile or so later, she managed to grab on to a rock at the edge of the water. She crawled onto it, shaking so hard, she could barely make her muscles function. She spat out the case. Her jaw ached with effort. Her teeth were going to fall out for the clacking.

She clung there, like a wet rag. Just trying to breathe.

Jack jerked to a stop at the skid marks, his heart thudding. He leaped out, staring at the trough the vehicle had made as it slid down into the water. His guts were a knot. His mind rejected the most probable outcome, but the rest of his being shook with fear.

He vaulted over the gravel slope of the road's shoulder and slid in the loose shale to the water's edge. He followed the current, hopping rocks, clambering on boulders, slogging through water. He had to swim through cliff-lined channels, prying himself out of the current's grip just before he got sucked into rapids. He finally spotted her, across the river. Spread out on a rock as if she'd washed up on it. Facedown, wet hair spread around her. He screamed her name, over and over. She did not move.

He dove back in, fighting the water. Got across, God alone knew how. He crawled up. Rolled her over gently, with shaking hands.

Her eyes opened, looked into his. He was so relieved, he burst into tears, and dropped his face against her chest. Her skin was ice cold.

She was alive. His soul shook.

It took them a long, staggering time to get back to his truck. He would have carried her if he could, but they couldn't go back the way he'd come, not with those channels, those sheer cliffs. He couldn't dump her into that current again, and the only alternative was to climb straight up, to the road far above them. They had to scramble and claw their way up slippery rock faces, and Vivi could barely keep upright.

Jack's relief at finding her alive was undercut by growing fear. Her face was so white, her eyes so shadowed. She couldn't stop shaking, kept falling down. She could hardly speak. When they finally crawled onto the asphalt of the highway, he picked her up.

She protested, weakly, but her voice was slurred.

He sped to town, squealed to a stop outside the emergency room at the hospital. They caused a big stir, and things moved with gratifying speed as the EMT techs got Vivi squared away. He was annoyed, afterward, to find some of the EMT techs wanted to fuss over him, too. Fucking waste of time. He'd prefer if they left him alone and concentrated on Vivi.

He begged a cell phone off one of the EMT techs, and called a guy he knew in the local cop shop. "Hey, Tim? It's Jack Kendrick."

"Holy shit, man!" Tim exploded. "Where the hell are you?"

"Later for that. That son of a bitch who was lying in Unit 42 of Evergreen Acres. Do you guys have him in custody?"

Tim hesitated. "Uh . . . are you okay, Jack?"

"I'm fine. What about the guy in Unit 42? He's a serial killer."

"There was no guy in Unit 42," Tim said. "Just a trashed room, blood on the floor, and a bunch of bullet holes. Whatever happened in there, we missed it. Would have been really helpful if you'd been around to clue us into the serial killer thing, because he didn't hang around, either. And the chief was unthrilled with you for fucking off before you could give a statement. What were you thinking?"

Jack blew out a long shuddering sigh, feeling the cold sink more deeply into his bones. "You have no idea," he muttered.

He hung up, passed the phone back, and ripped the IV needle out of his arm, ignoring the shouts and scolding lectures. He grabbed a chair and situated it outside the curtained cubicle where Vivi lay, a vantage point that gave him a clear view of both ends of the corridor plus the lobby entrance. Almost hoping the guy would make a move.

So he could fucking finish this, already.

Vivi drifted in and out of consciousness on the drive into Portland. She shifted in the seat, keeping her eyes closed. She didn't have the nerve to talk to Jack and ask him how he felt. What it all meant. If he had changed his mind about the two of them, or if he was just being righteous and heroic. A guy's gotta do what a guy's gotta do, yada yada and all that. His grim, taut face discouraged confidences.

He'd bullied the hospital into letting her leave after only twenty-four hours, and there had been a big kerfuffle. Lots of shouting about security and danger and attackers. The angry doctors made her sign a waiver accepting responsibility, which she'd been glad to do, though her fingers barely felt the pen, as she floated in a Demerol cloud. Even stoned out of her mind, she knew which side her bread was buttered on. When it came to the Fiend, EMT techs and nurses weren't enough protection, not by a long shot. Jack Kendrick was the man. Hands down. She'd stick with him.

Margaret had come by that morning, bringing Jack some clothes, and one of her own warm-up suits for Vivi. Eggshell blue, spattered with yellow daisies. Wow. Very special. But still, she was grateful.

"I'm flying to New York," she announced, bracing herself.

"That's the last place you should go!" Jack exploded. "John told you he'd hired an army. We've warned your sisters and their men. Do you want to face an army? Those guys weren't enough of a challenge?"

"It's not that," she said. "I can't live like this. I have to resolve this thing. No matter what. You do what you want. I'm flying to New York."

Jack muttered something foul under his breath.

The earliest flight they could find with seats available left the following morning. Too long to wait, but no choice. They checked into an airport Ramada. When they were locked in their room, Jack laid his pistol on the kitchenette counter. "I'm taking a shower," he announced. "I'm still cold, from that river. You all right out here?" He waited for her nod, his eyes still doubtful. "Don't open the door to anyone," he added.

As if. She rolled her eyes. He disappeared into the bathroom.

She felt like a puppet with the strings cut. Limp, now that she didn't have his hot, vital energy to struggle against. She curled up on the bed and thought it through.

She had to be realistic. She had nothing to offer Jack except a crushing burden of danger, financial drain, and constant, grinding stress. He'd already risked his life. Dodging bullets and knives, diving into wild water. A man couldn't marry a risk like that. Or have children with her. She'd be stupid to demand promises from him now.

This, however, did not mean she was going to deny herself the comfort of his body. Life was short and uncertain.

She listened at the bathroom door to the shower hiss. She caught a glimpse of herself, in the prim, daisy-spattered warm-up suit, and sputtered with laughter. Whoo-hoo. Seductive. She stripped it off, and waited for the shower to stop, shivering in the air-conditioned chill.

When she opened the door, his startled face made her smile, cat-like. She laid the gun on the counter by the bathroom sink. The room was a fragrant fog of steam. The bruises on his face were taking form.

Maybe she was presuming too much. Maybe he was too stressed, too injured and exhausted—or, um . . . maybe not. His cock was pointing straight at her, in seconds flat. "What's this, Viv?" he asked.

She touched the dripping, gleaming contours of his body. "Just living in the moment."

He flinched. "Don't throw that in my face. We need to talk."

"No, we don't," she said quietly. "No past. No future. Just now."

He looked worried. "How long do we have to play this game?"

"How long is irrelevant, when you're in the moment," she said. "Only now exists. You should know that. Aren't you the expert?"

He stared at her. "You're a real hard-ass, Viv D'Onofrio."

"I've had tough teachers." She gazed into his face, and relented. "Look, if I ever have a normal life again, with no axe hanging over me, and you still want to have a conversation about our future, we can have it. Until then . . ." She reached out, stroked his cock.

"Until then, you just want to fuck me?"

Her mouth twitched at his sulky tone. She sank gracefully to her knees. "I ask it . . . respectfully," she purred, trying not to smile.

He vibrated with laughter and pleasure as she swirled her tongue around his cockhead. "Oh, God. I've never gotten respect like this."

"It's about time," she murmured, then sucked him into her mouth.

With difficulty. He was so thick and broad and hard, but she was inventive, and hungry for his every shudder and gasping sigh. She used her hands, her tongue, and, bit by bit, pulled him deeper into her throat, long suckling strokes that made him quiver and groan.

She kept him trembling on the brink until the ache of her own yearning grew too sharp to bear, and then rose and turned to face the mirror. She parted her legs, arching her ass so he could see everything. How gleaming wet and eager she was for him. "Take me," she said.

He seized her hips. "I don't have condoms."

"I know. Of course you don't. You've been busy saving my life."

He looked worried. "But if you want to . . . Viv, this is exactly the kind of thing we need to talk about. I think we should—"

"No talk," she said. "Give it to me. Now. Before I start screaming."

He eased his penis past the initial resistance, sliding it around in her lube, and drove deep. She clutched the counter, staring at her own flushed face, whimpering at each slick, slamming stroke. They held each other's gaze in the mirror as if the fate of the universe depended on it. He reached around and toyed with her clit, building her up to a wrenching climax. When she had the strength to prop herself up, he was still waiting for his own release, his face tight with self-control.

"I want to come inside you," he said.

She thought about it for about half a second, and nodded.

His eyes widened. "You're sure? You're okay with that?"

"I want it all," she blurted. "Everything you have to give me."

His eyes flashed, and he gave it to her. One last shove, and he exploded. She hung over the counter, limp and soft. Light as air, soft as a cloud. One thought floating all alone in her mind, in a perfect bubble.

Of how much she would love to make a child with him.

Jack set the shower running again, and washed her tenderly, with great, sensual thoroughness. That interlude ended as one might have expected, with herself pinned against the wet tile wall, her legs draped over his elbows, sobbing with delight as he nailed her, deep and hard.

Not a thought about bad moments in her past. Not a thread of panic, of nausea. No "danger keep out" signs. Her old phantoms were gone. They could not withstand the bright light of Jack Kendrick.

Afterward, glowing and relaxed, Vivi sat naked on the bed and stared at the necklaces she'd retrieved from Ulf Haupt's briefcase. She laid them out on the bed, fiddling with them. Staring at the white gold lacework that decorated the top of each pendant.

Something about them tickled her mind. The lacework was different on each pendant. On her own, there were open spaces in the swirling coils of gold. On Nell's, the lacework was flat, and protruding on each side. Nancy's was more like her own, but with the protrusions extending toward the opposite side. A strange choice, for Lucia, whose taste in jewelry had run toward the classic. That asymmetrical, random element. More like something she herself would do. Angular, quirky.

In fact, it reminded her of a sculpture she'd done back in art school, one of the pieces that had been mangled in the Fiend's second break-in. Three female figures, made of motley chunks of glass, pebbles, and bits of plastic, all wired together. But their stylized hair swirled out like halos, hooking and tangling together. Linking the three figures.

She had entitled it *The Three Sisters*. Lucia had loved it. Had displayed it proudly, right next to her priceless bronze Cellini satyr.

Vivi placed the pendants side by side. Nancy, Nell, Vivi. She felt a strange, dreamlike feeling as she slipped the lacework of Nell's pendant into the open space in Nancy's. A push, and *click*, the openwork linked together. Seamless swirls of gold. Her heart pounded.

"Jack," she whispered, her voice shaking. "Come look at this."

He looked. His eyes widened. "The other one? Does it fit, too?"

"Let's see." She slid the protruding part of Nell's pendant into the openwork of her own. *Click.* The pieces were all united.

Jack held out his hand, and she passed the thing to him. He manipulated it, putting pressure on every point. One of the protruding bits on Vivi's pendant moved. At first she choked off a cry, thinking he'd broken it, but then she saw that it was a lever, moving smoothly down—

Click, once again, and something snapped out of the bottom of the three pendants. Three fine, shining sheets of white gold, flush to each other, as narrow and sharp as a razor blade. They leaned closer.

Something was written on them, in letters so small, she could not make them out. Jack dug into his pockets and pulled out a pocketknife with a multitude of attachments, one of which was a small magnifying glass. He held the thing up under the lamp and peered through it.

"*Salve Regina Mater Misericordiae,*" he read slowly. He turned it over and studied the back. "*Primus Modus Doricus.*" He looked up at her. "Latin, right? Can you make anything out of that?"

She shook her head. "No, but Nell could! She knows Latin!" She pressed her hand to her mouth. It was too soon for tears of joy, but finally, a window had opened up. A ray of light, at last. "This was the part that I was supposed to figure out," she said, with conviction.

Jack raised his eyebrows. "How's that?"

"In the draft of the letter we found, Lucia said it was our love of art, music, and literature that would solve the puzzle. I don't know the first thing about music or literature." Vivi thought about *The Three Sisters*, and tears sprang to her eyes. "But this part was just for me."

It felt almost as if Lucia had sent her a message. A wave of love, faith, and encouragement to her youngest adopted daughter.

"Oh, God. I'm losing it," she whispered. "I miss her so much."

"Go ahead," Jack said quietly. "You're entitled."

He stroked her hair while she hid her face in her hands. She raised her face after a moment. "I want to call my sisters," she blurted.

"It's three a.m., New York time," he said gently. "We'll be there tomorrow. We've waited this long. Can't you wait a few hours more?"

"Okay," she said, sniffling. "I guess."

Jack laid the united necklaces on the bedside table next to the gun, and slid between the sheets. He held the covers up. "Does being a hard-ass broad permit cuddling in bed?" he asked, warily.

"Duh," she said, sliding between the sheets and into the hot, lovely rush of his tight embrace. "I may be a hard-ass, but I'm not an idiot."

She let his warmth relax her for a few moments, and then stirred, to look into his face. "Thank you for coming back to save me," she said.

He gazed back. "Thank you for still being alive," he replied.

Tears prickled in her eyes, but if she gave in to them again, they might drown her.

Chapter
12

Duncan and Vivi's sister Nell met them at the airport. Nell was horrified when she saw the battered-looking, hollow-eyed Vivi and insisted on sitting in the back with her little sister and holding her hand while Jack and Duncan debriefed.

At one point, Jack looked back and found Nell's eyes sparkling at him. "So what does the Latin phrase mean, anyhow?" he asked hastily.

"Hail queen, mother of mercy, first Doric mode," Nell told him.

"Does that mean anything to you?"

Nell shook her head regretfully. "Not anything particular, no. It's just a common phrase from the Catholic liturgy."

They headed to Nancy and Liam's place, and Jack bucked up his depleted social energy to meet two new people. Fortunately, they seemed mellow and sensible. Liam was intelligent and canny, the older sister, Nancy, likewise. Besides being just as easy on the eyes as her two sisters. He felt at ease with both of them immediately.

Liam had prepared a juicy, appetizing pot roast with a mountain of gleaming potatoes and vegetables, and Jack dug into it gratefully. Afterward, they gathered in Liam's workshop, around an unfinished dining room table, upon which he had set the safe.

"So?" Nancy asked briskly. "Do we try just keying in the letters of the phrase? In Latin, or in English?"

"Try them both," Vivi said.

"You're sure it won't explode in our faces if we get it wrong?" Duncan asked nervously.

"Only if we try to crack the safe," Nancy reassured him.

Duncan looked far from reassured, but Nancy just got to it, frowning down at the keypad as she keyed in the long sequence.

The little button flashed red. The door remained locked.

"In English, then," Nancy said, undaunted. She keyed in the new sequence. The light flashed red again. "Nope."

They stared at the safe, discouraged. Nancy held up the linked pendants. "Hail queen, mother of mercy," she repeated softly. "I've seen this translation. First Doric mode is a musical term. This was sung, not . . . oh. Oh, my God. *Yes.*"

"What?" they all cried out, in ragged chorus.

"Just a minute. Let me get something." Nancy leaped to her feet and scurried out. She came back moments later, a CD in her hand.

"Novum Gaudium!" she said. "The Gregorian chant choir that I represent! I took Lucia up to see their concert last Christmas, at the Cloisters Museum concert series. She loved it! She even bought the disc." Nancy pried out the liner notes. "Let me see . . . it's a Marian antiphon. The phrase 'hail queen, mother of mercy' is the incipit. This is in Doric mode. I wonder if she meant for us to . . . but how?"

Jack spoke up, his voice hesitant. "I don't know about music," he said. "But could the tune have some sort of numeric correspondence?"

Nancy's eyes lit up. "Sure it could. In relation to the Doric mode, you bet it could. Liam, give me that CD player on the workbench."

The tall, laconic carpenter unfolded himself, grabbed the player, and plugged it into the wall socket near the table. She selected the track. A haunting tune began. Men's voices, deep and reverberant, in perfect unison. The sounds rose and fell in ancient patterns that sounded somehow familiar. Nancy listened to a fragment of the piece, brow furrowed. She hit "stop" after a few moments, and let it play again. And again. And again, scribbling numbers after each time.

Around the eighth time, she held up a scrap of paper with a long sequence of numbers. "Twenty-five digits," she announced.

"Try it," Vivi urged.

Nancy keyed it in. They held their breath. The light flashed red. Nancy sagged. "Hell," she said, dispirited. "I'm all out of ideas."

"Try adding PDM for *Primus Modus Doricus*," Duncan suggested.

Nancy shrugged, and punched in the numbers again. "Okay, guys. Here goes nothing. P . . . M . . . D," she concluded out loud.

The light flashed green. The door of the safe popped open.

Nobody could quite believe it. They stared at the thing, almost afraid of the thin seam of dark behind the crack of its opened door.

Liam touched the door with his finger, and swung it wide. There was only one thing inside. A piece of yellowed paper, in a plastic sleeve. Thin, limp, covered with cramped script. Nancy took it out.

"It's in Latin," she said. She passed it to Nell.

Nell put on her glasses and peered at the thing. "This must be Marco's treasure map," she said quietly. "A bunch of what look like flower names. Instructions that say to move from this flower to this flower, et cetera, et cetera. At the end, it says to go down into the ground four hand spans and turn three times counterclockwise. No wonder Marco thought the treasure was in the palace gardens. The gardener at the Palazzo de Luca said that they had to dig up the garden more times than he could remember."

She sighed, and laid it down. "Well, phooey. We've exchanged one puzzle for another. And I, for one, am burnt out on puzzles."

Liam got up. "I'll go get dessert," he said, sounding resigned.

Vivi got up to stretch her legs and wandered around Liam's workshop, touching various items with her fingertip. She turned to Jack.

"This is all Lucia's stuff," she told him. "Things that Liam and Nancy were able to salvage from when John trashed her house." She fingered a mangled thing made of glass, pebbles, plastic, and bent wire. "This is one of mine. *The Three Sisters*. I think Lucia meant for me to think of it, so it would occur to me to put the pendants together." She petted the twisted knot of materials and wire. "I'm going to restore this. In memory of her."

"Excellent idea. Liam's doing that with Lucia's *intaglio* table, too," Nell said. She laid her hand against the plane of a beautiful carved oak table that lay on the workbench. It was cloven in two splintered pieces.

"This is the famous table Duncan told me about?" Jack asked Vivi. "The one from the Renaissance that had the hidden drawer?"

"Yeah." Vivi traced some brutal scratches on the surface with her fingertip. "These marks were carved on it by the SS men, during the Nazi Occupation. Colonel Haupt's men."

Jack leaned down to take a closer look. "Amazing detail. I can tell in a glance what all these plants are. Common wildflowers, and whoever carved these spent hours looking at them. Look. *Centaurea scabiosa*. Here's *Achillea millefolium*, and *Linaria vulgaris*, and *Senecio jacobea*—"

"What did you say?" Nell demanded.

Jack looked at her, embarrassed. "Oh, yeah. Sorry. I meant, knapweed, yarrow, toadflax, and ragwort. And this one here is—"

"No, not that! Repeat what you said in Latin!"

"Oh." He was taken aback by the sharp, almost frightened look on her face. "Ah, let's see." He glanced down at the table for reference. "I just said *Centaurea scabiosa, Senecio jacobea*—"

"They're in it! They're in Marco's map!" She turned toward the door. "Duncan! Liam, Nancy! Get in here!" She collected the map in its plastic sleeve. Liam, Duncan, Nancy, and Vivi gathered around the splintered table, wide-eyed and breathlessly silent, to watch.

"The first one on the map is *Senecio jacobea*," she said. "Ragwort, did you say?" She waited for his nod. "It says to go from there to the nearest *Knautia arvensis*. Do you see that?"

Jack studied the table, and pointed. "Right here," he said. "That's scabious, in English. There are others, but this is the closest one."

"Okay. *Achillea millefolium*, then," Nell said.

Jack's finger moved down a few inches. "Yarrow."

A breathless tension was building. Jack was almost starting to feel scared by it himself.

"Do you see anything named *Anagallis arvensis*?" Nell asked.

"Scarlet pimpernel," he said, scanning the table. "Right here."

"And *Trifolium repens*?"

"Clover," he said. "Here it is. Down at the corner."

Nell frowned. "And this is where it says to turn to the earth, and go down four hand spans."

Jack looked at her. "Go down the table leg," he said simply.

Vivi looked at him, wide-eyed, and leaned over to give him a kiss on the jaw. "How'd you get to be so smart?" she teased.

"See if I'm right, first," he said dryly. "Then reward me."

"Count on it," she murmured.

Vivi's sisters exchanged winks and nudges at that interchange, but Liam was already at work examining the carved table legs that lay on another work surface. "I labeled them when I removed them," he said. "Relative to the direction that the flowers are growing, this one is the front left leg. Right under that clover." He laid it gently on the table.

Nell leaned over it. "Four hand spans," she said. "Let's assume they're a man's hands. Liam, measure four, please."

He did so, and his hand finished up right next to a carved knob adorned with a relief of climbing vines and morning glory flowers.

Liam looked up at Jack. "I'll hold it steady," he said. "Three full turns, counterclockwise. Want to do the honors?"

Jack seized the smooth knob, felt the texture of the morning glory vines beneath his hand, and applied pressure. It did not budge.

He tried again. Still nothing. "I'm afraid of damaging it," he said.

"It's been sixty-five years," Vivi said. "It's bound to be stiff."

He applied pressure, and felt a crack, a squeak. The leg began to turn. One time, two, three. Fragments scattered, but it came free.

The bottom part in his hand was hollow. Threads had been carved into it, caked with ancient, blackened wax. He tilted it, and a cylinder of parchment dropped out of the hollow. Ancient paper, yellow and brown at the corners. He held it gingerly in his hand, and passed it to Vivi.

"Here," he muttered. "I'm afraid to hold the thing."

"All this time," Nancy whispered. "Right here. In Lucia's table."

Vivi accepted it and laid it on the table, gently loosening the roll. The pieces of paper were not large, but very brittle, threatening to crack. Vivi widened the flat space, pressing them against the table as she unrolled them. She stared for a long moment. When she lifted her face, her eyes were huge. "Oh, you guys," she said. "This is . . . I think that this might actually be . . . oh, God, this is scary. I'm getting dizzy."

"What?" Jack snapped. "Out with it, goddammit!"

"The big *L*," Vivi said, staring first at Nell and then at Nancy. "Just look. At this sketch, of the angel. Look at that face. And look at this, the writing below it. That script. Backward."

Nell and Nancy gasped. "No way," Nancy whispered.

"I can't believe it." Nell's voice choked off into a squeak.

"Who the fuck is the big *L*?" Jack roared, maddened.

Nell turned to him. "*L* as in Leonardo. As in, da Vinci."

"Oh." Jack closed his mouth abruptly.

There was a moment of dead silence. "I need a drink," Liam said, turning toward the door.

"Bring the bottle back with you," Duncan called after him.

A few restorative swallows of fine single-malt Scotch took the edge off their collective freak-out, and a half hour later they were all sprawled on the couches grouped around the coffee table in Liam's living room, still stunned. Staring at the roll of parchment that sat in the middle of the table, as if it were an unexploded bomb.

Which, in a sense, it was. After all. It had almost gotten all six of them killed, at one time or another.

"We have to tell the press," Nancy said. "Get it on AP. All over the Internet. If the sketches are no longer secret, and that bastard knows that it's in the hands of experts getting authenticated, there'll be no more reason for him to attack us. No profit to it."

"Wrong," Vivi said, regretfully. "That would be true if you were dealing with normal, reasonable criminal buttheads, but John is special. He's totally over-the-edge insane. I don't think John even cares about the money anymore. He's just pissed. He wants payback. He wants blood."

"So we'll be looking over our shoulders for the rest of our lives?" Nancy flared. "I am so sick of it!"

"One thing's for sure," Liam said. "I will not have that thing in my house overnight. I've lost enough sleep lately."

"It's been in your house for weeks of nights," Nell reminded him.

Liam gave her an eloquent look and tossed off another swallow.

"I'll take it," Vivi offered. "My friend Jill has a big rare-book and antiquarian gallery in the city. She'll be able to tell us how to take care of it and get it authenticated. And how to find a safe place to store it. Somebody lend me a phone. I'll call her."

Vivi wandered into the kitchen to make her call, and Jack listened to the animated rise and fall of her voice as she told her librarian friend the crazy tale. He felt beaten down, exhausted. Scared. Impressed about the famous art and the big *L*, for sure. Very cool, zowie and all that, but only a tiny part of him really gave a shit. It was only paper, after all.

He was far more focused on the danger that bastard John posed to the living, breathing, beloved Vivi. And her sisters, of course.

Vivi came bouncing out, and tossed Nell's phone back to her. "It's all set up. Jill about had a stroke. She'll make arrangements for us for authentication, and she can store the sketches in her rare-book vault."

"The sooner you get rid of them, the happier I'll be," Liam said.

Nancy gave him a soothing kiss. The guy looked unsoothed.

Vivi was holding up the necklace to her sisters. "Should we detach these again? Do you want your necklaces back now?"

Nell and Nancy looked at each other. Nell took it from Vivi's hand, flipping the lever to retract the three planes with the miniscule writing. "Not yet," she said. "Let's stay united. When this is sorted out, we'll get the chains fixed and wear them again. For now, you keep it, okay? Like a talisman."

There were tears, at that point, and group hugs. Jack averted his eyes, until Vivi's voice caught his attention. "Nancy, can I borrow your Jetta to drive into the city?" she asked.

Jack's muscles seized up. "What? You're going to just stick the sketches in your purse? Carry them right out on the street?"

"I'll put them carefully into the table leg where they've resided for sixty-five years, put the leg into a big shopping bag. No one will know they're there," she soothed. "We'll all breathe easier when those sketches are safe in a vault."

"I'll breathe easier when that son of a bitch is dead," Jack said.

Vivi kissed the top of Jack's head. "Afterward, we'll drive out of the city. Find ourselves a hotel, okay? If Nancy can spare the car."

"Sure, but it's kind of unpredictable," Nancy warned. "The window in the back's come loose, so don't even try to roll it all the way up. It got smashed in by crazed crackheads one too many times."

"Can't be more rickety than my van was," Vivi said, wistfully. "My poor drowned van. I owe that van. It gave its life for me."

Jack's urge to fight drained away. Look at him. Pussywhipped as they came. Following that chick around like a panting hound, doing exactly as he was told. Jesus. Still, the thought of a night in absolute privacy with her alone in a hotel room was too inviting to resist.

He wanted to have that talk that she had promised him. To thrash things out between them, so he could relax, and buy her a goddamn engagement ring already.

He wanted to close the deal. Now.

But his pussywhipped patience reached its end when he realized that she intended to stop at Lucia's house in Hempton on the way. "There's something I need to pick up there," she insisted.

"At a time like this? What in holy hell could be so important?"

"It's a secret!" She frowned at him. "You'll understand later! Now just take this exit, turn to the right at the bridge, and stop arguing!"

He snarled obscenities as he flicked on the turn signal, and guided Nancy's battered, coughing little car off the highway, following Vivi's directions to the quiet street where Lucia's house was located.

He jerked to an angry stop in front of it. "So?"

"So what? So thank you," she said primly. "You're very obliging. So polite, too. Do you want to wait here while I run up and get it?"

"Fuck no. You think I'll let you go into a dark, abandoned house all alone?" He pulled out his gun. "Bring those goddamn sketches."

"As if I'd leave them in a car," she scoffed. "Let alone one with the back window held together with duct tape."

Jack kept hold of her arm. The street was quiet at this hour, just a few of the houses lit, the bluish flicker of televisions here and there. But his senses were buzzing, his hairs rising. No way could anyone know they were here—unless Lucia's house itself was watched. But who would watch an empty house? For weeks?

Get real, he told himself, as Vivi pushed the door open.

She didn't waste time in the sad, quiet house, just flipping on the light over the stairway, and then the light for the steep stairway leading up to the attic. Jack followed her up, fuming. His neck crawled. His discomfort grew as she pried open box after box. "What the fuck are you looking for, Viv? Christmas decorations?"

"Shut up and let me concentrate," she replied calmly.

She finally found what she sought, although she would not let him see it. She hid it with her body, wrapping it in a big plastic sack.

"Okay," she announced. "We can go now."

He led the way down the stairs, muttering imprecations as they went back to the car. Vivi frowned at him as he opened the trunk for her. "I wish you'd relax a little," she complained. "You're making me tense."

"I? I'm making *you* tense?" He opened the car door for her, and circled around, slid in, and started up the engine in one movement. "Let me tell you about *my* tension level, Viv."

That instant, he registered the smell. Already too late. There was a rustling sound, like a flock of bats. Panic exploded inside him—

Vivi's gasp choked off into a squeak. A heavy arm was clamped across her throat. A gleaming blade was pressed right beneath her eye.

John grinned from behind her car seat, a panting, stinking death's head, his face swollen, bruised and shiny. The point of the blade traced its slow, cruel way down over Vivi's cheek, leaving a thin red line in its wake. It ended up jammed against her throat. Point digging in.

"One move, and she bleeds out in forty seconds," John rasped.

Vivi's system was so burnt out from adrenaline, she barely reacted. She felt blank. Empty. No matter what she did, no matter how she fought, the way out of this trap was always barred.

"I'm sure it would be fascinating to hear about your tension level," John said, with a wheezing, giggling laugh. "We can compare it to your tension level while you're watching me cut your little fuck buddy here into bite-sized bloody pieces."

Jack's hand moved. John pressed the knife tip harder against her throat and clucked his tongue. "Not one muscle. Hands where I can see them. On top of the wheel. *Now!*"

Jack complied. Vivi wanted to look at him, but she was afraid the knife would jab right into her artery. Her voice box bobbed against it, stinging. "It's too late to get the sketches," she said, her voice thin and high. "I've told everyone. Curators at the art museums. Sotheby's, the press. I've scanned pictures of them to the *New York Times*, to—"

"Don't bother, you stupid bitch," John hissed. "I know you haven't done any of that yet. I watched you. I have vidcams all over Knightly's house. What a bunch of careless, stupid fucks you all are."

"Cameras?" She was startled. "At Liam's house?"

He laughed, and the hot cloud of his foul breath made her gag. "All that time they spent in Denver with Liam's dear old dad," he said. "I rigged his house. Saw every minute. You never called the press. Just that curator bitch—what was her name? Jill Rosseau. Is she cute?"

She gathered her nerve. "You still won't be able to sell—"

"You think I give a fuck?" His laughter was shrill and explosive. "If I can't sell them, I'll wipe my ass with them the next time I take a shit. I just want to make . . . you . . . scream." He jerked her head back, dragging the blade over her tendons. He stank, of sweat, and worse.

"So with Haupt dead, there's nobody left to pay you for the job, though, right?" Jack remarked, in a conversational tone.

"Oh. Haupt. That's another bone I have to pick with you, slut. You killed the old bag of bones before I got a chance to do it myself."

"You're doing this for revenge?" Jack sounded casually interested.

Vivi's hand clenched in the folds of the dress Nancy had lent her. It closed over the linked pendants that Nell had slipped into the pocket. She slid her trembling fingers inside, felt for the lever with her thumb.

"I'm doing it because you guys fucked me," John snarled. "Nobody fucks me. You have to pay."

His voice was shaking. So was the hand that held the knife. Vivi pushed the tiny lever of the linked pendants. The thin gold blade snapped out, pressing against her thumb, sharp as a box cutter.

"Must have hurt you quite a bit, with that head smash," Jack said. "You must have one motherfucker of a chronic headache."

"Fuck you," John said sullenly. "Shut your mouth."

"And that kick to the knee. Did I fuck up your knee? And don't you have a bullet wound? Your arm, or your shoulder, or something? Has it gone septic? Smells like gangrene, man. You should have somebody look at that. You probably need IV antibiotics."

"Shut up!" John shrieked.

"Come to think of it, you look like you've got a fever, too," Jack offered. "You should pop some Tylenol. That smell is intense. Whew."

"You fucking bastard! Shut the fuck *up!*" John whacked his hand across Jack's face.

Vivi used that brief instant of distraction to snap the pendant up, slashing it into John's face. He shrieked, jerked back. Jack twisted—

Bam, bam, bam. The pistol blasts were deafening in the small car.

The force of the bullets punched John back against the corner of the backseat. His big, heavy face went slack. Eyes blank.

His head tipped, slowly and heavily to the side. Mouth slack.

They waited, several heartbeats. Jack reached back, gingerly, and pressed his finger to John's carotid artery, for a long, cautious moment.

"Gone," he said, his voice hoarse and exhausted. The gun slid from his hand, thudded to the floor. He sagged, breathing hard.

"Oh, Jack." She lunged for him.

They rocked together, in a tight, trembling embrace. It was over.

It was several hours later, after a long, complicated, emotional stint at the police station, before Jack and Vivi managed to get to their hotel. They'd scrounged yet another car from Vivi's long-suffering family, since the blood-drenched Jetta had been sequestered, and it was long past dawn by the time they checked into their room.

Vivi's sisters had begged for her to come back to stay with them in Hempton, but Vivi quietly insisted on some time alone with him. Thank God. He was pathetically grateful for that small grace. Her sisters were lovely and great, and he liked them fine, but the conversation he needed to have with Vivi required privacy. No winking, nudging, or giggling.

Vivi flipped on the light, dropped her bags by the door and leaving blackout curtains closed against the morning sunshine. She sat on the bed, big eyed and solemn. She looked like a girl from another century, hair tangled and soft around her like a red cape. She wore a blue print dress that one of her sisters had lent her, but it was too big for her. The neckline drooped low over her bosom, showing off her tattoo. She followed his eyes, and smiled.

"Hey. You're staring at my *Eranthis hyemalis*, buddy," she said.

"Does it make you nervous?" he asked.

She reached up to touch the little yellow flower on her bosom, giving him a smile that made his crotch tighten. "Not in the least."

He fought his surging sexual hormones down, and sank to his knees in front of her. It seemed appropriate, considering.

"You promised me that if the axe got lifted, we could have this conversation," he said. "About us. And our future."

"So I did," she said demurely. "The axe is gone. And here we are."

He stared searchingly into her face. "Why were you such a hard-ass, Viv? Were you punishing me for being a dickhead before?"

She shook her head, and stroked his jaw. "Hell no," she whispered. "I was just trying to be a grown-up. How could you hook up with a woman who was nothing but a black hole of problems? What kind of a future could you possibly plan with a woman like that?"

He laughed, unbelieving. "I don't care. I'd marry you anyway. I'd marry you if those fuckers were banging on the door this very minute."

She pulled him closer, between her knees. He leaned forward against the swag of her full skirt, seeking more contact.

"I thought it would be better not to make plans, or get attached to the future," she said. "Since I thought I might not even have a future. Better to stay in the moment. Since you'd already taught me how."

"Ouch," he grumbled. "Would you stop with that?"

"I don't mean it as a judgment." There was a smile in her voice.

"The hell you don't." His arms slid around her waist, and he nuzzled her solar plexus, dragging in a deep lungful of her sweet scent, rubbing his cheek against a glossy lock of dangling hair. "This is the thing, about staying in the moment," he said, carefully. "There's a lot to be said for it, but certain things require a larger arc of time. Like planting a flower garden. You plant, you wait, you weed, you water, you enjoy. Takes months. Or waiting for those *Eranthis hyemalis* seedlings to take root and spread into a floral carpet. That takes time. That's not a momentary thing. They won't even bloom until February. Understand?"

"Oh, yeah," she whispered, her mouth touching his ear.

He was shaking, deep inside, in his core. "Or opening a gallery shop of wearable, usable art, for example," he went on, doggedly. "Or, uh, making a baby. Although I don't know. Now that you're a megazillionaire, things might be different. You might want to live a glamorous, jet-setting sort of life. What the fuck do I know."

"Megazillionaire, my ass." She tilted up her face, and shook her head. "If I ever do see money from that mess, the only difference it'll make to me is that I'll be able to hire a girl to spell me at the shop. So that I can have time to work on my art. And, ah, the baby. Of course."

He was grinning. Like a fool. He wanted to roll over backward for joy, wave his legs in the air. He controlled the impulse, with some difficulty. A proposal of marriage should be dignified, goddammit.

She slid both hands into the hair on the back of his head, leaned her forehead against his. Her hair fell down, fragrant against his cheek.

"You told me a few weeks ago that I'd pack up my van and drive away as soon as I realized what it meant to look at the same place, day in and day out. Or the same person," she said.

"I'm sorry." He nuzzled that fragrant hank of hair. "I was a dick."

"No, no. I wasn't roasting you. Let me finish. I just wanted to say that, um, I think I've definitely realized what it means, now."

He pulled away, gazing at her with narrowed eyes. "Yeah?"

"Yours is the face I want to look at for the rest of my life," she said quietly. "Day in and day out. And I want to see it in my children's faces, if we get lucky that way. While seasons turn. Rain and snow and wind and sun. While flowers bud and bloom and go to seed around us. While seedling trees grow way up into the sky. A big arc of time. Decade after decade. As long as fate gives us."

He hid his shaking face against her chest again, letting secret tears soak into her dress. "Just one more question, Viv," he ventured.

She smiled, against his silky hair. "And what's that?"

"What the hell was that thing you had to stop at Lucia's house to pick up last night? The suspense is killing me."

She froze, and then burst into startled laughter. "Oh! I forgot all about that! I'll show you." She retrieved the plastic bag from where she'd left it by the door and gave him an embarrassed look. "This makes me a little shy."

"Out with it," he prodded. "Don't make me wait."

"Thigh-high black lace-up boots," she said, whipping them out of the bag. "You said you wanted to see them. So, um . . . here they are."

He stared at them. He started to laugh. His tension started to unwind, into shaking convulsions. "Oh, God. I can't believe it."

"I no longer have the ripped fishnet stockings at the moment, unfortunately," she said. "I'll have to go shopping to complete the ensemble."

He wiped his eyes. "They're fine all by themselves," he assured her. "They're perfect. Put them on right now. I'll show you."

And he did.